AMAZULU

AMAZULU

Being The Many Divers Adventures
Of The Induna & The Boy
Among The People Of The Sky
In The Time Of
Shaka KaSenzangakhona, King Of Kings

by

WALTON GOLIGHTLY

Quercus

First published in Great Britain in 2008 by

Quercus
21 Bloomsbury Square
London
WC1A 2NS

Originally published in 2007 by Kwela Books, a division of
NB Publishers (Pty) Limited, Cape Town, South Africa

A CIP catalogue reference for this book is available
from the British Library

ISBN 978 1 84724 326 3

10 9 8 7 6 5 4 3 2 1

Typography: Nazli Jacobs
Set in Utopia
Printed and bound in Great Britain by Clays Ltd, St Ives plc.

For my father

In me you see one of the last of those wonderful men,
the men who were veterans when they were yet boys,
who learned to use a sword earlier than a razor,
and who during a hundred battles had never once let the enemy see
the colour of their knapsacks.

From "How The Brigadier Came To The Castle Of Doom"
(in *The Exploits Of Brigadier Gerard*) by Arthur Conan Doyle

Contents

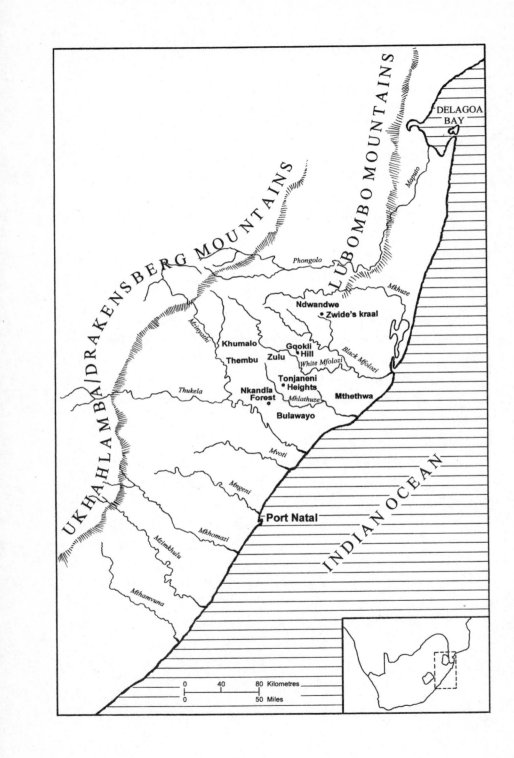

DELAGOA BAY

LUBOMBO MOUNTAINS

DRAKENSBERG MOUNTAINS

UKHAHLAMBA/DRAKENSBERG MOUNTAINS

Maputo

Phongolo

Mkhuze

Ndwandwe
• Zwide's kraal

Mzinyathi

Khumalo

Thembu

Zulu

Gqokli
Hill

Black Mfolozi

White Mfolozi

Thukela

Tonjaneni
• Heights

Nkandla
Forest

Mhlathuze

Mthethwa

• Bulawayo

Mvoti

Mngeni

INDIAN OCEAN

Mkhomazi

Mzimkhulu

Port Natal

Mthamvuna

0   40   80 Kilometres
0   50 Miles

Main characters

The Zulus

Shaka KaSenzangakhona	*King of the Zulus. Born in the 1790s. Seized the throne in 1816*
Mbopa	*Shaka's prime minister*
Mdlaka	*Commander in chief of the Zulu army*
Dingane } Mpande }	*Two of Shaka's half-brothers*
Nqoboka	*One of Shaka's generals*
Mabhubesi	*A shaman*
Senzangakhona KaJama	*Shaka's father*
Mduli	*Prime minister during Senzangakhona's reign*
Pampata	*Shaka's favourite concubine*
Nandi	*Shaka's mother*
Nobela	*A powerful female shaman*

The Mthetwas

Dingiswayo KaJobe	*Ruler of the Mthetwas, and Shaka's mentor*
Mgobozi	*Served with Shaka in Dingiswayo's army, then went with his friend to claim the Zulu crown and stayed on as Shaka's most trusted general*

The Ndwandwes

Zwide KaLanga	*King of the Ndwandwes*
Nomahlanjana	*Zwide's heir and commander of the Ndwandwe army at Gqokli Hill in 1818*
Noluju	*Zwide's prime minister*
Soshangane	*Leader of the army on its invasion of Zulu territory in 1820*
Zwangendaba	*Soshangane's trusted general*
Ntombazi	*Zwide's mother*

The Khumalos

Dondo	*A Khumalo chief*
Mzilikazi KaMashobane	*Dondo's nephew and heir of one of the Khumalo clans*
Nonhlakanipho	*Dondo's daughter, abducted by Zwide's men as one of the "spoils" of war*

Others

Stanley Boyd } Oliver de la Vere	*English ivory traders*
Jacob	*Their interpreter*

Prelude

Izindaba zami lezi . . .
These are my stories,
of long ago and far away.
Uma ngiqambe amanga . . .
If I have lied,
I have lied the truth.
If this is not the way things were,
it's the way they should've been.

PART ONE

The Royal Stool

The nations, Shaka, have condemned you,
Yet still today they speak of you,
Still today, the books discuss you,
But we defy them to explain you.

From the praise poem
Ushaka Ka Senzangakhona
by B.W. Vilakazi

They came from the north.

In the beginning there was a chief called Nguni. He it was who led his people out of Egypt and down to the great lakes of central Africa. Here, where the pasture was green and the game plentiful, and the land stretched forever beneath a sky the depthless blue of the Great Spirit's soul, one tribe became many. Clans broke away and over time evolved their own dialects and customs. Enough similarities remained, though, for this grouping to become known as the Nguni people, the Restless Ones.

Relative peace reigned. Disputes could be settled simply by taking one's family and moving on. Intermarriages occurred with the people encountered in the new regions and still more tribes were born. And the migration, this slow seeding, this quiet colonisation, spread – across the great Serengeti to the foothills of sacred Kilima-Njaro – the Mountain That Burns – and beyond.

With the Lala people leading the way, the Nguni tribes drifted ever southward, the men hunting and scouting ahead, the women carrying their possessions on their heads, herdboys driving the precious cattle.

In the sixteenth century a chief called Malandela – the Follower – found the country of his dreams on the east coast of southern Africa – fertile land, mighty rivers, good pastures and freedom from the tsetse fly that decimated livestock up north.

In time his son married and moved away to establish his own clan. The son's name was Zulu, and so the AmaZulu, the People Of The Sky, came into being. They remained a small tribe, but prospered, especially under Zulu's great-grandson, Ndaba Kaphunga, the Man Of Affairs, and then Jama, He Of The Stern Countenance.

By now the land of the great lakes was just a memory, to be recalled to this day by storytellers as mystical Embo.

17

Power struggles raged around the little tribe settled in among the green hills between the Pongola and Thukela rivers – the arguments and conspiracies of wealthier, stronger relatives, with the Mthetwas and the Ndwandwes emerging as the dominant forces in a land growing ever more crowded. Under Jama's son, Senzangakhona, He Who Acts Wisely, the Zulus allied themselves with Dingiswayo, ruler of the Mthetwas. Since the land occupied by the Zulus formed a buffer zone against the Ndwandwes, Dingiswayo allowed Senzangakhona much leeway when it came to military expansion. Not that the Zulu King could ever field more than five hundred men.

While still a prince, Senzangakhona fathered a child with a woman called Nandi. He later denied paternity and it was claimed Nandi's swollen stomach was due to an "intestinal beetle" called a "shaka". When the child was born, this was the name Nandi gave him, saying, "Here is your Beetle, come and fetch him."

Although Senzangakhona finally married Nandi and acknowledged Shaka as his first-born, their sojourn at the royal kraal was brief and unhappy. Nandi eventually left, taking the boy with her, and, scorned even by her own clan, the two lived the life of refugees, seeking succour where they could. Sweetened only by the devotion of his mother, it was an unhappy childhood the boy would never forget.

*

Senzangakhona KaJama died in 1816. A year later, Zwide, king of the Ndwandwes, assassinated Dingiswayo and defeated the Mthetwa army. All that stood between the Ndwandwes and total paramountcy was the small Zulu state under its new king, Dingiswayo's protégé, the Bastard Son, the Bull Elephant who had trumpeted his arrival by slaughtering all those who'd shunned his beloved mother – Shaka KaSenzangakhona.

1
The Fat And The Fire

"Shades of Agincourt, what!"

Oliver Valery de la Vere lowers his spyglass and favours his plump companion with a look of disdain.

Stanley Boyd, his rouge running down his cheeks, his forehead glistening beneath his battered shako, chuckles. "History, old chap. History in the making!" he says, his hand sweeping over the black armies arrayed before them.

"Aye, but who are we? The English or the French?"

"Oh, the English, old boy, always the English!"

De la Vere, who was with Saltoun's Grenadiers at Hougoumont, grunts something noncommittal and raises the spyglass once more.

The plain dips here, before rolling up to the slopes of this strange, flat-topped hill where the Zoolas sit idly on their shields. Only their officers – indoonas, De la Vere believes they're called – are on their feet, walking up and down, talking to their men.

"That must be him . . ."

De la Vere swings his spyglass in the direction his companion is pointing.

A tall, broad-shouldered black man, standing almost motionless on a large flat outcrop of rock on the hill's northern rim.

Shaka.

His kilt is a golden colour, and the cowtails that comprise his leggings are white. He also wears a fur collar and the long tail feather of a loerie rises from his headband.

"That's one savage that won't live to see sundown," sneers Boyd. When De la Vere mutters something that sounds like disagreement, he adds: "Oh come on! I'm no military man, but even I can see there's a distinct difference in numbers here!"

This is true and it's some consolation, supposes De la Vere. But dammit, that Zoola line only *seems* ragged: even he can see that Shaka's had his men crowd together on purpose, so their numbers seem even fewer.

And there's something about the way they're sitting. A complacency . . . Yes: the complacency of a disciplined fighting force. The languor of fit, well-trained men. The readiness.

By contrast, the Ndwandwes arrayed before them look more like a mob than the regiments of an army.

De la Vere captures the Zoola King in the circle of his spyglass again. Why has Shaka chosen to array his host in such an odd manner? If he's right about those ranks, the discipline he thinks he can perceive in the attitude of the men, that's evidence of an able commander. Why then *this*? De la Vere's never seen the like before.

He leaves Shaka, guiding the spyglass downward to examine the gradient. No overhang. The king's clearly chosen that spot as his command post. If he remains there . . . well, they have a chance.

When Shaka falls, the battle will be as good as won, the witch doctor has assured them. And as loyal servants of Zwide, king of the Ndwandwes, they'll be allowed to hunt for ivory to their hearts' content. "We will award no other White Men this right," the king has told them. "You will have my protection." Aye, and their fortunes will be made.

Allowing himself a grin, De la Vere lowers the spyglass, compresses it and slots it into the case dangling from his saddlebow.

It can be done, he decides. Provided the Ndwandwes are able to hold the Zoolas back long enough, and if they seem an unruly bunch, they *do* outnumber the Zoolas by about five to one. And these savages don't use arrows – can't find the right kind of wood for the bows, apparently – they prefer a short, stabbing spear, so when he gets out there, in the heat of battle, he won't have to worry about missiles coming his way. He should have a reasonably easy shot.

"Agincourt, old boy," says Boyd again. He's wearing a purple frock coat, britches that were once white, but are now a dusty brown colour with darker stains here and there, a silk cravat he produced for this special occasion and that shako he dug up somewhere in Cape Town. An Incroyable who makes Mr Brummel and his cronies seem like Sans Culottes, he spent the morning pouting until De la Vere retracted his promise to break his fingers one by one if he dared to don his make-up. Now his lipstick has gone the way of his rouge and white powder and he resembles a Grimaldi caught in a rainstorm, or a miller who's been eating cherries. He's known as Mafuta, the Fat One, an appellation that causes him much mirth.

"Agincourt!" he says, raising his gun. "And *we* have the longbows."

Oliver Valery de la Vere is more suitably dressed for the bush and wears a brown corduroy jacket over a collarless shirt, riding britches and boots, and a wide-brimmed straw hat. Because of his red beard and quick temper, the Ndwandwes call him the Fool Who Set His Face On Fire. However, preferring discretion to valour (or, in this instance, Valery) their interpreter's told him his "native" name means the Fiery One.

Boyd slaps De la Vere on the shoulder. "We're going to be rich, Oliver. Rich beyond the dreams of avarice!"

2
The Corn And The Cob
About eight months earlier

Regarded as a delicacy among the Zulu and other Nguni tribes, amasi is made when fresh milk is poured into a leather pouch or gourd and left to stand until the contents turn sour, a relatively quick process given the subtropical climate of the region. The containers are never cleaned out, and every morning fresh milk is added.

Strangely, for such hospitable people, amasi is never shared with anyone outside the immediate family. The fact that Dondo, the inkosi, or chief, of the Khumalos, offers the Induna some from his own stock is therefore a great honour.

He wanted to slaughter an ox, but the Induna dissuaded him, reminding the old man he was there incognito. Instead, the meal the women bring them as the shadows stretch into early evening comprises roasted mealies, samp and beans, phutu, boiled madumbes, beer and, of course, the amasi.

In his mid-twenties, the Induna is tall, broad-shouldered, with heavy arms and strong thighs. He wears a tasselled kilt and is barefoot. His only other adornment is his war necklace, comprising beads and stones interspersed with lion's teeth. The teeth are an indication of his rank and the other items are relics from the battlefields where he has fought.

Normally, on occasions such as this, he'd wear a civet collar and the tail feather of a blue crane in a leather headband, as an indication that he is Isithunzi SikaShaka, the Shadow Of Shaka, the King's representative, who speaks and acts with the King's authority. But this is a secret mission and he wants to pass himself off as a mere wayfarer.

With him is his udibi, a boy of eleven summers, who serves as his apprentice, carrying supplies and extra weapons. Right now he's beaming quietly, scarcely able to hide his pride at being permitted to sit with the men – who, along with the Induna and the chief, include Dondo's three eldest sons. And, although he doesn't much understand or like girls, he enjoys the admiring glances Dondo's daughter, Nonhlakanipho, keeps sending his master and the way she ensures that it is she who serves the Zulu.

Tempering his happiness, though, is the knowledge that his master is frustrated by the greybeard's obstinacy.

The boy sneaks a glance at the Induna. Paying Nonhlakanipho's ministrations no heed, he's eating without savouring, driven on only by good manners.

Why won't these Khumalos listen? To the boy it's all quite simple: Shaka is the Father and he would be the Father of these people too. With his protection no harm will befall them. Why can't they see that?

"This is good food, Nkosi," says the Induna after a while.

The old man shrugs. "Beef would've been better."

"Be here tomorrow, we'll have game aplenty," says Yanga, the chief's eldest son.

It's a provocative comment, for he's the one who's consistently argued against the chief heeding Shaka's warning.

"Even the finest beef would've been spoiled by my son's manners," murmurs Dondo. "For this I apologise."

"If it was just a matter of game I wouldn't be here," says the Induna.

"Perhaps that's all it really is." Yanga's voice is almost a snarl.

"Silence!" says Dondo. "How many times would you have me apologise for your manners? Be still."

The boy notes how the other two sons exchange grins. They have no opinion on the matter; they are only happy to see their father and their elder brother quarrel.

And, beside him, he senses the Induna grow ever more impatient, struggling to keep his anger in check. Yanga annoying the chief isn't making the Induna's task easier. The greybeard's irritation is likely to make him reject anything anyone suggests now.

But time is running out. The Induna and the boy have to leave this place at first light. Already they have been detained for longer than the Induna feels is safe.

Hoping the esteem Dondo has for him and the fact that they're the chief's guests will help stifle the greybeard's annoyance, the feeling he must have of being pestered from all sides, the Induna tries again.

"Will you not heed Shaka's warning?" he asks. "This is more than the King repaying you for the great service you did him. He regards you as a trusted friend . . ."

"Valuable ally, you mean," interrupts Yanga.

Before Dondo can respond, the Induna turns to the heir: "And what of it? So what if that is also true? Because the time will come when we will have to join together to fight this mad jackal or else he'll devour us one by one."

"Cha! Who would be the vassal of a vassal?" asks Yanga.

"We are beholden to *no one*!"

"What of Dingiswayo?"

"We did not serve him. We marched *with* him!"

"A lot of good your Zulu loyalty did him!"

"Enough!" says Dondo. "Leave the past alone."

There is silence while the old man munches on his mealie. Then he lowers the cob, balanced on the palm of his left hand.

"I hear you, Nduna," he says. "I hear your wise words, and beyond them, I hear Shaka's voice. I, too, regard him as a trusted friend. Shaka is a strong king. The Zulus are a strong, proud people. But this is what I have to ask myself with the welfare of my people foremost in my mind: Do you have the power?"

He raises his left hand.

"This is the way things are, my friend."

He has chewed the corn off one half of the cob, leaving only a few kernels on that side. He points to these.

"Your people. Strong, proud, brave."

His finger moves across to the other half: rows of maize clustered together on the cob; the ordered, impenetrable ranks of superior numbers.

"The Ndwandwes."

He regards the Induna.

"What can I do? This land becomes ever more crowded. Where can we go? Back north, where our cattle die? South, where we meet the Xhosa and the White Man? East, where the swamps will swallow our people?

"When Dingiswayo ruled things were different, it is so. He was a wise, just king and I happily forged an alliance with him. But my reasoning then was the same as it is now. We cannot rule this land, we do not want to rule this land, but if we are to stay here, we must make friends with those who do."

The Induna knows the chief has a point. With the subjugation of the Langeni and Buthelezi clans, the Children Of The Sky have gained more land and their army has grown, but the Zulus remain an insignificant part of the region's balance of power.

With Dingiswayo dead and the Mthetwas in disarray, the Ndwandwes have emerged as the dominant force. Chances are, Zwide would have ignored the Zulus, expected them to bend before him as a matter of course, were it not for the fact that, as a general in Dingiswayo's service, Shaka had administered thrashing after thrashing to the Ndwandwe army. Now Zwide is coming for them and the Zulus will have to fight for their lives.

"You speak of friends," says the Induna, "but, Nkosi, you must know Zwide can be no one's friend!"

"You might be right, Shadow Of Shaka, but don't you see? I have no other choice! I have no other choice than to take this invitation at face value."

"Nkosi, this is why I am here! It's not that you seek peace with the Ndwandwes. In his wisdom, the King understands your position. You do not anger him by seeking peace with the Ndwandwes. No! But he's sent me here, in his name, to warn you this is a trap. Zwide cares nothing for your friendship – because of past alliances, because you marched against him with the Mthetwas and the Zulus, and worse, because you warned Shaka that Dingiswayo had been slain and enabled him to withdraw with his forces intact, he seeks your head, Nkosi. Nothing less will satisfy him."

"Father, I would speak."

Dondo sighs and nods.

"Zulu, maybe you do not mean to," says Yanga, "but you impugn both our courage and our wisdom."

"That was not my intention."

"So be it. But tomorrow, we will meet for the hunt. This will give us an opportunity to gauge Zwide's intentions. Perhaps tomorrow evening we'll have a different answer to your pleas."

"I came here only to warn your father, Cub. And this is my warning: go to that hunt and you will not live to see the sun set!"

*

Early the following morning, the Induna and the boy take their leave of the chief. Instead of returning to the Zulu capital, the Induna leads the boy to where the two hunting parties will meet, and they hide amid the dense bushes on the slopes of a hill overlooking the clearing.

Dondo, his sons and a few other men and boys are the first to arrive. They settle themselves in the shade of a marula tree, and after a while the boys climb the tree to pick the fruit. The men wear leather kilts and are armed only with hunting spears.

About an hour later, the Ndwandwes arrive. There are seventy of them and they are dressed as for war. White stripes are painted across each soldier's body and they carry fighting spears, with extra assegais clipped to the insides of their shields. Unlike the oval Zulu isihlangu, which is the height of a man, these shields are smaller and rectangular, comprising hide pulled over a wooden frame and strengthened with additional crossbars.

Zwide has warned Dondo not to be alarmed by this readiness for battle – it's a necessary precaution, what with Shaka's impis abroad and spoiling for war.

The Khumalos rise and move away from the trees to greet their guests.

And before they know it, they're fighting for their lives, their flimsy hunting spears no match for the Ndwandwe assegais.

The massacre is over in a matter of minutes with the Ndwandwes suffering negligible casualties. The chief and his sons are beheaded and the warriors move away to join their comrades who have attacked the village. Already, the Induna can see smoke rising from that direction.

When he is sure they are alone save for the circling vultures, the Induna turns to the boy . . .

. . . who saw the Ndwandwes drift into a semicircle around the Khumalos . . . saw the old chief stride forward . . . the chief who'd shared the amasi with them, who'd laughed on greeting the boy, squeezed his arms and said how he was growing into a fine young warrior . . . he heard snatches of the ritual greeting carried up to where they hid . . . then, suddenly, the Ndwandwes hurled their spears . . . and the screaming began . . . rage, pain and helplessness . . .

"Do not be embarrassed to look on this with wet eyes," murmurs the Induna. "For, truly, this was an act of evil that could have been avoided."

"But *why*, Master? This inkosi – he wanted peace."

"This is the way some are, Boy. This is the way that Ndwandwe jackal is. Remember that too. This is what we face."

*

Seated on an ant hill amid the waving grass, Mgobozi watches as the Induna and the boy approach. In his mid-forties, Shaka's most trusted general is short and wiry, and white hairs mat his chest like ash. His thighs and arms bear the scars of many campaigns. He carries a long-handled war axe used to direct men in battle.

"So!" he says, grinning, after they've exchanged greetings. "Which of these fools did you see first?"

"No fools. Just a wise general."

Mgobozi laughs. "Do not let your own memories of life in the ranks cloud your judgement. This is for their own good. Remember that."

"I remember, too, the punishment would fall regardless."

"Better that than death in the field."

"Cha! There are those who would choose that alternative."

"At least they have that choice here."

"This is so."

Mgobozi raises his swallow-tail axe, twirls it in a tight circle. Zulu warriors rise up out of the long grass, move out of the shadows beneath the bushwillows. The general points the axe to the north. "Hambani!" he shouts. *Run!*

The warriors set off in the direction he's pointed.

"We have received word of what happened," says Mgobozi. Zwide, he adds, has taken the opportunity to devour all of the Khumalo clans. Only one of the heirs has managed to escape with a few followers: Dondo's nephew, a young warrior called Mzilikazi.

"He wouldn't listen."

"All we could do was warn him. The final decision was his."

The Induna nods.

"Which is scant comfort. But we are not ready to take on this jackal. We could do no more than warn the old man."

The Induna nods again.

"Come, the King awaits your report."

Mgobozi leads the Induna and the boy through the long grass to where a slight dip greets a flat-topped hill.

"He's up there," says the general.

As they watch Shaka appears, silhouetted against the sky, stepping up onto a broad rock.

Mgobozi lays a hand on the boy's shoulder. "You and I will wait here until those fools hide themselves again, then you will help me find them."

Breaking into a gentle trot, the Induna makes his way toward the hill.

3
The Three Maidens

Zwide KaLanga, ruler of the Ndwandwes and known throughout the land as the Devourer Of Kings, reclines against a mound of cowhides in his hut, picking slivers of meat from between his teeth with a twig while absent-mindedly rubbing his left foot against the breasts of a concubine. In his fifties, he has the ponderous corpulence of a big, strong man grown lazy. Heavy, almost womanish lips perch atop a double chin and his eyes lurk behind the crest of his cheekbones. His kilt of hide strips has ridden up to reveal genitals crushed in the crevice of broad thighs.

Embers in a circle of stones in the centre of the hut cast a pale glow, and the clutter around the fringes – shields and spears, axes and clubs, a pair of elephant tusks, clay pots – throw long, curving shadows up the walls, so that, in one place, the elephant seems to live again, crouched in homage to the Ndwandwe king.

Zwide examines a particularly large fragment of beef, daintily picks it off between his teeth and flicks the twig away.

"We need a reason." His voice is a low drawl.

"This is so," says his son and heir, Nomahlanjana, who's inherited his father's belly without first going through the muscular stage. He is sitting on the hard-packed dirt floor, warming his feet at the fire. The top part of his body appears to have sunk into the swollen waterskin of his belly, while that belly, in turn, seems to have trapped his heavy legs – slightly bent and stretched out in front of him.

"Our allies would become wary were we to attack without just cause," he adds.

Zwide snorts derisively. "These Zulus grow ever more annoying."

"And dangerous!"

Zwide couldn't capitalise on his assassination of Dingiswayo and annihilate the Mthetwa army completely because of the presence of Shaka's army on his flank, ready to strike – to avenge the death of the man who had become like a father to the Zulu King. Indeed, Zwide's soldiers returned home almost empty-handed. Now, to make matters worse, Dingiswayo's remaining legions have joined up with the Zulus.

All the same, Shaka's position is precarious. Aside from Zwide and the Ndwandwes in the north, he has to contend with the Qwabes in the south, who also regard the growing nation with envy and suspicion, and with the powerful Tembus in the west.

"These Old Women – what news have we?" asks Zwide.

He's referring to the Qwabes and Tembus. Nomahlanjana essays a shrug that wobbles his breasts. "Hot air and foul breath."

"Cha! I'll settle with them when the time comes."

Both Shaka and Zwide have been working to form alliances with the two tribes, but Zwide has cast the sincerity of his own diplomatic overtures into doubt by devouring the Khumalo clans.

Zwide grins at the memory of that day, three months ago. This one whose hard nipples tickle the sole of his foot, she was one of the Khumalo females his men carried off . . .

Nomahlanjana has his eyes on the girl too. She's on her haunches, leaning forward against his father's foot. Idly he wonders if he can tell her to fetch him a pot of beer without evoking his father's wrath.

Probably not . . .

But that gets him thinking about something else.

He straightens, pulling himself out of his gut. "Tell me this, Father," he says. "Did you not help this Beetle's father when he subdued the Buthelezis?"

Zwide nods. This is so: he had promised Senzangakhona his support.

"And did he not say you could have three Zulu maidens in return?"

Now it's Zwide who sits up, kicking the girl away as he does so. "Leave me," he tells her. "Go!"

She hurries out of the hut's smaller rear entrance.

"Three maidens, Father."

"This is so."

It doesn't matter that Zwide never actually fulfilled his obligation: the promises had been exchanged.

"And does a man not only inherit his father's estate, but his debts as well?"

"This is so," says Zwide again.

Nomahlanjana slaps his left knee. "There you have it, Father. Your excuse."

"Cha!" says Zwide. A clicking, spitting sound. But Nomahlanjana can see his father is pleased.

This is the pretext they need. A reason to go to war that might allay the fears of the other tribes that they'll be next. For that's the argument Shaka has been using with the Qwabes and Tembus, urging them to form a three-way alliance with the Zulus to protect themselves against Zwide. To date, though, the Qwabes and Tembus have ignored Shaka's overtures. With an acceptable excuse, an obvious provocation, Zwide can move against the People Of The Sky – and doubtless, the other tribes will then try to win his favour by refusing to aid the Zulus.

Short-sighted fools!

"Do you think this Bastard Son will honour his father's debt?"

Nomahlanjana allows himself a chin-wobbling chuckle. "Although they say we are of an age, he and I, I do not know him, but since you removed the head of his beloved mentor, I'd say that is unlikely."

"Then we will have our excuse!" exclaims Zwide, as if the thought has just occurred to him, and Nomahlanjana knows that by morning his father will have convinced himself the whole thing is his idea.

*

When Zwide demands from Shaka the maidens promised him by Senzangakhona, the Zulu King's response is swift.

"That impotent hyena is not fit to sleep with the ugliest sow in the kingdom! Never shall a sister of mine wed that sack of pustulence! He wants Zulu maidens? Let him come and fetch them!"

And Zwide begins mobilising his superior numbers in preparation to do just that.

4
The Inkatha

With war looming, it is time for the Inkatha. Shaka summons a sangoma called Mabhubesi, the Lion, to KwaBulawayo. He is renowned across the land as a shaman of great power, a favoured servant of the ancestors who can claim a lineage that stretches back to Zulu, the Father of the nation, and beyond. He will conduct the ceremony.

*

This KwaBulawayo, the first (and smaller) of two capitals to bear that name that Shaka will build, is situated on the right bank of the Mhodi, a tributary of the Umkumbane River.

Typical of most Zulu villages, it's placed on a slight incline, with the main entrance at the lowest point. The gentle slope means heavy rains will wash dung and other dirt into the vegetable plots below the settlement, enabling the bare ground around the huts to dry out quicker.

Two circular stockades surround the village, the outer fence made of cut acacia trees, with the thorny tops compacted to form an impenetrable barrier against thieves and beasts of prey.

Two hundred or so circular beehive-shaped huts are situated between the inner and outer stockades.

Zulu huts are made by sticking a row of saplings in a circular trench, fifteen centimetres deep and about five metres in diameter. Horizontal rows are then added. The saplings are tied together with grass where they cross and the lattice is bent over to meet at the top and covered with thatch so arranged as to lead off water. The doorway, closed at night by an isicabha, or wicker door, is small and low. The floor is made of clay beaten hard with stones and smoothed. About twice a week, this is covered with cow dung, which doesn't smell and can be made to shine.

The right side of the hut, or isililo samadoda, belongs to the men, while the isililo sesifazana is for the women; it's a division scrupulously adhered to. Right at the back of the hut is the umsamo, where the ancestors are thought to live.

During the day, sleeping mats and other articles are hung from the walls, along with baskets containing provisions and beer.

As in any other Zulu village, or umuzi, the largest hut in KwaBulawayo is the indlunkhulu. Built on the highest point furthest away from the entrance, it's occupied by Shaka's mother, Nandi, when she's in residence.

The King's smaller dwelling is to the right and a little behind the indlunkhulu.

It's a custom among the Zulu people that the hut of a chief's first wife will be to the left of the grandmother's, the second wife's to the right of the chief's hut, while the third wife lives to the left of the first wife, and so on. Shaka, however, is unmarried and will remain so. The twenty huts fenced off at the top end of Bulawayo, behind the royal compound, mark the beginning of a harem that will grow to house more than a thousand women.

Cattle are herded into the circular centre of the settlement at night and here, to one side, is the ibandla tree, where the King and his councillors meet to discuss important matters, since the People Of The Sky regard cattle as precious and the isibaya, or cattlefold, as a sacred place.

It is here that the ceremony of the Inkatha will be held.

*

The regiments gather in the cattlefold; ordered rows forming a semicircle around the ibandla tree, where the King and his most trusted advisors stand.

Shaka is thirty, tall, broad-shouldered, with high cheekbones and slightly sunken eyes that occasionally give him a gaunt look. A shade lighter than his skin, these eyes are capable of staring deep into the soul of a man and are said to shine with ubukosi – a natural state of ascendancy, of leadership, more powerful than any birthright. His body is the rippled rock of a warrior able to run all day without tiring and his powerful hands bear the callouses of shield strap and assegai shaft.

Like his soldiers he wears amashoba – leather thongs with long fringes made from a cow's tail fastened under the knees and over the elbows – and a kilt formed from two separate aprons. The isinene, or front apron, comprises skins cut into circular patches and strung together on sinews to form tassels, which are weighted to prevent the apron from opening in case of sudden movement. The rear apron, or ibheshu, is slightly longer, almost reaching the backs of the knees, and is made from soft calfskin.

In Shaka's case, though, both his isinene and ibheshu are fashioned from civet pelts, so that his kilt is a golden colour, and the tails of his amashoba are white. He also wears a collar of civet fur and the long tail feather of a blue crane in his headband.

Each of the regiments has added its own flourishes to this uniform – a practice encouraged by Shaka, since, from his own experience in the front line, he's learnt the loyalty comrades-in-arms feel toward one another will outweigh their loyalty to their masters. And such is the competitive spirit that exists among his regiments, they have to be kept separated when not on campaign, because fights erupt when the warriors encounter each other.

But the call has gone out. They are getting ready for war, and now their rivalry will be expressed only in a willingness to kill more of the enemy than the other impis.

They watch intently as the Lion sets about making the fire according to the old way. He inserts the pehla, or boring stick, into a small cut in a softer piece of wood. Holding this rectangular plank in place with his feet, he rubs the metre-long stick between his hands. When the friction has caused the softer wood to glow, he puts aside the pehla and goes onto his knees, gently blowing on the dried moss he's placed around the hole. Then he adds twigs . . . sticks . . . branches . . . and something else . . .

For suddenly the flames explode upwards into the sky – and the soldiers roar their approval, since this signifies the start of a new phase in the tribe's life.

The cries become war songs, each regiment getting its turn and trying to outdo the other impis.

Shaka watches his men intently. White Men are camping at Zwide's kraal and this has been regarded as a bad omen. Which is another reason for the ceremony. The regiments need to be reminded of their own strength. They need to be reminded that it's up to them; it's what they do that matters, not the machinations of outsiders.

The songs fall away. A hush descends. Wearing only a loincloth and a lion-skin cloak, the shaman raises his arms. The ranks part as a phalanx of four junior sangomas moves toward the clearing in front of the ibandla tree. Here, at Shaka's feet, they lay a thick grass coil about a metre in diameter.

The Inkatha, the symbol of tribal strength.

In turn, each of the apprentices kneels at Shaka's feet, carefully picks up one of the articles arranged there and proffers it to the King for his approval. On his nod, the youth stands, backs away from the King for six paces, turns and moves to the Lion. With his head bowed, his arms extended, the junior shaman passes the article to the chief sangoma. The Lion holds it up to the assembly, then empties the contents into a pot containing seawater and ox blood.

Sacred substances: straw from the royal huts, dirt from the floors, handfuls of soil from paths on which the King regularly walks, samples of royal vomit.

Mabhubesi himself fetches the last, the most precious talisman from the King. This is the ibizi, the King's faeces. It's wrapped in cabbage leaves, and after holding it up for the approval of the warriors, the sangoma places it in the pot.

Mabhubesi and his assistants will tend the pot through the night. Tomorrow, after the sun has passed its zenith, the impis will gather once more to watch as the sangoma smears the mixture from the pot over the coil. Palm fibre will then be wrapped tightly around the Inkatha, followed by a large python skin. Next, Mabhubesi will call on the ancestors to give the ring magical powers capable of dispelling danger and protecting the King and the tribe from evil.

Stepping into the centre of the ring, Shaka will be daubed with fortifying medicines while praise singers recount his brave deeds. He'll dip his fingers into a potion made from herbs, bark and human fat and, by licking the dark substance from his fingertips, he'll acquire superhuman powers. The Inkatha will be complete.

Now, though, while Mabhubesi stirs the pot, orders are shouted.

The warriors will leave the kraal and move into the bush, where trackers will lead each regiment to areas where herds of buck have been spotted. The warriors will then surround the animals and kill as many as they can. In this way, their assegai blades will be blooded and ready for war.

It is Ukugeza Izikhali. The Washing Of The Spears.

*

Shaka distinguished himself as warrior in the service of Dingiswayo, and later came to lead the Izicwe regiment. At Dingiswayo's urging, Senzangakhona had finally acknowledged Shaka as his heir, but there were other sons who felt Shaka had no right to the throne – not least because he hadn't lived with the Zulus since he was six. Thus, when Senzangakhona died, Dingiswayo allowed a strong contingent of Izicwe men to accompany Shaka, to help the Bastard Son claim the Zulu throne.

Declared King, the twenty-eight-year-old immediately set about reorganising the Zulu army. The tactics he had in mind required at least four regiments. A head and chest to engage the enemy and two horns to encircle them. This was the Way Of The Bull.

He called up all able-bodied males and grouped them in regiments – amabutho – according to age. Older, married men, who wore the isicoco, a fibre circlet woven into the hair and held in place with beeswax, went into the Amawombe, or Single Clash, regiment. A second group, comprising men a little younger, aged between twenty-six and thirty-one, who had taken the headring, but had not yet married, were forced to shave off the isicoco and became the Ujubingqwana, Shorn Heads. The remaining "bachelors" who had not yet taken the headring were organised as the Umgamule, Cut Through.

The youngest men formed the Ufasimba impi – the Haze. This was the one age group that would be trained in Shaka's methods from the start of its career, and the ibutho that would become Shaka's favourite. It was from Fasimba ranks that he'd choose his bodyguards.

In charge of these regiments, Shaka placed generals and indunas he had personally selected: men who were commoners and, in many cases, foreigners. It was a sly move. Hitherto clan and vassal chieftains had fielded and led their own "armies". It was one of the factors which meant the King's authority could never be absolute. Now, the commanders of the "new" army owed their elevation and therefore their allegiance solely to Shaka.

Having amabutho grouped according to age-sets and stationed at amakhanda, or special military kraals, also meant able-bodied males

were removed from the influence of their home clans. This strengthened their loyalty to Shaka, especially since they could see for themselves promotion from the ranks was within everyone's grasp, being
based on merit and not birth.

Next Shaka dispensed with the flimsy throwing spears favoured by the
tribes in the region and introduced a weapon he himself had adapted
while serving under Dingiswayo. This was the short, broad-bladed stabbing spear intended for close combat that came to be called the iklwa,
an onomatopoeic word mimicking the slurping, popping sound the
blade made when it was pulled out of a body. Shaka also had new cowhide shields made, shields that were larger and tougher than the old
ones.

While the spears were being assembled by the Zulu ironsmiths, Shaka
himself drilled his impis in the new tactics. He ordered them to throw
away their sandals and had them run back and forth across a parade
ground scattered with thorns to toughen their feet. Soon his men could
cover eighty kilometres in a day, trotting tirelessly across the veld and
the rolling, trackless hills.

Warriors at this time were expected to forage for themselves, and
another important innovation the new King introduced was having
twelve- and thirteen-year-old boys accompany the soldiers, carrying
rations, water gourds and sleeping mats. One boy would look after three
or four warriors, while indunas – senior officers – would have an udibi
to themselves.

*

"Remind us," says Shaka, indicating Mgobozi with a languid flick of his
hand, "remind us why we fight this crocodile!"

Mgobozi is from the Mthetwa tribe. He served with Shaka in the Izicwe regiment; fought shoulder to shoulder with the young Zulu. Soon
he too had discarded his sandals and was wielding the short stabbing
assegai Shaka favoured. He accompanied Shaka when the latter went to
claim the Zulu throne, and stayed on, helping to train the Zulu men in

the new tactics. Shaka put him in charge of the Fasimba impi. He would've made Mgobozi commander in chief of the Zulu army, but Mgobozi declined the offer. "I'll drill your men in peacetime, Father," he told Shaka, "but when it comes to war, I seek only to fight!"

All the same, much to the older man's chagrin, Shaka insists Mgobozi keep himself safe and stay out of the fighting as far as possible.

"Thrice did Dingiswayo have the Ndwandwes beneath his blade," says Mgobozi, "and thrice did our Father urge him to annihilate these animals, for many brave warriors had fallen in these campaigns and Zwide and his jackals were not to be trusted, but Dingiswayo did not heed our Father's counsel. A promise of loyalty was all he asked, for he was a kind man."

"It is so," murmurs Shaka. Words that are almost a growl.

"But kindness in these circumstances can be a treacherous concubine," adds Mgobozi. It is a necessary rider, since Shaka as King and Father of the Zulu people would also like to be regarded as a kind ruler.

"It is so . . . it is so . . ." murmur the indunas and warriors gathered around the fire.

Mgobozi goes on to tell how, after a period of uneasy peace, Zwide, without any provocation, fell on Matiwane and his Ngwanes, killing men, women and children and burning their kraals. Only the precious cattle were spared. When Dingiswayo angrily demanded the meaning of this massacre, wily Zwide claimed he'd received news the Ngwanes were plotting against Dingiswayo and had attacked them before they could bring their plans to fruition. He and his legions had been acting out of loyalty to Dingiswayo.

"It is so, my Brothers," says Mgobozi. "Zwide offered Dingiswayo a fine repast – of shit!"

Laughter ripples around the fire.

"And Dingiswayo saw it for what it was, and Zwide sent his sister, Ntombazana, daughter of Ntombazi Of The Skulls. She was to soothe the Wanderer's anger. Win his affections . . ."

Shaka smiles, shrugs: "She was a woman, this Ntombazana, my Children, and Dingiswayo was but a man. He was taken with her and she took him."

"Indeed," says Mgobozi. "She stole his seed."

A king's semen is regarded as the source of his power, a substance so precious it's not even used in the manufacture of the Inkatha, lest some of it be stolen for more nefarious purposes.

And this is precisely what occurred in Dingiswayo's case. Wily Zwide wanted once and for all to defeat his old nemesis and this was his sister's true mission. When she returned to her brother's kraal, the Ndwandwe medicine men went to work . . .

"And so brave and honourable Dingiswayo was cursed," says Mgobozi.

He takes a sip of sorghum beer and places the pot at his feet.

"Brothers," he says, "brave comrades-in-arms, you were there when, heeding Dingiswayo's call, we marched on the Ndwandwes! But the charm was already working. We were to march separately and strike together, but Dingiswayo neglected to send out his messengers to inform us of his movements."

The Mthetwa army halted close to KwaDlovungu, Zwide's capital. They were to await Shaka's impis, although Dingiswayo hadn't told them exactly where his forces would be. Instead, he set out accompanied only by five female bodyguards and was duly captured by a Ndwandwe patrol. The small group was escorted to KwaDlovungu, where Dingiswayo was cordially received by Zwide, who slaughtered an ox in his honour.

The following day, the ruler of the Mthetwas was executed.

"It is said his women fought bitterly to save him," says Mgobozi, "but he told them to desist. Do not grieve for me by fighting for a lost cause, he said. To his executioner he said: Drive your blade well and true, my son. And the deed was done. And his head was removed so that this Ntombazi might have another king's skull to add to her collection."

"And his women," adds Shaka. "His women, my Children – did they return home when Zwide told them to?"

"No, Father," comes the response.

"No. They encircled their fallen king and drove their blades into their own hearts! Will we be shamed by such loyalty?"

"No, Father! No! The jackal shall perish!"

The Ndwandwes fell on the Mthetwa army, which was unnerved by the disappearance of their king. The result was a rout. The only reason why the Zulus did not become involved was because Shaka and his men were intercepted by a messenger from Dondo of the Khumalos, informing them what had happened.

"Now all have become skulls for Ntombazi to gloat over," says Shaka. "Now this Devourer Of Kings would devour us!"

The men hiss.

"Know this, my Children: we fight for our lives! Death is the only mercy we can expect! He has sought and found a provocation and now he comes for us. For our women, our children, our cattle! But we have his measure. Believe me when I say this, my Children: the Bull Elephant has his measure. Let him come. He'll encounter a tempest the like of which this land has never seen. This land . . ." he whispers, gazing at the orange faces around the fire, the shadows of the warriors beyond, who loom up behind them, like pillars holding the sky aloft.

"Brave warriors about to go into battle are told: 'Be joyful, Embo awaits you!' And this is so. But I tell you this, my Children: do this, defeat these lice and *this* awaits you!" Shaka spreads his arms. "These green hills, these plains and swollen rivers! Standing shoulder to shoulder you have the power to win this land. To rule this land. Let this treacherous crocodile come – let *him* come! He will taste the gruel of defeat. And you are the ones who will do this. *You!*"

*

Early the next morning, before the warriors in the sky have extinguished all their campfires, a small group rises and quietly leaves the main body. It comprises the King, Mgobozi, a detachment of ten bodyguards led by the Induna and the Induna's udibi, who carries extra spears and water gourds for the party.

The King and his Fasimbas have been hunting to the southwest of KwaBulawayo. Now at the languid, loping jog trot favoured by the Zulu army on the move, Shaka leads the small group eastward.

5
The Englishmen

De la Vere and Boyd have come up from the Cape, where De la Vere was able to trade on his family name to finance their expedition. Even those who hadn't heard of the Sussex de la Veres were impressed by having a member of the titled gentry come calling, even if De la Vere was only a baronet.

Such snobbishness is common in the colonies. While portrayed as places where a man can make himself away from the class-conscious strictures of the motherland, the good burghers nonetheless crave the legitimacy their new-found wealth will acquire through dealings with members of the British aristocracy. The fact that De la Vere was also a veteran of Waterloo made his ingress into what passed for society in the Colony even smoother.

Boyd, on the other hand, is one of those dissolute younger sons a wealthy father has sent away, with a monthly stipend, to indulge his vices on distant shores. Putting his distaste aside, De la Vere had gone out of his way to befriend the fop – for investors were one thing, but a source of ready cash for sundry day-to-day expenses was also to be welcomed.

That distaste was the only obstacle in De la Vere's "courtship" of Boyd, for Stanley was like the lonely put-upon fat child at a public school, only too eager to win the school captain's protection.

They travel with three wagons, each pulled by six oxen, and the expedition – such as it is – is a combination of exploration and gain. They've heard of plentiful ivory to be found along the east coast. At the same time, they also want to explore the possibility of establishing a lasting relationship with a local tribe, who will supply them with tusks.

They're accompanied by a group of servants to see to the oxen and an interpreter they hired in King Williams Town. Of mixed blood, he speaks English and Xhosa, which language, their business partners in the Colony have assured them, is not much different to the dialects spoken by the tribes living in the territories around the bay of Natal. His name is Jacob, but they call him Tuppence, although they doubt he's worth even that . . .

*

Boyd slots the butt against his shoulder and, keeping the barrel lowered at a forty-five-degree angle, pretends to take aim at a distant spot. Actually, the gun, a two-bore flintlock, with a deep fish-belly curve on the underside of the buttstock to absorb the recoil, is so heavy, that's about as high as he can keep the barrel raised for any length of time.

"Bang!" he says. "Loud thunder! You kill many savages."

"Warriors," interjects De la Vere with a hiss.

"Right. Don't translate that. I mean you kill many warriors! Many, many warriors with this magic spear!"

Cha! growls Zwide. *How much beer has this fool drunk?*

"What's he say?" says Boyd to their interpreter.

Or perhaps, Father, we *have not drunk* enough *beer!* says Nomahlanjana.

The Nguni tribes along the east coast of southern Africa have long known about guns, which they call izibhamu. Portuguese sailors seeking a sea route to India – and harbours where their ships could replenish their water supplies and victuals – first introduced the locals to these "magic spears", and the tales have been passed down from generation to generation. Then there's the Colony in the Cape; since the late 1700s hunters and trappers have been making the two-month journey to this territory.

De la Vere pushes Tuppence forward. "Do your job!"

"No, wait," says Boyd, "let's start again." He balances the gun across both hands. "See? This gun. Ga-un. This magic spear. Mag-gick."

He turns his head toward their interpreter. "Go on . . ."

Tuppence sighs. *He's showing you his gun. He wants you to look surprised.*

And you, Half-breed? What are you doing with these simpletons?

Not to impugn your wisdom, Nkosi, but I am no half-breed. I am Xhosa!

Zwide squints at him. *And my cows have pricks!*

"What's he say?" interrupts De la Vere, grabbing Tuppence's shoulder.

"He is mightily impressed with your magic spear."

"Jolly good," says Boyd. Nodding at Zwide and his son, he says: "Jolly good!"

Look at those cheeks, my Son – have you ever seen such redness?

Aiee, no, my Father!

Reacting to De la Vere's glare and the bite of his fingers on his collarbone, Tuppence tells the two Englishmen that the king and his son are still remarking on the "magic spear".

What are you telling them, Half-breed?

That you are in awe of their magic!

Zwide rocks with laughter.

Boyd joins in with theatrical joviality. "That's the spirit, you Black Bastard! Lap it up!"

See, Father? He laughs too.

Cha! That is nothing! Watch – Keeping his eyes locked on the fat Englishman, Zwide curls his right arm, lays a fist over his heart, then extends his arm outwards . . .

With due solemnity, Boyd mirrors the gesture. When the Ndwandwe king wiggles his fingers, he does likewise.

Nomahlanjana snorts beer out of his nose and topples sideways in an avalanche of laughter.

"I do believe they have taken a liking to us," observes Boyd.

"Yes, you appear to have bowled them over."

De la Vere's sarcasm draws a quizzical glance from his companion. "What's the matter?" asks Boyd.

"I don't trust these savages."

"Neither do I, but they have their uses."

Nomahlanjana, meanwhile, raises a languid arm. Immediately two of the bodyguard arranged behind Zwide and his son rush forward and pull the prince upright.

You see? We can control these fools.

It is so, Father, says Nomahlanjana, wiping tears of mirth from his eyes.

"I think a little thunder is in order. Give me the gun . . ."

"A capital idea," says Boyd.

And you say these two come in search of ivory?

Tuppence nods. *That is so, Nkosi. It is a valuable commodity to them.*

And in return they would aid us in our war against these Zulu upstarts!

So it is true, Nkosi?

What is?

You would go to war against the Zulus?

We have no choice, Half-breed, interjects Nomahlanjana. *These Zulus do not honour their debts. They are cowards!*

De la Vere has turned his back to Zwide and his son and is loading the gun.

So! They would aid us against the Zulus, says Zwide.

Yes, Nkosi.

Fools! Do they not know we could fall on them and take their guns for ourselves?

Apparently not, Nkosi.

Zwide shakes his head in disbelief.

Or maybe, adds the interpreter, *they feel their guns would be worthless to you without their knowledge . . .*

You could show us.

I do not know how they work.

Liar!

"Tell them to watch," says De la Vere, stepping away from the group.

You are about to be amazed, Nkosi, says the interpreter.

The massive flintlock was originally intended for elephants, or so the

Dutch farmer who sold the weapon to them claimed, but De la Vere believes they've been duped. It's much too heavy to be lugged around on hunting expeditions, where one often needs to reload while on horseback.

However, it ought to provide for an impressive demonstration, so maybe their rix-dollars weren't wasted. Grimacing at the weight, De la Vere raises the flintlock to his shoulder, takes aim, squeezes the trigger and a tree stump explodes in a shower of splinters.

"Laugh at that, you sooty bastards," he says stepping away from the cloud of smoke.

Such a roar, observes Nomahlanjana.

And to what purpose?

Tuppence raises his eyebrows. *Didn't you see?*

See what?

The tree stump.

Zwide leans sideways trying to peer in the direction the interpreter is pointing. *What tree stump?*

Exactly!

Show some respect, Half-breed, says Nomahlanjana.

Tuppence inclines his head toward Zwide. *My apologies, Nkosi. But didn't you see? He shot the tree stump.*

Was it threatening us?

Truly, Father, chuckles Nomahlanjana, *I have always said that was a particularly sullen tree stump.*

No, Nkosi, says Tuppence. *He was merely showing you the power of his weapon.*

And when we are attacked by trees we will be sure to beg for the White Man's assistance.

It is so, Father! I have heard it whispered the acacias are growing restive. Although it may just be the wind. Aiee! Maybe they are plotting with the wind!

"What the hell are they saying?"

Tuppence turns to Boyd. "They are mightily impressed."

"Really?" murmurs De la Vere. "They don't look it."

Please, Nkosi, says the interpreter, *we Xhosas like a joke as much as the next man, but . . .*

Your masters grow petulant?

As children, Nkosi. Although they are not my masters.

May I speak, Father?

Zwide nods.

They have but a few guns and there are many Zulus, it is so, says Nomahlanjana, *but would it not be better to have their hot air blowing at our backs, rather than in our faces? Our magic is strong, but let us make it stronger by entering into an accord with these jackals. We lose nothing, and who knows? We may yet find a use for their arrogance.*

6
The Place

"What say you, Brave Mgobozi?"

The general scratches his head. Smiles ruefully. "It is audacious, Father."

"It is inspired!"

"It is mad!"

Shaka favours Mgobozi with a wry grin. "Do not be afraid to speak your mind on this matter, Old Friend. You need not be wary of my wrath."

"And indeed, Father, such wrath would've been warranted had I called your plan 'madness'. But I did not, Father. Truly, I did not. I said only that it was *mad*!"

"Cha! Those are two cows that stand very close together in the kraal."

"That may be, Father. But I remember a young induna who was called mad for going into battle with a broken spear."

"And bare feet!"

"Yes!"

"And when that induna ran too far, too fast after his hungry assegai, who was there behind him to protect his back?"

Mgobozi chuckles.

Shaka answers his own question: "Another mad one, I think!"

"Cha! Mgobozi could not let this Zulu outdo him!"

Shaka laughs and lays a hand on his most-trusted general's shoulder. "So – what say you, Old Friend? Let this be where the matter is decided?"

Mgobozi gazes around. Nods. "Let this be where the matter is decided."

It is almost mid-morning and the sun still has to chase the cold shadows from the groves and ravines. They are standing on a hill a little to the south of the White Umfolozi. Long gentle slopes curve up to meet the ridge of the summit. Skirting the summit, this ridge hides a shallow hollow. At its base, the hill has a circumference of about two thousand metres. It's surrounded by flat grassland, turning yellow now that winter's approaching; ant hills add smears of red and flat-topped acacias and ragged bushwillows are dotted here and there.

Shaka stands with his legs apart, his hands on his hips, gazing at the countryside. Down there, he's told Mgobozi, the Way Of The Bull will not serve us. There are too many of them. We will fight like lions and they will surround us, surround us without even trying, and victory will be theirs. But, if first we allow them to surround us and then fight like lions . . . Then, Old Friend, victory will be ours!

"Yes," he says, "this is where the matter will be decided."

He swings round. "What say you, Nduna?"

The Induna moves forward. This was where he found the King on his return from the Khumalos a few months ago. He peers out over the veld.

After a while he says: "I see no water, Father."

Shaka laughs, claps the young officer on his shoulder. "This is a wise one."

"This is so," grins Mgobozi.

"No water!" roars Shaka. "But *we* will have water. And food. And what will they have?"

"They will only have their fear to gnaw on," murmurs the Induna.

*

The grass domes of KwaBulawayo are in sight when Shaka, leading the way, stops suddenly. Moving up behind him, Mgobozi asks what's wrong. The King hesitates a moment, squinting at the huts in their circular orderliness. The cows grazing outside the stockades. The slender streams of smoke rising into the blue sky.

From this distance, the huts resemble upturned drinking bowls.

"It is nothing," murmurs Shaka, and moves on, the others trailing behind him.

But a short time later, when they have reached the broad path that leads to the main gate, Shaka holds up his hand. Immediately, the bodyguard detail commanded by the Induna runs forward, to line up on either side of their King in a V-shape with Shaka at the apex. The Induna himself takes up a position a little in front of the formation.

"Something is wrong," says Shaka.

7
The Messenger

It might just work. They'll be more involved in things than they had intended, but that also means the reward they can expect will be greater. Assuming this savage can be trusted, of course . . .

Then again, it's not as if they're after something these people regard as being especially valuable. De la Vere has already seen enough ivory lying around the place to fill one wagon. This Zwide might even think he's getting the better part of the deal. They rid him of Shaka and all he has to do is allow them to hunt for ivory . . .

The fact that this will mean travelling with the Ndwandwe army when they go out to seek the Zoolas *is* worrying, but De la Vere reckons it's worth the risk.

It was disconcerting when these savages didn't react quite the way they expected them to on being shown the "magic spears." The visions they had of firing a few shots and watching the heathen hordes turn tail and scamper away or drop obediently to their knees were a little optimistic. Clearly, though, Zwide had given the matter some thought – in itself a sign he does understand the potential of having guns on his side, even if one is not going to be much good against hundreds of the screaming bastards – and the cunning old savage had hit upon the one way a single gun could be of value to the Ndwandwes.

He'd approached the Englishmen with his plan during last night's feast. "Your gun shoots straight?" he wanted to know through the interpreter.

"That it does," had been De la Vere's reply.

"It shoots far?"

"Further than a man can throw a spear or shoot an arrow, old boy."

"And you want ivory?"

De la Vere had nodded.

Zwide spoke again and Tuppence hesitated.

"What is it?" De la Vere had asked.

"He says . . ."

"Out with it, man!"

"He says if you want ivory, you must kill Shaka."

"Fair enough. Tell me where I can find him." It was the beer that had replied for the Englishman.

Tuppence conveyed this to the Ndwandwe king who responded with a burst of that angular language of theirs, all clicks and hard vowels.

"What's he say?"

"He says you will come with the army. They will find Shaka for you – for he accompanies his men into battle – then you can earn your ivory."

*

Like KwaBulawayo, Zwide's kraal is built on a slight incline, but this settlement is horseshoe-shaped and surrounded by a palisade of roughly

49

hewn poles bound together with grass ropes. The king's compound is situated at the highest point and consists of the five huts of his wives with his larger dwelling in the centre.

A similar compound – of six huts surrounding a larger one – has been constructed about five hundred metres away from the main kraal. It's reached via a closely guarded side gate and houses Zwide's mother, Ntombazi, and her collection of skulls.

As Zwide's legions have hacked their way ever closer to hegemony, so has KwaDlovungu grown. Now it comprises more than five hundred huts and the tips of the horseshoe have reached the shallow stream that flows along the bottom of the incline. With the Ndwandwes preparing for war, regiments from surrounding villages and vassal tribes have come to the capital and they camp on the opposite rise.

But it's a young boy who's caught Oliver de la Vere's eye.

He must be about ten, scrawny, with skinny spider legs, and he's moving with a stubborn purpose, his skin glistening like mud.

"What is it?" asks Boyd, hoisting himself to his feet.

"I don't know."

As the two Englishmen watch, one of Zwide's officers, a warrior they recognise as Soshangane, moves to intercept the lad.

"Perhaps a messenger of some sort," says De la Vere.

They can see the boy's tiny chest heaving as he struggles to catch his breath. Another officer has followed Soshangane and now he hands the lad a gourd of water. Greedily, the boy snatches it, hoists it to his mouth with both hands – and Soshangane has to snatch the gourd back after he's taken a few gulps so he doesn't make himself sick.

Too late – the boy turns away and vomits.

He would collapse, but the second officer grabs him by the elbows and wheels him round to face Soshangane.

The Englishmen can clearly hear the words he barks at the boy – presumably telling him to pull himself together.

At last the boy can speak. Soshangane listens intently.

"Clearly a messenger," murmurs De la Vere.

"The Zoolas?"

"Must be."

Soshangane straightens, turns, sets off for Zwide's compound. Releasing the boy's elbows, letting him drop into the dust, the other officer follows him.

Zwide appears at the gate of the compound; obviously he's been told about the messenger's arrival. As the Englishmen watch, Soshangane begins to relay the boy's message. Zwide steps past the officer to get a better look at the boy. Soshangane bellows a command and the warriors who have gathered around the child with their questions immediately move aside. At a signal from the officer, one lifts the lad to his feet.

Zwide examines him, nods and turns his attention back to Soshangane. He says something, asks a question, perhaps. The officer nods vigorously. Zwide throws his head back and roars.

A bellow of triumph.

"Well, well, well," mutters De la Vere. "I wouldn't get too comfortable if I were you, old boy," he tells Stanley. "It seems as if this Shaka awaits us."

*

Zwide turns back to Soshangane. "Tell me again," he commands. "It is so?"

"Sire," grins the officer, "it is so. Nebo, your most trusted spy, saw this for himself and sent the boy to tell us."

"Then we have him! We have this Beetle for the crushing! Tell the men to make ready – we march at dawn."

8
The Outrage

The impis rise when Shaka enters the cattlefold.

Several paces behind him, the Induna extends both arms and the men who accompanied the King to the hill come to a halt.

Silence has the kraal by the throat. Assegais bristle like the fur of an angry leopard.

Shaka strides over to the circle of stones that mark the fireplace. The pot lies shattered, the King's precious bodily fluids spilt across the ground. The Inkatha itself has been hacked to pieces.

He can't let his anger show. Standing with his hands on his hips, he surveys this outrage, grateful the sun is behind him, leaving his face shadowed.

"Father?" whispers Mgobozi, about the only man who'd dare approach the King at this moment.

"What is it?" asks Shaka without turning around.

"This Mabhubesi, he tended the fire all night, as is custom. And this morning no one approached the cattlefold, as is also the way. It was the first soldiers who returned from the Washing, they discovered this outrage."

"They speak the truth, Father."

Shaka wheels round. Pampata has made her way past the huts between the inner and outer stockades and has approached Shaka and Mgobozi from the direction of the main gate. A slender young woman in her mid-twenties, with lean thighs and firm, rounded breasts, she wears a short skirt comprising strings of multicoloured beads.

She's been Shaka's lover and close confidante since the days he fought in Dingiswayo's army. Having killed in battle, it is a soldier's duty to sula izembe, cleanse the axe, by sleeping with the first woman he sees. Until he's done so, the warrior is considered unclean. No woman can refuse a soldier's request to sula izembe – and Pampata always made sure she was the first woman Shaka encountered after returning from a battle.

While he was away with the army, she'd visit his mother every day and help Nandi with the rituals meant to ensure a warrior's safe return. She'd also look after Shaka's hut, sweeping the floor and lighting a small fire every night.

When a warrior has gone to war, his sleeping mat has to be kept rolled up and leaning upright against the rear wall of his hut; if it falls over, it's believed the soldier will die. Pampata would tie Shaka's mat to the wall.

"Why are you still here?" growls Shaka. The women and children are in the process of being evacuated and Shaka's mother, Nandi, has already left with a contingent of bodyguards. Pampata was supposed to accompany them.

"I was about to depart when this thing was reported to me," she says.

"You were meant to leave two days ago, Woman."

"This is so, but one of the women was about to give birth. I stayed and tended her."

"Then you will go now."

"I will stay." Pampata smiles. "I will stay to spend one more night with you."

"Will you ever obey me, Woman, without an argument?"

"I live my life for you, Father."

It's mid-afternoon and the sun bakes the dirt. The cloudless sky shines like the finest silk. There's no wind and silence binds the men gathered in the cattlefold; shackles of fear and unease.

"Father," says Pampata, "I beg of you – keep your anger in check today. You know none could have prevented this, because none would've been allowed here. You know this, Father."

Shaka nods slowly. Then, remembering something, he turns to Mgobozi. "Where are his apprentices?"

As junior sangomas they would've been the only ones allowed into the cattlefold while Mabhubesi was mixing the special muthi.

Pampata answers for the general. "They are over there," she says, pointing to where a small group of men stand a little to the side of the main body. Two of the warriors are clutching a slender teenager between them.

"Where are the other three?" asks Shaka.

"The indunas of the first impi to discover this acted too late to prolong their suffering."

"Where are their bodies?"

"Where the vultures circle and the hyenas praise you for your generosity."

"Good." To Mgobozi, the King says: "Bring that dead man to me."

At Mgobozi's signal, the teenager is dragged forward. Gently, Shaka places the tip of his assegai under the boy's chin and raises his head. Puffy, swollen eyes, like big black beetles against his skin; lips knuckles have crushed; a steady stream of blood flowing from the nostrils of a broken nose.

"Where has your master gone?" asks Shaka softly.

The youth shakes his head.

"Taste the words I want to hear or your own testicles. The choice is yours."

Hanging limply between the two soldiers, the boy shakes his head again.

"Did your master think that he could harm me by breaking the Inkatha and desecrating it? Did he?"

The boy remains limp.

"As you wish. You would use sorcery on me, then you shall die like a sorcerer!"

To Mgobozi, Shaka says: "You know what to do . . ."

"It shall be a pleasure, Father!"

"Now go," Shaka tells Pampata, "I would address the men. Return to your hut. Wait for me there."

"Now *that* is a command I will gladly obey."

"Go, Sister!"

Mgobozi, meanwhile, has shouted his orders and three men come running. The one clutches several lengths of wood used to make the iklwa, the other carries a rock a little bigger than a man's fist.

Shaka steps forward. Raises his shield and assegai.

"Children! Are you angry?"

Cries of "Yes!" from the soldiers. "Yes, Father!"

"Are you enraged?"

"Yes!"

"Are you afraid?"

"No!" cry the men. "No!"

"Cha! You should be!"

The apprentice shaman is thrust face forward onto the ground. One of the warriors settles himself on the teenager's back, and leans forward to pinion the boy's arms away from his body. Two other warriors each grab hold of an ankle and pull the shaman's legs apart. Then they squat, resting their weight on the boy's ankles so he can't move his legs.

"You should be very afraid!" shouts Shaka. "This deceitful one, he hasn't destroyed the Inkatha. This is merely grass, merely a symbol of our power. But because he believes he can weaken us in this manner, by befouling our sacred ceremony, he has angered the ancestors. That is why you must be afraid! For woe betide you as surely as the coming of the dawn if you do not move to avenge this insult! The ancestors are angry and only we can appease them!"

Mgobozi takes the rock and, gripping one of the stakes in his other hand, steps between the teenager's legs.

"Children: this is not a curse on us! This is a curse on *him*! And those Ndwandwe jackals he doubtless serves. *They* are his masters, not the ancestors! He mocks the ancestors! So let us not cower! Let us add vengeance to the fires that burn in our chests!"

Mgobozi kneels and gently fits the sharp end of the stake between the boy's buttocks. The teenager tries to twist and turn, but the three soldiers hold him fast. Mgobozi takes careful aim – and, using the rock, begins to hammer the stake into the apprentice shaman's anus.

"Listen to me, my Children! We march at dawn . . ."

The teenager screams. The soldier sitting on his back pushes his face into the dust. "Silence!" he hisses. "The King speaks." Mgobozi is handed another stake.

"We march at dawn," continues Shaka, "and I'll show you a true ring of power! A ring of true unity! I'll show you the true Inkatha. For am I not your Father?"

Carefully, carefully, Mgobozi places the tip of the second stake on the flattened head of the first. Then, in case the boy moves, he quickly brings the rock down.

"Am I not your Liberator?"

A writhing, twisting scream. Mgobozi slams the rock down again.

"I *am* your Father! I *am* your Liberator! I *am* the Bull Elephant who will crush our enemies into the dust!"

The apprentice shaman sags into unconsciousness. Mgobozi stands, tosses the rock aside. "Take him away!" he says.

Two soldiers each grab an arm. They'll drag the dying youth to the Place Of Execution.

"My Children: we march at dawn, and I will show you true power!"

Mgobozi has retrieved his shield and spear; now, he raises the latter. "Bayede!" he bellows. "Bayede, Nkosi Yamakosi!" *Hail, King of Kings!*

The impis' assegais pierce the blue sky. "Bayede! Bayede, Nkosi Yamakosi! Bayede!"

*

While the officers march their men out of the cattlefold, Shaka calls the Induna over to him.

"Ndabezitha!" he says. *Your Majesty . . .*

Shaka moves up close to him, so close the Induna can feel the heat of his rage.

"Nduna," hisses Shaka, "you will find this creature. I would piss on his pelt before nightfall!"

9
The Search

The Induna orders five groups of twenty men to follow the major paths that radiate out from KwaBulawayo. Those who'll take the trail leading in the direction of Ndwandwe territory are warned to be especially careful not to engage any of Zwide's patrols.

After the warriors have left, the Induna turns his attention to the desecration: the broken pot, the dark stain in the sand that seems resistant to the sun's rays, the grass ring.

He sinks onto his haunches. This has been bothering him while Shaka spoke to the troops: Mabhubesi was here throughout the night, mixing the muthi, the strong medicine to bind the Inkatha – why didn't he do what he did then? He and his apprentices could have been far, far away by now . . .

Pampata was right. No one would've dared enter the cattlefold – only the warriors returning from the Washing are allowed to.

Mabhubesi did this thing. There's no doubt about that. It's *when* he did it that perplexes the Induna. Why didn't he do it at night when he would've had ample time to make good his escape?

And look here.

The grass circle lies hacked apart amid a welter of tiny indentations. A profusion of miniature crevices in the dirt.

The Induna stands. Toys with his assegai.

First he thrusts it downward in an underarm motion.

No, that's not right.

The angle is awkward, the twist of his wrist uncomfortable. He switches the position of his hand so as to employ a stabbing motion.

Yes!

Yes, this is what he did. On his knees, the sangoma stabbed at the ring. The tip of the assegai blade fits neatly into the indentations. He stabbed at the Inkatha.

And he was angry, because see how many times he missed!

Mabhubesi performed the first part of the ritual, accepting the sacred offerings from the King. He and his apprentices worked here all night, tending to the pot and the fire, none of them sleeping.

Then something changed.

The sangoma grew angry, broke the pot and attacked the ring, stabbing at it with an assegai.

The Induna frowns, marshalling his thoughts. The shaman performed the first part of the ceremony. Then, sometime during the night, when men are at their most vulnerable, when the tikoloshe come out, evil, wiry creatures with monkeys' bodies and dogs' snouts, bad thoughts entered his mind.

Cha! But a tikoloshe ought to be no match for a Zulu shaman! Could it be, then, this was a consummation of resentments long hidden? Could it be that his legs were already open, his mind the wet loins of a concubine awaiting her lover? He would not serve Shaka! Shaka who would clamp down on the power and prestige enjoyed by sangomas! He destroys the Inkatha, then flees . . . And because he is no fool, he must have known that, despite his age, he had a chance of getting away!

"Master?"

The Induna turns.

"We are ready."

The boy has packed supplies, filled their water gourds, rolled up two sleeping mats and is carrying the Induna's shield and a clutch of extra spears.

The Induna accepts the shield, but waves away the sleeping mat and gourd of water. "We will not need those."

"But the King . . ."

The Induna grins. The boy is not being impudent. Shaka has ordered the Induna to capture the sangoma by nightfall. If he fails, then, chances are, the udibi will receive the same punishment as his master.

Sending the soldiers off was merely a precautionary measure, however, and the Induna tells the boy not to worry. "We will find this creature," he says. "But not out there!"

"Master?"

"He is here, Boy. I smell him. He is somewhere nearby."

The boy looks around nervously.

"Not *here*. But nearby."

As another precautionary measure, though, the udibi is to round up a group of senior herdboys – they will do as he commands even if he is younger than them, because he is the Induna's udibi. "They know where they go to hide from angry parents, or when they would not do their chores. They are to search these places, as well as the empty huts. Do you understand?"

The boy nods, proud to be placed in charge.

"The guard at the gate and the King's compound will be doubled. They have instructions to listen to your call should you find this creature."

"We will find him, Master!"

The Induna chuckles. "I do not think so."

"Master!" says the boy, struggling to keep indignation out of his voice. "We *will* find him!"

"I think not, Boy, because I am going to fetch him."

"You know where he is?"

"I have an idea."

"But then, Master, let us . . ."

"No, Boy, you will obey my command. You will search every hiding place in this kraal. Because I may be wrong. And because I may be wrong, you will act wisely and with caution. You find him, you call for help. Do you understand?"

"Yes, Master!"

"Now go! I have a foolish lion to catch."

*

The Induna passes the warriors tasked with disposing of the apprentice shaman's body. They salute him, looking sheepish and nervous, and continue back to KwaBulawayo. He soon sees the reason for their guilty behaviour. They haven't gone all the way to the Place Of Execution; have simply rolled the corpse down a bank some distance from the cliff.

Shaking his head, the Induna continues along the path. The bank grows steeper until it becomes a sheer drop. All Zulu kraals have a place such as this, where criminals and sorcerers receive their just desserts, the former throttled first, the latter impaled like Mabhubesi's apprentice.

The Induna peers over the edge. A tangle of bones and skulls . . .

And the four apprentices, in their cowhide cloaks.

The Induna grins.

A second path branches off from the first. It leads to a natural stairway of roots and branches down a narrow defile. It's steep, but not so steep a man can't traverse it with a shield and spear. It's the route the slayers take to go and make sure the condemned are truly dead.

10
The Storm

Lightning tears the night. Boulders rumble across the sky. But it's a constipated sky and this is the restless flank of a storm to the north. When his eyes become used to the dark again, the figure pushes on. He's running along a tightrope, following a narrow strand of mud between the shallows of the stream and the gravel on the bank. Every now and then his foot slaps water, but he keeps moving, knowing the noise will be lost amid that of the night. He's already past the picquets, anyway, so he can afford to substitute speed for stealth.

*

Carefully, gently, not stabbing, not breaking the surface, the Induna pushes the tip of his iklwa into the cowhide cloak. Holds it there for a few seconds, denting the hide between the body's shoulder blades; a prolonged pressure, a steel fingertip demanding attention.

"Awake! Arise!" he says, lifting the blade away. Still keeping the cloak wrapped around himself, groaning and sighing like one aroused from a deep sleep to attend to trivial matters, the sangoma rolls over.

*

Another streak of lightning. The man drops onto his hands and knees, becomes a boulder beneath his cloak. An avalanche of thunder. He takes this moment to catch his breath. And hears something.

He raises his head above the cloak. Men grumbling about the weather. Another voice, from further off, telling them to quieten down. Some muttering, sinking like silt into the noise from the stream, then silence.

The shape darts forward again.

*

The Lion frees his right hand to shield his eyes as he gazes up at the Induna.

"You!"

The Induna, an ebony statue fringed by sunlight, nods.

"So it is true," says the older man, "what they say." When the warrior makes no response, he continues: "About your wisdom, your prowess . . ." His hand comes away from his forehead in a waving gesture. "Please! The sun . . ."

The Induna drops to his haunches; seems to lean against the haft of his spear. In reality, though, the weight of his body rests on his feet, his ankles, and he can bring the weapon into play easily and without losing his balance.

The sangoma hoists himself up onto one elbow. "An old man thanks you."

*

A minute or so later, where the bank dips, the man halts again. Listens. Looks around. There's a stagnant quality about the air, a tense waiting; even the crickets and frogs are silent. It's only men who make any noise beneath this lowering sky. Coughs. Groans. The whimper of a youth lost in restless dreams on the eve of his first battle. Over his shoulder to his right, the man can just make out the shapes of this sleeping army and knows more than one pair of eyes will be awake and, possibly, looking this way.

He leans against the broken bank and uses his elbows to worm his way up and into the grass. Without pausing, he crawls forward on his stomach. Elbows and feet; the grass stabbing his belly. Forward. Body twisting this way and that, in measured, sinuous movement; clods of earth scraping his elbows, his knees, the rustling insanely loud in his ears.

*

"How did you know?"

The Induna shrugs. "I asked myself where I would hide had I need to wait until nightfall, where no one would think of looking. And coming here I saw four fresh bodies, which I thought strange, since you had only four apprentices and the fourth body lies back there . . ."

"I didn't expect them to sacrifice themselves. I told them to run."

"Did you?"

The shaman chuckles. "I thought it. I willed it. It was foremost on my mind."

"As you slipped away."

"Yes."

"Because they couldn't know where you intended to hide."

"No. Shaka's questions have a way of being answered, no matter how fervent one's loyalty. But, truly, I did not mean for them to sacrifice themselves."

"They didn't have to. You did it for them."

"Can I help it if they stood around like old women wondering what to do next?"

"A harsh lesson."

"With a harsh penalty for failure. But this is not an easy profession."

"And one which has just got a little more onerous."

"This is so."

"Revenge has these hazards."

"Revenge?"

"Come now – did you not destroy the sacred Inkatha to avenge those of your profession whom Shaka has vanquished?"

*

When he's in the shadow of the stockade, the man stands. Brushes the dirt from his elbows. Removes a few thorns. He's plotted a course that's taken him diagonally to the wall and kept him out of sight from those who guard the gate. Keeping to these deeper, darker shadows, so no one on the opposite slope can see him, he follows the stockade up the shallow incline.

*

The sangoma sits up.

"No! No, Nduna, do not be misled as to my motives! I do not care for those fools! They debase the calling as surely as Shaka. No, Nduna! Slay me for the right reasons!"

The cowhide cloak falls from the old man's shoulders as he brings up his hands to emphasise his words. "Do you not see what this madman does to us? Blood is all we taste these dark days. The ancestors weep to see such suffering. And I am not alone, Nduna. Others feel likewise, but all live in fear. I speak for the ancestors and our words will spread across the land like the coming of spring."

"More like a pestilence, I think."

"Are you blind, Nduna? Yet again our men must march against the Ndwandwes! Who will it be next time?"

"We did not look for this fight!"

"Cha! Shaka would've found a pretext! Zwide they call the Devourer Of Kings, but his appetite is no match for Shaka's gluttony. He hungers for power and he would destroy his own people in the process!"

*

The man stops a few paces past where the stockade begins to curve inward. This is far enough. Reaching over his right shoulder with his left hand he removes the jewelled dagger from its scabbard. And begins to saw at the bindings that hold the poles in place.

*

"Yet when he called upon you to perform the Inkatha – a signal honour – you obeyed promptly. Or was there treachery in your heart all along?"

"Not treachery. Confusion. I would obey the King, but what is one to do when the King is not worthy of such loyalty, when by obeying you would hasten the demise of the nation?"

"Zwide promises that! Not Shaka!"

"Zwide we will survive. The same cannot be said of Shaka. He would debase our sacred ceremonies."

"This you know?"

"This the ancestors know!"

"Ah! The ancestors . . ."

"I do not expect you to believe me. I would only plant the seeds – Shaka's rain of blood will do the rest. You will see . . . One day, you will see I am right."

*

After cutting the bindings on four poles, the man sheaths the dagger. Pulling one pole toward him, he steps up close to the stockade and stretches his right arm sideways through the gap. Pushing the other three poles outward, he eases through the opening. Then, he repositions the poles so the gap in the fence won't be too obvious.

He's just finished when he hears a groggy voice asking who's there?

Smaller rectangular structures comprising thatch mats fastened over looped poles and used to store grain are built along the wall and he ducks down into the opening of one of these. Repeating its querulous question, the shape solidifies into a small head on a barrelled chest balanced atop bow legs.

The man stops alongside the low storage shelter.

Snorts.

Belches.

Farts.

Proceeds to piss.

A mighty torrent. The crouching figure feels the wetness seep between his toes.

"Come on, come on," growls the other man, clenching his buttocks.

Then, looking down at his crotch, his eyes drift to the side.

Before he can even gasp in surprise, a fist snakes upward out of the darkness. Knuckles find his chin and he's sent spinning into the next storage hut. A fist in the stomach knocks his shout for help out of his mouth, curls him forward, gasping for breath. Then a knee flattens his nose and night invades his head.

*

The sangoma they call the Lion shrugs. "It doesn't matter what I say. What will be, will be. The bones do not lie. Shaka will triumph, it is so, but it will be a false dawn. They will come riding their winged canoes." He lifts the sheathed dagger away from his chest. "We defeated the Arabi, it is true. The Feared Ones with their vulture noses and long hair who stole our children, took them to the land beneath the horizon – we bested them. But these ones, these pink Long Noses, they are more powerful. Already their spies are among us. They will come for gold, for ivory, for diamonds, but they will take so much more."

"All the more reason for a strong leader."

"The depredations wrought by Shaka will make it easier for them. And he will protect them!"

"*Protect* them?"

"Why not? They'll offer him even greater power. Or so it will seem. But these beasts from the sea are cunning."

"You speak of things to come, Old Man. The ancestors promise good crops, but where are these good crops if the people decide not to sow the seeds? See, some will say, a bad omen! We will lose this battle! But what of the victors? Would they say that was a bad omen? You destroyed the Inkatha, but if your intent was to destroy the King's power, you have failed. Cha! Perhaps we should be thanking you – you've bound the Children Of The Sky together in a way woven grass could never have."

The Lion grins. "Then let me go free! I have done Shaka's bidding."

The Induna laughs. "Only in the way Zwide does Shaka's bidding by offering his forces up to us for annihilation. Speak of things to come, but it is the hot air of a traveller telling of a country he's never visited – wild stories that fool only children. The future is a drum, but we, the drummers, determine the tempo. Speak of things to come, but I will concern myself with the present."

The Lion stands, his knees clicking. "Believe me, disbelieve me, it matters not. Now let us get this final calumny over with!"

"Where is your lion-skin, your medicine bag?"

"Hidden over there," says the Lion, pointing past the Induna.

In rising, he has casually gripped the sheath of his Arabi dagger, as though to stop it swinging away from his chest. When he points – and the Induna turns to look away – the shaman brings his hand back, plucks the dagger from its sheath, held steady by his other hand – and swings it outward, so that when the Induna looks back at him, it's to find the blade moving through an arc that ends in his jugular.

*

If Zwide's taken by surprise, he doesn't show it. His eyes hidden in the darkness under his brow, he examines the intruder. A tall man wearing a leather loincloth and a lion-skin cloak. The head, fangs bared and frozen in a roar, rests atop the man's head; a leather thong along his collarbones fixes the skin over his shoulders; the front paws hang down his chest; the tail and hind legs dangle behind him. Slung diagonally across his chest is a satchel made from a cow's udder – his medicine bag.

"Ha!" says the Ndwandwe king. "Your reputation precedes you and news of your most recent deeds is even fleeter footed."

Nomahlanjana's own surprise and terror more than make up for his father's equanimity, leaving his skin grey and his mouth dry. "Gu-ards!" he croaks.

Zwide holds up his hand. "Later," he says. "I would hear what this ghost has to say! This tortured spirit!"

"I am no ghost, Nkosi."

"Nkosi! Do you hear that, my son? A respectful ghost!"

"I am flesh and blood, Nkosi."

"Yes – flesh in the beak of a vulture, blood in the gullet of a hyena. How can it be otherwise? Every breath you take would be an affront to Shaka after what you did!"

"Nonetheless, here I am."

"Then my spies lied."

"They did not."

"And yet here you are."

The sangoma inclines his head.

"Flatter me," says Zwide, "and tell me you come to pledge your allegiance to the stronger king. That this discontent has long been a thorn in your heart."

"Would you believe me?"

"No."

"I owe my allegiance only to the ancestors."

"Then why are you here, Zulu?"

"Shaka is the enemy of our nation. You are the enemy of Shaka."

"Shaka is your king, Zulu."

"He is an affront to the ancestors."

"Shaka is your king, Zulu."

"A bastard son who stole the crown and is now a tyrant who lives off the blood of his subjects."

"How does this make him any different from your other kings?"

"These ceaseless wars, the wailing of widows and starving children – these are the things that set him apart. The agony of the ancestors is a roar louder than a thousand lions in my head."

"And here you are, paying court to the enemy of your enemy . . . Tell me, oh Sangoma, whose wisdom awes even our own medicine men, what would you say were I to return you to Shaka's aching bosom tomorrow? What would be the outcome of this noble gesture?"

Nomahlanjana's features harden. He'd be expected to lead such a mission into the arms of Shaka's impis – an angry Shaka and impis hungry for blood – and it's a prospect he doesn't relish.

"Would not old wrongs be forgotten and the enemy of your enemy become his trusted ally?"

"This is a path you could follow, it is so. But would not such a measure only serve to prolong your agony?"

"My *agony*?" hisses Zwide.

"I meant only your hunger pangs. How long would such a measure serve to sate your appetite, oh Devourer Of Kings?"

Zwide bares his teeth in a grin.

"Every day you tarry Shaka grows stronger," adds the shaman.

"As do we."

The Lion inclines his head – a gesture of polite agreement; deference to the Ndwandwe king over a dubious statement not worth debating.

"And you would prefer me over Shaka?"

"Anything is better than Shaka."

Zwide nods, storing the insult away for a later reckoning.

Nomahlanjana stirs beside his father, raising his chest out of the sack of his belly. "Perhaps when Shaka speaks this one's lips move, Father."

Zwide fixes a look of disdain on his son. Shaka is cunning, it is true, but to have the Inkatha destroyed almost in front of his troops – that is a ruse even he would not attempt. The effect such an act would have on his soldiers' morale would far outweigh the benefit of getting a treacherous shaman into Zwide's inner circle.

"I am here at your mercy, Nkosi," says the sangoma. "If you believe I cannot be of service to you, then so be it. The Great Journey awaits me – and better that than Shaka's tyranny. It is for you to decide. But these words are the twittering of birds that herald the dawn – the day you do battle with this bastard son."

"The day I defeat him, you mean."

"I have the medicine to make that a certainty."

"And I am now to value your loyalty? Cha! I would ask Shaka the value of your loyalty. About that, at least, the Beetle and I might agree."

"I do not offer you my loyalty."

"What then do you bring with you into the jaws of death? For I warn you – Zwide you will not elude as you have Shaka."

"I bring you my power."

"Power!" Zwide spits the word out. "Power," he sneers. "I say but the word and my mother will eat her breakfast porridge out of your skull."

"Would she not prefer Shaka's skull?"

"Why? Have you it with you?"

"No – "

"Cha! I thought not."

"But I have the power to attain it."

"So have I, Zulu!"

"I do not dispute that. You outnumber Shaka's army – but a cornered leopard still has sharp claws. Remove the head with one blow and the matter is ended instantly." The sangoma shrugs. "Pay too severe a price for victory and these Qwabes and Tembus might yet seize their chance. You outnumber Shaka's army, yes, victory lies within your grasp, but why have these tribes not allied themselves to you?"

"Because they are short-sighted fools!"

"Or perhaps they bide their time."

"The same thing!"

"Then make it so. Be *assured* of victory."

"And you have the power to achieve this?"

The sangoma nods.

"Don't waste my time with potions! I have my own medicine men!"

"But they do not have this – "

The sangoma slips his hand into his pouch. Removes a package wrapped in cabbage leaves. Speaks the one word that makes Zwide sit up and take notice, that silences the king's sarcasm, vanquishes his arrogance.

Ibizi!

*

Lightning. A fissure in the sky. An uneasy roll of thunder. Pampata's hand on his shoulder.

"Come back to me, Beloved."

Shaka slips his arm around her waist; she presses up against him.

"Does the storm toy with your plans?"

"A little."

Water – or rather, the absence of it – on the field of battle will prove an ever more powerful ally as the day wears on.

"It is not the rainy season and this will pass, Beloved."

Shaka grunts an agreement. He thinks so, too. Yet it is good to hear her echo his thoughts. He has granted her this power over him: to re-assure him, calm him.

Pampata is concerned about the news they've received of the White Men at Zwide's kraal. She wants to ask Shaka what he thinks of this de-velopment. Will they – can they – aid Zwide? But she knows this is not the right time to speak of these things. Nothing they say or do right now will change anything. It is better to leave it. But she is worried; a churn-ing in her stomach, a sense of foreboding looming over her like a shadow.

"Come inside, Beloved," she whispers. "Tomorrow you sleep with your impis under the stars, let me be your shelter for tonight."

*

Her lips curl in a scowl of disdain. "You are not Mabhubesi!"

Zwide follows these words, hurled like stones, to regard the sangoma with an expectant grin.

Ntombazi raises her walking stick and prods the Zulu shaman in the chest. "Did you hear me, Fool?"

Zwide's grin widens as he waits for the sangoma's response. He's clearly enjoying this. As is Nomahlanjana, who's eagerly awaiting an opportu-nity to add an "I told you so" to the conversation.

Zwide's mother jabs the shaman again. "Did you hear me? I said you are not Mabhubesi."

"I heard you, Crone."

It is a calculated insult, for Ntombazi is anything but crone-like. If she's older than she looks that's because she probably never actually looked young. Tall, angular, with breasts that are but flaccid folds of skin, there's something decidedly mannish about her. And from the way she carries herself, straight-backed, walking with long, firm strides, it's clearly an aspect of her nature she takes pride in and endeavours to cultivate.

"Does Shaka think he can thwart us so easily?"

"I cannot speak for Shaka."

"Why not? You are his creature."

"I am Mabhubesi. I answer only to the ancestors."

Addressing her son, Ntombazi says: "This is an impostor. And you are a fool for waking me, Boy. Did you not stop to think that this one is much too young to be who he claims to be? Are you blind?"

"I am my father's son," says the shaman. "Perhaps it is him you recall – although I do not think you two ever met."

"Liar!"

Mabhubesi holds the sheath of the dagger away from his chest. "Would an impostor have this?"

Now Zwide's expectant smile awaits his mother's response.

"Has age withered your tongue, Crow? This talisman is the mark of my family's power, snatched from the stiff fingers of the last Feared One we vanquished. And the Arabi came no more to steal our people, and ours is a dynasty that has outlasted all kings."

"A blade is just a blade."

"Many have thought that, many witches, too, but they soon had reason to regret their impertinence, for a blade between the ribs takes on a new meaning. Although of this I can't be sure, for there was little time to discuss the matter. I have only wide eyes and open mouths to go on. Perhaps you would like to see for yourself."

"And when was your father's passing?"

"But a few moons before Shaka indulged in his own impertinence, by expecting Mabhubesi to bless his tyranny."

"Yet, you answered the call."

"As the hunter follows the barking of his dogs."

"And why are you here?" asks Ntombazi.

The shaman sighs with forbearance. Says he has heard of what Zwide plans with the White Men.

"You have heard?" asks Nomahlanjana.

"I have ears everywhere. I have heard the guns. I know they can kill from a great distance. Shaka leads his men into battle. Cha! Even a child could make a fire from these twigs."

*

Mgobozi comes upon the boy sitting in the doorway of the Induna's hut. "You are awake, Little Warrior," he says.

The udibi stands. "I await my Master."

"He will not be back tonight."

"It is my duty to wait for him, General."

"You would not sit here while we thrash the Ndwandwes, would you?"

"But, General . . ."

"Your Master would not want that either."

"Where is he, General?"

"I do not know, Boy."

"I should be with him."

Mgobozi smiles. He knows how, when darkness fell, the boy had to be restrained from leaving the kraal to go and search for his master.

"Listen, Boy. The King has decreed that every officer take an udibi to aid him in his duties. This you know."

The boy nods.

"And you know, too, that I have no udibi. For I have twenty wives and warfare for me is a time of tranquillity; a blessed escape. I do not need someone to fuss over me."

The boy manages a grin.

"Well, you are different, Boy. I know this, because your Induna has often sung your praises to me. So, tomorrow, Mgobozi would have you as his udibi. Would you do me this favour until your Master returns?"

"He will return?"

"The Great Spirit willing. Now, what say you?"

11
The Watcher Of The Ford

The rains upcountry mean the White Umfolozi is running high and can be crossed only in three places, each of which is attended by a small contingent of Zulu soldiers. After his scouts report back, Nomahlanjana decides not to split his force or waste time following the river's course seeking other places to cross. He sends his men through the ford before him, which, anyway, seems lightly guarded.

Rapids lie below the narrow crossing and the current is strong; close to the opposite bank the water reaches shoulder height. The soldiers wade into the river in files four abreast; each man holds his shield and spears high in one hand, while gripping the shoulder of the man in front with the other. These human chains sway and sag, assailed by the current, the logs and other debris carried downstream, but remain unbroken as those leading the way move through the swirling brown waters. Rock gives way to mud and the men sink deeper and deeper.

Suddenly the Zulu force guarding the ford doesn't seem so insignificant. Led by Nqoboka, they wade into the shallows. With them is a warrior called Njikiza Ngcolosi. A giant of a man, almost two metres tall and with a chest like a mountain range, he wields a huge spiked club. The Ndwandwes fall like reeds beneath the mighty weapon and from this day on Njikiza will be known as Nohlola Mazibuko, the Watcher Of The Ford.

The other Zulus have left their shields on the bank; using the long spears they've captured, they crouch in the shallows and jab the assegais underwater into the unprotected bodies of the Ndwandwes. Two or three will fall and drag several others with them, the bodies rolling and tumbling to shatter against the rapids.

In this way, a company of fewer than two hundred holds off an army numbering eight thousand.

*

Shaka uses the time to see to it that still more supplies are brought to the hill. In addition to the precious water in earthenware pots, there's firewood, beer, maize roasted on the cob then shelled off and ground to meal, and some slaughter oxen. The udibis have also collected bark and ujoye leaves, to be used in dressing wounds.

Protected by a small force drawn from the Nkomendala impi, commanded by Shaka's half-brother, Dingane, the Zulu women and children and most of the cattle have been sent to the Umhlatuzi River, which marks the southern boundary of Zulu territory. Nandi and Pampata are with them. Shaka doesn't trust Dingane, and this is a way of ensuring he can't get up to any mischief; Nandi and Pampata, who command more respect from the people than Dingane does anyway, will keep an eye on him, and they in turn will be watched over by a bodyguard hand-picked by the King from his Fasimba impi.

If things go wrong here, they have orders to move into the dense fastness of the Nkandla Forest, close to the Umhlatuzi.

When he hears that action has commenced at the ford the King leaves to reconnoitre with five hundred of his Fasimbas. Mgobozi, who is supposed to remain with the main force, begs Shaka to take him along.

"My Father," he says, "must we sit here like a bunch of vultures atop this hill while brave men fall, or are we going to join the fight?"

"Mgobozi, it is impossible to argue with you!" chuckles Shaka. "You may accompany us – but for once I expect you to restrain yourself."

"Thank you, Father. And this I will do, for I would not want to deprive our warriors of their share."

The boy accompanies them, sticking with the general.

When they arrive at the ford they see that Nomahlanjana has with-drawn his men while he considers his options. The mud is red where the Zulus wait; bodies lie twisted about the rapids, broken on rocks that look to the boy like giant fangs.

While Shaka and his party are being regaled with accounts of the Watcher Of The Ford, messengers arrive from the other fords. The Ndwandwe prince has at last split his forces, but he has been held back at these places too.

Shaka stays to watch the enemy attempt another crossing.

"Why don't they just drown themselves and be done with it?" mutters Mgobozi.

"But, Old Friend, what are you still doing here? I thought you'd be down there with your hungry assegai."

"Cha! This is too easy, Father!"

"Something tells me you won't be able to make that complaint for much longer."

"Yes, I see it too, Father."

It's noon and the river is beginning to drop.

Shaka instructs Nqoboka to watch the level of the water and to return to the main body when the fords become redundant. He despatches messengers with the same orders for the officers commanding the other two detachments. Then, he and his party return to Gqokli Hill.

*

As it happens, Nomahlanjana prefers to remain on the other side of the White Umfolozi for the rest of the day, doubtless to lick his wounds and berate his commanders.

Nqoboka and the contingents from the fords rejoin the main force before dawn. He finds Shaka seated alone on a large flat outcrop of rock on the northern rim of the hill. Orderly ranks of soldiers asleep on the slope below him, Shaka is staring in the direction of the White Umfolozi and the Ndwandwes.

The general makes his report. The river has dropped further and is now fordable in many places. He has left picquets to keep an eye on the movement of the enemy. Shaka nods, thanks him.

"Listen to that –"

Nqoboka grins. Looks over to where Mgobozi lies, sprawled on his back, snoring.

"You try sleeping near that! It is a monster dragging dry hides!"

"He sleeps like a child on the eve of a feast day."

The sky is turning purple and the stars are vanishing. A cold wind climbs the slope. Here and there shapes rise up, as the warriors begin to awaken.

"Now, this is what I would have you do," says Shaka.

Nqoboka will take two hundred men from the Nkomendala impi – and one in four of the Zulu cattle. When Nomahlanjana crosses the White Umfolozi, his scouts will see this force driving a herd of cattle in the direction of the Tonjaneni Heights, some ten kilometres to the south. By splitting and recombining his units, Nqoboka will make his column seem larger than it is. The cattle will be a temptation too great for Nomahlanjana to withstand. Thinking that Shaka has divided his army into two almost equal bodies, the Ndwandwe prince will detach a large force to go after the livestock.

"Know this, Nqoboka – I do not expect you to sacrifice your men. Indeed, you must *not* sacrifice your men. The time will come when you must let these jackals take the cattle."

Shaka holds up a hand. "Do not worry, they won't retain our cattle for long. Allow the condemned some small pleasure, at least." When Nqoboka and his men find themselves too hard-pressed, then, they will relinquish the cattle. "Now you gain the advantage. They'll try to rejoin the main body, but they'll have our cattle with them. This will slow them down, hamper their movements."

"And my men and I will be cheetahs in the long grass!"

"This is so. Now go, may my faith guide you!"

"Bayede, Nkosi!"

And before the column returns, a decision will have been reached here, at Gqokli – either way. Shaka is confident he can last the whole day – certainly, his men have sufficient supplies. If need be, at nightfall, he'll form the survivors into a solid phalanx and fight his way out, rejoin his tribe in the Nkandla Forest.

The mountains in the east are rimmed with orange, the fires that announce the arrival of the sun. The clouds high up are streaks of red against a sky already turning blue. The Zulus call this time of early morning kuzempondozankomo: when the horns of the cattle become visible. All the warriors are awake now and the udibis are bringing them bowls of maize-meal porridge. Even Mgobozi has stopped dragging his dry hides and is sitting up, glancing around like a child already planning numerous acts of mischief.

It's a day in April, 1818.

12
The Scouts

There are four of them; four Ndwandwe scouts, led by a warrior named Tjello. Since they're under orders not only to reconnoitre, but also to find out what happened to the last group of scouts, they are not happy.

Away from the trees that mark the course of the river, the land unfurls itself into a plain: a rough, ragged carpet of thatch and lovegrass, sharp-edged blades that tickle the backs of the knees. Shades of yellow, white, grey and pale green in these autumn months; soil the colour of bread crust, dusty, lifeless. Flat-topped acacias, their slender branches holding grey-green foliage aloft, like women returning home with firewood balanced on their heads; ragged bushwillows with their sweet-scented flowers. Dongas, potential hiding places for warriors with hungry assegais. Ant hills, red castle keeps rising above the grass.

The party halts of its own accord without any signal from Tjello. Slowly, one by one, they drop to their haunches, resignation in their movements. No point in hoping the man is peering *over* the ant hill.

Tjello waits, then realises the others are waiting for him to make the first move. Reluctantly he stands. Takes a deep breath. Moves toward the ant hill. It is Ntabo. They shared a meal last night. His eyes are wide open, staring upward at a point slightly above Tjello. The scout pokes the forehead with the tip of his spear and the head topples backward off the ant hill.

Lowering his assegai, Tjello hesitates a moment, listening. The faint rustle of the grass. His own breath blowing a gale through his nostrils.

Where are they?

His hand squeezing the haft of his spear, the shield on his left arm suddenly feeling heavy, he moves forward, long decisive strides that take him around the ant hill and away from the head.

Grass. Trees. In the distance a low hill.

His eyes are like flies, buzzing this way and that, unable to settle.

Where are they?

He's gone ten paces when he suddenly stops. Wheels around. Curses. Running now, he retraces his steps. One by one the other warriors stand. At least they have the grace to look sheepish. Speaking in a low whisper, he curses them and their forebears. His mouth is dry. He breaks off his pejorative to take a gulp of water from his gourd. Wipes his mouth with the back of his hand. "Now follow me!" he hisses.

Grass. Trees. A sudden rustle, a ripping, tearing sound, and an impala breaks out of a bushwillow thicket and races diagonally away from them.

Have they disturbed it – or someone else?

Back on his haunches again, the other scouts crouching behind him, Tjello straightens his back – risks a peek above the swaying grass.

Nothing.

No one.

Or rather, no one he can see. Shadows beneath the thicket, long shadows in the early morning sun. Shapes in those shadows . . . or is he imagining things?

Tjello ducks down again. Wipes the sweat from his eyes. His face is a flood. He is melting.

Twisting his head, he makes a clicking sound with his tongue and stands. The other three follow suit.

They move forward again.

Grass. Trees. The distant hill, growing larger, stands out on the plain like a huge tree stump. The highest point for kilometres around. Tjello comes to a compromise with himself. He'll make for the hill, see what lies beyond it. No one can say they haven't obeyed their orders, then.

He looks down again. And, a few metres ahead, a donga becomes visible. It's as if the ground opens wider with every step he takes. A donga means cover. But he pauses on the brink. A body lies down there, on its back, disembowelled. A warrior whose name he can't remember.

The other men move up alongside him.

"Come, come," he hisses. He grabs the nearest soldier's elbow and pulls the man sideways. "Move!"

They skirt the donga, quickening their pace.

The hill, thinks Tjello. Move toward the hill.

Long shadows under the trees that harden into crouching warriors then become shadows again.

Where are they?

Where are these Zulus?

Unconsciously he's quickened his pace.

And when he looks ahead, again, it's as if the hill has leapt forward, for the ground dips suddenly here, and the hill is a lot closer than it seems.

But he goes no further.

He has found the Zulu host. And . . .

He can't believe his eyes. Clearly, the Zulus have gone mad.

13
The Host

Down there, Shaka has told Mgobozi, the Way Of The Bull will not serve us. There are too many of them. We will fight like lions and they will surround us, surround us without even trying, and victory will be theirs. But, if first we allow them to surround us and then fight like lions. Then, Old Friend, victory will be ours!

To this end, Shaka has drawn his men up in a circle that surrounds Gqokli Hill. It's a circle – of little more than fifteen hundred men – that he fully expects to be encircled in turn.

And Nomahlanjana obliges him by doing just that. His eight thousand men form up in a large crescent on the northeastern side of the hill, while their commander surveys the Zulu positions with a bemused, disbelieving grin. When his scouts return and inform him that, yes, the Zulu lines extend all the way around the hill, he shakes his head. "Do I dream?" he asks one of his generals.

The officer shrugs, at a loss for words.

The prince turns to his brothers. "What say you?"

"Where is this bull we have heard so much about?"

"Perhaps the bull is sick."

"Perhaps the bull is a cow!"

Grinning, Nomahlanjana issues his orders – and the Ndwandwes spread out to encircle the hill.

"It will be a massacre," murmurs Boyd.

De la Vere is not so sure. With the interpreter and the Zulu shaman tagging behind, the latter on foot, he and Boyd have come up with the rearguard. He's led his party to one side, where a grove of trees and bushes ought to shield them from sight. He spends a long time examining the Zulu host with his spyglass. When he finally lowers the instrument he wears a worried expression.

"Look at that line! How many men does he have up there?" he asks.

He gives Boyd a few seconds to raise his spyglass and focus the lenses; then: "Are you looking at the line?"

Boyd nods.

"How many ranks are there? How many do you see?"

"One . . . maybe two . . . It's hard to tell, they're bunched up."

"Precisely my point, old chap."

Boyd lowers the spyglass. "What do you mean?"

"He's bunched his men up. Got them sitting close together and on their shields. I'm willing to bet that when he separates them we'll see at least five ranks!"

Shaka's position has other advantages. Losses can be counteracted by drawing his men higher up the hill, thereby contracting the circle. Also, he'll never have to worry about his lines of communication. He has placed himself on a large flat outcrop of rock on the northern brim of the hill – from where he can see the tree where Nomahlanjana has settled himself. Nzobo and his indunas are on the southern end, while Ngomane and Mdlaka oversee the eastern and western fronts respectively. The result is a perfect liaison.

A broad ridge of stone circles the depression in the centre of the hill and, by moving along this, Shaka can inspect all the fronts in a matter of minutes.

Nomahlanjana, by contrast, has to make use of runners to find out what's happening on the other sides. Not for him the exertion of hiking around the hill; he'll stay in the shade, drinking beer and waiting for victory.

Appearances to the contrary, though, he is an able commander. He's given the Zulu positions a shrewd evaluation, trying to discern a method in this madness. But there's nothing he can see, nothing to counterbalance the indisputable fact that he has the superior numbers – particularly if you bear in mind this madman has split his army, and Nomahlanjana has detached a column of two thousand men to go after the Zulu cattle.

He gazes up at Shaka.

Shaka, in his golden kilt, with his white amashoba around his arms and knees, and his shield, also white, with a single black spot in the centre.

What do you have in mind, Zulu?

"The men are in position, Nkosi."

Nomahlanjana nods. "Have them advance two spears!"

A few minutes later, he discovers that superior numbers in this instance can have some disadvantages.

For when the Ndwandwe army tries to advance to a position two spears' throw away from the Zulus, they move from a circle with a circumference of more than three thousand metres into one with a circumference of fifteen hundred metres.

The result is a scrimmage that leaves the captains screaming in anger as they try to bludgeon the ranks into some kind of order.

*

"Yo! Yo! Yo!" laughs Mgobozi. "They look like ants whose hill has been disturbed."

"These are not ants," says Shaka.

"Which makes my heart glad, Father – for where is the pleasure in crushing ants?"

"And they surround us. Bear that in mind."

"So! Your cunning plan has worked, Father!"

Shaka grins. "You had your doubts, Old Friend?"

"Well, look at them, Majesty! Can these Ndwandwes be trusted with anything? Even surrounding a stationary force? Who knows where they might have blundered?"

"I think they can be counted on to try and kill us, Old Friend. I think that's one thing about which we can be certain: they *will* try to kill us."

*

Down below, hidden behind the trees, the Englishmen watch the Ndwandwe officers bring some order to their men. But the regiments remain muddled. And the great circle seems to be constantly moving, bristling, as warriors jostle for space, those in front leaning back, their leg muscles straining, tiring already with the effort of trying not to be pushed further forward.

But Boyd seems to appreciate this still-daunting sight that makes the Zoola lines on the hill seem skinny, fragile . . .

He turns to De la Vere: "Shades of Agincourt, what?"

*

"This is the message I need you to convey to the indunas while I speak with the generals," says Shaka. "They must remind their men of the necessity for absolute obedience. One is all, here. A single break in the ranks will tear us all apart! If we give chase the line must be maintained. No impi is to outdistance the others. The men must listen to the commands and obey!"

"This they will do, Majesty, but I'll see to it they are reminded."

"Above all, Mgobozi, warn them – warn them to guard against the gate that opens too easily, to beware of the load that suddenly becomes too light. For, sooner or later, it will occur to these Ndwandwes that the only chance they have to get us off the hill is to get us off the hill, understand? They will try to break our ranks by feigning a retreat and drawing our men to where their reserve awaits with the open jaws of a crocodile."

Mgobozi nods. "Wise words, Majesty. And your men will hear them, I'll make sure of that."

He sighs, stretches. Slaps his stomach. The day is a bright, gleaming bauble as yet unsullied by the bloody fingerprints, the foetid breath of screaming men.

"Truly," says Mgobozi, "this is a good day for dying!"

"Cha!" growls Shaka. "It is a better day for killing!"

14
The Challengers

An officer disengages himself from the restless, crowded circle and moves forward a few paces. "What are you waiting for?" he shouts to the Zulu warriors. "You cowardly dogs!"

The soldiers in the line bark raucously. They wear hide kilts and sandals. White stripes are painted across their chests and faces. Each man carries one long throwing spear and has three more clipped to the inside of his rectangular shield.

"Even – even your fleas are afraid!"

The Zulu warriors remain seated impassively on their shields; some nonchalantly offer their neighbours a pinch of snuff.

Another Ndwandwe steps forward further along the perimeter.

"Look at them, my Brothers – sitting there like baboons! Come down from your hill, baboons! Taste our steel!"

"I would call you Zulus cowards," bellows a third warrior. "Cha! But it is the same thing! See a Zulu, see a coward!"

From a fourth: "Your balls are pebbles! Your pricks are straw!"

"If you even have pricks!" shouts another warrior.

"Where are your women? They would make a better showing!"

"Ha!" shouts the first Ndwandwe. "But your women shit through their cunts!"

Now the Zulus are on their feet, the movement like the flexing of a giant muscle. A rumble of anger.

"Silence!" bellows Shaka. "Seat yourselves and be still!"

The order is repeated by the indunas, some of them seeking to restrain the soldiers by slapping their backs with the sides of their axes.

"The Beetle speaks! Tell me, Beetle – where are your champions?"

"Yes!" echo the other warriors. "Where are your champions? Bring forth your champions!"

With order restored to the Zulu ranks, all are seated again, glaring outward – all except one man. He has twisted around and is staring up at Shaka.

The Zulu King waits for the cries of the Ndwandwes to peter out, then he glances down toward the man. Nods.

Manyosi KaDlekezele stands, picks up his shield, and moves down the hill. When he reaches a point halfway between the lines, he halts.

The Ndwandwe officer turns, points to a warrior.

Standing next to Mgobozi on the hill's summit, the boy watches as a Ndwandwe soldier steps forward and in one, fluid motion hurls his spear at Manyosi.

Instinctively the boy ducks.

But the Zulu is ready. He raises his arm and the spear bounces off his shield with a "Thwuck!"

The Ndwandwe straightens up from his throwing crouch. Unclips a second spear from his shield. His right arm curled, his fist tight around the shaft, he appears to test the weapon's weight, raising and lowering his hand in short rhythmic movements.

"He will not throw," murmurs Mgobozi.

The boy glances up at the general and almost misses what happens next . . .

The Ndwandwe flings his right arm forward –

Manyosi ducks behind his shield. But it's a feint: the Ndwandwe pulls the spear back at the last second.

Then he hurls it, his arm a striking cobra.

In the process of lowering his isihlangu, Manyosi swings his arm outward, and swats the missile away, the blade scoring a furrow in the cowhide.

The boy hisses.

"Now!" says Mgobozi.

It's as if the Zulu warrior hears him, because he lunges forward. Covering the few metres between them as the other soldier frantically struggles to free his third spear, Manyosi brings his shield back into position – turns slightly to the right – hooks the outside edge of his isihlangu behind the inside edge of the Ndwandwe's shield, then swings his left arm outward again, wrenching the other man's shield away from his body.

The Ndwandwe arches, goes up onto his toes, as though trying to pull away from the blade that's entered his left armpit.

Manyosi twists his wrist – twists it again, like someone wringing water from a cloth – then withdraws his iklwa. The Ndwandwe flops into the dust.

The Zulu raises his assegai. "Ngadla!" *I have eaten!*

A blur to his right.

Instantly he drops into a crouch, raising his shield. The spear is hurled with such force it transfixes the cowhide.

"See what treacherous dogs these Ndwandwes are!" says Mgobozi.

The boy nods sagely, trying to ignore his swollen bladder. It feels as if he has enough piss inside of him to fill fifty gourds. Which is odd, since his mouth is so dry.

The fierceness of the throw has caused the Ndwandwe to overbalance. He's moving forward when the Zulu crashes into him, the spear stuck in the shield getting crunched between the cowhides. The Ndwandwe staggers back – helped along by the iklwa in his gut.

Manyosi halts abruptly – allows the other warrior to slide off his blade – and wheels to face the Ndwandwe ranks, lest another challenger try a sneak attack. "Ngadla!" he shouts, backing away from the crushed ranks.

Directly in front of him, two soldiers are shouldered aside as a third charges forward with a bellow. He's as big as Njikiza, the Watcher Of The Ford – maybe even bigger, decides the boy, although that's hard to believe.

This warrior has dispensed with his shield and wields his spear like a pike, gripped by both hands at waist-level, and comes at the Zulu like an enraged rhino.

A split second before their bodies slam together, even as the spear scrapes past the inner edge of his shield aimed at his midriff, Manyosi drops backward.

The boy gasps, thinking the Zulu has been bested; even Mgobozi's hand becomes a talon as it bites into the udibi's shoulder.

But as the Ndwandwe flies over him, his spear embedding itself in the ground to the left of the Zulu's head, the shaft snapping, Manyosi kicks upward, using his shield as a springboard. Kicks and thrusts upward, his iklwa cutting through the other man's exposed stomach. Kicks and thrusts upward and allows his own momentum to send him after the dying Ndwandwe in a backward roll that leaves him straddling the soldier's chest, facing the enemy ranks.

"Sho!" gasps the boy. And Mgobozi, too, grunts something that sounds like surprised approval.

On his feet, his back coated with dust, Manyosi raises his bloodied assegai.

"Ngadla!"

He lowers the iklwa, slaps the blade against his shield. "Who comes next?"

The Ndwandwe ranks seem to swell forward, but no one breaks through to challenge the warrior, as hisses and jeers rise from the impis on the hill.

*

From his position on the summit, Shaka raises his own spear. "Ayihlo-me!" he commands. *To arms!*

As one, the fifteen hundred Zulu warriors seated around the hill rise. As one, they rise and raise their shields. As one, fifteen hundred spears are beaten against fifteen hundred shields in rapid succession.

Then there's a moment of silence, holding the world at bay, the Ndwa-ndwes motionless, breath caught in bursting lungs.

Silence . . .

Then thunder, as the fifteen hundred stamp their right feet in unison. A thunder both heard and felt as the ground trembles.

The Zulu lines rearrange themselves, splitting into five ranks each separated by three or four paces.

Suddenly, this puny army of baboons seems to have doubled in size. And the disconcerted Ndwandwe circle swells outward as though pushed back by an invisible force.

Nomahlanjana, already apoplectic at the defeat of his champions, sees this . . . this cowardly hesitation, and screams at his generals to attack, attack, *attack*!

The order travels around the circle. The Ndwandwes are not cowards and they soon recover from their surprise. Obeying their officers, they advance. But as the circle moves up the slopes of Gqokli it shrinks yet again, from fifteen hundred metres to one thousand metres – or twenty-five long paces from the Zulu host – and confusion tangles the jostling ranks. Elbows fight to claim space; shields are locked against chests. Once more the regiments become a congested mob.

And Shaka seizes his chance.

He calls to his generals to ready the first two lines.

"And you, Boy," he shouts across to where Mgobozi and the Induna's udibi stand. "You make sure no harm befalls that old goat. Guard him well!"

The udibi gulps, both proud and nonplussed. The King has singled him out, given him a command – but what a command! He glances warily at the general.

"Hawu!" mutters Mgobozi. "Here I must stay, while these young bloods feast!"

"I hear you, Old Friend!" calls Shaka. "Your task is to watch the warriors fighting and see where improvements can be made!"

"I would lead by example, Majesty!"

"Then start now, by obeying my command, you cantankerous old goat!"

Mgobozi proffers a stately bow.

Turning his attention back to his lines, Shaka checks that the men are ready. They are – the indunas stand poised, looking his way. Shaka casts one more glance at the churning Ndwandwes, then shouts: "Bulalani!" *Kill!*

Movement becomes sound, sound movement; sound that seems to rise up out of the ground like a thousand angry snakes, movement that crashes down from above. "Si-Gi-Di!" roar the charging Zulus. "Siiiiiiiiiii-Giiiiiiiiiii-Diiiiiiiiiii!"

A war cry that turns into a hiss, carried and echoed by the lines remaining on the hillside. And the two ranks – some six hundred men – smash into the six thousand Ndwandwes. A wave of muscle and rage, discipline and fire, slams into the confused enemy ranks like a blade thrust into tangled intestines.

The Ndwandwes can't even throw their spears. Screams of "Ngadla!" reverberate around the hill as soldier after soldier drives home his iklwa again and again, stabbing the living and the dead, for such is the jam, bodies remain upright.

Shaka leaps off his rock and circles the summit. Everywhere his men are engaged in slaughter.

But their progress is slowed by their own success – the bodies pile up in a crumpled redoubt – and after two minutes the Ndwandwe commanders are able to pull their men backwards, opening the circle to give the soldiers space. Now they can fight back. Spears fly. The Zulus are held in check behind their shields; begin to suffer greater casualties.

A natural lull follows. The two forces are at a standstill: the Ndwandwes unable to move forward for fear of becoming congested again; the Zulus behind their shields, too small a force to continue their advance.

Back on his rock, Shaka orders the retreat.

Obeying their training, the Zulu warriors disembowel the fallen, friend and foe alike – to release the spirits of the dead soldiers – and pick up as many Ndwandwe spears as they can on their way back. Back on the slopes, the more seriously wounded are taken up the hill. The ranks reform, the first two, those who've just been in battle, moving to the rear. Udibis hurry among the men with gourds of water.

*

Close to a thousand Ndwandwes have been killed. Nomahlanjana summons his generals to him. It is decided to split the force in two. Half will remain on the hill spaced out appropriately; half will be withdrawn several paces to the foot to be deployed as a reserve.

If any remember the Englishmen and the Zulu sangoma, they quickly banish all thought of these strangers. They might be able to promise great magic, but the pride of the Ndwandwe army is at stake. Zwide has ordered them to make use of the interlopers' services, but they also know he'll never let them forget that outside help was needed. The generals are as angry as Nomahlanjana. The fallen must be avenged – and it is the Ndwandwe army who will do this. Not the White Men and certainly not this traitorous Zulu sangoma.

*

"Seems to me we've backed the wrong pony here," mutters De la Vere.

"It can't be," says Boyd, "it can't be! Christ, they outnumber the Zoolas almost six to one!"

"And yet these buffoons trip over their own feet! I've never seen the like!"

"Six to one . . ."

"Not any more."

"But still . . ."

"Aye?"

"The weight of superior numbers and all that . . ."

"Seen much action, have you, Stanley?"

Boyd's lips twitch with rare irritation. He's unsettled, in need of re-assurance, not De la Vere's nastiness.

"I was merely pointing out what logic dictates . . ."

"Logic! It's discipline that counts in these affairs. Discipline is worth a whole battalion! Did you see how those soldiers withdrew when a stale-mate threatened? How they moved to the rear, so the van would comprise fresh men? I tell you, this Shaka is a fly fellow. He has brought us here. He has lured us here! And now he awaits every opportunity. D'you think he meant to attack just now? Of course not. He merely saw his chance and grabbed it. With glee, I'm sure."

*

Deciding he won't be needed for a while, Jacob the interpreter guides his horse over to where the Zulu sangoma sits, seemingly uninterested in the course of the battle.

"What say you, Xhosa?" asks the sangoma, after the interpreter has dismounted.

"I say it will be a long day!" sighs Jacob, dropping down next to the shaman.

*

"What's this? What's happening?"

De la Vere raises his spyglass. "Ah!" he mutters. "Someone's using their brain."

They watch the Ndwandwes reforming themselves, becoming once more an army of orderly ranks.

"Much better!" says De la Vere.

"Hmm," says Boyd, "I think I'm still going to bank on those superior numbers, if you don't mind, old chap."

*

Reclining in the shade of his tree, Nomahlanjana accepts another calabash of beer from one of his attendants and comes to much the same conclusion. His men erred a little, let their enthusiasm get the better of them. A minor mishap. They still outnumber the Zulus greatly. This day *will* be theirs.

15
The Smoke

Shaka and Mgobozi clamber down the low ridge and move through the lines, the boy trailing after them.

It's like walking along the edge of a bushfire. The warriors exude a palpable heat; drenched in sweat, caked in dust and blood, they seem to seethe with the energy of flames that would devour the whole veld. Greedily they accept water from the udibis.

They would stand to salute Shaka, but he waves them down, tells them to rest. He stops to check that the dressings on the lightly wounded have been properly applied, speaks words of praise and encouragement.

Even Mgobozi cannot keep up his façade of feigned parade-ground sternness. "Aiee!" he grins. "What old fool trained you! But never fear, there are still many more down there for you to practise on!" Moving on: "Hawu, Simphiwe! Fix the bindings on your shield. You too, Naka!

You'd swear you've been in a battle, you two!" When other soldiers laugh, he turns on them: "Call this a battle? You slaughter cows here today!"

But where's the Induna? What's happened to him? Why won't anyone tell him?

The boy gazes dismally upon the rampart of tangled bodies down below . . . so many . . . yet many more standing by . . . where is his master? An udibi's place is alongside his master!

"What say you, Mgobozi?" asks Shaka, when the two return to the King's post.

"The lines are strong, Majesty. They will hold."

"For how much longer, though?"

"For as long as you want them to, Majesty."

"Cha!"

"I do not seek to flatter you, Old Friend. These are good, brave men. They will stand firm if need be, attack if you command it."

"They have to, Mgobozi. They have to stand firm."

"Father!"

A call from one of the other generals.

Mgobozi and Shaka both direct their attention to the slopes.

"They come again," says Mgobozi.

Shaka nods.

Standing beside them, the boy watches as the Ndwandwes advance. This time each warrior has more space. At a call from their officers, they halt within a spear's throw from the Zulus.

Another command, echoing around the hill – and the boy has never seen such a sight before. The Ndwandwe spears arc through the air. A stockade come to life. A wall of death, crashing down on the impis.

But the Zulus are hunkered behind their overlapping shields. A knocking, drumming sound circles the hill. It's a noise the boy will never forget. But it's more frightening than effective.

"Cha!" laughs Shaka. "See how they throw away their weapons? Such foolishness!"

The Ndwandwes themselves are a little disconcerted, and there follows a pause longer than the time it takes them to free a second spear from the fastenings of their shields. And they watch as Zulus from the rear ranks dart around collecting their spears – which are then handed to the udibis who carry the bundles up the hill. It's bad enough to see how little effect their assegais have against the Zulu shields – now this: having the Zulus confiscate their weapons. The line ripples as soldiers glance uncertainly at their neighbours and then glance back at the Zulus.

The officers shout new commands.

A second volley of spears flies at the Zulus. This time the Ndwandwe soldiers have been instructed to throw horizontally. Again the drumming sound reverberates around the hill. Here and there, a spear breaks through shields to impale a thigh, but the Zulu lines hold firm.

And knowing their men are growing ever more panicky, the Ndwandwe officers immediately order another volley. Now some spears fly high, some fly low, so that the Ndwandwe ranks become, for an instant, an enraged porcupine, shooting off quills.

And, their frenzy spent, the Ndwandwe soldiers are again left gaping at the immobile Zulus. Each man now has only one spear left.

"Truly," says Mgobozi, "they look like cows before a new gate. They know not where to go, what to do."

"We will show them," says Shaka. Moving to the rim of the rock, he raises his assegai. "Bulalani!"

Rising and running in one pouncing movement, the first two Zulu ranks sweep down the hill, spurred on by the hissed "Si-Gi-Di" of the ranks behind them, who have moved forward to take their place. The crash of shields is followed immediately by the screams of impaled men. The Ndwandwe lines shatter and the battle becomes a series of desperate duels. Warrior faces warrior; clumsy throwing spears try to parry the deadly thrust of the Zulu iklwas. Sometimes all a Ndwandwe warrior can do is grab hold of the haft, try to wrench the assegai away as he topples backward, so the soldier behind him can face an unarmed

Zulu. Blood rises above the grappling men in a dusty haze. Bodies underfoot, some seeking death in a foetal curl, others with limbs flailing uncontrollably . . .

*

. . . Shaka turns to the boy, notes his fear – wide eyes, clenched fists – and squeezes his shoulders. "Come," he says gently, speaking into the udibi's ear. "Come stand here."

He positions the boy away from the edge of the slab, so he can't see the howling, clawing clashes below, and points to a distant mountain – the Tonjaneni Heights. "See?" he asks. "See that smoke?"

Slowly the boy nods.

"I would have you do this for me," continues the Zulu King. "Watch that smoke! Do not let your eyes stray. When that fire is extinguished and smoke rises from the other side of the peak, tell me. Do not let your vigil be interrupted. You have the most important task of any here. Watch and tell me when you see the smoke move. Do you understand?"

His eyes already affixed on the distant mountain, the boy nods again.

"Good! You have my faith, Boy."

And the King moves away to oversee the progress of the battle . . .

*

. . . frenzied attack; desperate defence. Backwards and forwards. Here, a final spear flung in desperation finds a Zulu throat. There, two unarmed men wrestle amid the dead. Shrieks and bellows. A warrior sitting with his legs apart stares at his entrails. Run through, a Ndwandwe claws at a Zulu shield. A dying Zulu rises one last time to thrust his iklwa into his killer's groin. Here, towering Njikiza swings his club, scything a space around him; there, Manyosi adds to his tally . . .

Once more the rising mound of bodies enables the Ndwandwes to disengage and stagger back a few precious paces. The moment Shaka sees this, notes the way the Ndwandwe reserves are only too eager to move forward past their comrades and join in the fray, he orders a withdrawal.

This engagement has lasted longer than the first – about ten minutes – and as the Zulus back away it's obvious at least three Ndwandwes lie dead for every Zulu killed. But the Zulu casualties are high. Most of the leading line has fallen. Of the second line, almost a third are dead or seriously wounded.

If Nomahlanjana had immediately deployed his reserves . . . But no, his generals are gathering for another conference.

It's a delay Shaka heartily welcomes, for another factor is gradually making its presence felt. It's about midday and the sun burns down on the Ndwandwes – on the Zulus, too, but Shaka's men have something the Ndwandwe soldiers don't have: water.

Some of the enemy have already begun to wander off; now the exodus grows. Most of the exhausted soldiers throw themselves down at the feet of the reserves, but a significant number shoulder their way through the ranks and keep on going, oblivious to the calls of their officers. More than one man is brought down by a captain's spear between his shoulder blades, but this doesn't deter the others. Their thirst is too great. Some are already delirious, blundering through the long grass, then collapsing. Even attempts on the part of the wiser officers to organise parties of wounded to go and fetch the others water doesn't stop groups of men from wandering off by themselves.

All around the hill Shaka can see antlike processions moving away.

"Drink!" he calls to his own men. "Drink your fill, piss it out and drink some more!"

Leaving the boy watching the distant plume of smoke, he calls Mgobozi to him and they move along the ridge, inspecting the lines.

At least that's their intention, but they don't get far. "Look, Majesty," says Mgobozi, "they would die some more."

The two halt and watch the manoeuvres. The fresh Ndwandwe reserves are moved through the mauled front ranks, then split into three lines.

"The front lines," says Shaka to Mgobozi, "how many spears does each man carry?"

Leaving the general squinting down the slope, he runs to the southern brim of the hill.

"One, Majesty," calls Mgobozi. "I think each man carries only one."

"Yes," says Shaka, "here too."

At his signal the generals join him. Hurriedly, he briefs them.

16

The Retreat

Again, the Ndwandwes advance. This time it's been decided the first two lines will charge the Zulus, engage them in hand-to-hand combat – then the men in the third line will advance and, taking their chances whenever they see a break, throw their spears.

It's a change in strategy Shaka has anticipated – seeing the first ranks move forward with each soldier carrying only one spear – and the first two lines haven't advanced three paces when the Zulus charge them. Following the King's orders as relayed to them by their indunas, the first wave of Zulus simply crashes straight into the first rank of Ndwandwes, knocking them back into the second rank, which in turn crowds the third, so these men can't throw their spears. Following in close support, the second line of Zulus are the ones who deploy their iklwas. Crouching, gripping their assegais near the shaft ends to give themselves the necessary reach, they thrust the spears past their comrades. For the startled Ndwandwes it's as if spikes suddenly sprout from the ground.

But they still outnumber the Zulus!

The rear ranks join the maul, trying to halt the backwards roll, and Shaka is forced to send in his third line, leaving him with only one line in reserve, comprised mostly of lightly wounded men. And soon a living wall of death is being built on the slopes of Gqokli; a crush of writhing arms and legs. Some say it is here, at this time, on this day, the legend is born that you don't just kill a Zulu, you have to push him over as well. For, as the third line crashes into the thicket, the mortally wounded in the front ranks are kept upright, able to continue fighting. Driven forward again, dead men claw at faces, fingers gouging eyes and nostrils. A Zulu warrior just run through will fall on his slayer, his teeth tearing open the soldier's throat.

The ferocity of the Zulu assault, launched downhill, has driven the Ndwandwes back some two dozen paces when the inevitable lull creeps between the exhausted men. There's a disentangling, the uttering of final curses and then the Zulus allow the enemy to withdraw unimpeded, while they gather up more Ndwandwe spears and see to their wounded.

The air remains stunned, beaten like a dog, quivering. The day has become an invalid, too afraid to move. Torn, bedraggled, bleeding men return to their lines. The ground is black with blood. The bodies of the living glisten like wet stones; the dead are grey and red. And covering all: the heat. A soup of rotting entrails and shattered bones; sweat and fear; shit and piss.

High above, the vultures are wheeling.

Shaka watches as Nomahlanjana comes lumbering away from his shade to berate his commanders; then he turns his attention to his own force. Two of the five Zulu lines have vanished and many of the remaining warriors are wounded. He has little more than eight hundred men encircling the hill. Morale remains high, but will that number be enough?

Should he . . .? Is it time . . .?

Sensing his friend's vacillation, Mgobozi moves closer to Shaka. "No, Majesty," he whispers. "Now is not the time. See? The sun becomes an ever-more valuable ally. Look how more and more go in search of water. Our lines will stand a little while longer."

Shaka nods. Checks to see if the smoke from the Tonjaneni Heights has changed position.

It hasn't.

*

"Where's everyone going?" wonders Boyd.

De la Vere lowers his spyglass and glances around. A rustling of grass, moving away from the hill. The Englishman frowns. Wheeling his horse, he rises up in his saddle, surveying his surroundings.

"I'd say they're going to get water," he says, rejoining Boyd, before looking once more up at Gqokli, where Shaka can clearly be seen above the settling dust. "This black bastard has thought of everything."

"But, but they can't just desert!"

"Oh, I'm sure they're not exactly deserting, old boy. God knows what punishment they'll face for *that*. They're just going to fetch water. They'll be back."

"But by then it might be too late!"

"Precisely!"

"What is this idiot up to?" asks Boyd, meaning Nomahlanjana. "I mean, what happened to the plan?"

What indeed. For some reason the son has ignored the father's instructions – the old bastard finally realising how useful one shot, fired from one gun by a marksman like De la Vere, could be. Is the risk worth it this late in the game, though? The weight of superior numbers – there's a joke. It's only those superior numbers that have kept these buffoons in play, and even then they're only hanging on by their fingertips.

And if they turn their horses right now and gallop away, leave quietly amid the confusion? Something tells De la Vere even defeated Zwide's reach will be as long as his memory.

Damn this son with the unpronounceable name, this obdurate fool! The plan *can* work, and it's not too late!

One shot. That's all it'll take. Just one shot . . .

"There they go again," says Boyd.

As the Englishmen watch, one man in four moves forward to form two ranks ahead of the Ndwandwe reserve.

"Why so few?" asks Boyd.

De la Vere shrugs.

"He's up to something," says Boyd, his voice rising in excitement.

Perhaps he's right. Maybe Zwide's fat son *does* have a plan in mind. Something, some way to break those Zulu ranks. Because, break them and the day is won. Shaka now has too few troops to plug any holes effectively; and, of course, he *is* completely surrounded!

Although, heaven knows, that fact hasn't held him back. The man has pulled himself into a defensive position only to attack. Remarkable! And although they still outnumber these Zoolas the strain is beginning to tell on the Ndwandwes.

De la Vere's reminded of the Frenchies coming through the wood at Hougoumont, on yet another futile attempt to dislodge the defenders.

See how wearily they trudge up that blasted hill!

Yes – wearily and warily, for there's more than mere tiredness in their steps: they move like men expecting a blow at any minute.

And here it comes . . .

"Si-Gi-Di!"

That sound that's like sand poured down your back. A sinuous hiss that races through your ears to sting your teeth. That burns your eyes. The pounding of feet. The urgent, ominous whisper of moving bodies.

And once more the Zulu wave hits the Ndwandwe reef.

Entanglement. Shrieks and shouts. Thrusting assegais. Cries of "Ngadla!"

And then the Ndwandwes turn and run.

At first De la Vere thinks it's because they've had enough, these cow-ardly savages! But orders have been bellowed amid the crash and grunt, and the Ndwandwes are retreating en masse.

After a second's hesitation, a moment of startled confusion, the Zulu impis charge after them . . .

*

And up on the hill, Shaka's bellowing: "It's a trap! Call them back! It's a trap! Call them back!"

And the indunas from the remaining lines set off after their comrades . . .

. . . who are heading straight for the Ndwandwe reserve.

And the boy's at his side.

"Majesty, Majesty – the smoke! It's shifted!"

17

The Condemned

Nomahlanjana sends word back to where the Englishmen wait with their interpreter and this Mabhubesi. The one with the gun must get ready.

Thirsty soldiers streaming away from the battle watch aghast as the shaman proceeds to pour precious water from several gourds onto a patch of dirt. The captain sent to deliver the message screams at them to return to their lines, but they pay him no heed. Some can barely walk so dehydrated are they.

"Christ!" hisses De la Vere, as Boyd helps him undress.

"This was your idea, old boy!"

"Don't remind me!"

Naked save for his drawers, the Englishman presents a strange sight to the Zulu. The skin around his stomach and thighs is as white as milk, but his arms up to the elbow and his face down to his neck are a vivid red, with smears of brown, a mixture of sunburn and dirt.

After some insistent cajoling from Boyd, De la Vere sinks onto his knees in the puddle. Boyd begins to smear mud over his friend's shoulders. Tuppence moves forward to assist, but De la Vere waves him away with a curse.

They do not like black hands? asks the shaman.

The interpreter grins. Shrugs.

Except in toil. But with our women it is a different story.

"No!" says De la Vere, as Boyd hands him a borrowed loincloth. "Are you mad? There has to be a limit to this lunacy!"

"As you say. We'll keep the drawers on."

"Bloody right we will!"

"Hold still while I do your face."

"My eyes! Watch my eyes!"

"Don't worry . . ."

"And damn yours, Boyd – damn your eyes!"

The Ndwandwe captain returns.

The commander grows impatient!

Mabhubesi holds up his hand.

We are almost ready.

"What are they saying?" demands De la Vere, his eyes two pale circles in a mask of mud.

Aiee! grins the captain. *He looks like an owl!*

"Uhm. He wants to know if you are ready, Master," says Tuppence.

De la Vere hoists the kilt over his drawers. "Yes, goddamn it! We're ready. Let's finish this farce!"

Cha! Mabhubesi steps between the Englishman and the Ndwandwe officer.

"What does he want?" snarls De la Vere. "A whipping?"

The shaman turns his head to the interpreter, issuing a few rapid instructions.

"What is he saying?"

"He would have your gun. The gun you intend to use. Loaded. It must be ready to fire."

"What?"

"It is part of the ritual. He would ensure your aim is true."

"I'll bloody show him just how true my bloody aim is!"

"Oliver, give him the gun. Let him speak his incantations and let us finish this farce, as you call it."

De la Vere glowers at the shaman a moment longer, only to find his glare met with equanimity.

"Fine!" says the Englishman at last. "Fetch it, Boyd. It's by the tree."

Such a petulant Mud Man, murmurs the Lion, keeping eyes on the Englishman.

"What did he say?"

"Uh. He says you will make a fine warrior," says Tuppence.

Boyd returns with the gun before De la Vere can respond.

And somewhere, adds the shaman as the plump Englishman approaches him, *there is a giant dung beetle waiting to roll this one to its hole!*

"Only a pleasure, old boy," says the plump Englishman, handing the Brown Bess to the sangoma. "Don't mention it. Only, remember – it's loaded. We wouldn't want you accidentally blowing your own brains out, now would we, you black bastard?"

The shaman turns.

"Hey!" protests De la Vere. "Where's he taking that?"

"To perform the ritual," explains Tuppence.

"Come," says Boyd, folding a hand around his friend's elbow. "Leave him to it. There are a few spots I missed . . ." Sagging to his haunches, he scoops up some more mud.

Please, Comrade, whispers the captain, *we have not much time.*

I do not need much time, says Mabhubesi.

Clutching his medicine bag in one hand and the gun in the other he moves behind a stand of low bushwillows.

"You can do this?" hisses Boyd to De la Vere.

"Yes! Nothing to it. It's not like these savages use bows or even throw their spears! And I don't intend to get close to them. We will win the day for these fools!"

*

Up on the hill, Shaka is livid. Oh, it was a fine sight watching his impis outpace the fleeing Ndwandwes, and keeping in formation, too, never outrunning each other. Some even almost crashed right through the Ndwandwe reserve before they were killed. But they'd disobeyed his orders! The Ndwandwes had intended to lure them off the hill into the jaws of their reserve. Only the Zulus' iron discipline saved them at the last moment – those indunas from the remaining line, who raced off after them, had managed to halt their rush and get them turned around.

If the Ndwandwes hadn't been so thirsty and battered, they might have made more of the chase back up the hill. Because that's where their long spears had the advantage, whether hurled at the shoulder blades of a retreating man or used to trip him up, slice his ankles and cripple him. Although, yet again, the Zulus kept in formation, never breaking the line that circled the hill and ran with their shields behind their backs.

But still, they had disobeyed Shaka's orders!

One in ten men, including the officers, is chosen from the offending regiments.

"You know the punishment for disobeying my orders," Shaka tells them. "But I promise you this: you will not die by a Zulu's hand today."

Each man is made to stand well out in front of the lines. They'll engage the enemy first and will fight until they're killed.

When these men reach their allotted places, they turn around to face the King. Raising their assegais, they give the royal salute for the last time: "Bayede! Bayede, Nkosi, bayede!"

Then, facing the Ndwandwe ranks again, each man stamps his right foot and bellows "A-Yi-Ze!" *Let it come!*

*

Mabhubesi returns, the gun balanced across both hands. Bowing his head slightly he proffers the weapon to the Englishman.

De la Vere takes the flintlock from the shaman and almost instantly his nose twitches. "What the . . .?"

Now Boyd smells it, too. Pulls a face. "Jesus!"

De la Vere squints at the barrel. "Fucking hell!"

Mabhubesi turns to the interpreter. *What's he saying?*

Uh, he would rut . . .

Cha! Tell him the axe is cleaned after *the battle!*

"This is *shit*!" shrieks De la Vere. "You smeared shit over my gun!"

Aiee! I thought I smelled something! You smeared shit over his gun?

Tell the Long-Nosed heathen this is our way. This is our magic! Tell him now he cannot fail to kill Shaka!

18
The Battering Ram

It's a muted council of war; even Nomahlanjana has run out of invective. Mistaking his gloomy silence for the quiet that precedes a storm of punishment, his generals hasten to reassure him. See? they say. The Zulu lines weaken!

That he was told the same thing a few hours ago doesn't escape Nomahlanjana; yet they also speak the truth – the Zulu lines *are* growing ever more ragged. The fact that he's at last decided to put his father's plan into operation appears to have rallied his senior commanders. They bristle with outrage; their skill as leaders and strategists is being impugned. It remains a matter of pride for them. They don't need this Englishman . . .

They're blind to the growing numbers slipping away in search of water. When it's brought to their attention by concerned – and thirsty – captains their response is an irritated shrug: Water? But there's plenty of water. What are these fools talking about?

And there *is* plenty of water – for the generals are able to make frequent trips to the gourds zealously watched over by the prince's servants in the shade of the trees. The wellbeing of their men is not an issue.

Nomahlanjana's brothers know their father better. They are equally oblivious to the state of the men (those that have wandered off will be rounded up and punished once victory is assured), but they lack the generals' optimism. In fact, they guess rightly that the generals *have* to be optimistic; any other stance would be an admission of failure, a sign that one hasn't pushed one's men as hard as one could have. They can see the Zulu lines weakening – where there were five, there are now two – but they are not so sure the end of the battle is approaching as speedily as the generals believe.

Nomahlanjana agrees with his brothers, here. He is loathe to prolong the matter overnight and into the following day. That would give his father ample time to receive word of his army's many setbacks and casualties. Nomahlanjana has yet to send any reports back to his father, but it's a certainty that Zwide's own messengers are at this moment searching for the Ndwandwe army. And Zwide will be furious. But if Nomahlanjana can end this affair today, before sunset, he'll escape most of his father's wrath. A victory is, after all, a victory.

These are all factors in favour of deploying the Englishman, who promises a speedy end to the matter with his "magic" – and perhaps a reason for Nomahlanjana to curse himself for not using De la Vere earlier. At the same time, however, his brothers urge Nomahlanjana to be cautious. Since they also stand in the way of Zwide's wrath, Noma-hlanjana feels he can trust their counsel on this.

Who will gain the glory should the White Man succeed?

That's the question. If De la Vere succeeds, the princes believe this will enable their father to claim the glory. After all, it was he who hatched this scheme. This in turn will enable him to snatch a greater share of the loot – the cattle and women they'll round up while the Zulus flee. In fact, he might even leave Nomahlanjana and his brothers nothing at all, a humiliation too great to contemplate.

So – use him, they urge, use this White Man with his isibhamu, but be wise, be cunning!

Yes, thinks Nomahlanjana, and there is Mgobozi up there and other respected leaders – they might still rally the Zulu impis and prolong this matter, if given enough time . . . Yes, he decides, Shaka's fall must be accompanied by a last, all-out offensive. A final attack, wherein confusion will be a valuable ally. And afterwards who will be able to say whether it was the Englishman or the brave Ndwandwe soldiers who finally sent the Zulus fleeing like yelping dogs?

*

The smoke has shifted. Time is running out for Shaka. Soon, the Ndwandwe column will rejoin the main force. He, too, would like to settle this matter today. And this is another reason why he grew so angry when his regiments seemed about to run out of control. Even if the Zulus had succeeded in turning feigned panic into a genuine rout, the Ndwandwe army would've scattered. To pursue them Shaka would have had to split up his forces – and he doesn't have the numbers. The Ndwandwes could reform and pick off the regiments isolated by the chase – and they'd be strengthened by the column coming in from the Tonjaneni Heights.

No, this thing has to be finished today, while he has the bulk of the Ndwandwe army here below him, weak and ailing; and it has to be finished soon, long before sunset, before the two-thousand-strong column returns.

*

Two lines. Some six hundred men. That's what this Zulu has left. Nomahlanjana can still field close to three thousand troops.

Two lines . . . six hundred men, fewer even . . .

A shaky stockade. Perhaps a little push will do the trick . . .

Or, better still, a mighty shove!

Nomahlanjana briefs his generals.

*

"They come again," says Mgobozi.

"I see that."

"Surely they do not mean to trick us once more," adds the general, watching as one man in four moves forward.

"Father!" calls Nzobo from the southern rim.

"See –" he points, as Mgobozi and Shaka arrive at his side.

Here, one in four has moved forward. But the whole rear rank of the reserve is streaming sideways, heading north.

"Father!" calls Mdlaka from the eastern rim.

"Go see," Shaka tells Mgobozi.

The King meanwhile retraces his steps back to his rock, keeping pace with the shifting units below.

Mgobozi does the same along the eastern rim, where a large body of Ndwandwes is also moving north.

The two men meet back on the rock.

"What is this?" wonders Mgobozi, as they watch the men form up in ranks some metres behind the remaining reserve.

"Let us deal with this annoyance first," says Shaka – for the men that have come forward now begin to advance. Each Ndwandwe is carrying only one spear.

Shaka lets them come far up the hill, their tired thighs straining against the gradient, before he sends his first line in.

*

This is it! Suddenly, left by the mimosa tree with the interpreter and shaman, Boyd feels very lonely, very exposed. Oliver loaded his friend's musket before he left – Boyd being too afraid to keep the thing permanently primed – and now Stanley struggles to keep the gun balanced on one knee while he works the spyglass with his other hand.

No, this isn't going to work.

He tells Tuppence to remount and join him. Don't trust the bastard, De la Vere has told him, but Boyd's too nervous to worry about that now. He hands Tuppence his gun.

That's better!

He scans the advancing Ndwandwes – and picks out his friend. De la Vere's mud has dried grey and cracked, and he's not hard to spot.

Still, decides Boyd, he doesn't stand out *that* much. He's also relieved to see the Ndwandwe captain has been true to his word and Stanley is behind a wedge of warriors. They're supposed to protect him while he lines up his shot.

Speaking of which . . .

A blur of bodies, bloody soil and rocks as Boyd raises his spyglass. Speaking of which, there he is. Shaka, in all his glory. Nicely silhouetted against the sky.

The Zoolas haven't attacked yet and Boyd's pleased to see the line, with De la Vere's small party unobtrusively mingling with the others, climbing higher and higher. Such is the angle of the slope that Shaka will almost always be in De la Vere's sights so long as the king remains at his post. And it doesn't seem like he's going to be moving.

Boyd brings the spyglass down to find his friend again. Panics as he scans the black backs without spotting De la Vere.

Easy, he tells himself, lowering the telescope, easy . . .

He wipes his face with his cravat. Casts a glance to his left to make sure Tuppence is still there.

Christ, is this such a good idea, after all?

But one shot – that's all it'll take. Then, his task done, De la Vere will come back down the hill. And the Ndwandwes will do the rest.

A hiss from the Zoola ranks: "Si-Gi-Di!"

And down they come . . .

Boyd is reminded of a stormy sea, a wave racing to the shore – for this hiss is like the shifting of the pebbles in the wave's path.

Where *is* he . . .?

Boyd raises the spyglass to his eye once more.

Ah! *Yes*!

De la Vere leaps into focus. Cracked mud peeling from his back. That ridiculous kilt. As Boyd watches, he drops onto his knees. Raises his Brown Bess.

Then there's a flash and De la Vere reels away from his gun, hands up over his face . . .

What the . . .!

Instinctively, fat Stanley Boyd digs his spurs into the horse's flanks – he's going to charge in there to rescue De la Vere – but the animal moves forward without him, as a lion leaps out of the bushes, pulling the White Man from the saddle.

*

De la Vere's gun explodes in his face just as one of Shaka's "dead men" – one of the lone outposts he ordered to stand ahead of the lines – crashes through his protectors. Thrusting this way and that, the Zulu makes light work of the Ndwandwes; then, his iklwa plunges into the heart of the screaming White Man. Not that the warrior recognises him as such. He doesn't have time to ponder the presence of this mud-caked apparition with bleeding eyes, because he's moving on, leaping over the dead Englishman, pouncing on another Ndwandwe.

It's these "dead men" who almost single-handedly repulse the Ndwandwe attack, some hacking their way through the line, then turning and attacking from the rear. What's more, many survive to move back into position, a few metres in front of Shaka's remaining men.

*

Of the Ndwandwe ranks only the southern semicircle is left intact. From the new formation made up by soldiers pulled out of the lines, another begins to form. A column of warriors twenty abreast with three paces between each man. Rank after rank they come, so that by the time the column reaches the foot of Gqokli, it comprises seventy-five ranks and stretches a distance of almost two hundred metres. Rank after rank they come as this human battering ram begins to make its way up the slope.

"Now, Mgobozi? Now?"

The general nods. "Now!"

"You will take Njikiza and a few others of the Fasimba impi and you will kill the princes."

"Only the princes, Father?"

"Cha! Just do it, Old Friend!"

Turning his back on the Ndwandwes, Shaka steps toward the inner edge of the rock that has served as his command post.

A force of four thousand Zulus, fifteen hundred of which he had put to encircle Gqokli Hill . . .

"Brave Sons of Zulu," bellows Shaka, "your time has come! Awake! Arise! Attack!"

A force of four thousand, fifteen hundred of which started the day encircling the hill, while five hundred were sent off with the cattle so that Nomahlanjana would divide his army . . . And now two thousand warriors stand up in the hollow atop the hill where Shaka has kept them hidden.

The Zulu reserve: two thousand fresh men, who've been receiving regular rations of water and food from the udibis, two thousand rested men impatient to join the fray.

With five hundred held back lest Nomahlanjana's southern semicircle attack and the two lines left in place around the hill, the remaining fifteen hundred stream over the brow, splitting into two prongs, eight men abreast. The Fasimba impi led by Mgobozi is on the right; the Izicwe impi is on the left. These horns race down the hill on either side of the Ndwandwe ram, keeping a spear's throw away from the startled warriors.

Only when the first ranks reach the rear of the column do the Zulus close in. And the enemy is engaged before he even has time to realise he's been enveloped.

*

The interpreter's horse skitters sideways, turns in a tight circle. Reining the animal in, he regards the Induna.

"Clearly your subterfuge, if subterfuge it was, has worked, Zulu," he says, his left hand around the gun barrel, the butt pressed against his thigh. "Let my response be much simpler. I'm of a mind to pay a visit to my mother's clan, who lives many, many days' journey from this place."

The Induna nods. "Go well, Xhosa."

*

Mgobozi leads his party crashing into the rear ranks of the column. The men assigned to protect him make sure they take up positions on his flanks, two on each side, while Njikiza covers his rear. The general twists to the right, hooks the outer edge of his shield against the inner edge of the Ndwandwe's, then twists to the left, hooking the warrior's shield aside – but just as he's about to drive his iklwa home, Njikiza's club comes whizzing overhead, shattering the man's skull and knocking him sideways. Lunging forward, Mgobozi engages another warrior – hooks his shield aside and watches as the club strikes again, splattering grey porridge. After this happens a third and a fourth time, the general wheels round.

"Njikiza!" he bellows above the fray. "What are you doing?"

The big warrior crushes the head of an Ndwandwe about to run his spear through the general's spine and shrugs. "We are to protect you, General. The Bull Elephant has decreed it so."

Mgobozi is about to protest, but with a curt "Forgive me, General," Njikiza pushes him sideways. The big Zulu doesn't have time to raise his weapon; instead he simply stretches his arm outward and allows the Ndwandwe soldier to run into the club. It catches the man in the throat, and as he tries to jerk away, one of the spikes bites home, hooking him under his chin. When Mgobozi turns and pushes him backwards with his shield, the warrior leaves his lower jaw behind, dangling off Njikiza's club.

"You do not protect me," continues Mgobozi. "You deprive me!"

The jaw bone goes flying off as the big Zulu floors another Ndwandwe.

"My iklwa would join the feast! Now stand back!"

*

The Induna falls upon a group of soldiers returning from the distant river. One, then two go down, before the men flee.

Shaka had just issued his instructions – find and kill the Lion – when Mgobozi intervened. "You want vengeance, this is so," he told the King. "But let it be a quiet vengeance." Mgobozi's idea: the Induna will find the Lion, kill him and assume his identity.

"To what purpose?" asked Shaka.

"To trick Zwide, Majesty. Let the Induna approach the crocodile as the sangoma, offer to aid him in the coming battle. Zwide used sorcery on Dingiswayo. Let this crocodile have a taste of his own medicine!"

"Surely you do not expect me to . . ."

"No, Majesty! No. Not your seed! But something almost as potent . . ."

Now, a Zulu warrior once more, the Induna turns. Spies another party. Five men. Races toward them. As far as they know, he's a powerful sangoma in the employ of Zwide and they think he's come to berate them for cowardice. Even after he kills two of them, the others waver. He's meted out his punishment, now he'll send them back to the battle. When he rounds on them, though, they prepare to fight back. Will anyone know who slew this traitorous Zulu? What right does he have to discipline them, anyway?

While the one tries to keep the Induna distracted, the others move left and right to encircle the warrior.

He charges the man directly in front of him, turning at the last moment, using his shield to force the man to step away. In the same instant, he thrusts his assegai at the warrior to his right – but it's a feint. Twirling the spear, he straightens his elbow and drives the blade backwards, into the stomach of the man to his left who is now behind him. Then, riding his own momentum, he twists again, sliding his shield between him and the man to his right just in time to deflect the soldier's spear – and thrusts his iklwa to his left, guiding the assegai across his body in an underarm stabbing motion that drives the blade into the groin of the first man.

The third man turns and flees.

The Induna moves in the opposite direction, heading for the tree where Nomahlanjana has stationed himself.

*

The Ndwandwe princes fight bravely and die like heroes. Let their names be remembered: Nombengula, Mpepa, Sixoloba and Dayingubo.

*

"We must withdraw, General!" shouts Njikiza.

"Let me not stand in your way," says Mgobozi, bleeding from cuts in his side and thighs.

"Cha! The King . . ."

". . . is not here!"

And then they're thrown apart, as the Ndwandwe column descends on them. The desperate men have turned themselves around and the rear has become the van. They are now trying to fight their way off the hill. And it's all Njikiza and the other Fasimbas can do to stay on their feet, wielding assegai and club with a vehemence that is matched only by the hysteria of the fleeing Ndwandwes.

And they lose sight of the old general as he disappears beneath an avalanche of shields and falling men.

*

Most of Nomahlanjana's entourage has fled and those that remain are trying to persuade the prince to make his getaway as well when the Induna crashes into their midst. He kills several, before the others race away.

"Where is your lion-skin, your medicine bag?" the Induna had asked.

"Hidden over there," said the Lion.

And the Induna had foolishly turned to look in the direction the sangoma was pointing. And when he turned back, it was to confront the Lion's Arabi dagger . . .

He leant away, felt the blade nick his throat. His right hand closed around the Lion's wrist, forcing the dagger to continue in its arc. The sangoma was thrown against him, his back to the Induna's chest. The Induna slipped his left arm around the Lion's throat, and forced the shaman to thrust the dagger into his own heart.

Nomahlanjana regards the panting Zulu for a moment . . .

Then, without standing, he raises his head and parts his hands, moving them palm upwards away from his body.

The Induna drives his iklwa into the prince's heart.

*

Suddenly it's over. The Ndwandwe battering ram is destroyed. But there's that other column, coming in from the Tonjaneni Heights . . .

Shaka orders the thousand warriors who remain after destroying the human battering ram to move out and sweep up the Ndwandwe water parties. Then he withdraws his northern two-line semicircle, leaving only the "dead men"; these will form the horns who'll move to outflank the remaining Ndwandwe ranks on the southern side of the hill. The head will comprise every remaining soldier still able to fight.

The Ndwandwe commander, however, has seen the soldiers returning from the Tonjaneni Heights and immediately orders a rapid retreat. With a head start and by sacrificing his wounded warriors in a series of rearguard actions, he's able to reach the van of the returning regiments. Then, and only then, do the Ndwandwes turn and fight.

Shaka, who has personally led the pursuit, now orders his men to fall back in the direction of Bulawayo.

A bizarre running battle ensues. The reinforced Ndwandwes once again outnumber the remaining Zulus, but as they harass the retreating soldiers, so they are harried in *their* rear by the men of the Nkomendala and Fasimba impis who lured the Ndwandwe column away from the main force in the first place. Only four hundred of these men remain, but they have already counted for nearly twice as many Ndwandwes.

Outside KwaBulawayo Shaka makes a stand, and a thousand Zulus face the two thousand Ndwandwes returned from cattle rustling and the five hundred who have survived Gqokli. The fighting is fierce and Shaka himself moves up and down the ranks with a reserve, shoring up the lines where they seem weakest. Manyosi falls before the door of the royal hut itself, brought down by a spear in his side.

Then, just when things seem at their bleakest, the warriors return from rounding up the water groups and the situation changes instantly. Now the Ndwandwes find themselves surrounded.

In the end, fewer than eight hundred manage to escape east.

19

The Hill

Shaka leaves all his wounded at KwaBulawayo, guarded by a strong detachment, and returns to Gqokli with the main body of his men. Despite their victory, he knows they remain vulnerable. With his reduced numbers he can still defend the hill against a counterattack – and those reduced numbers also mean he still has ample provisions left. They'll spend the night here before commencing mopping-up operations and fetching the women and children back from the southern frontier.

The first thing Shaka does on his return is to pardon the men he ordered to place themselves ahead of the Zulu lines. "The Bull Elephant gave you his word you would not die at the hand of a fellow Zulu this day," he tells them. "You have redeemed yourselves. Return to your regiments and let your courage be remembered by praise singers across the land."

He then retreats to the outcrop of rock from where he conducted the battle. Nqoboka finds him staring down at the pile of corpses that marks the remains of the Ndwandwe ram. It has kept its shape and the bodies lie in a long rectangle that ends in a mound of shields and tangled limbs at the foot of the hill. An arc of four bonfires surrounds the crush where Mgobozi fell and Shaka can see Njikiza standing down there, a lone sentinel, obeying the King's commands to the last.

"Father?"

"What is it?"

"Your men . . . they wish to see you."

Shaka stands. He is momentarily surprised to see that while fires have been lit in the hollow there are no men around; only udibis watching the cooking meat.

He moves past Nqoboka and follows the ridge to the eastern side of the hill. Here, at the foot of Gqokli, the Zulu army has formed up, every fifth man clutching a burning torch. The general has stopped to light his own torch; now he holds it aloft and as soon as Shaka steps into the pool of flickering light, the men erupt in a cheer.

"Bayede, Nkosi Yamakosi, bayede! Hail, King of Kings! Hail, Shaka, the Bull Elephant! The Liberator!"

With Nqoboka following him, keeping the torch aloft, Shaka begins to make his way down the hill, stepping around the bodies, and stepping into history. For this is the end of the beginning. A great nation has been forged on this day.

*

And the boy is at last reunited with the Induna. The two stand staring at each other, the boy with trembling lips, the Induna with a faint grin.

"You are well?"

"I am well, Master. Are you well?"

"Ngisaphila," says the Induna. *I am well.*

Picquets have been posted and the rest of the men have gathered round the campfires. Their voices are muted as they drink beer and eat the meat prepared for them by the udibis. Tales of their courage will be told by others. Their morale is high, but these exhausted men know only that tonight they are alive, and that is victory enough.

"The King told me you have performed an important service for him this day. He says you have the makings of a great warrior."

"Master, it was nothing. He bade me watch for the smoke . . ."

"An important task, Boy."

"Yes, Master . . ."

"But?"

"I could have done more . . . I . . . I could have been with you, Master."

"Cha! Who then would have watched for the smoke?"

The boy lowers his head.

"Come," says the Induna, "let us find something to eat."

They move around the murmuring circles, faces, lit pale orange in the firelight, turning to watch their progress.

Logs snap and crack; sparks drift into the air. High up, the stars lie like splashed milk.

The Induna lays a hand on the boy's shoulder. "I am glad no harm befell you," he murmurs.

The boy looks up at him. "And I – I am glad you are well, Master."

*

There is one more thing to be done after the men have been dismissed.

"I would see where he fell," says Nqoboka.

The other generals murmur their assent and Shaka nods. They skirt the hill until they come to the fires guarded by Njikiza.

Nqoboka cannot restrain himself. "Didn't our Father instruct you to guard Mgobozi's life, to keep him safe?" he asks Njikiza, his voice quivering with anger.

The big man nods solemnly. "This I did."

"What do you mean?"

"Wait!" says Shaka, holding up his hand. "Do you hear that?"

The men listen with frowning concentration.

"Who is the only one to drag dry hides in such a manner?"

The snoring comes from under the pile of shields. All eyes turn to Njikiza.

"What is the meaning of this?" asks Nqoboka, his bluster getting tripped up by his grin.

"Why did you not say anything?" adds another general.

"My orders were not to leave him. What could I do when everyone went off to chase the Ndwandwes?"

"But to leave him in such a manner . . ." says Nqoboka, indicating the mound.

"I called to him, but he said he would rest for a while."

The snoring stops with a snort and a grunt. The shields begin to move as if the dead warriors are coming back to life.

"And now he awakens," says Shaka. "Help him, help the old goat so that he might continue to vex us with his chatter."

The men begin to pull away the bodies and shields, and finally Mgobozi rears up, his bloodied body glinting in the firelight. "Cha!" he says stretching. "Let us continue to feast. My assegai cries out in hunger . . ." Then he sees Shaka.

"Majesty!" he says, stepping over the bodies. He looks around. "Am I to assume this matter has been favourably resolved?"

"That it has, Old Friend."

Mgobozi glances at the other generals. "Did you not leave any for me?"

"You would take a nap in the middle of the battle, Mgobozi."

"Only so that I might conserve my strength, Majesty. And these lice were going nowhere."

"Mgobozi, must you always have the last word?"

"Me, Majesty? Not me!"

The two men embrace, and the other generals swarm around until Mgobozi shrugs them off. "A few flesh wounds, it is nothing. Please, Brothers – I have enough wives at home!"

"Which is why you need your rest, Old Friend."

"This is so."

"Do you see what I mean, Mgobozi? You must always have the last word. And it is never a 'Yes, Father!'"

"Truly, I do not know what you mean, Majesty."

"Mgobozi, you are incorrigible."

"Yes, Father!"

"See? Even when I do get a 'Yes, Father!' out of you it is pregnant with every other meaning but the one which those words signify."

"Well . . ."

"Out with it, Goat!"

"My 'Yes, Father' was a 'Yes, Father' of deference, Majesty. Of trust."

"Trust?"

"Trust, Majesty. For, truly, I am not sure what this 'incorrigible' means."

"What do you think it means?"

"I am hoping it is a malady that can be cured by a lake of beer, and if this is the case, then my 'Yes, Father' would be a 'Yes, Father' of unfettered enthusiasm, Majesty."

*

The boy is asleep, as are most of the men. The Induna stands alone on the flat rock, staring into the darkness. Down there, somewhere beneath the northern rim, lies the body of the Englishman who planned to assassinate Shaka. How the King had roared with laughter when the Induna had told him how he thwarted the Long Nose. And there, somewhere out there, lies the body of Nomahlanjana and, a little further away, by a grove of trees, lies the Englishman's fat companion. Already the bodies that could be seen in the glow of Njikiza's fires at the foot of the hill have vanished, dragged away by hyenas. And growls and grunts can be heard – and the sound of breaking bones and tearing flesh – as the animals feast.

Then he's no longer alone.

He turns.

It's Dingane, Shaka's half-brother, who arrived a few hours ago, seeking news of the battle.

"Greetings, Old Friend," says the Prince, for they were soldiers together once.

"Greetings. You are well?"

"I am well. And you are better – if my brother is to be believed."

The Induna shrugs. "I did as I was ordered."

"Aiee! Not many would enter the leopard's lair in such a manner."

"And you? You and your men – you were not intercepted?"

"No. You kept them too busy here. I bravely parried the whining of women and the mewling of children."

The two men stand in silence, watching the darkness.

"It is done?" asks Dingane after a while.

"For now," murmurs the Induna.

"So yet more Zulu blood will flow." He keeps his voice low.

"We did not pick this fight."

"Cha! Do you not know? The more a man drinks, the more he *must* drink."

When the Induna remains silent, Dingane glances at him, trying to judge his reaction.

"Many brave men died here today," says the Prince, lowering his voice still further. "Yet all he can talk about is his shit! How powerful, how blessed his shit is that it felled the assassin."

"Forgive me, Old Friend, but I am tired. I would sleep now."

Dingane's hand closes around the Induna's elbow. "You are loyal and wise, Friend, but one day soon you might find these are two masters you cannot always serve at the same time. And then what will you do?"

Dingane looks around to make sure no one's in earshot. "And understand me well, Brother. I do not talk of treachery. That would be –"

"Imprudent?"

"Misleading."

"Ah."

"Because is it treachery when the fate of a nation hangs in the balance? Can it be treachery when a legion of brave men rises up to end tyranny?"

So it was you . . .

Familiar words. It was Dingane, this Needy One, who tipped the scales of the Lion's precarious conscience. Or perhaps it was the other way around, but the Induna doubts it. It's more in Dingane's nature to manipulate – and from a distance too. Moving ceaselessly, invisibly, like a current in a stream. The Induna doubts he had a definite plan; just like that current, he simply went to work to disrupt and destroy where he could. No definite plan, but a goal: to usurp Shaka by undermining his authority.

Dingane shakes his head. "Brave men have died today, many brave men, and all he can talk about is his shit . . . Sometimes the family must be protected from the father."

"Where will such a path take one? The heir who has usurped will in turn fear his heirs. The tribe will eat itself. What good can come of such a situation?"

"And if the father is mad – what then?"

"Who is to make that decision? Certainly not the heir."

"Agreed. Which is why I speak of a legion of brave men . . ."

"Brave men are loyal men."

"This is so. But what if they believe their loyalty lies with the tribe, not the King?"

120

"Is not the King the tribe?"

"Only if he would serve the tribe and not himself."

"We vanquished a near-invincible foe today. Did we start this matter? No. But we finished it. What more could we have done? Who could have served us better?"

"I ask you to look beyond today. That is all."

"Cha! But first I must shut my eyes. They are weary."

"Rest them, then. But remember what I have said."

The Induna nods. "Sala kahle," he says. *Stay well.*

"And you – you go well, my Friend."

*

Treasonous talk to be sure, but no one, least of all Shaka, expects anything less from the Needy One, and as the Induna moves through the darkness he has a smile on his face.

So! The King is enamoured of his own shit. Such potent shit. Shit that choked the Devourer Of Kings. Blessed shit!

Shit he'd used to block the White Man's isibhamu, a plug he forced down to hold in place the sand he'd first poured into the barrel of the gun.

And when one of Shaka's servants returned accompanied by a group of bodyguards and nervously handed the Induna this sacred talisman Shaka believed was necessary if the Induna was to fool Zwide into thinking he was the shaman, the Induna accepted it with due reverence. And, a few hours later, when he was far away from KwaBulawayo, he buried this shit with due reverence. And the gnawing of a guilty conscience.

But the smell was greater.

For although winter is approaching, the days remain hot, and any man's shit, even a King's, will begin to stink under such circumstances. Especially if in a large quantity – and, truly, Shaka was enthusiastic in his collaboration. It was as if he wanted to ensure the downfall of ten kings.

He buried the King's shit and ran on, preferring to draw on his own resources when he got nearer to the enemy's kraal.

PART TWO
In The Service Of Shaka

In the adventure book of the story of mankind in South Africa there are some chapters which far surpass even the most extravagant fiction. Thus it is with the story of Shaka, a man whose career was drenched with the blood of endless conflicts; a man whose courage and resolution and intelligence made him loom as a giant in a cringing African world; a man whose shadow fell, although he scarcely knew it, from the Great Lakes to the Cape; a man who built a nation from a patchwork of insignificant clans and left them a legacy of world-wide martial renown and a pride based largely on the glamour of his name.

From *Shaka's Country* by T.V. Bulpin

It's a night in late 1815 and men from Dingiswayo's favourite Izicwe regiment are dancing. Flames reflected in their sweat make their bodies glow, as they crouch, their hands waving grass, their eyes on their prey. With the drums marking each movement, they creep through the shimmering grass. Then they leap – leap and kick . . .

Resting on his elbow, Senzangakhona reaches across his chest to tap Dingiswayo's shoulder. The Mthetwa ruler leans back.

"Who is that one?" Senzangakhona's voice is a rasp. "Do I know him?"

He's pointing at a tall, muscular warrior dancing in the centre of the first row.

Dingiswayo twists his head to speak into the old man's ear.

"He is Zulu," he says, loud enough to defeat the drums.

Senzangakhona nods and Dingiswayo has to stifle a grin. Clearly the old fool has misheard him.

*

A brave warrior with some outspoken notions as to how battles should be fought, Shaka would've come to Dingiswayo's attention in due course. That their relationship should have soon deepened into something beyond mere respect and admiration, however, was due to the fact that Dingiswayo saw in the young Zulu a kindred spirit.

The Mthetwa ruler had also been an outcast. He was born Godongwana and it was said he and a brother conspired against their father, Jobe. The plot failed, the brother was put to death and Godongwana fled. Others say the traits that would one day make him a great ruler revealed themselves at an early age and Godongwana became Jobe's favourite. Jealous, some of his brothers said Godongwana was plotting to overthrow their father. Upon receiving the summons to Jobe's kraal, Godongwana chose to flee rather than see his father shame himself by believing the lies of others.

Whatever the reason, the young nobleman found himself among the Hlubis, people of Lala and Swazi stock, where he soon distinguished himself through his bravery and initiative and became a headman in the tribe. By this time he'd taken to calling himself Dingiswayo – the Wanderer.

One day a White Man came to the kraal. Possibly he was one Dr Cowan, the last survivor of a mission sent by the governor of the Cape to explore the hinterland in 1806. What is known is that he had a gun and a horse, for these Dingiswayo claimed for himself after the White Man's death.

Deciding it was time to venture homeward, Dingiswayo agreed to guide the White Man to the coast. As they neared Mthetwa territory, however, Dingiswayo murdered the White Man and took his possessions. At least, that's the story Zwide told, seeing it as yet another instance of his rival's treacherous nature.

Others say the White Man was stricken with fever and Dingiswayo nursed him until he succumbed.

This is more likely, for Dingiswayo would always speak highly of the White Man. Somehow they overcame the language barrier – not so difficult if the White Man could speak Xhosa, a dialect that would've been comprehensible to Dingiswayo as the Mthetwas were also of Nguni stock. And sitting around the campfire at the end of the day, the White Man told the young warrior of the settlement at the Cape, the great empires across the waters, talking not just of war and conquest, but of industry and trade as well.

It was the White Man, Dingiswayo later said, who gave him the idea of uniting the tribes in the region. But it wasn't to be conquest for the sake of conquest. Dingiswayo envisaged what was in effect a commonwealth that would be able to deal with the White Men on its own terms. For that was something else the White Man told Dingiswayo – the Long Noses were coming, and in greater numbers than he could ever imagine. And their actions would gradually begin to impinge more and more on ways the tribes thought were timeless and immutable.

When Dingiswayo heard that his father was dead, he immediately rode to the Mthetwa capital to claim the throne. He was a dead man come to life, reborn, renamed, and cut a fine figure with the horse and musket. Here was one truly blessed by the ancestors – resurrected and sent back to his people. It mattered not that the horse soon died, for these were not healthy environs for such creatures. Neither did it matter that the gun was next to useless, lacking ball and powder – it was perceived as a powerful talisman all the same.

The year was 1809. Few had the courage to dispute Dingiswayo's claims – certainly not his conniving brothers, who also believed he was blessed by the ancestors, and quietly moved away with their families.

Dingiswayo set about building his army and Shaka's age group was duly called up. Shaka had been eleven when he and his mother sought refuge and found lasting happiness among the Mthetwas.

*

Leaning sideways, Dingiswayo studies Senzangakhona for a moment. The old Zulu King is clearly ailing – hunched shoulders, trembling hands, withered limbs, a mockery of his former self. Dingiswayo wipes his hand across his mouth to hide his grin.

Oh yes! Senzangakhona definitely misheard him. He thought he said "He is a Zulu."

The old fool. This warrior he thinks he knows is more than a mere Zulu; he is Shaka, he is Zulu, of the Bloodline.

Dingiswayo waits for Senzangakhona to savour a mouthful of beer, before leaning forward again to speak into the old man's ear.

"Would you like to meet him?"

Senzangakhona shrugs. Why should he want to? Because this strong man is a Zulu? Cha! He is no Zulu if he lives among Dingiswayo's people!

Dingiswayo however takes that for a yes. He despatches one of his servants. As the boy approaches Shaka, the drums fall silent, for all of this has been carefully planned ...

The Wrath Of Shaka

Moving through the morning mist, chased by the taunts of their pursuers, the woman and the boy can scarcely see three paces ahead of them. The rattle of a pebble dislodged by a warrior's foot. The clink of steel against stone. The sense of dark shapes moving through this grey world. The woman turns to grab the boy's elbow, the better to hurry him along, but he snatches his arm away. It's easier to make your own way over the slippery boulders, glistening green and black in the cold air.

Around and over the rocks clamber the two: the boy, ten, and clad only in a loincloth; the woman in her mid-twenties, bare-breasted, wearing a bead skirt with a cowhide robe thrown over her shoulders. Both carry an iklwa. The boy slips on some moss, bangs his knee – has to bite his lip to stop from crying out. The woman looks over her shoulder; he waves her on. He can look after himself.

Their breath burns in their chests as they chart a zigzag course up the gorge. The mist is wet, sullen, as much a foe as an ally.

How close are their pursuers?

How much further to the top?

The spears hinder their progress, interfere with their balance, but they are necessary, for these two will not be taken alive . . .

*

Her name was Nandi, the Sweet One, and sweet was her song, so sweet he thought he'd stumbled upon Marimba, the goddess of music, who taught our people the secret of many beautiful sounds.

She'd been bathing, stood up to her knees in the stream. Her breasts were firm, her thighs voluptuous lips waiting to part in a smile of welcome. Her face was round and her eyes were almond-shaped. And it was *she* who surprised *him*.

He stood motionless beneath the trees that craned over the water and when she saw him, alerted by the intensity of his gaze, as palpable as the current caressing the reeds, she showed no fear – or modesty.

She simply straightened up, placed her hands on her hips and regarded him with a look that said: Well?

*

Uneven steps. Straining thighs. Cold sweat.

The woman places her spear on the ledge, then hoists herself up. It's only waist high, but her arms are as tired as her legs – and she's suspended a moment on locked elbows, her shoulders shuddering. Just as it seems she might slip back, waste precious seconds trying again, she finds the strength to lean forward and raise a knee. The boy follows her example – lays his spear on the ledge, hoists himself up onto his arms – and worms forward, dragging his legs after him.

The woman helps the boy to his feet and they hurry on, following the ledge to where they can scramble up a bank of dirt. The incline rises to meet them and they're on their stomachs before they realise it. Hard to crawl carrying a spear – but they pull themselves onward and upward.

Now the boy is grateful for her outstretched hand. He takes it and allows the woman to pull him over the rock. Bites his lower lip to stop from crying out as jagged ridges scrape his stomach and thighs. Leaving him, the woman attacks the next slope . . .

*

Of course, she knew who he was. Senzangakhona, son of Jama, king of the Zulus, escorting his mother on a visit to her home clan.

She knew who he was, had felt his eyes on her at other times, on her and her alone, while she helped serve the food, chattered with the other maidens, went to fetch water . . .

Hawu, but it had taken him a long time to find her alone. She was running out of excuses to escape the company of the other girls, chores she could do that would take her away from the village.

Silly man! For all their bluster and swagger, their stern self-importance and feigned indifference, men were like children in these matters. No – cattle. Cattle that had to be led. Guided. *Shown*.

Prompted, too. For look at this one, standing there like a lost calf.

"Aiee!" she grinned. "Would you speak with your eyes and listen with your lips?"

He mirrored her grin and moved to the water's edge.

"I know those words," she said.

"Cha! You are too young!"

"Not so young that I can't understand the language of your eyes."

"Language?"

"I was being kind. Or perhaps I am wrong. Perhaps only a baboon might find such hunger eloquent."

"It is refreshing to see my being a prince doesn't induce shyness and diffidence in you."

"These being qualities you Zulus prize in a maiden?"

"In which case you have nothing to worry about."

"My breasts are bare. I am a maiden!"

The prince laughed. "This is not what *your* eyes tell me."

Nandi, the Sweet One, bent forward to place her hands in the water, fingers splayed. Senzangakhona watched the swing of her breasts, the way they settled back into a proud firmness when she straightened up.

"So it's true . . ." she said, running her wet hands over her belly.

"What is?"

"That you Zulus prefer your women as meek as your beer."

"Cha! Have you tasted Sweet Innocence?" asked the prince.

Nandi laughed. "No, but you would."

"I like what I see, it is true . . ."

"But not what you hear. How sad!"

"No. An observation. When you interrupted me, I was about to say I like what I see, but looks can deceive."

"You are right. I know whereof you speak."

"I am right? You agree? Let us slaughter an ox to celebrate this occasion!"

"How would a Zulu prince resolve this dilemma?"

Senzangakhona leant forward in a slight bow. "By trusting in your wisdom."

"There are two paths we can take."

"Enlighten me."

Nandi pointed past the prince. "We can return to the village, with me following obediently behind you. A familiar path you have walked many times."

"And the alternative?"

Nandi turned, pointed behind her, to the opposite bank. "*You* can follow *me*. A strange path, for you. A new path. But one that leads to a place where the shade is cool and the grass is soft . . ."

Senzangakhona grinned. "Lead on!"

*

They're at the top.

The woman tosses her spear ahead of her and hauls herself up. On her knees she leans sideways and tells the boy to give her his hand. Too tired to protest, he obeys.

The woman pulls him after her. His feet slip against the wet rock. For a moment he fears he'll drag her off the ledge. Then a final spurt of adrenaline allows his feet to find purchase in a crack and he's able to propel himself upward toward the woman. They fall in a tangle and instantly roll apart, the woman rubbing her breasts and cursing his knees.

They're above the mist, now; it lies below them in the ravine like smoke. But it's an overcast day, threatening rain, the sky the colour of slate, pressing down on the hill that rises before them.

The Tonjaneni Heights.

A path skirts the foot of the slope, heading east and west. But the woman chooses a route that'll take them straight over the hill. It means another climb, and reluctantly the boy goads his aching body into motion.

*

Senzangakhona was drinking beer with some friends when Mduli, the prince's uncle and chief elder of the tribe, found him. When at last he was spotted and Senzangakhona alerted to his presence, Mduli raised his right arm and pointed to the prince. Then he turned and walked away.

Senzangakhona rose unsteadily to his feet. With Jama ailing, Mduli had taken over the running of the tribe's day-to-day affairs. He was forever singling the prince out for chastisement, so while he knew he was in trouble, Senzangakhona was not unduly concerned. He was used to it. Doubtless Mduli was going to lecture him, yet again, on the impropriety of enjoying himself while his father lay on the threshold of the Great Journey. It appeared to be of no matter to Mduli that the tribe had been holding itself in readiness for the departure for several moons now, as Jama rallied and then sank, drifted in and out of moments of weak lucidity.

Senzangakhona, however, became decidedly less sanguine when he caught up to the old man in front of the latter's hut.

The fact that no one was around, that the beehive-shaped huts in the immediate vicinity were temporarily deserted, was ominous enough, but it was when the prince saw his uncle's face that he felt his stomach twist in dread. The older man's features were set in a mask of stony rage. Mduli was ill-tempered by nature, but the prince had never seen his uncle's anger accompanied by such calm before.

Truly, this was the moment of stasis beneath clenched clouds that preceded a terrible storm.

*

"Hssst!"

Finishing his piss, Themba turns round. Njabulo motions his companion to join him on the flat rock.

Crouching low, Themba moves toward the older boy.

Njabulo points.

Themba sees a woman and a boy scrambling up the slope across the way from them. Both carry spears and are clearly desperate to reach the summit as quickly as possible.

Njabulo meets his companion's quizzical expression with a grin and a shrug.

As they watch, the two make it to the top of the hill. They stand silhouetted against the grey sky, the boy bending over to catch his breath. The woman gives him a few moments, then touches his shoulder. He straightens and they disappear from sight.

Themba makes to stand, but Njabulo grabs his arm. Pulls him down. "Look!" he hisses.

This time he points to the mouth of the ravine below them.

A man hoists himself up. Then retrieves his assegai and shield. He's followed by a second man and then a third.

The boys can tell they're Zulu warriors from the oval shape of their shields and the strange, shortened spears they carry.

"I told you I heard shouting," whispers Njabulo.

After conferring for a few moments, the men move along the path, heading west, away from where the two herdboys lie.

*

"You fool!" hissed the old man. "You irresponsible fool! I've overlooked your many transgressions in the name of youthful vigour, but this . . . You have gone too far!"

"Uncle . . ."

"*What*?"

"I would only know what it is I am accused of."

"*Accused*? What am I accused of? he asks! As if there might be any doubt! And I have watched you, Boy. This seems to be your sole talent: moulding doubt like clay into a reprieve. Well, there is no doubt here! You are accused of nothing, so sheath your bluster! It will do you no good. The clay is dry. You are accused of nothing. Instead, you stand condemned! Do you hear me? *Condemned*!"

"Of what?"

"Know you not?"

"No!"

"Then you are a bigger fool than even I realised!"

"Stop talking in riddles, Uncle, and tell me why I have angered you so. And please remember, I am my father's son, I am the heir."

"Then act like one, Boy! Cha, but what am I thinking? That is shutting the gate after the cattle are gone. You will get no respect from me, Boy, because you have acted in a way fit only for censure!"

"Am I not to be allowed to defend myself?"

"In this matter, you have no defence!"

"Let *me* be the judge of that!"

"Your liking for sweetness has betrayed you, Boy."

"There you go – speaking in riddles again."

"And this fondness you were idiotic enough to indulge in while escorting your mother to the Langeni."

Senzangakhona frowned. He hadn't exactly forgotten his encounter with Nandi; it was simply that, with his father growing weaker by the day, the prospect of succession had consumed his thoughts.

In fact, despite a real unease that, this time, he had committed a major transgression, or maybe because of that unease, Senzangakhona was more concerned with fanning the flames of his own anger than discovering what it was he was supposed to have done.

How dare Mduli treat him like this! He was soon to be king; he was owed respect! Let *that* be his defence!

"Frown all you want," growled Mduli, "you cannot charm your way out of this!"

"For the last time, Uncle, tell me what has happened!"

"A messenger from the Langeni, Fool. This morning I had the pleasure of entertaining a messenger from the Langeni – although, truly, mine must have been a pale shadow of the pleasure *you* enjoyed."

"A messenger implies a message, Uncle . . ."

"Ah! Impertinence! A sad defence. But I will indulge you. A Langeni mai- . . . No, that is not right. A Langeni *female* is with child. I nearly said 'maiden' but you have taken care of that side of things. Yes, look alarmed, look bewildered, it will not change the facts. You made her pregnant."

*

Zulu warriors.

The two herdboys have listened to the talk of the men in the village, have heard of the great upheavals in the small Zulu Kingdom – the coming of Shaka with Dingiswayo's legions to claim the crown; the Bastard Son who has forbidden his warriors to marry and expects them to devote all their time to preparing for war, while the women are left to tend the fields.

War? What war? Able to field an army of fewer than five hundred and surrounded on all sides by wealthier, stronger tribes, what does Shaka think he's doing?

It's said that if dust can be seen rising above the Zulu kraals, it's not the army on the move, but the stamping of madmen infected by their king's delusions of grandeur, an insanity that will drive them into the ground.

Doesn't this Zulu fool, this upstart, who by cunning won Dingiswayo's trust, know that in arranging the assassination of Sigujana, the son the dying Senzangakhona chose to succeed him, he has sealed his own fate? For how can it be otherwise? How will Shaka ever be able to sleep? Who can he trust? By killing an heir, you show your own heirs a quicker path to your throne.

Madness! The house of Zulu is doomed!

Njabulo and Themba are too young, too callow, to note the unease in the voices that discuss these matters. For the very things that make for mockery are cause for concern. Add to this the fact that the Zulus are a proud, brave people – and who knows what they might achieve with a resolute madman at their head?

All the same, both herdboys are quiet for some moments after the Zulus have disappeared from sight.

There was something about the way they carried themselves. A self-confidence. A strength, a fitness, a swagger Njabulo and Themba have never seen before, even among the brave men of their own clan.

And if their men seem diminished by comparison, they, too, being almost men, are diminished. Perhaps this is why Njabulo, who at fifteen is the elder of the two, breaks their reverie and suggests they go after the woman and the boy – an unconscious need to regain their sense of manhood by doing *something* . . .

Or perhaps it's simply a desire to do mischief, to break the boredom of long days spent tending the cattle. Besides, the fact that the woman and the boy are fleeing the warriors means they are izilahlwa, *rubbish*, and, therefore, fair game . . .

No one will care what happens to them.

*

Ukuhlobonga – or the Pleasure Of The Road – was a form of loveplay sanctioned by Zulu society that allowed for the release of sexual tension among the young and unmarried without conception resulting. The woman kept her thighs together while the man stimulated her clitoris with his penis. In this way both could achieve an orgasm.

A Zulu warrior who had been in battle was considered unclean until he could sula izembe, *clean the axe*, by sleeping with the first woman he laid eyes on upon returning home, and none could refuse his request. In this instance, Ukuhlobonga was also practised.

Naturally, it often happened that both parties lost control and penetration occurred. If a pregnancy resulted, the girl's father could demand a fine of cattle from the man. Marriage was not mandatory.

Later they'd say Nandi had miscalculated, overreached herself. These were the women of her own clan who claimed to know her best, better, certainly, than the men who were bewitched by her arrogance: the flaunted reminder of that which they would never have.

The grandmothers saw in Nandi a rebellious nature that would challenge the way things were supposed to be. The wives she made uneasy with her flirtatious ways. It seemed to them she'd choose a man for herself, and once she'd made up her mind, nothing would stand in her way. And even if she ended up as a man's third or fourth wife, theoretically subordinate to the first wife, there was no telling to what lengths she'd go to ensure she became the favourite. Girls her own age, meanwhile, shook their heads at Nandi's aloofness, but were secretly bothered, for there was censure in Nandi's attitude, as though they were fools for following the traditional route of marriage and motherhood.

There was no doubt about it: Nandi's was a pernicious influence. And the older women regarded her name as an apt irony: the sweetness that beguiles, invites gluttony and leaves one clutching one's stomach and howling at the moon.

Were they right? What happened in the glade where the shade was cool, the grass soft and Nandi's thighs warmer than the sun? Had she, in the Zulu prince, found the man who'd satisfy her ambitions, her sense of being better than the others? Was there passion when she opened her legs – a loss of control amid his caresses? Or was it calculation – let him sample the wares and he'd never look away?

If that was so, then she *had* erred. For although Senzangakhona was willing to use her with equal vigour, he had a more immediate goal in mind: mere pleasure. A tale of conquest to entertain his friends with back home, something to save this tedious journey with his mother from being a total waste of time.

He was after all a Zulu, from a people who called those from other tribes and clans izilwane, *beasts*.

*

Themba has been complaining – they've strayed too far from the herd; if any cattle go missing, they'll be in big trouble. Although he's a baby who can still taste his mother's tit, his warnings have nonetheless pricked Njabulo's conscience. They *have* left the herd far behind in their pursuit of the two Zulus – well, not two, really; Njabulo only has eyes for the female.

But now it's okay, because these izilahlwa have at last stopped to rest.

The woman sits hunched up in her cowskin cloak, seeking shelter in the lee of a large rock.

So tired. So afraid. Never mind: Njabulo will warm her! Oh yes!

Slowly, carefully, he comes up behind her.

Where's the boy? Probably off collecting firewood. No matter. Themba will take care of him.

Reaching out, Njabulo snatches away the cloak – only to see a small stone topple off a boulder.

Before he can even register surprise, he feels the broad, flattened blade of a Zulu spear tap his left shoulder.

"Little boys who don't take care of their father's cattle deserve a good thrashing," whispers the woman. "Now turn around."

Njabulo obeys. Lets his eyes rise up her body in what he believes to be a sardonic appraisal.

"You are far from home, Girl."

"But you are close to my blade. That should concern you more."

Njabulo's eyes flick past the woman's shoulder. He grins, fixing her with a stare. "Really?"

He has seen Themba.

The path follows the contours of the hill, and Themba has stepped into view from an outcrop of rock above the track a few paces behind the woman.

*

"It was Ukuhlobonga, Uncle!"

"How can that be, Boy? If it was the Pleasure, she would not be with child, would she?"

Senzangakhona shrugged. "These things happen."

"This is your response?"

"Hawu, Uncle, your feigned amazement does not do you justice."

"Boy, it is bad enough you spill your seed with no thought to your standing, the Bloodline you represent, but this I agree I can do little about . . ."

"For you were young once!"

"This is so. I concede this happily, for all the insult implied, for I would not hasten to place myself in the same kraal as *you*, Boy. But, yes, I was young once. But I also wasn't so stupid or so lustful as to commit incest!"

"Incest?"

"Yes, incest! For that is your crime, here. Not impregnation, but incest! Fool! To lose control is one thing, to lose control with one of your mother's clan – that is an idiocy I thought beyond even you!"

Well, yes, his lust had blinded Senzangakhona to this aspect of Zulu law. He had a sudden, overwhelming desire to sit down. He felt dizzy. His knees were water, his surroundings a blur. Only his uncle, glaring at him, remained steadfastly in focus, like a toothache you couldn't drink away with all the beer in the world.

"What . . ."

"What was my response to the messenger?"

The prince nodded.

"I asked him how are we to know that you were the bull involved. How are we to even know this bitch is really pregnant . . ."

Mduli held up a hand to forestall his nephew. "Do not even think to thank me, Boy. Do not thank me for doing my duty. You left me no choice and I acted out of respect for your father. Not you. Do not delude yourself I had your interests at heart. Cha! My heart aches! You are as a maggot to me now. Go! Return to your layabout friends. It burns my eyes to look upon you. And no, your father will not hear of this! But know this, Fool: this matter is not over. Let that knowledge accompany your dissolute enjoyment of the days to come. I have fought a delaying action today, nothing more. Now go! Get out of my sight!"

*

He has seen Themba. But Njabulo's grin fades the moment it forms. As Themba steps down onto the path, the boy appears above him, moving into sight from behind the rock, his assegai at the ready.

"You have him?" asks the woman, without turning around.

"I have him," says the boy.

"Good."

*

In due course, Nandi's pregnancy became visible, obvious, undeniable, and a delegation was once more despatched to the Zulu royal kraal at Esiklebeni.

In the interim Jama had died and Senzangakhona had become King. Such was the nature of the accusation levelled against him, though, this change in his status was immaterial.

It was left to Mduli to deal with the messengers once more. Despite his own distaste for what had transpired, his loyalty lay with the Bloodline. "You say she is pregnant," he informed the Langeni delegation, "I say impossible! You say her belly is swollen with the seed of a Zulu King, I say rubbish! This female is ill. If she says she is with child, a Zulu child, her mind is diseased. If her belly is swollen, her stomach is diseased."

Her enlarged midriff, he told the delegation, was due to an intestinal beetle that caused swelling of the stomach and suppression of the menses.

The Zulus called this "insect" a "shaka".

"That is what is in her gut," sneered Mduli. "A shaka!"

*

Themba's been sent back to look after the cattle, while Njabulo leads them to the village. It's a strange procession, the herdboy in front, the woman and boy several paces behind him, walking alongside each other, their spears pointed at the teenager's back.

The village is a wide semicircle of beehive-shaped thatched huts built around a clearing of hard-packed dirt on a slight incline. The incline leads to a narrow stream, then climbs once more to a ridge. As they come over the ridge and make their way along the path, they're soon spotted. The inkosi is summoned and, by the time the trio arrive at the clearing in front of the huts, the villagers who aren't working in the fields or out hunting are waiting for them.

"Now find your father and seek out the thrashing you deserve," hisses the woman to Njabulo.

She had to take him as a hostage, because she didn't want the villagers forewarned of their approach. She couldn't risk one of the herdboys running on ahead.

She reaches for the boy's hand, takes a deep breath, and tightens her grip on the haft of the spear. Then they move forward to where the chief and his advisors wait, accompanied, she notes wryly, by some armed men.

It's only a few metres across rock-hard dirt the colour of dried maize, but with all eyes on her and the boy, a mixture of expectation and amusement – the expectation of dogs before a meal; the sly, mocking amusement of siblings who know you're in trouble, but won't tell you why – those paces seem to stretch across wide ravines, over perilous mountain passes . . .

*

There was shame.

Shame, because she'd set out to seduce a Zulu prince only to be rejected by him. Shame, because in doing so she'd fallen pregnant. The Langeni women saw this as a fitting comeuppance given Nandi's wily ways, and her airs and graces.

Such a foolish girl.

"See?" said the elders, after the child had been born, and named Shaka in mocking reference to the Zulus' dismissal of Nandi's claims. "There is your beetle! Come and fetch him!"

And Mduli complied, telling Senzangakhona he had no choice in the matter. But there was still shame – because Nandi was quietly installed as the new King's third wife without a wedding ceremony.

And Nandi knew only coldness and sniggers and whisperings, knew only shame. Even a fleeting reconciliation with the King, which saw the birth of Shaka's sister Nomcoba, did little to quell the tongues of the vipers. Only Mkabi, the King's first wife, showed the young woman any kindness.

And then there was her love for her son . . .

She threw herself on her husband when he wanted to beat the six-year-old for letting a dog kill one of his sheep, and Nandi, the boy and his sister were sent back home to the Langeni.

And more shame.

"Look at her!" they said. "Even when she gets what she wants she cannot retain it."

By now Shaka was old enough to suffer the shame and mockery, too. Especially the mockery. For had not his mother told him time and time again, as if to reassure herself, that he was of royal blood and heir to the Zulu throne? But the others, his playmates and the elder Langeni boys, laughed when he solemnly revealed to them his true status. They'd heard the story from their parents and saw the boy as fair game, especially as he was so easily riled and beaten.

And being so stubborn in his declaration of his own royalty . . .

There was no escape. When he baulked at their vicious ploys he was forced to participate. To lick the porridge spoon was a treat for a child; but the elder boys would bury the spoon deep in the pot, where it was hottest, then force the spoon upon Shaka. "Come," they'd say, "let us see if you have the courage to be a king!"

When he returned home hungry after tending the cattle, they'd hide his bowl and force him to accept his supper in his cupped palms. And invariably he'd starve, because invariably he'd drop the hot food, which they then wanted him to eat off the ground, like a dog, an indignity he rejected – despite their blows – his defiance making them even more vindictive.

And when he retaliated, the boys would complain to their parents – this Shaka was a bully. Never mind the fact that he was unafraid to fight boys older than himself. For this was his defence – to become stronger than the others.

Yet his body betrayed him there. He could soon run faster than the others, was stronger and braver than the rest – but see, they said, see the little earthworm!

A crushing blow for an eleven-year-old supposedly on his way to becoming a man, but not yet allowed to wear the isinene that covered the genitals. And the earthworm was there for all to see and mock.

Yet always, always, there was Nandi, herself trying to carve a life amid this bitterness. "Never mind, my Little Fire," she'd tell Shaka, "one day you'll be the greatest King in all the land."

And only Mkabi, Senzangakhona's first wife, and Langazana, his fourth, would visit Nandi with gifts and words of support. It was a great kindness Shaka never forgot: when he came to power he installed the two women as veritable queens of his most powerful military kraals.

But that was far off into the future, many were the hardships still to come . . .

*

She stops a respectful distance away from the inkosi and bows her head. Makedama, chief of the Langeni, folds his arms and fixes her with a steady glare.

"Nkosi!" she says. "We come in peace, seeking sanctuary."

"Yet you are armed."

"There are those who would do us harm."

"Zulus?"

The woman nods.

"What was your crime?"

"There was no crime, Nkosi."

Makedama's chuckle is echoed by his advisors. "Then why do you flee your tribe?"

"In the eyes of the Great Spirit – and the ancestors, too – I believe I have committed no crime."

143

"But such appeals will not satisfy Shaka?"

"It is so. You guess right, Nkosi. He is my persecutor."

"Cha! There is no guessing involved. Such is the way of Shaka. He has been your king for only a few moons now, but already we have heard much of him. He growls like an empty stomach and would be a law unto himself."

"It . . . He wasn't always so, Nkosi."

"The runt of the litter doesn't grow stronger, it only becomes more cunning! But you are a woman, what do you know of the affairs of men?"

"I am Pampata. Perhaps you have heard of me . . .?"

Eyebrows arched in surprise, Makedama seems to sway back under the weight of this revelation. A hiss of surprise snakes through the gathering as the news is passed on.

Pampata! Beloved of Shaka; the King's favourite, more courtesan than concubine. Now that he's assumed the throne, she's a trusted advisor, holding as much sway with him as his beloved mother . . .

Pampata.

"Please, Nkosi," she murmurs, "we seek your protection! Your mercy!"

*

In 1802 came the great famine of Madlathule – Eat And Be Quiet – and Nandi was no longer able to feed her children, and no help was forthcoming from her own people. The three were forced to roam the dying land like refugees. The King's wife, his heir and his daughter, made to live like beggars.

It was even said that when Nandi sought refuge with Gendeyana of the Amambedweni, Senzangakhona sent messages to the chief suggesting he'd win the Zulu King's favour if he were to make his guests vanish like the lakes in the drought-stricken valleys. Gendeyana refused – but whether the story was true or not, there came the day when he told Nandi he could no longer offer them protection.

A long trek to the coast brought them to the Omadla clan, the Fish

Eaters, whose chief made them welcome, and where Shaka developed a taste for seafood.

When Shaka was eleven, they went to live with a clan of the Mthetwa tribe – and their fortunes began to change. For Shaka's bravery in battle would attract the attention of Dingiswayo, king of the Mthetwas . . .

*

"Why do you ask this favour of me?"

"Because you are no friend of Shaka's."

"That is not quite true," says Makedama. "I have had little to do with the Zulu."

Shaka may be an upstart, but you still don't want to antagonise him with careless pronouncements.

"And," Pampata hastens to add, "because you are known for your mercy." She nods. "And your courage."

Makedama's eyes narrow. His ego isn't so big that he can't detect the trace of a taunt here; the implication that it might be deemed cowardly were he to send her and the boy packing.

And that wouldn't necessarily be so. He has the welfare of the tribe to think of. Does he want to risk a quarrel with Shaka and his barefoot impis over these two?

"How come you flee the one you once loved?"

"I love him yet!"

"Then why are you here, Daughter, quaking in fear?"

Pampata folds her hand around the boy's elbow. "My son," she says.

The calculations furrow Makedama's brow. It's only been four summers since they first heard of this brave Zulu warrior in Dingiswayo's legion, and Shaka's been king of the Zulus for less than a year . . . So even if he and Pampata had been lovers for five, six seasons in total, the boy is still too old to be Shaka's son. Indeed, he seems almost too old to be Pampata's child.

"Your son," says the Langeni chief, "but not Shaka's."

"No, Nkosi. A youthful indiscretion. Before I met Shaka."

"A very youthful indiscretion," observes the chief, casting his eyes over the boy.

And isn't it just like a woman to be flattered, even under circumstances such as these, decides Makedama – for Pampata smiles demurely. "He is younger than he looks," she says.

"Indeed."

Pampata nods.

"But he is not Shaka's," muses the chief.

"No, and I was able to keep his existence a secret."

"But your beloved found out?"

"Yes."

"And he fears an heir – even one who isn't, but who might be so mis-construed."

"Truly, you are wise."

It's about the only thing that Zulu baboon fears – and with good rea-son! No house can endure the usurpation he has begun. And never mind any sons he might have, he has many half-brothers who would learn by his example.

"Very well," murmurs Makedama. "You may rest here. But do not overstay your welcome!"

"Thank you, Nkosi, thank you! We need but a few days for our pursu-ers to tire and seek some other sport!"

"Go now – my sister will show you to a hut. You will be safe here. You have my word."

*

It had all been discussed and planned beforehand. The leader of the drummers had been told to watch for the moment when the serving boy went up to Shaka; then the drums were to fall silent. Dingiswayo stood as Shaka approached. Acknowledged his bow and reached for his hand. It was quite natural for men, whether Zulu or Mthetwa, to hold hands; it was a sign of friendship, and a sign of the esteem Dingiswayo had for Shaka.

146

"The years have made you strangers," Dingiswayo told Senzanga-khona, "but surely you must see in this one the man you once were."

Senzangakhona's response was an uncertain smile signalling polite indulgence more than anything else. Dingiswayo had said this one was a Zulu. Well and good. So what? What did his ally want from him? This was a brave warrior, but the fact that he'd chosen to live among the Mthetwa – well, Senzangakhona couldn't look kindly upon that. Why hadn't he remained with his own people? Eh?

"A brave warrior," said Senzangakhona. "I greet you."

"More than that, much more than that, I think."

Senzangakhona frowned, wondering the reason for Dingiswayo's smirk.

"Sawubona, Baba," said Shaka. *I see you, Father.*

"Your first-born and heir," grinned Dingiswayo. "How pleased I am to bring about this joyful reunion."

*

Pampata and the boy have scarcely the energy to unroll their sleeping mats; the exertions of their flight have worn them out and both are asleep within minutes. They are awakened in the early evening by the chief's sister: Makedama has requested they join him for supper.

The Langeni chief's questions are openly probing as he strives to discover from Pampata the strength of Shaka's new army, what his plans for the future might be, how deep the discontent of the people.

For hasn't he forbidden his warriors to marry and even ordered some of them to shave off their headrings? Surely this must have caused *some* resentment.

Pampata and the boy are by no means the first Zulu "refugees" to pass through Langeni land, and Makedama has heard how Shaka and his favourite general Mgobozi, himself not a Zulu, but a Mthetwa who'd fought alongside Shaka in Dingiswayo's legions, have forced the men to discard their sandals and march across a parade ground strewn with thorns to toughen their feet.

Madness!

And those who do not stamp with sufficient enthusiasm are summarily executed as an example to the others.

But, according to Pampata, if there are dark mutterings among the older men, this is outweighed by the enthusiasm of the senior herdboys answering their first call to arms. They adore the new King, who promises them a future filled with many heroic deeds. They have happily thrown themselves into learning the new tactics and how to use the iklwa Shaka has equipped his army with.

Answering Makedama's questions as best as she can, Pampata leaves the old chief and his advisors even more troubled than before.

*

The Induna and six other warriors arrive at the Langeni kraal at mid-morning the next day. They are all big, strong men, and their amashoba – circlets comprising dangling tufts of cowtails worn around their upper arms and below their knees – make them seem even more imposing. Each carries a large oval shield made from toughened cowhide and a broad-bladed iklwa.

Warned of their approach, Makedama, his advisors and a group of twenty armed men are waiting to receive the Zulus.

"You have come," says Makedama.

The Induna inclines his head. "Your messengers are fleet-footed."

"It is just as well, for this affair pains me."

Makedama makes a signalling motion with his left hand. Two warriors drag Pampata from around the back of the squad of bodyguards. Beaming, Njabulo and Themba bring up the rear, holding the boy between them.

"But see," continues the Langeni chief, "we have rounded up your stray calves!"

Pampata struggles, trying to tear herself free from the fists that hold her.

"You offered us succour," she hisses. "You offered us protection!"

148

Her words are flies the chief swats away with a careless flick of his hand.

"Take them," he tells the Induna. "Shaka is welcome to them! Let him see this as a pledge of our loyalty!"

"But did you not give them your word?"

Makedama's obsequious smile freezes. It is not the Induna who has spoken, but one of the other Zulu warriors. After a moment of rigid indecision, while he waits for the Induna to issue a rebuke and finds none forthcoming, the Langeni chief continues, resolved to pretend he has not heard this impertinence.

These Zulus! They truly are baboons: ill-mannered, savage and scarcely worthy of the name Abantu. But if this is what he has to endure if he's to make his way safely through the treacherous new terrain opened up by Shaka's ambition, so be it!

"We will not allow those who have crossed your king to seek refuge here. Shaka will find us a valuable ally!"

"But did you not give them your word that they would be safe here?"

This is too much! Scrupulously ignoring the tall Zulu warrior, Makedama addresses the Induna: "What is this? Do you allow your men to disrespect you in this manner? To disrespect a chief?"

The Induna's spear is a striking cobra as the flat side of the blade slaps Makedama's shoulder, causing him to stagger sideways. "Silence! The King of the Zulus speaks!"

The Induna's tone, as much as what he has said, is enough to halt the Langeni men surging forward to protect their chief. But the Zulu warriors have raised their shields and their short stabbing spears are ready.

The tall warrior smiles. "Don't you recognise me, Old Man?"

Leaving Makedama to stare in shocked disbelief, Shaka turns his head toward the Induna. Nods.

The Induna raises his spear. "Ayihlome!" he bellows. *To arms*!

And a Zulu impi stands up out of the long grass on the slope overlooking the village. As the order is repeated, more soldiers appear atop the crest of the ridge. Dogs bark and women and children surge ahead of a third contingent as they move between the huts. The men of the chief's bodyguard wheel round in time to see that they are surrounded. At a signal from the Induna, two Zulus pull Pampata and the boy away from their captors.

Shaka has handed his shield and assegai to one of his men; now he folds his arms and regards the Langeni chief. "You have not answered my question," he says softly.

Makedama's hands rise, palms upward. "It's been many years since I last saw you . . ."

"Did you not promise these two they would be safe with you? Did you not offer them your protection?"

While other soldiers look on, their assegais at the ready, some move through the villagers, pulling this man forward, pushing that tearful wife away, until two distinct groups begin to form.

There is sweat on Makedama's brow, but he daren't wipe it away. It occurs to him to suggest that since they – this woman and this boy – lied to him, his own lie was justified. But he quickly decides that wouldn't be the right thing to say just now.

"I thought it was more important to demonstrate my loyalty to you."

"Which is worth what?" asks Shaka. "You lied to them, why would you not lie to me? You had no need to lie to them. A girl and a boy! Such a threat to your brave warriors! All you had to do was take them into your custody, summon a few brave men to hold them for you until your messengers found my impis. But, no – you lied to them. You lied when you did not have to. Clearly treachery comes naturally to you."

Shaka raises his chin as if he's just remembered something. "And tell your men to lay down their weapons. My warriors' assegais are hungry."

Makedama issues the order. Langeni spears drop.

"I offered you," continues Shaka, "what you never thought to offer my mother. A second chance. Let us see, I thought, what this crocodile does when another frightened woman and her son seek his protection. Let us see, I thought; the past is a distant valley, you can afford to be merciful, here. But you have proved yourself worthy only of my wrath!"

*

A fateful meeting, that night in 1815. One longed for by Shaka, but somehow an anticlimax. He could never feel anything other than hatred for Senzangakhona, but he was disappointed to see the revelation left the old man bewildered more than anything else. It was the illness, of course, this genet curled up in Senzangakhona's gut, gnawing him from within – it left him floundering in the face of Shaka's stony glare.

Such an anticlimax. Even his half-brothers kept their distance only because they feared Dingiswayo's displeasure.

Dingiswayo had warned him not to expect too much of the encounter. Even the promise they were to extract could not be counted upon. But it was essential all the same. Senzangakhona had to publicly acknowledge Shaka as his heir. And this came to pass, the old man nodding and mumbling. Shaka was his first-born and therefore his heir. And when the old man duly broke this promise on his deathbed, Shaka was able to move in and claim the crown as the first-born and no mere usurper.

*

Shaka is naked. He has shed his aprons and amashoba and he steps out of the shade of the Gathering Tree growing in the top corner of the cattlefold.

More warriors have arrived, driving ahead of them the inhabitants of the surrounding kraals, so that almost all of the Langeni are gathered here.

They have been divided into two groups. The larger stands under guard beyond the low palisade that surrounds the cattlefold. The second group has been herded into the enclosure itself and comprises those old enough to have known Shaka as a boy, about one hundred men and women. Using their shields, the warriors have arranged them into ragged lines.

Stepping into the sunlight, Shaka raises his arms. "See?" he bellows. "The Earthworm has become a Bull Elephant!"

By his mid-teens things had begun to acquire their natural propor-
tions, much to the young Zulu's relief. So much so, in fact, that for a
long while he refused to wear the isinene of manhood. Let those who'd
mocked him see how wrong they had been! Finally, his mother intervened, reminding him that a certain amount of propriety was in order
when it came to such matters.

He grips his penis with his right hand: "Would you laugh now? Would
you mock? Why don't you laugh? Why don't you mock? I would laugh, I
would mock, when I think of how I could fuck all your women five times
over and leave them sated and limp. Yet here you stand, chewing your
teeth. Hawu! You are a strange people."

He begins to move through the ranks, telling this man to stand over
there to the right, that woman to join him, this man to remain where he
is, until this group has in turn been divided into two groups. The larger
stands to the right; the smaller, about thirty men and women, stands to
the left.

"I can recall no specific incidents you were a party to," says Shaka,
addressing those on the right. "But I know this: you looked on in silence
while my mother and I suffered countless indignities at the hands of these
others. You looked on in silence, refusing to intervene. Therefore, before
this day is done, you will die. Before sunset, you will eat dirt. But your
death will be swift, and first I want you to see what I do to these other
lice, so that you may go to meet the Great Spirit praising my kindness!"

Shaka turns to those on the left.

"Yet, even with you," he says, "I am of a mind to show mercy."

He pauses, watching with amusement as some of the faces flare with
hope.

"Your ears do not deceive you. Let those who can prove to me they
did my mother an act of kindness come forward."

Almost instantly, an old woman steps out of the first row. She looks to
her left and, realising she's alone, turns and pulls her companion, also a
woman in her sixties, up alongside her; then she squares her shoulders
and allows her eyes to meet the King's with a look of icy hauteur.

A man pushes forward from the rear. He is joined moments later by another man. Both are in their mid-thirties, about four years older than Shaka.

When it's evident no one else is about to move Shaka shrugs his shoulders. "Is this all?" he asks.

Stalking forward, he addresses a fat man in the second row. "What of you, Zihle? Was not the hot spoon a lesson in humility? And have I not learnt that lesson? You should be proud of the great service you and your friends did me!"

Turning to another man: "And you, Hambile? What of you? All heirs to the throne should be expected to eat their food off the ground, like a dog! Then they will not abuse the privileges they later attain! Do not be modest – step forward! No? So be it! And you?" he asks, moving to the first woman who came forward. "What did you do for my beloved mother?"

"My sister and I were very good to your mother! We did many things for her, gave her many things."

Shaka nods. "This is so. But is it not also true you gave only so you could criticise? Do not deny it! For I have heard you. You and your sister were like these hyenas who'd trip a small boy and mock his clumsiness, who'd goad him into fighting and then beat him for his arrogance in daring to retaliate!"

Shaka circles around behind the woman. "Your charity was bile!" he hisses in her ear. "You offered so you might mock our neediness. You gave so my mother, the wife of a King, might be beholden to you."

He moves in front of her again, bringing his face up close to the woman's: "I heard you, Bitch! To your husband, to your friends, to this one, your sister, who lacks the intelligence of even an ant hill, you were a praise singer praising your own kindness, my mother's humble 'thank you' only ever a victory for your armies of spite!"

Shaka straightens. "Now rejoin these corpses!"

*

Pampata's hands bite deeper into the boy's shoulders. He finds her grip comforting. It anchors him. Anchors her, too. For Shaka's words are the smoke rising from the cooking fires of your home village. It's a village ravaged by the indignities of an unhappy youth, but it's still home, all you once knew, and you cannot help but return there, he cannot help but return there, guided by his own words. And Pampata wants to go to him, offer him the comfort once only Nandi could provide, and then only sparingly, because she too was beaten down. But, of course, she can't reach out to him. Later, yes, but not now. Now he must face the memories alone. And she holds onto the boy to stop herself from doing anything foolish . . .

*

And Shaka is naked. His spine is a river flowing through a ravine to the delta of his shoulder blades. Muscles swell his thighs, his arms; the power of a warrior-king who can outmarch and outfight even the best of his soldiers. Now he towers over the Langeni man who came forward from the rear rank.

"And you?" he asks. "What kindness did you offer my mother?"

The man bows his head. "As a herdboy, Sire, I found your mother a grinding stone. And I would tend her cow with my father's own livestock while you were still too young to do so."

"And you?" asks Shaka, moving to the next man.

"I am Milyani. It was I who rescued your sister's goat."

Shaka runs the palm of his left hand over his chin. He remembers this incident, he says. "But Milyani," he adds, "you were a herdboy at the time, were you not?"

The man nods.

"And in rescuing the goat, were you not merely doing your duty – that which was expected of every herdboy?"

The man's shoulders seem to collapse around his paunch as he shrugs.

"So, Milyani," says Shaka, extending a hand, "I think you should rejoin your fellow corpses."

Returning to the first man, Shaka says: "The grinding stone, I remember too. You did not have to offer it to my mother. Indeed, you were courting the disdain of your peers when you did so. You will be free to go. You can select the best ox from your chief's herd and long may you prosper. But for now, I bid you stand aside, for you will see how much you owe to that one act of kindness."

Shaka extends his right arm to the side – and the Induna moves forward with a bowl of water.

"You punched me, you tripped me, you whipped me, you mocked me – such were the seeds you sowed. Now it's time to gather in the crop."

He takes the bowl from the Induna. Very deliberately, keeping his eyes on those gathered before him, he pours the water over his head. After returning the bowl to the Induna, he runs his hands over his face.

"You are uthuvi!" he says. *Excrement!* "To look upon you is to be swallowed by the stench." Sliding his hands down his torso. "This is why I must wash myself."

There's thunder and darkness in Shaka's words, the faces of the condemned a cowering, storm-beaten landscape.

"Friends of my youth, I will tell you how you will embark upon the Great Journey."

The poles forming the palisade around the cattlefold will be sharpened.

"One for each of you," says Shaka. "You will each be led to a pole and impaled on that sharpened pole."

Lifted into position by four Zulu warriors, the condemned will be left there until they die.

"And the vultures will sing my praises," adds Shaka. "And let all know this is the fate that awaits those who would oppose me!"

It is custom when two Zulus have met, and conversed, for the one moving on to take his leave by saying "Sala kahle." *Stay well.* The other will respond with "Hamba kahle." *Go well.*

Now Shaka takes his leave of the condemned by saying "Hlalani kahle!" *Sit you well.*

Mgobozi and his men move forward.

As the first shriek slices through the air, Shaka motions for Makedama to follow him. Accompanied by the Induna and ten Fasimbas, he leaves the kraal.

Pampata takes the boy's hand and they follow the men.

*

Outside the chief's hut, Shaka makes the old man wait while he dresses. The Induna crouches by the cooking place and makes a fire with the flints he keeps in a pouch around his waist.

Screams fill the sky.

"Do not think I have forgotten you," Shaka tells Makedama. "For I suffered at your hands as well. You were a young man, and the heir, and you should've known better, but I was your chief entertainment on lazy afternoons. How you encouraged the herdboys to greater exertions! You hear those sounds? That was your laughter to my ears."

Shaka sighs. "Even when your father rewarded me with a goat for protecting Langeni cattle from a mamba, I got no respect. Cha! I would have happily given that goat back, because it only made things worse."

He nods. "Now you will know suffering! The endless suffering I endured!"

Turning to the Induna, he asks: "Is the fire ready?"

"Yebo, Baba!"

"Good," says Shaka. "Burn his feet. Burn them well. I want to smell the meat cooking!"

Two Zulu soldiers grab Makedama and drag him toward the fire.

"And after the third full moon," says Shaka, "after your medicine man has healed your wounds, my men will come again, and you will feel the fire again. And after that, they will come again. And again! Many moons did I suffer, we shall see how long you last!"

*

It is late afternoon. The impalings are complete.

"Kill the others," Shaka's said, "but make their deaths swift! And when you are finished, kill the ones you have impaled. I would be finished with this place!" Then he went with Pampata to supervise the division of the Langeni livestock, most of which will be taken back to the royal kraal as booty. The boy is sitting alone in the shade of a tree some distance away from the village when the Induna finds him.

"Truly," he says, "Pampata made the right choice when she chose you, for you acquitted yourself well!"

"Thank you, Master," says the boy, standing.

"You have every reason to be proud, yet you are sad."

The boy shrugs.

"We are still a small nation, Boy. This, Shaka will change, but for now, we will have to bark loudly and bite viciously! And better this, Boy, than Zulu blood being shed! A few warnings now might give our enemies pause for thought. While we grow stronger."

The Induna smiles. Lays a hand on the boy's shoulder. "And we *will* grow stronger if we have brave warriors like you in our ranks!"

The warrior drops onto his haunches so he's face to face with the boy. "Now I would ask you this . . ."

Herdboys march with the Zulu army as udibis, apprentices who carry weapons and food for the soldiers, with one udibi taking care of four men – and Shaka has decreed that officers might have an udibi to themselves.

"This you know," says the Induna.

The boy nods.

"Well, I would have you as my udibi."

The boy's eyes widen in surprise. He had thought he was too young, too puny to ever be chosen as an udibi, let alone one who serves an Induna.

"Yes, Master!" he gasps.

"Good!" the Induna straightens. "You will serve me well."

"I will try my best, Master."

The Induna chuckles. "That was not an order, Boy. I merely describe

157

what I see in your eyes, where wisdom kindles the flames of courage. You will serve me well."

*

Cha! But you would know what happened to Mduli, the uncle who claimed Nandi had a stomach beetle. He was among the first Shaka put to death after taking the Zulu throne. He asked to die like a warrior, with an assegai thrust, and Shaka acceded to his wishes, and the old tales tell of how Mduli died praising Shaka, prophesying his greatness. For had he not looked into Shaka's eyes and seen everything Senzangakhona was lacking? Here was a King truly worthy of the Bloodline . . .

*

"Tell me, Boy," asks the Induna, as they make their way back to the village, where the impis are forming up, "did you enjoy your sojourn with Pampata?"

"Sho!" says the boy. "It was hard!"

"How so?"

"She kept on telling me no one would believe I was her son and that I must act younger!"

"*Younger?*"

"Younger, Master!"

"What did you say to that?"

"That it would be easier if *she* acted older, for after all, she *is* old!"

"Aiee!" says the Induna, when he's able to stop laughing. "You are truly brave, Little One."

"That's what Pampata said, Master."

It is 1817. Following the subjugation of the Langeni, Zulu territory has grown somewhat, as has Shaka's army. Other clans have allied themselves with him – although he doesn't need Nandi's warnings about their loyalty. He's well aware that, although some chiefs have seen in him the same sense of ubukosi noted by Mduli, most have joined the Zulu nation out of fear – and because their lands adjoin Zulu territory and lie within easy reach of Shaka's ambitions. Consequently, these vassals need watching, although, chances are, they won't do anything too provocative, for behind Shaka stands Dingiswayo. But Shaka wants them under his control, not Dingiswayo's. Let the Zulu nation grow until it can be treated as an equal by the Mthetwas.

As it is, Dingiswayo continues to shrug off Shaka's suggestions that they destroy Zwide once and for all. He might be his beloved mentor's favourite, but the Zulu King still feels as if Dingiswayo treats him as an impetuous younger brother, not to be taken seriously. Even more frustrating is the way he has added his voice to Nandi's urgings about the Ubulawu.

This is the King's talisman, supposedly bringing him power and good fortune. It's destroyed on the death of the King and the heir is supposed to seek out his own, unique Ubulawu. It can be almost any object and supposedly it finds him, in that the King will recognise his Ubulawu as soon as he lays eyes on it.

He might be King of the Zulus, but given his treatment as a child, Shaka is not well disposed to honour Zulu traditions. As his men stamp the thorns, so he would stamp out the past – which only contains bad memories for him.

When he has sought to mollify Nandi by saying he's already found his Ubulawu – in his army – she hasn't listened, however. And now Dingiswayo has also begun nagging him.

Nandi's motives he can understand. His position remains precarious and she fears for his safety. Discovering his talisman will go a long way to silencing those who still see him as a usurper and it'll add to his strength when it comes to facing Zwide's army.

But why is it so important to Dingiswayo? Dingiswayo helped him claim the throne – which was rightfully his, anyway, as he was the first-born – and the support of the Mthetwa ruler is more powerful than any thing in ensuring Shaka retains the throne.

Is the Ubulawu, then, not a bone tossed to a dog, in the hopes he'll become distracted?

Why won't Dingiswayo take his warnings about Zwide seriously? Why does he want to see the People Of The Sky kept hemmed in, forever weakened?

Trying to put these worries aside, Shaka's turned his attention to the Buthelezis. The clans are old rivals and the enmity between the two is legendary. The young Zulu King reckons crushing these lizards will be just the practice his army needs before they face Zwide and the Ndwandwes, a clash Shaka knows to be inevitable . . .

The Way Of The Bull

But even now, called to Shaka's side to witness the might and prowess of the Zulu army, Dingiswayo can't leave the Ubulawu alone!

"There it is," he says, pointing to a smear of green that marks a ravine in a distant cliff face.

And how like an old lady he is becoming these days. If it's not nagging Shaka, it's fussing, like now. For all know of this place, jealously guarded by the Buthelezi sangomas, there's no need to point it out.

"That is the place you and your men must make for," Dingiswayo tells the Induna.

"Our spies have been watching them," adds Mgobozi. "And clearly their arrogance blinds them, for none have tried to flee."

The men are on a low ridge. Fashioned from civet pelts, Shaka's kilt is a golden colour, and the tails of his amashoba are white. He wears a collar of civet fur and the long tail feather of a blue crane in his headband. His cowhide shield is white with a single black dot in the centre. He ignores the other three, turning away, his attention elsewhere. He has granted his mentor this favour – although, in truth, it was one of those requests that are really commands – and right now he has more pressing matters on his mind. This is, after all, an auspicious day – the day they crush the Buthelezis once and for all . . .

And Dingiswayo is here to witness the power of the army Shaka has created and trained in such a short space of time. He is here to marvel at the Zulu King's tactics, the discipline of the men. He's here so he can see for himself what Shaka had meant all the time he was pestering him about spears that are thrown away, the sandals that slip . . .

Yet, yesterday, Dingiswayo had stood on the ridge not listening to Shaka as he pointed out where he'd be placing his regiments. Instead, he interrupted the young King, saying: "That is where you must go."

Misunderstanding him, thinking he was speaking of the Buthelezi kraal, Shaka grinned and said that was where he intended to go.

"No," said Dingiswayo, pointing to the ravine.

He was referring to the sacred place protected by the Buthelezis.

"Send your most trusted induna and some men there," he said. "Let us see what they have kept hidden there all these years! Who knows! That might be where you find your Ubulawu!"

Shaka couldn't believe his ears! All Dingiswayo could talk about was the Buthelezi treasure.

Now the ruler of the Mthetwas twists his head to address Shaka: "I need your men to get there as soon as possible. The Buthelezi sangomas must not be allowed to destroy, or remove, anything!"

"They will do it," says Shaka. "But let us not forget – before we can get there, there's the little matter of the Buthelezis to resolve."

The other men glance downward. Arrayed on the gentle slope across the way is the Buthelezi army. Plumes and shields; spears and clubs.

"Truly, Old Friend," grins Mgobozi, "they are but a little matter."

*

The night before the battle, partly to help calm the udibi's nerves and to remind the others of the importance of their mission, the Induna tells them of the coming of the Ma-Iti so long ago . . .

A hot day: a shimmering sky over the singing grass. The Zambezi River is an old sow lying on her side, too lazy to seek shade; languid waters smoothed by a breeze that's more like the panting of a dog. Three boys, each about ten summers old, stand up to their ankles in the mud on the river's broad banks. Freed from their chores in the heat of the day, when most adults ask only to be left alone to enjoy their naps, the boys have come across a crab. Not one of those small ones that scurry across the mud, but a big fellow, the size of an adult's cupped hands, that's somehow got stranded away from the water's edge – for the sea is less than a day's walk away, and the river has its tides, shares the ocean's moods.

Mulumbi – stronger, faster and more daring than the others, and therefore the leader of the trio – lowers a wet twig towards the crab's pincers. He is facing the other two, who have their backs to the river. All eyes are on the crab at their feet. Its carapace is orange in the centre, fading to white around the edges. The same pattern is repeated on its limbs and claws, orange close to the body, becoming muddy white at the extremities. Mulumbi taps the twig against the outer arc of the crab's left claw. Its walking legs twitch, but its tiny eyes and antennae remain motionless.

Bored before discovering this distraction, itchy and irritated in the heat, the boys want to believe the crab will, somehow, pounce – and force them to leap away. Now Mbimba makes to use his twig. Although shorter and smaller than Mulumbi, he would usurp the latter as leader of the group, for he feels it won't be long before he can run faster than Mulumbi. Already he can almost beat the other boy whenever they have a foot race. Now let him see if he can rouse this creature – for any opportunity to best his rival must be seized. And there –

Well, even he's surprised as the crab's claw snaps off the end of the stick.

And he takes a step back – his head jerking up – but as he's about to ask the others if they saw that, he realises they aren't paying attention. Mulumbi is looking past him – and isn't that just like him, seeking something else to interest himself in so he doesn't have to acknowledge that Mbimba's got the better of him. Even slow, dim Luba has turned and is looking in the same direction.

Mbimba swallows his words with a scowl. Turns.

Mulumbi was watching the crab, then he happened to look up –

And there it was, sliding by.

A glaring angry eye. A mouth curled in a snarl. A beak cutting through the water. These are the first things Mulumbi spots, and for a heart-stopping moment he thinks he's looking at some kind of river monster. But then he realises, no . . . this is something else . . .

And now all three boys are gaping at the strange, frightening apparition.

A winged canoe.

A gigantic winged canoe, drifting past them . . .

*

The orderly deployment of his forces has a soothing effect on the Zulu King. This is a glimpse of meaning beyond petty emotions, a higher purpose.

This is me. I brought this about.

The western side of the ridge drops to a shallow stream, with fast-flowing water, but only an ankle deep. From there, the ground slowly rises to where the Buthelezis are arrayed, about five hundred metres away. The gradient is negligible; that his soldiers will be moving uphill when they attack will have little effect on the outcome of the battle. Although – and Shaka notes this with a smile – from the relaxed posture of the men in the front ranks, it's clear the Buthelezis believe this high ground to be an advantage to them, for will not their spears fly further?

But then, of course, they have not learnt the lesson of the reeds.

Convinced though he was that his tactics – and the new spear they required – would work, Shaka realised he had to persuade his soldiers. He needed to instil in them the same kind of confidence, for if they didn't embrace his innovations with enthusiasm, they were lost. Subtlety was called for.

He called his regiments together and had the udibis cut reeds. There were two sizes: one the length of the short, stabbing spear he himself carried and the other as long as the incusa, the throwing spear the men were familiar with. He then selected two groups of soldiers. The smaller contingent came from his Fasimba regiment, who had already started practising with the iklwa; to these he handed out the shorter reeds. The larger group, of veteran warriors, was equipped with the longer reeds.

A mock battle was staged, with Shaka urging the older men on, telling them here was their chance to chasten the arrogant youngsters. Yet it was soon apparent to all that once the veterans had thrown their "spears" they were left unarmed. The others had only to lower their shields and charge – and deliver a thrashing that showed why Shaka had such high hopes for the Fasimbas. The message was clear: if a soldier wanted to survive in battle he had to learn how to use the iklwa. And for the older warriors there was an added incentive: let them learn quicker and show the young Fasimbas.

The reeds. It's a lesson the Buthelezis will learn today.

And from the reeds will emerge the Bull . . .

And things will never be the same again.

Once more, an artist gazing upon his masterpiece, Shaka lets his eyes roam across his ranks. These disciplined ranks.

There, closest to the Buthelezi van, is the Fasimba regiment, forming the head of the Bull. The men sit complacently in the long grass; each has his shield next to him, his arm through the straps, and an assegai clutched in his other hand. Rows of rippling backs, spears aloft like stalks; a crop of death. The Bull's head that will slam into the enemy.

Behind the head is the Amawombe, the regiment that comprises the Bull's loins. These ranks mirror those ahead of them, with the indunas the only men standing – but there's one difference. They are the reserve to be sent in after the Fasimbas and they sit with their backs to the enemy, facing Shaka. This is so they cannot follow the progress of the battle and grow excitable or dejected, states that would make them harder to control. Instead, their eyes remain on Shaka, for it is he, and he alone, who'll give them the order to join their comrades.

But a bull also has horns . . . Shading his eyes, Shaka scans the rough terrain half a kilometre to his right. Dongas and bushes. He grins happily. The Ujubingqwana regiment moved into position there early this morning and he is pleased that he can't spot them. On his left flank, the ground is more open, and his Bull's left horn – the Umgamule regiment – is squatting behind this very ridge. When the Fasimbas attack, the Umgamule will come out of hiding and advance in a wide arc. Let the Buthelezis see them. Shaka doesn't care. It's part of the plan, anyway. Let them think he means to outflank them and flee in the opposite direction. Where, of course, they'll encounter the right horn moving out of its hiding place.

The young King's first taste of true power.

Ranks of Zulu muscle forming a vision of meaning, a glimpse of a higher purpose; the light in the darkness he was moving to all this while, through the desert of his childhood, the stinging sandstorms of mockery, the hunger of loneliness, the thirst of despair . . .

Hai! But they are more than that, these ordered ranks lusting for glory, they are both the prayer and the answer to that prayer . . .

Shaka turns to Dingiswayo, his mentor, his father. He has some men standing by to whisk the Mthetwa ruler to safety should things go wrong here today. As for Shaka, he'll join his warriors, for if things do go wrong it matters not what happens to him, he'll at least die as a soldier.

Dingiswayo grins, seeing these thoughts flicker across Shaka's face. "I do not think that will be necessary, do you?"

Shaka's smile is tinged with guilt – to think that, a few moments ago, he was railing at this man in his mind, petulant at being ignored.

"So be it," he says.

*

"It's true, Father! This is what we saw!"

Having just been aroused from a sweaty nap, Lumbedu isn't so disorientated he doesn't notice the urgency in his youngest son's voice. So when one of Mulumbi's older brothers grabs the boy preparatory to cuffing him, the chief tells him to let Mulumbi go.

"But we are sick of this one's tales," growls the brother.

"Silence! Let him speak." To Mulumbi he says: "Tell me more . . ."

Mbimba and Luba had run away. Mulumbi followed them, but only until he reached a vantage point from where he could observe the giant canoes. There were three of them, the others soon moving into view.

And he valiantly tries to describe what he saw . . . They were floating, so they were like canoes, only much, much bigger . . . and they had wings . . . and spikes . . .

What he had seen were three galleys, gingerly navigating the Zambezi, their oars raised, their sails unfurled . . . but his vocabulary fails him . . . and he resorts to drawing in the sand with a stick . . . and, fortunately, Mbimba and Luba aren't so embarrassed by their cowardice that they won't back him up, help to convince the adults they did in fact see something . . .

But, from his hiding place, Mulumbi saw more. Saw men moving about on the deck. Shaggy men in robes, in shades of blue and red – and although their skin wasn't albino-pale it was nonetheless a few shades lighter than any colouring Mulumbi had ever seen before. As he watched, some of the oars slapped the water to slow the galley's progress, and he could hear distant shouts when men in the stern hailed the other ships. Small steel vessels were lowered from ropes to collect water. Some men even stripped and jumped into the river, where they swam and splashed as if they'd never heard of crocodiles . . .

The older brother's shaking his head, rolling his eyes at this preposterous story, but he and the other doubters will soon see Mulumbi is telling the truth. For it's five hundred years before the birth of Christ, and the Ma-Iti have arrived in southern Africa.

*

Across the way, the Buthelezis are growing ever more fractious. Their taunts are becoming louder, more insistent. Walking among the men of the Fasimba regiment, the Induna warns them to stay calm. Let the Buthelezis waste their breath. "They are barking like dogs," he tells the men, "and like dogs they are barking because they are afraid."

Or at least unsettled. Why haven't the Zulus risen and come to stand opposite them? Why are they just sitting there?

"All is well?" asks the Induna when he reaches the group he'll be leading on Dingiswayo's mission. There'll be four of them: Maweru, Njikiza, Dingane and the udibi. Maweru and big Njikiza both nod and shrug. The Zulus will be able to accomplish anything they set their minds to today. Dingane is sulking. As a Zulu prince, his place should be with his regiment. But, although Dingane's proven himself to be a brave and re-sourceful warrior, he does have a reputation for laziness and Shaka wants to ensure he remains in the thick of things. There'll be no skulk-ing in the rear for the young nobleman today. Instead he'll take his place in the Induna's party, who will move forward with the third rank of Fasimbas in the Bull's head.

As for the boy – that he is to remain among the men while the other udibis are sent to the rear fills him with pride, but, when his eyes and mind shift to the waiting Buthelezis, his stomach hurts, he would gag his mouth is so dry.

The Induna drops to his haunches, clasps the udibi's shoulders, draws him closer. Last night, to distract the boy from thoughts of the coming battle, he'd told him the story of the coming of the Ma-Iti, these stran-gers from long ago and far away, whose precious artefacts obsess Dingi-swayo and others.

Now the boy must be as brave as Mulumbi . . .

The udibi nods. He is ready.

The men will surround him when they go forward, with the Induna in front and Njikiza in the rear, and he is ready. Aiee, he is ready, even if the Buthelezis won't be carrying reeds today.

*

Lumbedu swallows. He would very much like to run away, knowing that, right now, his legs will give him the speed of a gazelle. It's only pride and a certain amount of annoyance that keeps him moving down the path at the head of the party. He is the chief. He can't let his people down. Yet – and this is where the annoyance comes in – those selfsame people, whose best interests he most assiduously guards, have begun to grow restive.

The strangers' ships haven't moved on. They have remained where Mulumbi first saw them and this has had an unsettling effect on the tribe. Which is understandable, Lumbedu supposes. It's the way they've come to blame him for the strangers' presence that confuses – and angers – him. No one would dare say anything to his face, but the chief is no fool. He's heard the whispers: Is Lumbedu a coward? Why doesn't he confront these men?

But he's also had a chance to examine their doings, these men in their gigantic canoes – for he's ordered they be watched at all times. More to the point, he's seen their weapons . . . So far they haven't disembarked on this side of the river, haven't done anything that might be seen as threatening, but with weapons like those, their leader can afford to relax and bide his time.

And the spears of Lumbedu's people are flimsy sticks with crudely shaped points made of bone, and their circular shields are small and fragile – they rely on traps when hunting, and flee their village when neighbouring tribes go on the warpath. Not that they have anything to attract a conqueror's attention. Their village is a red sand clearing in a jungle whose tangled foliage surrounds them; their huts are twigs and grass.

All the same, he's a chief. He'd rather die than be regarded as a coward, and with a sense of resignation, Lumbedu leads a delegation of ten armed men to accost the strangers . . .

*

Across the way, atop the gentle incline, the Buthelezis grow still more impatient.

Let us test the mettle of these arrogant Zulus, who will not learn from the past and instead come for yet another beating. Let's see what they are made of. Where are their champions? Who will come forward?

The first time the question is bellowed the Zulu officers sink to their haunches wherever they stand. The second time the question is shouted, a low, ominous hiss sizzles through the Zulu ranks. The third time, the Induna rises, turns toward Shaka.

On the ridge, watched by Dingiswayo, Shaka steps forward – points his iklwa at the Induna, then at the Buthelezi lines.

The Induna jogs forward. Comes to a halt a few paces before the Buthelezi van.

Like the other Zulus he carries an iklwa and a war shield, an isihlangu. Oval, made of strengthened cowhide, it's one and a half metres high and a little under a metre across at its widest point. Strapped to the inside of the isihlangu are two more short stabbing spears and an incusa, a longer, throwing spear.

He taps the iklwa's broad blade against his shield. "Who will die first?"

A warrior almost as tall as he is steps out of the Buthelezi ranks. His cowhide kilt reaches to his knees and he carries only a spear, no shield.

Weighing the assegai in his right hand, he sinks into a crouch and moves sideways. The Induna turns to follow him. His eyes are on the man, but in particular he's watching the warrior's free hand. In his crouch, the warrior keeps his left hand low, almost at knee-height, the fingers splayed.

When those fingers curl inward, the Induna readies himself, his shield part of his arm, as light as a sleeve . . .

There's a "Thwuck!" And the spear bounces off the cowhide. Now the Induna's attention is on the men behind the warrior, lest a coward try to throw a second spear. He steps forward, transfers his iklwa to the hand holding his shield and drops to his haunches in a straight-backed posture that means he can still bring the isihlangu into play. A quick glance downward and the Buthelezi spear is in his hand.

He straightens. Takes another step forward. "Here!"

With an extension of his arm and a flicked wrist, he tosses the assegai back to the warrior, shaft first.

The man is stunned, but manages to snatch the spear out of the air.

His own assegai back in his free hand, the Induna retreats a few paces, parting his arms to bare his chest. "Let us try again."

The man is shocked and shamed; better a Zulu iklwa in his guts than this . . .

Better still to bring this arrogant bastard down.

Yes!

Again the crouch.

Again the twitching fingers that give away his intent.

And for the second time, the Induna tosses the spear back at him.

On this occasion, though, the Buthelezi is quicker. He throws his weight onto his right knee and hurls the spear as the Zulu backs away.

Expecting a move of this nature, the Induna swats the assegai sideways with an outward swing of his shield.

He has to move further to pick up the spear and when he tosses it back to the man, the Buthelezi grabs the assegai and charges, catching the Induna with his iklwa in the wrong hand. But the Buthelezi's momentum down the slight slope proves his undoing, as the Induna leans sideways, dropping low. The other warrior can't stop himself, or turn. He flies past the Induna, tripping over the Zulu's outstretched leg, and keeps on going, in a helpless sprawl that takes him far into the no-man's-land between the two armies.

Whirling around, the Induna moves after him. Here, out of the reach of any spear that might be thrown from the enemy ranks, he has room to manoeuvre. It's time for the kill.

The Buthelezi warrior has had enough, however. He first darts to his right. Then realises – and the Induna can see the thought rippling across his features in a look of panic – that'll bring him closer to the Zulu impis.

He changes direction so abruptly he slips. The Induna darts forward. The Buthelezi rights himself and keeps on moving, in a diagonal course that takes him away from Shaka's men and closer to his own. He is scared, but daren't turn and run. Instead he backs away.

The Induna is a lion, keeping his distance, waiting for the chance to pounce.

The men on both sides are silent. Spellbound.

The Buthelezi is an owl, trying to swivel his head, so he can look behind himself, make sure he doesn't trip again, then swinging his head round to check on the Induna's position. Wide eyes; the spear limp in his right hand, forgotten.

A name is shouted. Both warriors turn toward the Buthelezi ranks, the

Induna's opponent to meet a spear hurled into his gut. He drops his own assegai, grabs the shaft of the spear and topples backwards.

"Forgive us, Zulu," calls the Buthelezi general who threw the assegai. "We did not mean to insult your courage with such a buffoon."

The Induna straightens, bows in the man's direction.

"But know this, Zulu," says the man, pointing at the Induna, "you – you *will* die today!"

"What?" replies the Induna. "Would you have your women left inconsolable?"

"Laugh, hyena! Laugh! But you will die today!"

As soon as the Induna has resumed his place in the ranks, Shaka gives the order: "To arms!"

And the Bull's head rises.

"Up, my Children, brave Children, proud Children, up!"

But where is Mgobozi?

There he is, lurking in one of the middle ranks, trying to appear inconspicuous.

Shaka steps over to the edge of the ridge and calls to one of the udibis: "Go and fetch that Old Goat, Mgobozi, tell him to report to his King! Tell him," adds Shaka, "his stubbornness delays matters!"

"Aiee! That one!" chuckles Dingiswayo.

Shaka nods.

"Now you have a taste of what I have had to endure! But only a taste! For imagine that Goat with a young barefoot Zulu!"

Shaka examines the Buthelezi ranks once more. Are they really going to wait for him to make the first move? Aiee, in handing him the initiative, they deliver themselves to be slaughtered.

He lowers his gaze. The long grass of the gentle slope. A few boulders here and there, but nothing that will hamper the movement of his men. The first ranks, calmly awaiting his order. The indunas prowling up and down, keeping one eye on the ridge and talking to their men all the while.

And there's Mgobozi, shaking his head, warding off the udibi's pleas, snatching his hand away.

But then Mgobozi looks back toward the ridge, and somehow he knows the King's eyes are on him. The argument flows out of him. He says something to the udibi, and the boy turns away, to be followed by the general, lagging several paces behind, like a wilful child called to order and summoned to his father's hut.

Shaka's attention returns to the Buthelezis. They have arranged themselves along the slope in a long, ragged rectangle. There is no order, no discipline. Rows bisect one another in knots of spears and shields. Here, Shaka can count seven rows. A little further along, these merge to become five, with a group of men standing a few paces away from the rest at the back of the tangle. And there's a bulge in the centre, where men have been pushed forward.

As the Buthelezis number more than four thousand to the Zulus' two thousand, this rectangle is wider than the formations that comprise the head and loins, who number five hundred respectively, each arranged in ten ranks of fifty men. However, Shaka's not too concerned about the enemy flanks enveloping his van. He used reeds to show his men the efficacy of their new weapons, now the enemy will become as reeds, parted, thrown aside by the charging Bull. Confusion and the approach of the horns will send the Buthelezis packing. All the same, he has ordered the loins to spread out on a larger front, with ten ranks becoming five, when they are sent into the fray.

"Majesty," growls Mgobozi.

He has taken the long way round, following the ridge to where it peters out some two hundred metres on Shaka's right flank, instead of clambering up the low bank at Shaka's feet.

"You were inspecting the troops?" asks Shaka with a wry grin.

"Majesty – I am a soldier, it is as a soldier that I can best serve you!"

"No, Old Friend, I have told you before, you serve me best by remaining at my side."

"But Mdlaka . . ."

Mdlaka will be made commander in chief, says Shaka, since Mgobozi has declined the post. But that is neither here nor there.

"You will serve me best by remaining here and observing the battle."

Dingiswayo holds up his hand to counter the general's imploring glance. "It is true, brave Mgobozi, my army is the poorer for your absence, but, Old Goat, my days! My days are more peaceful! You serve Shaka now. It is him you must obey. And torment!"

Mgobozi straightens. "Very well!"

"Aiee, Shaka, beware," says Dingiswayo. "He is grinning again!"

Shaka's eyes narrow with suspicion. "What is it, Mgobozi?"

The general's shield comes away from his body as he shrugs, all innocence. "I apologise for my petulance, Majesty."

"Yes, and . . .?"

"Perhaps you will allow me to redeem myself . . ."

Shaka turns his head to follow the direction of the general's meaningful gaze. He sighs, "So be it."

Mgobozi can accompany the reserve when they are sent into action.

"Now," he says, inclining his head, "perhaps you will allow me to crush these lizards!"

Mgobozi beams. "Nothing will give me greater pleasure, Majesty."

*

The indunas relay Shaka's orders. The Head moves forward. Five paces and the men are jogging. Another five and they're running. Then they're sprinting, each rank keeping the correct distance.

"Siiiiii-Giiiiii-Diiiiii!"

The war cry is like a stick thrust into an ants' nest. It causes a churning in the Buthelezi ranks, as some men decide they no longer want to be at the front and others try to ensure there are at least four or five men ahead of them. The officers are screaming, but that only seems to add to the panic. Then the first wall of shields hits the squirming mass . . .

The Way Of The Bull.

*

The boy has sunk to his haunches, as he waits for the others to finish searching the ramshackle huts. Suddenly he feels drained. Tired. More than that, he feels as if he no longer quite inhabits his own body. A floating sensation. Inaction has caused the past few hours to open up before him, a vista seen from a mountain top.

One moment he was waking up – warriors stirring around him, shapes in the morning mist – then there was movement and waiting, a lot of waiting, then they were facing the foe, and his master was running forward to meet the challenger, then . . . a bad dream.

A blur.

Running and keeping his eyes fixed on the Induna's kilt. And the men around him – Dingane, Njikiza, Maweru and his master – were suddenly giants, twisting and turning. Thumps and grunts, a spray of blood speckling his face, his chest, Dingane almost bumping into him as he parried a clumsy spear, Njikiza at his rear, pushing him forward . . .

Then they were free of this human swamp. Were running even faster. Overtaking fleeing Buthelezis, paying no heed to these screaming soldiers, who, anyway, were no longer warriors, just frightened men . . .

All in one day, a few hours . . . It's almost too much to comprehend.

But perhaps it doesn't have to make sense! For right now, this udibi who serves his master with pride and who wishes time would hurry up and make him a man, feels so like a child, and right now, with the wisdom of a child, feels that's not such a bad thing to be . . .

*

The Buthelezis are routed within a matter of minutes. In fact, so quickly do they break up and flee, they almost elude the horns.

But only almost.

Unhampered by sandals, armed with weapons they will not be foolishly throwing away, Shaka's impis are soon among them, the loins led by Mgobozi taking over the chase when the head tires.

The Induna and his men fight their way through the Buthelezis and then make for the ravine, which is about two kilometres from the battlefield. The sangomas who live here have watched the progress of the battle and fled, abandoning three huts and a kraal of five cattle.

They soon find the Ma-Iti relics and the Induna can only shake his head when the others have finished arranging the objects in the sunlight. A rusty sword. A dented bronze breastplate. Some goblets.

The Buthelezis are not alone in prizing these things so highly, but it's something the Induna's never been able to understand. It's said the Ma-Iti relics are powerful, they have to be kept hidden to protect the people. But when does awe become veneration?

These are the scat, the spoor. The beast has moved on. But it seems to the Induna there are many who would like to see that beast return and set upon their enemies.

They were voracious, these Ma-Iti. They befriended Lumbedu's people and the old stories tell of how they tunnelled into mountains to pluck the stones from the rock. And then there was gold too, the tears of the sun.

The people of Lumbedu brought a lot of what happened on their own heads, through their greed and lust for power, but that doesn't detract from the horror that ensued . . .

For unborn generations would suffer as children grew up knowing only hunger and slavery, fear and suffering.

The land was cursed and when the Ma-Iti were finally overthrown, the evil only went into hiding, to be reborn centuries later . . .

In the distance shrieks fill the air; dustclouds rise. There's no stopping the Zulu Bull. It tramples everything in its path. The Buthelezis will not be allowed to surrender. On that score Shaka is most specific. Pleas for mercy are to be ignored. Neither does he want the chief and his sons brought before him. Let them be slaughtered where they stand.

*

As it turns out, the Induna never gets a chance to tell Dingiswayo the truth about the ravine. By the time he and the others rejoin the main body of men, the ruler of the Mthetwas has set off for his home kraal.

It's only because he seeks him out to make his report that the Induna notes the Wanderer's absence; the others don't care. They have won the day, destroyed the Buthelezis once and for all – that's all that matters. Huts are ablaze and slaughtered cows are being hacked apart by drunken soldiers. Shaka himself proceeds to get very drunk very quickly – and misses most of the festivities. It's only a few days later, when the euphoria's worn off and the men are back under control, that the Induna learns why Dingiswayo declined to take part in the feasting.

It's Mgobozi who tells him about the Wanderer's rage, how he could scarcely control himself and surprised even Shaka. It seemed the methods of his protégé, now allowed to be put into unfettered practice, horrified the Mthetwa ruler. He was aghast by the way Shaka refused to call back his impis even when victory was assured, but instead had let his soldiers rampage through the Buthelezi settlement, killing all who stood in their way. It was a form of total warfare Dingiswayo found barbaric and he lost no time in castigating the young Zulu King. And what could Shaka do but let the mentor he sought to impress, and whose praise meant so much to him, leave and then drink himself into a stupor and stay drunk for three days?

"Hai," said Mgobozi, "but if this was how Dingiswayo dealt with Zwide we would not now have the Ndwandwes sharpening their blades and waiting to fall on us."

And although relations between Shaka and Dingiswayo remained cordial, they never patched up their differences. Shaka never got the chance to point out this was how the Ndwandwes fought and how, as a consequence, they had risen to be a very real threat to the Mthetwa alliance. And then it was too late.

It's late afternoon, and three children of the Omadl'izinhlanji clan are out collecting mangoes. The two older boys have climbed the tree and are tossing the fruit down to the youngest. It isn't long before they grow bored, and by the time they've clambered up the second tree they've taken to throwing the mangoes at the boy, who happens to be the one's younger brother.

When the child starts to cry, big brother has to climb down and comfort him. There'll be a hiding for him if the seven-year-old returns home in tears. Apologies proffered, reassurances made, the little boy is pacified and the other two help him carry the fruit to the trunk of the third tree.

All too soon the older boys start throwing the mangoes further and further away from the tree, watching the little one scrabble about in the undergrowth, while they shout directions, offer encouragement.

"Over there! No, over there! See? Are you blind, Little One? Can't you catch? Mama will beat you if you let the fruit run away . . ."

A great game, much laughter – until one of the bushes swallows the seven-year-old.

At first the other boys think the little one is playing the fool – or maybe he's tripped over his own feet as he's wont to do.

Then they see it.

It's obviously been there all along, but only now that it's moved do they spot the rock python. More than six metres long, the reptile has dry, scaly, tan-coloured skin with brown markings outlined in black and a black V atop its wide, flattened head.

The little boy was on his haunches reaching under the bush when the snake struck: a brown blur knocking the child over and biting into his right shoulder. With its prey pinned, it twists its head, turning the body into its coils, gradually, relentlessly enveloping the seven-year-old. His struggles only seem to make things easier for the python. Round and round the coils go, tightening every time the child gasps for breath. The boys in the tree clearly hear the little one's ribs crack like twigs in a fire. His legs stop kicking. The python's coils clench tighter than a fist, then it unhinges its jaw.

Aghast, clinging to the branches like sailors to the mast of a storm-tossed ship, the boys watch as the snake unwinds itself, twists, turns and slithers back to the child in a wide arc that brings it frighteningly close to the tree.

Its mouth opens wide, then even wider. There's a lurching, swallowing gulp and the child's head disappears. The python's jaws swing open again . . .

Rows of recurved teeth hook into the child's flesh, forcing it inwards with each contraction. Coils a man can wrap his hands around swell to the size of a barrel to accommodate the prey.

Finally, all the boys can see are the child's tiny feet, dangling limply from the snake's mouth. Then these too are sucked inward.

It has lain in wait, patiently biding its time, the heat sensors in its jaws tracking its prey . . . The rock python, known to the Zulus as the inhlwathi, truly a creature to be feared. And the boys remain in the tree all night. Now and again they hear voices calling for them in the darkness, but they're too afraid to respond. They think those voices might be the snake trying to trick them.

It's only some hours after daybreak that they're discovered by a search party from the village.

The Snake That Swallowed A Village

The Omadl'izinhlanji, or Fish Eaters, are a special clan to Shaka. The chief was one of the few to offer Nandi shelter when Shaka was a boy and they were reviled by all. It was while with the Omadla that he developed a taste for seafood, for the grunter, blacktail and crabs caught by the men of the clan. When he came to power and declared Zulu cuisine to be bland, not fitting for such a powerful people, Omadla women were among those Shaka summoned to his capital at KwaBulawayo to teach the nation how to cook.

Shaka is well aware of the old chief's cantankerous exaggerations and his request for help has come at a bad time – the Zulu King has other, more pressing matters of state on his mind. Somewhat reluctantly, it seems to Shaka, Dingiswayo is preparing for a new campaign against the Ndwandwes. Although things have cooled between Shaka and his mentor, it goes without saying Shaka will march with Dingiswayo against Zwide. It's time they finished off that old jackal! He's therefore been concentrating on drilling his impis. The Buthelezis were one thing – Zwide's army they'll not find such easy going, and Shaka won't have his men shamed by Dingiswayo's regiments.

For all this though, when news finally reaches him that yet another child from the Omadla clan – this time a babe in arms – has been taken by the python, Shaka sends the Induna to investigate.

With him, of course, goes his udibi. The boy carries two gourds, the one filled with water, the other with sorghum beer. His straw sleeping mat and the cowhide cloak that can also serve as a blanket are rolled up and tied diagonally across his chest. Fixed to the bedding at the back is a cooking pot. Inside this is a sack of victuals – dried maize meal and beans and sweet potatoes. He also carries a spear. It's a heavy load for one approaching his eleventh summer, but the boy will not complain.

This is the furthest he's yet travelled with his master, and pride vanquishes fatigue on the two-day journey.

Aside from his own bedroll and a gourd filled with water, the Induna carries a spear and a shield. Wrapped in cowhide and fastened to the inside of the shield is a bundle of three more short, stabbing assegais and an incusa, a longer spear used for hunting.

The umuzi of the Omadla clan is situated at the mouth of an estuary, where the beehive-shaped huts look out from under their thatch across a broad beach of white sand. Inland, beyond the village, the ground becomes a wetland of swamp figs, their roots like stilts, lifting the trees above their marshy surroundings, powder-puff trees, dangling their long strands of white flowers, and eleven-metre-high white mangroves, tall, pale trees with greyish leaves.

Mudhoppers and water scorpions, fishing spiders and fiddler crabs, the males with their enlarged and brightly coloured claws, move through the shallows and across the muddy ground. A sense of teeming life, like a disturbed ant hill, but also, somehow, trapped, mired in this sweaty, stultifying tangle.

As they near the village, in the early afternoon on the second day of their journey, the boy is relieved to spot crude funnels made from folded banana leaves hanging from trees along the path at regular intervals. Because it hunts here, the lair of the python must be somewhere nearby and these baskets contain muthi, medicine mixed by the clan's shaman to protect travellers.

It's some consolation to the boy who, like most Zulus, does not like snakes of any kind.

His neck is sore and he has a headache from trying to watch both sides of the path at once, eyes flicking to the left and right, constantly focusing and re-focusing – but he can't stop himself. Ants of fear crawl through his mind, his hand aches, so tightly does he grip the haft of his assegai – and when he hears the shrieks, it's as if his fear has broken loose, and is now running madly down the path.

Only, the shrieks are coming toward them.

When the Induna stops, the boy moves as close as he can to the warrior without bumping into him.

It's a woman. Her face warped and glistening, she drops onto her knees in front of the Induna.

"You have come!" she wails. "You have come to find my baby!" Beads and breasts quivering, she waves her hands. "The beast has it! You must find it! You must find my baby!"

Earlier, they stopped and the Induna slipped the blue feather into his headband and donned a collar of civet fur, adornments that identify him as a representative of the Great Shaka, so she knows who he is.

"Shadow Of Shaka," she begs, clasping her hands in front of her. "You must help me! These fools do nothing! You must help me find my baby! You are brave and strong! You can kill this monster! Kill it and rescue my baby!"

The Induna raises his left arm, bringing up his shield, and makes a sweeping gesture, like one parting reeds.

"Out of my way, Woman."

*

These Fish Eaters are indeed strange people, decides the udibi. As if this breach in etiquette – daring to approach Shaka's envoy before he's been properly greeted by the chief – isn't bad enough, he's dismayed to see that the official meeting place is on the bank of the river. The ibandla, where the chief and his advisors gather to discuss matters, listen to grievances and sort out squabbles, is normally in or near the cattlefold, regarded by the Zulus as a sacred place. But these people have only a few cows in their kraal; clearly they do not value cattle. Instead, rows of dried fish hang from wooden racks outside the huts. And even the sea air does little to dissipate the smell of fish, while the river alongside the ibandla tree seems to be more mud than water, and that adds another layer to the pervasive stench.

Now he knows why most people avoid these swamps. This heavy air is evil, seems almost to have a life of its own. He can well understand how it might make one ill, with the Trembling Sickness that burns the body.

What's more, the chief, a short, wiry old man, devoid of finery, wearing only a loincloth, looks as if he has spent most of the day rolling in mud.

"So!" he says, after they dispense with the traditional greetings. "The Grumpy One has at last seen fit to answer my calls for help!"

The boy gapes to hear such casual disrespect.

But the Induna grins. "Mnumzane," he says, using the new form of address Shaka insists upon for village or clan leaders. They're no longer to be called "inkosi", he has said, for there can be only one chief in the nation: Shaka. Instead, headmen are called "umnumzane", an honorific meaning *gentleman* or *highborn*.

"Old Friend Of Shaka, the King has instructed me to inform you, your complaints are like silt in his bowels."

"And, truly, it is a dark day for the kingdom when the King can't find fulfilment in a good shit."

"Shaka intimated as much."

"Ha! His problems are tadpoles compared to what we face. I tell you: this snake eats my village!"

The Induna glances over his shoulder, at the huts in the clearing beside the estuary, the muddy villagers waiting expectantly for the outcome of the meeting.

"I think you exaggerate, Mnumzane."

"If I do, my words are lightning needed to illuminate our predicament for you."

The Induna laughs, raises his hand, turns his head. "Too bright, Friend Of Shaka!"

"Cha! Have you come to help us or taunt us?"

"Why, to help you, of course."

"And where is your impi?"

The Induna taps his chest. "I am your impi." He indicates the boy standing behind him. "We are your impi."

The boy pushes his shoulders back, tries to stand up even straighter.

"You? Him?"

"We are all you need."

"Ha!"

"You have heard of me, I think."

"This is true . . ."

"Well, then . . ." says the Induna.

*

He asks the headman how many villagers have been killed. Six is the answer. Six in seven full moons. Three women, one with child, a young boy out collecting mangoes and now, most recently, but a few sunsets ago, an infant. The umnumzane has one of his councillors fetch the two boys who hid in the tree. It was what they saw that helped solve the mystery of the first four disappearances.

"We suspected, but we hoped we were wrong," explains the chief.

The Induna questions the two boys closely, elicits from them an account of what happened, while his udibi looks on with growing alarm. He's been hoping the tales that have brought them here will turn out to be false. Better an ageing leopard who has taken to hunting human prey than this!

The chief then describes how they found the boys and confirmed their story by examining the tracks left by the python.

"Did you not follow those tracks?" asks the Induna.

"Cha! I did not become a greybeard by being foolish."

"And your young men also preferred to live to see their own beards grow grey?"

"We know only the moods of the sea, Shadow Of Shaka, the seasons of the river. We felt we lacked the necessary . . . expertise."

"What expertise? You follow the tracks, you slay the creature."

"Ah! See how you enlighten us! That is precisely the kind of expertise I mean."

"Old Man, that silt grows ever thicker!"

"Believe me when I say this, Nduna, nothing would give me greater pleasure than to bring relief to the bowels of the Grumpy One. And this is, of course, why you are here."

"Of course."

And now the shrieking woman they met on the path does the truly unthinkable, forcing her way into the meeting place of men without being invited. The boy is shocked. Clearly the females in this village do not know their place. He cringes as the woman throws herself on her knees in front of the Induna and hugs his legs.

"My baby!" she gasps, her voice hoarse. "These weaklings do nothing! But you, Shadow Of Shaka, *you* will help me!"

The Induna raises a hand, halting the two men who come forward to grab the woman. Placing a hand on her shoulder, he gently pushes her away, and takes a step back, freeing himself from her embrace.

"Stand up, Woman."

Trembling, sobs rocking her breasts, the woman obeys.

"Tell me what happened."

Two days ago she'd been out gathering firewood. She had left her infant in the shade of a tree; when she returned, the child was missing.

"The snake took it, Nduna, and these ones . . . they do nothing!"

The Induna nods to the two men.

"I apologise for this," says the chief, after the woman has been led away.

"She is not of your clan?"

"No."

"No one's wife?"

"Aiee! Who would have her?"

"Then how comes she to be here?"

The chief grins. "Ukuhlobonga."

The Induna nods. The Pleasure Of The Road.

The umnumzane tells how he despatched an impi to join Shaka's mopping-up operations against the Buthelezis. Their march took them to the land of the Dladla clan, where they were to wait for the other regiments . . .

185

That would make the child about seven moons old.

"So she is of the Dladla clan?"

The headman nods.

"And the warrior?"

"Honour for him involved making the Great Journey."

"Convenient."

"That's what we thought. Who was to say who planted the seed?"

"But did you not offer a haven to the Queen Mother under similar circumstances?"

"We knew of Nandi's situation, her fire burnt bright, there was no smoke to blind the eyes. She and the little one came here and accepted our way of life. Unlike this creature. Who only knows how to complain. Whose fire is more smoke than flames. If she is unwelcome here, it is because she has made herself unwelcome."

"Why has she not left then?"

"I have often wondered this myself. After all, according to our way, no woman with child can become a man's first wife – not that any have shown an interest."

"Yet that is her ambition?"

"So the other women claim."

"Perhaps unhappiness is the soil in which she grows best. There are many like that."

"This is true. I think, too, she stays because she is unwelcome in her own clan."

Significantly, explains the chief, her father hasn't come seeking lobola.

"Truly, I do not think she is wanted there. After all, if this is how she acts as a guest . . ."

The Induna nods. He turns to the boy and instructs him to go and prepare a sleeping place for them.

"No, you will stay with me."

"Many thanks, Honoured Friend Of Shaka," says the Induna, laying a hand on the old man's shoulder. But, he adds, he and the boy will sleep on the beach. In that way they'll avoid the worst of the omiyane, the mosquitoes that plague this place.

After dismissing the udibi, he turns back to the chief. "Now, while there is still light, show me where your men bravely captured the tracks of this creature."

*

The boy is running.

Panting, open-mouthed, his skin pulled tight around his skull as he tries to suck in air.

The ground trembles. Creaks. Tilts. Cracks open, fissures chasing his feet.

Running, his head now thrown back, his mouth wide, biting at the acrid air, now bent forward, his chin pressed against his chest. Running.

The ground growls. A distant anger, like a leopard trapped deep in a cave.

But then another noise attracts his attention. He swerves, almost slips . . .

Looks up. In the branches of the mango tree, a bundle. He catches a glimpse of tiny hands . . .

He stretches, reaches up, fingers straining . . .

Clutching the baby to his chest he starts running again . . .

A cave.

With a final surge of adrenaline, teeth clenched, he lunges into the darkness.

And falls on his side on the floor . . .

The wet, slimy floor . . .

And the walls are ribbed . . .

And they seem to expand, like a skin filled with water . . .

And the boy screams.

A dreadful mistake.

This isn't a cave. It's a mouth, and the jaws are closing, crushing them . . .

*

The Induna shakes him awake.

The boy sits up, wide-eyed and trembling.

The Induna hands him the gourd containing the sorghum beer.

The boy takes a mouthful of the pinkish liquid, wipes his mouth with the back of his hand. Passes the gourd to the Induna.

"Who were you fighting?"

"Inhlwathi."

"Ahh! Tell me about inhlwathi."

"Nduna?"

The Induna's features are streaks of ebony in the flickering flames. "Tell me a story, Boy. Tell me why we, the People Of The Sky, fear these creatures . . ."

*

A long time ago, before the Abantu, the Human Beings, before Mame-ravi, the Mother Of Nations, when the world was new, there dwelled a race of golden-eyed, hairless people. They lived in peace, according to the laws of the Great Spirit. No animal died in vain. No hand was ever raised in anger. No woman wept in the night. No child starved.

Then one of their women, called by some Nelesi, by others Kei-Lei-Si, gave birth to a son, deformed in both body and soul.

"Kaaaaaaauk!" said the wise Kaa-U-La birds. "Kill this monster! Kill it at once!"

But Nelesi fled with her child, into the bowels of the earth, where they lived off mud and bones. She called her child Za-Ha-Rrellel. His arms and legs were shrunken and his head was bigger than his body, and he had but one eye, and his soul was twisted and his mind diseased.

"You are nothing but a female beast obeying the natural law," he told his mother one day. "Now I have grown up I have no need of you any more."

And he called forth the Ore from the earth, and the Ore became a sharpened snout with vicious teeth, dragonfly wings, grasshopper legs and a tail with a crystal sting on the end. And the creature of iron tore apart Nelesi, who realised too late that the wise old Kaa-U-La birds had been right – the child *was* evil.

And Za-Ha-Rrellel conquered the world, telling the Peaceful Ones he'd been sent by the Great Spirit to free them from ignorance and savagery – the ignorance of love, the savagery of peace.

Those who followed him lived a life of great ease in huts of pure gold. If they desired warmth, fires were lit of their own accord. Crops planted and harvested themselves. No longer need one even raise a drinking pot to one's lips – think the thought and the pot lifted, ready to obey your whim.

Time passed and the followers of Za-Ha-Rrellel became so lazy that even chewing their food was too strenuous – and so Za-Ha-Rrellel gave them the power to wish the food into their stomachs. Soon, the men and women even gave up trying to walk. They slithered across the ground, when they bothered to move at all. This is how they came to be called Izinhlwathi – Bellycrawlers, Those Who Go Where There Is No Path.

And Za-Ha-Rrellel sent out his iron monsters to capture wild animals. These, he crushed into a pulp and from the remains created the Bjaauni, the Lowest Of Low, creatures of rotting flesh and dead blood, who became the servants of the Bellycrawlers.

"Enough!" said Unkulunkulu, the Great Spirit. And his voice was thunder. Lightning flashed again and again. His tears became rain and the waters rose. Za-Ha-Rrellel and his slothful followers took to rafts of iron and gold, floating cities where they feasted and mocked the thunderclouds.

Then Ma, the Mother Of The World, who had created the stars, the sun and the earth at the command of the Great Spirit, grew angry, and her breath turned the ocean into a boiling cauldron so hot it melted the rafts and the metal monsters, and so Za-Ha-Rrellel and his followers perished in blood-red waters.

"But some survived," says the Induna.

Yes, agrees the udibi. Some of Za-Ha-Rrellel's minions survived. These ones who could only crawl and could scarcely chew their food. Some learnt to marshal the venom of their hatred: these became the mamba, the tree snake, the cobra . . . Others, like the python, developed a taste for human flesh.

"Some say they seek to create their own Bjaauni, mindless servants who will rise up one day to destroy the Human Beings."

"So some say, Master, but I prefer not to think of that possibility. Better a thirsty assegai to drink my blood!"

"Better a greybeard and nothing to do all day except wear out your women and count your cattle, Boy."

The Induna takes a sip of beer and pushes the gourd into the sand by his feet. "But these are the stories they tell."

"These are the stories they tell," agrees the boy.

"Now tell me, Boy: you fear the python, but do you not also fear the lion?"

"But the snake is cunning in a way the lion is not."

"Would the impala or the zebra agree with you?"

The boy ponders that.

"And the anteater?" asks the Induna.

"The anteater, Master?"

"Do you fear the anteater?"

"Aiee!" The boy laughs, shakes his head. "No, Master!" He presses his nose against his wrist and waggles his hand in front of his face, mimicking the creature. "Aiee," he giggles. "Who fears the anteater?"

"The ant."

That brings him up short. He lowers his hand.

"Fear is ignorance, Boy. It is easy to fear the other side of the mountain when you do not know what lies there. We need to climb the mountain and see for ourselves."

"But the old stories . . ."

"Are perhaps the tales of those too afraid to climb the mountain. And I ask you this: did not the Goddess Ma, mother of the sun, stars and earth, destroy Za-Ha-Rrellel and his impis by boiling the waters?"

190

"It is so, Master."

"How then could this spawn survive?"

"Because it is evil."

The Induna chuckles. "No, Boy, it survives only because we are ignorant."

The boy nods his head slowly.

"Now, let us get some sleep."

The boy rearranges his cowhide cloak, snuggles down on his sleeping mat.

The Induna sits watching the flames amid the comforting, restful sigh and hiss of the waves at the water's edge.

"Boy?" he says, after a while.

"Yes, Master?" An instant response; a sign the boy is still far from sleep.

"We have spoken – but you are still afraid."

A pause; twigs crackle in the fire, sending more stars up into the velvet night. Then: "Yes, Master."

"It is all right to be afraid."

"Yes, Master."

"Now, get some sleep."

*

The chief is able to supply forty men and some boys. The mango trees where the tracks were spotted are down a path that runs inland along the river bank; the tracks showed the python to be moving away from the river. The Induna gets the men spread out two arm lengths apart down the path, facing the trees. Every second man is armed with a long hunting spear; as they move forward, these men will use the spears to sweep the long grass and prod the undergrowth. The others carry short, stabbing assegais.

With so few men the Induna can't cover as much ground as he'd like to, therefore he has placed senior herdboys in trees on either end of the line. They're to watch for sideways movements, away from the approaching warriors, and any hippo that might have wandered close to the settlement. Other, younger boys walk up and down the line with gourds of water.

After about four hours, the Induna calls a halt. Women bring porridge and fruit from the village and the men breakfast where they stand. The line has long ago moved past the mango trees. The eelgrass has given way to rougher country, tangled branches, muddy pools gradually connecting to become swampland. At times the men sink up to their knees. Mosquitoes are here, so many it's easy to believe the heat is generated by their buzzing wings. Every so often, the Induna has the boys move forward to climb trees a little ahead of the men.

They can now see the path that leads to the village. It has angled away from the shore and forms the left-hand boundary line of the search area. The Induna sends some of the younger boys to stand on the path, lest the snake try to escape in that direction. It's a possibility he feels is unlikely, though. The bushes on the seaward side of the path soon give way to the low dunes of the beach, and he suspects the python will not be happy in the sand with no thickets to hide in. But he wants all potential escape routes guarded.

The Induna slips two fingers into his mouth and whistles once. The udibis slide down from the trees and run ahead of the line again.

The boy is on the side closest to the path. His shins are scratched and his feet are a dark grey from dried mud. He dodges the sharp leaves of a cycad and spots a tree, an umdoni waterberry, he can climb. He's so anxious to get from one tree to the other, as quickly as possible, that he doesn't notice he's moved further ahead of the line than the other boys.

What he does notice is the smell.

He comes to a halt.

Sniffs.

Glances around anxiously, wishing he had an assegai with him.

The waterberry has fluffy white flowers that give off a strong scent, but this smell overpowers even that.

The lair of the python will smell like this. The stench of rotting meat.

He glances upward and sees the bundle in the lower branches, but it doesn't immediately register as something out of the ordinary; it's not the python and all the boy wants to do is get into the tree and survey the surrounding area for the source of the stench.

So it's only when he has a foot on the branch and his back against the trunk that he looks down at the bundle . . .

. . . and shrieks . . .

. . . and yanks his foot away . . .

. . . and loses his balance.

*

Night's stars flicker and flash in his skull. His dream has come true, except he doesn't have the baby in his arms.

Initially, though, the Induna is more concerned with his wellbeing. He checks the boy's limbs, gently bending each one. Then he runs careful fingers over the boy's skull.

When he's satisfied the boy isn't injured he lets him stand. After allowing him a few moments to get his breath back, he sends the udibi to fetch the village shaman. It's a considerate gesture, allowing the udibi to find a secluded spot where he can throw up without embarrassing himself in front of the other boys – although several who've approached the tree to see what the commotion is about have turned away to plant their breakfast porridge in the soggy ground.

The Induna reaches up for the bundle. Carefully gripping the front fold, he lifts it off the branch and steps back, holding it away from him. It sags like a waterskin. Dropping to his knees, the Induna places the tiny body on the ground.

The maggots are white, bloated. An army of flies attends the corpse. A ragged wetness encircles the infant's mouth where the lips should be. The skin around the tiny cheekbones has begun to crack. The baby has rotted in the heat that collects here during the day and only the cowhide coverlet wrapped around it gives the corpse any substance.

The Induna shakes his head sadly. Mutters a prayer for the child, and then a cleansing prayer for himself.

Then, still on his knees, he looks away . . .

Amid the shadows beneath a low tangle of bushes, a collection of tan and brown spots suddenly coalesce.

And the Induna sees it.

The python.

It lies almost paralysed by the large lump halfway down its thick body, for such is the way of the inhlwathi. After taking its prey, it slides away to its lair, where it'll remain inactive for up to four weeks while its intestinal juices go to work.

As the Induna watches, the snake's heavy, flat head rises and turns toward him, so that man and reptile are staring at each other. The stench of the tiny corpse, the muttering of the men, the chirping of the weavers, the rustlings and disturbances, all fall away and the Induna sees dark shapes moving through a murky world – strange beasts with long necks and the squat legs of the elephant, birds with spears for beaks and leather wings, animals with crocodile tails, the sharp peaks of mountains on their backs. In turn, its ancient senses reaching out, the snake feels the trembling ground of a thousand feet – screams and war cries, sweat in your eyes, madness in your heart, shrieking assegais, bodies falling away – and its tongue slips between its lips as though to taste the blood . . .

The Induna allows his own lips to twist in a wry grin.

"Not today," he tells the tiny black eyes.

*

When the two elders bring the woman to the ibandla tree, the Induna has washed the mud off himself and is wearing the blue feather and the fur collar.

The woman is weeping and struggles to break free from the men who hold her.

"You have found him?" she asks.

194

"Yes," says the Induna softly, so she has to quieten down if she's to hear his words properly – and he's not the kind of man you ask to repeat himself. "We have found him."

"Is he safe?"

"Yes," says the Induna. "He is safe."

The woman's mouth drops open. She stops struggling. "He is safe?"

"He is safer now than he ever was with you."

"Shadow Of Shaka, I . . . I do not understand," she stammers.

Even the old chief is looking at the Induna in a strange way. The boy, too, is puzzled.

The Induna raises his assegai and presses the tip of the broad blade between the woman's breasts. "Why did you kill your own child?"

The chief stares at the Induna, then at the woman with raised eyebrows and wide eyes.

The woman's knees give way. The men have to hold her up.

The Induna waits for a response, but the woman remains with her head bowed, her chin almost touching the blade of his assegai.

"My iklwa thirsts for your blood," says the Induna, at last, "but it is not my place to dispense justice. It is to him," he says, motioning to the chief, "that you must appeal for mercy."

He tells the men holding her to take the woman away and keep her under guard.

"Your counsel in this matter will be greatly appreciated, Nduna," says the chief once they're alone. "What would you do if you were an old man weary of death and madness and wanted only to care for your own people?"

The Induna smiles wryly. "If that were me and I were faced with this situation, I would send the woman back to her own clan and have done with her."

"Yes . . . Yes, that is good advice, I see now why the Grumpy One values you so."

"Send her back now, Mnumzane. Let them start the journey before sunset. Have done with her. But be sure to select wise greybeards for her guard, lest she beguile them with her wiles. This one is clearly capable of anything."

"I will do even better," says the chief. "I'll send two of my sons and their mothers – *they* will see she arrives where she belongs!"

"Shaka salutes your wisdom!"

"Cha! That'll be the day when the Great Waters fall still and the fish herd themselves into our nets!"

"Then *I* salute your wisdom."

"*That*, Nduna, is a compliment more precious than all my wives."

"I think not, Mnumzane. But I will treasure your words nonetheless."

*

The boy puts aside the remains of the crab the women of the village have prepared for them. It was far tastier than he expected.

The fire dances between them and, across the sand, the waves are a warm wall of sound. A lullaby heard just the other side of sleep.

"Master? How did you know?"

"Why would a mother leave her child unattended while she collected firewood? Is it not the way of our women to carry their infants on their backs?"

"So you knew even then?"

"I was suspicious."

"What made you certain, Master?"

"When you made your discovery. No creature would do that."

"What do you mean, Master?"

"The way the baby was wrapped up. It was dead, this is true, but only a mother would've cared enough to have ensured it would not grow cold on its Great Journey."

The boy ponders these things for a few moments. Picks at the remnants of the crab. Gazes at the stars.

"Why would she do such a thing, Master?" he asks at length.

"I do not know. Perhaps she wanted to be someone's first wife, which would've been impossible with a child, such is the way of this clan."

196

"She is evil, Master."

"Perhaps."

"How can it be otherwise?"

"Sometimes I think evil is a fork in the road. But perhaps, for this one, there was no fork. Her name ensured that."

It is a tradition among the AmaZulu to name their children after an incident that immediately preceded the child's birth, or the emotion felt by the parents at the time of birth. The woman's name is Unolusizi, which means Bitterness.

"Is this why you were so merciful, Master?"

"A stone rolls down a hill, Boy. As it rolls, it picks up speed of its own accord. But did it start rolling of its own accord? Let her clan, her parents, reap the crop they have planted. Unolusizi," whispers the Induna. "That is not a name, Boy, that is a curse."

The boy nods sagely. He is thinking of Shaka, scornfully named after a beetle . . .

"Now let us get some sleep," says the Induna. "We have a snake to catch tomorrow."

*

And praise singers across the land could add another verse to the legend their words had already begun to weave around the Induna's exploits when, the following morning, with the uncanny instinct of one favoured by the Great Spirit and the ancestors, he led the men of the Omadla clan straight to the lair of the python and with a single thrust of his assegai and a cry of "Ngadla!", he slew the reptile that had terrorised the village for so long.

Whereas the praise singers disseminate the tribe's history, revelling in heroic deeds and great battles, the Izazi Ezigcina Izimfihlo, or Men Who Know, are guardians of the tribe's secrets and are found in most clans. They are the ones who know the locations of the old Ma-Iti mines, for example, and they also protect the Ma-Iti and Arabi artefacts and precious items from other cultures that have come into the clan's possession, and which are regarded as having extremely potent magical properties – so potent, in fact, they're best kept hidden.

These secrets are passed down from father to son. Four times a year, the guardian will retrieve the artefacts from their various hiding places and convey them to his hut. Here, he'll examine each one in turn, reciting its provenance – in effect, doing an inventory, making sure none of the precious relics are missing or damaged. He'll also name the locations of the mines and any other secrets he might have been entrusted with. For the ceremony, he'll wear a cloak made from the skin of a hyena, which is deemed a secretive creature.

The only other people present during this observance will be the guardian's eldest son and heir and his eldest son and heir, even if a babe in arms. That is to say, the guardian's son and grandson, and the onus is on the first-born male to produce his own heir as soon as possible. This is to ensure continuity. The ceremony is also the time when the guardian can pass the secrets on to his successors, for it's the only occasion the secrets may be spoken and the artefacts viewed. And even then the secrets aren't told or shared in any overt manner – the heirs learn them by "overhearing" or listening in on the guardian's litany.

The headman is then summoned and the process is repeated – with one exception. Even he is not allowed to know where the various artefacts are kept hidden.

An heir only officially becomes a guardian on his father's death, even if senility or some other affliction means he's been standing in for the guardian for several years already.

The identity of the guardian family is supposedly known only to the headman of the clan (and how the family came to be chosen is lost in the mists of time). If the clan's territory is overrun by invaders, the guardian will simply vanish along with the other refugees and the clan's secrets will be safeguarded, and will remain so even if the clan is subsumed into another tribe. Although, if this happens, the observances stop, and unless the clan is able to regain its "independence", the secrets will die with the last guardian. However, because the guardian and his heirs are exempt from military service and allowed various privileges, it's fairly easy to guess who the Izazi Ezigcina Izimfihlo are in smaller communities. Yet, since those secrets are partly what define the clan's own special identity, the Men Who Know are unlikely to be betrayed. The whole community will suffer as a result and this isn't a matter of belief or superstition; it's a fact, as unassailable as the knowledge that a man who sticks his hand in a fire will get burnt.

By the same token, the guardian and his entire family, including relatives by marriage, face death if any of the artefacts go missing, or it becomes apparent that others have been told the secrets . . .

The Man Who Was Bewitched

Guinea fowl pick at the grass on the fringes of the hard-packed dirt. A cow gazes over the branches that form the small cattlefold directly opposite the hut; long lashes, eyes surrounded by two brown patches, a steady appraisal that takes in and dismisses the slender man with the protruding stomach. And his own brown patch, a clearing like a splash of mud on the upper left side of his skull, where the hair no longer grows. The guinea fowl scatter as a young girl, the sangoma's daughter, comes along the path from the homestead a few metres further down the slope. Paying Zondi no heed, she slips into the shaman's dwelling.

A slender stream of smoke rises from the hut and, following its course into the sky, Zondi is jerked from his reverie. The sun is low – it's late. He'll have to spend an extra night in the veld. Instinctively, his hand rises to his chest, fingers closing around the small leather sack hanging there from a leather thong. It's part of the treatment, the muthi, the sangoma has given him. And he should be safe.

Hai, but he's forgotten what it means to be safe, in the same way a sore throat will, after a very short while, cause a man to forget what it's like to swallow without pain. Carefully, his fingers squeeze the sack, compressing the dried herbs and the dung, then his hand drops. Finds the satchel at his hip, the other potions the sangoma has prepared for him, wrapped in leaves.

If he doubts the efficacy of these muthis, it's the consequence of what he's gone through. Nervous days. Terror-filled nights. A man has a right to wonder if the medicine will be sufficient under such circumstances – for it seems so little and he has endured so much.

Then this long journey, more perilous for him than any can know. Obviously, he couldn't consult a sangoma from his home village, and had to travel far enough to ensure he outstripped news of the theft – and even then he knew he was taking a risk, for news of that nature travels far. But he is a desperate man, fast running out of sanity.

To the sangoma he presented himself as a supplicant come following the shaman's reputation, knowing flattery would go a long way in distracting the healer.

Anyway, it was perfectly natural for a man to be bewitched without knowing why, and this was the guise Zondi adopted. He even went so far as to resurrect his dead friend when the sangoma asked him if he had any suspicions as to who the culprit might be. And he didn't have to lie when he told the sangoma of how Siyafunda haunted him in his dreams, because that was the truth. The grim truth.

"But this friend of yours," said the sangoma, "he is clearly dead."

"Uh, y-yes," stammered Zondi, "yes, he is." He should have known the sangoma would divine that fact. It was a near-fatal error, one guaranteed to make the shaman suspicious. Why hadn't Zondi told him this in the first place? More importantly, why had he implied Siyafunda was still alive?

"This is a delicate situation," said the sangoma. "I understand your reluctance to confront this occurrence."

And, while Zondi breathed a sigh of relief, the shaman went on to probe for signs of enmity between the friends. Of course, there hadn't been any, not while Siyafunda was alive, and there was no need for Zondi to feign perplexity.

Now that ordeal is over. He must face the infinitely greater terror of the trip home.

*

He stops once more. Listens.

The footsteps continue for a few paces before falling silent.

It's as if the person wants Zondi to know he's being followed.

And he can hear the footsteps, because, whoever it is, they aren't on the path. He – it – is moving among the trees, through the long grass behind Zondi and to the left. He can hear the crackling of twigs and dried leaves.

Or can he? Those noises might simply be small animals, the whisper of the breeze.

But it sounds as if someone's scooped up a handful of dried twigs and is breaking them within earshot, then rustling dried leaves together.

Zondi starts running. Gripping the necklace to stop it from flapping around, clutching his spear tightly in his other hand, he's soon sprinting. Branches leap out trying to grab him before being brushed aside. The path has been worn into a narrow trough, with clumps of grass along the shallow rim waiting to trip him up, but his feet never err. For a few exhilarating seconds he feels like the wind: free, unfettered. Then the path begins to climb out of the bushes and he has to slow down. Stop. As he bends forward to regain his breath, the fear slams into him again, squeezing his lungs, for there, several metres to his rear: a shattering, snapping sound, falling silent even as he wheels.

His chest heaving, the tangled bushes rising and falling, Zondi scans the greenery looking for something: a shape, a shadow, anything.

"Who's there?" he gasps, raising his assegai. "Who's there? Come out! Come out and face me like a man!"

His free hand finds the pouch around his neck. Why isn't it working?

The sangoma's voice echoes inside his head: "These things take time."

How long, though? How long?

Zondi's eyes scan the craning trees, the thickets . . . A rustle to his right, catching him by surprise even though he's on guard. A splatter of squeaking bats spilling across the orange sky.

He resumes his journey, following the path out of the ravine. When he's above the trees and bushes, he turns for another look. There *is* movement down there, but it's just the veld, readying itself for sunset.

*

Zondi stares into the flames of his campfire and grimaces. In a way, the journey outward had been easier, for he'd brought along four cows as payment for the sangoma. He at least had some form of company. Now he's alone. He keeps his eyes on the flames, doesn't bother to look around. After too much stress the mind shuts down, what will be will be. He doesn't bother to look round, because he doesn't have to. That thing, whatever it may be, is out there, watching him.

*

He sleeps . . .

. . . and dreams.

First there's the sense of unease, burning brighter than the campfire. It squeezes the inside of his skull, pushes fingers out through his eye sockets and twists his head this way and that. It's a ghost animating his limbs, causing him to run; a vain flailing that serves only to kick off his wildebeest cloak. It's a voice that pries apart his lips, to tell the night, "No, no, no, no!"

Then: a coalescing. The unease, the fear, the sweaty flailing become a hyena's head, peering down at him.

A . . . what?

His eyes are open.

There's a hyena . . .

No, not a hyena . . . Blinking, his eyes get the perspective right. It's too high, too far above him to be a hyena. It's a man . . . A man with the head of a hyena, standing over him, peering down at him.

Zondi shrieks.

Sits up.

Dives forward, away from the hyena-man. Has to twist to avoid the fire.

He's panting.

His spear . . .

Where's his spear?

Unable to find it, he rolls over, an arm raised to ward off the attack.

But the night is empty, save for the crickets and the bullfrogs.

There's his spear!

Zondi lunges for it and gets up. Turns, assegai at the ready, turns and turns until he makes himself dizzy.

When he drops down his wails fill the night.

*

After an uncomfortable night, with sleep finally coming to him while he sat hunched up by the fire, Zondi rises unsteadily to his feet. Kicks sand over the grey embers. Retrieves his belongings.

A few paces away from his camp site, when he's once more on the path that leads to his village, he spots something hanging from a branch that arches over the trail.

His hand leaps up to his chest.

There's nothing there!

He hadn't noticed it was missing, and there's nothing there, because the muthi talisman the sangoma gave him to protect him from the evil spirit is hanging from the branch.

*

Footsteps and footprints.

Yes, there have been footprints as well. A scratching at the thatch late at night; rushing out, his spear at the ready, calling to the thief to show himself. And the next day there'd been footprints around his hut, close to the thatch, spoor that belonged to a stranger. Well and good, he'd thought, he had seen off a thief in the night. But two days later he was again sitting up in the darkness, tilting his head, trying to identify the noise that had awoken him. The impudence of this person! That was his thought as he once more charged out of the hut.

Aiee, such boldness was a faint memory by the fifth night it happened. Even more disconcerting were the nights he wasn't disturbed, when he'd wake up with relief, only to find fresh footprints . . .

His wives were bemused when he took to sweeping the area around his hut, once, twice a day. It became a compulsion. Perhaps by removing the footprints he could obliterate his nightly visitor altogether.

But there was also a more sane motivation.

The frequency with which he took to sweeping soon got out of hand, the desire irresistible, even though he knew there couldn't have been another visitation because it was still daylight. *That* he couldn't control, but a part of him also saw this as a necessity, a way of destroying the evidence. He couldn't let it be known that he'd been singled out. It was too soon after . . .

Footsteps, dogging him.

Footprints to remind him he wasn't imagining things.

And there'd been footprints around his camp site. He'd seen them as he gathered up his belongings, another reason he didn't immediately notice the necklace was missing. Someone really had been standing over him. And had returned later to remove the medicine . . .

Aiee, this being, this creature had been close! Had *touched* him!

A realisation with ominous implications that sets his head spinning. He'd retrieved the muthi, with trembling hands, but now he has to doubt its efficacy.

Perhaps he has no protection, no defence, because he is being justly persecuted.

*

Later, they'll ask him why he didn't simply return the amulet. Although it would not have made up for his crime, it might have afforded him some relief.

"I tried!" Zondi will say. "I did!"

But the hut was closely guarded lest the thief return to steal the rest of the treasure, and he couldn't – daren't – carry the amulet with him, hidden about his person, in the hope of seizing a chance to enter the dwelling . . .

*

No defence. No protection.

It doesn't bear thinking about – and as a consequence Zondi is doubly glad to spot a fellow wayfarer further along the path. Not only will he provide Zondi with some company on his last night in the veld, the idle chitchat of two men sharing the same track will free his mind for a little while.

Quickening his pace, he catches up to the man about thirty minutes later. From a distance, a hobbling, slightly bow-legged gait spoke of an elderly individual, but up close, Zondi sees the stranger is a little younger than he expected. The grey hair that mats his chest, the numerous scars on his thighs and arms disguise his true age and Zondi judges him to be approaching his forty-fifth summer.

Zulus are assiduous about greeting whoever they encounter on the road. Unless on a pressing errand, no traveller will forego the opportunity to chat a while. Often they'll rest together and take snuff. It's a sign of bad breeding to pass another without some form of salutation.

Since they are headed the same way, the two do not tarry for long. There's no need: they'll travel together, share a fire tonight.

The stranger's name is Umfo.

"Igama lami nguZondi," says Zondi, introducing himself.

"We are untying the distance to your home village?" asks Umfo.

Zondi nods. Says he's been to visit relatives.

"Aiee," sighs the stranger, who's fallen in behind Zondi, "my journey is of a similar nature, although little pleasure awaits me at its end."

"It is a pleasant village, not a destination to be dreaded."

"I do not doubt that. That is not whereof I speak."

"Then who are these unpleasant relatives?" asks Zondi, shooting a grin over his shoulder. "Maybe I know them."

"Yes," says Umfo, his voice brightening, "I did not think of that!"

Something about the man's tone, a certain optimism, causes Zondi to glance over his shoulder once more.

"I am going to visit my nephew's grave," says Umfo. "Did you know him? His name was Siyafunda."

Zondi stumbles.

"Be careful," says the stranger.

Zondi stops and turns. Stops because he's not sure he can walk any further; turns to examine this man more closely. "Yes," he says, forcing a grin, "I knew Siyafunda. We were the same age, and playmates once."

Umfo's delight is obvious. "You knew him?"

Zondi nods.

"I have questions . . ."

Zondi interrupts him. He'll be happy to answer Umfo's questions, but let them untie more of this distance, for they still have a way to go.

And he needs time to think!

Umfo is amenable to this and they continue their journey.

*

Later, they'll ask him why he did such a foolish thing.

How can he explain it? It was so beautiful, had bewitched him from the moment he laid eyes on it. It didn't matter he'd only seen it that one time. And the two boys were risking more than merely the wrath of Siyafunda's father. Had they been found out, they would've been brought before the chief, and who knows what might have happened. Their parents would have faced punishment as well – Siyafunda's father for being lax in his guard, Zondi's for raising such a dangerously irresponsible and disobedient son. But the time of the observance was drawing near and Zondi had always been slightly in awe of his friend, of the special status he'd one day inherit. And both boys were at just the right age – to ask awkward questions and to have the courage to seek the answers on their own, no matter what the risks.

It was Zondi who did the asking, the pestering and wheedling, and it was Siyafunda who had the courage to show his friend the treasure, as though that might help Zondi explain to him why he was different to the other boys – for although only a few moons separated their birth, Siyafunda looked up to Zondi as a brother years older. And, yes, Zondi was flattered, strove to play that role, but it also irked him that his friend, who seemed so much younger than he, should have been singled out, by a mere accident of birth, for such an auspicious role. But all of this was forgotten when his eyes fell on the amulet . . .

*

"It was a sudden death?"

Zondi nods, keeping his eyes on the fire.

"An accidental death?"

"A tragedy, Brother," whispers Zondi.

"A snake, they say."

"A tree snake, Friend."

Umfo shakes his head, clucks his tongue. "A painful death."

"A horrible death," murmurs Zondi.

He'd been in the fields with his wives, on furlough from his regiment and making a token attempt to help the womenfolk with the weeding, when Siyafunda's youngest son came racing past, shrieking something about his father . . .

"It is as they say, then?" says Umfo. "No cause for suspicion?"

Zondi straightens, takes a deep breath. "Is that why you've come? Have you heard anything to the contrary?"

"No, I merely seek reassurance."

"For he was my friend. I will avenge him if . . ." Zondi's voice tails off. "I will avenge him," he murmurs, watching the flames, these orange blades, once more.

"I see that."

Zondi's head snaps up. "See what?"

"That you were close."

"It is so."

"Since childhood, you say?"

Zondi nods.

"It's just that . . . my brother and my nephew were not quite like other men and the possibility has to be considered . . ."

"It *was* considered, Friend," says Zondi. "And I know whereof you speak."

"You know?"

Umfo shakes his head at such recklessness.

"I suppose," he says, after a moment spent glaring at the flames, "in some communities . . ."

"Yes, yes," says Zondi, happy to allow his nervousness to become irritation, "we each have our own way, and we are a small village. But rest assured, secrets were protected and this matter was thoroughly investigated."

"Then why has Shaka despatched one of his indunas?"

He knows about the induna!

Somehow Zondi manages a calm response. "News travels far and wide."

"Your chief sent a messenger to inform me of this development."

"Then you know it was *he* who sought Shaka's aid."

"Because something was missing, was it not?"

Zondi nods. A guardian's sudden death means the heir will hold an observance as soon as possible, and that's how Siyafunda's son discovered the amulet was missing.

"This is why some things should not be spoken about, no matter how small the village."

"There was trust!" And now you are hissing like a tree snake, thinks Zondi. Calm. He has to stay calm.

"Apparently not!" says Umfo.

"Have you thought of this," says Zondi. "Perhaps the two events are not connected!"

"Come now! It is more likely they are. A death and a theft. Rain and mud! How can they not be connected!"

"Perhaps we'll find out tomorrow."

"The induna . . ."

"Yes. He has been there long enough."

But it is not him you fear, is it?

"So I will be in time to speak to him, to hear what he has to say, this Isithunzi SikaShaka!"

209

Probably more of the former than the latter, thinks Zondi, managing a wry grin. "Perhaps," he says.

*

No, it's not the induna and his questions he fears. Indeed, Zondi can't quite see what the man hopes to accomplish. His investigation will be hampered by the strictures surrounding the Izazi Ezigcina Izimfihlo and the position the Men Who Know occupy in the community; it would be optimistic even to think an investigation is possible. These special circumstances might mean that one of the tribe's secrets has to be shared with Shaka's induna, but he, in turn, couldn't reveal this to his men or the villagers.

In fact, news of the induna's imminent arrival had sparked much debate among the villagers. Was he allowed to know what had been stolen? Was it right and fair that he should be told what the members of the clan were not permitted to know?

"After all, it is our future that is threatened," said some.

Was the induna even allowed to know that something had been stolen? Old-timers were urged to search their memories for tribal lore pertaining to such a situation – and no one could remember anything similar ever happening.

But whatever the headman decided to tell this Shadow Of Shaka, his investigation would anyway be curtailed because there were some questions he'd be unable to ask if he chose to interrogate any of the villagers.

And lurking in the background of all the heated discussions was the suspicion that the induna had not come to investigate the "theft". That he and his men were there to execute Siyafunda's family, as custom dictated. The family was much-liked and there were many who thought the punishment was too harsh, who, if the truth be told, couldn't see the point of such a fuss over what were mere things. Hadn't Shaka overridden so many of the old traditions and, through his conquests, given his children so much more to value? But no one said anything.

For Zondi's part, an investigation is but a paltry annoyance, given what he's facing. Although, if he wants to be honest with himself, the induna *is* a threat. Of course he is! The punishment he can conjure in the name of Shaka is not to be contemplated lightly.

But that which stalks him is far more fearsome.

*

Watching Umfo turning the meat on the fire, the older man having caught them a dassie for supper, Zondi feels a surge of anger. He has these moments – when his mind rebels, rattles the cage of fear. Let this thing come! Let it face him! Better a fight to the finish than these cowardly taunts.

Let it reveal itself – and even if he is the loser, as he is sure to be, he'll at least have had the chance to speak his mind.

Yes! You would punish me for taking the amulet, you would condemn and terrorise me, but it is true! I value it more than you ever did! For you it was merely a thing, part of a calling you sometimes wanted to reject!

You may have forgotten this, Siyafunda, but I remember – how you envied me going off to join my regiment, while you remained tethered by your family's obligations.

So yes – I valued the amulet far more than you! Do you now have the right to haunt me?

Reveal yourself! Let's end this . . .

Umfo is gazing at him. "Did you speak?"

Zondi stands. Says no. Says he will fetch more water.

He knows he can afford the luxury of such rebellious thoughts right now, because Umfo's with him. For all his awkward questions, at least the older man's presence means Zondi doesn't have to face the night alone.

*

Later, they'll ask him why? Why did he do such a foolish thing?

How to answer that question? How to describe the strange effect the amulet had on him, rubies mounted on a simple bronze band nestling among the other artefacts in the sack. *That* was the day he was bewitched! All that has transpired since is simply the culmination of a process started years ago, that day, when he was eleven summers old. The crescendo of a wail of desire that has been flowing out of him for so long. Why he stole it is a question that has no meaning for him. The theft was an inevitability, a natural consequence. He sees that now. It was going to happen from the moment he set eyes on the amulet. He was trapped. But why that specific artefact? What is it about the amulet? And why him? Why should it have such a profound effect on him? *Those* are the questions he'd like to see answered!

*

Birdsong awakes Zondi. Seconds later, blinking his eyes, stretching, he's grinning . . .

But wait!

His hand snakes up under his cloak to find the pouch. It's still there!

His grin widens.

It's still there and he's slept through the night.

He's conquered the night!

"Give it time," the sangoma had told him. Clearly he was right!

Wise sangoma!

Zondi sits up, savouring the cool air.

Sweet air!

He stands, arching his back and running his fingers down his ribcage and over the mound of his stomach. The world has a crispness about it, a freshness. The green leaves seem brighter, the birds more melodic; he feels the sand beneath his feet, the coolness of the morning air is invigorating and even his first piss of the day is sublime. And his cock soon hardens again, reminding him of one of the other pleasures that have eluded him these past few weeks. And although he would linger, enjoying the moment, the desire to get home and resume his life is stronger.

He even feels a surge of compassion for Umfo, as he moves over to where the older man lies, still fast asleep. The muthi might be working, but his presence also helped. Zondi feels an urge to thank him, although of course he won't, because that'll only confuse Umfo.

He's lying on his side, facing away from Zondi. Crouching, Zondi shakes his shoulder.

A grunt. A groan.

"Come," says Zondi, grinning indulgently, "we must be on our way."

Umfo rolls over and sits up.

And Zondi recoils in horror.

It's not Umfo!

It's a much younger man. A stranger.

Zondi springs backward and slips. Lands on his arse.

"Who are you?" he shrieks, kicking up sand as he slithers further away.

The man rubs his eyes. Frowns. "What's the matter?" he growls, his voice foggy with sleep.

"What have you done with him?" Zondi's eyes are wide.

"Who?" asks the man, clearly grumpy at being awoken in such a fashion.

"Umfo! What have you done with him?"

"Umfo? But I am Umfo!"

"No! You're not him!"

"What nonsense is this?" says the man, making to stand.

"Don't move!" Zondi casts about anxiously, trying to find his spear.

"Have you gone mad?"

There it is! Zondi lunges sideways, rolling over his wildebeest cloak.

Divining his companion's intent, the man has reached for his own spear and rises to his feet at the same time as Zondi.

"Don't do anything foolish, Friend!"

"Who are you?" hisses Zondi.

This man is definitely not Umfo. Umfo was older, had grey hair and scars, walked and stood with his legs slightly bowed.

"I have told you! I am Umfo!"

No! This man is younger, taller.

"You are not Umfo! Where is he?"

"Put that spear down, Friend, lest I do you an injury."

Zondi shakes his head.

"Do you mean to rob me, is that it?" asks the man.

The words bite home. But he is not Siyafunda! Who is he?

"Do not move, Demon!"

The man's response is a snort of disbelieving laughter. "Demon? What madness is this? I am Umfo! We shared supper last night!"

"Not you! No! What have you done with him?" asks Zondi, taking a step backward, as the man comes forward. "Don't move!"

"No," says the man. "*You* stay where you are!"

Keeping an eye on Zondi, he gathers up his belongings.

"I will leave you now," he says when he is ready. "I'll leave you to your madness, and you – you will leave me alone! I will make my own way to your village. Do not try to overtake me or you'll rue the day. And when I reach your village I will find your sangoma. Maybe *he* can make sense of your madness. But stay out of my way, for I restrain myself only because you say you were Siyafunda's friend!"

*

It's more than an hour before Zondi himself resumes his journey. His eyes are bloodshot from the tears, his knuckles bleeding from where he pounded the ground. He has screamed himself hoarse. Wails of anguish, of desperation. He has clawed at the sky and rolled in the dirt. He has thrown away the necklace, and the other muthi the sangoma gave him. Useless! He has sat slamming his fist against his forehead. He has ripped up grass and torn apart bushes, in a frenzy of pain and frustration.

Earthly punishment will be a release now.

*

He couldn't help himself . . .

He truly couldn't help himself. From the moment he saw the amulet he was doomed. He sees that now, but back then, on that fateful day, he was entranced. He carried it with him in his mind, to be recalled and clasped while waiting to be sent into battle, enduring the privations of a forced march through hostile territory, helping still the pain of his wounds . . . It was a presence, a balm, the warm fire burning outside your hut, beckoning you homeward on a cold night. Often he thought of asking Siyafunda to show him the amulet again; tried to work out how he would broach the subject, what he would say. But he knew it was to no avail. That had been a childhood transgression, which they never spoke about, and which doubtless Siyafunda hoped he had forgotten. He was the guardian now, had been for many years, conducting the observance with his son and grandson, who was already ten summers old.

Later, they'll ask him how he could do such a thing, commit an act that effectively condemned his best friend's family to death, and he'll try to explain how he was moved by forces beyond his control.

In the end, did he really have any choice?

He remembers that day, seeing one of Siyafunda's younger sons come rushing by, weeping and calling for the sangoma. His father! Something about his father and a snake. Running to fetch his spear, Zondi found himself outside of Siyafunda's hut. Every morning for three days in a row Siyafunda had left the village. It was precisely the kind of behaviour that might lead one to suspect he was one of the Izazi Ezigcina Izimfi-hlo, although of course the other villagers turned a blind eye to such activities. Not so Zondi, who always found himself watching Siyafunda whenever he was home from his regiment. And on this visit he suspect-ed an observance had taken place and Siyafunda was surreptitiously returning the artefacts to their hiding places.

And he was right.

Somehow he'd entered the hut unnoticed by the others who were rushing to his friend's aid. It was as though he drifted in through the walls. He couldn't remember deciding to enter; he was simply there, gazing upon the sack he knew contained the relics.

Was the amulet still in the sack or had Siyafunda already returned it? Zondi couldn't help himself.

Just one look . . .

Had he meant to take the amulet?

No!

Yet he had.

And then he was running with the artefact clutched to his chest . . .

And the Ma-Iti amulet was his. He wasn't stealing it. He was merely correcting an imbalance, for the amulet was meant to be his!

*

The man he knows as Umfo is waiting for him on the path just before the umuzi. The grey-haired man with the scars tries to tell Zondi how his concern got the better of him and he decided to hang back and wait for the younger man. Has he recovered himself? But Zondi ignores him, as he ignores everyone he encounters in the village. He retrieves the amulet and goes to the chief's hut and hands the artefact to the induna.

Later, they'll tell him how they did it. The Induna's udibi, chosen for the task because he was small and could hide easily, was the one following him so noisily. Mgobozi, enjoying every minute of this adventure, was the man Zondi knew as Umfo. Mzilikazi was the one who took his place before Zondi awoke. The Induna wore the hyena's head, which he has returned to Siyafunda's grateful son.

"Will you at least show mercy there?" says Zondi.

The Induna nods. "Never fear. Nothing will be done because there is nothing to be done. Your clan's secrets remain safe."

"I salute your wisdom, Shadow Of Shaka."

"You too were wise in bringing this affair to a conclusion."

"And my relief knows no bounds! Death will be bliss!"

"There can be no other way."

"I understand that, Shadow Of Shaka."

It's clear Zondi believes his guilt was always apparent and the headman had sought Shaka's help some time before he announced to the village he was sending to KwaBulawayo for assistance. The announcement was clearly a ruse agreed upon when the Induna was ready to reveal his presence.

This is not true. The chief had only asked for help after Zondi's odd behaviour – seen in a sudden furtiveness, the endless sweeping – alerted the umnumzane's suspicions. Why should the dead man's best friend suddenly start acting so strangely? But the Induna will lie when Zondi shakes his head and says: "So it was you who taunted me in my hut those long nights!"

Knowing Shaka must be seen to be all-powerful, the Induna will lie and say: "Yes."

The Zulu day begins early, for daylight is a precious commodity not to be wasted. In the winter months the pre-dawn darkness is icy and bodies have to be prised from the warmth of bedrolls; the sun is a saviour, soothing creaking limbs. During the summer, however, these hours are bliss, the coolest of the day, to be welcomed as a brief respite from sweaty nights and a glowering sky.

As the light slips between the distant peaks to touch the horns of the cattle, the herdboys are up and about, hissing and whistling, guiding their families' livestock into the veld. Each wears an umutsha. Given to them when they reach puberty by their father, the garment is a kilt comprising a frontal covering of tails or strips of skin – the isinene – and the ibheshu, a rear flap made of soft calfskin.

If harvest time is close, younger brothers will make for the fields, where they'll remain until evening, chasing away birds and baboons, who are particularly fond of stealing mealies.

Their sisters, meanwhile, go to fetch water. There are giggles and greetings, snatches of song – and once her pot is full, each girl will drop a pebble into it, so that no other stone will trip her on the way home, causing her to spill water, or worse, break the pot. They'll be bare-breasted and wear short skirts decorated with beads.

Back at the kraal, mothers and wives sweep and dust, tend to babies and grandmothers. They're helped by their younger children and it's common to see a girl of six carrying a baby brother or sister strapped to her back. Married women cover their bodies more fully, as a signal to other men that they're taken. They wear knee-length skirts, which hide the back of the upper thigh, and an antelope skin covers the upper body. Coded beadwork decorates the front with a message understood only by the husband.

In summer, the morning's domestic chores will be more cursory, as the women head to the fields to hoe and plant.

Crops – which include maize, pumpkin, watermelon and calabash – are planted in August, when the Pleiades appear in the early morning sky. Mothers and daughters, some with babies strapped to their backs, scatter the seed in all directions, then turn the soil with hoes. When the plants get to be about forty centimetres high, the ground is weeded. Often the men will take over at this point, inviting their neighbours to come and help.

Each wife has her own hut, fields and cattle, given to her by her husband. These remain her property, to be inherited by her eldest son.

*

The sun is well up when the herdboys bring home the cattle. First the head of the kraal's cows are milked, then the rest. A grass cord, called an umkhala, is introduced through the nostrils of the animal to keep it quiet. A calf is allowed to suckle for a short while, then it's pushed away and the herdboy begins the milking, squatting on his heels with a wooden pail between his knees. Younger boys keep the calves away with sticks. The milker talks and whistles all the while, reassuring and encouraging the cow.

After milking, the first meal of the day is eaten. This usually comprises amasi and a maize-meal porridge. Afterward, the herdboys take the cattle back to pasture, while the females busy themselves with mat-making or beadwork. Pottery is left to women skilled in the art. The pots are made from red clay mixed with soot or umsobo leaves, moulded by hand and left to stand and dry out for a few weeks before being fired.

When the sun has passed its zenith, and the heat of the day is over, the women return to the fields or go and collect firewood.

The men are either with their regiments – organised according to age – or home from the wars, resting. Because of this they no longer help the women in the fields, as used to be the case, although certain chores remain their province, such as woodwork, hunting, preparing skins and building huts.

*

Just before sunset, the time of day the Zulus call selimathunzi, when the shadows lengthen, the herdboys lead the cattle back to the safety of the kraal and the women return from the fields to prepare supper.

Each wife must cook enough for her own household as well as a portion to be sent to her husband. The wives take turns in attending to his needs – but even if a wife is "off-duty", she must still send food to her husband.

All sit on mats to eat, for it's considered bad manners to do otherwise. If the husband is present, he'll sit near the door on the men's side of the hut, while other males take their places according to seniority. The children sit at the back of the hut on the women's side.

Before the meal begins a young girl or boy will offer a bowl of water to the father, so he can wash his hands. The other members of the household wash when he's finished.

Two pots of food are then brought in – one for the men, one for the women. Each family member will have his or her own wooden spoon.

After supper, the men will play games with the children, or tell stories.

*

Languid days. If the men often seem to be at war, this is simply the way Shaka ensures his children can prosper and enjoy these days in the time of the Imbizo, the Great Coming Together, when all know the protection of the Bull Elephant, the Sitting Thunder who left Zwide howling for mercy and united the clans under the Umthetho, the Law.

Shaka's Court

"Majesty – I do not understand this story of yours!"

"Cha, Mgobozi! I have told you: it is not my story! It was told to Dingiswayo by the White Man."

"And I wonder if this story told to you by Dingiswayo, who heard it from the White Man, has not . . ."

"Has not what, Old Friend?"

"Well, if something hasn't, perhaps, gone missing – a calf wandering off, here, some grain spilling, there – in the course of its journey to our ears this fine morning."

"Seek you to cast aspersions on my memory?"

"These things happen, Majesty."

"Before you fall over trying to apologise for doubting my memory . . ."

"Majesty, I assure you . . ."

"Be still, Old Goat. I was merely going to say this was my very response when Dingiswayo told me the tale."

"What? Did he impugn your memory, Sire? I do not see what that has to do with the story . . ."

"Mgobozi?"

"Majesty?"

"Shhh!"

"Please, Mgobozi, I, too, am not sure I understand this strange tale."

"Thank you, Nqoboka. Now, as I was saying: this was my response when Dingiswayo told me the tale. Truly, I could not understand it."

"I am honoured to find myself in such esteemed company, Majesty."

"Mgobozi . . ."

"Majesty!"

"And Dingiswayo – even he was forced to admit he could not understand it."

"For where would one find such a large cow, Father? It would have to be bigger than your biggest cows – and, truly, I cannot imagine such a creature."

"This is so, Nqoboka. And Dingiswayo said the White Man first spoke of a horse. And Dingiswayo allowed that in other lands men rode these creatures and so became fast and powerful, but horses also, to him, seemed puny creatures."

"Aiee! These naked zebra do not last long in these parts!"

"That is so, Nqoboka. And Dingiswayo at last got the man to admit it may have been a cow."

*

It's a bright, sunny morning in August 1818. The Zulu army has grown in the months following Gqokli Hill, a clan is becoming a nation, and Shaka KaSenzangakhona, the Bull Elephant and Conqueror, the King of Kings and Father of that nation, is holding court.

As usual, the day has commenced with the inspection of the cattle, when the incidents that have occurred among the King's herd overnight are reported. The White Men who'll later visit the capital will be amazed at the precision of these reports, where even the twist of the horns of individual animals is described.

Shaka himself is capable of surveying his many hundred head of cattle and noting those that are missing when the herd is paraded before him in KwaBulawayo's great inner enclosure. He then selects the number of beasts required for the day's consumption, usually from six to twelve. These are for honoured guests and the King's inner circle. The inhabitants of KwaBulawayo as a whole consume so much beef that the capital has become the nation's chief repository of shields, which are, of course, made from cowhide. Representatives from regiments stationed in far-flung areas regularly come to beg izihlangu from Shaka.

Each beast he selects is instantly put to death with a long spear called the Umkhontho Wamadlozi, or Spear Of The Spirits. Every Zulu household has one, and the blade is never cleaned – to do so, to remove the nsila, or gore, is considered the worst form of desecration.

After the bulls have been led out, the soldiers, who've been in the enclosure all along, begin to sing and dance, as the cows are never milked until they've been danced for. Whenever a beast lows, the soldiers praise it loudly, saying the cow is praising the King. Then the regiments retire to their huts to break their fast and the royal milkers enter the enclosure in a long line, holding their pails above their heads to keep the dust out.

It was while watching the milking in the company of Mgobozi and Nqoboka that Shaka mentioned the tale his great mentor had told him . . .

"This is where my comprehension begins to falter, Majesty. A cow, you say?"

"A cow."

"They offer this cow as a gift? Just the one cow . . ."

"Yes, Mgobozi."

"There were two great and mighty tribes who fought and, finally, the one tribe, these Amagliki, encircled the other's kraal. But both tribes were equally fierce, equally strong, and the Amagliki could not break through the walls of the kraal. So they waited. Let hunger be our ally, they said, for they were strong enough to ensure the other tribe could not leave their kraal."

"That is the story, Mgobozi."

"Let these jackals starve, they said . . . But they were trapped too. Soon they had to seek victuals further and further afield, which meant weakening the regiments that surrounded the kraal."

"And so they decided to trick the other tribe, Mgobozi."

"So you say, Majesty."

"This is the story Dingiswayo told."

"Yes, Majesty. But, Majesty, they do this by sending their enemy a gift . . ."

"Yes, Mgobozi."

"Of one cow, Majesty."

"It was a very big cow, Mgobozi."

"Hai, even if that cow had been an elephant . . . No! If I had been a general in the other tribe I would've looked upon this lone cow, and I would've said, there are many of us and we are very hungry, yet these jackals send us the loneliest cow in the world – what manner of insult is this? I would not have let such an affront through my walls!"

"But it wasn't for slaughter! It was a . . ."

"What, Nqoboka? What was it? A token of the other tribe's esteem? One cow? How can that be?"

"Majesty – perhaps Mgobozi has a point . . ."

"But you are right, Nqoboka. He is right, Mgobozi. This beast was not intended for slaughter . . ."

"Well, then, Father, this is the other thing I cannot comprehend. How did these warriors get inside this cow?"

"This is what Dingiswayo asked the White Man."

"What was the White Man's reply, Father?"

"He said it were better if they were to talk of other things."

"Aiee! See? It was his tale and even *he* did not know!"

"Dingiswayo said perhaps the warriors rolled themselves in grass . . ."

"But how many, Majesty? How many could fit in a cow, even a cow as big as an elephant? Not enough to destroy a city!"

"Yet this is what came to pass."

"Perhaps it is true what they say, Majesty – that the sun shrivels the brains of these White Men and leaves their necks aglow."

"Nonetheless, General, we must never underestimate their cunning." It's Mbopa, come to brief the King on the morning's proceedings.

*

When Shaka and his councillors and generals have settled themselves under the great ibandla tree in the two-hectare yard in front of the King's Council Hut, Mbopa summons the izimbongi. Their stage is the swathe of hard-packed dirt between the tree and the rows of people, supplicants and spectators, squatting on their haunches, and the praise singers range about here, reciting the great deeds of Shaka and the People Of The Sky.

Many have travelled a great distance to seek Shaka's wisdom and mercy, and this is part of the spectacle they expect to find at KwaBulawayo. But for those who are veterans of the King's court – some of whom, for a fee paid in the form of a cow or a collection of skins, will advise newcomers on how best to state their cases, make their claims – it provides an opportunity to gauge the King's mood. If he sits in silence, listening closely to the praises – that's a bad sign. It's almost as if he's hearing these things for the first time and in hearing them, relives them. He listens and frowns – these are praises, it is true, but they cannot allay his pain. His rage. These things that have come to pass – they are not enough to avenge the indignities he and his beloved mother suffered. There must be more blood. An ocean of blood. A torrent. And these who prostrate themselves before him with their crimes and petty squabbles become ingrates . . .

Today, though, the King sits on the pile of rush mats that comprise his throne under the wild fig tree, chatting easily with Nqoboka and Mgobozi, and Mbopa, who's to all intents and purposes Shaka's prime minister. He doesn't pay much attention to the praise singers, is clearly in a good mood – and more than one litigant can breathe a sigh of relief.

At a nod from Shaka, Mbopa stands, raises his hand, and the praise singers fall silent.

He's a short, stout man, with the heavy buttocks the Zulus regard as a sign of nobility. "Who will approach the King?" he asks.

It is a rhetorical question. He and Shaka have already discussed the order in which the litigants will appear.

"Who will approach the King?" asks Mbopa again. But this time he answers the question himself, calling forth the headmen of two villages who're bickering over grazing land.

*

An hour later, it's the Induna's turn. His is the first major case today.

Leaving the accused standing between Njikiza and Thando, he moves forward at Mbopa's command.

"Nduna!" says Shaka. "Are you well?"

"Ndabezitha!" says the Induna. *Your Majesty.* "I am well."

"This is a very serious case!"

"That it is, Father."

"While that one there," says Shaka, meaning the accused, "chews his teeth, tell me of the circumstances leading to his death . . ."

*

It was said the day didn't begin until she went by, on her way to fetch water from the river. When her shadow fell over them, old men were young again. Her status as a bride-to-be made the younger men cautious, but her innocent friendliness, so devoid of dangerous flirtation, disarmed them, and they found themselves envying the one who would be her husband without feeling resentful or jealous. She was too open, too kind, too gentle, and malicious thoughts were as a thirst soon vanquished by her intoxicating presence.

It was said this was so despite the darkening sky that attended her days. But she was not to be blamed for the trouble. Better to point a finger at her father for encouraging two suitors. It was said he should have consulted with his daughter, this treasure he claimed to value so much. Was that not a way out of any deadlock? True, a maiden was expected to follow her father's counsel in these matters, but where two clans have begun sharpening their blades, a sign from her would have allowed for an honourable withdrawal by one of the suitors. However, her father was too greedy to allow matters to be taken out of his hands in such a manner.

And she was just sixteen summers old. With full heavy breasts and firm wide thighs destined to welcome many strong warriors into the world.

Or so they said.

But it was not to be . . .

The Induna shook his head.

It was not to be.

*

She lay at the foot of a precipice, her body buckled over jagged rocks. Her left knee was bent and raised. Her head was thrown back in a spray of blood. Her right arm was outstretched, the fingers curved over the palm. Her left arm rested against her side, the fingers splayed.

The Induna and a group of warriors were returning to KwaBulawayo after a foray into Zwide's territory to meet with a messenger from a spy Shaka had in the Ndwandwe court when they'd encountered the envoy. He too was heading for the capital. After questioning him and hearing that a dispute between two families was about to turn violent, the Induna'd told Maweru to continue to Bulawayo with the spy's message, while he led the rest of his men to the village.

They arrived the previous evening and were told the matter was resolved.

Clearly they had been misinformed.

After instructing big Njikiza and the other warriors to keep the crowd back, the Induna clambered onto the rocks and stood a moment surveying the body. The spirit had gone, embarked on the Great Journey, you could see that by her skin. A certain lifeless quality. A greyness. Her mouth was open and her eyes shut – which, taken together, the Induna regarded as signs of a violent death. A scream of shock, the eyes shutting in capitulation in the face of the inevitable.

The boy, meanwhile, confined himself to what he hoped resembled an astute evaluation of the precipice itself. It wasn't revulsion that made him avoid looking at the dead girl. It was something he couldn't put into words. The sense of great beauty there the one moment, gone the next. Gone and, in its going, taking part of the world with it, so that things would be forever other than they might have been . . .

The Induna turned to face the crowd's distressed faces. "Who found her?"

Dakla stepped forward. "I found her."

He was of medium height with tiny eyes, hollowed cheeks and a face that seemed to end in a dollop of fat. He'd raced to the village to summon help and was sweating, his attire dishevelled. His kilt was twisted awry around his waist, there was a gash on his right knee and his leggings were tangled, speckled with yellow pollen and burrs.

He was one of the suitors in this matter that was supposed to have been resolved.

"Did you touch her?" asked the Induna.

Dakla shook his head.

The Induna went down onto his haunches.

"What is it, Master?" asked the boy, peering over the Induna's shoulder, managing somehow not to actually look at the body.

The Induna shifted onto his knees and leant forward. "See?" Without touching it, he let his finger glide over the four streaks of blood. "What does that tell you?"

"She moved," whispered the boy.

The Induna nodded. "She suffered. The fall did not kill her."

He stood. Turned to scan the crowd once more.

Then he was leaping off the rocks, shouting orders, telling Njikiza, Thando and the boy to follow him.

*

The Induna and his udibi were waiting in the shade of the village's ibandla tree when Thando and Njikiza brought Dakla to him. They were followed by the village headman, the girl's father and a group of armed men. The latter were clearly there in support of Dakla; to a man, their eyes were bloodshot, their movements jerky, signs they had sought courage in dagga. The Induna made a point of ignoring their presence.

Calmly, while Dakla fumed and tried to pull away from his captors, Shaka's envoy issued instructions to the udibi. The boy was to go and tell the sangoma and the women they could prepare the body for burial.

Two of the Induna's warriors were to remain with them, the others must return with the boy to the ibandla tree.

Only after his udibi had left on his errand did the Induna step forward to address Dakla.

"I was led to understand this matter was resolved."

"I thought the same thing, Nduna."

"Yet here my men must waste their time restraining you and your playmates while there's a murderer afoot."

"I would catch that murderer!"

"Know you who he is? I thought you merely discovered the body."

"She may be a body to you, Nduna, but I look upon her and still see my beloved."

"But that is not why you and your friends slipped away, is it?"

"No, I would avenge her death."

"I'll say it again: I thought you merely discovered the body . . ."

"Any fool can see who killed her!"

"Then I am a fool. Enlighten me!"

"Nduna! It is obvious. Mzane! He's the one!"

"But did he not withdraw his claim?"

This was what the Induna had learnt upon arriving at the village: Mzane had retracted his marriage proposal.

"He tricked us!" snarled Dakla, trying once more to pull away from Thando and Njikiza. "And here we stand, chattering like old wives, while he gets away. Let me hunt this dog down! Your men need not even exert themselves. I have my own impi."

"Your brothers and her brothers – truly a group disposed to dispense a fair justice!"

"Do not speak to me of fair! You saw her! You saw how she died!"

"But if you are right and this Mzane is responsible, then we will find him very easily. For truly he is a foolish crocodile! A little forethought would have told him suspicion would fall on him as surely as a piss follows beer. If he still went ahead – well, such a one can be counted upon not to hide his tracks very well."

The boy and four warriors moved past the others to stand behind the Induna.

"It is done?" asked the Induna.

"It is done, Master."

"Good!"

He turned back to the men arrayed before him, the three groups – Dakla between Thando and Njikiza, the mob of brothers, somewhat subdued now, and the headman and the father. He called the father over.

"It is true, Nduna! What Dakla says. That treacherous dog! It is true!"

"Shut up. Fetch me your daughter's mother and her sisters."

The father bowed, retreated.

"Now," said the Induna, addressing Dakla, "you and your friends will keep my men company while I consider this matter."

"Cha! We –"

The Induna's hand came up. "Court my anger, Cub, and wrath will be the consummation. Now do as I command!"

*

Two suitors come to a beautiful maiden's village to conclude marriage negotiations. Her father is a greedy scoundrel and he plays the one party off against the other. The lobola increases, it seems, every time he leaves the hut. Finally, one of the men – this Mzane – decides he's had enough. He withdraws; has left the village by the time the Induna and his men arrive.

Why did he retract his offer? Had the price become too dear?

In which case he might still have harboured designs on the maiden. Designs of a more nefarious kind, his yearning to marry the most beautiful girl in the region perverted into a spiteful desire to ensure no other man would have her.

In which case Dakla is right.

In which case Mzane is very silly. As the Induna pointed out to the enraged Dakla, Mzane had to have known the finger of suspicion would point to him. Even if he got another to act in his place and could prove he was in the company of reliable witnesses from the moment he left the village he had to know this would send the Induna looking for the one who had done the deed in his name. Such a man would not be hard to find; this was the kind of dangerous task one gave to a sibling or trusted friend, whose identity would soon be known by his absence among Mzane's cohorts.

Then again . . . Jealousy drives a man to do strange things.

Yes, there's that aspect to consider.

Jealousy might have meant Mzane wasn't thinking straight.

The Induna and the boy are atop the cliff. The grass is ragged here; a ledge of smooth rock juts out in an overhang. It is a popular meeting place, there are many signs that people come here – so looking for tracks would be a waste of time.

The maiden's sisters said she had left the umuzi straight after her early morning chores.

Dakla said he went looking for her – and found her broken body at the foot of the precipice.

When the maiden's sisters asked her where she was going, she pretended not to hear; said: "I have to go somewhere, I won't be long." She was already moving away, could later claim to have been out of earshot when the others asked her where she was going.

And she came here. To this spot, where maidens met their suitors. It was reached by a steep path, which meant they were unlikely to be disturbed by mothers and grandmothers, yet it was also close enough to the village for them to feel safe. The path below was always in use and crying out would have brought a rescuer should one of their young admirers get too eager.

She came here to meet someone.

Mzane?

Perhaps.

The other things the maiden's sisters told him worry the Induna, however.

Then he looks over to where his udibi sits in the grass. The boy's palms and fingers are yellow, because he's been sliding his hands up and down the short stalks of the grass that produces a pollen the Zulus call "monkey snuff". The Induna glances down and sees his own leggings are speckled with the same pollen . . .

*

Now, in the shade of the mighty ibandla tree, Shaka says: "Ah!"

The people sitting on their haunches are a tranquil lake, with ripples here and there, as heads turn, for what is being said under the tree is quietly being relayed to those in the furthest rows. The soldiers standing with the accused are reeds on the shores of the lake.

"Yo! Yo! Yo!" says Nqoboka.

"An astute observation," adds Mbopa. "And this was the only place where the snuff was to be found?"

"Doubtless there were other places, but none close by," replies the Induna.

"Nduna," says Shaka, "your wisdom is as great as your courage!"

The Induna inclines his head. "Your praise gladdens my heart, Father. But I simply saw what was there for all to see."

"Nonetheless, you were the only one to note the snuff on that fool's leggings," says Shaka.

"But, Nduna," interjects Mgobozi, for this is the Zulu way – all those present at a hearing are entitled to ask questions, express an opinion. "Why? Why would he do such a thing? The other suitor had left the field of battle. He had her. She was to be his bride!"

"Hawu, Mgobozi," says Shaka, "even I, who was not there, know the answer to that question. He had her, but she would not have him."

He turns to the Induna. "Am I right?"

Indisputably a question to which there can be only one answer, but the Induna need not lie.

"You are right, Father," he says.

This was what the maiden's sisters had told him. She favoured Mzane and had been distraught when he gave up his claim.

"It was Dakla she went to meet that morning," says the Induna. "He will not say what transpired between them, but I believe she told him it was Mzane she loved."

"But she would abide by her father's wishes and marry Dakla if he refused to withdraw his proposal," says Mbopa.

"This is so," says the Induna, "for she was a dutiful daughter."

"And doubtless she would have done her best to be a dutiful wife. All the same, I cannot help but wonder whether this wasn't her way of beseeching Dakla to give up his claim."

"A warning?" suggests Nqoboka.

"In a manner of speaking," says Mbopa.

"More a plea, I think," says the Induna.

Shaka, who's been following this exchange, shakes his head. "You are not saying this is a reason for mercy!"

"No, Majesty," says Mbopa. "It is mere speculation. I, for one, do not pity that creature, for all the disappointment he must have felt. There is no excuse!"

"I agree," says Shaka. "Let him come forward."

Thando and Njikiza guide Dakla a few paces, then release him. Immediately he drops to his knees. With his head bowed, he crawls toward the King. When he reaches the mat at Shaka's feet, he stretches out onto his stomach.

Shaka gazes at the back of the man's head for a few moments. Then he says: "Look upon your Father."

Dakla raises his head.

"You have nothing to say in this matter. You will not waste my time and anger me with excuses. Do you understand?"

Dakla nods.

"I am finished," says Shaka.

At a signal from Mbopa, two of the King's slayers, cloaked in hyena skins, come forward and take Dakla away.

"But," says Shaka, when the condemned man has been dragged from his sight, "I am not finished with these other two."

Mbopa, who's been making ready to call the next case, is clearly taken aback. "The other two, Majesty?" he asks, skilfully turning his dismay into a mild query.

"Yes," says Shaka. "You know whereof I speak, do you not, Nduna?"

The Induna inclines his head. "They are both here, Father, for I thought you might want to question them."

"For this matter doesn't quite end with that one's demise, does it, Nduna?"

"That is so, Father."

*

Shaka regards the heads at his feet. "Look upon your Father," he tells the younger man.

Mzane obeys.

"Are you a Zulu?"

Mzane nods.

"Hai! Would you lie to me?"

"No, Father!"

"Then tell me how you can be a Zulu. For would not a true Zulu fight for the woman he loves?"

Mzane's chin brushes the dirt as he nods. "You are right, Father. And – truly – I loved her!"

"Then your actions were even more despicable than I thought – and you cannot be a Zulu!"

"You are right, Father. I see that now. My decision will haunt me for the rest of my days."

"Which might be fewer than you realise."

"Then I thank you, Father – for putting an end to my suffering."

"But why did you not fight for her?" asks Mgobozi.

"I thought this way was better."

"For who?" asks Shaka.

"For her, Father! I saw how this bickering was affecting her and I thought I was sparing her further anguish by retracting my suit."

234

"Did you not know it was you she loved?" asks Nqoboka.

"No! She was a dutiful daughter, willing to abide by her father's wishes. To have chosen one of us even surreptitiously would have been to disobey her father."

"Yes," murmurs Shaka. Then, "You," he says, addressing the maiden's father, "look at me and tell me what you have to say about this sorry event."

The father raises his head. "Majesty, I wanted only my daughter's worth to be acknowledged."

"Has her worth now been acknowledged to your satisfaction?"

"Majesty! I – no! Would that I could have foreseen this!"

"Was the fact that two families were sharpening their spears not enough of a warning?"

"To sow discord was not my intention, Majesty."

"As that dead man, Dakla, was not intending to murder your daughter when he went to meet her, yet kill her he did."

"Majesty . . ."

"Be still." Shaka points to Mzane. "You! What was the last bride price you discussed with this lizard?"

"Seven cows, Majesty."

"You and your family will go to this lizard's kraal and fetch his cattle. You will take seven for yourself and bring the rest to me. You and your family will go to Dakla's kraal and fetch all of his cattle. Seven you will keep, the rest you'll bring to me. Do you understand?"

"Yes, Majesty."

"Honour, not cowardice, guided your actions, therefore you may profit from this affair. Let that bring you some small solace for your loss."

As for the father, he is to get out of the King's sight and thank the ancestors he is still able to thank the ancestors.

*

The Induna straightens, is about to salute Shaka when the King holds up a hand. "Wait, Nduna! While you were resolving this matter another arose in your absence. The miscreant is here, awaiting my wrath, but it is not too late to seek your counsel. Come and join your comrades and bring your boy, perhaps he will learn something."

"Perhaps he will even see the smoke our old eyes miss!" chuckles Mgobozi.

"*Your* old eyes, Friend. But you are right. Join us, Nduna . . ."

*

A few paces from Shaka's throne, Mzilikazi hangs back, lets the youth stagger ahead of him, then raises his left leg and rams his foot against the prisoner's arse. Sends him sprawling in front of the King.

"You seem perturbed, my Son," observes Shaka.

"Lack of success has this effect on me, Father. I have caught the cub, not the hyena."

Shaka's brow lowers. "I had hoped I was misinformed," he says softly.

"Nothing would've given me greater pleasure than to have surprised you, Father."

Shaka glares at the youth, who has snaked forward and stretched out so that he is lying prone at the King's feet. "You!" says Shaka. "You know my ruling?"

The youth nods.

"What is my ruling?"

"Hai!" shouts Mbopa, as the youth raises his head. "Did your Father say you might look upon him?"

The youth quickly lowers his head.

"What is my ruling?" asks Shaka again.

"Those who would answer the Calling . . ."

"What? I can't hear you!"

Mzilikazi kicks the youth's feet. "Speak up!"

Trembling, sweat dripping off his nose, the youth repeats Shaka's law – that since they are exempt from military service, those who are training to be sangomas are to sleep outside their master's kraal, so they might experience some of the privations faced by new recruits in the Zulu army.

"Yet where did you sleep?" asks Shaka.

"In-... inside the kraal, Majesty. In ..."

"In?"

"Inside, Majesty."

Shaka looks up.

"Mzilikazi ..."

"Majesty!"

Mzilikazi steps onto the youth's buttocks. The youth yelps. His hands come away from his sides to claw at the dirt. Mzilikazi steps off the boy and kicks the side of the teenager's head.

"Majesty," whispers Mbopa. "Some consciousness on the part of the condemned would be desirable at this time."

"Yes," says Shaka. He waves Mzilikazi aside. Leans forward. "You were saying?"

"Majesty ..."

"Where did you sleep?"

"Inside ..."

"Where?"

"In ... in my master's hut."

"What? Did you sleep in *my* hut?"

"No!"

"No? Am I not your Master?"

"Majesty – no! I meant the hut of my teacher!"

"Who is your master ...? Who am I?" Shaka glances at his generals and the Induna, at Mbopa and the boy. "Am I a ghost? A spirit? Am I no longer the Father Of The Sky? Would that I had heard this sooner! To be free of the burdens of my Bloodline! What bliss!"

"Alas, Majesty, such bliss is to be denied you," says Mbopa, "for you are still our Father."

"But how can this be? I forbid these herb-pickers to sleep in the kraal, yet I am not their Master."

"You are our Master," says Mgobozi.

"You are their Master," says Mbopa, sweeping his arm to take in the rows of spectators.

"But not this one's master. For he has another master. One who would tell him otherwise. And clearly I am also not the Master of that master. Still . . . you would live as a sorcerer, then you shall die as a sorcerer."

Shaka signals his slayers. "I am finished," he says. "Impale him."

As soon as the youth has been led away, the King turns on Mzilikazi. "And the sangoma?"

Mzilikazi bows his head. "We lost his trail."

"Know you the penalty for failure?"

Mzilikazi nods. "Yes, Father."

"Majesty," interjects Mbopa – and before Shaka can voice his annoyance at the interruption, he hurries on: "We share your anger. These sangomas grow ever more wilful, ever more disobedient. And, claiming to speak for the ancestors, they encourage others to be disobedient. Set your wrath loose on *them*, Majesty! This sangoma will have achieved an even greater victory if you do not show mercy to these loyal warriors."

"Father," says Mgobozi, "Mbopa's words are wise. I would go further, though. Perhaps these men have not failed you."

"How so?" grunts Shaka.

"If they had caught this wizard and brought him to meet the fate he deserves, there the matter might have rested. While elsewhere – elsewhere, Father, the wizard's brothers and sisters would have continued to gnaw away at your authority. As they do even now, inciting others to disobey you."

"Let one go, so we may catch the rest," adds Nqoboka.

"For it is time to hunt out these evildoers," says Mbopa.

Shaka turns so he can see the Induna. "What say you?" he asks.

"It is time, Father."

Shaka strokes his chin. Nods. Waves Mzilikazi away. "Your brothers have done you a great service this day," he says. "Do not forget that."

*

The question is how. These sangomas need to be taught a lesson, but they occupy a special place in the tribe. It's the sangomas who have the

Calling – and, in a way, the people fear them more than they fear the King, because the Calling makes sangomas guardians of the tribe's well-being in both a spiritual and a physical sense. Through their knowledge of herbs and roots, sangomas are able to heal the sick and through their divinatory powers they would also govern the tribe's destiny, protect the nation against evil. Since these two functions so often blur into one, the servants of the ancestors have all but become masters of the tribe, with the power of life and death.

Let the crops fail and it is they, not the King, who will come to the tribe's aid. A gathering is held wherein sorcerers are smelt out – and put to death without question. In fact this seems their solution to any hardship that befalls the tribe. But Shaka has often interceded to rescue those accused of witchcraft. Which has angered the sangomas even further.

More importantly, in doing so, he has won the loyalty and gratitude only of the victims and their families. The rest of the people have reacted to these acts of mercy with unease – such is the power of the sangomas.

"With all I have given my Children," growls Shaka, "you'd have thought they'd learnt to trust and revere me."

"But they do, Majesty, they do," says Mbopa.

"Yet they turn, time and again, to these herb-pickers."

It's mid-morning and Shaka is performing his ablutions – in public and surrounded by his intimates. First he smeared a paste of minced beef and ground corn over his body, the three boys in attendance helping him with his back and legs. Then they fetched water so that Shaka could wash himself. Now the boys are rubbing red paste over his body.

Patiently Mbopa explains that just as the people can see and enjoy the fruits of Shaka's power every day, so the sangomas are able to show off their powers regularly, by healing the sick.

"Would that was all they did," observes Shaka.

"Which is precisely the problem, Majesty."

The Zulu King grunts an agreement and raises his left arm so one of the boys can go to work on his flank.

"They lie low," he says, "waiting in the long grass."

"This is so, Majesty," says Mbopa, "and see this as a further sign of your power, your greatness. Your conquests force them to remain silent."

"Silent?" says Shaka, raising his right arm. "I think not! I hear the champing of their jaws, the gulping of their gullets, for they would feed off my success."

"That is another way they stalk loyalty. By not speaking out against you at this time, your victories become their victories. They can claim to have guided you."

But let one bad season follow another, as is likely in this region, and the sangomas will be the first to turn against Shaka, claiming his high-handed manner has angered the ancestors.

After the red paste has been applied, the King is shaved – a perilous undertaking for even the most experienced barber. The sangomas are forgotten for the moment and Shaka is entertained with jokes and small talk. The shavings are carefully collected in a basket. They'll be burnt in the isigodlo, the royal compound, and the ashes discarded in running water.

When the barber is finished, a short grey-haired old man approaches the group. Bowing to Shaka, he says: "Father, I am sick of cooking! I can cook no more!"

It's a ritual formula, informing the King his breakfast is ready. If one of his cooks were to dare to tell Shaka that he was finished cooking, or that the meat was done, his words would be met with a sneering reply: "What? Are all the King's cattle slaughtered?"

Shaka rises and leaves the ibandla tree. Normally he eats alone, with his serving girls in attendance, but this morning he indicates that Mbopa, the generals and the Induna are to join him.

When the King and the others have entered the eating hut, one of his servants takes up a position a few paces away from the structure and begins to knock two hoes together in a rhythmic "Thock . . . Thock . . . Thock . . ."

This is to warn the people, for no one may spit, cough or sneeze while the King eats.

Breakfast consists of isithubi, a porridge of mealie meal and milk; isinkwa, a form of bread made by boiling crushed mealies; ibonsi, an apricot-like fruit; and water fetched from a place no one else has access to.

But Shaka's good mood has faded. Although he urges his men to eat their fill, he barely samples the dishes placed before him.

It's Mbopa who returns to the topic that's uppermost in their minds. "There is but one way to assuage your anger, Father. Move against these mambas!"

Shaka nods, acknowledging Mbopa's suggestion, and glances at Mgobozi. "Say you nothing, Old Friend?"

"My silence is the best counsel I can offer in this matter, Father."

There is no need for him to elaborate. His hatred for those of the Calling is well known.

"Killing the Lion who desecrated the Inkatha – that was a lesson to all," interjects Mbopa. "But, alas, it was not the lesson you intended, Father."

"Yes, they learnt only to become more cunning." Shaka places his bowl of porridge on the mat. "What say you, Nqoboka?"

"Majesty: this is but one of several occurrences. These things are happening more frequently, although I do not believe these creatures have any immediate plan to move against you."

"Not yet," murmurs Mbopa.

"Yes," agrees Nqoboka, "not yet. But the threat is there all the same. That's why I say now is the time to crush them. For soon we must deal with the Ndwandwes again. Ensure you face that campaign with a clear mind, unhampered by these meddlesome ants."

"Nduna?" asks Shaka.

"The ancestors will be grateful, Father. Maybe these hyenas once received the Calling, but now they hear only what they want to."

Waking up is like falling into an icy lake. It's the coldest time of the morning – just before first light, when there's a faint glow on the horizon, but the sun's rays have yet to trickle across the sky. Mzilikazi pulls the skins that cover him back over his shoulder. Any other movement will awaken his bladder and he's not yet ready to leave what little warmth he's managed to accumulate.

Through the gloom, the cold making his eyes burn, he spots one of his men walking his beat on the far side of the compound. And there – the other sentry passes the warrior, moving in the opposite direction. Both men are too weary to do little more than exchange a nod.

Mzilikazi clenches his teeth: Aiee! This piss! He's going to have to rouse himself.

They were lucky – and luckier still! As punishment for their failure to catch the sangoma, Mzilikazi and his men have been set to guard the King's inner enclosure.

Is it true what some of the other officers whisper behind his back? That Mzilikazi of the Khumalos, who threw his lot in with the Zulus after Zwide murdered his uncle, Dondo, and his father, can count himself as one of Shaka's favourites? Ha! They had not seen the rage burning in Shaka's eyes that day when Mzilikazi had to tell him the sangoma had eluded them. It was only thanks to Mbopa and the generals that Mzilikazi had escaped a fate that, while it undoubtedly involved death, would have been worse than death. And now he *must piss!*

The Blood

Walking in opposite directions, two sentries have been set to patrol the inverted U of the fence. At each end is a basket, one of which is filled with pebbles. When a sentry reaches that basket, he'll take out a pebble, retrace his steps, passing the other sentry in the process, and drop the stone into the second basket. When all the pebbles have been transferred from one basket to the other, the shift has ended and it's time to change the guards.

Another two men walk a beat that takes them past the Council and servants' huts. There're also guards around Nandi's hut – although she isn't in residence – and Shaka's harem, but Mzilikazi's men are only responsible for the King's area.

However, when Mzilikazi returns from his epic piss, he notes none of the men are where they're supposed to be . . .

All nine are awake.

All nine are standing in a cluster a few paces from the entrance to the King's hut.

All nine are gaping.

More than that, Mzilikazi notes as he runs over, all nine are afraid. It's in the way they've hunched their shoulders, unconsciously twisted away from the hut as though to protect themselves from an inevitable blow; in the way their spears dangle limply in their hands, blades pointing downward.

Mzilikazi runs, not daring to wake the King with a loud shout – although chances are, Shaka's awake already, which makes this little gathering even more of a cause for alarm. Let him come out of his hut and see these men cowering like children . . .

Roughly, Mzilikazi shoulders the warriors aside. "Fools!" he hisses. "What are you doing? Move! Move!"

But they merely part like cattle, their eyes on the hut.

One of the men points.

And then Mzilikazi sees for himself . . .

The King's hut is glistening in the early morning light.

A terrible premonition – confirmed by the faces of his men – tells Mzilikazi what he'll find.

What the dark substance is . . .

But he drives himself forward, dry-mouthed, his heart in his throat . . .

Reaches out . . .

Touches the thatch.

A wet stickiness.

Glistening.

Blood.

The King!

Is the King safe?

Once more Mzilikazi finds his heart in his throat, choking him. Time becomes a swamp and although he knows he's moving fast, it's as if he's wading through mud.

The King!

He almost collides with Shaka coming out of his hut.

"What's going on? What is the meaning of this?" asks the King, his eyes on the gaping men, who back away before his words.

"Majesty!" pants Mzilikazi out of breath, as if he's been running for hours. "Majesty!" he gasps. "You're alive!"

Now it's Shaka who draws away. "Would you have me kick you so you may be assured of this fact?"

"No, Majesty! No! It's – look!"

*

The Induna is alone when Shaka's messenger finds him. He has just seen off Njikiza and a detachment of the Fasimba impi who are to escort Pampata to the kraal where Nandi is staying. With them went his udibi. After a few seconds of trying to understand the messenger's babbling, he waves the man aside and sets off for the royal enclosure at a run. Mbopa and Mgobozi are there already. Mzilikazi is with them. His men now guard all entrances to the isigodlo with orders not to let in anyone who hasn't been summoned by the King.

"Nduna," says Shaka. "Observe, examine, tell me what you think."

The Induna circles the hut, looking for footprints and anything else untoward that might help explain this occurrence. Back at the entrance, he pulls free a handful of thatch. Sniffs it. Drops to his haunches and places the stalks on the ground – one doesn't discard anything one finds in the royal enclosure. Even rubbish has to be disposed of in a special way. Standing, the Induna presses his hand against the rough wall of the King's hut.

There's not much he can tell Shaka. The ground is too hard for footprints to be visible. The blood has been splashed on; only the uppermost part of the domed roof is untouched. Now that the sun has left the mountains, you can see layers of differing thicknesses, alternating bands of light and dark, exactly as if someone moved around the hut splashing blood from a bucket and wanted to make sure he covered all the thatch he could.

"So it *is* blood," says Mgobozi.

The Induna nods. "The blood of an ox."

"But who? How?" stammers Mzilikazi. He turns to Shaka. "Father! My men and I, we did not betray the trust you placed in us!"

Shaka lays a hand on his shoulder. "Have no fear, my Son. I do not believe you and your warriors were anything other than conscientious in the execution of your duties. No," he says, turning to Mbopa, "it seems as if we are dealing with witchcraft, here. What say you, Mbopa?"

"Yes, Majesty. A message, perhaps . . ."

"A message?" asks Mgobozi.

"Yes," says Shaka. "Why not? Here I am, surrounded by my most trusted men, what better way to remind me of my mortality!"

"Give me ten men, Father. I'll find the creature responsible and deliver my own lesson in mortality! And it will be a long lesson, Father!"

"Aiee! I almost feel sorry for the wretch," says Shaka. "But no, Mgobo-zi. For do we not have among us those well versed in the ways of smelling out sorcerers and witches?"

"But, Father . . ."

"Perhaps I was right to stay my hand. Now let them earn their keep."

"You can't trust them, Father!"

"Let this be their chance to gain my trust."

Shaka turns to Mbopa. "Do this: send out messengers to all the san-gomas in the Kingdom. They are to come to KwaBulawayo immediately. Someone seeks to bewitch me, I would have them tell me who. Tell them to come, or Mgobozi and his ten men will teach them about the importance of obeying my orders!" Shaka grins. "You might yet have a chance to deliver your lesson, Mgobozi."

But Shaka's old friend can only shake his head, concern lowering his brow.

So called because part of their training involves living off herbs and roots in the wild, izangoma combine a knowledge of herbalism with divinatory powers. When widespread disease breaks out, when cattle are lost, omens appear or a wizard is suspected of having caused things to go wrong, it's the sangoma who is consulted. Some use bones to foretell the future or divine the source of current unhappiness and are known as amathambo. Others talk to the spirits, who respond to questions in a whistling voice. These are called abalozi, or whistlers. The amabukula-zinti use sticks, which leap about in answer to questions.

It is those sangomas who specialise in the smelling out of evil whom Shaka has his eye on and it is these who are summoned to the capital. As for the rest, the izinyanga – herbalists – with their valuable medicines, the rainmakers and those who guard the People Of The Sky against lightning and hail, they are left alone so long as they have not associated themselves with the sangomas Shaka's identified as troublemakers.

*

Neither the inyanga nor the sangoma uses, or claims to use, magic. Their wisdom and power comes from the ancestors. Those who use magic – or witchcraft – are regarded as evil, as abathakathi, those who must be smelt out and destroyed. To be called a sorcerer – or umthakathi – is the greatest insult, not least because one's life will instantly be in danger.

Only the sky-herders can use magic – and as a result they live a monastic life of taboos and strict observances. They are so called because they go to work much like the boys who herd cattle. When a storm breaks, they'll rush out with their weapons and rain-shields to remonstrate with the lightning, whistling and shouting, telling it to go elsewhere.

*

There is one other who is allowed to use magic, who is even expected to use magic.

The King.

And it is this special status that lies at the heart of the tension that exists between Shaka and the sangomas. He has not only challenged them on a political level, seeking to curb their secular calumnies – by virtue of being King he is the one sorcerer they cannot touch, an affront to their world-view whose edicts they must obey.

A commoner accused of being an umthakathi faces death if the charge can be proven. Call the Zulu King an umthakathi and it's the greatest of compliments. The King has a right to be a great sorcerer and there is no question of using these powers for evil, for whatever is to the King's advantage must be to the advantage of the tribe.

Indeed, the titles Inkosi Enkhulu – Great King – and Umthakathi Omkhulu – Great Sorcerer – are used interchangeably.

The Great Smelling Out

"This is an outrage!"

"Indeed it is!"

"That is not what I meant!"

"Beware, Crone, you address the King," cautions Mbopa.

"These are trying times," says Shaka. "Let us practise a little patience. What concerns you so?"

Nobela glowers up at him. Of indeterminate age, she's like malaria, always around, visiting herself upon you at inopportune times, and an aggravation even when expected. The various pelts she wears – baboon, hyena, lion – give her a bell shape and appear to have long ago become part of her body, so that she resembles something not quite human – a useful attribute when your profession rests partly on scaring people shitless. Amid this covering, her face seems shrunken, only a little larger than the monkey skulls that hang around her neck; an exaggerated comparison, but that's how she seems to Shaka this morning. Her nose is flat, and is matched by heavy lips. But for all her undoubted age – and some say she'd already passed her child-bearing years when Shaka's grandfather was king – her face is untouched by the passing seasons.

"That's because if she has any power, it's to leave *others* frowning with vexed, wrinkled faces," says Mgobozi.

Maybe. But she *does* show signs of ageing. Below her cowhide skirt, her legs are skinny, bowed, like the sides of a pot and, although she tries to keep it hidden among the dangling paws that cover her breasts, Shaka has noted the fingers of her right hand are gnarled, twisted into a talon that no longer remembers how to hold. Hai, perhaps she *is* changing into another being!

"We cannot work like this," she says, her voice rough, grating. "It is not our way."

"We? Our? Speak you now for your brothers and sisters in the Calling? Are you their queen?"

If Shaka is expecting confirmation of what has always been tacitly acknowledged, he is disappointed – not that he expects her ever to speak plainly.

Nobela dismisses his question with a backward-forward motion of her staff. "You know this is not our way."

"My soldiers are trained to act in a certain way," observes Shaka placidly, "but sometimes circumstances dictate they should act in other ways, and they are fully capable of doing so. This is what makes them good soldiers."

The adjective he employs is a Zulu word that can also mean "adept", a word usually used to describe the capabilities of sangomas.

A clucking of her tongue is a sign his pun hasn't been lost on Nobela, and by the way her lips curl, in what could be a snarl of derision, she manages to convey the fact that she finds such wordplay childish, without openly rebuking the King.

"The Calling is otherwise."

With a sweep of his arm Shaka indicates the crowd gathered in Bulawayo's large central enclosure. A sullen collection of drooping shoulders and bowed heads. "I seek merely to hasten the process," he says.

"Hai! But you spoke of patience, King."

"Indeed I did. And the word was the deed. In speaking of the need for patience I was exercising patience. Now that time has passed!"

"It cannot be done!"

"What? Are you – and your brothers and sisters, here – not the most powerful, the most revered sangomas in the land?"

"Even the hut built by the most . . . *adept* craftsman will collapse if he's not allowed to practise his art in the correct and proper manner."

"We are not talking about huts here!"

"Aren't we?"

"Crone," snarls Mbopa, no longer able to restrain himself, "if it were simply a matter of huts and ox blood we would have no need for your services. Such as they are!"

Nobela leans forward on her staff, her eyes glittering – and despite his anger, Mbopa feels a prickling sensation run up his spine.

"And know this, Crone," he continues, speaking to swallow the foul taste of his momentary fear, "you are here at the King's command. You know the punishment for disobeying his orders!"

Again her eyes lock on his, looking through him. He knows this is about power, about the exercise of power, vying with Shaka over whose claims to power are more legitimate – the Zulu Bloodline or the whispers of the ancestors; the supremacy Shaka has acquired through his conquests and a loyal army, or the strength attained through knowledge of the secrets of the veld. He knows this. Yet, he is still a Zulu, raised to respect these Chosen Ones . . . their power. Evidence to the contrary is only that; it isn't quite proof, can't quite supplant the sense of knowing you had as a child that these Chosen Ones were to be feared. Just as her milk forms and strengthens one's bones, so the myths imbibed at a mother's breast shape one's attitudes and can never quite be relinquished.

And a part of Mbopa is relieved when Shaka speaks and snatches away Nobela's glare.

"Yes, Crone," says the King, "perhaps it is the punishment for failure you fear."

"No, King," says Nobela, with a sudden disarming humility, "it is your displeasure I fear."

Shaka's grin is one of disbelief. "What?"

"It is true," she says. The King is bewitched. About that there can be no doubt, and here a gloating tone creeps into her words. Shaka is bewitched. And she will find the abathakathi – the wizards – responsible. About that there can be no doubt . . .

Shaka interrupts her. Abathakathi? There is more than one?

Nobela shrugs her shoulders. Shuffles her feet. Pushes her staff outward. In another time, another place, she'd be a peddler hypocritically apologising for not being able to offer a lower price.

"This is what concerns me," she says – and both Shaka and Mbopa notice the slight pause. She was on the brink of adding a "Your Majesty", before realising such a sudden and uncharacteristic stab at deference would have made the two men even more suspicious of her attempt at sincerity.

"Out with it," says Shaka. "Enlighten us!"

"I fear you will not like the answer to your question."

Shaka nods. Frowns. Rubs his chin, as though giving Nobela's comments some consideration. When he speaks, it's to show her two can play the sincerely concerned game.

"Yes," he says. "Yes. I understand your misgivings. But have no fear. These wizards must be vanquished. Find them for me. I do not care who they are. It's the welfare of the tribe that matters. Find them! Find those who dare to challenge me in such a manner! My slayers have sharpened their stakes."

Nobela nods. "As you wish. This evil must be exterminated."

Shaka waits until she has turned around and is moving away from him to rejoin the other sangomas. Then he speaks: "But you *will* obey my other command. I want smaller groups and this matter resolved by nightfall."

*

Some fifteen sangomas – the most revered practitioners in the land – have been summoned to KwaBulawayo. Each is accompanied by a group of six or seven others, comprising those still learning the craft and ex-students who have decided to remain with their masters. In a Smelling Out, these will work with the gobela, or chief sangoma. It's a ploy which adds to the terror of the suspects. However, because they will have to examine all the residents of Bulawayo, including young children, Shaka's ordered the sangomas to divide themselves up into smaller groups to save time. Hence Nobela's complaint.

Splitting up means some will be with those whose methods they're unacquainted with. But they have to obey Shaka's command and now it's more important to choose who they're going to work with – and for several minutes there's a confused milling. This man is sent there, and then told to come here, and then, instead, chooses to go somewhere else altogether; a woman bickers with another, demanding that her favourite pupil stay with her . . .

Only Nobela stands aloof.

When the groups have at last been reformed, and the fifteen has become twenty-six, she informs Shaka she has no need for any helpers, only her two attendants, who are not sangomas anyway.

The King shrugs, gives Mbopa a nod.

The hefty man steps forward. "Let us begin, so that we may conclude this unpleasantness."

They are a motley crew, these sangomas. All wear a variety of skins. Some have painted their bodies white . . . red . . . yellow . . . Some wear plaits of hair over their faces, others masks made from the skulls of bulls, with the horns in place; still more sport plumes of feathers from leather headbands. Adornments include horns, hooves, swollen bladders, tails from genets and monkeys, baboons and leopards; one, Shaka notes, even has a long pouch made from the skin of an unborn calf.

They move into the waiting crowd, desperately trying to regain control of the situation, hissing and chanting, calling up the frenzy that will subdue their victims.

The truth is, though, those they seek to subdue are in their thrall already. They have gathered here to be judged and there can be no escape.

Is this not further proof that Shaka's power is the greater? They have obeyed his summons knowing some will not leave here alive. It doesn't matter who will be chosen – or how, or why. The fact that Shaka can call them to their deaths is surely more important. The sangomas who do the choosing – the Smelling Out – can they say the same thing? They might be powerful, but they still need the King to bring them their victims.

The pleasure Shaka feels at this realisation, however, is soon tempered by the looks on the faces of these loyal subjects who have obeyed this other calling. He even feels a twinge of shame.

Look at them.

Smell the fear.

They cringe. They quake. They are diminished.

Hai! Then they deserve this! This is not the way Zulus behave, decides Shaka.

Let them suffer! Let them learn!

In their fear, in their bowed heads, their nervous shuffling, their entwined fingers, they betray him. It is him they should fear, not these sangomas!

*

Shaka's entourage is on the opposite side of the cattlefold, where the condemned smelt out by the sangomas will be placed. Two regiments stand in close formation to the right and left. Men from a third regiment line the walls of the enclosure, facing the crowd with their shields and spears, while a contingent guards the main gate at the far end. No one can get to Shaka and no one can escape.

Leaving the sangomas to pull and pluck, hiss and stamp, leap and croon, Shaka moves along the front rank of his entourage. He's followed by one of his body servants, a teenager carrying a shield he'll hold up to shade Shaka from the sun should the King desire it.

Shaka's half-brothers Mpande and Dingane are among the "guests" Shaka has summoned along with the sangomas. Mpande, who will one day ensure the Bloodline remains unbroken and who'll father the mighty Cetshwayo, is fifteen at this time and acting as Dingane's udibi. Stopping by them, Shaka inquires after their health, the status of Dingane's crops, his cows, his wives.

"And you, Old Friend," says Shaka, moving on to Mgobozi, "what ails you?"

Mgobozi's eyes are wet, but he shakes his head. "I am well, Father."

There's a hovering, a hesitation swollen by the ululations of the female sangomas. Both men recognise in each other a desire to speak, to say more, but it's Mgobozi who breaks the connection. Forces a smile. He assumes the King would try and explain to him why this is necessary, to justify this injustice, and he doesn't want to hear it. Nothing Shaka – his old friend and comrade – can say will help him see the necessity for this. If someone is working against the King, why, he and a few of his men will "smell out" the culprit soon enough and the innocent will not suffer.

Against his better judgement, Shaka wants to tell his old friend how wrong his presumptions are, but even as he swallows the urge, he's distracted. Has the sense of someone watching him. Eyes are often on the King, but this is different, an intensity strong enough to touch him, the way he feels Pampata's breath on the back of his neck when they lie together.

Even as he turns, he knows who it is.

Nobela.

Her two attendants have retreated a few paces and she stands alone, uninterested in the Smelling Out, her eyes on Shaka.

Cunning, calculating eyes.

To show his lack of concern, Shaka continues wheeling, so he has his back to Mgobozi and is facing the enclosure. He has warned the guards in the cattlefold to be gentle with those the sangomas have chosen and he's pleased to see his commands are being obeyed. Not that there's much call for pushing and shoving. Deemed abathakathi, those in the fold believe themselves dead already and the guards have merely to move and rearrange them as new bodies are added.

Shaka notes how the large mass of people has shrunk back. Gaps in their ranks, left open, mark the movements of the sweating, shrieking sangomas. Shaka's children will not flee, but the soldiers along the walls and at the main gate will be hard-pressed to push them forward again. Suddenly, the sorrow he feels is once more transmuted into anger. Hai! They cower. They withdraw, like tortoises. Do they not trust their Father? Let their anguish be the punishment for this lack of faith.

But now that he's aware he's under Nobela's scrutiny, he also knows he has to marshal his emotions. It's for the sangomas to announce themselves with painted faces and skull necklaces. He must remain impassive. A rock.

Turning back, Shaka addresses the Induna. "Are you well, Nduna?"

The Induna bows his head. "I am well, Father."

"Keep an eye on this Old Goat," says Shaka, meaning Mgobozi.

"As ever, Father!"

"Good."

Shaka moves on.

*

"She's taken a liking to you."

Hai! The boy knows *that*!

After Nandi sent word to KwaBulawayo asking Pampata to join her, Shaka entrusted the travel arrangements to the Induna. When the Induna informed her he'd be sending a detachment of ten Fasimbas under Njikiza with her, Pampata remonstrated. She could make the journey with fewer men. "I'll be safe," she told the Induna.

"But I won't be should some mishap befall you," he replied.

"Hai!" said Pampata. "I can look after myself!"

The Induna admitted this was so and perhaps it was *she* who was being sent with the soldiers to look after *them*, not the other way round.

"Such honey," said Pampata to the Induna's udibi. "His mouth is a hive!"

Very well, she added, so be it. She would not argue. This was a matter of some urgency – and importance. But she would need an induna of her own. Perhaps he'd consent to lend her his udibi . . .

"You are needed here," she said, "so let the shadow become the tree."

The Induna acquiesced – and was mildly surprised when the boy put up only a token resistance when they were alone again. "Why me?" he'd asked.

"She's taken a liking to you," said the Induna, grinning. And with a grunt and shrug, the boy set about gathering up his belongings.

The truth is, Pampata's obvious affection for him has ceased to embarrass the boy, who's almost thirteen now. He still feigns annoyance when the Induna, Mgobozi or one of the other men tease him, but now their words please him. He enjoys the fact that Pampata likes him. That this has been noticed by others too, adds to his pleasure.

Yet there're times when these confusing emotions coalesce into an assegai blade, pricking his heart. When Pampata laughs and plays with the other udibis he knows he's expected to join in, but even when he's held back from them and Pampata has called him, he still feels annoyed. Left out. And Pampata's attempts to cajole him only make him more angry. It's like falling and knowing there's nothing you can do. He can't stop himself. An anger that leaves him speechless, that makes him turn his back on her and walk away, walk until he's out of her sight, then run. Trying to outdistance these feelings. Hurt, anger, abandonment, all mixed up in a stew of self-pity.

And only Pampata can make him feel better.

Better than better, in fact.

Like two nights ago – their first night away from the capital – when she told him to unroll his sleeping mat next to hers.

However, the following evening, when they made camp, some evil voice inside him told him not to put his mat next to hers, so he might once more experience the joy of having her ask him to join her. Fortunately, the better side of his nature intervened – he at least knows the first impulse was wrong, a spiteful temptation – and he settled down next to her.

Today, he's gone out ahead of the main party, with the three scouts, led by Thando. It's a way of removing himself from Pampata and the weird, contradictory emotions she evokes in him.

Also, he's still very much a boy, eager to explore. And, as the Induna's udibi, he feels he should take an active part in the expedition.

They're following a river up a valley to a cluster of rounded peaks, still another day's journey away. They've left the oppressive humidity of the plains and the air is cooler, sharper. The vegetation is a luminous green, coating the slopes of the valley, branches arching over the narrow path. A smell of mulch, rotting leaves; the ground on either side of the track is soggy, black. The boy's feet sink to his ankles in the wetness when he leaves the trail to bypass the others and join Thando.

He's come to a stop – is poised, leaning slightly forward, between his shield and spear. Listening.

The boy knows enough not to disturb Thando with questions. Instead, he tries to hear what the soldier has heard. Hard to discern anything amid the rush of the water several metres below them, though. Then the boy realises it's not a sound that's caught Thando's attention. It's the smell of burning. A fire.

Other wayfarers?

But it's midday, too early to be making camp, too late to be setting out.

Thando turns. Issues whispered instructions. He and the boy will go forward. The other two will wait – and follow them.

Several minutes later, they can see the smoke drifting in the air a few metres down the path. There are no man-sounds, though. Only the birds and the river can be heard.

"We are going where we are going," says Thando softly, meaning they won't lie about their destination. "But we are just us."

The boy nods and they move on, in single file, Thando in front, with the udibi behind him. Careless and carefree travellers who know they won't reach the end of their journey today.

Soon they can see the smoke is thicker, hanging over the path several paces ahead of them.

A fallen tree has created a clearing which rain has eroded further, breaking down the river bank and allowing access to the fast-flowing waters. Flames leap in a circle of stones. Nearby is a large cooking pot. Next to the pot is a leg and an arm. It's only as they make their way down to the fire that they spot the rest of the man. His body lies on its back amid the ferns on the other side of the tree trunk.

The sound of breaking branches, rapid movement through the undergrowth.

With long lunging steps, Thando and the boy regain the path. Bending, they see two, three shapes blundering through the trees on the slope above them, moving diagonally away from them. Almost the instant they spot them, they lose them again amid the tangled greenery.

"Cannibals!" hisses Thando.

The boy nods.

Droughts in the region have periodically led to outbreaks of cannibalism, but as Shaka has discovered, in his efforts to stamp out the practice, rumours exaggerate the prevalence of these creatures. Consequently, although they've heard the stories, this is the first incidence these two have come across. He is the Induna's udibi, though, and knows his master will expect a full account of this discovery. More than that, there's a desire to emulate his master, to put aside his fear and look and see, observe and learn. So while Thando watches, the boy moves about the camp site. The fire is burning high, he notes, with a big log in the centre. It's not ready for cooking – a sign it was lit shortly before they first saw the smoke. The boy touches the arm. The skin is cool, firm. This man has been dead for a while, but not too long, for the skin hasn't turned grey. There are cut marks in the thigh. A further indication, surely, the man-eaters had only just begun to prepare their feast.

The arm and the leg are things. They're somehow easier to examine. But the boy forces himself to approach the naked corpse. The grim reminder that this was after all a human being. Not that the udibi goes too close. He contents himself with a brief examination, standing on the other side of the log by the fire.

The boy searches for the man's clothing, his baggage. But clearly these have been dumped in the river. Following the deep footprints to the water's edge, he spots a piece of leather tangled up in some exposed roots just out of reach. Calling Thando, he gets the warrior to grip his arm while he steps into the icy water. The current leaps at him, almost snatching away his legs. With Thando leaning backwards, his feet embedded in the mud, the boy stretches in the opposite direction. His fingers brush against, then snag the piece of leather. Now, working against the current, he feels his legs swept away and Thando has to pull hard to tug him back to safety.

"Haibo!" hisses Thando, who's dropped onto his backside. "Are you mad, Little One?"

Lying between the warrior's legs, the boy gives him a grin. Brandishes the piece of leather, which is in fact a loincloth. "It's my Master's way to see everything," he says.

Thando shakes his head – and looks up as the other scouts arrive. Leaping to his feet, he tells them to go and fetch the main party and warns them to be extra vigilant. "We will wait here," he says. "And wonder if we'll ever be able to eat beef again!"

The boy looks up – he's been twisting the tassels of his apron to wring out the water. "Thando!" he says.

"What?" asks Thando.

"That is an ox I do not want in my kraal," says the boy, meaning it's something he doesn't want to think about.

He casts a glance at the severed limbs. People die because they want to kill you, which is warfare, or because you want to kill them, which is murder, a crime – with a reason, a motive, extenuating circumstances perhaps. Hunger isn't a motive. It's an aberration.

Thando chuckles. "Never fear! When your stomach grumbles you will forget this thing."

The boy rubs his arms, moves closer to the fire – but turns away from the log so he can't see what lies behind it.

When Pampata and the others arrive she insists on examining the scene, seeing for herself that this was no mere robbery. "What's in the pot?" she asks.

"Water," says Thando, kicking it over.

"And his belongings?"

"Just this," says the boy, showing her the leather loincloth.

"I've heard the tales," says Pampata, "but this is the first time . . ."

THE GREAT SMELLING OUT

"Yes," says big Njikiza. "I, too, have never seen the like."

They can't stay here, says Pampata, but they'll need to find a place to camp for they won't reach their destination until late the next evening. Somewhere safe, she adds.

Njikiza nods his agreement. According to the stories, cannibals either work alone or in small groups – and hadn't Thando and the boy seen three men fleeing? – and attack smaller groups, or stragglers. Therefore they are safe for now. There's very little ten armed Zulus, veteran warriors all, can't face with equanimity. But come nightfall they might be vulnerable. They'll continue on their way, sticking close together, and hope they can find a place that's easily defended.

*

Dust rises. Ghost-men. Animal-women. A glare. A nudge. A sniffing. A circling. Two, three creatures moving around the man, the woman, the child – pushing, prodding, pawing. The smell of animal fat, sweat, fear. A face against yours. A nose in the nape of your neck, brushing your cheekbone, pressing against your eyelids. Dog-like snuffling, foetid breath. Encircled. Entrapped. Then . . . a shriek. A finger pointing. You're pushed from behind. You stumble. You're on your hands and knees. Alone, as the others shrink away and the diviners move on. Dust rises.

The shrieks and howls are echoed by the crowd, as if this will convince these others of their innocence. It's all they can do. Nowhere to run. Nowhere to hide. The ancestors are angry. The King has been bewitched. Someone must pay. And the sangomas dance and sing, calling on the spirits to guide them. Here, an old woman slaps a young wife with the wildebeest tail she has hanging around her neck – another one found! There, a sangoma wearing a mask made from a bull's skull, slams the mask against a man's head, knocking him backwards, with a bleeding nose – another one! Disconcerted they might have been by Shaka's decree, but they soon recovered themselves. The frenzy and the fear make up for not having trusted assistants to work with. The fear and the frenzy are all they really need.

261

By late afternoon, it's over. Some three hundred abathakathi await their death in the cattlefold.

The sangomas stand swaying in the settling dust. They are spent. Exhausted. Let Shaka see how they have exerted themselves in his name.

But Shaka barely gives them a second glance. Instead, he sends one of his servants to summon Nobela to him.

"Your brothers and sisters pant like dogs, but your mouth remains full of spit. Would you distance yourself from these proceedings?"

"No. That would be to disobey you."

"Indeed." The sweep of Shaka's arm takes in those gathered in the cattlefold. "Do you then dispute . . ." Nobela shakes her head vigorously and Shaka interrupts himself. "What, then?"

"My brothers and sisters have surpassed themselves in obeying your command."

"But?"

Nobela shrugs.

"Well," says Shaka, "is the curse lifted?"

"No, not a curse . . ." Nobela squints past Shaka, her eyes fixed on the middle distance. "No," she murmurs.

"Was I not bewitched?" asks Shaka.

"It is not clear." She straightens, her eyes on Shaka. "I cannot be certain."

"I have not the Calling," says Shaka, "so allow me to untie this knot you bring me in my own way. My hut was covered in ox blood, even while trusted soldiers stood guard. To me, although I have not the Calling, this was an instance of witchcraft. I summon the most revered sangomas in the land. We stand in the sun while they wear themselves out. Now you tell me . . . Well, might you not have expressed your doubts sooner? Before we burnt our shoulders and swallowed dust? Truly," he adds, indicating the tangle of sangomas, "those plants are wilting."

"I do not doubt some . . . trickery is involved here."

"Trickery?" hisses Shaka. "The King's hut is defiled and you speak of trickery!"

"Witchcraft, then. Sorcery! I will not bicker over names!"

"The King does not bicker," says Mbopa.

Nobela ignores him. "There is thunder. There is lightning. The farmer looks to the horizon, thinking of his crops. And so he doesn't see the thief in the night sneak past him."

"Hai! Another knot! My fingers are weary!"

"I merely mean we are looking one way, when we should be looking another."

"Where would you look?" asks Shaka.

Nobela turns –

The King follows her gaze.

"No," he says. "You know my ruling. My soldiers are exempt from your meddling! You will leave them alone!"

"You trust them?" asks Nobela, mild disbelief seasoning her words.

"I trust them," says Shaka, ignoring her tone.

"Well then . . ." says Nobela. Now her speculative gaze is on the councillors and others standing behind the King.

"Ah!" says Shaka. "Think you the malcontent is in my herd?"

Nobela shrugs.

"Given the magnitude of the affront, I fear you may be right."

Nobela's head comes up, her eyes meet Shaka. She is taken aback. Clearly she was expecting bluster, outrage from the King.

"I will not stand in your way," says Shaka, stepping aside. "Find him! Fetch me the one who sought to bewitch me! One or many, it doesn't matter, the King's slayers are ready."

Is *she* ready, though? Watching Nobela, Shaka has to fight hard to suppress a grin. It is as he suspected – her complaint about the groups being made to split up didn't apply to her. It was a way of reminding him the other sangomas looked to her to speak for them. She has no need for shrieking theatrics and the like. And why should she? That piercing gaze is enough to melt any man's kneecaps. Yet Shaka's sudden invitation has disconcerted her, just as his earlier order had disconcerted the others.

She's been given an opportunity, here, one she'd dared not hope for – therefore she suspects a trap. Aiee, but this opening is too precious to reject! Trap or not, she'd be a fool if she didn't seize her chance. And if it is a trap – so what? Does Shaka really think he can trick her?

"I will not stand in your way." Yes. Arrogance, pride, these are the things that will be Shaka's undoing, here, for they lead him to believe he is too clever by half.

"I will not stand in your way." Yes. The people of Bulawayo have stood where they stood and have seen fathers and sons, mothers and daughters, brothers and sisters condemned. It will surely try their obedience if Shaka sets her loose among his inner circle, then intervenes to rescue his favourites. Has he considered that? No. He seeks merely to humiliate her, but here, today, he will not succeed. Never have so many been smelt out – and anguish is but a clenched fist away from being rage. And even if he intervenes, even if he is so stupid, how will that harm her? The people will see and remember . . .

And portents can always be found: See – the curse remains. You have made your sacrifice, but the King and his sycophants sneer at the ancestors – and the curse remains! What will you do about this?

Caution, though . . .

Caution is called for. The ground is shaky.

Shaka watches her move along the line. At his command the men have spread out into a single rank, which even Mbopa has joined after a quizzical glance in Shaka's direction. It's a wonder she isn't drooling, he decides. For these are the highborn, members of the Bloodline and Shaka's most trusted advisors and councillors . . .

She has waved away her attendants and is alone. She has no need to cavort and chant. She moves down the line, keeping several paces away from the glowering men, doesn't even seem to be looking at them.

*

An old woman and a younger wife wail and shriek at the sight of the loincloth the boy produces. It's the woman's son, the wife's brother, who's been missing since this morning, explains the headman of this small, impoverished homestead. Including himself, the clan only comprises five able-bodied men, four now they know the fate of the one who went missing – what can they do to defend themselves? How could they even go searching for the missing man? There are too few of them to make up a strong search party and leave enough men behind to guard the women and children.

Who, the boy notes, outnumber the men greatly. Once the coming and going that attended their arrival has settled down, he is able to count eight young women and the old granny and twice that many children, the eldest being a girl in her early teens.

"Our life is bad enough," says the headman, "without these monsters to fear. But this is their way, is it not? To pick on the weak and defenceless!"

They're standing in the clearing in the centre of the homestead – five huts almost hidden by tall thatchgrass. The trail had gradually taken them away from the river, onto open ground. Then flattened grass around a fork in the path had alerted them to the fact a settlement was nearby.

Njikiza has sent four of his men to go with some of the children to fetch water. The old mother and the sister have retreated to their hut, attended by the other females, all wailing.

"Aiee!" says the headman. "But you are here, now! Shaka's lions! Together we will hunt down this vermin!"

Njikiza nods. He won't disappoint the greybeard just yet. They have to meet up with Nandi as soon as possible. They can't be detained here. Anyway, the greybeard's disappointment will be short-lived. Njikiza will not let this matter rest. Nandi has some five hundred soldiers with her. He will get Pampata safely to her destination and return here with a contingent drawn from those men. Then they'll teach these cannibals a thing or two about Zulu justice. Now is not the time to discuss these matters, though. They have to get through tonight.

But the headman has thought of that too. "Tonight our women and children can sleep in safety," he says. "This is thanks to your presence! Let us repay your kindness. You and your men have travelled a long way, you must be tired. My men will stand guard tonight, while you rest – they would prove to you it's merely a lack of numbers, not courage, that sees us squatting here, unable to venture far."

Njikiza agrees, not wanting to insult the headman. Although his men will bed down around the fire tonight, he'll set up a series of shifts so there'll always be two soldiers awake.

Pampata, meanwhile, pulls the boy aside. There's an empty hut and they want her to sleep there; the boy must join her. When he remonstrates, saying it would be better were he to share the hardships of the other men, she grins. "You have not seen the hut!" she says. "It is *they* who will praise *you* for your endurance!"

She's right. The hut is dilapidated; the thatch loose, frayed, the interior dusty. The mats are awash with fleas.

"This is one ordeal I will not suffer alone," says Pampata.

She cannot turn down the offer of the hut for that would be an affront to their hosts, who have already shown an eagerness to share whatever meagre supplies they have with the new arrivals. Gingerly, she and the boy roll up the sleeping mats that are there already and dump them in a far corner; then they go off ostensibly to look for firewood, but Pampata wants to find something she can use to sweep the floor of the hut.

*

The people in the main enclosure have eased forward. In a momentary reversal of roles, it's the sangomas who have had to get out of their way, scurrying with as much dignity as their thirsty, aching bodies can muster to position themselves by one of the regiments.

But it's as if what has gone before never happened. Moving forward, the crowd ignores even the condemned squatting in the cattlefold. Their eyes are on Nobela.

Can it be?

Are there sorcerers amid Shaka's inner circle?

Is such a thing possible?

Nobela reaches the end of the rank. Turns around. Standing in the sun for several dusty hours, she's had to draw on reserves of energy she didn't know she still possessed. She will not let Shaka see her sit or show any other sign of weakness. It's been a fierce struggle, she's as tired as if she'd been out there, dancing amid the cringing lines. Her knees and ankles ache. The leaves she chewed this morning to help ease the pain have worn off. Her skins – tails and paws, pelts and swollen bladders – weigh her down, but these eyes . . .

How she loves these eyes.

They lift her . . . buoy her . . . sustain her . . .

Yes, a little dagga wouldn't go amiss right now, but these eyes are almost as potent . . .

Even the disdain, the hate, she's glimpsed – even these things are testament to her power . . .

Remember, though: you walk on uneven ground. One false step . . .

What is Shaka up to?

And what is this other thing she can glimpse? It lurks in the corner of her mind, moving closer when she ponders the riddle of Shaka's behaviour, retreating when she turns on it, snatches at it.

"Trickery," she whispers, gazing down the line to where Shaka stands.

The King's hut bleeds ox blood. He is bewitched.

But is he?

Do we assume that because that's what we'd like to see? Does our arrogance, our pride at being proved right at last blind us?

"Trickery . . ."

Nobela moves to the centre of the line. She summons her attendants, who fetch her water. She drinks. She speaks . . .

"The ancestors guide me. Yet they are wary today. There is a great evil here. An evil the like of which I have never before encountered. The ancestors are not cowed. No, never cowed. Yet they speak of the need for caution. Caution must guide us, if they are to protect us. For we are all in danger. They cannot help us if we do not heed them."

Turning her head in Shaka's direction: "And I cannot help you, if you do not heed me. No!" A shriek from deep within her. She falters. Raises her chin. Shuts her eyes. A hiss. "Trickery."

She brings her staff around, to her side. Extends her right arm, pushing the stick away from her body. Tell me, she commands the darkness behind her eyelids.

Tell.

Me.

An empty hut. Her awareness is a glow, spreading fast, vanquishing the gloom, illuminating the interior. But the thatch is alive. The thatch is moving. The thatch is entwined serpents, writhing, becoming a dark mass. Blood. The insides of her eyelids. Red. She lurches forward. Acting almost of its own accord her right arm moves, planting the staff before her again. Something to lean on.

She opens her eyes to the glare of the sun, so painful all of a sudden.

And all is quiet. Motionless.

All eyes are on her. Staring.

"Caution!" she shouts. "It is with caution we will cross the swollen river. But there is one who crosses that river time and time again without fear. There is one who, with the heart of a lion, defeated the Lion. Let him come forward!"

Without hesitation, the Induna steps out of the line.

"No!" hisses Mgobozi, but the Induna ignores him, turns to face Shaka.

"Nduna!" says Shaka, dismay in his voice.

Although the Induna is more than a soldier, Shaka might have argued he is exempt, protected by the King's ruling that sangomas are to have nothing to do with his warriors, but he is obviously too stunned to think clearly. "Nduna," he whispers. Then he straightens, becomes the King once more.

"Since you have served me well, Nduna, you will die a warrior's death. My slayers shall not touch you."

The Induna is to stand to one side, by the cattlefold.

But Nobela is speaking again, the words coming of their own volition.

"What do we say of the man who has travelled far? Let him come forward!"

This is a pun on Nqoboka's name, which means the Weary One, and without hesitation he, too, steps out of the line.

"Nqoboka? You?" Shaka's voice is a hiss.

Yet, like the Induna, he will not face the slayers . . . Shaka has just issued the order and the general is moving away when Mgobozi blunders forward.

"Majesty! Father! What are you *doing*! Would you condemn your bravest, most trustworthy warriors? How can you listen to this, this *bitch*! Can you not see she seeks only vengeance? How can you do this, Father?" His voice is a child's wail of anguish.

"Mgobozi," says Shaka, "I have been bewitched. We must smell out the culprits!"

"But your friends, Majesty . . . Think you now your friends plot against you?"

"Not until the ancestors spoke."

"The ancestors? No, Father! This one – it is not the ancestors that speak, only her own bitterness. Her spite!"

"She has the Calling, Mgobozi."

"Think you that, Father, then I, too, will join my friends! I spit at her," he says, putting deed to word. "I will not be condemned by this bitch. I will choose my own fate." And he does the unthinkable, walks past Shaka, cutting in front of him. But before Shaka can respond, a cry from one of the men in the line wheels him round . . .

Nobela is on her hands and knees. Coughing. Choking.

She raises her head. "No!" she pants. "No!" She is fighting with herself, trying to hold back words that will come out, words she would force down again.

"There," she pants.

Shaka moves closer, bends over her so he can hear her more clearly.

"There. Is. One . . . Blood."

Head bowed, she sucks in mouthfuls of air. Her nails claw the dirt. A shudder shakes her body and the words come quickly, like buck before a veld fire: "Blood of your blood, he will destroy you, for he is needy. He wants what you have."

Dingane, the Needy One, looks to his left, looks to his right, and sees the others have moved away from him.

Shaka also realises Nobela is referring to his half-brother. "No!" he says. "My family you will leave alone!"

He steps aside. Signals Nobela's attendants. They rush to help her to her feet.

"Fetch her some water," orders Shaka.

Nobela tucks her withered arm out of sight again. Leans heavily on her staff. Sweat stings her eyes. Her throat is burning, for those words were fire. The knowledge flaring up, knocking her over. And she fought the words. For they were fire and very, very dangerous. Not just because warning Shaka against an assassination attempt is the last thing she wants to do. Let him die! But now she has made an enemy of Dingane, betraying him, albeit unwittingly. How is he to know how desperately she fought to silence herself?

Yet . . . her breathing back to normal, her heart no longer beating like a drum, the water soothing her sore throat . . . she realises all is calm.

Shaka seems quite sanguine, as he waits for her to recover. Her revelation has had little effect on him.

When her eyes meet his, he even has a smile for her.

"Are you done?" he asks.

And the foreboding returns.

What is he up to?

But all she can do is nod her head.

*

The boy is lying on his side, gazing out of the doorway, listening to Pampata patting and slapping herself, scratching and squirming, quietly cursing. He watches one of the men from the clan stepping between the soldiers, carrying a large bundle of sticks and twigs – which he dumps

270

on the fire. The soldiers are huddled under their cowhides, their spears within reach, and there on the far side of the leaping flames sits Njikiza – no mistaking that gigantic form – and Thando, still awake. For a moment the boy thinks of joining them, but it is warm in the hut, the small fire they had built in the centre massaging his back . . .

*

"My Children," says Shaka, "brave Children Of Zulu, loyal Children Of The Sky, you have heard how the Bull Elephant awoke one morning to find his hut drenched in blood! Guarded though he was by his most loyal men – soldiers beyond reproach – he still awoke to find the thatch sticky! And then I summoned the most revered sangomas in all the land. Men and women of whom praises echo through the valleys! I summoned them here and I told them: find the sorcerer, find the villain. Your praises echo through the valleys, you are revered throughout the kingdom, find the one who stole past my guards, this ghost, who would mock my power. For you have the power, I said. You can do this. Yes, Father, they said. Yes, Majesty, they shouted. We have the power! Then do your work, proud sangomas! This is what I told them. Do your work! We would smell out this evil, they said, for this is our way. This is our way! Summon your people, they said, summon the people of Bulawayo! My people, I asked, would you have me summon my people? My loyal subjects? My precious Children? Yes, they said."

Shaka pauses, nodding his head.

"Yes, they said. And again, yes! For this is our way. But my Children are loyal, I said. My Children love me! This is not so, they said, these sangomas. There are those among your Children who are evil! *Evil*! Summon them, Oh Mighty King! Let them suffer! We will find the evil ones. And this I did, my Children. For are we not to trust these Chosen Ones of the Calling? Do they not speak for the ancestors? Are they not guided by the ancestors? This is so, they told me. We speak for the ancestors. We are guided by the ancestors. We are the Chosen Ones. Summon them, Majesty, summon your Children so we may smell out the evil. And I summoned you, my Children, and you came. Came to meet your death. For see the evil ones!"

Shaka points to the cattlefold. "See the evil ones! See how many! And yes, there are those of my inner circle in that herd. All evil. All smelt out by these all-knowing sangomas. The most revered, most powerful in the land! But here is something I don't understand, my Children . . ."

Nobela is instantly alert. Her eyes narrowed, holding Shaka in their glare.

"Here is something I don't understand. I summon these sangomas and I ask them: who was it that smeared ox blood over my hut? And they move among you, saying this one, that one, him, her – evil! All evil! Yet here I stand!"

Shaka spreads arms.

"Here I stand!"

He shrugs.

"Here I stand, my Children! For it was I! I was the one who smeared ox blood over my hut!"

A gasp. Heads turn in amazement. The sangomas gape. Nobela shuts her eyes.

"I was the one. Not those over there, who have been condemned! It was I!"

A signal from Mbopa and, before they know it, the other sangomas are surrounded by armed men. Only Nobela and her two attendants are left alone.

"It is true that we have some powerful sangomas in the land – but clearly these are not they. They have failed me – and the punishment for failure is death!"

A cheer explodes from the crowd. Even those in the cattlefold – who are still by no means certain of their fate – join in.

"Bayede, Nkosi! Bayede! Ndaba Uyazitha! Ndaba Uyinkosi! Bayede, Nkosi! Bayede!"

"The punishment for failure is death!" says Shaka. "But I would not see my slayers waste their energies. Perhaps my Children, here," he adds, indicating the condemned in the cattlefold, "would oblige me by ridding the kraal of this dung!"

More cheers. And the crowd surges against the fence to watch those who were about to die turn, barehanded and snarling, on their accusers.

Striding over to Nobela, Shaka says: "Never fear, Cunt – you will have your chance to leave this place on your hind legs."

*

All is quiet. The boy is still lying on his side, but he must have drifted off for a moment.

For longer than a moment, in fact. He pushes himself up on one arm. Morning must be near, for a low mist has gathered in the clearing between the huts, cloaking the sleeping soldiers so that they have become vague shapes.

The boy considers crawling outside to examine the sky, see how close dawn is, but thinks better of it. Instead, he twists his head to look over his shoulder to make sure Pampata is sleeping peacefully – which she is, on her side, facing away from the fire.

He rolls back onto his back.

And tries to pin down the thing that's been worrying him. It was Pampata who set him gnawing at this bone, trying to get at the marrow. Something she said while they were out collecting wood. Actually, she said a lot of things, such as that perhaps they'd be better off in the dark forest than fighting fleas in that hut, and that she wouldn't be eating anything these people served them no matter how hungry she might be – did he see how dirty they were – and where were their crops, they hadn't passed anything that even vaguely resembled a vegetable patch, and their cattle? Stolen! It was hard to believe these were Zulus! Yet this was how their people lived before Shaka claimed the crown – the boy must never forget that. Never! And then the headman accosted them. He was with two women. No, no, he blustered, they were honoured guests, they weren't to collect firewood! Here, they were to return with him, his women would find the firewood.

And the boy was left frowning. Something Pampata had said had flared amid the tinder in his mind, but before he could fan the flame he had been distracted.

What was it?

Something important. He knows that.

Sho! His head hurts!

He coughs. Frowns. Sits up. Coughs again.

The mist is inside the hut now.

A throbbing behind his temple. And his eyes are sore.

He stands, sees how thick the mist is: a heavy, sluggish morass at his feet. And it seems thicker in the centre of the hut, where the fireplace is.

Dropping to his hands and knees, the boy scrabbles blindly about in his belongings until his left hand closes over one of the waterskins.

On his feet again, every breath now a cough, he steps toward the fire-place, judging its position from the hole in the apex of the roof, and empties the waterskin, squirting out the liquid and hearing an answering hiss.

Pampata!

He can't see her! The mist – or is it smoke? It has a fragrance mist lacks, it must be smoke. The smoke covers the floor. He circles the fire until he comes to the place where Pampata should be. Yes – here she is.

He hesitates a second, dreading to re-enter the thick, stifling mass. Then he takes a deep breath and drops to his knees. And it's while groping for Pampata, hoping he doesn't touch her somewhere . . . private, that he remembers! Remembers what's been pestering him so. And he's a fool! But there's no time for recriminations. His hands find Pampata's thigh. He digs his nails into her flesh. There's no time to waste!

She sits up with a squeal, trying to pull her leg away, trying to turn over. "Pampata! Wake up!"

Her head lolls as he shakes her, but gradually, groggily, consciousness reanimates her features. And she's coughing. "What's happening?"

"We must get out of here."

When he's sure she'll remain propped up on locked elbows, he stands. Starts tearing at the thatch of the walls with his bare hands.

Within moments Pampata joins him, handing him an assegai from the bundle in her left hand. Gripping the haft close to the broad blade, the boy hacks away. Cool night air. Refreshing mouthfuls.

Soon the hole's big enough to push the spears through and, using the assegai she's retained, Pampata joins the boy in making the opening wider. Stopping to savour the fresh air, the boy turns. Killing the fire has helped, leaving a core of wet blackness around which the smoke now swirls, but a grey thickness is pushing in through the entrance of the hut. Simply putting out the fire would not have helped them.

Pampata pushes through the hole, sprawling into the wet grass. The boy follows her. Knowing they need to keep their wits about them, he is more careful. Steps through the opening. Steps to the side. Leans against the thatch, swallowing mouthfuls of air.

Pieces of dried grass dropping down his neck. A scuffling, scraping sound.

The boy pushes away from the hut and turns to meet a shape hurling itself at him from the roof.

Arms, legs and bared teeth.

The udibi just has time to raise an elbow as he's thrown backward. And teeth bite into the flesh of his forearm. But the boy's shriek of pain is truncated as he realises . . .

No! It can't be!

The boy forces himself up, scuffles backward into the long grass. It's a child! He's being attacked by a child. A male child of seven or eight years! A lion cub trying to bring down its first zebra. The udibi twists to the left and right, frantically trying to loosen those teeth, before he realises this will only cause his flesh to tear more.

Using his free hand, he forces himself up onto his feet. Fingers claw and scratch his face. And all the time, those teeth, biting deeper and deeper. Like some ravenous animal. But not an animal. A child. A male. And any male, even a child, has . . .

The boy's hand snakes forward, a striking cobra, his fingers fangs embedding themselves in the child's genitals. Tiny worm and pebbles, gripped and twisted!

The teeth fly free – but the boy tightens his grip, and flings the thing away from him. A child, yes, but only in form. This clan has left the human race a long time ago to hide and lie in wait for luckless travellers, the only flesh that will satisfy their inhuman appetites.

And Pampata's struggling with one of the men. He straddles her, snapping at her throat. It's all she can do to hold him at bay; she daren't buck her hips – that'll only bring those teeth closer to her jugular. The iklwa blade slices through the man's side as the udibi hits him, knocking him off Pampata.

The boy rolls away, taking his spear with him and rises in time to see Pampata on her knees by the man, driving her own blade through his throat.

"It is I who will eat tonight," she hisses.

On his guard, the boy moves away from the huts. Several metres from the dwellings, two fires burn. Orange faces become dark shapes leaping the flames, racing toward the two Zulus.

Pampata has seen the fires, too. Fires that await their flesh. And she has seen the shadows coming for them. Gripping an assegai in each hand she tells the boy to go and rouse the others. And she's stepping past him to meet another attack. It's the headman. He's wielding an axe. Before the udibi can respond, Pampata parries the axe with one iklwa and plunges the other into the headman's exposed stomach. "Go!" she screams at the boy.

Pampata turns, rams her back against the headman to loosen her blade and drops into a crouch. "And you, little sister?" she whispers. "Would you also taste my steel this night?"

The girl mirrors Pampata's crouch, raising fingers curled like claws. Her upper body moves from side to side in a sinuous motion, like a reed brushed by a crosswind, but Pampata keeps her feet firmly planted, waiting for the girl to come to her.

Then, perhaps because the girl freezes, seems to gather herself for a leap, or because she hears the sudden rush behind her, Pampata wheels – and extends her left arm to meet the man's charge with the blade of her assegai. Extends her right arm as the girl springs at her from the opposite side. But, mortally wounded, the man blunders past Pampata and into the girl, knocking her off course, so that Pampata's blade only penetrates the little one's shoulder, hooking against her collarbone, before the girl's momentum deflects it, so that both girl and spear fly in opposite directions.

And Shaka's beloved is left without any weapons, as the woman following the man moves in for the kill . . .

Cutting between the huts the boy circles the perimeter of the gathering place so as to avoid tripping over the unconscious men. The wood . . . There must be something in the wood the headman insisted the women and children collect for them. Because they were honoured guests! Hai! Honoured only as the soldiers honour Shaka's cattle gathered in Bulawayo's large inner enclosure. Something in the wood that when burnt causes those nearby to fall into a deep sleep. Now, moving past the huts arranged around the clearing, the boy spots something else he should've noticed earlier. Only the entrance to the "guest hut" faces inward, faces the fireplace. The other huts have their entrances on the sides, so far around they're almost at the back. And this smoke is heavy, it settles only around the fireplace, which means those inside the huts would be safe from its effects.

Although tonight their hunger had obviously made them impatient – and the adults had gone off to prepare the fire, the pots, the knives, leaving only the younger children perched atop the thatch, herders ensuring none of their precious cattle stray, these big, meaty Zulu bulls!

The mighty Watcher Of The Ford is a mountain range draped in early morning mist. The boy shakes him. A grunt. He shakes Njikiza again. A groan.

Water! He needs water! But where . . . The smoke is a thick lake that reaches to his knees, there's no time to fumble blindly for a waterskin.

277

There's only one thing the boy can do. Using both hands, he pushes Njikiza over onto his back. Standing, he pulls aside the tassels of his front apron – and pisses on the big man's face.

Coughing, spluttering, wiping his face, Njikiza sits up. The boy tugs at him. "Up," he pleads, "get *up*!"

Bewildered, blinking, smacking his lips with suspicion, Njikiza allows the boy to help him to his feet. "What's going on?" he grumbles. He runs his fingers over his cheek and sniffs them, but even as the angry realisation dawns on him, the boy shakes him.

"You must wake up! We are under attack!"

"What?" Njikiza glances around, noting the smoke for the first time. The shapes amid the dense greyness, men turned to stone.

Then the boy slaps both hands against his chest, pushing him aside, and leaps in the opposite direction. The clan's grandmother blunders between them, her knife stabbing air, causing her to overbalance. The boy helps her along, hitting her rump with his shoulder. Orange fingers enfold her, pulling her into the palm of the fire. She shrieks, kicks wildly, tries to rise, but the palm has split open, become a mouth, the flames becoming fangs tearing open her chest, her stomach, and enfolding her at the same time.

The indignity of being summarily knocked over is enough to restore Njikiza's senses – and the movement has disturbed the smoke at their feet. Spotting his club, he pounces on it with an enraged roar.

The woman has Pampata down, but even as her back crushes the wet grass, she's twisting violently. Throws the woman off her. Rolls on top of her. Straddles her, sitting down hard on the woman's groin. The woman's hands claw at her face. But Pampata ignores this. Leans back a little, to give herself some space – and rams her left fist into the woman's face. Straightening again, she rams her right fist into the woman's face.

He should've known! He should've remembered the night they captured a Xhosa bandit.

"What's wrong?" the Induna had asked, seeing the boy looking down at the body and looking puzzled.

278

And he'd pointed to the man's penis . . .

Another of the soldiers is coming to his senses, crawling through the smoke, coughing and retching. But as the boy moves to help him, a shape slithers down the roof of the hut, kicking away at the last minute, to leap onto the man's back. The udibi darts forward, snatching the child's legs and pulling it off the man before it can sink its teeth into his neck.

"Here!" calls Njikiza. "Send that one here!"

The boy tosses the child over the screaming, writhing granny – Njikiza swings his club and the tiny broken body spins away into the night. Then the big Zulu brings the weapon down onto the back of the old woman's skull to shut her up.

The boy meets Pampata coming between the huts.

Is she well?

Yes. She grins. She is well. Has she not said she can take care of herself?

*

The cattlefold is a lake of blood, gleaming in the rays of the setting sun. The slayers have dragged away the broken bodies of the sangomas and their helpers; the skins and necklaces, masks and other regalia have been gathered into a pile, which will be set on fire as soon as night falls. The condemned have been allowed to rejoin their families, and now the crowd waits silently, all eyes on the gathering under the ibandla tree.

Back in the King's party, Mgobozi is looking somewhat deranged. Shaka hasn't yet had a chance to speak to his old friend – to ask for his forgiveness – and he hopes Nqoboka and the Induna have had an opportunity to pour honey into his ears. Shaka knows if it had been him tricked like that, he would be livid. But, hopefully, Mgobozi will understand the necessity for keeping him away from their plans.

At Shaka's request, the Induna had started a fire. Now he stands and says: "Majesty! It is ready!"

"Good," says Shaka, grinning, having just thought of a way he might soothe Mgobozi's anger.

He turns to Nobela.

"I promised you a chance to leave Bulawayo on your hind legs, and I am a man of my word."

Nobela stands flanked by Shaka's soldiers. A second group, to her rear, keeps a watch on her attendants. She stares at Shaka.

"It is true!" says Shaka. "And what is more – you will remember this! For it is a test you of the Calling devised yourselves! It's fallen into disuse since my grandfather's time, but – hai! – if it worked once, it will work again. And it always worked, didn't it?"

Nobela gazes past Shaka.

"Didn't it?" he hisses.

She watches the Induna rise, lifting the assegai blade out of the coals. Her eyes shift to meet Shaka's. Her lips curl.

"Aiee! A snarl! How it becomes you!"

The Induna is alongside Shaka.

"You will have to remind me, though – is a burnt tongue a sign of guilt or innocence? I have forgotten."

When it's clear Nobela isn't going to respond, Shaka tosses the question over his shoulder. "Mbopa?"

"Guilt, Father. Always guilt."

"Nqoboka?"

"Guilt, Father."

"Nduna?"

"Guilt, Father."

"Ah! Then let us begin."

Gripping the assegai shaft in two hands, the Induna raises the blade.

"Open your mouth, Cunt," whispers Shaka.

"Umthakathi!" hisses Nobela.

Shaka grins. "No, Umthakathi *Omkhulu*! Now open your mouth!"

Nobela's lips part.

"Pass this test and you walk free," says Shaka. "Nduna . . ."

Gently, the Induna guides the blade into Nobela's mouth.

"Bite, Cunt!"

Instantly, Nobela's mouth becomes a bursting blister. She staggers backward, leaving her lips behind on the red-hot blade. Her hands over her mouth, she drops onto her knees.

"What say you, Nduna?"

"Guilt, Father."

"Nqoboka?"

"Guilt, Father. I smell the burning flesh from here!"

"Mbopa?"

"Guilt, Father. Or perhaps you might like to try one more time to be sure."

"No," says Shaka. "That would be cruel."

He watches as Nobela rocks back and forth, her eyes glazed, a keening sound escaping from her fingers. The bitch! Even now she will not give him the satisfaction of seeing her suffer.

"Mgobozi!"

"Majesty," says the general, appearing at Shaka's side. His salutation is almost a murmur and there's something wary about his demeanour, his bearing.

"Old Friend!" says Shaka, laying a hand on the general's shoulder. "When we first saw the blood on my hut and this distasteful affair began, you said give me ten men and I'll sniff out this miscreant. Well . . ." Shaka indicates Nobela. "I have found her for you. But I'll still let you have your ten men."

He turns, issues an instruction to one of his boys.

Moments later, the servant returns with ten assegai shafts. Shaka takes them from him and throws them in front of Nobela.

"There," he tells Mgobozi, "there are your ten men. I have seen you admiring one of my black bulls – hai, do not deny it! Well, that bull will be yours if you make those ten men disappear into this Cunt!"

Mgobozi breaks into a smile. "Then that bull is mine!"

*

Something else he should've noticed! They had cleaned the hut – he and

Pampata – as best they could, and with the dust gone they had seen the furrows, tiny furrows scored in the hard-packed dirt, left by those being dragged to their demise.

But the other thing . . .

"What's wrong?" asked the Induna. And the boy had pointed to the dead bandit's penis. And the Induna had laughed and told him about the Xhosa circumcision ritual undergone by young men, seventeen, eighteen summers old. Once Zulu males had been forced to undergo a similar ritual to prove their manhood, but the practice had been abolished long before Shaka's time – and Shaka had dispensed with what remained of the old Zulu initiation ceremony altogether. Let service in the army be a test of manhood, he decreed.

The dismembered body by the river . . . The boy had noted that the man's penis was missing the top quarter of its foreskin. Which should've told him the man couldn't have been a Zulu. Which meant he didn't belong to this clan, as they had claimed!

The boy would tell the others this, shrug off their praises, but before he can speak he absently tries to bend his right arm – and passes out from the pain.

*

The Induna was somewhat taken aback when Nobela's words reached out to ensnare him – and he wonders how much of Shaka's dismay was feigned. That Nqoboka should have been chosen next – aiee! Nqoboka and the Induna had collected the ox blood. While Mbopa provided a distraction for Mzilikazi and his sentries – their punishment a convenient way of ensuring the King's enclosure did not have its full complement of guards – the Induna conveyed the pails to Shaka. "No," said Shaka, taking them from the Induna, "this is something I must do alone. You keep watch."

Thus it was the King himself who had splattered blood on his own hut in the darkness. But Nqoboka and the Induna had been involved in the scheme, and they had been smelt out by Nobela.

What is one to make of that?

What of Mbopa, though? He was not called out. Maybe he would have been had not Nobela been distracted, and Shaka had not moved to put an end to the charade.

Charade it might have been to the King, and the others in the know, but it wasn't for Nobela.

The valley with its rolling hills is still in the dusk, the sky is orange turning gold on the horizon, but the Induna sees Nobela again. On her hands and knees, wrestling with the sudden revelation, a vomiting dog, a wounded hyena, fighting the words – and the Induna has no doubt this was one revelation she would have preferred to keep to herself.

Aiee, and what a revelation! That Dingane is not to be trusted – that's hardly news to the King. But Nobela saw more, didn't she?

Blood of your blood, he will destroy you . . .

Sooner or later, Dingane will move against Shaka and he will succeed! Is this not what Nobela's words mean?

Yet to know an enemy will attack means one can prepare oneself.

Zulu cows dot the hillside and the valley. Many times a Zulu impi has concealed itself by having the men spread out and hunker down behind their big cowhide shields so that they resemble grazing cattle from a distance. The Induna wonders if things are as they seem in this instance. Might there not be another path over this mountain?

Nandi's summons to Pampata had provided a timely pretext, but Shaka would have found another excuse to ensure his beloved was away from the capital when the Smelling Out took place. For she isn't his wife, a family member he could protect if Nobela had pounced on her.

The fact is, one doesn't need special powers to know in advance who Nobela might have smelt out if given the opportunity (as she was) to range among Shaka's entourage. Mgobozi, Nqoboka, Mbopa, they were sure to be smelt out. Mzilikazi, too, if he hadn't been sent off to one of the war kraals. Neither is it surprising she should have chosen the Induna, given his reputation. And why shouldn't she seek to sow further discord between the brothers by pointing out Dingane as one who would seek to assassinate the King?

These are the things the Induna has spent much time mulling over since the events of five days ago. But ultimately it doesn't matter that in her last hour, with almost her last breath, Nobela might have provided proof of her powers. This was never the issue. Whether or not Nobela really was guided by the ancestors was not Shaka's concern.

This was about who was the more powerful, and Shaka's triumph was real.

*

When the boy comes to, he's shocked to find himself on Njikiza's back. The shame! His protestations that he can walk with the others only serve to waken the pain in his arm, however, and he falls silent. It's day and they're almost at their destination. When they stop to rest Pampata tells him how they roused the men last night, made sure the cannibals were dead, and then, after making some torches, they set off into the darkness, seeking to put that evil place as far behind them as possible.

When they stopped to break their fast Pampata collected the herbs she needed to treat the wounds of those who had been bitten. The boy has vague recollections of movement, being lifted and put down and lifted again, of orange leaves, shifting shades sliding past, of Pampata tending to his arm – yes, and of collapsing against her in tears as the poultice started doing its work with a sudden sting that was every bit as painful as the original bite. But she says nothing of this – and the boy remembers something else: how she rocked him, holding him gently but firmly, and how good that felt. The shame!

But he is a hero. All the praise is his. If he hadn't awakened Pampata and sounded the alarm . . .

He wants to tell them how ashamed he is, how he should've realised sooner what was happening, but no one will listen to him. They merely laugh and shake their heads and ask him to tell them again how he roused Njikiza . . .

And what of Pampata? How bravely she fought? Aiee! She was a lioness! But when they have their destination in sight and the boy has insisted on being put down so that he might at least walk this last distance like a man, Pampata falls in step alongside him. Asks to see his arm. Makes to adjust the fastening so the others pass them. "Listen to me," she hisses, crouching before the boy, looking up at him, "you will not exaggerate my role in last night's battle."

"But . . ."

"No," she whispers, pressing a finger against the boy's lips. "Remember, our Father said I was to be protected. And no, no one failed me, but perhaps Shaka will not take that view of things. Do you understand?"

The boy nods, understanding at last why the men looked away whenever he tried to speak of Pampata's bravery. It wasn't that they doubted him, or refused to believe a woman could have done those things. They were afraid of what Shaka might say should he hear his beloved had been put in a position where she was forced to prove her bravery.

"I will say nothing," says the boy. "But I will not forget."

Pampata grins. "Neither will I, Brave Warrior."

*

The Induna bows as Shaka clambers to the top of the ridge.

Retrieving his spear, the King holds up a hand. "Sheath your concern, Nduna. I am well aware Mbopa will swallow his tongue when he learns I came out here alone. But I knew I would be in the company of one of my bravest warriors!"

Shaka sits cross-legged on a large rock and invites the Induna to join him. Messengers arrived at midday with news that Pampata and her party were close to the capital and both men have come to await their return.

They sit gazing at the cattle, Shaka pointing out this one and that one by name, discussing that bull's shortcomings as a sire, this cow's capacity to produce milk. Cattle are precious to the Nguni people and valuable booty for invaders. When the Zulu army goes to war, every effort is made by their foe to conceal their own cattle. By contrast, the Zulu beast is allowed to roam free. "Khala, nkomo yakwaZulu, wena ongase-ze waya ndaye," boast the Zulus. *Low on, Zulu cow, for you will never tread a foreign soil!*

"Aiee!" chuckles Shaka, as they watch a group of herdboys move in on a cow and take turns to drink milk straight from the udder. "I remember my time as a herder! Such carefree days!"

It's dusk, the time of day Zulus call selibantubahle – when all people are beautiful.

PART THREE

The Lair Of The Baboon God

As at all times of privation, a flock of social vultures –
profiteers, food hoarders and black marketers – appeared
among the Sotho. One of these ingenious, if distasteful,
gentlemen went by the name of Raboshabane, and
there is a proverb about him which the Sotho still quote:
"The rock of Raboshabane is slippery."

From *Myths And Legends Of Southern Africa*
by Penny Miller

"He did what?" roars Shaka.

"It is true, Beloved! He pissed over Njikiza!"

Shaka rolls away from her, laughing.

"I cannot believe it!" he gasps.

"Neither could the Watcher Of The Ford. He said he was on the point of throttling the little fool when some killing intervened."

"Not a fool! That one is no fool."

"I know that. As does Njikiza."

"And the Induna, most of all."

"Yes, Father."

"Aiee! Poor Njikiza! Mgobozi will never let him forget the night – yes, I can just hear him now, he'll never let Njikiza forget the night the Watcher became the Ford!"

Pampata giggles.

"You are right: poor Njikiza. But tell me," she says, growing serious, "what of Mgobozi? Has he forgiven you your treachery?"

Sitting up, Shaka grunts. Runs a hand over his face. "Yes," he murmurs, "that is the way I felt – I, the King – that I had betrayed him!"

"But it had to be that way."

"Yes, and he knows this now. Mgobozi, I told him, Old Friend, you were a part of my plan all along! What could I have done without your indignation? Indignation the like of which you never could have feigned! For this reason I told you nothing of my plan. I didn't have to. I knew you would play your part without question."

"And his response?"

"He was fresh from impaling Nobela so he was of a mind to be generous!"

"And now she is finished."

*"And her kind." Shaka reaches for a drinking bowl. "But for how long?"
He swallows a mouthful of beer. "How long before others take her place?"*

*"Beloved, I think you have put paid to these sangomas for a long, long
time to come. They'll stick to their muthis for a while."*

*"Hmm," grunts Shaka, passing the bowl to Pampata. "But what of this
one my mother found?"*

"He is not a sangoma. You will see that for yourself soon enough."

*"Why? Must I now face Zwide yet again so that I might speak to this
Truthsayer?"*

"Hai! All that means is at least something will come out of your efforts."

"Yes, that one and his Ndwandwe jackals continue to annoy me."

"Besides, this is something you must *do."*

"Must I?"

"Beloved," says Pampata soothingly, "you know whereof I speak."

"Drink! For I am thirsty."

Pampata takes a sip of beer, hands the bowl back to Shaka.

*"What," he says, after taking another drink, "what if this one is another
tall tale?"*

*"Nandi will not allow herself to be so deceived. In my presence she
questioned the Honey Man's emissary yet again. She is much too wise to
be tricked by deceitful tongues!"*

"That she is!"

"Besides, the Honey Man is your ally. Your most valuable spy, is he not?"

Shaka grunts his agreement.

*"He is real, this Truthsayer – and he is one who might be able to guide
you. And he is not a sangoma, Beloved. About that the Honey Man's emissary was most clear, and knowing your aversion to these Chosen Ones,
Nandi questioned him on this point. This Truthsayer was a brave warrior
who was once severely wounded, and upon recovering discovered he had
the ability to dream of things to come, to find the path others seek."*

*"Yes," sighs Shaka, lying back next to Pampata, "I will get to him and
hopefully I'll be able to step over Zwide's body to do so. But first we will
visit these Sothos who believe themselves safe in their mountains . . ."*

1
The Encounter

Even Mgobozi was rendered speechless. In turn, as though obeying a command issued by their beloved general, five hundred Zulu warriors fell silent, greeting the bizarre spectacle with a mixture of gaping disbelief and bewilderment.

This detachment of Shaka's Fasimba impi was conducting a reconnaissance in force deep in Sotho territory. They moved through the waist-high grass in a long rectangular formation five men wide. To guard against ambushes, platoons of ten men moved in a parallel course out of sight on the right and left flanks while others made up a rearguard trailing the force by about a kilometre. Another complement of warriors scouted some way ahead, and it was one of these men who came running up to Mgobozi at the head of the column.

The general raised his swallow-tail axe high, signalling a halt. Accompanied by his udibi, the Induna joined Mgobozi. "What is it, General?" he asked.

"Who knows!" growled Mgobozi. "Perhaps these fools have lost their way again."

"General!" said the scout, coming to attention.

"What is it?"

"General . . . I am not sure . . ."

"Are we being attacked, Nkondo?"

"No, General!"

"You have grown lonely and have come to seek the warmth of my company, the comfort of my foot up your backside?"

"Hai! No, General!"

"Then I am truly at a loss, Nkondo. Spare me from the misery of not knowing the cause of your foolishness."

"General?"

"Nkondo," interjected the Induna, "the general would know what you have to report."

Nkondo met the Induna's eyes. "Nduna . . ." he began. Then he turned and pointed: "Look!"

"At what?" asked the Induna mildly.

Nkondo turned back to him. "You will see, Nduna," glancing nervously in Mgobozi's direction, "General . . . You will see . . ."

What they saw, a few moments later, was five of their scouts heading towards them . . .

Five Zulus and three others. A boy, a man and a greybeard.

As the group drew closer, it soon became apparent the three strangers were moving at their own infuriating pace. The Induna could see by the gait of the warriors – the way the one behind repeatedly stepped sideways to avoid bumping into the soldier in front and the way the scout bringing up the rear would pause, wait for the party to get ahead before striding forward again – that the Zulus were impatient at the slowness of that pace. Why didn't they hurry the strangers along? It was as if they were guarding them. Were they dignitaries come to meet the Zulus? Not likely. As far as the Induna knew, there were no settlements in the area.

"What nonsense is this?" growled Mgobozi.

"I – we – know not, General. We encountered them a short while ago," said Nkondo.

"Did you not stop them?" asked Mgobozi. "Question them?"

"We tried, General."

"You tried? What do you mean – you *tried*? Either you did or you didn't!"

"We tried, General. But . . ."

"But?" asked the Induna, taking pity on the scout's stricken expression.

"We tried, Nduna, but they . . . They ignored us."

"What?"

"General, it is so. They were not threatening. They just . . . It was as if they could not see us!"

"What nonsense is this!" growled Mgobozi once more.

It was the last thing he said for several minutes.

*

Shaka has sent his army north over the Drakensberg mountain range, known to the People Of The Sky as Ukhahlamba, the Barrier Of Spears, saying: "Let us see who skulks on the other side of the stockade."

They are now in the foothills of the Maluti Mountains. The highveld: rolling prairie, green and singing in the summer, dead and frostbitten in the winter. With the cold months approaching, the grass is fading into the brown of dying wheat. Sandstone cliffs recline in the distance; sculptured by the wind, worked by the water, eroded into deep gorges and valleys guarded by towering precipices.

This is the land of the Sotho. Whereas the Nguni people reached the southern tip of the continent by moving due south, the Sothos came in diagonally, from the west, settling first in what would later become known as Botswana. Like the Nguni nations they existed chiefly by hunting, tilling the soil and rearing cattle, but their language was incomprehensible and their beliefs alien. They said humans and animals had emerged from a hole in the ground, the humans last, obliterating the tracks of the animals, thereby reducing their numbers. They also venerated totems, a practice unknown among the Zulus and Xhosas. Thus, those who revered the life-giving fokeng, or dew, became the Bafokeng. Those who became adept at working metal took the name of Morolong, the chief who legend said taught them the craft, and became the Barolong. Those whose totem was the crocodile became the Bakwena. In order to propitiate the gods and spirits of a people they had defeated, another group adopted those spirits as their totem, took the name of the tribe they had bested and became the Bapedi.

Then there were the various clans comprising the Bahurutshe who built their settlements on steep slopes and revered the baboons who roamed their villages . . .

*

On and on they came. Closer and closer. A father, a son and a grandson. The greybeard bow-legged and hunched beneath the skin of a wildebeest. The son tall, slender, wearing a ragged loincloth, with a cloak rolled up and slung diagonally across his chest, a satchel made from the udder of a cow hanging from his shoulder. The boy, as skinny as his father, carrying a sack over his shoulder. Both of the adults clutched a bundle of long hunting spears.

On and on they came, walking slowly, but with purpose, wayfarers who still have a long path ahead. There was nothing threatening about their demeanour. They seemed oblivious; unconcerned with anything but their journey.

And there was something else: the two adults were talking. Talking in low, anxious tones in the strange language of the region. Tones at odds with their manner.

As they drew nearer the column, the scouts halted, leaving the strangers to come on alone.

Mgobozi opened his mouth to say something, then shut it – in disbelief.

Clearly he'd noticed it, too, decided the Induna. For as they drew closer it was obvious the three weren't simply unaware of the Zulus' presence, they weren't blind, they were actively trying to ignore the warriors. It was particularly evident in the two adults – they were looking everywhere but at the men. No mean feat, as they came ever closer to a column of warriors five men wide.

With the child it was different. The child, noted the Induna, kept sneaking glances, then looking away. He also saw that, when the father spotted this, his tone would become urgent; eventually he laid a hand on the boy's shoulder, fingers tightening, as though to keep him walking in a straight line.

Because that's what they were doing: walking straight at the Zulus, muttering all the while.

It was Mgobozi's action that governed the way the men behind him reacted.

Making to step forward to intercept the three, then thinking better of it, he seemed to have been rendered mute. A remarkable state for the cantankerous general.

And if the Induna had not been there to witness for himself what happened next, he wouldn't have believed it.

Mgobozi gaped, made to stop the trio, and then . . .

He stepped aside.

And first Nkondo, then the Induna followed suit, pulling the udibi with him.

And the three strangers walked past them, almost brushing them.

Walked past them – and *through* the Zulu ranks, the warriors jostling each other to move aside.

The Induna stared down the gap that had opened up. Without exception all the warriors had turned to follow this strange passage.

Standing next to the Induna, Mgobozi had his hand raised, like someone who's just forgotten what he was about to say. And the Zulus parted, shields scraping against bodies, spears raised, the blades pointing skyward, wavering like long grass in a sudden gust of wind. Toes were stamped on, curses hissed, elbows jabbed sides, but the ranks parted and the three strangers made their way down the centre.

Then the greybeard, the son and the grandson were beyond the column – and only the child looked back, briefly, before his father's hand closed over his shoulder again.

Five hundred heavily armed Zulus, give or take, stood staring for many long minutes until the three strangers were lost in the distant greenery.

It was Mgobozi who broke the reverie.

"Well, fuck me," he said.

*

The Induna started issuing orders. The boy was to go immediately to the rearguard and tell them to wait for the three travellers. They were to hide and, if they saw the trio pass, they were to leave one of their udibis

295

behind and follow the strangers until nightfall. If the soldiers didn't encounter the group, then obviously that would mean the three had turned off somewhere between the main column and the rearguard.

This would make it easier for the Induna to pick up their trail when he went after them – and follow them he knew he must. For this reason, his udibi had to run quickly, skirting the three and remaining unseen. When he'd delivered his master's orders, he was to return immediately, once more avoiding the travellers.

The Induna also instructed two other udibis to go and find the skirmishers out on the left and right flanks, who were to halt, go to ground and wait for further instructions. Nkondo and the five men he sent back to the scouting party with the same orders.

Then, with the help of his fellow officers, the Induna restored order to the ranks of the column. They would leave the track and take up a defensive position about a kilometre to the east, where distant bushes fringed the plain and they could vanish amid the greenery and shadows.

"We will not be taken by surprise," said the Induna, reporting back to Mgobozi when the column was in place and picquets had been posted.

"*Again*, you mean," muttered Mgobozi.

"That is true, General," grinned the Induna.

"Nduna – speak the truth! Perhaps it is best I retired and allowed my wives to terrorise me into the grave. Did my eyes deceive me?"

"That," said the Induna, "was exceedingly strange!"

"Aiee, Nduna! Strange is . . . Strange is . . ."

"A weak brew in the circumstances?"

"Yes. What we have just witnessed . . ."

The general shook his head. "After that, I would welcome strange. I would embrace it as a comely maiden!"

"They were talking, General – did you hear?"

Mgobozi nodded. "We have some who can understand this savage tongue, I believe?"

The Induna turned, signalled. The warrior hovering nearby, but out of earshot, jogged forward and came to attention.

"Thando, son of Khahlamba, the Hunter," said Mgobozi. "Yes . . . You speak this language?"

"A little, General, for my father hunted in these parts."

"He did more than that, for he was a man who hankered after open spaces. Hunting was simply an excuse. He longed to explore new territory."

Thando agreed this was so – and he'd accompanied his father on these expeditions, some of which had lasted several months.

"And you understood what these three were saying?" asked Mgobozi.

He could make out a little, said the warrior. "They are Sothos, General. Of this region. Hunters, possibly."

"Are you sure they were Sothos?"

"Yes, General!"

"I had my doubts," said Mgobozi, addressing the Induna. Izilwane they might be, he added, using the Zulu word for beasts, an epithet applied to all those who were not Zulus. But if they were indeed Sothos that meant they weren't . . .

"Otherworldly?" suggested the Induna. Or ghosts, he might have added, but he wasn't going to encourage such speculation. There were many other paths to explore before one sought out that route. The men were unsettled enough.

"Yes," said the general. "An acceptable supposition, surely, given the way they reacted to us."

"Or didn't react," added the Induna.

Who hadn't heard of the Zulus? Who didn't fear them? Certainly, most of the tribes that comprised the Sotho people had come into contact with Shaka's mighty empire.

"Yet, these three . . ." Mgobozi shook his head.

"What were they saying?" asked the Induna.

Thando shrugged. Said it was mere chitchat. They gave no indication they were aware they were walking through a heavily armed Zulu impi.

The two officers stood in silence a while after dismissing Thando. A gentle breeze rustled the leaves. Nothing moved on the plain. High above, an eagle rode the thermals, its wings outstretched.

"It was as if they didn't see us!" said Mgobozi.

"Or didn't *want* to see us, General," murmured the Induna.

2

The Boy

The dry leaf slides over smooth rock, suddenly picking up speed, for the water flows rapidly here – crackling, streaked with silver. The leaf tilts, then spins into the pool. Sent sideways by the current, it twirls past the boulders that buttress the bank, and gets caught up in a clump of twigs and other detritus that's followed the same path. Plump fish doze in the dappled light. If disturbed, they'll make a break for it, shattering the surface as they skate over the slippery rock to drop into the next pool.

Sepeng reckons he can catch some of those fish if he can find the right spot – a pool with a shallow outlet he can dam with a few rocks. Then the fish will have nowhere to go.

He's done his chores, collected firewood and left his father and grandfather wading in one of the pools higher up with their spears. Now, out of sight of the adults, he too wants to catch some fish. It's the kind of challenge any little boy might set himself – to match the accomplishments of the grown-ups and show that he, too, is a man – but it's also a welcome distraction.

What he saw earlier today . . .

Those men . . .

Warriors, with shields and spears . . .

Broad shoulders, fierce faces . . .

And his father, pulling him along. Not seeking to assuage his fear, ignoring his questions, pretending it never happened.

Which confuses the boy. Because they *were* there. He saw them.

His father and grandfather may have acted like the men weren't there, but they couldn't hide their fear. Their unease. They've both been quiet since the incident, but their alarm and apprehension have been obvious, undercutting their attempts to ignore the whole thing.

Perhaps this pool . . .

There are several fish, plump and immobile on the bottom. Sensing movement, Sepeng looks up.

And sees the Induna squatting on his haunches on the other side of the pool, less than two metres away.

In his shock, Sepeng topples backward. Tries to stand. But Thando's behind him, gripping his shoulders. As the child struggles, twisting this way and that, Thando tightens his grip while, across the way, the Induna raises his finger to his lips.

Be quiet, little one. Be calm! whispers Thando, speaking a Sotho dialect.

Sepeng kicks out, splattering mud across the water and causing the fish to dart away.

Then he remembers to scream –

Takes a deep breath –

Instantly, with a roughness the Induna had hoped to avoid, Thando clamps his left hand over the child's mouth, smothering the scream.

"Tell him again," says the Induna.

Be quiet, little one. We don't want to hurt you.

Sepeng goes limp. Almost passes out, in fact. The shock. To hear one of these strangers – these men who don't exist – speaking his language, speaking to him, is like suddenly being able to understand the sounds a dog makes.

Fearing the child might have fainted, Thando releases his grip somewhat – and Sepeng comes alive again.

Easy, easy, whispers Thando.

Gently, he twists Sepeng to the right.

Another boy, a few years older than him!

"His name," says the Induna.

Be quiet, little one. We don't want to hurt you. We just want to talk to you. Tell us your name. I will let you speak, but you must be quiet and tell us only your name.

The udibi nods encouragingly.

Will you be quiet, little one? Can I take my hand away? Will you speak only to tell us your name?

His eyes fixed on the older boy, Sepeng nods, his chin bumping Thando's forearm.

Carefully, Thando moves his hand.

Tell us your name, he whispers.

Sepeng.

"He says his name is Sepeng, Nduna."

He will see me. He will see me . . . talking . . . Because He is everywhere. Knows all. Controls all. We live in the palm of His hand. All is His. Except . . .

"Who?" asks Thando. "Who will see you?"

The boy is limp in his arms.

They are here, he whispers. *And if they are here, where is the Other? Is this a test? How can they be here without the Other . . . without the Other knowing? Is it my fault?* Sepeng asks the udibi. *Have I done something wrong? Am I being punished? But it is they who talk to me. What can I do?*

About what? asks Thando.

"Thando?"

"Nduna, I can't be sure, but I think he's speaking about us. But there's someone else who's watching him." Thando glances around nervously. "Perhaps watching *us*!"

"Cha! There is no one. But he will be missed!"

"I understand, Nduna."

Addressing Sepeng once more, Thando asks who is watching him.

Does he watch us, too?

He is everywhere. Sees all that we do. Knows our thoughts. He is everywhere!

Who? asks Thando.

They are asking questions, says Sepeng, still speaking to the Induna's udibi. Maybe he can explain it all. *They want to know these things. Why?*

What do they want? He is all, He is everything, but they are here. Did He send them?

No one sent us, says Thando.

They say no one sent them, but this cannot be! Nothing can happen without His knowledge, His permission. Nothing exists beyond Him. His realm is all.

Yet here we are, says Thando. *Who are you talking about?*

How can they ask such a question? Those who are of the Other would not ask such a pointless question. Yet . . .

Who are you talking about? asks Thando. His voice is insistent. He knows they don't have much time.

The Other. The Baboon God. The All. The Everything and Everywhere.

Slowly, falteringly, Sepeng tries to explain as best he can.

*

"I am not sure I understand him, Nduna," says Thando later, after they've sent Sepeng back to his father and grandfather. "He uses their word for a god, then he speaks of a baboon. It is as if the two are one . . ."

"A baboon god?" asks the boy.

"Yes. And they have no need to worship him, Nduna. Because he is everything. And everywhere." Thando shrugs. "That's what the child seemed to say."

"Meaning, perhaps, this god exists despite and in *spite* of their beliefs," suggests the Induna.

A baboon god who is everywhere. A god who has chosen these people. Whether they like it or not . . . They can do nothing without his sanction . . . He did not tell these three the Zulu army would be there, so they ignored the warriors.

Yes! The Induna nods to himself. Mgobozi said he thought they might be ghosts – but we were the ghosts in that encounter! We were the supernatural creatures because we were beyond their experience.

The Zulu warriors were not of their world, the world of this baboon god.

How confused they must have been! How bewildered! How frightened!

Except for the child, Sepeng. He's still too young to be fully a part of this god's world. So he could "see" the warriors in a way the adults could not. The warriors were more real to him.

It's almost enough to make one roar with laughter – the way five hundred heavily armed Zulus meet three Sothos – and both parties think they've encountered something otherworldly. And the Sothos merely keep on walking, talking all the while to vanquish their fear, while the five hundred look on, open-mouthed . . .

Almost enough to have one rolling on the ground with laughter. Except for that fear.

*

Sepeng knows they are following, and twice he starts to dawdle, slowing his pace until his father and grandfather are out of sight among the low, twisted trees and squat aloes. Then he stops and waits for the Zulus.

"Having once tried not to see us, this young one is now trying to avail himself of every opportunity to feast his eyes!" chuckled the Induna, after the first time they persuaded Sepeng to hurry on and rejoin his family.

When it happened a second time, however, the Induna grew impatient. They were never going to reach the Sothos' destination at this rate.

They wait with the child. Soon enough, they hear Sepeng's father calling. Gently, the Induna nudges the child, indicating he should go to his father.

Who comes to a halt further down the path. The Induna grins with satisfaction: this time there can be no mistake. He has seen them. Indeed, his gaze has drifted past Sepeng and now it's as if he's trying to hold the Zulus in place with desperate, frightened eyes. The Induna's grin evaporates. Such fear! Such naked terror! Yet the father does not move. He doesn't try to call his son, tell him to come here quickly! He doesn't try to rush over to Sepeng, bundle him up and carry him away to safety. Neither does he try to accost the Zulus, get between them and his son . . .

"Tell him," whispers the Induna, "tell him we are friends."

Thando nods, calls out to the father.

We are friends, says Thando. *We mean you no harm.*

The man remains stricken.

It is true, Father! says Sepeng. *They have spoken to me. They are not Him!*

At this, at the mention of this "Him", the father darts forward, grabs Sepeng by the arm and pulls his son away.

*

It's hours later and the ridge they've been approaching looms over them. The man and the greybeard are waiting in the shade of a tree. The three Zulus stop some distance away. They watch as Sepeng tries to speak to the two adults, gesticulating, pointing at the Zulus, begging and pleading. Ignoring him, the father starts up the path that zigzags among the rocks on its way to the top of the ridge. The greybeard lingers longer, though, studying the Zulus while Sepeng babbles away. To the Induna it looks as if he's about to address them. But then the grandfather thinks better of it and, saying something to the child, sets off after the younger man.

Sepeng is trembling and confused when the Zulus reach him.

What did the old one say? asks Thando.

Sepeng gazes up the path, at the hunched back of his grandfather. *He says we are all dead.*

3
The Caldera

A giant has reached into the rocky earth to scoop out this caldera, his fingernails scoring furrows in the cliffs even as they were being formed.

As far as the Induna can see, lingering atop the ridge while the others make the descent, this is the only route in and out. A large butte dominates the centre of the depression and the Induna is surprised to note some dwellings on the flat-topped summit. Six structures: one large, thatched, circular hut and five smaller rectangular buildings made of stone.

The vegetation on the floor of the valley is sparse. Threadbare brown grass struggles to survive amid stony swathes the colour of old leather. There are no trees – merely strangely shaped outcrops, with rounded contours, like large dollops of dried mud. Shelves of rock, resting askew, create an impression of incompleteness, of windswept abandonment.

A second, larger settlement is nestled in the northwestern arc of the basin, where the slope is shallower, sandier. Stone houses with flat roofs made from poles lashed together. A kraal housing a dozen head of cattle; a small herd given the size of the umuzi. Rectangular vegetable patches barely discernible amid the surrounding soil.

The Induna redirects his attention to the butte; here, he can make out a cluster of figures standing on the rim. They appear to be drinking – passing gourds back and forth – and such are the acoustics of the caldera, he can hear echoes of laughter. A strange contrast to the lethargy of the village . . .

It's a long, strung-out procession that makes its way down the path that zigzags to the valley floor. The two Sotho men stride ahead with new-found energy and the determined gait of those whose journey is near its end. Several metres behind them come Sepeng, the boy and Thando. Even further behind, only just now leaving his vantage point, is the Induna.

Once they reach the floor, the Sotho men slow down a little. Perhaps they want to give Sepeng one more chance to catch up to them and cease his foolishness. But they don't stop and when Sepeng and his companions reach the trail that runs along the foot of the cliffs to the village, the two men are still some paces ahead.

The boy falls in step alongside Sepeng.

"Ask him, Thando," he says, glancing over his shoulder, "if this is where his village is."

Thando obliges and the udibi is looking expectantly at Sepeng when there's a whistle, a strange, squelching "Thwuck!" and Sepeng's head jerks sideways. Almost at the same time there's a distant crack. But the boy barely notices it. He's staring down at Sepeng. Staring at the wide, unseeing eyes. The open mouth; lips glistening with blood. The neat hole in the side of his head.

Thando has dropped into a crouch, raised his shield. "Here!" he hisses. "Over here!"

The boy leaps over the body and drops down next to Thando.

The body!

They were walking along –

And then that sound –

That horrible sound –

These three things happening almost simultaneously – a whistling hiss that became a sickening impact – a squelching "Thwuck!", strangely truncated, like a pebble thrown with great force into a puddle of mud – that became a force, an invisible force, knocking Sepeng sideways . . .

"Thando," whispers the boy. "What was that?"

"I don't know," says the warrior, his eyes seeking movement among the boulders and outcrops.

Shouting.

It's the father, sprinting towards them.

Thando and the boy stand. Maybe the danger has passed – the father's behaviour seems to indicate that; and Zulus will not cower while others show no fear. Nonetheless, Thando keeps his shield half-raised, his iklwa at the ready.

The father is cradling his son, weeping and crooning, when the Induna arrives at a run.

"What happened?"

Thando shrugs. "We do not know, Nduna."

The Induna gazes up at the butte. Further along the path and higher than the others, he'd heard the crack more clearly. It had been like a snapping twig. And he'd seen a puff of smoke from the edge of the pinnacle.

More shouts. The grandfather is returning with the villagers. There are a few women – one, obviously Sepeng's mother, joining her husband with a wail – but most are men, and all are armed with long hunting spears. These are, of course, far flimsier than the Zulus' short, stabbing assegais, but they're no less dangerous for all that.

And within seconds the Induna, the boy and Thando find themselves encircled on three sides by a lethal, shifting palisade.

The Induna waits until the father has carried Sepeng away, then he speaks. "Tell them, Thando," he says, raising his voice, "tell them we would happily accept the hospitality they proffer, but then we Zulus would be obliged to reciprocate in kind!"

Thando is just about to speak when an elderly man makes his way to the front of the Sothos. Taller than the others, he has a lean, broad-shouldered body and grey hair. "Hai, hai, hai," he says. "Easy! Easy! Easy, Brothers!" Pushing aside a spear he positions himself between the Zulus and the bigger group of men.

The Induna steps forward. "You speak our language."

"And why not?" says the man. "I am Sakhile, son of Dumane, of the Khulani clan. Or I was, until Jama's anger suggested I seek my fortune elsewhere."

He is speaking of Shaka's grandfather.

"Yes," says Thando, "my father knew you. I am Thando, son of Khahlamba."

Sakhile beams with recognition. "I knew him well and now I see him in you. He was a young man when I showed him the trails that led to plentiful game."

"Now you are here," says the Induna.

"Yes, here to warn you. Fight and you *will* die!" Sakhile holds up a hand. "I do not impugn your courage. Far from it. You will slaughter all these calves, and they are like calves. For all that they outnumber you, they tremble in fear."

"As they should!"

"Yes, Brother, but it is not *you* they fear."

The Induna's eyes narrow. "Speak you of those . . ."

"Aiee, do not look there. Do not even turn your head! Look at me, look at the trembling spears behind me, but do not look there! Know this: slaughter these you might, but that will not be the end of the matter! You will die, regardless. Yes, I see the anger in your eyes. But you *must* listen to me! These calves behind me, they come not to fight – although fight they will, fight they *must*, if you would have it so. But that is not their intention. They would take you captive . . ."

"Captive!" hisses the Induna.

Sakhile's hands come up. "In a manner of speaking, Brother. I will see to it that you are not disarmed. But you must go with them. You must go with them *now*! Every breath you take here might be your last! You are in grave peril. More than that, we are *all* in grave peril!"

"Cha! So speaks an outlaw and refugee!"

"You suspect treachery – hai, then I will position myself so that mine is the first body your assegais feast upon. Let that allay your suspicions! But you must come with us now!" Sakhile's voice is low, urgent.

The Induna nods. "So be it! Blood spilt now or later, it doesn't matter to me. We will accompany you."

Sakhile says something to the gathered Sothos in their own language. They appear to relax. But as Sakhile leads the Zulus into the crowd, the men part and then surround them.

"Master!" says Thando nervously.

"Stay calm, but be alert," whispers the Induna.

As they draw nearer the village, the Induna leans closer to Sakhile. And says a single word: "Isibhamu?"

The older man nods. "More than one, alas!"

4
The Baboons

"Look! See? They return," says a cousin called Phopho.

"What? Get out of the way!" Kamohelo, also known as the Baboon God, and in fact wearing a headdress made from the skin of a baboon, the skull intact, with fangs bared, pushes aside two other cousins.

"Ho!" he says. "And see how they stagger underneath the weight of all the buck they've killed."

He raises a gourd to his lips, drinks, swallows some of the beer, and spits out the rest over the edge of the precipice. "Slovenly fools! Lazy ingrates!"

"Weren't they merely seeking spoor?" inquires a nephew called Labang.

"Shurrup!"

Handing his gourd to Phopho, Kamohelo turns to address the others. "What say you, Brothers, we teach them the error of their ways!"

All except Labang nod enthusiastically.

"Thabo!" bellows Kamohelo. "Bring it!"

One of the weapons carriers, and always expected to be ready, Thabo comes running, carrying two muskets. Kamohelo hops off the ledge, takes one of the guns from the teenager and moves along to where the ledge merges into a low, flat rock. Awkwardly, holding his head back so the baboon's arms and legs don't flop across his face, Kamohelo lowers himself onto the rock. Slotting the stock against his shoulder, he rests the barrel on a log. It's been placed there for just such a purpose and is held secure by a pile of stones.

Now the limp arms and legs obscure his vision. Kamohelo first shakes his head and then wrenches the headdress off, tossing it aside. "Which one is it to be?" he asks.

"The little one," suggests one of the cousins, nudging another cousin, his brother. Kamohelo is just drunk enough to permit such facetiousness.

"Yes," says the brother. "The little one."

Hearing the sniggers in their voices, Kamohelo glares at them over his shoulder. "You would test me?" he growls.

The culprits shrug. "You asked," says one innocently.

"You think I could not drop him from this distance?"

"No, no! It is merely a feat we would dearly like to witness."

"Show them," says Phopho. "Show these fools!"

Kamohelo sights down the barrel. "Ha! You would have to tell me which little one, for there are two."

Phopho looks, sees Kamohelo is right. "The littlest one!" he says. "Show them!"

Kamohelo grips the gun tightly – the White Man's weapon the Zulus know as isibhamu – aims, sucks in a breath . . .

And squeezes the trigger.

Instantly, he's on his hands and knees, peering through the smoke.

"Did I drop him, Phopho? Did I drop him?"

"Indeed! See how the others panic!"

"Yes! You're right! What say you to that, eh?" says Kamohelo, turning around triumphantly. "What say you?"

"I say you are a fool, Big Brother." Takatso has joined the party. He stands with his arms folded. Only he can address the Baboon God in such a manner.

Kamohelo chuckles, trying to make light of the chastisement. "What do you mean, Little Brother?" he asks.

"See for yourself!"

Kamohelo turns around to survey the scene below.

He shrugs. Stretches his arm in Phopho's direction. Accepts the gourd. Takes a swallow. Shrugs again. Turns back to face his brother. "A cunning riddle, Little Brother. Enlighten us!"

"You see nothing unusual?"

Kamohelo's features harden. He values his brother's intelligence too much to lift a finger against him, but sometimes Takatso goes too far. "As I said, Little Brother: enlighten us!"

"Three left, Kamohelo, seeking spoor. See how many have returned . . ."

Slowly, almost solemnly, Kamohelo regards the figures on the path once more. How many . . .? Counting's never been one of his strong points – but there *do* seem to be more people down there than there should be.

Seeking to spare his brother more embarrassment, Takatso shoulders his way through the others and joins Kamohelo on the rock. "There are more than three, aren't there?" he says softly.

Phopho lets out a low whistle, a sign he too has at last spotted the discrepancy.

"Thabo!"

Takatso grimaces at the bellow, lays a hand on his brother's shoulder. "What are you doing?"

"Let us work our way back to three again," says Kamohelo.

Takatso brings his lips close to his brother's ear. "No," he whispers.

"No?" asks Kamohelo.

"No. That would be . . ." Takatso lowers his voice even further: "Foolish!"

"Who are they?" asks the nephew.

"Strangers," says Kamohelo.

"Maybe," says Takatso.

Kamohelo shoots him a frown. "Who else could they be?"

"If they are who I think they are, then there are many more where those come from. Many more!"

*

They were led into one of the huts halfway up the slope, and two men were chosen to stand guard outside, which the boy considered pointless since they had still not been disarmed.

Thando also noticed this absurdity and asked Sakhile about the guards.

"Things have to be seen to be done," was the Zulu's cryptic response.

Then Sakhile was on his hands and knees, digging by the rear wall of the hut. Was he also, suddenly, a prisoner?

Soon he had uncovered an opening that might have been a rear entrance before shifting sand blocked it. He then shouted something in Sotho and a few minutes later, gourds of water and a pot of porridge were pushed through the hole.

The boy was puzzled. The dwelling had a perfectly good doorway . . .

"And some things ought not to be seen," said Sakhile, handing the Induna a gourd.

The shadows lengthened and darkness came fast to the valley. Sakhile had just lit a small fire in the centre of the hut when the guards outside shouted a salute and the older man ducked through the door.

Sakhile stood immediately and the other three followed his lead.

*

"Zulus?"

Takatso nods. "It was only a matter of time."

All except the sentries have gathered in the main hut amid the stone structures atop the rock.

"Only a matter of time," says Labang, who regards himself as one of Takatso's favourites.

They know of Shaka's kingdom, of course, have to trek through part of his territory to reach the White Men who trade at Delagoa Bay.

"Well, then," says Kamohelo, "let them come!"

"It is not a case of you letting them come, Brother. Or . . ." Takatso allows his gaze to take in the others, ". . . of anyone being afraid. Come they will, regardless! Of that there can be no doubt!"

One of the sentries appears at the door.

Takatso looks up. "What is it, Zeba?"

"The strangers remain under guard in one of the huts."

"Have they given them food? Water?"

Zeba nods. "They thought they were being clever, but we saw them."

"Good. Report to me at sunset. I would know the situation."

The sentry nods and returns to his post.

"At least our little sheep still fear their shepherds!" says Kamohelo.

"Yet they allow the jackals into their kraal."

"That *is* worrying," agrees Labang.

Kamohelo cuffs him. "Fool! Did not my brother say they were not to be harmed!" Then Kamohelo frowns. "Yet, Takatso, you seem to be saying another thing now."

"I suggested *you* take no further hand in the matter, Big Brother. With those down there, that is a different story. They took the Zulus captive and in this they seemed to show loyalty to us – but why did they not slaughter the Zulus then and there?"

"Because they are cowards and layabouts," says Phopho. "You know that, Takatso. They have to be goaded, prodded into doing what is expected of them."

"This is so," says Takatso. "But who is doing the prodding now?"

"Prodding?" says Kamohelo. "I'll do more than prod if they presume to turn against us."

"Do you think that's a possibility, Takatso?" asks one of the other cousins.

"But we have their totem!" says someone else.

"Yes," adds Kamohelo. "And am I not the god of that totem? And what is our power, compared to those Zulu savages?"

Takatso nods absently. That's just the problem: the answer to that question might not be as self-evident as his brother believes it to be. He might exercise a restraining influence on his older brother, but just like Kamohelo he's grown lazy. Careless. They've all underestimated the villagers' discontent. Those who would speak out against the Baboon God remain a minority, but now that they have strangers in their midst their influence will have grown even more baleful.

A little later he has more kindling to add to his unease. Zeba, the sentry, returns with a report from one of their informers in the village: "He says they talk."

"With who?" asks Takatso. "That old troublemaker?"

"Yes."

"We should have fed that old bastard to the vultures a long time ago," grumbles Kamohelo, after Zeba has returned to his post. "Now he fills their ears with lies!"

*

It was in the time of my father's grandfather and a great drought was upon the land (says the old man). We faced many enemies. There was the sun, blazing ceaselessly, drying the soil, making ash of our crops. We had a waterhole, but how long would it last? We had a little food, but marauders roamed the land. And worse –

Yes, my friends, it was the time of the cannibals. Men whose hunger had driven them to eat the flesh of other men. But their hunger was not to be sated. Once they had feasted their fill, a new hunger came over them. They found they liked the taste of human flesh and would not be satisfied with anything else.

One day, a large band of these monsters attacked and we were sorely put to defend ourselves. By sunset we would be torn apart and in the bellies of the mad ones. So it would have been, had not a band of wanderers come to our aid. Catching the cannibals by surprise, attacking from the rear, they helped us to defeat them.

We were grateful. And afraid. Perhaps these newcomers were merely clearing the way. And, indeed, those who thought this, suspected this, even at the risk of being deemed ungrateful, and my father's grandfather was one of these – well, they would be proved right. In time.

At first the headman thanked the strangers, sang their praises, and they laid aside their weapons and we rested our spears against the walls of our huts and we feasted with what little we could muster. Then the strangers sang our praises, thanked us for our generosity, the sacrifices we'd made so they could dine well. At which point the headman did a foolish thing – but how was he to know? The strangers' praise shamed him, for had they not saved the village? Perhaps he felt the need to boast a little. Whatever the reason, he told them of our waterhole, which ran deep, beyond the reach of the sun's rage. Although it wasn't much, we were able to feed ourselves if we were careful enough.

Now these strangers . . . They comprised a clan, a family, of many brothers, mainly, with their sisters and wives. Their leader, their father, was a man called Raboshabane. He it was who built the dwellings atop the tall rock. He it was who said they would settle here and watch over us. Together we would be strong enough to see off any number of cannibals and marauders! Our supplies of food we would store on the rock, in his safekeeping. There no one could touch it.

Aiee! Was a truer word ever said? But we knew not what horrors awaited us. We did not think to examine our saviours. And guided by fear – and yes, the beguiling tongue of Raboshabane – we agreed.

We agreed, friends, even though the rock was a sacred place to us. It was the home of the baboons, in whose form the Great Spirit had chosen to reveal himself to us, and the place where the life-giving water rose to the surface. But what better place, urged Raboshabane. The stronghold of the baboons would become our stronghold. And despite the warnings of others, my father's grandfather included, the headman even handed over the sacred totem – the Baboon God.

*

Takatso gives the rhino horn that's fallen off the heap a desultory kick. Look at this! Once they could gather a mountain of ivory within a few months – which is partly why they built this fortified compound at the northern base of the huge outcrop. Now it's as if the elephant and rhino know to avoid these environs and their hunters have to range further and further afield, increasing the risk of coming into contact with other tribes – strangers who might lead them to question their continued devotion to this Baboon God.

Meanwhile, their patrons, the Portuguese at Delagoa, have grown increasingly impatient, ever more distressed at the low yields brought in by their investment – of shot, muskets and alcohol, mostly.

Perhaps it's time to move on. After all, when the ground grows barren, you seek fertile soil elsewhere.

Takatso chuckles – the ground here is certainly barren.

Move on.

These villagers – layabouts and cowards, Phopho called them – they can keep in check. Invaders from other clans – well, none are left in the region, they put paid to that threat years ago. But the Zulu army – that's a different prospect altogether.

Their fortress will become their tomb. They have food aplenty, oh yes, but the villagers won't help them and sooner or later their supplies will run out. That's assuming the Zulus even bother to wait. They command the heights – fifty, a hundred men they can see off, but a sustained assault by the thousands who swell Shaka's impis? No.

But in moving on, they'll become the refugees they despise. Shiftless. Homeless. Prey to anyone whose path they cross.

Then again, perhaps the decision is no longer theirs to make. The Zulus are here already. An advance party to untold numbers.

Maybe all that's left is to stand their ground – and die like men.

*

How cunning this Raboshabane was. He listened to the headman and heard how precious the totem was. More precious than food even, said the headman. How Raboshabane and his sons must have laughed when they were alone. Mirth louder than thunder. For, of course, they saw that this was not so. As valuable as the talisman might have been, the food that sustained us was worth more! Besides, what would the totem have been worth were we all dead from hunger and there was no one to revere it? Raboshabane realised this and having already taken our precious food into his safekeeping, it was easy to persuade the headman to hand over the talisman. Where better than his stronghold to place the valuable object?

Aiee! That's another thing. It was what finally convinced my father's grandfather his suspicions were correct. Somehow, this stronghold that Raboshabane had said would protect us all became *his* stronghold!

And, of course, the totem *was* precious. Food and water, these were more valuable, it is so, but the totem was valuable in another way. It inspired awe, instilled loyalty, commanded obedience. Raboshabane realised this, too. But he would bide his time. And, for a while, it seemed we were blessed. More cannibals came – they were killed. As were marauders from other tribes, who were but one missed meal away from being cannibals themselves. Then the drought passed. The rains came. We rejoiced. Gave praise to the Baboon God, our Protector. And many were those who began to confuse the Baboon God with the men in the stronghold.

Aiee! We had been too busy looking beyond these cliffs to note what had been going on under our very noses. My father's father was one of those who rebelled, who refused to turn over his hard-won produce to the family on the rock – and, along with the others, he was killed when the brothers came down from the rock to collect what they now claimed was rightfully theirs. And they sneered, called the rest of the village ungrateful for daring to challenge the Baboon God.

So the years passed. Raboshabane died and was succeeded by his eldest son, who, on his deathbed, handed the totem to *his* eldest son . . . There were more droughts, this valley became ever more barren, and we were forced to become hunters. This pleased the men on the rock, the Baboon God, and the tribute they now demanded was ivory. So the years passed, and there were other interlopers to fight off, and some of us lost sight of the fact the brothers defended us only in the way a man and his sons defend a herd of cattle; a matter of protecting wealth, rather than lives. Some, many, too many, friends, saw them as the saviours they claimed to be. And this is so today. We are prisoners here, but many would deny that fact. Born into captivity, captivity is all they know.

Dark days, friends. But do not think too harshly of us. It is difficult to see the bonds that hold you in place if they have always been there. Even I, for a while, refused to listen to my father. I wanted to be like the brothers on the rock, for they have let some of us join them. Then my father asked me this: where are the baboons? For, as I have said, the rock was a sacred place, home to a tribe of baboons. Where had they gone? Were those who were there now baboons?

"Hai," said my father. "You have seen baboons before. Are these they? Are they? Are you such a fool?" he asked. "There are no baboons on the rock – only men!"

5

The Promise

And these men have chosen a fine stronghold. Sheer drops, each with a slight overhang, mean the butte is virtually impregnable on three sides, even on the eastern flank, where the giant who cleared out this valley tried to split the stump. A narrow fissure has cracked the rock, and weathering has created a shoulder about a metre below the main summit. But even this is beyond the reach of all but the most skilful climber, as is the fissure, which peters out halfway down, so the shoulder remains part of the monolith. The summit is roughly rectangular and sentries patrolling the four sides will make light work of anyone who tries to scale the heights.

The only way up is on the northern flank, where a narrow chute drops in steep steps to the ground. A series of short wooden ladders make the climb easier. But a few men armed with guns, with some to load while the others fire, could hold off a multitude, could ensure that many would be sacrificed before the first attacker reached the summit.

Neither are the men at the top of the ladders the first line of defence. A compound comprising six huts and surrounded by a stout stockade of pointed poles has been built at the foot of the rock. A low watchtower guards the gate and at night, if need be, three huge bonfires situated in a semicircle several metres beyond the gate will be lit. This hasn't happened for some time, but now that the Zulus are here, both Sakhile and the old man agree this practice will be resumed.

The stockade is not only meant to guard the way to the summit. The water hole is here, too; a muddy wetness in a smear of green. The stockade is also where the clan's females reside and the ivory the villagers collect for the clan is stored – no sense in dragging it up to the top of the rock when you only have to bring it down again. Still, if heavier objects have to be hauled up, there's a ship's pulley mounted on a wooden frame at the top of the cliff – a gift from the Portuguese.

It's still light, but night is already hiding in the folds, furrows and dongas of the valley, and the western wall is engulfed in shadows when the Induna comes to the butte. Unarmed and without his shield, he wears the blue crane tail feather in his headband and the civet collar which identify him as a representative of Shaka. His udibi is with him.

Warned of the strangers' approach, the men have readied themselves for a suitable welcome. Ten arrange themselves along the northern rim, four cradling muskets; crouched out of sight are the weapons carriers with extra guns, ready to pass them on and start reloading the others should the need arise.

Wearing his baboon headdress and clutching the tribal totem, Kamohelo stands on the top step of the chute. A step below him, holding a gun, is Phopho.

The females are in the huts in the compound and Takatso has arranged a group of twelve men in a semicircle in front of the gate. Some are clutching bundles of spears, others are armed with heavy clubs and axes.

Takatso steps forward to greet the delegation. "What is this, Sakhile?" he asks. "Have you at last remembered you are a Zulu?"

"No, Master. I am merely here because I understand both tongues."

"And what are we speaking now? Did you not tell them I understand their language? Indeed, did I not learn it as a child at your knee, just as I learnt to read the spoor? It was one of many things you taught me."

"This is so. I was your humble servant."

"My father's perhaps. Never mine. To me you were as an uncle. Which is why I have shielded you many times from my brother's wrath. And is that why you are really here? To stir the pot, maybe even to gloat, now that your countrymen have found you."

"I am merely here –"

"Because you understand both tongues. Yet you know I speak your language . . ."

"I wasn't sure if you would want to reveal that fact."

"Why not, Sakhile? Surely I would not be revealing anything you haven't already told them. Neither would I be so rude as to converse in a tongue they did not understand."

He smiles and, switching to Sotho, adds: *Would I, you treacherous old leopard?*

Then, turning back to the Induna, he says: "But already I have been lured into rudeness. Where are my manners, leaving our guests standing here while we prattle on . . ."

"Indeed!" says the Induna. "I am impatient to meet this mighty Baboon God."

Takatso turns and points to Kamohelo, who stands scowling down at them, the totem – a baboon carved out of wood – resting against his shoulder.

"That is He."

"The Other, who sees and hears all?"

Takatso nods.

"Sho! He is a big baboon! And the others – are they also baboons?"

"Only when the beer flows!"

"There are many under my command of whom the same might be said," says the Induna.

"Many?"

"Many."

"When we were children, we would play a game," says Takatso. "You picked up two stones. One, you would throw at the target. If you hit it, you would place the second stone on a pile at your feet. He who had the most stones won. Would you have me start piling stones?"

The Induna shrugs. "You would prefer us to speak plainly?"

"That is the best way in these circumstances. Let us assume we can both throw with accuracy."

"Very well. You begin. For, that one up there, if he is either a baboon or a god then my shit smells sweet," says the Induna affably. "We will speak plainly only when you cease to speak of gods, or baboons, or baboons who are gods. For we are not ignorant savages."

"Stern words for one who is outnumbered."

"Cha! When I feel I am outnumbered I will stay my tongue. Maybe! But you are the one who suggested we speak plainly . . ."

Takatso inclines his head. "You are right!"

"In which case," says the Induna, "allow me to offer you my praise."

"A rare commodity, I think."

"And deserved in this instance. For this is a rare accomplishment."

"And you say this, speaking as Shaka?"

"That is so."

"Well," says Takatso, "you – and he – have my thanks. And I might say the same of Shaka's great accomplishments. And then we stand here, exchanging praises . . ."

"A tedious ritual."

Takatso spreads his hand. "Pointless."

"Yes."

"So then, Zulu, why are you *really* here?"

"Happenstance. Why does the path lead us where it does?"

"Destinations are decisions, Zulu. You decide to stay, or move on. What is your decision?"

"For now I have decided merely to slake my curiosity."

"For now."

"Yes."

"And has your curiosity been satisfied?"

"It has."

"Then you would retire to consider your options."

The Induna nods. "A good suggestion."

"Very well, you may do so, and," Takatso holds up his hand, "yes, I know you Zulus rarely need anyone's permission to do anything. I seek merely to reassure you that you may do so without fear of waking up with an assegai blade through your chest."

The Induna inclines his head. "For this I am grateful."

*

Thando returns at midday the following day. He is accompanied by two herdboys and they are driving five head of cattle. It takes them a while – using ropes tied to the horns – to guide the animals down the path that leads into the valley, and their efforts, shrouded in dust, are watched avidly by those on top of the butte.

Takatso curses.

Where is that impi?

But it is too late to send out scouts. He has a feeling that, very soon, every man will be needed.

For the same reason – and barely able to restrain his temper – he stops his brother from shooting at the new arrivals. Kill them all, even the cattle. That's Kamohelo's solution. But Takatso suggests they spare the ammunition.

"Do not whine," he says, no longer in any mood to pander to his brother's pride, "you will get your chance. And soon!"

They watch as the cattle are herded into the kraal. How much bigger they seem than the villagers' scrawny beasts. A few hours later, while the Induna looks on, the cattle are slaughtered. A crowd gathers and Takatso assumes the animals are being gutted and cleaned.

He's right – because the carcasses are then tied to poles, hanging by their hooves, and a slow procession staggers toward the rock. The animals are so well fed, it takes four villagers at each end to lift the poles and carry them at shoulder height.

Takatso is waiting at the stockade gate with five men when the Induna comes forward. "We will see what this Zulu is up to," he has told Kamohelo and the others, "then we will strike!"

"Accept these as a token of our esteem," says the Induna, indicating the swinging carcasses, "slaughtered as is our custom."

"Is it also your custom that the condemned are to enjoy a fine meal before meeting their fate?" Takatso raises a hand. Proffers a rueful grin.

"No. No need to respond. I was merely thinking aloud and would not want to seem ungrateful."

"I am not offended."

"And why should you be? We have your esteem – but not, I note, your goodwill. Still, it is better than nothing."

Takatso turns, calls for men to ready the hoist. A rope is dropped down as the villagers carry the first cow between the domed huts to the base of the precipice. One end is tied to the pole and, with the villagers helping them, the men pull on the other end, jerking the load ever higher. At the top, arms reach out and haul the carcass in. After some struggling and cursing, it's untied and the rope is dropped, ready for the next animal.

"Such fine cows!" says Takatso. "The tales we've heard have not exaggerated your wealth. And, I wonder, is that not a custom, too? Leaving some alive so that they may frighten the others with the stories they have to tell of the mighty Zulus?"

"Cha! Tall tales told merely to excuse the cowardice of the teller. And even if it were a custom – perhaps it would not apply here."

"For there are no cowards here!"

The Induna shrugs.

"Or survivors," adds Takatso. "But we have a custom too, Zulu. Ferocity in defeat. Ensuring we have many companions with us on the Great Journey."

"That I can believe. An opponent would not want it any other way."

"I envy you. For there is something that eludes *my* understanding. Something I cannot believe . . ."

"Seek you my counsel?"

"Why not? Perhaps you might enlighten me, being yourself a Zulu."

"What is it, then?"

"Why would Shaka, this mighty Bull Elephant, who tramples all underfoot, and who now rules a vast empire – why should he concern himself with an insignificant hole, where the people are somnolent and even the water tastes foul? This I cannot believe – that Shaka would risk many brave warriors to annex such a place."

"I am not privy to Shaka's motives."

"But . . .?"

"Even the tiniest thorn may cause the strongest man to limp."

"Hai! But you Zulus do not concern yourself with thorns. Your feet are tough!"

"That is *why* our feet are tough! Because we *have* concerned ourselves with thorns!"

"And a thorn remains a thorn."

"This is so. Yet a man might still survive without being deemed a coward. A wise man, a brave man, might yet win Shaka's favour."

"How? By betraying his own kind?"

"No. It is not Shaka's way to reward traitors."

"I didn't think so. How, then? How might a brave man, a wise man, win Shaka's favour in these circumstances?"

"By still being alive at the conclusion of the matter."

"Ah! Changing one's mind rather than one's allegiance."

"In a manner of speaking. In this way both parties win each other's respect."

"And the brave, wise man?"

"Will become Shaka's brave man, Shaka's wise man."

"Something to think about, Zulu. And there – see? I have thought about it. And if this man is truly wise, truly brave, he would prefer to eat his own shit than any scraps Shaka might toss him."

The Induna watches the last carcass being hauled aloft. "Indeed," he says.

6
The Stronghold

It's close to midnight when Takatso comes round to check on the sentries. Sakhile and the old man were correct: the bonfires have been lit and they blaze an arc of light around the stockade gate. Up on the rock –

Takatso climbing the ladders yet again, irritated, annoyed at the exertion, but knowing it's necessary – a sentry patrols each side. In what he knows is a vain attempt to ensure they stay awake and alert, Takatso has instructed them to keep moving. They have to check on each other. In this way Takatso hopes to ensure none go missing – "missing" in this case meaning either being overwhelmed by someone climbing up the rock – which is unlikely – or napping at his post – a very real possibility, unfortunately, for many refuse to be alarmed by the threat posed by the Zulus.

While the shifts are changed, grumbling men climbing out from underneath their warm cloaks, Takatso moves to the shelter where the carcasses have been placed. If they feast tomorrow, he'll make sure the Zulus eat first. Although he doubts they'll stoop to presenting poisoned food as a gift.

No, thinks Takatso wryly, it's something *I* might have done, not them; no, they are too arrogant . . .

Fine cows. Plump beasts. As sure a sign of Zulu wealth as anything. At least we will eat well, decides Takatso.

He strides over to where the sentries of the second shift wait, sullen and bleary-eyed. He will tell them what he expects of them – to keep moving, keep checking on each other – and try to make them see the necessity of being extra vigilant tonight.

"You will know," the Induna had said. "You will know when the time is right . . ."

The summit is a rough rectangle. The stone buildings are arranged in an L-shape, with two built along the southern rim, the one at an angle, and three down the longer western flank. Crudely constructed, they are used for storing the grain and other victuals the villagers hand over for safekeeping. The structure where the carcasses have been placed – the middle one along the western edge – simply comprises three walls. Only one, the building closest to the southwest corner, has a roof, and it is here that the clan's four weapons carriers sleep.

The large thatched hut has been erected toward the northeastern corner and stands slightly apart from the stone structures, leaving an open area in the centre of the summit. A waist-high wall of rocks circles the hut, to hold the framework in place and protect the structure from the wind.

The village is to the northwest, and a broad ledge forms a parapet down the western flank, which merges into a wide slab of rock in the northwest corner. It's from this point the men of the clan observe the comings and goings in the village and on the path that runs along the caldera's western wall. It's also where one begins the descent down the steep ledge that leads to the stockade.

Beneath the southern edge there lies the shoulder, about a metre lower than the rest of the summit: a wedge-shaped adjunct to the monolith.

The rest of the clan's men, save for those in the stockade, sleep in the large thatched hut. Lumps beneath animal-skin cloaks; beery breath mingling with the flatulence in the gloom. The fire in the centre has burnt down to a few orange embers.

Kele, patrolling the southern rim, can just make out the smooth shelf of rock about a metre below him; beyond the rock's rim: blackness.

"You will know . . ."

Takatso will spend tonight in the watchtower. With him is Labang, who would presume to be his favourite. His questions, suggestions and observations might be annoying, but he has his uses. He has agreed to remain on watch until morning and Takatso knows Labang's irritating desire to impress will at least mean he'll do his utmost to stay awake. Gingerly, Takatso stretches out on his sleeping mat – sighs with resignation. It's as he suspected: the poles lashed together that comprise the floor are uneven; lumps prod his spine, his buttocks. He eases onto his side, pulls the wildebeest skin up to his shoulders. That's better, but not much. His feet are exposed . . .

"You will know when it's time . . ."

Thando was sent to find Mgobozi and tell him what the Induna had in mind. When the general had finished chuckling, men were set to work.

Skilfully weaving and plaiting grass, they made a long, thick rope. To hide the rope in plain sight, it was looped around the horns of the five cattle Thando and the herdboys brought into the valley.

Now a section of that rope has been wrapped around the boy's waist and the rest lies in a coil wedged behind him. He is in a foetal position; curled on his side with his head bowed and his knees up, pressed against the rope. His arms are bent, forced together, as though tied by invisible bonds. The Induna broke a spear, leaving just enough of the shaft immediately below the broad blade so one could grip it. This is what the boy clutches in his right hand, the wrist bent awkwardly. Pain is a fire that burns along his forearms, down his back. His neck aches – and with his head bent, his chin pressed against his chest, the rope wrapped around his midriff and his knees up, it's a struggle to breathe.

Kele moves along the edge – and there's Mavhusu, waiting for him. Mavhusu spent a large part of the afternoon drinking beer, surreptitiously and away from Takatso's censorious glare. As a result he can scarcely keep his eyes open. Twice he's realised he's been walking with his eyes shut in a half-doze, not something you want to do on the edge of a sheer drop – and here, on the eastern flank, there isn't even a ledge forming a low parapet as there is on the opposite side.

Who can climb this mountain? Only a baboon! And are they not the only baboons, here? Takatso is a nervous old woman.

The boy's eyes snap open. He had drifted off for a few moments. How long? He begins to panic, but then the Induna's words come back to him: *"You will need to move fast, but there will be time for you to be careful. Do not rush."*

Cringing with pain, he straightens his right wrist. Pokes at the smothering, wet darkness with the tip of the blade. Weak jabs. But the blade soon snags something.

His fingers are numb, it doesn't feel as if he's holding anything, which means he's got to be careful he doesn't drop the blade. He bends his right wrist forward. The tip of the blade has definitely caught on something. But as the boy exerts even more pressure, the tip slips free. The boy shuts his eyes, trying to squeeze out the tears of frustration. Raising the blade so it's more or less in the same position as it was before, he tries a thrusting motion. He feels the blade press against something, then break through. Bending his wrist toward himself, he frees the tip. Is about to try again. Then has another idea. Slowly he runs the blade downward. A lump. No – guiding the tip sideways – a ridge.

Yes!

He has to fight a sudden desire to hack and saw and break out, just so he can vanquish this searing pain. But such wild movement isn't an option, anyway. He is trapped, pressed, crunched together.

He guides the tip of the blade onto the ridge – then he thrusts again – and feels the tip break through.

Fat Kele settles himself against the wall of one of the stone huts. After a moment, he decides he'll be more comfortable if he lies down . . .

The boy pushes the blade further. Moving his right hand back and forth, sweat in his eyes, pain howling down his back, he starts sawing.

Takatso tries lying on his stomach. *Ow!* He shifts sideways. That's better. "Are you awake, Uncle?" asks Labang. Takatso ignores him. Watches one of the sentries in the stockade move away from the gate.

Through! A sudden slackness. The blade loose. Through. Now he can let go of the blade. Blind fingers grope their way to the opening, pull it further apart.

Fresh air!

Tala will not leave his corner as Kele has done. But he decides he'll be warmer and more comfortable if he stretches out in the shelter of the low ledge that forms a parapet along the butte's western flank.

The slit was stitched up and then a mixture of blood and mud was smeared over the hide to disguise the cut. The mixture was then smeared over the same area on the other carcasses, so none of them would stand out as different. The boy was in the fifth carcass carried to the rock, for the Induna had rightly assumed it would end up on top of the others when it was finally stored. And the men working the hoist and carrying the carcasses atop the rock would be too tired to notice it was heavier than the others.

And the Induna was sure they'd store it on top of the rock. They'd want to impress the Zulus with their ingenuity, as though the hoist was their own invention.

The boy is about to panic because he can't get at the blade – it's somehow slipped under his side and he can't reach there – when he remembers what the Induna told him. The cow would be hung upside down from the pole, and its spine would take the boy's weight, therefore the stitching holding the gut together didn't need to be strong. All the boy had to do was cut it once, then by pulling on the twine, he could undo the stitching.

Groping, he finds one of the severed ends. Begins to tug on it.

Takatso watches the sentry return, his spear dangling in his right hand, the tip almost touching the ground. A moonless night, the sky speckled with stars. A breeze bringing with it the reminder that winter is near. The glow of the bonfires below the northern face.

Free at last, the boy lies on his side, shivering. This is what the Induna has told him to do. Once out of the cow, he mustn't try to move. As soon as possible he must resume his original position. This way the bite of awakening muscles will be lessened and then, gradually, he can straighten his legs, stretch his back. It'll also give him time to listen for any movement.

The boy's fingernails scrape against the stone floor, he bites his lips, as the blood returns to his limbs and a stinging replaces the burning.

Labang shakes his head to stay awake. His tiredness is causing him to draw shapes in the dark, see movement beyond the flames of the bonfire.

On the floor of the watchtower, Takatso wonders where that impi is. Not far, judging by the time it took the Induna's man to fetch the cows. He turns his head and suddenly finding himself in a comfortable position, is asleep.

The udibi clambers to his feet. Stands swaying as a dizziness ripples through him. Then he checks the rope, slips his right arm through the second coil, hoisting it onto his shoulder.

He steps out of the stone shelter.

"Look for the glow of the bonfires," the Induna had told him.

He is lucky, the open side of the structure faces the next building along. Crouching, he moves a pace away from the stone structure. He sees the big hut, the low entrance like an open mouth. Turning, so he's looking north, he sees the bright glow of the bonfires, staining the night orange.

Look for the glow . . . then move in the opposite direction . . .

Still crouching as best he can with the rope wrapped around his midriff and the other coil tugging him sideways, the boy moves a few paces to the south. Stops just before the doorway of the second stone hut, the one with the roof, where the weapons carriers sleep. The sound of soft snoring tells him it's occupied. He daren't retrace his steps and go around the back of the structure. That would take him along the parapet that runs down the western flank of the rock, where there's likely to be at least one sentry.

He has no other option: the boy takes a breath, steps past the door, and halts again.

Listening.

Sleeping sounds. A groan. The faint rustle of the breeze, chilling his blood-soaked skin. He peers around the corner of the structure: this segment of the parapet is empty. He tries to merge with the shadows and waits.

Nothing. No movement.

He darts forward . . .

7

The Climbers

The rope is pulled sideways, to the left. Then, as someone takes up the strain on the right side, the rope goes taut.

The boy is lying just as the Induna showed him: prone on the rock, with his feet wedged in the fissure that separates the shoulder from the main outcrop. The rope runs across the crook of each elbow. His arms are smeared in cow blood, allowing the rope to slide easily over his skin. The pain is in his elbows, as the rope bites downward.

The first Zulu crawls over the edge. The rope goes slack. The warrior relieves the boy and takes up the same position. The shoulder is a metre lower than the rest of the summit and the boy retreats into the shadows by the fissure to stand guard with the spear the warrior had passed him.

The rope goes taut again. The second warrior comes over the right-hand edge, the western flank of the butte. He's soon followed by the Induna, slithering over the left-hand edge.

Crouched low, he moves to the boy. Lays a hand on his shoulder. The boy nods. The Induna squeezes his shoulder. His iklwa is tucked into his kilt at the side and he draws out the weapon. The boy points his blade in the direction of the sentry he spotted as he crept toward the shoulder.

The Induna stands.

Peers over the edge.

Waits.

Listens.

In the meantime, two more warriors have pulled themselves up. From his mountainous bulk, the boy recognises Njikiza with his large spiked club. He takes the place of the soldier holding the rope. The boy reckons he can haul up all the others single-handedly.

The Induna is atop the main summit. After listening again, he moves toward the sentry . . .

Straining his ears, the udibi hears only the faintest rustle. Then the Induna's back, moving to the southeastern corner, keeping low until he reaches one of the stone buildings. It's built at an angle, with the entrance facing inward.

Stepping carefully, so as not to dislodge any pebbles, the Induna peers around the corner, looking northward along the eastern flank of the rock.

Kele, who's been dozing in the deep shadows right alongside the wall of the building, only a few paces away from the corner, watches the shape withdraw. Frowning, shrugging off his cloak, he picks up his spear. Stops for a moment to look around, to think – something woke him up.

A noise.

Movement.

Tala, going for a piss?

And then looking for him?

Has Takatso come up to check on them?

He follows the wall, turns the corner and steps past the Induna.

Who rises out of his crouch. Clamps his left hand over Kele's mouth. Drives his iklwa blade into the sentry's side.

"Ngadla," he whispers into the man's ear, as he twists the blade. Thrusts it deeper.

When Kele goes limp, he carefully lays the dead man on the ground.

Returning to the step, he pulls the boy up. The udibi whispers something in his ear. The Induna motions to four warriors, sends them to throttle the sleeping weapons carriers, for although they are young, mere teens, they can wield a spear as lethally as any man.

Some of the warriors have brought up kindling and torches, and they start a fire behind one of the structures along the southern rim . . .

The sky is purple. Dawn is coming.

8
The Battle

The shrieks of dying men. Takatso sits up, eyes on the smoke billowing off the rock . . .

"Let's see if these baboons can fly," says the Induna. The warriors who have disarmed the remaining sentries toss them over the edge . . .

Flailing limbs and screams cut short as Mavhuso crashes through one of the huts below, while a body slaps the ground. Two things happen at once: Takatso shouts for the stockade guards and Labang shouts for his uncle . . .

The thatch of the large hut is ablaze, Zulu warriors cut the men down as they push their way out. The guns are in there, but everyone is too panicked, they just want to escape the flames; everyone except Kamohelo . . .

Finally, even as the sky was lightening, Labang fell asleep, resting his body against the railing, while his feet dangled over the edge of the watchtower. The shrieks behind him jolted him into consciousness – but he comes awake looking outward. And sees a Zulu impi calmly sitting in three long ranks about two hundred metres beyond the remains of the bonfires. He sees and doesn't believe his eyes. It can't be! He blinks. Looks again. The Zulus are still there. In one hand, each soldier carries an iklwa, the blade pointing skyward; his other arm is pushed through the straps of his shield, which is horizontal, balanced on its edge and resting against the man's shoulder. "Uncle!"

Kamohelo has picked up one of the guns. It's loaded, but even as he slots the butt into his shoulder, part of the burning roof drops onto him. The shot goes wide and he careens into someone else as he tries to shrug off the fire . . .

"Get up there!" shouts Takatso, only vaguely hearing Labang's call. "Save your kinsmen!" But the guards have come together in a bunch and they're not interested in what's happening to the men atop the rock – they're peering over the stockade. Takatso turns to follow their gaze. He sees Labang's ashen expression, sees him pointing, sees the Zulu impi, a dark mass amid the early morning shadows . . .

It's Phopho. He bumped into Phopho, who's looking for another gun. Screaming, Kamohelo pushes him aside and crashes through the burning thatch . . .

The guards hesitate, then they throw down their spears and flee. Past the watchtower – Takatso too stunned to say anything – out of the gate, and along the path that runs parallel to the Zulu lines . . .

Kamohelo sprawls. Rolls on his back. Rolls over. Stands. And is felled by Njikiza's club. The boy's watching – and sees how the blow stretches the Baboon God's body out, so he's prone before he even hits the ground, bits of grey matter splattering around him . . .

Takatso finds his voice: "Come back, you cowards!" But the assorted cousins and nephews ignore him. Blood might be thicker than water, but it can run just as fast. "Come back!" And why aren't the Zulus moving? Takatso soon sees why. The villagers have formed up in a semicircle at right angles to the impi and, as Takatso watches, they intercept the fleeing men . . .

The hut suddenly collapses, falling on Phopho, turning him into a mass of burning flesh.

The Induna kicks Kamohelo's body to ensure he's dead. It's almost over. With the boy at his side, he moves to the northwestern corner and watches the villagers dispense with the remaining men . . .

The women are wailing. Some have the presence of mind to chase the rest back into the huts. The villagers surge forward, trampling the bodies of their former captors. They wrench a shrieking Labang off the tower. Spears pinion him to the ground.

Some of the men clamber onto the tower, where Takatso makes ready to defend himself, but, from the top of the rock, the Induna bellows: "Leave that man alone! He is mine!"

The villagers hesitate, responding to the commanding tone. Then Sakhile comes forward, translating the Induna's words, shooing the villagers away. Takatso lowers his spear.

It's over.

9
The Decision

"You and your men have liberated us from this tyranny!"

Mgobozi waves Sakhile's words away. "Not me! The Induna deserves your praise and thanks."

"This is so. Nduna . . . we can only thank you and revere your name so that future generations might remember how you saved us."

"I serve Shaka," says the Induna.

"Then Shaka has our thanks, too."

The clan's women and children have been led to the village. All males over the age of thirteen have perished; the younger boys will be watched over for a long time, lest they contemplate foolhardy thoughts of vengeance. But they will be allowed to join the tribe if they so desire. With the women things will be easier. All were taken from the village and this return represents a happy homecoming for most.

"Will you stay here?" asks the Induna. "The baboons will return to their stronghold."

He means the real baboons, honoured by the tribe's totem.

"It will not be for me to make that decision," says Sakhile. "But I think we will move on. Go and look for those baboons."

"It is better that way," observes Mgobozi.

"This is so."

"By your words," says the Induna, "are we to assume you will remain with these people?"

Sakhile nods. "I have grown accustomed to their misery. Now I would help them find contentment."

"Know this," adds Mgobozi, "the mighty Shaka will pardon whatever outrage Jama claimed you committed. Hai, in Shaka's eyes, this would make you an ally, for you have walked the same path Shaka and his mother walked when the King was a boy."

"Truly, this pleases my ears. But my place is here." Sakhile smiles. "Besides, I might yet serve Shaka, for I remain a Zulu."

"That may well be so," says Mgobozi. "Come now, I'm sure it's been a while since you tasted Zulu beef." The general turns to the Induna. "You would see to the other one first?"

The Induna nods. "Yes, General."

Mgobozi calls to the boy: "Come," he says, "you have done a man's work today, let us see if you have a man's appetite."

The Induna watches as the three – Mgobozi, Sakhile and the udibi – walk over to the fires where the carcasses are being roasted; then he makes his way to the watchtower. Dismissing the guards, he climbs up and joins Takatso.

He is looking away from the rock, in the direction where the impi had taken up their position in the darkness a few hours before. In this way, he avoids seeing the bodies of his kinsmen, disembowelled by the Zulu warriors.

"I will see to it that you die a warrior's death, with an assegai thrust," murmurs the Induna.

"A kindness I thank you for."

"But if it's a warrior's death you crave, why not seek it out? March with us. A warrior's death today or sometime further along the path, does it really matter? If the end is inevitable, enjoy the journey. March with us. You know this land, you will be of much value. And you will be one of us. The general, Mgobozi, he is a Mthetwa. He served under Dingiswayo with Shaka. Yet he is a Zulu. It is not about blood . . ."

"More about bloodshed," grins Takatso.

The Induna chuckles. "This is so. It's a man's actions, his courage, his pride – these are the things that make him a Zulu, not the woman whose legs guide him into the world."

"I had resolved to die like a man."

"You will have other chances."

"With you?"

"As one of us."

Takatso sighs. "Why not?" he says. "The seasons will come, the seasons will go . . ."

"Many moons. Many plantings. Many harvestings."

"Many battles?"

"Yes, those too," says the Induna, grinning.

"Then consider your ranks greatly enriched, Zulu."

PART FOUR

The Fortress On The Plain

I shall be mad if you get smashed about;
We've had good times together, you and I;
Although you groused a bit when luck was out,
And a girl turned us down, or we went dry . . .

Yet there's a world of things we haven't done,
Countries not seen, where people do strange things;
Eat fish alive, and mimic in the sun
The solemn gestures of their stone-grey kings . . .

From "The Soldier Addresses His Body"
by Edgell Rickwood

A granite sky and a wind that brings with it a whisper of snow and ice. It avails the Induna little to hunker down on the ledge, for he's facing into the wind. His eyes are stinging, his lips are chapped, but deep inside Ndwandwe territory, just a few kilometres away from Zwide's capital, vigilance must fight numb fingers and toes.

He's above the steep southern side of a shallow depression. His six men are spaced out in twos around the rim, one man peering outward, watching for the enemy, the other with his eyes on the Induna, awaiting any signal the warrior might make. Mgobozi squats with a young boy in the shelter offered by some boulders in the middle of the depression. The boy can't be older than eight summers and he is gesturing and pointing, while Mgobozi leans on his spear shaft and listens.

The Induna's udibi lies prone on the ridge above the warrior. A second contingent of soldiers led by Njikiza is hidden in a thicket about a kilometre away. If something goes wrong, if they're betrayed or discovered by a Ndwandwe patrol, Mgobozi will convey what he has learnt to the udibi, who'll race off to find the others. Njikiza will escort him home with the valuable message, while the Induna and his men discourage pursuit.

But here comes Mgobozi now, eating up the slope with high steps . . .

The Induna stands, raises his spear horizontally and twists his wrist, so the blade points backwards over his head. The men nudge their companions and begin to disappear off the rim of the depression. They'll circle around and meet at the foot of the slope behind the Induna.

He extends a hand, pulls Mgobozi up onto the ledge. While the general leans forward to regain his breath, the Induna watches the boy Mgobozi was talking to – one of this Honey Man's younger emissaries – collect a calf that's almost as big as he is and make his way up the depression's shallower northern slope. This will be his excuse should he be stopped and questioned: he has gone looking for a missing calf.

The Induna watches until the boy has disappeared from sight, then regards the general.

"They come?" he asks, his words milky vapour in the cold air.

Mgobozi straightens. Nods. "They come."

The Ndwandwes

Where are the Zulus?

Soshangane stands in the blazing sun in the centre of the umuzi's inner enclosure. The village, one of several smaller settlements dotted around KwaBulawayo, is deserted. Over the ragged thorn-bush fence he can see his men moving between the huts. Frustration siring destruction, some have taken to hacking at the walls as if grain might be secreted amid the thatch. With a sigh he returns his attention to the excavation going on a few paces away.

The Zulus keep their grain and other foodstuffs in small raised shelters built among the huts, but there's also a special storage area in the circular central enclosure. This is for emergencies – should the kraal be razed, the conflagration is likely to destroy the food stores along with the rest of the dwellings, leaving the villagers to face starvation.

A large cistern-style pit is dug in the enclosure with an opening just big enough to allow a child to get through. A boy is then sent down. He plasters the walls and floor with clay and piles up mealies in lattice-like layers. When he's finished, he climbs out and the hole is covered with a flat stone. Within a matter of days this is in turn covered by a layer of cow dung – since the enclosure also doubles as the cattlefold. Hardening, the dung not only hides the entrance to the chamber, but also seals it so the contents are preserved and will stay edible for years.

Hundreds of tiny holes bear testimony to the men's search. They found nothing the first time and had to retrace their steps, sticking their spears deeper into the dried dung. Once the stone had been uncovered and removed, they set about making the opening wider. But their Zulu hosts, wherever they might be, have been cunning.

Soshangane watches as one of his soldiers is hauled out of the storage pit, shaking his head.

Oh yes, the Zulus have been cunning. Here, and in the other villages the Ndwandwe army has visited, the pits have been emptied, covered up and disguised again, made to seem undisturbed. So the hungry invaders will waste time looking for them. And they conduct a search at every kraal, even though the Zulu strategy has become evident – for hungry men must be optimistic men, seeking food wherever they can.

Soshangane calls his officers to him. Hunger has made his soldiers eagle-eyed, even as it's weakened their bodies; if they haven't found any food, there's none to be found. "Order the men on," he says, "and have the rearguard set fire to the village."

Where are the Zulus?

Another deserted village. Another empty grain pit. Zwangendaba, one of Soshangane's most able generals, sits in the shade of the ibandla tree drinking water and watching how yet another disappointment has caused his men to wilt even further. The desperate enthusiasm of a few minutes ago has waned; now they are listless dogs, panting in their own fragments of shade.

No food. No grain. The vegetable gardens situated by the main gate have been hoed over, left to the weeds. Even the game has fled, it seems. A few buck and some zebra – that's all the Ndwandwe hunters have been able to account for.

Zwangendaba pushes himself up against the tree trunk. They do still have a little grain left in their food bags. As for the absence of wildlife – a sustained hunt such as the Zulus must have undertaken will have had that effect, causing the game to move away. The Ndwandwe hunting parties will simply have to roam further afield, even though this will be more risky. He'll have to send out larger groups lest they stumble on the Zulus.

Zwangendaba stares at the plumes of smoke in the distance, marking the positions of other Ndwandwe regiments in other Zulu villages.

Where are they?

Where are the Zulus?

Soshangane stands atop a rise, surveying the surrounding countryside while two hundred of his men enter the next umuzi. Nothing moves down there. All is as still as death. It was the same at KwaBulawayo, which Soshangane has decided to leave intact. Not only will searching it thoroughly take some days, it can serve as a supply post once they start finding food.

He gazes at the shimmering hills. Knuckles of rock, shaded precipices, streams glinting in the distance, smears of red, marking erosion furrows, trees like lone sentinels. And the veld: almost white in these dry winter months.

Where are they?

He would laugh were their situation not one meal – two at the most – away from being desperate.

They crossed the White Umfolozi, Zwide's reconstituted army, following in the footsteps of their fallen comrades. They passed Gqokli Hill with its necklace of skulls and bones, the officers chivvying the men on; no good could come of dwelling on this, the site of their defeat. Soshangane, however, lingered with twenty men until the long lines had snaked away. Telling the soldiers to keep watch, he climbed to the summit of the hill. He saw where Shaka had hidden his reserve and stood on the large flat rock where the Beetle had stood and directed his forces. You could still see what remained of the mighty human battering ram Nomahlanjana had sent up the slope in a last-ditch attempt to secure victory. Amid the long grass the bones kept their ranks, perhaps more disciplined now than on the day, when those bones were flesh and blood, living, screaming men. Brave men, to be sure – but that's what enabled Shaka to withstand their repeated onslaughts. His men were brave, too, but they were also disciplined. Bravery sends men into the fray, discipline is what keeps them there, ensures they stand their ground.

And at Gqokli Hill, this place of skulls, Shaka showed he understood the true meaning of discipline. For discipline is not fear. Fear only makes a king's soldiers obey their orders. What happens when the officers fall and there's no one left to give orders? Many a proud general has seen his army annihilated because he hasn't understood this.

Soshangane was there that fateful day, a humble lieutenant, whose regiment had found itself on the southern side of the hill – the segment Shaka had saved for last, attacking only after his hidden reserve had destroyed the human battering ram. He'd seen how the Zulus encircled the flat-topped promontory and allowed themselves to be encircled, in turn – as sure a sign of their discipline as any. The way the Zulu warriors sat on their shields, idly taking snuff, while a force of superior numbers surrounded them so completely there didn't seem any way they could escape – that was remarkable. And Soshangane had found himself examining the Zulu positions with foreboding.

When the order came to advance, he urged his section forward – and saw how entangled the ranks became, men crushed against each other, unable to throw their spears. And then Shaka launched his first attack. And again Zulu discipline was in evidence. For in that sally, and all others, the soldiers kept their ranks. If they swept down the hill with fire in their eyes, they were also careful enough to ensure none outpaced the others. Even when the Ndwandwe generals tried to lure the enemy off the hill with a feigned retreat, the Zulu officers were able to call their men back in time. Yes: fear, bloodlust, fatigue – discipline could harness all of these.

Soshangane was there that fateful day and was one of the few Ndwandwe officers to escape with his reputation not only intact, but bolstered. He'd led the final retreat from KwaBulawayo, organising a series of ferocious rearguard actions that ensured the Zulus could not destroy the Ndwandwe army totally. And it was his spear that felled Manyosi at the door to Shaka's hut in Bulawayo. Earlier in the day, he'd been delivering a message to Nomahlanjana's command post, and had seen the Zulu champion come down to face the Ndwandwe challengers. Rage exploded in his heart when Manyosi bested the first man and Soshangane tried to fight his way through the ranks to get to the front so he could avenge this insult, but the men were packed too closely together. In fact, they seemed to be pushing *against* him, as though trying to back away from the hill. He shouted and punched, but this was a thicket he wasn't going to break through. And he'd come to his senses – there was, after all, the message he had to deliver. Besides, he reassured himself, fighting his way out of the sweaty mass, he'd get his chance. Fool that he was, he still believed the Ndwandwes could win simply by swamping their opponents.

It was not to be, of course. And although he finally got his chance to face Manyosi, it was a bittersweet triumph. For how many Ndwandwe bodies lay at the Zulu's feet? How many had the champion accounted for before he was finally made to eat dirt?

Soshangane learnt a lot that day and as the new commander in chief has tried to instil in his men a sense of discipline. Columns and troop movements are now more orderly and the regiments have been broken down into smaller groupings, each under a junior officer, thereby ensuring in any engagement there's always likely to be someone to issue orders. And Soshangane certainly won't spend any battle lolling in the shade of a tree as his predecessor was wont to do. He'll lead by example. True discipline comes with time – and endless repetition – but he feels he and his officers have made a good start. They are at least at a stage where they're able to ensure their superior numbers remain an advantage.

More importantly, it's thanks to him that of the three assegais Ndwandwe soldiers carry, one is a short stabbing spear much like the Zulu iklwa – and their flimsy wooden shields have been replaced by tough oval cowskin shields similar to the Zulu's isihlangu.

But this is why, right now, standing on the hill, watching his soldiers scurrying like ants through the deserted village, he has to suppress a bellow of mocking laughter.

They have come, thirsting for vengeance, ready for the close-up combat Shaka's men favour – and where are the Zulus?

Nowhere to be seen!

*

Zwide, Devourer Of Kings, Ruler Of The Ndwandwes, shuts his eyes and hisses as the warm, wet loins of his favourite concubine begin to draw release from his cock. He lies on his back; she straddles him, sitting upright, her full, heavy breasts almost obscuring her face from his view. Her rhythm is regular, measured; cruelly regular, cunningly measured, for here and now to obey is to disobey, and she ignores his grunts, his impatient growls. The release is hers to control and, despite his urgings to the contrary, she knows this is the way her master likes it. His hands fold over her breasts. He squeezes them. He digs his heels into the ground, tries to rise, push himself deeper into her. He has the scrunched-up face of a baby wailing silently.

Then . . .

He sags, his face flaccid with release.

"I am pleased to see you are at least able to finish *one* thing."

Zwide stiffens, even as his penis shrinks. Pushing the concubine aside, he hoists himself into a sitting position – and glares up at the intruder on the other side of the fire that burns in the centre of the hut.

"Or maybe I am mistaken. I see by this one's hungry eyes your pleasure has not been hers. You have led her to the gate, but, for her at least, it remains shut."

"Can I help you, Mother?"

She makes a clicking sound. "Cha! You take after your father in this respect."

"Mother . . ."

Tall, flat-chested, a collection of sharp angles, Ntombazi Of The Skulls addresses the girl. "Begone!" she says, jerking her head sideways.

Kani rises to her feet. Stands, slightly crouched, her eyes on Zwide. Unlike the others of his harem, who would have needed just a glance from Ntombazi to be on their way, she's waiting for him to confirm the command: a fact which pleases him and one of the reasons why she's his favourite concubine.

He nods. She may leave.

Still crouching, her eyes downcast, Kani scurries past Ntombazi, and ducks through the hut's smaller rear entrance.

"I don't trust her!"

346

"State your business, Mother. Or is spreading misery something you now do in your spare time, as well?"

"Your indolence is my misery!"

"Indolence? Ha! Have I not given you many skulls to add to your collection?"

"Paltry additions, barely worth the effort. Shaka's scraps!"

A sneer curls Zwide's lips. "One day, Mother, you will go too far!"

"That is because *you* never go far enough!"

"I warn you. I am my father's son. I am king. Who are you, old woman?"

"Perhaps if you learnt to finish what you started you would be left in peace."

Zwide's response is a derisive snort. He's more concerned with how he might stand, get himself up, so he can face his mother, eye to eye. Normally, pulling the hefty king to his feet is a servant's task, but Zwide knows what his mother's reaction would be were he to summon someone to help him. Unfortunately, though, there's no other dignified way he can hoist himself upright.

"As it is, everyone else is made to suffer for your indecision."

He could roll onto his side and then push himself up onto his knees – but then what?

"You have gathered the largest army this land has ever seen. At least this is your boast."

She has his attention again.

"No boast," says Zwide, leaning back on one elbow and crossing his ankles. Blithe insouciance will anger his mother more than a panting ascent – it's also less effort.

"But where is this army? Is it a whirlwind rampaging through the Beetle's lands? No. This army of yours has invaded itself. For your soldiers hunker down eating our food, eating enough to feed three such armies. They have been here for two moons now, exercising their gluttony and little else. And your people grow restless."

Zwide shrugs. "They will reap the rewards of their sacrifice soon enough. Besides, if they are unhappy, let them bring their complaints to me. I'll ensure there're fewer mouths to feed."

"An army that sits picking its nose is not an army. The sharpest blade is useless if never used. Your soldiers have become locusts devouring your own crops when they should be pillaging the Beetle's villages. Your soldiers have become indolent, believing the boast to be the deed."

Zwide shrugs again, trying to picture an indolent locust. It takes time to organise the largest army this land has ever seen. Being a woman, his mother wouldn't understand that. Still, her criticisms cut a little deeper than he wants to acknowledge. The two months it's taken to call in the regiments, and ensure they're equipped according to Soshangane's exacting specifications, *have* been a drain on the capital's resources.

"Have you lost your way, Blood Of My Blood? Has your liver shrivelled? What price a strong arm if it remains shackled by your fear?"

"Fear?" growls Zwide. "I fear *nothing*!"

"Yet you do not move against this Zulu upstart."

Well, for one thing, that's an inappropriate description right there. Shaka can scarcely be called an upstart any longer. Which is another reason for careful planning. Waiting to ensure things are just right. Like those shields, for example. They have too few craftsmen schooled in making shields the Zulu way, and to accrue enough for the army has taken time!

"Or perhaps that's precisely the problem. For this Beetle can no longer be called an upstart, can he?"

Zwide pushes his lips out. Examines his fingernails. His mother's always had an uncanny knack for divining his innermost thoughts.

"Is this what stays your hand?" continues Ntombazi, who also has a mother's aptitude for spotting when her words have struck home. "Weak rulers with their cowardly armies – these you are happy to gobble up. But a worthy adversary . . . No, wait. Perhaps, it is these weak ones who are a measure of your worth. Shaka is the lion, you are the vulture, happy to feed off his carrion. Is that the way things are?"

She turns to warm her hands over the fire. "Or maybe . . ."

348

"Aiee, are my shortcomings so numerous?"

"I was merely wondering . . ."

"Aloud, unfortunately."

". . . whether you have at last decided to act as the child you never were."

"How so?"

"To heed the thrashing Shaka gave you and not be a naughty boy again."

Ntombazi frowns. "Why are you grinning? Are you about to add incipient idiocy to your list of failings?"

"On the contrary, Mother, my grin salutes your shrewdness."

Ntombazi's eyebrows rise, but she says nothing. Folds her arms and waits.

Zwide's grin widens. "Very like a child," he says. "I am a lake, mirroring the sky of my youth. Where you loomed as large as a baobab. Aiee, with as many arms as that tree has branches and each one a slap or a smack aimed at me. But was I cowed? No. Oh no!"

"First-born you might have been, but you always were the runt of the litter."

"Yet, here I stand, Mother. Can the same be said of my brothers?"

"Or your sons?"

Zwide glares at her. A malevolent, angry stare. One day . . .

Ntombazi's gaze is unwavering, however. "Strange that we should talk of your childhood, for I have seen that look often enough when you were a boy."

"When you tried your brutal best, but failed, to cow me."

"This is true. You only got more cunning in your transgressions."

"Exactly! At last the old sow understands!"

And she needn't worry, adds Zwide – although it's strange that she should suddenly interest herself in the welfare of his subjects – their sacrifice really is almost at an end. "Tomorrow I meet with Noluju and Soshangane to plan our campaign against the Zulus."

"I don't trust him," hisses Ntombazi.

It's a weak riposte, decides Zwide. Her way of hiding her astonishment. He feels a glee almost as pleasurable as the orgasm he experienced a few minutes ago. Let her see there are things set in motion she knows nothing of. Oh how she must be seething inside!

"Why?" asks Zwide mildly. "He is a most able commander . . ."

"I don't trust him, either. But I was referring to Noluju."

No surprise, there. His chief councillor is one of those who set things in motion, while she sulked in her hut.

"You trust no one, Old Woman. Not even me. And see? I have surprised you! Now go – leave me. Make some space in your collection for Shaka's skull. It will be yours forthwith. And then you'll have to find something else to champ your gums about. Although I'm sure you're up to *that* task. Just as my men are up to the task of crushing this Beetle once and for all."

*

Zwide's hut has two entrances, a large front entrance called "the mouth" – from which the king's commands and proclamations issue – and a smaller rear entrance called "the anus" – an appellation devoid of scatological connotations, for the Ndwandwes regard that orifice with a certain amount of reverence, seeing it as the source of regeneration. For does not cow dung become the fertiliser that feeds the plants that feed the cattle?

Outside the rear entrance high palisades made of poles lashed together run from either side of the main hut to two smaller huts set adjacent each other. The one hut is a storeroom, the other houses whoever might be the king's favourite concubine. There are gates in both walls and should the king choose to leave by one of these he is theoretically incognito. However, this only means he's not engaged in matters of state and cannot be pestered by petitioners; Zwide never goes anywhere without a troop of bodyguards.

Aside from the king, only his personal cook and his concubines are allowed here. It is a back yard, an inner sanctum, where he can go and relax, sun himself away from his councillors and generals.

Even his bodyguards are posted beyond the palisade. As with Shaka's royal enclosure, this compound is situated within a larger section walled off from the rest of KwaDlovungu. Bonfires encircle the king's sanctuary and are kept burning throughout the night, ensuring no one can approach unseen.

Kani, the concubine, crouches in the deep shadows that have collected in the corner where the palisade meets the curved wall of the royal hut. She doesn't move, scarcely dares to breathe. A few paces away from her, a man is trying to peer over the poles. She can just make out his shape against the glow of the fires beyond. Her fists are clenched to stop her hands from trembling. Sho! If he hadn't pressed against the wall, causing the bindings to creak, she wouldn't have spotted him. But he would have seen her the moment she stepped away from the hut . . .

Who is it? Is he eavesdropping? Or trying to see who else might be listening in on Zwide's conversation?

She tries to draw herself still deeper into the corner, pulling the darkness around her like a shawl. At least there's no question of him even attempting to open the gate. No one would dare! In fact, he's taking a chance simply by lingering near the wall. Both are transgressions punishable by death.

And there's a clue as to his identity, right there – he must hold some sway with Zwide's bodyguards, the elite company whose sole duty it is to protect the Ndwandwe ruler.

Which means . . .?

She hears her master's sneering laugh. Seconds later the man at the palisade is joined by another, one wearing the ostrich plume of Zwide's bodyguard.

"Beware! She comes!"

The almost frantic warning is followed by the sound of Ntombazi calling for her escorts. At the same instant, the soldier darts from the concubine's view.

The first man lingers a little longer. Kani watches as his shape seems to shrink and realises he's now trying to peer between the poles.

Then, with a start, as though suddenly remembering where he is, the peril he's in, he straightens and moves away.

Seizing her chance, Kani darts across the yard, moving diagonally and ending up at the far corner, where the palisade passes the wall of her hut. There's a log, here, and she stands on it. Her guess was right. On this side of the outer enclosure there's a smaller gate that leads to the area where Zwide's councillors reside. And that's where the man is headed. He's circled behind the two smaller huts of the king's sanctuary and, even though he's now moving away from her, there's no mistaking those hunched shoulders, that hurried walk.

It's Noluju.

As Zwide's chief councillor, he's also the commander of the king's bodyguard – and therefore the only one who could sniff around the king's sanctuary with impunity.

As she watches, he disappears into the darkness beyond the furthest bonfire – and he might as well be invisible, for the sentries ignore him, turning away whenever their paths seem about to intersect.

Noluju. But was he listening – or looking for others who listened?

*

They spent a bleak, miserable night on these slopes – now this. But perhaps it's just as well. A timely reminder that they've grown careless, become too concerned with finding food.

"Please, Master," whispers the man kneeling before Soshangane. "We were taken by surprise. They came out of nowhere!"

The Ndwandwes had brought a hundred head of cattle with them, mainly to supply the troops with fresh milk. As the army spread out, however, the herd was left far to the rear. Late yesterday afternoon, a Zulu impi had ambushed the small detachment guarding the cattle. They timed their attack well and were able to disappear into the encroaching darkness with most of the animals. Smaller units had then harried the regiment who raced to the first group's aid, continuing to exact high casualties late into the night.

"Please, Master! We were outnumbered, but we fought like lions. Only four of us remain – and it was the Zulus who retreated!"

Soshangane nudges the man's shoulder with his foot. "Go," he growls. "Rejoin your regiment."

The man scurries backwards on his knees, mouthing profuse thanks – but Soshangane isn't listening, he's yelling for his generals.

They came with each man carrying enough rations for three days. Another of Soshangane's innovations, a lesson learnt at Gqokli Hill when thirst and hunger had proven Shaka's most valuable allies: now each man carries a food pouch and a waterskin. It took them four days to reach the White Umfolozi – and during that time, while still in Ndwandwe territory, they were fed by the villages they passed. It's true they expected to live off the land and the spoils of their conquests once they were in Zululand and having been here for two days already they're fast running out of food, but . . .

The generals form a semicircle around Soshangane.

"I am pleased," he says. "I am pleased this happened. For we have lost our way, here. We have not come to this accursed land seeking food! We have not come here to burn empty huts! We are not wayfarers come to barter skins and sample another nation's beer! Do not bemoan the missing cattle! Let us rejoice, for we have at last encountered the Zulus! For are we not soldiers? Hardship is our companion! Hardship . . ."

Soshangane pauses. Frowns. Strides forward, pushing his way through the assembled officers.

"Do my eyes deceive me?" he says, as the men turn to see what has caught his attention.

"Look!" he bellows, pointing with his spear. "Look!" he hisses.

Figures are moving on the slopes of the Sungulweni Heights. Men and cattle. Men with shields and spears, herding cattle.

A hiss snakes through the group. Immediately there's a stiffening and a straightening. Last night's misery is forgotten as some add their laughter to Soshangane's. He wheels back to face his men. "We have them! Our carelessness has become theirs!"

The officers disperse, charging down the slope, calling for their subordinates.

Soshangane turns to watch his prey again. Merely a foraging party, not more than twenty men, but that means the main force can't be far off.

Soshangane pivots, strides to the opposite slope. Long, eager steps. The Beetle will pay for the arrogance he showed in stealing Ndwandwe cattle. Although Soshangane immediately despatched a regiment to chase down the raiders, he was more concerned with pulling his column together again. No easy task, with the Zulus abroad, and very often several messengers had to be sent before one got through. But it's paid off. Soshangane believes he managed to turn the skirmish to his advantage.

He has brought his army together again, and now in the shallow valley below him, there seethes a brown sea as eighteen thousand Ndwandwes prepare for battle.

*

Kani is returning from visiting her younger brothers and sisters. Because she's proven herself most able – and energetic – in pleasing him, Zwide has graciously granted her siblings a plot of land and a hut. This amounts to citizenship in the nation, and is a rare honour. Usually, captives – spoils of war – spend the rest of their days as slaves. Even women fortunate enough to be taken as a wife will remain as servants in their husband's household, at the beck and call of the other wives. For males, the Ndwandwe army remains the only escape, but even there they're likely to be used as porters or as the expendable skirmishers sent in to test an enemy's strength.

Needless to say, Kani and her family remain in a precarious position. What the king gives he can take away as well, and the concubine doesn't relish the time when Zwide tires of her – as, inevitably, he must.

The path she's on is the lower of two parallel tracks. It runs through the bushes along a ravine before climbing to meet the other trail, which eventually leads to a side entrance of the kraal. The top track follows the ridge to Ntombazi's compound – five huts encircled by a palisade and watched over by a contingent of the king's own bodyguard.

When Kani drops to her haunches, she can't be seen by the man who's just left the queen mother's enclosure. She's hidden by the long grass and, headed back to KwaDlovungu, the man is moving away from her. She heard him haranguing the guards at the gate, urging them to be extra vigilant; now, half rising out of her crouch and peering up the slope, she catches a glimpse of him.

Noluju.

Again!

What was he doing with Ntombazi? Had he been on official business, he would've been accompanied by his attendants.

Kani plucks a blade of grass, chews on the sweetness. Zwide believes Noluju is his creature – hasn't she been present when the two have discussed strategy and hasn't she seen how eagerly Zwide eats up the ideas his councillor serves him? Yes, these ideas become the king's own on their way to fruition, but he values Noluju – and Kani's often heard Zwide complaining about Ntombazi to the councillor. Aside from her, he's the only one Zwide will discuss his mother with, for such discussions invariably reveal how much of a hold the old crone has over her son, for all his snarled assertions to the contrary.

So why would Noluju pay a private visit to the queen mother?

Kani stands, brushes her knees and wonders how she might use this information to her advantage.

*

Ntombazi puffs on her long-stemmed pipe. Puffs and paces. Short, agitated puffs; long, angry paces.

Finally she wheels, approaches the cage. It's one she's had specially constructed for the Truthsayer. A high, stiff collar, made of leather and sewed together at the back with hair from a zebra's tail, keeps his head raised and almost immobile. A rope has been wrapped twice around the collar and each end has been tied to the upright of a frame shaped like an H. A strap made of rawhide encircles his chest and ropes looped through the strap are tied to each upright; his hands and ankles are also bound to the uprights of the frame. His upper body therefore has limited mobility; he can't lean forwards or backwards or to the sides. He's never freed. Ntombazi herself feeds him, and collects his shit and piss, which she believes are valuable substances. She drinks the latter and mixes in the shit with some other ingredients to make a paste she smears over her face and breasts before going to sleep every night.

Laying a hand against the left side of the Truthsayer's face, she exerts a gentle pressure. "Look," she whispers. "See."

Again her palm presses his cheekbone. "Listen. Hear . . . Dream!"

The Truthsayer expels a soft, low growl.

"Will my son outlive Shaka?"

A soft, soft whisper: "Yes."

"Will my son defeat Shaka?"

Almost a purr: "No."

Ntombazi clicks her tongue in irritation. "Will *I* outlive Shaka?"

"No."

"How can this be!" She turns away abruptly, slotting the stem of her pipe between her lips, but the pipe's gone out and she tosses it aside.

"How can this be?" she says again, as she faces the Truthsayer, her hands on her hips.

His lips are dried, cracked, seem to creak apart as he speaks: "I see what I see."

They've been through this before. The past is charred land; black ash. The present is a raging veld fire that consumes the future. He cannot always see through the smoke. And when he does see something, his words become the wind that might cause the wall of flame to veer away so that thing does not come to pass.

Suddenly Ntombazi has an idea. Approaching the Truthsayer again, she places her hand against the side of his head. "Look," she whispers. "See. *Dream*! And tell me this: Will I kill you?"

356

"No."

"No?"

The Truthsayer swallows. A clicking sound. "I will not. Die. By the hand. Of a Ndwandwe."

Ntombazi folds her arms. "We'll see about that!"

"Mother Of The King, I seek your indulgence."

Ntombazi's head whips round. What does that snake want?

"We are not done," she tells the Truthsayer.

Ducking her head, she stalks out of the hut.

"Do you still bother yourself with that abomination?" asks Noluju, in his supercilious way.

"And how is it your concern, Minion?" growls Ntombazi.

"It is not a matter that keeps me awake at night, I confess. But I trust he has foretold our victory?"

"What do you want?"

"The king has sent me."

"What for?"

"He has told me to tell you he will put two hundred of his bodyguard and myself at your disposal. We will escort you to the highest vantage point on the banks of the White Umfolozi, so you might see with your own eyes the smoke from the Zulu villages our men have set ablaze, for apparently you seem to doubt the abilities of our mighty army. I said this cannot be, Your Highness. But he said alas, it is so."

"I'm not interested in burning thatch."

"Quite. It's skulls that set you aquiver. You will have these shortly."

There's a pause while the two regard each other. Ntombazi's servants have taken Noluju's arrival as a sign as powerful as any omen that it is best to repair to their huts and stay there. Even the sentries have decided to patrol other sections of the palisade.

It's the councillor who breaks the silence. "Am I then to assume this is a journey you will not be making?"

"You do not like me, Noluju, and this does not offend me – I deem it a compliment, for I believe you are a slavering sycophant who is more manipulative than any wife. Truly, the world was deprived of a fine cunt the day you grew teeth in your mouth. However, for whatever reason, you and my son have decided to get me out of the way for a while . . ."

"Mother of the king! This is not so! I must protest. The king doesn't need a cause. The thorn provides its own reason for removal."

"You want me gone? Very well. But instead of marching four days closer to Shaka, I'll travel four days in the opposite direction and visit my home clan. Does that satisfy you?"

"Do you doubt our ability to crush this Beetle?"

"With you and my son in charge, what do we have to fear?"

"There *will* be a reckoning," says Noluju, his eyes narrow, his voice hard.

"I do not doubt that."

"Good." The councillor grins. "Now, would I be correct in assuming you wish to take your pet with you?"

"Yes. I will need porters."

"I'll make the arrangements. You can leave at dawn."

*

The Ndwandwe army has gone to ground in part of the Nkandla Forest, a ragged eastern outrunner, not as dense as the primeval fastness that lies a few kilometres to the west, but unsettling enough to men used to the rolling hills of the plains. Night has fallen. An eerie night of shapes and sounds. Strange sounds that sit you upright, reaching for your spear. Shapes that twist around you, lean over you, so it feels as if you've blundered into an ancient army of giants – gnarled, twisted giants – formed up and waiting for orders that have long ago been lost to the wind. Fires give these creatures life, shuffling, shifting, fidgeting movement, but the orange glow also seems to hold them back.

Sitting on his sleeping mat in the large clearing he chose for his command post, Soshangane's thinking of how a sea became a river. A wide and mighty river in flood, flattening bushes, swallowing boulders and dongas. He's pleased with the performance of his regiments, the way the broad ranks, two hundred men wide, with five paces between each row, kept their integrity, their discipline, slowing and reforming as the terrain demanded.

He knows several of his officers are angry with him, but he considers the day a success – for they are alive, aren't they? Things would have been very different, he feels, had he bowed to the demands of his more impetuous generals. Oh yes! He was cunning, not timid. Shaka called, saying: "Come, little Ndwandwes, oh come, let me eat you all up."

Shaka made his move – but Soshangane responded by not responding. Shaka called and he ignored the Beetle.

Come, little Zulus, oh come, play our game for a change . . .

For the first time since crossing into Zulu territory, Soshangane feels he is the hunter and Shaka the hunted. If some of his officers don't see it that way, so be it – as long as they do as they're told.

The detachment of five hundred he sent racing ahead of the main column in hot pursuit of the Zulu herders very nearly caught them. Zwangendaba led his men up the heights – and there the Zulus were! Shouting at each other, desperately trying to hurry their cattle along, the men and boys almost assured their own massacre by remaining with the beasts even as the first Ndwandwes were loosening their throwing spears from their shields.

"Aiee!" laughed Zwangendaba, when he reported back to Soshangane. "Did they think they could make their cattle outrun us?"

And when they fled, Zwangendaba wisely stayed his hand, set his men to rounding up the cattle. There was no need to follow the Zulus for he knew where they were headed.

"It is so," he told Soshangane. "I myself heard what they were shouting. We were the leopard by the watering hole and they were as young girls, running this way and that, shrieking and not caring who heard them!"

They were making for the Thukela, the mighty river that lies to the south of the Nkandla Forest.

Soshangane raises his porridge bowl to his lips – let his men see he's swallowing the same watered-down blandness they are! Insofar as he clearly wanted to see the invaders go hungry, Shaka's plan has worked. Although they caught their first sight of a Zulu impi waiting to do battle with them today – as opposed to the raiding parties they've had to deal with – lethargy soon rejoined the column. The shapes he can make out around the campfires move ponderously, rising and settling with great difficulty; men hovering while they try to remember what they're supposed to be doing and endeavour to force hungry limbs to co-operate.

As they drew ever closer to the Thukela the cattle tracks became more numerous. The grass was trampled, eaten, dung was everywhere; it was clear herds had converged in a mass exodus towards the river. There were three fords in the vicinity and early that afternoon the Ndwandwe invaders got their first sight of a Zulu force willing to stand its ground and fight.

But, moving rapidly from ford to ford, Soshangane was perplexed. Why had Shaka left so few men to guard these vital crossings? They seemed many because the fords were narrow, but a closer examination revealed otherwise. And hadn't Soshangane seen this before?

"Attack," said the generals. "Attack now!"

But Soshangane was thinking of another river, this one in flood . . .

He lays his bowl aside. The fools. Some of them had been there, as well. Yet they were willing to repeat Nomahlanjana's mistake . . .

The White Umfolozi running high, and Zwide's son not bothering to split his army, and trying to take all three fords at once. No, he simply sent his men through the crossing before him, which was in any case lightly defended.

But rapids lay immediately below the narrow ford and the current was strong and the water close to the other bank got deep – and disaster ensued. The Zulus waded into the shallows and slaughtered the Ndwandwes as they struggled to maintain their footing. One man would go down and take with him several others, the bodies rolling and tumbling to shatter against the rapids.

Soshangane snaps his fingers. Instantly two men crouching by the fire a few paces away clamber to their feet. The one comes immediately to the commander, bows and picks up the bowl. After a brief detour, the second servant approaches with a calabash. He bows and extends his arms. Soshangane takes the calabash from him.

"Will that be all, Master?"

"Yes," says Soshangane, "sleep if you can."

It's the last of his stock of beer. Soshangane swallows a mouthful. Smacks his lips.

"Attack! Attack now!"

The fools! They were the finest generals Shaka had, these Ndwandwe officers.

Soshangane stood gazing at the Zulu ranks across the river – and between them the fast-flowing Thukela. Aiee! This could scarcely be called a ford! A man crossing here would need to do so by walking alongside his most docile cow, so that the animal's bulk broke the current. Even then there was a chance the cow would lose its footing . . .

Soshangane turned back to his generals. Did they think they were impressing him by pawing at him and urging him to send over his soldiers?

"Silence!" he hissed. "Look you again and tell me what you see!"

That had them frowning, sneaking glances at each other, clearly feeling they were being tested.

Soshangane scowled. "I'll tell you what you see. You see cattle!" He pointed to the ground; the mud churned up by hundreds of hooves. "You see the tracks this side and you see they have crossed the river. You do not care for those sitting in your way. You'll happily trample them to get to your beef."

Tapping his assegai against his knee, Soshangane waited for his words to sink in. Waited as mouths opened to disagree, then shut.

"I'll tell you what I see. I see a trap! The Beetle *expects* us to go after the cattle!"

"Master?" said one of the generals.

"Speak! You will not anger me!"

"If you are right, Master – and I do not doubt that you are – what of it? We are many. Let this Beetle try and stop us. We'll crush him!"

"Answer me this, then – who is your leader?"

"You are, Master. And I did not mean . . ."

"Who is your king?"

"Zwide!"

"You do not mean to challenge my authority, and I do not mean to insult your courage, but cross this river here and now, and Shaka is your leader, Shaka is your king, for you are doing exactly what he wants you to do, as surely as if you were Nqoboka, Mgobozi or one of his other mindless jackals!"

"We are many," said one of the generals. Well, they were many at the Umfolozi, too. Shaka is not scared of a fight – so if he leaves a pass or a ford poorly defended there has to be a reason.

Soshangane takes another sip of beer.

There has to be a reason.

And whatever that reason was, it wasn't, as one of his generals suggested, that those soldiers were a rearguard meant to buy Shaka time so the Zulu King could make good his escape.

"Are we Shaka's enemy or his slaves?" Soshangane had asked his sullen officers. "Must we do what he expects us to do, as if it's a royal decree?"

"There lies disaster!" added Zwangendaba, showing Soshangane was right to regard him as one of his ablest generals.

"I agree," said Soshangane. "He knows we are hungry and he expects us to go after the cattle! He wants us to cross this river. Why? I cannot say, but I don't intend to find out!"

What they would do instead came to him in a flash as he was glaring at his men. They'd do the one thing Shaka didn't expect. The one thing he *couldn't* expect. They would make for the Nkandla Forest.

"Where we'll go to ground and await the Beetle's next move," added Soshangane. "Let him come to us for once!"

There were tense moments as some of the regiments at the fords had to be almost forcibly turned around, the officers moving through the ranks, slapping and punching, pulling and pushing hungry men who wanted to cross the river and find those cattle.

This wavering made the force vulnerable, and Soshangane was enraged, would have had men put to death were his anger not balanced by a certain giddy joy at the brilliance of his inspiration, but finally the army was on its way to the forest.

Let Shaka chew on that! Let him think they were retreating!

Yes, decides Soshangane, let's see what he does now! For Shaka is unlikely to allow an invading army so deep into his territory, burning villages as they go, and then let them wander off again.

You thought you had us today, thought we'd stupidly make the same mistake again, but you were wrong, Beetle. And now – where are you? What are you thinking?

*

"Before you go, Noluju – this matter with the Old Sow . . ."

"Yes, Highness?"

"You were . . ."

"I was there to see her off."

"Your position has its rewards."

"This is so, Highness."

"And she said nothing?"

"Not a thing, Highness. Although, as much as it pains me to admit it, I am not her confidante."

"As I said – your position has its rewards. But did she give no indication for her sudden decision to visit her home village?"

"She said nothing, Highness."

"I should be happy, but even when she is not here she vexes me."

"If I may, Highness . . .?"

"Speak!"

"This abomination . . . this *thing* they call the Truthsayer – perhaps you feel it, *he* might have told her something, and that this is not so much a journey, as a fleeing . . ."

"Think you that?"

"Highness, if you're asking whether I would put much faith in this thing's ability to see into the future, then my answer would be no."

"He is quite hideous, is he not?"

"Quite!"

"An affront to the way things should be."

"Indeed!"

"Perhaps, she seeks merely to annoy me. To mock my coming achievements."

"Now, Highness, there I feel you are on the right path."

"To goad me, then to act as if I had accomplished nothing – that is very like her."

"Very, Highness!"

"Good. Leave me now, Noluju."

"Your servant, as ever, Highness!"

Zwide slips his hand between her thighs and Kani, who's been feigning sleep, pretends to come awake.

*

Yellowwoods rise fifty metres high to hold up the sky. With their smooth-barked trunks and cream-coloured blossoms, ironwoods are their rivals in this ceaseless fight for the light, this quietly ferocious struggle of ravenous root systems and interlocked foliage wrestling in the breeze. Battles measured in centuries, victories in seconds – the sudden creak, the sharp crack that heralds the crashing death of an old monarch.

It's as if the trees and the lichens and monkey ropes have entwined to become a giant web that ensnares the night, pulls it to ground in deep, dark shadows. Aren't those squeals and coughs, shrieks and shiftings, the sounds of the night struggling to break free?

Pull your skins tighter around your shoulders, move closer to the fire, keep your assegai close . . .

For Zwangendaba, the forest poses problems of a more prosaic sort. The regiments have been arranged in a crude semicircle around Soshangane's clearing, while the commander in chief's Guards detachment encircles the clearing itself. Or rather, that was Zwangendaba's intent when Soshangane gave him the task of organising the disposition of the force. The very nature of the forest makes such neatness impossible. The regiments have become as entangled as the foliage that surrounds them and some contingents can't even see the campfires of their immediate neighbours.

The men were weary, went to ground where they stood when the order to halt was given – an order that came none too soon, as the regiments were in danger of losing each other in the deepening gloom – and it's more luck than judicious manoeuvring on Zwangendaba's part that they are, more or less, arranged around Soshangane's command post. Although in some places the platoons of one regiment have camped down ahead of the picquets posted by another.

Still, the very things that are causing them problems will affect the Zulus should they decide to launch an assault. It will be impossible for Shaka's disciplined impis to keep their ranks coming through the trees.

Much to his embarrassment, Zwangendaba couldn't find his own regiment for several anxious minutes after going out to inspect the lines. It was only his cook bellowing for him that enabled him to guide his escort back to their campfire.

For an hour or two there's a constant movement, a breaking of twigs and dragging of branches, as the men build their fires, ensure they have enough wood to last the night, and settle down to eat what remains of their rations. Finally the man-sounds subside, are consumed by those of the forest.

Zwangendaba dozes off. A few hours later – it feels like seconds to the general – he's sitting up again, calling to his cook, who's chosen to remain awake, watching over his master.

Noise. The hissed, anxious queries of sentries met by the growled responses of tired men. A blundering. A crunching and crackling. A stamping and stumbling. Bleary voices rise from the ground to curse the elephant who stumbled over a sleeping man, kicked his feet in the darkness, stood on his hand. But these others do not care; some even make a production of arriving, calling for their regiments, finding sleeping forms to kick accidentally on purpose. They have not yet had a chance to sleep, or even to rest.

It's nothing to worry about, says the cook. It's simply the hunting and foraging parties returning.

"Let's hope they've found something for us to eat," mutters Zwangendaba, before slipping back into sleep once more.

Elsewhere, other officers are shouting at the new arrivals to settle down and be still. Never mind finding their regiments – they are confusing the sentries; they must shut up and sleep where they are.

"Did you catch anything, Friend?"

"Not our party."

"Aiee! This Shaka has really chased the game away!"

"So it seems."

"I do not know you. You are not of my regiment."

"And you are not of mine."

"Never mind. Let me make space for you. The ferns are soft here."

The two men lie in silence a while. Gradually, the sounds of movement, the growls and threats tail off.

"At least it is warmer here than where we were last night," whispers the one.

"This is so," sighs the other.

"This is so," echoes the first man drowsily.

When next he opens his mouth it's in a howl of pain as the Induna's assegai blade slams into his gut. For the Zulus are here. The Zulus are among them.

*

"Let them come," said Shaka. "Let them come . . ."

And immediately after the May harvest, he ordered all those living in a sixty-kilometre-wide belt, from the Kingdom's northern boundary to the Thukela River in the south, to remove their grain, their cattle and themselves to the Nkandla Forest. The rest of the nation was to seek refuge in the Edlinza, Dukuduku and other forests.

"Let them come," said Shaka.

And they came, a Ndwandwe army of eighteen thousand, crossing the White Umfolozi. And by harrying the invaders at night, guiding them with cattle spoor during the day, Shaka led them down the corridor he had cleared.

They had waited until the harvest and had expected to find the Zulu granaries full. Instead, they found deserted villages – eerie and depressing – and no food to replenish their dwindling supplies.

Shaka's one fear was that the hungry Ndwandwes might turn back too soon. Hence, the raiding party that snatched away the last of their cattle and the lure on the Sungulweni Heights. By stealing the cattle Shaka ensured that even if they decided to withdraw, the Ndwandwes would run out of food before reaching the safety of their own territory; by having a small detachment of his men being seen to herd cattle over the heights, he offered Soshangane a more immediate solution to his dwindling supplies, a reason to go on.

And those men were to relinquish their beasts the moment the Ndwandwe skirmishers made their appearance, and in fleeing they were to "tell" their pursuers where they were headed.

And so it was that Shaka brought the Ndwandwes to the banks of the Thukela, where he ensured the fords were lightly defended.

And all this time Shaka's main army of ten thousand men was behind the Ndwandwes, waiting in the Nkandla Forest. He and his generals were watching from a hill as Soshangane hesitated at the river. The plan was to fall on the Ndwandwes from the rear when they tried to cross the Thukela.

Then, in a manoeuvre that left the Zulu King speechless, Soshangane withdrew. And came to the forest.

And settled his men a mere four kilometres to the east of the Zulus.

"I may live forever and never forget what I am seeing," said Mgobozi. "He comes to us! He brings himself to us!"

"He is cunning, this one," said Shaka. "He saw the trap."

"But he is not as cunning as you, Father."

"Hai! No! Let us not deceive ourselves, here. I did not plan for this to happen – and now I almost feel sorry for him."

*

The night explodes in sound and movement, running and shouting. The Induna impales two more Ndwandwes before they are even fully awake. Elsewhere, other Zulu warriors are going to work. Sentries are brought down with spear thrusts from behind. One Ndwandwe falls upon another; while waiting to slaughter the one who wins this struggle, Thando kills two more. "To arms! To arms!" shouts the Induna, sending a group of Ndwandwes blundering into Zulu spears; he's followed them, urging them on, telling them to attack, so that when two manage to turn back, he's there, waiting to block their escape. He charges both, ramming one man with his shield, while his iklwa leaps sideways to impale the second. The first man staggers backward then darts to his left, trying to crash through a tangle of bushes. The Induna gives him a moment to realise he's trapped, as surely as if he had stepped into quicksand, then drives his spear into the man's spine. Shapes come crashing toward him. He wheels, his shield and spear raised. "Ndwandwe!" he calls. "Qobolwayo!" comes the response. "Ndwandwe!" says the Induna again, relaxing, telling the Zulus to follow him. "Ndwandwe!" calls Mzilikazi. "Yes! Yes!" comes the panted response. "No! No!" says Mzilikazi as his blade strikes home. Shouts of "Over here! Over here!" Shouts of "This way!" The trees have come alive . . .

*

While his men ate well and prepared enough food for the following day, Shaka briefed his generals. A contingent of four hundred was to circle around the invaders and approach them from the eastern side. They would be the Ndwandwe hunting and foraging parties returning. Because both sides spoke the same language and this "new" army of

Zwide's carried similar shaped shields and short stabbing assegais, such a deception was possible in the darkness. Indeed, because they themselves might find it difficult to distinguish friend from foe, the Zulus would use passwords: the question "Ndwandwe?" followed by the response "Qobolwayo!" with the first man confirming his own identity by repeating the word "Ndwandwe!"

Qobolwayo meant "it is so" or "indisputably"; by answering in this way, one was, in effect, saying: "I am a true Ndwandwe."

This, believed Shaka, would only heighten the confusion – for if questioned in this manner, an enemy soldier was at most likely to respond by saying "I am a Ndwandwe." He'd see no reason to affirm that he was a true Ndwandwe.

When the officers finished explaining this to the men, Shaka moved among the four hundred.

"When their fires have become embers and all are asleep," he said, keeping his voice low, "you will rise up and stab them where they lie! And you will not stop until the approach of dawn!"

*

The trees have come alive. The night has grown teeth. The darkness has claws. Whenever a resourceful Ndwandwe officer manages to rally his men and send them racing to where the screams seem the loudest and most numerous, the Zulus are lying among the Ndwandwe dead, waiting for the formation to pass before springing up and attacking from the rear.

But Soshangane has kept his head. Several officers and their men have managed to hack their way to his clearing – a feat accomplished only by killing anyone in their path, be he Ndwandwe or Zulu. Now he sets some of these men to building up the fires in the clearing, while his Guards regiment stands to, their shields overlapping, their spears ready. Then he sends out his officers again. They have torches and their orders are to call the regiments back toward the clearing. To bring in the semi-circle, such as it is.

"To the fires!" they shout. "To the fires!"

A shattering of twigs; branches and leaves flying apart.

"To the fires!" shouts the Induna. He trips the third Ndwandwe who blunders by, drops onto him, his knee pressed into the soldier's back, and allows the next Ndwandwe to impale himself on his assegai. Then, without rising, using his shield to push the dying man off his blade, he spins the spear – and drives it into the back of the neck of the man on the ground. And immediately lies down next to him as one of the torch bearers and his escorts come crashing through the undergrowth . . .

There are demons here! Otikoloshe! Creatures who ride out at night astride hyenas. They are here! It's the Zulus who start the call, but it's soon picked up by the Ndwandwes. Because it makes sense. Who else could have infiltrated their lines, sneaked past their picquets? The Zulus play dead, thrusting their assegais at the legs that stumble past them, and the hysterical Ndwandwes see this as further proof they're being overwhelmed by otikoloshe, because the attacks seem to come from the direction of the ground, from below the waist, exactly as if the spears were being wielded by tiny creatures atop hyenas. The wounded can testify to this. It's they who spread the rumour most vociferously, for few have actually seen – and grappled with – the Zulu raiders.

"Fools!" bellows Soshangane on hearing the yells. "Cowards!"

Quickly he makes a tour of the human wall formed by his Guards, alternately threatening and reassuring. It's the Zulus, of course it's the Zulus – and fear them more than any supernatural creature! If any man breaks ranks, he'll personally see the coward run through. "Stand firm!" he urges. "Stand firm!"

Lights flicker amid the pandemonium beyond this island of order, as officers desperately try to get their men back. And even when the regiments are clustered around the clearing and the Zulu assault peters away, they are forced to listen to the shrieks of the dying, out there in the dark. The pleas for help.

As soon as he spots the morning star, Soshangane orders his regiments to leave the forest, so that when Shaka comes to inspect the battlefield a few hours later, not a Ndwandwe remains standing.

370

While his men move about dressing the wounds of the raiding party, dis-embowelling the dead and delivering the coup de grâce *to their mortally wounded comrades, Shaka takes the Induna aside.*

They could hear the shouts from where they were camped, he tells the Induna. The marauders killed many Ndwandwes, but more importantly, they ensured Soshangane's army had a sleepless night. That, coupled with a lack of food, will go a long way to neutralising his superior numbers.

"Now I must beg your forgiveness," says Shaka.

"Majesty?" asks the Induna, taken aback.

"You have served me well, but now I must tax your loyalty."

"I am yours to command, Majesty."

There is an important mission he has to undertake for the King. He must take four others and go and fetch the Honey Man.

"Treachery can be a valuable ally, as it has been here, and the Honey Man has served us well, but I do not believe treachery should be rewarded," says Shaka. "However, my mother extracted a promise from me that when victory was assured I would make an attempt to rescue him. I must keep my word and you will help me to do so."

Nandi has made an arrangement with the spy through his emissaries: every full moon after the Ndwandwe army has crossed the White Umfolozi, the Honey Man will watch for a fire burning in the hills that surround KwaDlovungu. That will be the sign for him to make good his escape and to follow the road that leads to Zululand.

"I would leave him to fend for himself," says Shaka, "but I have given my word."

"And your word is mine," says the Induna. "We will save him."

The Honey Man

"Sleep. You are safe now – and even the bravest warrior needs to rest."

Zenga shuts his eyes. It's cool here in the shade, and the grass is soft, and he's home.

Or almost home. They are only about five kilometres away from Kwa-Dlovungu.

And it *is* cool here, and the grass soft.

The fourteen-year-old has been running for three days. He could have – indeed, should have – made the journey in two, but he was so famished he fell on the food offered to him by the first Ndwandwe village he came across, overate and was plagued by an upset stomach that night and most of the following day.

But he has made it, is most certainly better off than the comrades he left behind: he is away from the Zulus and has eaten.

Listless soldiers slouching over hollow bellies, Zulu spears sprouting from the winter grass, cold nights spent shivering around a coughing fire – these all seem like fragments of a bad dream.

Will he be forced to return?

He supposes he'll have to. The king is bound to have a message for Soshangane. And the prospect of having to find the army again fills him with dread. He had an escort coming out of Zulu territory – although, truly, that was no reason for complacency, given the roaming Zulus, appearing out of nowhere to pounce on parties who dared to leave the main group – but going back he'll have to find his own way.

But the grass is so soft, here, in the cool shade, and he's no longer hungry: put that thought aside, push it away. Roll over onto your stomach, your full stomach, smell the grass, enjoy the softness, forget everything else.

Soshangane's briefing was very precise. Zenga must tell Zwide only what the commander in chief has instructed him to. And Zenga is already proud of the way he evaded the anxious questions at the village that fed him.

Soshangane is no fool. It's not beyond Zwide to send out a replacement whose first job will be Soshangane's execution. As a result, his message, composed after thorough consultation with Zwangendaba and the other generals he trusts, is a careful mixture of lies, wishful thinking and smidgens of the truth. Soshangane needs to let Zwide know things haven't gone according to plan; needs, in effect, to prepare Zwide for the bad news, the day when the army comes limping home and lies will be pointless. But Soshangane also exaggerates the Zulu numbers, downplays his own casualties and doubles the number of kraals his men have destroyed. The Zulus flee them, but continue to harass them with cowardly hit-and-run tactics. They won't stand still and fight, and this, Soshangane admits, is wearing his army down. This is the crucial part of the message: if the Ndwandwe army returns it will not be retreating, but merely coming back to replenish its supplies.

Zenga will not let his commander down. Lost in the ranks, never seeing the full picture, he anyway believes what he has been told to tell Zwide. And after Soshangane had given him the message, made him repeat it and left, Zwangendaba warned him to watch what else he was inclined to tell anyone who asked.

"This is war," said Zwangendaba. "War has its setbacks, its hardships. But those at home won't understand this. Neither will they want you to tell them the truth. They'll want to see a brave warrior. Be that warrior. Tell them there have been hardships, but also tell them how you and your comrades have triumphed!"

The deeper Zenga moved into Ndwandwe territory, the truer these words seemed to become. The escort had left him at the White Umfolozi and his initial reaction, once he'd crossed the river and the others were out of sight, had been to throw himself down under the nearest tree and bawl his eyes out. The days of living in fear had finally crashed through his desire not to be seen as a coward. Only the intense hunger and the knowledge that he was less than a day away from a decent meal kept him going. The urge to weep had returned with his first mouthful of beef at the village, but eyes were on him and gradually the wisdom – the *truth* – of Zwangendaba's words had become apparent. He *was* a brave warrior to these stay-at-homes. See how the maidens were eyeing him!

There *were* concerned questions from the elders, but he was looking at the maidens when he replied in the offhand manner he felt fitting for a brave warrior.

In fact, knowing he was now so close to KwaDlovungu, he'd been in the middle of a fantasy, reshaping one of the many stories he intended to tell them – where terror became wry acceptance and fear was a grinning admission – and he hadn't seen the soldiers squatting in the shade alongside the track.

When they rose, calling to him, he'd almost fainted from fright, instantly hurled back into that other realm of hunger and fear and marauding Zulus; that unreal reality.

But, of course, they were Ndwandwe soldiers, members of Zwide's bodyguard. They fed him, gave him water, said he could sleep if he wanted to, while one of them set off for KwaDlovungu.

And a few hours later, when the cool shadows have become colder, awakening Zenga – sitting him up; terrified, disorientated – Noluju is solicitude itself, as he first inquires after Zenga's wellbeing. What regiment is he with? Who are his parents? Where do they stay? It is only after these kind questions, and after Noluju has told one of the soldiers with him to give the teenager some beer, that Zwide's chief councillor takes Zenga aside and asks him to relay Soshangane's message.

Noluju listens impassively, and Zenga is mildly surprised when the councillor doesn't ask him any questions. He supposes these will come later, during his audience with Zwide. Aiee! He'll be meeting the king! Another honour!

Noluju calls the captain of the guard. "I have heard enough," he says.

The officer nods. He runs his spear through Zenga and calls for two men to carry the body away.

*

It's mid-morning when the Zulus catch up to the Ndwandwes, who are waiting for them east of Sungulweni. They outnumber the Zulus, can still muster more than sixteen thousand, but the men are tired and hungry and their mobility is further hampered by their loose-fitting sandals. Shaka's ten thousand, by contrast, are rested, well fed, in good shape. All the same, the terrain here is flat, and favours Soshangane's superior numbers. His orders are relayed by his officers and the Ndwandwes spread out, offering the Zulus a front some six hundred metres wide and several lines deep. The men stand shoulder to shoulder, ready to raise their shields and spears to meet the Zulu charge, for Soshangane has decreed the enemy must come to them. The two armies are about two kilometres apart and his men need to conserve their energy. More importantly, his regiments should be able to envelop the Zulus by sheer weight of numbers; in attacking, Shaka will become the boy ramming a stick into a bees' nest and Soshangane's bees will cover him, overwhelm him.

Shaka issues his orders. His generals raise and wave their swallow-tail axes and the Izintenjana and the Ukangela, two of the King's younger regiments, move out to the right and left of the main body, each forming a column five men abreast.

Thinking these are the horns of Shaka's Bull seeking to outflank him, Soshangane extends his front by ordering the rear ranks to move to the right and left and come forward.

Marching at a steady pace, the Tenjana and Kangela regiments continue on a course almost parallel to the Ndwandwes, veering in occasionally, before drifting away again.

Soshangane extends his front even further. Once, twice, the orders echo, until the Ndwandwe commander in chief realises that if this continues his front will become dangerously attenuated as more and more men from the rear ranks are called forward to fill in the gaps. His centre will then be vulnerable to attack from the main body of the Zulus, still arrayed opposite him.

He examines the horns again. The Tenjana is on his left, the Kangela on his right, and for every two steps forward, the columns move five steps sideways. Somehow both are keeping in pace so that neither has moved ahead of the other. Soshangane despatches his messengers . . .

The outermost regiment on each of the wings breaks away and the Ndwandwe centre contracts again. Shaka grins when he sees this. It's what he was hoping for – and the officers leading the two columns know what to do. He gives the order to charge – and the Zulu centre races forward in silence, their hardened feet crushing rough, winter-dry grass so that it suddenly sounds as if the veld has caught fire. The Ndwandwes ready themselves – but the Zulu centre stops two spears' throw away from the enemy. Only the flanks carry on to engage the Ndwandwe flanks.

There's a loud crash as muscle-driven cowhide tests the straining thighs and tendons of the waiting warriors. The Zulu momentum curls the Ndwandwe line inward at each end. Soshangane bellows frantic orders: the men in the centre must stand firm. On no account must they turn and try to aid their comrades. But even as the regiments on each end of the line recover themselves, soldiers from the rear ranks surging forward to take the places of the fallen, and his men begin to push the Zulus back, Soshangane realises what Shaka's intent is – and there's nothing he can do about it!

The Tenjanas and Kangelas have each drifted so far to the side that the regiments Soshangane detached to shadow them have wheeled. And as the Zulu flanks curled the Ndwandwe line inward, two columns of Fasimbas streamed out from behind the battling ranks, one column going right, one going left, charging straight for the exposed rear of each of the regiments facing the Tenjanas and Kangelas – who mark time until the Fasimbas are close enough, before attacking as well.

Each Ndwandwe regiment is trapped, sandwiched between two Zulu impis coming at them from opposite sides, and Soshangane can only watch the slaughter that ensues.

He daren't weaken his centre by despatching reinforcements – after all, the main force of Zulus is right here in front of him, just fifty metres away. Anyway, guided by the Zulus as surely as herdboys lead cattle, the detached formations have each moved about seven hundred metres away; they're out of reach.

Soshangane can only hope the two doomed regiments manage to hold out for as long as possible.

And they do. Crushed together, trapped, tripping over each other's feet, they fight back ferociously, with a courage that has Shaka praising them. When their annihilation is complete it's clear they've killed enough Zulus in the combined impis to render these too weak to threaten Soshangane's flanks. And he seizes his chance. As Shaka breaks off the holding action that kept the ends of the Ndwandwe line pinned back, Soshangane gives the order to attack . . .

*

"Yes. Yes, that *is* good news!"

"I thought you'd be pleased, Highness."

"We *have* suffered losses . . ."

". . . but not as many as the Beetle, Highness."

"Hmm."

"Who appears to be on the run."

"So it seems."

"Soshangane is an able leader, he'll not let his ruler down."

"If he knows what's good for him."

"Quite."

"So the Beetle flees before our mighty army, and comes creeping back at night . . ."

"Rearguard actions, Highness. To slow us down. At least this is my opinion. Highness."

"It is not like Shaka to run. He is many things, but not a coward."

"But can he fight off the inevitable, Highness?"

"Where is this messenger? I would reward him."

"Highness! My apologies! But I sent him to visit his parents. Let that be his reward – after all, he merely carries the good news! And, Highness,

I thought it would be good for the people to have a brave warrior fresh from thrashing the Beetle's dogs walk among them."

"Yes. Let them hear for themselves."

"And the heroic tales he tells will be built upon the truth, no matter how much he embellishes, Highness."

"This is so."

"However, I can have him summoned, Highness. If that is your wish . . ."

"No. Let him enjoy the attention. Let that be his reward."

"A wise decision, Highness. But perhaps I'll have him fetched for you in a day or so."

"Yes. Thank you, Noluju. Leave me now."

"Your servant, as ever, Highness!"

Zwide is sitting astride an upturned log, his belly sagging between his thighs. After Noluju has left, the king of the Ndwandwes leans back against one of the wooden pillars that support the thatch of his large hut. It's early evening and gloomy. Time to light the fire . . .

Zwide allows himself a derisive snort. Turning his head toward the smaller rear entrance he calls Kani.

Can it be? he wonders. Can it be?

*

The Ndwandwe front surges forward, howling for Zulu blood.

And the Zulus retreat.

Worried that Shaka might be up to something, not quite trusting the discipline of his own men, Soshangane calls a halt after they've advanced a hundred metres.

And the Zulus halt, too, fifty metres from the Ndwandwe front ranks.

Convinced now that this Beetle is up to something, Soshangane orders his men forward five paces – and watches as the Zulus retreat five paces.

In this way, a strange, staccato war dance ensues. The Ndwandwes advance and the Zulus retreat. When the Ndwandwes sprint forward, the Zulus run from them. When they walk, the Zulus walk. The discipline they show is remarkable. For it isn't a case of every man simply turning and racing away. When the Ndwandwes come forward, the Zulus in the first row peel off and move between the ranks to form up behind what was the rear row. They'll be followed by the men in the second row, and so on, so there's always at least one line facing the enemy.

So it goes for about a kilometre, until Soshangane calls a halt to this foolishness. His soldiers are starving, weak. They no longer even have the energy to taunt the Zulus.

Shaka watches the Ndwandwes withdraw, then orders his generals to have the men sit.

*

After lighting the fire, Kani sits at Zwide's feet. Runs a hand along his thigh. "You are perturbed, Master?"

Zwide looks down at her. "And you? You were listening?"

"As you instructed, Master."

"And?"

"I look to you for guidance, Master!"

"Cha!"

"I am a woman, I know little of these things."

"But?"

Kani shrugs, seems fascinated by the tracks her nails leave in Zwide's skin. "But . . ." she murmurs. "I am afraid."

Zwide brings his knees together, almost trapping her hand, curls his fingers under her chin and lifts her face so he can see her eyes. "Afraid? Why?"

"Zwide is my master now. I . . . I will have no truck with those Zulu hyenas!"

"This was not your father's attitude."

"I am not my father. And you are my master now."

"But you are afraid?"

She nods. "What will happen if they come?"

"Cha!"

379

Zwide pushes her backwards and stands.

Kani shuffles sideways. "I have angered you."

Zwide runs a hand along the elephant tusk leaning against the wall of the hut. "Are you surprised?" he asks. "Such treachery!" he adds, turning.

"No, Master!" says Kani, rising to her feet. "No! Not treachery. Never treachery! Just fear, Master."

"But you heard Noluju! We are crushing the Beetle."

Here they are again. This is an old bone, one they've circled many times. Many times, Zwide wary, yet perturbed by her carefully chosen phrases, waiting for Kani to give him an excuse to accuse her of disloyalty and send her away – that being the simplest, least taxing manner to deal with the doubt she has scattered in his mind. Zwide commanding her to eavesdrop on Noluju's report was a sign she's getting somewhere, but she still needs to build on that, daren't squander what she has gained.

"Yes, Highness," Kani agrees. "With little exertion, it seems."

"Hai! There have been setbacks! Losses . . ."

"Yes, Highness."

"Call me Master. I like it better."

"As you wish. Master."

"And as you have admitted: you are a female. What do you know of these things? You should be rejoicing, not pestering me with your complaints."

"I know Shaka is powerful, Master."

"But no match for me!"

"Of course not, Master!"

"He is a worthy adversary, though."

"But you have him, Master. Defeat him and this land is yours."

"Hai! How he will hate to see that!"

Kani smiles. "He will do anything to stop you."

"This is so."

"Yet his troops run . . ."

Zwide stiffens. "What do you mean?" His voice is the snarl of a dog facing shifting shadows.

"I do not know," whispers Kani.

Zwide's arm whips out, his fingers closing around the concubine's arm. "What do you mean?" he hisses, squeezing her flesh.

Fighting a desire to pull away, Kani shakes her head. "I don't know, Master." She bites back a gasp of pain. "This is why I seek your guidance."

Zwide lets go of her arm. A *concubine*! Has it come to this? That he listens to the plaints of a concubine?

But as Zwide's favourite, doesn't she have even more to lose than Noluju? Might not her concerns be justified, then, her suspicions reasonable? Without Zwide she is nothing. Whereas Noluju might have brokered a deal with Shaka . . .

Kani's hands curl over his tense shoulders: pressure, release; pressure, release. Zwide shuts his eyes, rolls his head.

Outside, the moon is full, shining brightly in the sky, edging the huts with silver. In the hills to the east, one can just make out the glow of a bonfire.

*

Zwide will be enraged when they return empty-handed. That Soshangane has burnt kraals and kept the Ndwandwe army intact will matter little to the ruler. But these are passing thoughts as the commander trudges along amid his Guards regiment. Right now, Zwide and his wrath are the lesser of two evils, for Soshangane doubts that Shaka is finished with them.

After withdrawing a sufficient distance from the Zulu host Soshangane had rearranged his army into a wide front, with each of his sixteen regiments forming a single line, giving him an impressive formation sixteen men deep. There's no way the Zulus, who have eaten, and are once more in sight – a black mass several kilometres to the rear – can outflank them. But they are there, nonetheless, tailing the Ndwandwe army, which still outnumbers them! Not that this fact is apparent in the hunched shoulders and bowed heads of the Ndwandwe soldiers. The once-mighty army has become an ailing elephant pursued by patient hyenas. Six of them in fact, for Shaka has split up his force into that number of compact, separate bodies.

And now even the terrain turns against Soshangane. The open, undulating veld that favours his formation is breaking up, becoming furrows and dongas, ravines widening into dry depressions with high walls. Gaps begin to appear in the Ndwandwe ranks. Soon the army becomes a series of columns each trying to negotiate its own way through and around these obstacles.

And exactly like hyenas, the Zulu regiments pounce, eating up rear-guards and stragglers. And there are the Tenjanas and Kangelas, each still bolstered by a contingent of veterans from the Fasimbas. In destroying the two regiments Soshangane had foolishly detached, they suffered heavy casualties; but they are still a force to be reckoned with, lurking ahead of the Ndwandwes, stalking and killing the scouts sent out by Soshangane.

*

Two days later another messenger comes trotting along, clutching his spear and with a waterskin strung diagonally across his chest. The Ndwandwe soldiers are mildly surprised; this one must have been despatched on the heels of the other. Or perhaps Soshangane sent several messengers each with the same message to ensure his report got through, and this one lost his way.

They rise from their resting place in the shade and hail the youngster. The leader of the trio sends one man jogging off to KwaDlovungu and the other to a nearby stream to fetch fresh water.

"Come, rest," he tells the messenger.

"Is the news bad?" he asks.

"For you, yes," says the Induna's udibi.

The Ndwandwe soldier looks down at the spear embedded in his gut. Looks up at the boy.

"Ngadla!" whispers the udibi, tightening his grip on the iklwa as the soldier topples backward, sliding off the blade.

Moments later, Njikiza ambles up the path from the stream, his mighty club bloodied.

Thando and the Induna emerge from their hiding places and join the boy.

The four were watching when Zenga was waylaid, noted the procedure that was followed and saw what happened after the group from KwaDlovungu arrived. Since then, they've discovered three bodies disposed of in separate locations and evidence of a fourth, which had been torn from its hiding place by hyenas. Clearly, being a messenger in Zwide's army is not conducive to longevity.

*

Positioned behind his Guards regiment, Soshangane can't see the mistake he's making; standing on a rocky outcrop overlooking the ford, Shaka spots it instantly.

He'd eventually called his men back as the sun began to set and the terrain opened up again and Soshangane was once more able to concentrate his forces. The Ndwandwes camped in the open; sixteen long lines, with no food and scarcely enough fuel to light more than a dozen fires. The officers had the men up and moving at daybreak. Now it's mid-morning and they've reached the Umhlatuzi River. Still able to field more than eleven thousand men, Soshangane was ready for battle – but when they made their appearance, the Zulus remained atop the ridge looking down upon the river, Shaka in his white regalia, clearly visible among his generals.

The Ndwandwes had reached the Umhlatuzi in formation, presenting a front some two kilometres wide. Soshangane retains this and places his Guards regiment in a phalanx between the Zulus and his main force, directly opposite the ford. The Zulus remain sitting on their shields and after waiting an hour – judging the passing of the time by the position of the sun – Soshangane gives the order to begin the crossing. The ford can only accommodate twenty men abreast, and the rear rank of the main force begins moving into the water, twenty men from the right,

twenty men from the left; the long line gradually shrinking. But Soshangane is too low down to see the problem he's creating for himself; or
perhaps he only has eyes for the Zulus perched above him.

His bodyguard regiment remains a compact mass, but he's not short-
ening his ranks to make up for the lines crossing the Umhlatuzi and
thereby preserving the density of the formation. It remains strung out
over two kilometres, but gets thinner and thinner as sixteen ranks become fifteen, fifteen become fourteen . . .

"We cannot let them get away again," Shaka had told his generals the
previous night. "We must not allow the praise singers and our own pride
to blind us, here. At Gqokli we only saw them off. Now we need to crush
them! Crush them once and for all! Remember, we have other enemies.
If we falter here, we will have still more!"

And here's his chance: with the Ndwandwes wading into the water
and the main formation growing ever more brittle, a log eaten away by
white ants.

It's time to feed the vultures!

Time to make the crocodiles sing his praises!

Shaka issues his commands.

When half the Ndwandwe army has crossed the river, he throws six of
his eight regiments at Soshangane.

"Up!" he bellows, raising his spear. "Up, Children Of Zulu – your day
has come! Kill them! Kill them all!"

Ranks of Zulus pour over the ridge and down the hill, leaping over
boulders and bushes.

"Si-Gi-Diiiiiiiiiiiiiiii!"

The Ndwandwe Guards bring their shields up and prepare for impact.
At the foot of the hill, the two regiments on each Zulu flank peel off
slightly. The two regiments in the centre keep coming forward. What the
Ndwandwes don't see is how one of these hangs back, allowing the first
to race ahead.

The collision shakes the ground and the Ndwandwe Guards are driven
back two, three, four paces in a mist of blood. And then, in the moment

of inertia before their superior numbers can recover and begin to push forward, the first rank of the second Zulu regiment crashes into the tangle. Following closely behind them are two rows of men. The soldiers in the first group are only carrying shields. As the Ndwandwe phalanx again staggers backward, these men raise their shields. Each chosen for his height, they wedge themselves between their comrades and send their shields sliding face down over the bobbing heads. Then they crouch and lean forward, hands on knees to brace themselves – as the second group comes racing up. These men are carrying only spears. Stepping onto the proffered backs, the warriors throw themselves onto the shields – and go crashing into the Ndwandwe rear ranks. They are a punishment platoon, soldiers who have been singled out by their indunas for dereliction of duty. This is their way to redeem themselves and all seize the chance. Many will die even before they can use their spears, impaled as they come crashing off the shields, but the effect on Ndwandwe morale, not to mention the vital cohesion of the rear ranks, is devastating.

Meanwhile, the two regiments on each flank have skirted the Guards to fall on Soshangane's long extended front on the river bank. They cannot match the width of that front, but it's become so denuded it doesn't matter where they hit it and there's little chance of them being enveloped by the ranks left free on either side. Zulu shields send men flying into the river. The Ndwandwes have no room to manoeuvre and there's a surge inwards, toward the ford. But, of course, there're men here, too – the shallows are choked with lines of soldiers trying to cross and there are those awaiting their turn. At the same time, the Guards' phalanx is being pushed backwards, beginning to break up. The result is a screaming tangle. The warriors in the water – those who've just begun to cross – turn and Ndwandwe fights Ndwandwe as men throw themselves into the water, trying to pull their comrades out of the way.

Chaos. Pushing and shoving. Kicking and shouting. The Zulu impis have turned Soshangane's orderly withdrawal into something that makes a rout seem like a parade.

Soshangane's only option is to bellow to his Guards to stand firm! And even then that's because they need to halt their backwards drift so they can resume it in a more orderly fashion.

Across the river, Zwangendaba realises fleeing soldiers are the least of his worries – the other two Zulu regiments have made their appearance. They've crossed the Umhlatuzi higher up and now they bear down on the Ndwandwes who are already disconcerted by the slaughter going on behind them. Or is it in front of them? That's how disorganised they've become, more a mob than a military formation, with some men facing the river while the others look longingly in the opposite direction, contemplating flight. The Zulus put paid to that notion, however. Running hard, they're among the Ndwandwes before they even know what hit them.

*

It's only out here, in the open country, that one realises just how oppressive the atmosphere in KwaDlovungu has become. The fact that Zwide has forbidden free movement and ensures the gates and walls are guarded day and night, contributes to the tension, but it's not the main cause. It's an order he would have issued anyway, even if he knew beyond a doubt victory was his, for he wouldn't put it past Shaka to send an impi to KwaDlovungu in a last-ditch attempt to stave off defeat. No, it's something that merely exacerbates the sense of foreboding that's settled over the capital. The longer the army has been away, the longer the people have had to sit and think. While the army was being called together and was quartered at KwaDlovungu, the many extra mouths to feed were of more immediate concern – and cause for endless complaint. One didn't have time to consider the wider implications. Now, though, with almost all able-bodied males gone, minds are free to contemplate the future.

You don't have to be a general to know this is an endgame. Shaka can't – and won't – tolerate Zwide sitting on his flank, plotting and scheming. The matter will be decided once and for all, over there, across the hills, and the outcome will change the lives of both tribes. One will be enriched, the other obliterated, for Zwide and Shaka have this in common: both know the other cannot be left alive to rebuild. It has to be all or nothing.

And the people are talking about the fires they've spotted on three consecutive nights. What do they mean? An omen? A warning? Even Zwide's concerned – and this morning he's told Noluju to send platoons out to find the source of the fires.

Despite being worried, however, he was still able to enjoy the effect his second order of the day had on Noluju. He understood the need for secrecy, he explained. It was a good idea to keep the messengers away from the kraal until they had been thoroughly questioned by Noluju; rumours flare up so easily in times of war. However, continued Zwide, since Kani felt she could do with the exercise, she was to accompany Noluju and his men on this occasion.

The councillor had spent a lot of time bowing and saying "Yes, Highness" around Zwide and disguising his true feelings, but he couldn't stop his jaw from dropping.

Zwide snorted and let Noluju know he chose to regard his councillor's aghast expression as one of surprised delight, delighted surprise. "She will surely brighten your mundane journey," he added.

"Indeed, Sire," said Noluju. "It's just that I fear for her safety."

"Why? Your men are able. *You* are able. And we have the Beetle on the run . . ."

"Shaka is cunning."

"Well then – a little danger will only add to the pleasure of the journey for her."

At first Noluju set a blistering pace, hoping to tire out Kani, but he was the one who faltered and surreptitiously returned them to a brisk walk.

And Kani's enjoying his chagrin as much as she enjoys the lightness that comes with being away from the capital. He and a captain lead the way, while she strolls behind them, followed by ten men. She can just imagine what the councillor is thinking. The ignominy! It's bad enough having to involve a woman in the business of men – but the ruler's con-

PART FOUR: THE FORTRESS ON THE PLAIN

cubine? Aiee! That is too much! And see? She has even armed herself with a spear! Who does she think she is?

Well, he knows the answer to *that* question: she is Zwide's spy!

Their pace quickens when they spot the men waiting on the path by a stand of trees. Then the captain grabs hold of Noluju's arm, pulling him to a stop.

"Master," he hisses, "those are not our men!"

Noluju's response is a querulous "What?"

"See – there are three when there should be two!"

Unnoticed, Kani moves to the side so she can look past the two. There are indeed three men standing on the path, two with shields and spears, the third a big, hulking brute carrying a club. With them is a boy. He, too, carries a spear.

"They are waiting for us," says the captain.

So it would seem, agrees Kani silently. The strangers will have spotted them, but they make no attempt to move.

"Zulus," murmurs Noluju.

"Yes," says the captain.

"I am intrigued."

"Intrigued?" asks the captain.

"Yes," says Noluju. "What do they want? Clearly, they do not mean to invade us."

"They are armed."

"As are we!" Noluju swivels to confront the captain. "Do you mean to say you fear three Zulu warriors and their herdboy?"

"No," grunts the captain. "I am merely . . . *intrigued* to know where the rest might be hiding."

Grinning, Kani eases past the men. "Let us see what they want," she says.

"See?" says Noluju. "Even Zwide's concubine is unafraid. Have your men follow us – and be alert."

He jogs to catch up with Kani and strides past her, so he is in front, as befits his status. "Stay behind me and don't say a word," he tells her.

*

Shrieks of fear. Screams of pain. Zulu assegais on both sides of the river striking again and again. Dust. Blood. Blazing sweat. Writhing, screeching, seething death.

Mgobozi, atop the ridge with Shaka, says: "You throw the shield, Father! And let me fly into those jackals."

"Be still, Old Goat!" Shaka replies, his eyes never leaving the battle.

Assegai blades are black. Shields are torn, cracked, discarded. Fingers become talons; teeth fangs. Wet dust. Dusty blood. The two entangled armies have become a third creature, sliding around in the slick mess of its afterbirth, looking to stand, struggling to breathe, howling in pain; a creature that lives only to die, to devour itself.

"At least let me go after the princes again," says Mgobozi.

"There are no princes here today," growls Shaka, "only brave warriors."

The Umhlatuzi is running red. Tangled bodies form a low parapet on the upstream side of the ford; downstream, they spin away, turning over and over in the current.

Then, as suddenly as the sucker punch to the solar plexus that takes your breath away, there's a lull . . .

A panting silence . . .

A wary watching, a weary waiting, as the Ndwandwes on both sides of the river find themselves temporarily protected by a redoubt of bodies.

The Zulu indunas look up to where Shaka stands.

"What say you, Mgobozi?" asks the King.

The general surveys the scene below them. The bodies entwined like thatchwork, piled up like logs, squirming like crushed frogs. The blood red river. The waiting men.

"Truly, I love war," he says, "it spares me from the lethal ministrations of my wives. But a surfeit can be as bad as a lack, as the child who has stolen his mother's amasi skin can tell you."

"It is time to end it, because it is ended."

"Yes, Father."

"Do it, Mgobozi."

Mgobozi raises his axe, twirls it in a tight circle, moves the swallow-tail blade back and forth over his head twice, signifying the King's command is for the regiments on both sides of the river, then he jerks the axe once more over his head, a short, sharp gesture.

Orders smother the groans of the wounded and dying, and the Zulu regiments back away from the Ndwandwes, giving themselves space to pick up enough speed to leap atop and over the human bulwarks should they attack again.

The Ndwandwes remain motionless, crowded together on the bank, standing knee-deep in the red water of the crossing, as though a single thoughtless movement will once more unleash the Zulu lions.

*

"Aiee! Invaders! I am quaking with fear! What do you want, Zulu?"

The Induna grins. "We have come for that which is ours."

"And what's that?" asks Noluju.

"Know you not?"

"All I can offer you is death."

The Induna looks past him. He sees there's a woman with Noluju – armed with a spear, no less – and considers her presence to be out of the ordinary, but he pays her little heed, lets Noluju see the disdain on his face as he examines the captain and his ten men.

"And where is the army which can bring this about?"

Noluju's laugh is theatrical. "Such arrogance," he says, grinning.

The Induna shrugs. Noluju is a metre away, with Kani a step behind him; the councillor's escort has spread out, so that the men are standing abreast about five metres from the Zulus. The Induna's flanked by Njikiza, on his left, and Thando, on his right; the boy stands a pace behind him and to the side.

The boy has allowed his gaze to linger on Kani – precisely because one doesn't expect to see a woman with soldiers under these circumstances. And because he soon realises he's seen her before.

"No," says the Induna, "the arrogance is yours if you think those men are enough to make my knees tremble."

"But you are so far from home," smiles Noluju.

Yes! She's Nonhlakanipho! One of the daughters of Dondo of the Khumalos! She had served them while the Induna tried to convince the old chief not to trust Zwide.

"Where a Zulu stands is where Shaka rules. Maybe *you* are the interloper."

She had served them, the boy remembers, and had scarcely been able to take her eyes off the Induna.

"Why are you here?" asks Noluju.

"Cha! I have told you."

Noluju opens his mouth, is about to speak, when, behind him, Kani lunges forward, and her feminine grunt precedes his gasp by a fraction of a second. It happens so quickly, the Induna is still watching the councillor's face, waiting for his response. And he sees Noluju's mouth drop open. Sees the other man's eyes widen in shock. And both he and Noluju look down at the same time, to where the blade of Kani's spear has popped out of the councillor's stomach. Noluju's expression is frowning, quizzical when he looks up, as though the Induna might be able to explain why this has happened. Then Kani tugs on the spear haft, freeing the blade, and Noluju topples forward.

"Aiee!" she says, stepping over the body. "Are these all the men you have? Where are the others?"

"Who –" begins the Induna.

"Don't you know this is Ndwandwe territory?"

"– are you?"

"Now we are five against eleven – and you are supposed to be rescuing me!"

"You are –"

"The Honey Man. Yes. Why else would I be here?"

"But –?"

"I am a woman. What of it? Men find me sweet. I am as honey to them."

391

"I know you," says the Induna.

"This is so, but do you think this is the time to renew our acquaintance?"

"Master," murmurs Njikiza.

The Induna pushes the concubine aside. "Well, what are we to do, Njikiza?" he asks loudly, his eyes on the soldiers, pinpointing those likely to flee and those spoiling for bloodshed. "Are we in a generous mood today? Will we grant these lizards their wish? For truly, it seems as if they would dearly like to die today."

"Get them!" shouts the captain.

Two paces. That's how far he gets before Thando's throwing spear hits him. One more step, and he crashes into the grass.

The spear embedded itself in the place where the neck meets the shoulder – and Njikiza chuckles.

"Aiee! You nearly missed!"

"Cha!" snaps Thando, unclipping another incusa from his shield, "I meant to hit him there."

Glancing at Thando, Njikiza sees he is holding a second throwing spear. He grins, turns his attention back to the Ndwandwes.

"You can't do it again."

"Would you test me?"

"Are you afraid?"

"Only of your shame on being proven wrong."

"Do not worry about things that will not come to pass."

"Aiee," says Kani to the Induna, "are all Zulus this talkative?"

"You are the Honey Man?" It's both a disbelieving question and a bemused statement.

Kani turns to the boy. "You are the one who met my brother?" she asks.

The boy nods, keeping his eyes on the Ndwandwes.

"Very well," says Thando. "So be it. You choose the one you would have me impale."

"And is your arm healed?" asks Kani.

Now the udibi looks at her.

"For did you not encounter cannibals on your journey and was it not your bravery that saved your companions?"

"Uhm," says Njikiza, taking a casual step forward, his club resting against his right shoulder.

The Ndwandwes shrink behind their shields. Those on the side closest to the big Zulu take a step back.

The boy nods. He would correct her statement about his bravery, but now is not the time. He doesn't believe he was brave then and he certainly doesn't feel courageous right now.

"Yes," says Njikiza. He extends his right arm, as if the club were a mere walking stick. "That one over there."

"The one with the black and brown shield?" asks Thando.

"Hai, no! That would be too easy. The little one next to him."

"Then am I the Honey Man?" asks Kani.

The boy nods. "You are also Nonhlakanipho, daughter of Dondo, and you are indeed very sweet."

Kani inclines her head with a grin. "Not as sweet as your words, Brave Warrior."

Leaving the boy beaming happily, oblivious as to where he is for the moment, she turns to the Induna: "Now are you convinced?"

"The little one, then," says Thando. "Come," he calls, "come to me, Little One!"

"Come, Little One," says Njikiza, advancing another pace. "You must charge, or else our contest will be pointless. And if you duck, you will get further than this other one."

"Don't listen to him," says Thando. "My spear will find you whatever you do."

"Not if you use your shield," says Njikiza, "and you do know how to use your shield, Little One?"

The step he takes means he has only another to take before he can bring his club into play.

It's the moment the Induna's been waiting for. "Now!" he shouts.

*

Soshangane moves through the remaining ranks of his Guards regiment and says something to one of the men in the front row. As Shaka and Mgobozi watch, some Ndwandwe soldiers start pulling bodies aside to make a path for Soshangane. These men would follow him once the way is clear, but he waves them back.

Striding forward alone, carrying only a spear, he approaches the Zulu ranks. Once more the indunas look up to the rock where Shaka stands. Stepping away from Mgobozi, the Zulu King spreads his arms.

And the Zulu ranks part to allow Soshangane through.

A few paces away from the foot of the shallow slope, Soshangane halts. His eyes on Shaka, he breaks his spear over his raised knee and flings the fragments into the dust. There's anger in the gesture, in the way he throws the broken spear down, and contempt, too. The anger of a brave and capable leader forced to admit defeat; contempt for his own action, for choosing this way instead of dying like a warrior.

Shaka raises his spear.

"Go well, my brother in arms! Let the praise singers remember your name! Hamba kahle!"

Soshangane turns and makes his way back to the remains of his army. Fewer than three hundred are left standing and it doesn't take long for Zwangendaba to hustle them through the ford.

Soshangane is the last to cross.

But history hasn't finished with him yet. Eventually making his way north, Soshangane, son of Zikode, will settle in what will later become Mozambique. He'll father the Shangane nation and establish a mighty empire to rival Shaka's on the east coast of the continent, stretching from Delagoa Bay to the Zambezi River.

*

"I said you'd get your chance," Shaka tells Mgobozi, "and here it is: fetch me Zwide!"

And Mgobozi and one thousand warriors make their way to KwaDlovu-ngu, killing the journey in two days. They are joined by the Induna's men on the outskirts of the kraal and approach the capital singing Ndwa-ndwe war songs. But Zwide has already fled, and Mgobozi and the Induna have to restrain the soldiers from taking out their wrath on the remaining inhabitants of KwaDlovungu.

"For they are now our brothers and sisters," Mgobozi tells the men.

It's a change in status the rest of the Zulu army ignores. Sweeping through Ndwandwe territory with Shaka they kill every man, woman, child and dog they encounter, burn every kraal and capture all the cattle, sheep and goats they can find. Still, Shaka respects his old friend's decision when he arrives at Zwide's capital. KwaDlovungu will not be razed; instead it will become a war kraal in this new "province" of Zululand and these new brothers and sisters will be expected to keep the regiments stationed here supplied with food.

In early 1906, angry at unfair taxation, a Zulu chieftain of the Zondi clan, Bambata KaMancinza, led an uprising against colonial rule. His impi attacked a police patrol, killing four men, one of whom had his genitals removed so sangomas could make a medicine that would protect the chief's followers against White bullets. Bambata and his men then took refuge in the Nkandla Forest and proceeded to conduct a guerrilla campaign against the Zululand Field Force, a volunteer militia raised to combat the rebellion.

The chief's luck finally ran out in June when he and his men were ambushed in the Mome Gorge. Of fourteen hundred men, less than half managed to survive the dumdum bullets poured down upon them by the militia, who refused to accept any surrender. A head cut off from one of the bodies was later identified by a number of Zulus as Bambata. But some say the pugnacious chief had the last laugh: those questioned by the authorities lied and Bambata was safely smuggled into Mozambique.

Dinzulu KaCetshwayo was King of the Zulus at this time. He had spent ten years imprisoned on St Helena and, after assuming the throne, was forced to watch as white settlers encroached on Zulu land and colonial authorities sought to stifle Zulu nationalism once and for all. He was therefore no ally of the Crown. But although he had granted Bambata an audience with him, he did not take an active part in the uprising.

However, Dinzulu was duly summoned to Pietermaritzburg, capital of the Natal Colony, to meet with the governor, Sir Henry McCallum, and prove his nonparticipation in the rebellion. Obese, alcoholic and not officially recognised as the King of the Zulus, being instead "employed" by the colonial administration as "government induna and advisor", Dinzulu was nonetheless feared by the authorities. He was after all the son of the mighty Cetshwayo. One word from him and every Zulu in Natal would have risen up in support of Bambata. And, a year later, his many nervous enemies would eventually ensure he was convicted and imprisoned for the lesser charge of having harboured Bambata's wives.

But on this occasion he was accompanied by his prime minister, Mankulumana. And it was Mankulumana – the White Rhino – who acted as his spokesman and who, through his eloquence, saved Dinzulu from a trial that could well have led to the gallows. He convinced everyone of the King's innocence and, on leaving for home, Dinzulu was presented with a musket and a shotgun.

Mankulumana, the man who saved the Zulu King, was Zwide's grandson.

The Shongololo

The millipede is black, ten centimetres long and flows across the red sand on legs like eyelashes, leaving a tiny furrow in its wake. Then – a rolling rumble shakes the ground. As it's swallowed by dust, the millipede rolls its cylindrical, segmented body into the tight coil that gives the tiny armour-plated invertebrate its Zulu name. The ground trembles, shudders, as the impi moves past – rustling amashoba, shields rising and falling; a thousand men on the march. And, miraculously, the shongololo remains untouched by the rhythmic drumming of bare feet . . .

*

It has to be the boy.

Of all of them, he's the lightest, the most agile. He's also more or less the right height.

"Are you ready?"

A nod that's perhaps a little too vigorous. "Yes, Master."

He's scared, but he'd rather die than show it. All the same, his fear is there for all to see, in a certain sternness of expression, the kind of careful concentration that a man trying to hide his drunkenness – and fooling no one – might employ. The Induna's faith goes a long way to bolstering his confidence, but it can't quite still the churning in his gut, the faint tremble in his hands as he checks the sack, making sure it's in the right position, dangling within easy reach against his left hip.

Deep, with a wide opening, the sack is made out of cowhide. It's filled with broken spears, each comprising the broad blade and about thirty centimetres of shaft. Skin from six slaughtered cattle has been cut into long thin strips and plaited together to make a series of ropes; the end of one of these is tied around the boy's waist.

"Do not rush," says the Induna. "We do not *need* you to rush."

"Yes, Master."

"Here –" says Njikiza.

Gratefully, the boy accepts the waterskin, gulping down several mouthfuls of water. He's already sweating; his mouth a bowl of ash.

He hands the waterskin back to the Watcher Of The Ford, nodding his thanks. Njikiza pats him on the shoulder.

Feeling like a warrior striding out of the ranks to meet an enemy's challenger, the boy approaches the rock face. He reaches into the sack and removes the first blade. In a stabbing motion, he rams the blade into the crack at the height of his knees.

Without looking back, he places his left foot onto the broken haft. And reaches into the sack for the second blade. This he forces into the crack about a forearm's distance above the first blade.

Leaning against the rock, he brings his right foot up onto the first haft. It's wide enough to accommodate both of his feet – the Induna saw to that when the spears were broken – but he daren't rest all his weight on it for too long. As soon as he's sure of his balance, he places his left foot on the second shaft.

After reaching into the sack, he fits a third blade into the crack. As best he can, given the position he's in, he checks that the broken assegai is embedded firmly.

It is.

His right arm stretched across the warm rock, he twists so that his chest is pressed against the rock face, and places his right foot on the second shaft. And instantly spreads his weight again by putting his left foot onto the third shaft.

He reaches into the sack . . .

Leans forward . . .

This is where his height helps him. It matches the crack's angle of ascent. If the thirteen-year-old were any taller – as tall, say, as the Induna – he'd have to bend too far forward – and down – to ram the blades home.

A fourth rung.

And a fifth.

A sixth and a seventh.

Sweat in his eyes. Scrape of rock against his cheek as he tries to wipe away the perspiration.

He loves this rock. It's warm and solid. He wants to become one with this rock; wants to stick to it like his shadow.

Dry lips. How many hours has it been since he drank from Njikiza's waterskin? He's breathing through his mouth, each inhalation the gulp of a hungry man. And there's a wind blowing in his ears, even though the air hangs around him like a heavy cloak.

Eight . . . nine . . . ten . . .

Yet somehow it doesn't matter. The sweat . . . the dryness . . . the sun burning his shoulders . . . the chafing on his knees . . . the ache in the arch of each foot . . . None of these things matter. A strange detachment has gripped him. Every fibre of his being is focused on reaching for the blade, reaching up, ramming the blade into the crack, transferring his feet, and dropping his hand into the sack, which is growing agreeably lighter . . .

The Induna's voice, behind and below him: "Easy . . . don't rush . . ."

Rattle of wood and steel . . . fingers closing around another haft . . . Left foot up, knee bent; right leg extended . . . Reach . . . Slam the blade home . . . Clenched teeth, as you bang your elbow again, scrape your knuckles . . . Test the haft . . . Bring your right foot up . . .

A second of tilting firmness, then nothing, as the blade dislodges itself under the pressure of both feet.

Somewhere far off, he hears the clatter as steel scrapes stone, but he's too busy falling . . .

. . . trying not to fall.

Somewhere far off, he feels nails tearing away, but it's someone else's fingertips, because his own have become claws hooked into the crack.

Somewhere far off, feet are scraping stone, desperately trying to find some purchase, but he knows only that his fingers are claws . . .

. . . hooked into the crack.

And he hangs, suddenly remembering to breathe.

Hangs, his arms two parallel sticks, pressed against his ears.

A slender stream of blood passes within millimetres of his eyes. Raising his chin, he sees the trail is coming from the crack . . .

From one of his fingers.

He sees something else . . .

He's only about two metres from the summit.

Calmly, he raises his left foot and pushes down. The hardened sole finds purchase where there shouldn't be any, and allows him to pry loose fingers that no longer seem to belong to him and move his left hand further along the crack.

He raises his left foot again . . . another split second of release and he's able to move his right hand to where his left hand was.

He's vaguely aware of pain, a whole lot of pain, hovering on the fringes of his senses, waiting to come crashing in, but right now he's got this to finish.

And he's going to finish it because he has no other choice.

It's as simple as that.

And his foot finds a narrow bump in the rock.

Without thinking he uses it to power himself upward, so he almost leaps toward the summit, hands groping for the bushes that grow along the edge.

And suddenly he's lying amid the foliage, smelling first the sap of broken stems, then the tang of his own vomit.

*

News of the Zulu victory and advance through Ndwandwe territory has given the Pepetas a chance to gather supplies and retreat to this isolated village, so ideal for a long siege. It's built on a large plateau that's part of a chain of mountains that rise ever higher to the northwest. Separate from the rest of the range, though, it towers above the surrounding countryside, a solid lump of sandstone with sheer drops on three of its sides. A long-ago subsidence has turned the fourth, western side into an inclined trough, a ramp between high walls. This was where the tribesmen led their cattle up to the top of the escarpment – and, in an acknowledgement that this is the natural fortress's weakest section, large boulders have been rolled into place to create a battlement about three-quarters the way up the ramp. More boulders line the walls on either side, ready to be dropped onto attackers.

Shaka knows there has to be at least one other way down, a secret path that will allow the women and children to escape if invaders seem about to break through the defences – but his scouts, who've been watching the settlement for three days, have yet to spot it.

This means they have to take the fortress the hard way, and time is in short supply. Shaka's men are weary after their rampage through Ndwandwe land; they want to return home, to rest and count their booty, the livestock they've taken. This is understandable, and under normal circumstances Shaka would've withdrawn his army, turned his attention to choosing new chiefs for the conquered territory.

But these aren't normal circumstances. Shaka has to honour his promise to his mother and retrieve this Truthsayer from Ntombazi's clutches. More importantly, there's Ntombazi herself to be dealt with. She's a goad to her son, perhaps the real power behind the Ndwandwe throne. She can't be allowed to rejoin Zwide, who, Shaka's sources tell him, has fled north across the Inkomati River. Her end will be especially painful, given the part she played in Dingiswayo's murder.

With his men impatient to get home, a siege is out of the question. Such an undertaking would be folly anyway, for those laying the siege are as trapped as those they besiege; Shaka can't afford to have his regiments tied up in such a manner. And these Pepetas have a spring and cattle and probably grain and other supplies up there – who knows how long it would take to starve them into submission?

Shaka has to see them routed as soon as possible. Nandi will never forgive him if Ntombazi kills the Truthsayer.

Three nights ago, under a full moon, he led a small band of men through the bushes covering the low ridge opposite the plateau's western flank. They settled themselves in the shadows to give what would soon be the scene of their assault a final once-over. The ground below the precipice was a sandy expanse; they couldn't advance any closer without being seen by sentries atop the plateau.

"What say you?" said Shaka, addressing Takatso the Sotho. "For you have some experience in such matters."

"There has to be another way up and down," murmured the Sotho.

"Yes, yes," said Shaka, his voice tinged with impatience, "but we have yet to find it. We must eat the dish we have been served."

"If we can get to the boulders," said Mgobozi, meaning the battlements about three-quarters the way up the sloping ground, "we can get over them."

"Yes," added Mdlaka, commander in chief of the army, "but it's getting to them, there lies our problem."

"We attack, they drop the rocks on us," said Shaka, "but they cannot get these rocks back, and soon they will run out of stones –"

"And spears," added Mgobozi.

"And spears . . . Hai, but many men will die before that happens."

"Many men, Majesty," said Mdlaka, "for we will be bunched up as we make for the barrier."

"Yes. I am not sure if this is a sacrifice I am willing to make."

"Majesty?"

"Yes, Takatso?"

"Perhaps . . ."

"Speak! We would see this matter settled before we grow much older."

Takatso pointed his spear. "See you those cliffs, Majesty?"

He was indicating where the wall curved inward to follow the ramp to the top of the plateau.

"Where they have piled the stones?" asked Mdlaka.

"Yes, General. See you how they jut outward?"

Shaka nodded. Takatso was right, there was an overhang on either side, shadowed now in the moonlight.

"They have not planned this properly," said the Sotho. "They have not thought about it, Majesty."

"Yes!" whispered the Induna.

"Nduna?"

"I see what he means, Majesty."

The Induna nudged Takatso surreptitiously, for one did not put the King in a position where he had to admit his own ignorance.

"Yes, Majesty," said Takatso quickly. "Those rocks are heavy. It will take two men to push them over the edge, but when they are pushed over the edge, Majesty, they will simply drop."

"Straight down!"

"Straight down, Majesty."

"Father? I do not understand."

"Hai, Mgobozi, it is obvious – so obvious those fools up there missed it," said Shaka. "They have gathered many stones ready to crush us – like ants, they think – but don't you see, Mgobozi?"

The cliff face was sheer, curving inwards as it reached the ground; boulders pushed off the top would plummet straight down – they wouldn't hit the sides, there was nothing to set them bouncing or rolling.

They could send a narrow formation of men, with, say, ranks ten soldiers wide, up the centre of the ramp, keeping away from the sides.

"It will rain rocks and leave our men dry," murmured Shaka.

And the ground immediately below each wall was sandy. When a rock landed the sand would hold it fast, or at the very least slow its momentum, reduce the distance it might bounce.

"They still have spears," observed Takatso. "A man throwing a spear downward can do much damage without exerting himself."

"Never fear," said Shaka, "I have a remedy for that."

*

His fingers on fire, the boy lifts himself and crawls through the bushes, the rope tied around his waist trailing after him. In the distance he can hear shouting. He raises his head as high as he dares. Beyond the greenery, the ground dips and huts are clustered around the spring in the centre of the depression. Sentries who should be manning this side of the escarpment have moved to join their comrades at the site of the Zulu assault. Not all of them have gone, though – and the boy ducks his head. About three hundred metres along the northeastern rim there's a low tower; it's built close to the edge and three men stand watch. The defenders clearly feel the other sides of the plateau are inaccessible and this is a sufficient precaution. The boy moves forward again, keeping low.

His shoulder bumps the trunk of a tree. He stops, leans against the squat tree. The trunk is unyielding. He circles the tree, moves back the way he came, then turns and crawls toward the tree – and circles it again. The rope tightens after he's crawled a metre back the way he came. He stops, turns, and circles the tree once more. His head bowed, dripping sweat into the sand; he's moving without thinking.

The rope pulls tight. He swivels round so that his back is to the precipice. Reaching for the other end of the rope, the loose end that dangles over the cliff, he gives it two tugs – waits – then tugs once more. It's a signal answered by two pulls on the rope a few seconds later. His feet against the tree, the boy braces himself. The rope alongside him snaps taut . . .

. . . as down below the Induna begins his ascent. He has his shield tied to his back; in his mouth he clenches the haft of a broken iklwa; a rawhide rope is tied around his waist. It's a rapid climb, made easy by the assegais the boy inserted in the crack.

When he reaches the place where the boy slipped, the Induna pauses. Removing the broken spear, he wedges the blade in the crack. Stepping on it enables him to reach the summit without much exertion. Letting go of the rope, he hoists himself up and crawls toward the boy.

The rope goes taut for the second time.

*

Upon arriving here from KwaDlovungu, Shaka had arrayed his men along the plateau's western flank, in a show of force out of reach of the defenders' spears or stones. Then he sent the Induna forward. Unarmed, the warrior approached the precipice at the corner, where it turned inward to guard the ramp. Calling up, he conveyed Shaka's request for a parley.

This was granted and Shaka and Mgobozi came forward to join the Induna; with them, hovering a few metres back, were a hundred men, ready to snatch Shaka away should these Pepetas turn treacherous. For his part, Shaka wanted to see how Mshika and his escort would descend from this fortress, as that might give him an idea as to how to breach its natural defences.

As it turned out, a ladder was lowered down the left flank, a few metres below the boulder battlements, and it was the chief's son, Wandwana, who came forward to meet the Zulus. Arrogantly alone, thought Shaka with a wry smile, although he also noted Wandwana stayed near the cliff face and didn't come too close to the Zulus.

Up above him, men stood guard, spears raised – and Shaka wouldn't have been surprised if the chief himself lurked somewhere up there. As they had to raise their voices to communicate, those directly above were in earshot.

"Sho!" said Shaka, craning his neck, twisting his head and making a show of examining his surroundings. "Do you like living like baboons?"

"What do you want, Zulu?"

"You know what I want – and I ask you," he raised his voice to make sure those above them heard, "is a dried-up old hyena sow worth the annihilation of your people? Hand her over and we will leave you in peace, so that you might pick fleas off each other and climb trees to your hearts' content!"

"Peace? Zulus know nothing of peace!"

"Hai! Tell that to those who have joined us and now prosper as a result. But your stupidity is of little interest to me. Give me that female hyena – yes, and her pet – and I'll let you live."

"And you think that's in your power?"

"Not think, know, little monkey."

"You outnumber us, Zulu, but I think we'll remain where we are for the moment."

"For the moment? Would you not prefer to live a little longer?"

"Let your men come, Zulu."

Shaka inclined his head. "Brave words – for which I salute you. And your father. But are you sure you would sacrifice everything for that miserable old bitch?"

"I might ask you the same question, Zulu."

Shaka grinned. Nodded. "Enjoy the last word, brave warrior, for soon you and your people will know only pain."

That was four days ago.

Shaka had withdrawn his regiments to the other side of the ridge. Let the enemy wonder what they were up to. A day later, Mdlaka arrived with reinforcements, bringing the contingent's strength up to two thousand men. After he and his officers had decided on a course of action, Shaka spent two days drilling a thousand of his men in the tactics he intended to employ, while others were set to plaiting rawhide ropes.

A frontal assault was all very well, but Shaka also needed to put a group of warriors atop the plateau as quickly as possible on the day of the attack. To this end, the Induna and the boy were sent to seek a spot that could be climbed. This they found on the northwestern edge, where a crack in the rock ran almost to the top of the escarpment.

Sentries patrolled the rim, but the Induna counted on these being withdrawn as soon as the Zulus' intent became obvious – because with that would come the realisation that they might just succeed in storming the plateau and every available Pepeta male would be needed to repel them.

The fact is, the main assault isn't intended as a feint – with the tactics Shaka has in mind it has every chance of succeeding. The Induna's task is simply to capture Ntombazi and hold off the Pepetas until the defences have been breached. There's also a secondary objective. Shaka believes that once he realises the Zulus are about to take the plateau, Mshika will at least want to see his women and children escape. Shaka, therefore, hasn't sought to surround the plateau. He wants them to escape, so his men might at last discover the secret way onto the mountain. Before identifying Ntombazi's hut and moving to capture her, then, the Induna and his men will watch for an exodus, see where they run. Word will then be relayed down below to Mgobozi, who stands ready with a reserve of five hundred men. They will move in and make their way up the path.

Last night, under the cover of darkness, the Induna and fifty Fasimbas crept into position below the cliff wall they intended to scale. There were still sentries in place and they had to wait for dawn and the attack before the Induna's udibi could be sent up the precipice.

*

He has chosen well. The tree remains sturdy as the rope cuts into the bark. He doesn't have to use himself as a counterweight. When the Induna reaches him, the udibi is lying on his side, shivering as though with a fever, his hands extended away from his body. The Induna examines them, sees the cuts on the inside of the boy's fingers, sees the udibi is missing three fingernails, sees his fingertips are glistening red.

"Easy, easy," whispers the Induna, his mouth pressed against the boy's ear. "It'll pass."

"Aiee," pants the boy, "it hurts, Master!" An admission that's as sure a sign that the boy's not himself; normally, he'd never admit to feeling pain or discomfort.

"Rest," whispers the Induna.

Thando comes slithering through the bushes. Detouring past the two, he finds a second aloe and wraps his rope around it.

"Here!" hisses the Induna, undoing the rope around his waist. "Tie this one as well."

In the distance, the shouts have become shrieks.

*

While the Pepeta men watch, an impi of five hundred Zulus emerges around the ridge and jogs in a course that takes them parallel to the plateau's western edge. They halt directly opposite the natural ramp. Orders are shouted and the contingent wheels and rearranges itself into a column ten men wide. Standing atop the ridge with Mdlaka, Shaka raises his spear and points the blade in the direction of the wide gorge. Indunas in the ranks bellow the order to advance and the column moves forward.

Ready for action atop the plateau, the defenders watch this and shake their heads. These Zulus are mad! They will be crushed. Literally!

The column halts a hundred metres away from the start of the ramp, still out of range of spear or stone.

An order is issued.

The soldiers in the outer ranks on either flank raise their shields to shoulder height, to form a cowhide wall down each side.

A second command – and the soldiers in the inner ranks raise their shields over their heads. There's some shuffling amid further shouted instructions and the column contracts until the shields overlap.

Now the defenders gape in astonishment.

What is this?

The Zulu soldiers who spent two days practising the formation call it Shaka's Shongololo.

"Forward!"

The column begins to advance. Learning how to move while crouching under their shields has been the hardest aspect to get right – but finally they mastered it, after Mgobozi had shouted himself hoarse. The Shongololo's progress is slow but steady. It's already halfway to the boulder battlements when the defenders manage to shrug off their amazement.

Urged on by angry officers, groups of men attack the rocks. First one, then another, then an avalanche of boulders and stones topples off the cliffs on either side of the Shongololo.

But each flank of the formation is at least five metres away from the walls and the stones drop and shatter, plummet and crack, and do almost no damage. Only in one place does a large stone careen off a bigger boulder to shatter a warrior's leg. As the man drops, screaming in pain, the soldiers in the surrounding ranks rearrange themselves to ensure the shields remain overlapping.

"Your spears," shrieks Wandwana, "throw your spears!"

His officers pick up his cry, running up and down the ranks, slapping and punching men out of their shock.

And shocked they are. Those boulders they manhandled into position, rocks and stones they sweated to fetch and carry up here – they were supposed to crush the Zulus, and fill the trough, making it even more inaccessible.

But it's come to nothing . . .

And Shaka's Shongololo climbs ever higher.

"Your spears," roars Wandwana, "use your spears!"

*

"Now what do you say, Truthsayer? Will you still tell me you'll not die by my hand?"

"You will not kill me."

"You sound like the wind – and even the wind dies!"

"You. Will. Not. Kill. Me."

"Why? It'll be so easy!"

"No!"

"Did you feel that? What did you see? Answer me! Will you sulk like a spoilt girl? What did you see?"

"You will not kill me."

"Listen! Can you hear? Something tells me screaming like frightened children was not part of their plans. I do not have your powers, but something tells me the Zulus will be here soon . . ."

*

A swarm of spears crashes down on the human Shongololo. Here and there, a lucky throw pierces the overlapping shields, and a man goes down, but the ranks soon reform to close up the gaps.

When they reach the boulder battlements, the men drop to their knees, and even fewer spears are able to pierce the Shongololo.

Mshika sends warriors down the ramp to the boulders. But these are intended to serve more as a barrier than anything else. Although they're higher up the slope than the Zulus, the Pepeta men can't see over the rocks. To hurl their assegais with any accuracy they have to clamber on top of the boulders, which means they'll then be exposed, should some of the Zulus be equipped with throwing spears.

Wisely, Wandwana, who's joined the troops, orders his men to stay down and has them withdraw three paces. Let the Zulus come over the rocks, let the Zulus be the ones to expose themselves. If they are patient and wait, they'll be able to pick the Zulus off and, hopefully, the bodies will cause a congestion behind the boulders and force the Shongololo to break up.

What Wandwana can't see is that a second column of five hundred Zulus has come up and positioned itself opposite the ravine. It's a little narrower than the first, comprising eight ranks of Fasimbas.

Indunas amid the Shongololo shout their orders, and the first row of ten men – those against the rocks – stands up. The second and third rows follow suit. Keeping their shields overhead, they form a step in the column. Men from the fourth and fifth rows squeeze in between these warriors, to "strengthen" the step with their shields.

Just as a herdboy comes running to inform Wandwana of this development, the second column begins to advance. And men on the cliffs shout at him to get ready.

"Siiiiiiii-Giiiiiiii-Diiiiiiii!"

A trot becomes a run, a run becomes a sprint – and the Fasimbas are atop the shields.

Are running over the overlapping shields.

Onto the step.

Onto the rocks.

Those in the first few ranks have one goal in mind – to get over the boulders.

Keeping low behind their shields, they pour into the Pepetas, using the cowhide to push their foe backwards. It's those who follow who bring their iklwas into play.

*

Although there are clear signs of panic from the Pepeta defences – men scurrying to and fro amid a lot of shouting, with some even fleeing toward the settlement – the Induna can't see what's happening in the niche. Zulu soldiers have yet to emerge on top of the escarpment, and knowing when to move forward is key to the success of their mission. Enough Pepetas have to be sucked into the melee, so the Induna and his men can easily hold their own against those who remain.

Then the sentries atop the tower spot them. Which is not unexpected – the bushes are too low to hide a body of fifty men indefinitely. However, the guards yell their heads off without being able to attract the attention of their comrades.

What's more, as the Induna despatches five men to deal with the screaming sentries, he notes a general movement toward the eastern side of the escarpment. Those fleeing the battle have passed the huts, inciting panic, and now have eagerly "volunteered" to escort the women, children and old-timers to safety. Some have already reached the rim and are disappearing below it. That's where the secret path must be . . .

The Induna calls Thando. Points. When the warrior has his bearings, the Induna sends him down the ropes to summon Mgobozi's impi . . .

*

. . . and Njikiza is waiting at the foot of the precipice, anxious to join the action. While Thando races off to Mgobozi, the Watcher Of The Ford takes it upon himself to follow the cliffs until he comes to where the Pepetas are scrambling down.

*

By this time, the five Zulus have reached the tower and accounted for the sentries. In doing so, they've been spotted by those fleeing the hill-top, but they're ignored by the Pepeta soldiers, whose numbers are growing as more and more men flee Shaka's Shongololo. Women and children are yanked aside as the warriors force themselves into the queue. The steep narrow fold in the cliff face permits only a single file and this is a column of ants compared to the mighty Zulu Shongololo . . .

*

Njikiza simply swats at the men as they stumble toward him. Most are unarmed and have discarded their shields. Since the trail is almost a tunnel, bounded on both sides by high walls, those who still have their spears are unable to use them until they reach the bottom. A few manage to escape the sweep of Njikiza's club, but they're soon intercepted by Mgobozi's men . . .

*

Up top, someone at last has the presence of mind to send a herdboy to warn the chief that there are already Zulus on the escarpment.

Seeing this, the Induna gives the order to charge.

His men rise up and crash through the bushes. Their target is the large hut standing to one side of the main cluster. It's clearly the abode of the chief's mother, when she's in residence, and the Induna assumes that's where Ntombazi will be.

That she hasn't chosen to flee isn't surprising. She's no fool. She knows her day is done.

As the Induna's warriors surround the hut, the first soldiers from Shaka's Shongololo appear at the top of the ramp.

*

The first men over the boulder battlement come crashing down behind their shields and race up the incline to engage the Pepetas, using their shields to push the enemy back. They're immediately followed by other waves. These men use their iklwas, thrusting the assegais between their comrades, so that the Zulu wall grows spikes. Wandwana tries to rally his troops, but within minutes the Pepeta ranks disintegrate. Those in the rear flee, leaving the front lines to hold the Zulus. The attack becomes a series of individual skirmishes and the Zulu advance is held up longer than necessary. It's Mzilikazi who finally urges the impis onward, leads the way to the top of the escarpment.

*

Torches are ablaze, turning the inside of Ntombazi's hut into a sweaty broth. Trapped in the cage Ntombazi has made for him, barely able to move, the Truthsayer regards the Induna with equanimity, a contemptuous smile curling his lips as he notices the Zulu's stiffening.

The Induna's never seen the like before. Privately, he'd dismissed the stories as exaggerations. But now . . .

The Truthsayer had been a soldier in Zwide's army. There'd been no Calling for him; the ancestors hadn't spoken to him. Then one day, during an encounter with a band of Ancient Ones, those who the White Man will later call "Bushmen", and who are treated as vermin by all and sundry, to be hunted down and exterminated, the man had been shot with one of their arrows.

The arrow had entered the warrior's left eye and embedded itself deep within his head.

And he had survived! To the horror of his companions he had regained consciousness and sat up, the shaft of the arrow protruding from his eye.

It was while the Ndwandwe medicine men examined him that the visions started. As soon as someone touched the left side of his face he'd see things . . . things that were yet to pass. But he hadn't been called by the ancestors! This was sorcery! He was possessed!

It was Ntombazi who saved him. Saved him only to imprison him in such a fashion that he couldn't do himself any harm. For with the glimpses into the future came pain and the man had begged to be killed.

He would have done it himself, pushed the arrow even deeper into his brain to put an end to his suffering, were he not restrained in the cage.

And the Induna is staring at this bizarre apparition – of a man, living and breathing, with an arrow shaft protruding forty centimetres out of his left eye socket – when Ntombazi comes at him.

The udibi has his shield, is waiting for him outside, and the blade of Ntombazi's spear slices a furrow in the Induna's side as he turns to face her. Dropping his own iklwa, he grabs her assegai with his right hand and punches her, the knuckles of his left hand connecting with her chin. It's an almost delicate blow; he merely proffers his fist and lets Ntombazi's momentum do the rest.

*

Thirty minutes later, the Pepetas have been subdued. Only a few of the men have managed to escape. The rest lie dead, their bodies disembowelled; Mshika and his son are among them. The women, children and cattle have been rounded up. Shaka has decided he'll keep the cattle for himself. His men have gained sufficient booty from the Ndwandwes, and anyway, he has resolved to offer them a further reward for their bravery and loyalty. He'll allow the men from his two older regiments to take wives. He's well aware that his refusal to let his soldiers marry has been a source of discontentment – aiee, but his children can annoy him at times; he gives them so much, yet they still find something to complain about – and not only will such a gesture be hugely popular, it'll serve as an incentive and reassurance for the men in the younger regiments: their turn will come. Those who are willing can choose their wives from the Pepeta girls.

Accompanied by Mdlaka and Mgobozi, Shaka tours the battlefield, and is pleased to note the Zulu casualties number fewer than fifty killed and a handful wounded.

"You are well?" he asks the Induna, when he reaches the spot where the officer and his udibi are being tended to by Zulu inyangas.

"No," he adds, when the Induna tries to rise. "You have earned your rest."

A grin disguising his grimace of pain, the Induna nonetheless climbs to his feet. His wound has been bound; strips of leather wrapped around his waist hold the poultice in place.

"I am well, Majesty."

"And your brave udibi?"

The boy's hands are swaddled in leather strips, but he too manages to come to attention.

"His courage has cost him, Father, but he will heal."

Shaka nods. "The wounds will heal, but the praise songs telling of his deeds this day will echo forever."

"So too will the tales of Shaka's Shongololo," says the Induna.

"Hai, but what will they say about Mgobozi?" grumbles Mgobozi. "They will say he was on the other side of the mountain chasing women!"

"Be still, Goat! You know you had another important task – perhaps the most important of all! Now tell me, was this task accomplished?"

"That it was! A perilous undertaking, but it was done. And all is ready for you. There is the hut . . ."

"Good!" Shaka turns to the Induna: "You have earned your rest, but would you like to see the end of that evil old witch?"

"Nothing would give me greater pleasure, Father. And she awaits *your* pleasure, guarded by my men."

"You kept her out of sight? She has not seen Mgobozi making the hut ready for her?"

Ntombazi knows nothing, says the Induna. He had her taken some distance away from the settlement.

Shaka sighs. "And the other one?"

The Truthsayer remains in his cage in Ntombazi's hut, says the Induna.

"Very well, let us finish with the one who thought she could add my skull to her collection."

*

And the old stories tell of how Shaka approached Ntombazi Of The Skulls and how, when he asked her what she had to say for herself, she spat in his face. Restraining Mgobozi, who wanted to strike the old hag, Shaka smiled. Wiped his face with his hand. "Your poison is weak," he said, regarding the spittle glistening on his fingertips. "Have it back."

And, so saying, he rammed his palm against her nose, knocking her over.

"Is this any way to treat one who would reunite you with your kin?" he asked, peering down at her.

And the stories tell of how Ntombazi's scowl vanished. She forgot herself in that instant. "You . . . you have my son?" she asked.

"Oh no," chuckled Shaka, "it is a blood relative who is even closer to you than that. Much closer."

He signalled his men and they helped the bewildered crone to her feet.

"Go," said Shaka, his eyes on hers, "go and be reunited!"

And the stories tell of how Ntombazi was dragged to the hut Mgobozi had made ready, and thrown inside. Cowhide had been draped over the smoke-hole in the centre of the roof, and two soldiers moved to block the doorway with their shields.

It was dark inside the hut. Ntombazi was temporarily blinded. Arms outstretched, she tottered forward.

"Who's there?" she asked.

A blood relative, Shaka had said. Go and be reunited!

"Who is it? Who's there?"

A shifting in the gloom. A tensing of muscles. And then the hyena Mgobozi's men had captured leapt through the darkness to tear her apart.

Rain falling.

A depthless blur; wire-thin steel icicles shattering on the hard-packed dirt. Coffee-coloured puddles, like scabs, speckled and growing. Huts lose their shape in the gloom, seem to sag into mounds of waterlogged thatch.

And the rain is falling sideways, a swarm of mosquitoes, stinging your skin. You tilt your head, wipe your face.

You tighten your grip on your iklwa, the wood burning your hand. Where is your shield?

You move forward, toes pressing into the puddles. A softness underfoot. Your vision is blurred as droplets catch on your eyelashes. You wipe your face once more. An instant of clarity, before the swarm surrounds you again.

Where are the sky-herders? Why do they not come to chase away this deluge that threatens the crops? What is wrong?

"There is one . . ."

Something is wrong . . .

An irritated sweep of your arm.

A brushing away that, miraculously, reveals the body in front of the hut.

It's as if you have remained immobile and pulled the tableau towards you.

The body. A big man, lying on his side, his back to you.

"There is one, blood of your blood . . ."

You move forward, knowing instinctively it's no use. He is dead, this man. There's nothing you can do to save him.

And you see yourself drop to your knees.

A statue of mud slowly being eroded away by the rain.

You are watching this as a third party might, having blundered onto this scene – and that's confusing. But it's a brief flailing, a momentary frown, for like this other, who is also somehow you, you want to reach out . . .

    Your hand on the man's shoulder. A stiffness in the wet. Cool skin.

    You pull, rolling the man over.

    This big man, lying on his side.

    You pull on this stiffness.

    And you also think: I can end this!

    Even as the horror reverberates through your body, like a silent scream, a mute howl of anguish, you think: I can wake up.

The Herald

A moonlit beach late at night on the southern tip of Africa has a special resonance.

Behind you loom forests and jungles, savannah and badlands, hills and mountains, rivers and lakes, dunes and wadies; a vast, rippling musculature. This continent, so like a slumbering giant, tossing and turning, taunted by fleas and bad dreams, colonial imperatives and tyrannical excesses. Spread your arms and feel the push of history, thwarted ideals and brave hopes. And before you, the sea, a shifting vastness, prey to its own bad moods, its own tides of illusory change. Spread your arms and feel the pull of a birthright even older than Mother Africa, hear the call of the moon, the secret messages of the stars.

And in between, this strip of sand, ivory becoming glistening steel at the water's edge, the blade and the handle: a nexus in these late-night hours, a meeting place.

For a moonlit beach late at night in Africa is at once eerie and comforting, silent and teeming, the waves the very engine that seems to produce the silence, and the space that surrounds you, the soaring openness, also causes the soul to clench and be reminded of its temporal boundaries, these sinews and veins. And strange thoughts bloom like ozone-scented orchards. Revelations and epiphanies, fragile spider webs that disintegrate all too soon, leaving only the memory of their momentary resilience.

*

The Induna emerges from the arched branches of their temporary shelter and moves down the beach; he's still in the grip of the dream and his gait is slurred. He woke up with a start, forgetting in that instant that he'd forced himself awake, that the real end of the nightmare was the realisation – a slender lifeline – that this was in fact a dream and he could, and should, wake up. Awash in horror, he reached out for Kani, sleeping next to him – but was glad, even as his fingers touched her arm, that he hadn't disturbed her. The dream was too vivid, too disturbing for talk. He needed to think.

Like a man finally consenting to let the desert have him, he drops to his knees in the sand. And because he is inadvertently mimicking his motions in the dream, he feels momentarily like a ghost. A word stripped of its meaning floating amid a haze of endless sound.

Sound.

Sighs and hisses; the waves massaging the wet sand.

What is the sea trying to tell him?

There is comfort there, or at least the promise of comfort, but he would shrug it off, even as he would've shrugged off Kani's concern had he awoken her. He wants to – needs to – has to immerse himself in the dream again, try to fathom its meaning.

A rainy day.

Cold, grey.

The rain blown sideways in silver streaks . . .

*

Later, wet-eyed, he stands and moves to the water's edge. Foam around his ankles. The tug of the retreating tide. When the water tickles the back of his knees, he throws himself forward, gives himself up to the waves, rolling and turning, letting the ocean wring the pain from his soul.

*

Kani comes awake with the Induna on top of her, inside her. Her pleasure is the sea's pleasure, her sigh, the sigh of the languid ocean on a moonlit beach, late at night in Africa. His strokes are the waves brushing the shore, measured, timeless. A rising tide.

*

Shaka laughed and gave her the skirt. "If you are going to do this thing," he said, "you must do it properly."

She had looked to Nandi, seeking confirmation, and the old woman nodded benevolently, signalling her consent.

"It is decided, then," said Pampata, grinning.

"But, of course," said Shaka. "Now I will leave you females to scheme and plot. Hai – would that my advisors were so crafty. And able."

"You are worried?" asked Pampata, after the King had departed.

Kani shrugged. There was always a chance . . .

"Haibo! How can he refuse you? And if he does, he is a fool."

"And will have me to deal with," added Nandi.

"But he is not a fool," said Pampata softly.

"For I am not a fool," whispered Kani – and the other women nodded and smiled.

*

He is the sea breaking over her. She is immersed, wondering, faintly surprised that she can still breathe. A new sensation. She is the sand, welcoming, revelling in, his measured motion. Susurration. Fingers pressed into his shoulder blades, her nails leaving hermit crab trails. Release deliciously close; a moon, forming and reforming in the shifting waters, yet always out of reach, just out of reach. But he, this one above her, inside her, he can bring the moon to her.

*

She had made her decision on the way to Bulawayo, where Nandi awaited her. The Induna had tasked some of Mgobozi's men to escort her and when they arrived, she left her brothers and sisters in Pampata's care and went straight to the older woman's hut.

On her knees in front of Nandi, she said: "I have been in hiding, Mother."

It was the statement a young girl would make upon reaching puberty. When she starts menstruating for the first time, a Zulu maiden will run off and hide somewhere near her home kraal; her girlfriends then report the matter to her mother, who informs the father. The situation here was a little different – Kani had long ago gone through the Umgonqo ceremony – but Nandi immediately divined the reason for Kani's choice of words.

Clapping her hands, she summoned her servants and sent them to cut wood for the Umgonqo. Usually the father would oversee the construction of the partition behind which the girl would rest in her mother's hut, completely hidden from view for a period of between two weeks and three months, the duration of her seclusion determined by her father.

"It is your heart that bleeds in this instance," said Nandi.

Kani nodded. "This is so, Mother."

"You have endured much to serve my son and now you would be cleansed."

"It is so, Mother. I can still smell his breath, that crocodile! I can still feel him inside me . . ."

Nandi reached for her hand. "Do not dwell on the past, Daughter. It is gone forever. You are safe now and my son will reward you."

"That was not why I served Shaka."

"I know that, Daughter – you would see the killer of your family eat dirt. But you will let my son's generosity elevate you, for you have earned all the largesse he has to offer."

"But I have failed, Mother. He still lives."

"Is that not a better punishment? Let Zwide roam the land, haunted and hunted, let him remember what he has lost. Truly, that is an agony worse than a merciful execution."

"You are right, as always, Mother."

There was another reason why she wanted to go through the Umgonqo, though; another reason why she wanted to cleanse herself – and be seen to cleanse herself. She wanted to offer herself to the Induna.

She had died when her father and brothers were murdered by Zwide's men. Only the realisation that as a favoured concubine she'd be in a position to aid in Zwide's downfall had sustained her – that and the need to care for her younger siblings. Gradually she had crept into a position where she had become indispensable to Zwide and could ensure her brother and sisters were better taken care of. And in her dealings with Nandi, her first step had been to ensure her siblings would be looked after, no matter what happened to her. She'd stopped caring about herself. Had things been different, she would have delivered the remainder of her family to the Zulus and set about finding Zwide again, so that her revenge might be complete. Instead, she'd encountered the Induna . . .

She'd attempted to suppress all else save the mettle needed to appease Zwide's bad moods and spy on him, but the moment she saw the Induna again she realised she had failed. He had been a talisman – both the solace and the spur – she'd carried locked away in her mind all along.

How angry she'd been that last visit, when her oldest brother had mocked the Induna! He'd come to warn them and had been met by insolence, her father – even her father! – bowing to the demands of the heir. Let's see what Zwide has to offer us! Well, they'd learnt the hard way that all that old crocodile had to offer was treachery and death.

And she thought she'd been incapable of love, that the girl who'd admired the Zulu officer who regularly visited her father was gone forever. But, seeing the Induna again, she realised she wasn't lost. She could be that young girl again – but only in his arms.

Now she needed him to see that she had been cleansed; had left her more recent past behind.

And so, in a version of a Zulu girl's puberty ceremony, she remained in seclusion in Nandi's hut until Shaka's victorious army returned home.

Then Nandi and Pampata went to work on the King. Not that he needed much persuading. He found it hugely amusing that it was a woman who had helped bring about Zwide's downfall – even as it was a woman, Ntombazi, who'd encouraged Zwide to ever greater calumnies – and Shaka found it easy to forget his disdain for traitors in this instance. He'd already decreed that his older regiments could take wives and he extended this ruling to the Induna without complaint.

More than that, he entered into the preparations with enthusiasm.

He would give her the isidwaba, the leather skirt she needed to wear in the courtship ceremony. Usually this was stolen from the father's kraal – and, said Shaka, it was right and fitting that the skirt should come from him. "Your father, Dondo, was a loyal friend. I am the Father of the Zulus, and now I would be your father," he said.

*

She holds him tight. He thrusts deeper, the sweat silver on his chest. He would lose himself in her, for just a moment, seeking an affirmation of life in the process of creating life – to banish the dream. Let his prick, her cunt, become the world. For just a moment.

*

The most common form of marriage negotiation, or courtship ritual, is the ukucela, in which the man's family opens negotiations and formally asks for the maiden's hand. But, because boys can be morons in such matters, there's also a way in which the female can initiate proceedings. This is called ukubaleka. After stealing a leather skirt from her father's kraal, the girl, accompanied by her best friend, travels to the boy's umuzi, which she enters on the right hand-side, as a sign she wishes to become part of the boy's family.

Kani donned the isidwaba and, with Pampata standing in for her sister, who was still too young to play the role of "best friend", she journeyed to the kraal where Shaka and his officers were staying.

It was a small umuzi of ten huts on the coast, and one of the King's favourite retreats. He'd invited Mbopa, Mgobozi and the Induna to accompany him on this furlough. Mdlaka and Nqoboka would also be joining them, after they'd seen the regiments safely back to their kraals with their booty. Thanks to Shaka's ruling, there'd be numerous marriage ceremonies across the kingdom, but the frontiers had to be guarded and the amabutho at the war kraals needed to be reminded to stay alert.

Once Shaka had rested, he and his most trusted advisors would huddle together to discuss his next move. He was of a mind to turn his attention southward, to the land of the Xhosas and, beyond that, the ever-expanding domain of the White Men. Mbopa, Mdlaka and the rest, meanwhile, were relieved to see the King had shrugged off his bad mood.

Shaka's face had been thunderous when he emerged from the hut where the Truthsayer was kept. All his faithful generals could do was move aside and let him pass. What had happened? What had transpired between the King and the Truthsayer to leave Shaka in such a rage? But the Truthsayer wasn't about to answer any questions. When at last Mdlaka and Mgobozi ventured into the hut, armed with torches, they found him dead. Strangely, although standing outside the door, they hadn't heard the wretch cry out. But dead he was: Shaka had pushed the arrow deeper. And for the next few days the King was best left alone – and avoided altogether, if possible. To catch his eye was to court instant death . . .

They still wondered what it was the Truthsayer had said to him, but the King's participation in Kani's baleka ceremony had lifted his spirits – and that was all that mattered.

Although the two women had begged Nandi to accompany them, to see through what she had helped initiate, the Queen Mother demurred. She was to stay at Bulawayo and keep an eye on things in her son's absence. Besides, she had done all she could. It was up to the youngsters now.

Hanging back, Kani and Pampata arrived in the late afternoon, a few hours behind their party, which included Kani's brother and sisters and the ten Fasimbas the King had ordered to escort the group. All those present except the Induna were awaiting their arrival. Strictly speaking, when a baleka was enacted, villagers not belonging to the family retired to their homes; instead, as was invariably the case on such occasions, mere lip service was paid to this rule, with people lingering around the doorways of the huts closest to where the maiden was due to be greeted.

Even Shaka, red-eyed and grinning, sat outside his hut on a tree stump. Shielded from the setting sun by an isihlangu held aloft by one of his servants, he had a clear view of the proceedings. Sitting at his feet was Mbopa. The two men were passing a rhino horn back and forth and the sweet scent of marijuana filled the air.

It was Mgobozi who came forward with the ritual greeting: "Ukhwela ngobani?" *Who will raise you from girl to wife?*

Kani spoke the Induna's name.

Mgobozi nodded. Stepped aside to show the women a hut that had been cleared for this purpose.

Kani shook her head. She would refuse to enter until offered a gift.

At Mgobozi's summons, the Induna's udibi moved between the huts, leading a goat. Called an indlakudla, such a gift is an important part of the ukubaleka and a sign of how welcome the girl is – even though she's initiated these proceedings herself. The gift, however, goes to the girl's companion, which is partly why she chooses her best friend to accompany her. In this instance, Pampata would give the goat to Kani's sister.

Once the goat had been handed over – and Kani's sister had come forward and led it away – Mgobozi turned and called for the Induna.

This was the part everyone was looking forward to, and the cause of a certain amount of trepidation for Kani. Usually, the baleka ceremony occurs with the connivance of both parties, the boy and the girl, as it's a way for a woman to choose a suitor who might not be as well off as her father would like him to be. Here, though, the Induna had been kept in the dark as to what was going on.

Snatched out of a nap by Mgobozi's bellowing, he came running up.

And stopped.

Stopped and stared. At Kani and Pampata, the latter lowering her head to hide her grin. At Mgobozi and his udibi, who looked away sheepishly. At Shaka and Mbopa. At the others lurking by the huts. At Kani again.

*

Silken softness – then, a trembling. A widening, welcoming his ejacula-

427

tion, as his release becomes her release. And he arches his back, pushes himself up on locked elbows. And her mouth is open and her eyes are shut. But she comes alive when he moves, makes to ease off her. "No," she whispers.

And draws him toward her, holds him tight against her breasts, her belly, so that she becomes the sea and he at last finds the solace he was seeking when he gave himself up to the waves a short while ago.

*

Her eyes fixed on his, Kani strode forward, the certainty of her steps belying the fluttering in her stomach.

"I have come for you," she said, looking up at the Induna. "You will have me?"

It was only a little later, when he at last had time for bemused contemplation – snatched from the raucous feast held that night – that he realised this was not necessarily a question.

"I will have you," said the Induna.

"You will take me?"

"I will take you."

"You will love me?"

A grin edged past the Induna's solemnity. "How can I do otherwise?"

"But the lobola," called Shaka, "can you afford the lobola? For be warned – it is I who set the bride price!"

In answer to the Induna's quizzical glance, Kani stepped back and pulled on the hem of her skirt.

"Oh yes," bellowed the King, "it was from me that she got the isidwa-ba."

"For he is my father now," said Kani.

"The bride price, Nduna!"

The Induna turned toward the King and bowed: "The bride price, Majesty!"

"This is what you will owe me before I hand over this precious daughter, Nduna. You will serve me well, Nduna, risking life and limb in my name. You will be my shadow, bringing honour to the house of Zulu wherever you tread. Your assegai arm will always be strong and your aim true. You will obey without question and none will question your loyalty. Your wisdom will be worth a hundred impis and your courage priceless."

Shaka stood, swaying somewhat, and spread his arms: "And see – you have paid me already. In full!"

Mgobozi laughed and applauded. "Bayede, Nkosi, bayede!"

It was a cry taken up by the other men in the kraal and the Induna bowed to the King once more.

*

After she's held him awhile, the Induna is mildly surprised to discover he is hard again, growing once more to challenge her warm tightness. He raises his head. Kani's smile is as wide as the sky.

"Again?" he murmurs.

"Again," she says.

*

Since they were now to be betrothed, said Shaka, it was right and proper that they should go off and be alone together. After all, he said, they had much to discuss.

"Aiee," added Mgobozi, "be warned: this will be your last chance to have your say!"

"Be still, Goat, your wives have your measure!" Shaka turned to the Induna: "You know where I go to be alone and think – go there! You have my permission."

The Induna knew the spot well, knew there was a place on the edge of the sand, where the trees formed a natural shelter . . .

*

The sun is high when Kani and the Induna awaken once more. She's up first and has a bowl of porridge waiting for him. He lies a moment, listening to her singing by the fire. The dream is still there, a barely healed wound. And it stays with him for the rest of the day, as a sense of foreboding. It's especially worrying to him that he recognised the kraal in the dream, but can't quite identify its location. He knows the effects of the dream will dim as time goes by, but that's not necessarily a good thing. He needs to remain on his guard.

On more than one occasion, Kani asks him if anything's bothering him and he has to reassure her everything is fine. It's not that he doesn't want to tell her about the dream – he still needs time to digest it all himself. Time to understand its meaning. And later, after the apparition has passed from their sight, he wonders if the two things are connected . . .

*

It's twilight. Shadows dapple the sand and Kani and the Induna are sitting on a rock gazing out across the waves when they see it . . .

Strolling along the water's edge a few kilometres up the beach Shaka, Mbopa and Mgobozi also see it. They're discussing where the location of the new capital should be, for Shaka's conquests mean that Kwa-Bulawayo is now on the fringes of the Kingdom, when the Zulu King stops and points . . .

"What is that?" hisses Kani. She's reclining between her lover's legs, resting her back against the Induna's chest; now her fingers dig into his knees and she stiffens.

The Induna has his arms around her waist; he squeezes her to prevent her from rising. "Do not be afraid," he whispers into her ear, his eyes on the horizon.

"But . . ."

"Shhh. I have seen the like before. Do not be afraid."

Further up the beach, Mgobozi shakes his head. "These are truly strange people!"

"I have said it before and I'll say it again," murmurs Mbopa, "this is one tribe you must not underestimate. Do not let their strangeness fool you! I'll grant you, they seem insipid creatures, but mark you their courage."

"Madness," hisses Mgobozi.

"Yet there they are! You say madness, but I say courage, for who knows how far they have come!"

"Yes," agrees Shaka, his voice low.

The Induna can feel Kani trembling. "Do not be afraid," he whispers again and presses her against him.

The soft breeze that cools them on the shore is a spiteful wind further out at sea, kicking white caps off the waves and pushing the brig in a diagonal direction toward the coast, so that it seems to have suddenly popped up over the horizon.

All of the men watching have seen sailing ships before; these winged canoes and floating houses. And have seen them more often in recent years, as they ply a passage from the settlement at the Cape to the Portuguese in Delagoa Bay. Their strangeness having abated, they now invite a curious scrutiny, a musing and a wondering . . .

Shaka, for one, is sitting again alongside the fire, listening to his beloved mentor. Dingiswayo would always return to his sojourn with the White Man and his tales of these other nations across the waters. How they'd learnt to ride the waters as they did their horses and were gradually moving outward, away from the tired lands of their home kraals. Tales of musketry and grapeshot, conquest and treachery. Tales of wondrous cities of stone, teeming ant hills of humanity. Tales of wheels and mortar. Of commerce and industry. These last were concepts Dingiswayo could certainly grasp; it was the scale of the trade, the variety, that beggared belief.

Do not underestimate them . . .

No, never. For those the Zulus have already encountered are merely the vanguard of an unstoppable invasion – about that Dingiswayo's White Man had been most adamant.

As with most of the other ships they've seen, this one has been driven out to sea by fierce storms further down the coast – where the continental shelf lies but a few hundred kilometres offshore. This tiny craft has been hit harder than most and even the Induna can see it's in a state of disrepair.

Sitting low in the water the hull has the soggy aspect of driftwood – a large log washed out to sea. The brig's backstays hang from the masts like creepers. Yards are missing from the mizzenmast and the spanker gaff has snapped off, leaving that sail collapsed over the poop like a shroud. As the ship draws nearer, the Induna can see tiny figures hauling in the canvas over the stern. Then, just when they can make out more detail, see the naked backs aloft, the bare feet, the bandanas and caps, can hear the shouts, the wind must change direction, for the ship begins to veer away from the shore once more.

"You would see us allied with these beasts?" growls Mgobozi, watching the brig seesaw as it fights the waves.

"It may be a way to blunt their claws," says Mbopa.

"And the old stories, Mbopa? Do you not listen to the old stories? Do you not heed their warning?"

Yes, thinks Shaka. Befriending the White Men might be the only option they have if they are to survive. And who knows? They might profit by such an arrangement and learn a few of the White Man's secrets . . .

But Mgobozi also has a point. The old stories . . .

"The Ma-Iti," he murmurs.

"Yes!" says the general. "Have you forgotten how the Ma-Iti tricked and enslaved our people, Mbopa? Fight them, I say! Destroy them before they gain a foothold! For like the Ma-Iti and, yes, those who came after them, the Arabi, they will hold out the hand of friendship and stab us in the back. More than that, Mbopa, they will steal our children and our children's children!"

*

For a while there, confronted with this thing, he had forgotten all about the terrible dream. This is not comforting, for the sense of foreboding remains. If anything, it's heightened. And this the Induna takes as a sign that if what he witnessed in the dream comes to pass, it will be only the beginning, a tiny rock fall lost amid an avalanche of change.

But then Shaka's dreams will more and more frequently lead him to this place. There's a sense of a journey, a long journey – ducking to dodge branches, sweeping aside leaves. A dull throbbing behind the eyes, the consequence of constant focusing and refocusing, best to walk with your head down, but so easy to slip into a trudge, then, and the King's impatience flares like a moment of pain: he is the King, why must he trudge? The sense of a journey, then, muttering, a phase that causes Shaka to toss and turn on his sleeping mat – frustration and annoyance forcing him to the brink of consciousness – then a calming, as the wayfarer, driven by something he cannot quite understand, comes to a halt.

An arrival.

This place.

Filling the mind.

Seen from afar the rocks resemble crocodiles sunning themselves, half-hidden in the long grass. Something reptilian about those rocks, those walls – crude bricks like scales. Move closer and the crocodiles vanish. The rocks rearrange themselves, become something else.

Circular walls creating enclosures.

Walls curving and ending.

Walls worn down by time and the elements to become rocky paths in the grass.

"You must go there," a hiss, an exhalation blurring the words, "where you belong. Where you belong. You."

Now it's anger that drives the King upwards toward the fragile meniscus that separates sleep and consciousness.

A final glance over his shoulder.

There they lie, those walls, baking in the sun.

A curse awaiting the awareness of words to give it life. A childhood

433

taunt, lying in the long grass of memory, seemingly discarded, but never forgotten. An evil that beckons, but is willing to bide its time, knowing its time will come. A final glance – is he running? Does the King flee like a coward? Who says the King flees? And he is awake, eyes burning in the darkness.

Awake.

The Crocodile

The Induna's udibi sits on his heels, sulking. His body all but shimmers like a desert horizon in the blazing sun, for this roiling rage has consumed him. His forehead is a sheen; sweat drips off his chin. But he welcomes the discomfort. Revels in it.

The Induna has placed him here. Well and good. Here he will remain. Right here, on this very spot, in the sun. He will not seek the shade that taunts him a few metres to his left.

No. He will stay . . .

Right . . .

Here.

*

A crocodile has made an appearance in the river from which the umuzi draws its water. That this village happens to be one of the Queen Mother's retreats is the reason why Shaka has despatched the Induna and some men to hunt down the reptile, which has already killed a woman and a child. Nandi, currently in residence at Bulawayo, and terrorising her son's harem, insisted he send only his best warriors and the King has complied with her wishes.

Crocodiles are evil, loathsome creatures. The People Of The Sky call them izingwenya, vicious criminals, and it's an apt description. The ingwenya is crafty. It will hide itself in the shallows, ready to pounce without warning. Goats, dogs, buck, baboons, humans, it'll eat anything – tossing its head from side to side to drive its conical teeth deeper into stunned flesh. On their way here, Njikiza told them how he once saw a crocodile attack a rhino . . .

The ingwenya reared out of the water at the rhino's feet, locking its jaws under its neck. The teeth bit deep and the rhino was dying before it could even retaliate. Its horn useless, it backed away in a stumbling, drunken gait, dragging the crocodile through the mud. Then it was on its side and the ingwenya was joined by three others, who proceeded to tear the rhino apart.

Njikiza said if he hadn't seen the attack for himself he wouldn't have believed it.

"That *is* strange," conceded Thando, "but not, perhaps, as strange as what I myself have seen."

"And what is that?"

"I have seen these creatures eating rocks!"

"Rocks?" scoffed Njikiza. "No!"

"Yes!"

"Yes, then," said Njikiza, "by all means – rocks. But a rock is not a rhino."

"But it *is* a rock, Njikiza. These creatures eat rocks – is that not more strange?"

"I have seen it, too," added Jabulani.

Later, after the heat of the day had passed and they resumed their march, the udibi asked the Induna and he said he, too, had seen a crocodile eating rocks.

Yes, these ingwenya with their horny plates like ancient bark and their vicious tails are truly hideous creatures. To be involved in hunting one and perhaps even being the warrior who delivers the fatal spear thrust – that would be something special. A true test of his manhood . . .

He is close to being fifteen summers old; he is no longer a child. Has he not served his master well? How can the Induna deprive him of this chance to prove his mettle?

It's not fair.

*

"Hai!" says his companion, moving away from the shade. "It is hot today!"

And this . . . This adds insult to his injury . . .

His companion is a herdboy from the village. He's just thirteen summers old and therefore a child.

436

How can the Induna do this to him?

The *men* have gone off to hunt the crocodile in the deeper, murkier waters downstream, where the reptile is more likely to be hiding – it's for the children to keep watch elsewhere.

The men have gone off, laughing and joking, already hearing their names in praise songs – it's for the children to stay out of harm's way.

And this is right: the udibi happily concedes that. Let the children keep watch, while the men hunt.

But he is not a child!

Yet, here he sits, while Sagila crouches at the water's edge, studying the lazy tilapia dozing at the bottom of the stream – a child all too easily distracted from the matter at hand.

"Come away from there," growls the udibi.

Glancing over his shoulder, Sagila gives him a bemused look that says: You're not my father, or one of my older brothers . . .

The udibi jerks his head to the side and scowls.

Slowly, reluctantly, making it seem as if he's doing it only because he wants to, Sagila stands.

Speaking has reminded the udibi he is thirsty and as Sagila approaches him he too stands. He will, he decides, assert his authority still further by insisting Sagila keeps watch while he goes to the water's edge. It's pointless, keeping watch, but it's a chance to put the child in his place.

He's turning to issue his instruction to the child, when he catches a glimpse of movement in the reeds behind them.

*

The spot where the Induna has placed them can only be reached by crossing the stream. It's a smear of dried mud bounded on all other sides by a wall of reeds. To the udibi's left is a lone fever tree, an acacia with pale yellow bark.

There's a split second of movement in the reeds behind them. A rustling that attracts the boy's attention because it's lower down, somehow more purposeful than the usual shiftings and murmurings that comb the reeds.

How long has it been there – creeping forward slowly, carefully – waiting – watching – how long?

Then the reeds are thrown apart – a snout speckled with teeth, lethal jaws, bent forelegs, a heavy body . . .

They – the "children" – have found the crocodile.

More to the point, *it* has found *them.*

And a crocodile can outrun a man over a short distance . . .

And even before his mind registers what's happening, the udibi has pushed Sagila away from him.

He pushes Sagila aside. And moves in the opposite direction.

But the ingwenya is a crafty creature. Even as its head and body turn to follow the shrieking Sagila, it whips its tail sideways, knocking the udibi off his feet.

Still managing to keep hold of his spear, the boy rolls and is upright again, as the crocodile swings round to face him.

The best that can be said for this predicament is that the beast's momentum has been halted, but, despite its bulk – and this monster is almost ten metres long – a crocodile is capable of leaping . . .

Pouncing.

"The tree!" shouts the udibi. "Climb the tree!"

Panting, his eyes wide with fear, Sagila remains immobile.

And the boy can't worry about him – he has no time.

The reptile moves its head from side to side as though sniffing out the udibi. Or it could be the ingwenya is toying with him. Waiting for him to make the first move, safe in the knowledge whatever this human meat does it's trapped.

"The tree!" shouts the udibi.

Yes, but the question is: how is *he* going to get to the tree?

Unbidden, a story told by Thando flashes in his mind. Two hunters suddenly finding themselves the prey, as a pride of lions advances on them. "What are you doing?" asks the one man as the other turns.

"I'm going to run away," says this man.

"But you can't run faster than a lion!" says his companion.

"This is true, but here, today, I just have to run faster than *you*!"

"The tree!" shouts the udibi again. "Get to the tree!"

Suddenly Sagila can move – and he surprises the udibi. Glancing around, he sees a rock in the water and darts forward. Straightening, he throws it at the croc.

It bounces off the reptile's head and, as the ingwenya turns toward the source of the missile, the udibi darts sideways.

He moves around the crocodile to the edge of the stream. There's no point in calling to Sagila and making a break across the water – that's the ingwenya's home! Instead, what's uppermost in his mind is the knowledge that whichever way the croc turns, it'll have to swivel its body right around to get at him.

As it happens, the reptile swings away from Sagila and the tree, following the boy's passage. This gives the udibi a little time. His feet splashing through the water, he grabs Sagila and pulls him toward the acacia.

The crocodile is now facing the stream, which means it still has to keep turning to follow the boys.

At the tree, the udibi drops to his haunches. "Hurry," he shrieks.

Time enough to worry about sounding frightened in front of the child later, assuming there is a later.

Sagila steps onto the udibi's shoulders and the boy rises, pushing Sagila upward into the branches. He feels the pressure vanish as Sagila gains a foothold, then he's following the herdboy, his spear clamped between his teeth. Desperation gives him the agility of a monkey, but in his mind he can already feel the jaws of the ingwenya closing around his ankles.

The crocodile comes lumbering over, picking up speed – and hits the trunk at an angle.

"Your spear," wails Sagila, as they watch the ingwenya waddle away from the tree. "Why didn't you use your spear?"

"Shut up!" hisses the udibi, keeping his eyes on the croc.

Fourteen summers he might be, but he doubts he has the strength to kill an ingwenya with one stab of his spear. And even though the reptile's flank had been exposed at the time, he reckons one stab was all he would have been able to get in – and he ran the risk of losing the assegai in the process.

But there's no time to explain all of this.

The crocodile has wheeled and launched itself forward again.

Suddenly, without knowing how, the boy realises what the creature has in mind. Even as the ingwenya picks up speed, he slips his spear through his kilt, stands and clambers past Sagila, who's one branch higher than he is.

Using its momentum and the solidity of the trunk, the crocodile rears. Jaws bite twigs and leaves where the udibi had been sitting. Sagila screams and the udibi has to grab him to stop him from falling out of the tree. Balanced on its tail, the crocodile hovers for a few moments, its jaws snapping.

Then it topples sideways.

Retreats.

That was close – too close – and the udibi decides they should climb higher.

He shakes Sagila, tells him what they need to do.

The crocodile prowls the clearing morosely, an angry man trying to calm down – but only so that his next move will be more successful. It shows no sign of leaving them.

"Do you understand? We must get higher!"

At last, his face warped by tears, Sagila nods.

The udibi eases aside and lets the child climb past him.

"That branch there . . ." he says. "Get to that branch."

Sagila straddles the branch and, guiding himself with his hands between his skinny thighs, begins to shuffle forward to make place for his companion.

The ingwenya's sinuous, sideways lope is deceptively laconic, and before the udibi can reposition himself, the jaws are back, even closer than before. The boy has to swing out, away from the trunk, to avoid those conical teeth. In doing so, he loses his spear.

Biting back tears of frustration, he settles himself again and watches as the crocodile moves to where the assegai fell.

"Help," whispers Sagila.

The udibi jerks his head around. The child is at eye level, hanging upside down, still straddling the branch, still holding on with his hands between his thighs.

The udibi grabs his shoulder and, hoping the croc doesn't attack again, pushes . . .

After much grunting and groaning, he manages to get Sagila upright again. While the crocodile circles the tree, the udibi settles himself next to the child.

"Now we must call for help," he says, noting Sagila's ashen expression. "Do you hear me?"

Sagila nods. And together they shout their heads off.

"Don't worry," says the udibi, when they pause for breath. He puts his arm around the child's shoulders. "They'll come for us. We'll be safe until then." A chary glance at their feet dangling in space: "Don't worry. We'll be safe."

His other hand curled around one of the smaller branches above them, the udibi squeezes Sagila's shoulders.

"Do you hear me?"

But Sagila doesn't have a chance to reply, because at that moment the branch they're sitting on breaks.

*

The men will be talking about it for many years to come. Initially, though, their attempts at good humour were a little forced. Not only had the crocodile outwitted them all – and all are supposed to be adept hunters – it had also attacked two children. And the Induna's udibi was temporarily placed in this category. However, relief is a fuel for laughter and it wasn't long before they were shaking their heads and chuckling. The

Induna's udibi was heartily praised for his "prowess" as a hunter; perhaps he could take his place among men, after all.

"Do not let their playful words wound you," said the Induna later. "Hear the truth behind their jokes. They treat you as one of them. You can be proud of what you did today. Shaka will be most pleased –"

Yes, when he's finished laughing, thinks the udibi.

"Do not doubt that. And you have learnt an important lesson, have you not?"

"Master?"

"Yes, you have. I think, after today, you'll always know this. That when tracking your prey, be sure to look *behind* you from time to time."

The udibi nodded, his right hand folded around the pouch that contained the teeth of the crocodile, his reward for killing the reptile. That *was* true.

All the same, although he knew the others were teasing him – knew, too, they were genuinely relieved he'd come to no harm – he still felt obliged to risk further chaffing by pointing out he *had* managed to stab the crocodile numerous times.

"Of course!" said Njikiza. "Of course!"

But, he added, the boy's masterstroke had been to first stun the ingwenya by falling on top of it from such a great height.

Prester John. King Solomon's Mines. The Queen of Sheba's gold. Such is the power of this place, proffering itself, all things to everyone. The dust and decay merely an illusion, to be shed like old skin when the time is right. Ancient evil calling the greedy and the venal. A chain of whispers, winding through the bush. A sly beckoning.

"On the plain there is a fortress," wrote Joao de Barros in 1552, recounting the rumours, "built of large and heavy stones. It is very curious and well constructed, as according to reports no lime to join the stones can be seen. One of the structures is a tower twelve fathoms high . . ."

And from Sofala they came, seeking this fabled place, lured by gold. The Portuguese never found it, found their gold elsewhere, but the stones could wait. The stones could bide their time.

And these others are footsteps on the path in Shaka's dream, fading before the final vista, leaving the Zulu King to shoulder his way through the undergrowth for those final few strides that span centuries. Twigs and thorns cut his arms, his face. But the pain is a welcome respite from the hiss of the abomination who set him on this path and whose words are a charm, bewitching him, driving each foot forward.

Rage.

A final flailing.

A last casting aside.

"There! I have done it! Now what?"

"Your destiny."

His destiny.

No!

A jolt, knocking him out of his anger, causing his legs to kick away the covering.

"You must go there."

No! Never.

"You must go there."

No . . . stones in the sun, reptilian scales, a basking, a patience, a smiling evil . . . never!

Cold. Growing cold, now.

Shivering.

So cold.

A groggy groping.

Skins tangled up at his feet.

Awake.

A groping, this time with burning eyes seeking out familiar shapes.

His hut . . . Still in his hut. But knowing this . . .

"On the plain there is a fortress, built of large and heavy stones . . ."

The First Betrayal

"They'll be here soon, but it's not too late. And I would know one thing, and one thing alone, Brother: why? Why are you doing this? The serpents at KwaBulawayo speak and they say you are proud and stubborn, as wilful as a child. They spit poison, these snakes, but are they right in this instance? Or did you fall out of the tree and now you are mad? I have seen this happen before – but, Brother, I was there that day and I did not see you fall!"

"Hai! Perhaps I should count myself lucky that's all they say."

"What do you mean?"

"About the tree! Or are you being kind in neglecting to tell me they also say I am a coward?"

"A coward?"

"For climbing the tree!"

"No! None dare call you a coward, for they know that is a falsehood."

"But I am proud and wilful. Or perhaps mad . . ."

"And stubborn."

"Yet none will come stand where I stand so that they might see things from my vantage point!"

"But that is why I am here, Brother."

"Your mind is made up, like all the rest. Like his!"

"Now *you* do me an injustice! I would not be here were I not willing to stand where you stand – but I do not like this vantage point. I would find us a more congenial spot."

"Honeyed words. Tell me this: who sent you?"

"My head is bare, I am here . . ."

". . . of your own volition? Then what's the point? We waste our breath, for it's clear to me he has decided."

"Things are not that simple, Brother."

"From where I stand they are, Brother."

"But you do not stand alone! And you will not fall alone. And perhaps such loyalty feeds your pride, but think again! Would you visit suffering on your people? Is that how you seek to repay their loyalty?"

"No! But I don't have much choice in this affair."

"Now you *are* speaking like a madman, for this path is forked."

"Yes, like a serpent's tongue! Truly, I have no choice in this matter. Shaka has seen to that. My men and I have fought shoulder to shoulder with his soldiers, we are owed this! But Shaka says no! Now I can only go this way!"

*

Mzilikazi KaMashobane makes his way between the huts. He does not take the shorter route to the main gate by cutting through the cattle-fold, because there's a bitterness in his mouth, anger in his chest, and to cross the isibaya clothed in such a mood would be to defile it.

The kraal is being enlarged here. The outer stockade has been moved further outward to accommodate more huts. Many are still in the pro-cess of being built, are slender sticks, bent over and tied – singing women are polishing the dung floors, working on the thatch, while men bellow to their sons to pull here, tie there. All this under a blue sky and a sun that warms the shoulders with the promise of summer.

And all for nothing!

Nothing!

The thought clenches Mzilikazi's teeth.

It's a sign of their faith in him – the faith of the band who went with him to seek Shaka's protection on the eve of Gqokli Hill, and the others of the remaining Khumalo clans who have since rallied to his shield – that his home village, abandoned for so long, has not only to be repaired, but expanded. A sign of their faith that they continue with their labours, even though they know a terrible storm is gathering below the horizon.

He will be their sky-herder in this affair, they think, whistling and stamping and chasing the clouds away.

Their faith . . .

Is it misplaced?

He greets some greybeards, holds up a hand to silence his bodyguards as a group of boys cluster around him. Although still too young to venture far from their mothers, they're eager to regale him with tales of their own exploits. They push and shove and all talk at once, much like his own thoughts these days.

He listens without hearing and when he laughs it's another man's mirth.

But isn't this another reason, perhaps the main reason, why he has to do this? Here – in these round, shining faces, these eager little fingers, these chubby legs – here is the answer to charges of vanity.

As for the adults, it's *because* they have faith in him that he has to do this!

He would not be worthy of that faith if he acted in any other way, chose another path, even if it seems easier.

And the pain that'll fall upon these faithful ones – let it be the pain of birth. Yes, let it have a purpose. A goal.

That other path, Shaka's way – it'll bring pain, too, and this is something he needs to keep in mind. Yes! It'll bring pain, too – but the pain of torture, that takes away and rewards with scraps.

Scraps!

No more!

Never again!

Smiling, patting heads, Mzilikazi wades through the children, his guards moving to shoo the more persistent ones away. "Gently, gently," he chides the warriors, with a grin, "for one day these will be bigger than you!"

It would be so much easier if Shaka decided to be more reasonable. And this is his last chance to bend a penitent knee before the Zulu's anger. And any man – any wise man, that is – must dread reaching the point of no return, making the decision from which there is no turning back.

Hai, but clearly he and Shaka are brothers in this matter. This is the third official demand the King has issued; clearly he too is wary of committing himself to the irrevocable.

"You are one of his favourites," the Induna had said.

So? Has he not earned that status? Doesn't he bear the scars, some freshly healed?

I was in the van at the Umhlatuzi, and again when we went to fetch Ntombazi – yes, and this Truthsayer who seems to have angered Shaka so. Was I not the one who led the charge onto the top of the hill?

Mzilikazi shakes his head. He does not seek to conflate his role in these affairs, and the other times he has served Shaka with unswerving loyalty. He was only one of many brave men, but do not say he hasn't earned his standing . . .

And Shaka has simply stayed his hand! The blow *is* coming, make no mistake about that.

*

"Hai! But you *do* have a choice. For surely you don't expect the King to back down. He will not back down."

"Better to say he can't! He could, but he can't – there's a difference!"

"Then enlighten me!"

"He could very well back down, but he can't, because he doesn't want to seem weak. Am I right? You know I am right. But don't you see? That in itself, being afraid to appear weak, is a sign of weakness."

"What? Would you be a sangoma now? Share the King's glory when the Kingdom thrives, turn against him when the droughts come? And there you are mistaken, anyway – there are no droughts. Shaka rules this land!"

"The strong man . . ."

". . . is unafraid of appearing weak. Yes, yes, I know the saying. But you are blundering here, Brother, groping about in the darkness of your guilt. Strength, weakness, these have nothing to do with the matter at hand."

"I have nothing to be guilty about!"

448

"Then you have decided treachery is an ox you'd welcome into your kraal!"

"Do not talk to me of treachery. I am not the Needy One."

"The King gave you a chance to elevate yourself, but now you would go higher, spitting in his face as you climb! How is that not a betrayal?"

"The King offered me my birthright! Now I must grovel? It was not his to offer or withhold in the first place."

"This is true, Shaka would not deny that, Fool! But was he not the one who protected your birthright, who protected these lands? Zwide would not have left you alive to spit in his face as you do with Shaka."

"I have repaid the King for that generosity, many times over. Surely he would not deny that?"

"No, and this is why he sought to reward you!"

"Reward me? He gave only so that he might withhold!"

"He asked for a few cows, Brother."

"A few?"

"The King is our Father, yours too, Brother, and we must show him respect!"

"I will not be treated as a vassal! You mistakenly speak of treachery and betrayal – but I do not seek to usurp Shaka! No, never! I am the one who was betrayed in this matter and I want only justice."

"I do not seek to place you in the same kraal as the Needy One, but I still see in your actions a certain cunning that mocks the motives you proffer. And I wonder how you would have reacted to the King's reward had the Truthsayer not muddied Shaka's mind . . ."

"What do you mean?"

"Hai! You know whereof I speak. The King is distracted, perhaps he'll ignore my tantrum, my disobedience, my treachery! Is that not the stream your thoughts follow?"

*

Mzilikazi's slipped through an opening in the palisade and stands on the lower end of the parade ground near the main gate. He turns his back on the three Zulus waiting with a group of his men so that he might gaze upon the village resting on the slight incline. Turns his back and smiles. Aiee! He has to concede the Induna's right. Whatever the Truthsayer said left Shaka in a foul mood for several moons – and there were whisperings that the abomination had told him about his Ubulawu, which made Shaka's anger even more incomprehensible – and Mzilikazi *had* thought it would be a good time to make his move.

Like a cowardly rustler moving in to steal the cattle when the menfolk are away at war?

Not quite. In his defence, this is something he would've done sooner or later. After all, it's something he *has* to do. Something he owes his people.

His eyes rove over the domed huts, and he knows his men are there, waiting for his command. His warriors crouch, muscles coiled, assegais at hand, ready to serve him as they did that day.

That day . . . They did him proud, made his blood sing that day!

*

"Go!" said Shaka.

It was June 1821, and after consolidating his power south of the Thukela, he'd turned his attention to the northwest. With the Ndwandwes defeated it was at last time to make use of the information brought back to him by the reconnaissance force Mgobozi had led deep into Sotho territory, and various other smaller expeditions. Accompanying Mgobozi that time, the Induna had undone the Baboon God – well, let us see who else might be undone with Zulu steel, said Shaka.

"Go!" he told Mzilikazi. "Go to the land of Chief Ranisi, go in my name and offer him the compliments of the Bull Elephant, then impale him on the bluntest pole you can find; let his screams ring out across the valleys as a warning to the others who would spurn our protection!"

Mzilikazi thrust his spear into the air, the two regiments arrayed behind him on the parade ground at Bulawayo following his lead.

"Bayede, Nkosi! Bayede!"

450

It was a cry picked up by his men, iklwa blades raised – "Bayede, Nkosi! Bayede!" – then lowered, to drum their shields, a hailstorm rattle of steel against strengthened cowhide – "Bayede! Bayede!"

They were happy and Mzilikazi was happy, because there was more. Not only was this to be his first independent command – and at the head of two amabutho comprised almost entirely of men from his own clan – but Shaka had also decreed that on the successful completion of the task, Mzilikazi could lead his people back over the White Umfolozi to the rolling hills below the Ngome Forest . . .

This was the real reward for Mzilikazi's bravery in Shaka's legions – they could go home! Could return to the land of the Khumalos from which they had fled in the face of Zwide's treachery, a little more than three years previously.

And if there were those like Dingane who grumbled over such generosity being shown a "foreigner", others, like Mbopa, took it as a sign that the Zulu King was at last beginning to shrug off the bad moods that had plagued him since his encounter with the Truthsayer – although the prime minister soon saw that that was wishful thinking.

A few kilometres outside of KwaBulawayo, Mzilikazi came upon the Induna and his udibi. With them was a small band of warriors that included Njikiza, Thando, Takatso and five others. All were ready for a long journey.

They would join their brother on this, his first campaign as commander. "Having fought alongside you, we would now happily be led by you," said Njikiza.

"We ask nothing more than your permission to let our assegais join yours in the feast you have planned for Ranisi!" said the Induna.

There was also this, he added, leading Mzilikazi away from the main body. They knew before him how Shaka intended to reward the young Khumalo – and, truly, they'd been so pleased, it had been hard not to spoil the surprise – and had already asked if they might be permitted to join their old comrade. Then, earlier today, the King had suggested that Mzilikazi would also need a guide.

"Hai!" said the Induna, holding up a hand to interrupt Mzilikazi's protestations. "Not in killing, or leading men – you have proved yourself
in these things time and time again!"

No, Mzilikazi was not to be offended. But before he could exercise his
prowess as a warrior, he first had to lead his men to the land of Chief
Ranisi.

And here Takatso the Sotho would be of assistance.

"He will take you – us – right to the leopard's lair!"

"But our Father didn't mention the need for a guide to me," said Mzilikazi. "What made him change his mind?"

The Induna grinned, laid a hand on Mzilikazi's shoulder. "I do not
know, Brother. But perhaps the need for a guide occurred to Shaka when
he saw you take your singing impis along the road that leads to the sea!
For, Brother," he added, pointing past Mzilikazi back the way they'd
come, "it is true, you will find Ranisi in *that* direction!"

Mzilikazi's aghast expression quickly gave way to laughter that echoed
the Induna's. "Let us say," said Mzilikazi, wiping his eyes, "that my men
needed the exercise."

"Yes, for they feasted prodigiously during their stay at Bulawayo."

And did they not owe Ranisi an extra day or two to enjoy his wives,
given the great entertainment he was to provide them?

"This is so," said the Induna.

"But tell me this," said Mzilikazi, as they returned to the ranks, "has
my cousin proven to be like Mgobozi's wives, pestering you so that you
must seek peace in war?"

"No," chuckled the Induna. In fact, if anything, the opposite was true.
"Kani says *I* begin to pester *her* if my iklwa grows too indolent."

Besides, he added, as he had said before, he would share this moment
with Mzilikazi.

Really? And already, despite the laughter, despite even his pleasure
at having his old friends with him, for he valued their counsel, a tiny
seed had been planted. Even if their reasons for joining him were as they
said – and he did not believe the Induna would ever lie to him – he had

452

to ask himself why Shaka had been so happy to acquiesce to their request. Could it be the King wanted to place spies – albeit unwitting ones – in Mzilikazi's ranks?

A tiny seed – of discord, anger, loathing – awaiting the sustenance of further suspicions, but forgotten for the moment, as they drew closer to their destination, forgotten amid the preparations for battle.

And the Bull rampaged through Ranisi's settlement, the horns swinging out to encircle the kraal, the head and loins slamming straight through the main gate.

*

And then there was this, too . . .

Alerted by a sudden eruption of indignant birds from some bushes several metres down the path, the Induna told Njikiza to wait where he was, and then follow smartly. The big man nodded and cast about for a boulder to sit on and rest.

They'd taken the village, the Bull's head with Mzilikazi in the lead had smashed through the huts, then split up to chase down bands of fleeing men, while the loins made a more careful sweep of the settlement, hauling out those who had chosen to hide and herding the women, children and old-timers into the cattlefold. The horns, meanwhile, had gone in search of the livestock, along with Takatso, the Induna's udibi and the Khumalo herdboys who'd accompanied the expedition and who'd be responsible for looking after the cattle on the return journey.

In the process of pursuing the group trying to lead Ranisi to safety, and eating up the rearguards the chief threw behind him, Mzilikazi had got separated from his men – and the Induna and Njikiza went to find him. It wasn't a difficult undertaking, all one had to do was follow the bodies, but the Induna had been growing ever more concerned. Although there were two or three, or even four of Ranisi's men to every dead Khumalo, there were still far too many Khumalo bodies for the Induna's liking. And there was a chance Mzilikazi might find himself alone, isolated from his soldiers.

The path skirted the contours of the hillside; at the place where the Induna had spotted the birds, it dropped into a tunnel of entwined branches, becoming a broad swathe of sand in the shade.

Slowing down, the Induna moved into the cool gloom.

Five paces . . . six . . . seven . . . until twigs and leaves shattered behind him.

A man, pouncing like a leopard.

The Induna turned, leant into his shield. A split second after impact – the jolt sending the man staggering one way, his spear flying the other – the Induna wheeled to face the second assailant, who'd been hiding further along the path. Wheeled and charged, twirling his iklwa, forcing the man backwards with his shield; ensuring he couldn't bring his assegai into play. Then, in a short, sharp jabbing motion, the Induna poked the haft of his iklwa into the man's solar plexus, pulling back his strike before the wood could pierce skin.

The man buckled – and the Induna dropped onto his knees in time to deflect the spear with his shield. Clearly surprised at the Zulu's quick reflexes, the third man hesitated long enough for the Induna to come out of his crouch. A bounding leap – a lunge – and the man was down, his stomach a mouth opening to release the Zulu's blade.

The first man was on his feet again: broad shoulders and heavy stomach, blundering toward the Induna. The Zulu dodged sideways, ducking low, sweeping his blade. Grabbing air, entrails unravelling out of the gash in his side, the first man crashed into the second, his momentum carrying both of them into the undergrowth.

A fourth assailant, a young herdboy, sprinting up the path, his spear clutched like a pike: twirling his iklwa, the Induna stepped sideways, whacking the teen on the side of the head with the haft.

Another whack, louder, more liquid than the first. The Induna spun round.

"Ngadla!" grinned Njikiza, the second man lying at his feet, his head spilling porridge.

"Hold him!" said the Induna as the herdboy scrambled to his feet.

Njikiza dropped his club and grabbed the boy's arm, almost yanking the latter off his feet.

"You would question him? Hai, but these are izilwane! We do not speak their language."

The Induna's reply was a noncommittal grunt. He'd forgotten that, and neither Takatso nor Thando were anywhere near.

"Let him go," he told Njikiza. They were wasting time.

"Nduna?"

"You heard me. Let that be the reward for his courage."

"I was not about to disagree, Master. I merely suggest we allow this little one time to sleep off his bloodlust."

The Induna nodded. "Do it."

After Njikiza had knocked out the teenager and dragged him into the undergrowth, the Induna said they would continue as before, with the Watcher Of The Ford lagging back to provide support when needed.

Bloodlust! The same malady had affected Mzilikazi, leading him to outstrip his soldiers. It was understandable – he surely wanted to prove himself worthy of his first independent command – but no less annoying for all that.

The Induna didn't much relish having to inform Shaka that something had happened to one of his favourites.

*

But he comes upon them a few minutes later . . .

. . . and isn't sure he should believe his eyes!

Some twenty or so of Ranisi's men are gathered around a tree. The tree is not tall, but it's sturdy, with a broad trunk and dense foliage as thick as thatch. A tangle of leaves that appears to have sprouted assegai shafts. Some men mob the trunk, craning their necks and shouting instructions, while others have moved into the sunlight and make ready to throw their spears.

There's no time to waste. Knowing Njikiza is only a few paces behind him, the Induna rushes forward. Many of the men have used up all their spears or haven't yet bothered to retrieve those that have fallen to the ground, and the Induna's bellowing orders for an impi to charge as he dispenses with the first few warriors . . .

And then Njikiza's there, and thinking they're being attacked by a regiment, Ranisi's remaining men scatter, leaving behind ten of their comrades, dead and dying.

After taking a few mouthfuls of beer from the calabash proffered by Njikiza, the Induna approaches the tree. Stands peering up into the foliage, his hands on his hips. "You can come down now, Brother!"

*

"Hmm . . ." The Induna holds the smoke in his lungs, then exhales. "I am put in mind of the shongololo," he says, handing the rhino horn to Mzilikazi.

"The shongololo?"

"The shongololo. That hard shell, those little legs, always moving – valour and discretion."

An arrow of smoke leaves Mzilikazi's pursed lips. "Discretion?" he chuckles. "No. Wisdom, Brother. Valour and wisdom. The wise man must on occasion withdraw so he might live to fight again, in more propitious circumstances."

"This is so," says the Induna, eyeing the tree. "But on *this* occasion, might it not have been wise to withdraw a little further?"

Mzilikazi hands back the horn. "You are right, Brother, and this was my intention, for my men were not far away. I merely sought to gather some fruit to sustain me on the journey."

"Aiee, Mzilikazi! You sound like Mgobozi! That is a tale worthy of the most enthusiastic praise singer!"

"Between you and me, Brother, I have to say I hope not! For . . ."

"These songs are sometimes open to interpretation?"

"And misinterpretation!"

"Very well, then let this remain here, between you and me, Brother!"

"Hai, I jest, Brother! You saved my life. That cannot be ignored!"

"They would've lost all their spears sooner or later, then your iklwa could have feasted!"

"Perhaps. But I am still grateful to you. I will not forget you saved my life this day."

"Good. Would you pick more berries, or can we return to our men?"

"I've had my fill. Let us go."

Just then the udibi arrives, looking for his master. They have captured the cattle, and Ranisi, too.

"Very good," says Mzilikazi, patting the boy on the shoulder. "And the stake – ?"

"It is ready, Master," says the udibi.

*

The three indunas are dressed in all their finery, with amashoba, necklaces and blue crane feathers curving above their heads. Three udibis serve them, although these linger outside of the kraal, with the officers' shields and spears.

Mzilikazi is interested to note he knows none of the men. Clearly, they've been summoned from Shaka's furthest kraals, and consequently feel elevated, are awash in self-importance.

Two extremes, muses Mzilikazi. The King has sent the Induna through the back gate, these three preened baboons through the front . . .

Mzilikazi's ordered that they be detained here, at the main gate. He will not receive them at the ibandla tree, and he's taken his time getting to them. All calculated insults.

Now – another. "What do you want?" he says brusquely, cutting across their traditional greetings.

A momentary bristling, then the middle induna steps forward.

"The King would know: what has happened to his cattle? Why have you not paid what is his due, owed to him for the protection he provides?"

"Seize them!"

Before the three can even turn, Mzilikazi's men have them from behind, gripping their elbows.

"Do not fear, Little Brothers," says Mzilikazi, moving forward, "I mean you no harm."

He has something far worse in mind. Swinging the blade of his assegai, he knocks the blue crane feather out of each man's leather headband.

"Release them," he says, stepping back, "so that they might wipe away their tears."

The three stand glaring at him, unmoving.

"I have said this before," says Mzilikazi, "and I grow tired of repeating myself. So let this be the last time. If Shaka thinks I owe him cattle, let him come and fetch them!"

With a languid flick of his hand, he dismisses them.

They turn and stride out of the gate, leaving their feathers in the dust.

*

When the Zulus and their udibis are out of sight, Mzilikazi whistles. Instantly, he's surrounded by his lieutenants. Shaka is coming! They must issue the order. The people must pack up all the provisions they can carry, they are to leave this place.

His officers nod their agreement. They know to stay and fight would be futile. They are not cowards, but they're also not stupid.

Shaka and his advisors might see in Mzilikazi's actions pride and stubbornness, even perhaps a hitherto unsuspected suicidal streak – but they'd be wrong. Ultimately, Mzilikazi has done what he's done to ensure the survival of his clan.

The impis Shaka will send will merely be attempting to complete by force a process that's already begun – the eating up of the Khumalos.

After the lieutenants have left him, Mzilikazi gazes around. It's precisely because this is an umuzi that they have to leave. As he told the Induna: haven't they earned the right, through fighting alongside Shaka, to be treated as an ally?

Instead Shaka would regard them as vassals, with Mzilikazi the umnumzane of an umuzi. Just one of many – paying homage, feeding Shaka's army.

The time has come for Mzilikazi to prove himself worthy of the faith, the trust his people have shown him, by giving them what they deserve.

Let them move away, then, an arduous trek, full of dangers, but one worth the risk, the hardships, for they will find a place of their own, where they can build an ikhanda, a royal kraal, not merely a village, and Mzilikazi can be their inkosi, their king, and no mere servant of another ruler. And if they must fight, they will fight viciously, for they'll be fighting for themselves for once, and not for the aggrandisement of another; they'll be fighting so that a brave clan might be allowed the space to grow into a tribe, a nation.

*

Mzilikazi heads back to his hut as the village springs to life around him, a dismantling, a gathering in, a readying. Once more he finds dread in his steps, for there's still his unfinished discussion with the Induna, who arrived late yesterday afternoon incognito, by a different road to the one the other three took.

Too late, too late, thinks Mzilikazi, trying to step over the dread of what he knows has to be a final goodbye . . .

Yes, and if we meet again, it will be on the field of battle!

But when he arrives at his hut, the Induna and his udibi are gone.

Silence ushers the Zulus into the stand of trees and silence is their companion as they move through this strange fruit. Men, women and children, strung up by their wrists. The stench of rotting meat is overpowering, a current ridden by an army of flies in a constantly shifting haze, swarming to cover faces and ripped-open guts.

No one knows where the Ancient Ones come from. They were simply here when the Nguni and others drifted down from the north. Their own name for themselves was "Khwai", or "Men"; the Khoikhoi, to whom they were closely related, called them "Souqa"; others called them "Bosjesmans", or "Bushmen".

They worship the wilderness as an all-powerful presence called Kaang and regard the praying mantis as sacred. They hunt with bows and poison arrows – and N'go, the caterpillar, is another creature they pray to, as crushed caterpillar heads provide them with one of their most lethal poisons.

Small, light-skinned, wizened before they're old, they're regarded as not quite human, and the invaders from the north forced them into the caves of the high country and the deserts of the Kalahari. Unable to hunt game freely, they've taken to stealing cattle and are ruthlessly hunted down and slaughtered.

For all that they're regarded as vermin, the Induna's udibi is surprised at the effect this sight has on him. It's almost as if, in being slaughtered and hung up like animals, these Ancient Ones have at last revealed themselves to be Abantu, human beings.

The Induna, he notes, also wears a bleak expression. Some of the men remain unaffected by the grim sight, but Njikiza's also scowling – and the big warrior silences a flippant comment made by one of the others with a menacing growl.

But they are *different, these Ancient Ones – isn't it said they can converse with baboons? And woe betide those who cross them! The boy finds himself staring at one of the bodies. This one shows signs of being punched and kicked. Thundercloud bruises cover the ribcage. There's a deep wound in the body's side, but the flies seem to prefer the hole where the man's nose used to be. The udibi's examining the busy mass when something draws his gaze to the man's eyelids.*

And at that very moment, the man, this corpse, opens his eyes . . .

The Tikoloshe

Some two hundred or so angry men crowd around the Zulus in a bristling circle of hungry spears. The Induna, Njikiza and Thando, meanwhile, have backed themselves into their own circle, so they can keep all sides covered while leaving each other enough room to manoeuvre. They stand waiting; big Njikiza with his club, the Induna and Thando with their oval shields and short stabbing spears.

"Hai!" grunts Njikiza, his eyes on the men, straining, yet reticent, with no warrior willing to lead the charge. "See? We have them surrounded!"

The Induna chuckles. "In a manner of speaking," he says.

*

They laid the frail man down in the shade of a boulder, where the boy was waiting with a waterskin. The Ancient One's eyelids flickered when the Induna slipped a hand behind his neck and raised his head. His lips peeled apart as the Zulu squeezed some water into his mouth. A few drops, that's all, before the dying man gagged. His breathing shallow, the Ancient One stared up at the Induna.

Hard to tell his age. His skin was like leather; cracked, lined. Creased. Tight curls of hair sprouted from his chin.

He tried to move. To roll onto his side. For this is their way, these Khwai. A dead man is buried on his side, with his face pointing toward the rising sun. Seeing the determination in the man's stirrings, the Induna helped him shift position.

"Fetch me a spear," he told the boy. "A hunting spear."

The boy obeyed and the Induna lay the long assegai next to the man. Gently closed the fingers of the man's right hand around the haft.

"For wherever he is going," he told the boy, "he is a hunter and it is right and fitting that he goes armed with a hunter's spear."

Njikiza joined them. "It is done?"

The Induna nodded. "They will do the rest."

"So you feel it too."

"Yes."

Seeing his udibi's perplexed frown, the Induna grinned. "Eyes, boy. Eyes are upon us. We are being watched."

Njikiza chuckled as the boy's head swivelled, trying to look everywhere at once – the acacias that covered the surrounding slopes, the boulders and crevices.

"Do not strain yourself. You will not see them."

*

"What?" bellows Njikiza. "Will you not fight?"

His legs are crisscrossed by bloody scratch marks from the spears of those who foolishly tried to duck under his club. A gouge in Thando's thigh is bleeding profusely and he has the beginnings of a black eye. The tip of a spear blade has connected with the Induna's hipbone and skidded off, leaving a long cut around his left side, just above his kilt; the last frantic lunge of a dying man has sliced through the flesh on the inside of his left upper arm.

Yet no one's in a hurry to lead a charge against the three Zulus. They growl and mutter, shift their feet, test the weight of their long spears, but there's a hold-me-back quality to their actions. As a result, movements meant to be threatening look suspiciously like nervous fidgeting.

*

Lumisani, the chief of the clan, sat on an ornately carved wooden throne, toying with a whisk. To his right and left stood his advisors. Behind them was a wall of shields and spears twenty men long and five men deep. A guard of honour – and show of strength.

Wearing their amashoba and carrying their shields and spears, the ten Zulu soldiers spread out behind the Induna, in their own show of strength – which, the Induna's udibi decided, was a little more impressive, given the warriors' noble bearing and the way they ignored the glares of Lumisani's men, as if these were of no consequence.

At a look from the Induna, the boy accompanied his master and Njikiza as they went forward to meet the chief. Neither man was armed, but the boy carried the Induna's shield, resting the bottom tip on the ground when they came to a halt, keeping the three iklwas he was gripping out of sight behind the isihlangu.

"So – here we are!" said Lumisani, with an imperious wave of his whisk.

The Induna and his men had arrived early the previous afternoon, but the chief had kept Shaka's envoy waiting for almost a full day.

Let these arrogant savages flex their impatience for a while, he'd said. It'll do them good!

"Yes, here we are," said Lumisani again. "Now tell me: what is it your master wants of me?"

Our master? thought the boy, lowering his eyes, so that none could see the rage flaring there. He is your master too, Fool!

"How goes the drought?"

The chief tilted his head, a dog hearing a strange sound. "What?"

"This is what the King would know," said the Induna. "How goes the drought that ravages these parts?"

And now the udibi's bowed head hid a smile.

"Drought? What drought?"

The Induna shrugged. "Why, the drought that destroys your crops and kills your cattle."

"Drought?" Lumisani's head swivelled so he could bestow a quizzical glance on the advisors standing either side of him. What is this Zulu babbling about? "There is no drought."

The Induna allowed himself to straighten, as though taken aback by this pronouncement. "No drought? How can this be?"

Lumisani levelled his whisk. "Do not try my patience, Zulu!"

"That is not my intent. I am merely confused."

"Surely a familiar state for a Zulu."

The Induna merely inclined his head in polite appreciation of the witticism and said: "Yet it *is* perplexing, is it not?"

"Is it?"

"It is."

"And again you try my patience!"

"But how can there not be a drought?"

An angry swish of the whisk and Lumisani leant forward. "Listen to me very carefully, Zulu. There. Is. No. Drought!"

The Induna turned his head, as though grappling with a complicated conundrum.

Given what they'd seen that morning, he was finding it hard to converse with Lumisani with even a modicum of politeness, and when he looked back at the chief all such pretence was gone.

"Then where is the tribute owed Shaka?"

*

The huts are placed very close together, almost touching each other, with narrow paths between each row. It makes pursuit very difficult, a fact the Induna was counting on when he led the others among the dwellings.

"Now!" he shouts.

Njikiza is behind him, the last in the line. He wheels round, swinging his club, knocking a warrior sideways into the curved wall of one of the huts. The Induna, who's also turned, crouches and jabs his iklwa past Njikiza, catching the thigh of the soldier who managed to duck the big man's club.

Ahead of them, Thando and Maweru dispense with the few soldiers coming down the row in the opposite direction, killing two and sending the other three fleeing.

Njikiza's club finishes off the man the Induna wounded. The Induna straightens, peering past the Watcher Of The Ford. The next two men have both turned and are using their shields to push their comrades back; there is no way they are going to face that club.

The Induna taps Njikiza's shoulder. "Let's go," he says.

Maweru and Thando move forward, leaping over the bodies of the men they've slain. The Induna is next, increasing his pace as Maweru and Thando start to run. Then comes Njikiza.

*

"The Xhosas over the hills there have not come and killed you," continued the Induna, his eyes firmly on Lumisani's. "And Zwide, whose appetite you thwarted by seeking – and receiving – Shaka's protection, he has not come slinking back to feed you your own entrails. So there must be a drought . . ."

*

Seeing the kind of hospitality they could expect, the Induna had warned his men to be on their guard. None were to leave the hut. They ate of the rations they carried and took turns to stand watch through the long night. Then, that morning, they'd become aware of a growing commotion. Young and old, male and female, had dropped what they were doing and were moving toward the gathering place. The Induna ordered his men to be on guard – nothing too provocative; they were merely to ensure their shields and spears were close at hand. After waiting until the scurrying had died down and it seemed as if almost everyone was at the gathering place, the Induna told Njikiza and the boy to follow him.

A large group of men – who probably saw themselves as a hunting party, thought the Induna wryly – had just returned. Several pairs carried poles between their shoulders. Tied to these poles by their wrists and knees were Khwai men, women and children.

Not all of them were dead.

*

"There must be a drought, for what else could explain such a feckless oversight? Your crops and cattle can only be dead. And, yes, now that we are speaking of these things, I see a certain weakness, a certain withered appearance in your men that must be a sign of empty bellies."

The boy grinned again as an angry rumble moved through the ranks of Lumisani's men.

"Yes! There! I hear it!" said the Induna. "The sound of aching stomachs."

*

After untying the Khwai, the warriors put down their spears and went to a large pile of stones. The Induna had wondered about that pile of stones, almost as big as a storage hut. Now he knew. And as he and the other two watched the brave warriors set about pelting the Khwai men, women and children with the stones they'd picked up.

And the rest of the clan cheered the men on.

And there was one old Khwai man, older than old, who remained aloof, who refused to join in the vain scramble of the others, knowing it was pointless. They had been freed only so that their suffering might be prolonged. And he stood his ground amid the storm. Incredibly, he went unnoticed by the warriors for a time. Only the Induna spotted him.

And the old man was the last left standing, and even then, dwarfed by the soldiers, he stood his ground, his gaze unwavering. A stone to the head felled him as a prelude to an angry avalanche, for in his eyes the warriors had seen their own shame and were now eager to obliterate him. But, even then, he made not a sound. He fell and died in silence. A silence that grew and infected the spectators, a poison that spread, killing their earlier excitement, and one by one, they turned and shuffled away . . .

*

"Yes, you are right, Zulu, we are sorely plagued," said Lumisani, "but it's not a drought that causes our annoyance. It's a beetle!"

The udibi couldn't help himself: his head jerked up.

"Yes, a beetle," said Lumisani, noting the fifteen-year-old's look of shock and outrage. "But never fear, Zulu, do not concern yourself on our behalf. As you have surely seen, we have a way of dealing with vermin!"

*

Thando's interlinked fingers form a step the Induna uses to scramble atop one of the huts, while Njikiza's club swats a warrior sideways and, on the other side, Maweru hooks his shield inside his assailant's, rips it away and sends his iklwa to feast on the man's entrails. Using his heels to buy him purchase in the thatch, the Induna extends his hand to take Thando's shield and assegai. Leaning backwards, he places them behind his head, on the flattened apex of the hut. Njikiza swings his club and fells another warrior – then lunges forward, to bring down yet another, his club shattering the back of the man's head. On Maweru's side, the attackers have backed away. The Induna reaches for his own shield and spear, places them atop Thando's – then he pulls Thando up.

As soon as the latter's secured his own footing, the Induna retrieves his shield and spear – and leaps across onto the neighbouring hut. The men on Njikiza's side are now below him, and the Induna manages to drive his iklwa into the shoulder of one before the others can react. With a shield and a spear, the Induna can't get too low, or else he'll slip off the sloping roof of the hut, but the villagers don't seem to realise this – and they back away even further, so that a hut now separates them from Njikiza.

Who's arguing with Maweru.

He will hoist Maweru up.

But Maweru is adamant. Njikiza is too big, too heavy to pull himself up.

"Hurry!" shouts Thando, who's leapt onto the next hut down, the one on the side Maweru was defending.

"Come!" says Maweru, entwining his fingers.

Reluctantly, Njikiza pushes his club onto the roof of the hut. They totter and teeter as he steps onto Maweru's hands – then, his fingers digging into the thatch, Njikiza manages to pull himself onto the hut. Immediately he twists himself sideways, extending a hand. Maweru mustn't bother passing him his shield and spear; all Njikiza needs is an arm, he'll do the rest. But now two men on Thando's side see their chance. While the one makes to stab at the Zulu's feet, protecting himself with his shield, the other charges past – and throws his spear.

Maweru's eyes bulge as the blade enters his exposed back.

"No!" bellows Njikiza. But even as he desperately tries to pull the warrior up and over him, Maweru's body goes limp, and Njikiza has no option but to let his comrade slide off the hut.

*

"What say you, Master?" asked Njikiza, as they moved through the lengthening shadows. "This one is not fit to serve our Father!"

The Induna nodded. They have to spend one more night here. On dismissing them, Lumisani had said he'd have a response for Shaka the following day. Ominous words. When they finished eating – touching no food they hadn't brought with them – the Induna called Njikiza. The men were to be extra vigilant that night.

"There is evil afoot," said the Induna. "The pot stands to boil over."

*

They run, leaping from hut to hut, easily knocking down the occasional spear sent their way with their cowhide shields. If villagers clamber atop the thatch, Njikiza just has to jump their way, landing on an adjacent dwelling, for them to dive off again. When the Induna sees a slender stream of smoke rising in the distance, he calls on Thando and Njikiza to follow him. Springing from hut to hut, they head for the gathering place where they had their audience with the chief.

*

Lumisani sits up. Coughs. Spits. Stiffens. Something has roused him. A shifting. A noise.

He frowns. The fire in the centre of the hut has burnt down, but it gives off just enough of a glow to show that . . .

No, it can't be.

There's something, *some thing*, hovering above the embers.

Hovering!

A tiny, monkey-like creature . . . as his vision becomes accustomed to the dark, Lumisani can make out skinny legs . . . skinny legs, bowed, dangling about half a metre off the ground . . . a body, and shoulders, and the angle of an elbow . . .

Lumisani loses himself for a moment trying to look, to see what this creature is, precious seconds that might have meant the difference between life and death . . . For as he recovers himself, realises what this creature is, and opens his mouth to call his guards, there's a soft hiss, a slicing of the darkness and he topples backwards, gurgling, choking, coughing . . . Sounds that roar in his ears, but which barely penetrate the night's silence. *Tikoloshe! Tikoloshe!*

Screams that are stillborn in the blood that bubbles between his lips.

And Lumisani dies raising his hands, trying to bring them up to his throat, to wrench away the pain.

Tikoloshe!

*

One of the servants found Lumisani's body earlier this morning, his horrified screams calling forth pandemonium, a wild dog shaking the village by the scruff of the neck. The ensuing panic, growing as the news spread through the huts, gave the Induna and his men a little time. Flight wasn't an option, for this would have been an admission of guilt. Besides, Xoli, Lumisani's son and heir, had ordered all the gates guarded as soon as he'd recovered from the initial shock of the discovery. Even a concerted dash by the Zulus would have proved futile. All the same, they were ready when a group of warriors came for them. It was clear this was no delegation arriving to tell them what had happened during the night. Neither were they there to question the Zulus. Their aim was to disarm their guests and take them into custody. The Induna was having none of that – and a running battle ensued.

Now, bleeding, bruised, but ready to fight, Njikiza, Thando and the Induna stand in their tight circle, surrounded by the larger group. They are all that remain of the original party; the bodies of the rest lie scattered about the village, each inevitably accompanied by five, six, seven dead men. Small wonder, then, that no one's quite willing to make the first move, to brave Zulu steel and the casual swipe of Njikiza's club.

Shoulder to shoulder, with their shields and spears, trying to give the impression they're only waiting for the order to unleash them, each of Xoli's soldiers knows many will die before the Zulus are brought down – and who wants to be one of those unfortunates? Certainly not the men in the front row, who are, naturally, most at risk; indeed, they know they are expected to distract the Zulus by dying, allowing those behind them to move forward and bring this affair to a conclusion.

Consequently, these men are not only more than a little wary, they're also annoyed. For they're being pushed from behind, as the others use their hesitation to hide their own fear – if they can't get at the Zulus it's because of these cowards in front of them.

And meanwhile the Zulus regain their breath, grip their weapons tighter, test muscles and joints, check to see their mobility isn't hampered – and wait, eyes on the foe.

*

Xoli pushes through his men. "Is this the way you repay our hospitality?" he snarls.

"Is this what you call hospitality?" says the Induna, straightening.

"Cha! We welcome you into our midst – and this is your response?"

"We come in peace – and this is *your* response?"

"Peace? You came here with treachery in your hearts, cunning in your eyes."

"We came merely to talk to your father."

"Cowards! You had to resort to sorcery to kill my father!"

"Your grief has made you thirsty. You would drink from the first watering hole you come across and deem it good."

"So speaks the Beetle's sorcerers!"

"We came in peace!"

"What do you Zulus know of peace?"

"Hai, but this is a pleasant path you walk!"

"What does *that* mean, Zulu? Explain yourself. Entertain me before you die."

"Blame the strangers! Truly, this is an easy path around the mountain."

"Do not fool yourself. You are not strangers to me! I know you too well, know you for the cowardly killers that you are."

"Yes, but do you know how Shaka will react to these baseless accusations?"

"Let him come! We do not fear him!"

"Many have said that – and so our Kingdom has grown."

"Yes – through sorcery and cowardly acts of treachery!"

"Our Kingdom was won in battle. But think that and it's Shaka's impis who'll have an easy path to follow!"

"Enough talk!"

"Agreed! Set your men upon us; those who would die today. But know this – the murderer moves among you. You might even be next!"

"Do you threaten me?"

The Induna shrugs. "I have no need to. I'll leave that to the murderer of your father."

"I know who murdered my father. Your tikoloshe, summoned to do your evil deed."

"And if you are wrong?"

"I am not afraid."

"Can you say the same of your men?" For look, adds the Induna, see the doubt, the concern on their faces! "If you are wrong and we are not the killers, then you and the village remain cursed!"

"Are we then to apologise and let you go? Do you think we're that stupid, Zulu?"

"I intend to go nowhere," smiles the Induna.

That surprises Xoli. "Oh?" he asks.

"Show me your father's hut, show me where this deed took place, and I'll show you the murderer."

*

It's an option that allows Xoli to protect his pride. Will his men even obey him should he scream at them to attack these Zulus, who have already killed many today?

He grins, as if hugely amused, and agrees to the Induna's suggestion.

Let's see what tall tale this jackal can concoct . . . This will at least break the bizarre impasse, three men holding off a horde of others. He'll have time to gather some trusted officers from his own regiment and then it'll be a matter of waiting for an opportunity to fall on the three Zulus. Finish them off quickly and without much fuss – and let that be a lesson to the other men! Oh yes, when this matter is resolved he'll make them rue today, the cowardice and ineptitude they showed.

And he can do this because he is the new chief. What with all the panic, the shouting and screaming, he hasn't really had time to process this sudden change in status and all it entails – and, truly, he believed the old bastard would live forever, just to spite him.

*

Some say the tikoloshe is a water sprite, who loves the company of old women, especially if they feed it milk. Its body is covered in ochre-coloured fur. It has black piggy eyes and a dog's snout, and its hands and feet are small, like a monkey's. Its tail is its penis and it will do a witch's bidding if she allows it to fuck her. Some say the tikoloshe will ride out at night astride a hyena on its wicked errands. Others claim it can render itself invisible and slip bad medicine into the spoon even as one is raising it to one's mouth. However, like it as not, the time will come when this malevolent dwarfish creature turns on its master or mistress and returns to its hiding place in the river.

"See?" says Xoli. "You smirked when I said a tikoloshe did this. But I ask you: who else could be responsible? Look you and tell me – who could have done this, if not a tikoloshe?"

The chief's dwelling was well guarded, with four men at the entrance – the only way in and out. What's more – and this added to the horror of the villagers – the entrance was barricaded with a wooden screen. And this "door" had not been moved.

The men who were guarding the hut are still there, looking like a bunch of revellers the morning after, except it's dread, not the effects of alcohol, that shades their faces. While Xoli makes a great production of showing how difficult it is to move the wooden screen, the Induna studies them. They are afraid, he decides. They are afraid because they know they're likely to be blamed – if not for the deed itself, then for dereliction of duty. They are afraid because something strange happened here last night, right under their very noses – and they believe the tikoloshe was involved. And although they were left unharmed, to have come so close to the creature, albeit unwittingly . . . that's enough to give the bravest man sleepless nights. What they are not, the Induna decides, is afraid of being caught out. Whatever happened here last night did not involve them.

"Is something wrong, Zulu?"

The Induna shakes his head. Says he'd like to make a circuit of the hut.

"I would echo my father and say, be my guest," grins Xoli, "but I would not like to wake up dead."

The soldiers around him chuckle.

"Just one thing," says the Induna, wheeling.

"What is it?"

"I would ask these men a question," says the Induna, indicating the guards.

"We are satisfied they were not involved," says Xoli. "After all – they are not Zulus."

"Know they the difference?"

"Of course!" A guffaw.

"Very well, then," says the Induna, addressing the officer who's clearly in charge of the guards. "Did any Zulus approach this hut last night?"

The captain casts a nervous glance in Xoli's direction; a look that asks whether he should lie or tell the truth.

"No," interjects the Induna, "I asked the question."

"Tell him," says Xoli with a shrug.

"No," says the captain.

"Did you see *any* Zulus last night?"

"No."

"Did anyone else come to see the chief?"

"No one," says the captain.

"And the chief was alive at this point?"

"Most definitely. He called upon me to make sure the men were vigilant."

*

The chief's dwelling is in a walled enclosure, separate from the village. The northern portion is shaded by a large tree. Its trunk is beyond the wall and its branches spread over the roof of the domed hut. His eyes on the ground, the Induna scrutinises the tracks of the guards: many footprints overlaying each other, describing a circle around the hut; no unexpected deviations; no footprints coming in from another direction. He sets Thando and Njikiza to check the thatch for signs of a hidden entry point.

Xoli watches with bemusement, occasionally muttering something to his men that elicits spasms of laughter.

Aiee! Such a show! He could almost admire the Zulus, the diligence they display in what they must know is a futile activity. Because, after all, they are the murderers – or at least the ones who called forth the tikoloshe – they know what happened and how. Yet here they are, probing the thatch the way one baboon will groom another, picking off fleas.

"Nothing," murmurs Thando, dusting his hands.

"And you, Njikiza?"

The big man shakes his head.

No one has cut their way through the thatch and then tried to disguise the opening.

"I would now like to see the body," says the Induna, with an imperiousness he knows will anger the younger man.

Xoli snorts. "But of course. Of course you would."

The Induna asks for a torch to be lit. He's crouching next to the body when he sees it: the small, jagged wound in Lumisani's throat.

That's how he died. Something went in and something went – was pulled – out.

Standing, the Induna moves to the centre of the hut and gazes at the circular opening above him – in effect the dwelling's "chimney" or smoke-hole.

He turns his head. Thrusts the blazing torch in Xoli's direction – a gesture that causes the heir to step back. "Would you know how your father was murdered?"

*

The tree is stout, says the Induna, its branches strong enough to allow someone to climb out over the chief's hut. In the darkness, that person would be invisible to the guards below him.

Two or more people were involved, adds the Induna. The one who climbed the tree was small enough to fit through the smoke-hole. He had a rope tied around his waist. His accomplices positioned themselves at the tree trunk, where they could not have been seen by the guards on the other side of the wall. They then proceeded to lower the smaller man – or boy – through the smoke-hole. Thando found markings on the tree where the rope had scraped against the bark.

Lowered into the hut, the smaller man then stabbed Lumisani with a spear – in the throat, so he could not scream – and, tugging on the rope to let the others know he was done, he caused himself to be raised again.

"And who did this incredible thing?" sneers Xoli, conscious of the fact that his men are exchanging looks that show they are impressed by the Induna's reasoning.

"Not a tikoloshe! Although, perhaps that's what you were expected to think."

Since no one's questioned, or indeed spotted, his lie, the Induna's happy for Xoli to believe this was a murder intended to look like the work of the much-feared creature.

Not that Xoli's about to believe anything he says. But the new chief's roar of theatrical laughter is by and large ignored by his men. They are thinking it through, thinking: Well, maybe . . .

And Xoli sees this, realises a sneering dismissal of the Induna's suggestion isn't going to work – but then he suddenly remembers something and his grin of triumph is for real.

"Two men, you say?"

"At least two. More likely three or four."

"Hmm," says Xoli. "And one small, a boy even?"

Seeing where this is leading, the Induna contents himself with a nod.

"Ah! But did you not have a boy in your party?"

A shifting among the men, as spears are gripped more tightly and shields are lifted higher, tells Xoli he has them back on his side.

"Yes," he continues. "A servant boy . . ."

"Not a servant," murmurs the Induna. "And not so small!"

Xoli holds up a hand. "Have it your way. He was a boy, nonetheless, and that is all that concerns us here. That and the fact that this boy seems to have disappeared – for I do not seem to recall seeing his body among the others."

"Disappeared?" says the Induna. "I think not."

"What do you mean? Where is he?"

"He's over there. With a few of his friends."

Xoli wheels round to see where the Induna's pointing.

Turns to see a Zulu impi of two thousand swarming over a ridge about a kilometre away.

A Zulu impi of two thousand in a line five hundred men wide, running at full tilt, eating up the veld.

*

Good old Mgobozi, who understands the need for a certain amount of alacrity in this matter!

Intended as a back-up measure should things turn nasty, the impi – comprising men from the Fasimba and Wombe regiments – had hidden itself several kilometres away. Suspecting the time for diplomacy was past the moment the commotion erupted in the village, the Induna had immediately sent the boy for help. This was before Xoli thought to post guards and the udibi was able to leave the village unnoticed in the panic.

The smoke the Induna had spotted rising in a slender plume to the east had been the sign that the boy had arrived safely and Mgobozi was on his way. From then on it was a matter of buying themselves some time . . .

*

On Xoli's orders his men surround the three Zulus once again. The Induna must be of some value to Shaka – therefore, says Xoli, let's see if the king is of a mind to save his servant's life. Thando and Njikiza look at the Induna – they would fight and are taken aback when the Induna tells them to lower their weapons. A last stand under these circumstances, with help so close, would be foolhardy.

Njikiza will stay behind with one of the greybeards – to open negotiations with the impi when it arrives.

"Tell them," says Xoli, "tell them if I see the smoke from a single burning hut, these men die!"

And, prodded by spears, Thando and the Induna allow themselves to be hustled away from the village.

*

478

They have been hurrying along for about an hour when the path enters a narrow gorge . . .

And the Induna had lied. Lumisani wasn't stabbed with a spear.

Xoli's bringing up the rear, casting anxious glances over his shoulder to check that they aren't being followed and that his warning has been heeded and no huts are ablaze. The rest of his men are more concerned with putting as much distance as possible between themselves and that Zulu impi. They can scarcely be bothered with Thando and the Induna except to ensure they keep up the pace. It's only Xoli's hectoring from the rear that forces them to chivvy their captives on . . .

As soon as he realised what had happened, the Induna had lied. Had lied so that lives might be saved. Now he sees that wasn't necessary. They are capable of looking after themselves, these Ancient Ones . . .

. . . and Xoli is the first to fall as soon as the party is safely trapped within the walls of the gorge.

The Induna had lied: Lumisani wasn't stabbed with a spear, he was shot through the throat with an arrow. The wound was too small for it to be anything else. Of course, the Ancient Ones knew nothing of the tikoloshe. In their cunning they had merely spotted a chance to strike at the chief who had ordered the massacre of so many of their number . . .

. . . and Xoli topples over backward, with an arrow through the heart. Is dead before he hits the ground.

And that's the prelude to a whispering death, as arrows rain down upon the men.

And somehow the Induna knows that he and Thando will be safe. If they get shot it will be by accident, which is why he tells Thando to stand upright and steady, while all around them shrieking men crouch and scurry for cover.

And die.

And when it's all over, the Induna and Thando unscathed, the only ones left alive, the Khwai melt away, as quietly as they came.

*

The village is obliterated, the men and older boys killed, the young children and women taken captive and Shaka's herd is increased by several hundred head. Let no one else seek to imitate Mzilikazi and challenge his authority.

PART FIVE

The Ring Of The Lords

We found him sitting under a tree at the upper end of the kraal, decorating himself, and surrounded by about two hundred people . . .

A servant was kneeling by his side, holding a shield to keep off the glare of the sun . . . Ornaments made from dried sugar-cane, carved around the edge, with white ends, and an inch in diameter, were let into the lobes of his ears.

From shoulder to shoulder he wore bunches of the skins of monkeys and genets, twisted like the tails of these animals. These hung half down the body. Round the ring on the head were a dozen tastefully arranged bunches of lourie feathers, neatly tied to thorns stuck into the hair. Round his arms were white oxtail tufts, cut down the middle, so as to allow the hair to hang about the arm . . . Round the waist there was a kilt or petticoat made of the skins of monkeys and genets . . . He had a white shield with a single black spot, and one assegai . . .

Henry Fynn's account of his first meeting with Shaka,
circa August 1824

They are all dead. Dingiswayo. Mgobozi. All, all dead. Even Mzilikazi, once his favourite, he too is as good as dead. Dingiswayo, his mentor, betrayed and captured, then executed like a common criminal. Mgobozi, his old friend, killed in battle, the way he would have wanted it, but that doesn't lessen the sense of loss. Mzilikazi, corrupted by greed, and dead to him. Dead. All dead.

And now his mother too.

His beloved mother.

*

Vague symptoms – flatulence and stomach ache; intermittent diarrhoea giving way to constipation – accompanied by a loss of weight, a wasting, had suddenly grown violent. Sweats and chills. Nausea and vomiting.

Shaka sent for Fynn, but even the White Man's medicine couldn't help Nandi. Fynn could see straight away that it was dysentery and the Queen Mother was unlikely to live through the day.

For the two hours it took for Nandi to die, Shaka sat in silence in the sun. When he received the news, he told the men with him to dress as for battle. He disappeared into the hut he used whenever visiting the kraal and did likewise. Meanwhile, the other inhabitants removed every item of ornamentation they had on.

Then Shaka re-emerged. "For about twenty minutes," writes Fynn, "he stood in a silent mournful attitude, with his head bowed upon his shield, and on which I saw large tears fall. After two or three deep sighs, his feelings becoming ungovernable, he broke out into frantic yells, which fearfully contrasted with the silence that had hitherto prevailed."

His howls of anguish were picked up by the villagers and those streaming in from the nearby umuzis. All through the night the shrieks and wails continued unabated, with no one daring to stop even for water. More and more people and regiments kept arriving. By morning twenty thousand mourners had gathered at the kraal.

"The cries now became indescribably horrid," writes Fynn, himself doubtless fighting hunger, thirst and fatigue.

Hundreds had fainted and were lying where they fell. The carcasses of more than forty oxen, slaughtered for the ancestors during the night, lay in a heap. Then Shaka ordered the execution of several men and "a general massacre ensued".

Some were killed even as they were killing others.

"Those who could not force more tears – those who were found near the river panting for water – were beaten to death by others who were mad with excitement." Fynn estimates that more than seven thousand were killed. The stream "became impassable from the number of dead bodies which lay on each side of it; while the kraal in which the scene took place was flowing with blood."

Shaka finally put a stop to the carnage at sunset, but the lamentations continued through the night, bolstered by the voices of fresh arrivals.

*

Dead. All dead.

And she is dead.

She has set.

His beloved mother, buried in a sitting posture in the hut where she died, which was then collapsed over her grave.

Nandi is dead . . .

1
The Father

She'd gone into labour just as the night was soaking up the last splatters of the day. Lizile, the midwife, and her daughter were there already, for they knew Fazi's time was due. Abu was told to go and wait, as though everything was as it should be.

Except he knows better. Sitting in the darkness, leaning his back against the mud wall of the hut across the way, the home of his third wife – watching the firelight glow that haunts the inside of the dwelling where the birth is taking place, the occasional shifting shadow – he knows better. Must steel himself for what is to come.

A cry. A gasp. His head jerks up. His wife . . . It's near. Almost time . . .

Three times the dream had come; three nights he'd dreamt there was a white bird trapped in his hut. He was awoken by the fluttering and, although it was dark, he could see quite clearly, had thought the bird was a dove. As he stood, turning, twisting his head to follow the bird's panicked this way and that, it had grown larger, as big as an eagle, and he began to fear for his safety, instinctively knowing those powerful wings could knock him down, cut his face.

And he'd awoken with his hands thrown up to protect his eyes.

Then, the last night, the bird had become aware of his presence. Space and perspective betrayed Abu, because the bird stretched its mighty wings, fully wider than a man's extended arms, and banked, as though the mud wall of the hut was a cliff face, no longer a barrier trapping it, but a place where thermals could replenish its flight . . . It banked and came right at him, a white shriek, its hooked beak open . . .

The next morning he went to see the midwife. "It is bad?" he whispered, after telling her of the dream.

"It is bad," she nodded.

Now he waits. Usually friends join one on these occasions, but Abu's told everyone Lizile said the baby is not lying properly; it'll be a difficult birth, with both mother and child at risk. To drink beer and laugh would be unseemly. At his instruction, his other wives have taken the children and gone to visit their home clans – as if this curse is constrained by distance and time, and spreading his family out will give them a greater chance of survival.

But he had to do something.

Had to fight back somehow.

Somewhere down the road, a dog barks. Shadows slide past the open door. He strains his ears, but his wife's fallen silent.

The village comprises sixty rectangular mud huts with thatched roofs clustered around a river crossing. The river is young here, more of a stream, and its source lies atop the cliffs that tower over the settlement. On a clear day, you can see where it cascades down the sheer rock face, a slender thread of white against the broader band of dark wetness.

Abu's a wealthy man, has five wives, twenty-five children and many cattle. The years have been good to him, but now he has to pay the price.

"A curse," he'd hissed. "Am I being cursed? Has a jealous, envious mind turned its attentions toward me?"

The midwife shook her head. "You know that is not the crop that grows here."

Lizile was right. Such a curse could have been combated, but this? There was nothing he could do in this instance.

"You know this is about balance," said the midwife.

A successful man will have to pay a price sooner or later. Because who knows the cost of his climb to wealth, how many of his successes were the price others finally had to pay for their own advancement?

It's to be expected. And accepted.

But why *this*?

Why not something else?

The midwife understood the import of the dreams immediately, and by her shocked reaction – seen in a looking away, a flailing for words – she scared Abu even more, reminded him just how terrible this thing is.

What will happen to his family should the word get out? Banishment is no longer practised, and the village headman is a relation, but the consequences will be just as dire. They'll be shunned, no longer welcome at feasts and festivals. To move away will, in fact, be their only option. Yet no matter how far they travel, tongues will be longer. Contentment will never be theirs.

He looks up again.

Short, staccato gasps. A coughing-barking-whimpering. The baby is coming . . .

. . . and it's her fifth child, and the birth is relatively easy, although, of course, the pain is shiny new, as ever a stranger, shocking her, but before she allows fatigue to claim her, Fazi is sure she hears the baby cry, that first spluttering wail, which can't be, because they later tell her the infant is stillborn . . .

Abu raises his head: a sky prickly with stars; a silent, last-minute plea, desperate, but wholly irrational, for this thing is here. It has come to pass.

*

The same stars twinkle over Shaka's kraal, many, many days' walk to the south, but the King of the Zulus lies on his face on the hard-packed dirt outside his hut. Hot, so hot, he had to find some fresh air, and he screamed at his guards, told them to leave him alone, to go away, go away, and let the assassins come tonight, he'll gladly bare his chest. And then he dropped to his knees, and stretched out, pressed his face into the dirt, extended his arms, spread his legs and arms, leaving crescents in the dust. And then, finally, succumbing to an overwhelming urge, he opened his mouth, let his tongue taste the sand, the grit . . .

*

The midwife is a hunched shadow, detaching itself from the doorway. "Here –" she says, handing Abu the bundle. "You know what to do."

There is a way, she'd said that day he brought the dream to her.

"No!" he hissed.

Lizile clucked her tongue in annoyance. "You have heard the stories," she said. "Who hasn't? And mothers use these tales to scare their children. But these tales malign him. He is no monster – know that."

Abu nodded.

"Know this too," she added, "you would not be the first father in this village to seek him out."

He hadn't thought of that.

"It is so," said Lizile, seeing his surprise.

Abu searched his memory for babies reported stillborn; could think of three . . . no, four . . . And he had even consoled . . . Fazi had made beer for the family, a gift to help them with the influx of relatives from neighbouring villages . . .

"You mean . . ."

"No," said the midwife. "Do not snatch at the fruit because it seems to hang low. I can neither deny nor confirm your suspicions. My calling involves discretion. Never forget that. It's a quality you might yet give thanks for."

Abu nodded. "I understand."

The baby's face is in shadow, the bundle forming a tiny hood.

"You know what to do," says Lizile again. It is not a question.

Abu looks up, meets her eyes. "It is as the dream foretold?"

"Yes." Her voice is an impatient hiss. He must go!

Abu feels the baby squirm. Almost drops the bundle. Of course it would be alive – what was he thinking?

"It's so quiet," he whispers. "I heard it cry . . . but now . . . it's so quiet."

"Such is their way."

Abu's eyes try to find the infant's features; the fingers of his right hand discover an arm amid the folds of the leather – a tiny branch.

"Is it . . . is it a he?"

"Is it important for you to know?"

Abu swallows. Shrugs. The maniacal laughter of a baboon; dogs in the village picking up the challenge with indignant barks.

"Would it make things easier for you? Besides, you already have an heir, do you not?"

"Yes," murmurs Abu.

Well then, he must go . . . Lizile's daughter has given Fazi something to make her sleep, but he has to get back before she awakes.

"She will want to see it, see for herself," whispers Lizile. "And it's better that way. I've told you this before."

The baby shifts again in Abu's arms. He will have to walk with this . . . this thing; has some way to go, not too far, but the darkness will add to the distance. Something he hasn't considered: being with this thing . . . being alone with this thing for a prolonged period of time.

The midwife pushes his shoulder. "Go," she hisses. "Go!"

*

"Father . . .?"

It's Pampata.

Shaka grunts, but doesn't move.

Why can't she just . . .

The taste of the sand is somehow comforting; it coats his tongue, and when he closes his mouth, his teeth crunch tiny crystals.

Why can't they all just . . .

"Father?"

She's crouching by him.

"Leave me!" A muffled voice, lips scraping the dirt.

He can feel her hand on his shoulder, but he's thinking of another's hand. A mother's hand. "My Little Lion, your fire burns bright, never forget that . . ."

Words of comfort to be heard nevermore.

"Father . . . she . . ."

Was always there. Swallowing her misery to comfort him, wiping away his tears. Angry tears. Frustrated tears. But she was a haven, always there to remind him of what the others wanted to deny. "Never forget, Little Lion: you are of noble birth . . ."

"Leave me!"

Her hand strokes his shoulder blade. Pampata, his beloved – but even she can't gauge the depth of his suffering – no one can!

"Very well then!"

He hears her shifting position.

She's sitting . . . no, lying, stretching out alongside him on her back, and when she next speaks, her voice is close to his ear.

"I will watch the sky."

*

The water bites his balls. He gasps, raises the bundle higher, and lunges on. He's about half a kilometre downstream from the settlement. He can't use the main ford, because that would entail moving through the village – and huts lie on both sides of the crossing. He daren't risk the chance of someone seeing him. Why would Abu be leaving the village on the night his child was born – and carrying a bundle? Curious eyes provide their own illumination on even the darkest night.

The icy current curls around his ankles and legs. He wasn't thinking; should've stopped to remove his sandals first. Now his feet are numb, and loose, slippery rocks lie like snares in his path. The water reaches his chest. He has to raise the bundle above his head. A momentary fear that the baby will come awake writhing like a wildcat and he'll drop it; then his thoughts are focused on the opposite bank. The water teases his navel – drops away from his leather kilt – twirls between his legs, then smacks his balls once more as his feet sink into the mud. But he's across.

"There is a way," the midwife had said. And self-preservation, the need to protect his family, had beaten aside his fear. He would do it.

"It is the only way," the midwife had said.

Abu wasn't to worry, she would contact the Nightman. And, later, he realised that was reassuring: if she had regular dealings with the man – well, perhaps he wasn't such a monster, after all.

Wet, shivering, turning sideways to protect the infant, he shoulders his way through branches and twigs. He's a herd of elephants, but he no longer cares. He wants to finish this thing.

On the other side, he pauses to get his bearings. A gentle slope to his left will lead him to the main road that runs through the village. Long grass brushes his knees as he begins the ascent. Once he's on the track, he'll be able to move faster.

Follow the path: that's what he was told. The Nightman will meet him somewhere along the way . . .

*

I will watch the sky.

An emphasis on the "I".

The implication isn't lost on Shaka. He is the Father Of The Sky. She will watch over him and the Sky, and his Children, the People Of The Sky.

Let her!

What does he care!

These People, his Children, they have grown fat and indolent, what do they know of suffering, his suffering? Why can't they just leave him alone?

No one, not even Pampata, lying quietly beside him, understands the depth of his loss. No one!

Only the dirt is comforting.

*

A moonless night, but not a cloudy one. He can see well. This is, after all, a familiar road. At least he hasn't had to go up into the mountains, or follow secondary paths which even the canniest of eyes might lose on a night such as this.

"What if I miss him?"

The question he'd asked the midwife a few days later, when she returned to tell him the arrangements.

"That will not happen," she'd told Abu. "Keep moving, concentrate on not getting lost, and he'll find you."

The nearest settlement on this road is a day's journey away. It makes sense that the Nightman would want to meet him this side of the village.

He's scurrying, his shoulders slightly bent. He daren't run, for fear of waking the baby, and his hips are aching from the controlled motion.

And why hasn't the baby stirred?

Should he be relieved?

Yes. A baby's wail is all he needs right now.

The midwife probably smeared something on its gums to help it sleep.

*

The dirt . . . to be under the dirt, to burrow under the dirt, to claw his way deeper and deeper, to feel the dirt close over him, dust and rock becoming sand, a cool moistness to soothe the pain that burns through him . . . Away from the babble, the silences – which are even worse, if the truth be told – these anxious faces waiting for a sign, a word, always waiting, let them think for themselves, but they can't, he has spoilt them . . . He must go deeper, away from them, far, far away, away from Pampata too, for she would remind him of his duties. Ha! Duty! What does she know? Does she think that'll cure him, does she think that's the incantation to bring him back? All is gone, all is lost, so – deeper and deeper, he will go.

Only the dirt is comforting.

*

When he looks up again, the darkness proffers a shape where there wasn't one before . . .

Abu stops, fear squeezing his heart for all that this is to be expected.

The shape moves across the road. "Come with me."

And Abu is following before he knows it. Jogging to catch up to the man. Instinctively clutching the baby closer.

They step off the track, heading north. Long grass. An incline, growing steeper, so that Abu's out of breath when the figure turns right and leads him on a course parallel to the road.

Seconds later, the figure moves off the path and upward once more – but diagonally, this time. They're heading toward a thicket; a tangle of bushes, black in the darkness. Abu wonders how he's expected to fight his way through and protect the baby at the same time. But the figure merges with the blackness, and Abu, following with trepidation, realises there's a passage through the bush.

Leaves and branches brush against his arms. More than once he has to duck. There are twists and turns so that the fire in the clearing is hidden almost until you step out into the open.

The figure turns.

"You are he?" Abu's voice is hoarse.

"Yes," says the Nightman.

Abu squints, trying to make out features, but the firelight only shows the man to be wearing a cowhide cloak of sorts.

The Nightman extends his arms – and at the last minute, his ordeal almost over, Abu hesitates.

"I know what you are thinking," says the Nightman, softly. "But this is not your flesh and blood. This is an aberration truly not of your making."

Abu finds himself nodding. This one who they call a monster is speaking sense. This infant in his arms – is it truly his?

An aberration.

Not of his making.

Abu hands over the bundle.

The Nightman steps back, tilts the cocoon toward the flames. "Look you upon this one last time and know no regrets."

Abu finds his eyes drawn to the tiny face revealed by the firelight.

An aberration, not of his making.

Straightening, the Nightman directs Abu's attention to a second bundle just visible in the flickering glow. "That is yours."

Abu nods. Stoops to pick up the bundle.

493

Did he really think his ordeal was over? Stiff limbs. A dead weight. He will have to carry this small corpse all the way back to the village.

But he is saving his family, he is doing this for them, and most of all, for Fazi. She will be spared this horror.

Clutching the bundle tightly, Abu blunders through the thicket without a backwards glance.

*

Pampata comes to her senses to find him standing, looking out over Bulawayo's large central enclosure, where his cattle are docile in their kraal, the ibandla tree their silent sentinel.

Pampata clambers to her feet. Finds Shaka's hand. "Come, my King, my Father," she whispers.

Meekly, he allows her to lead him back into his hut.

Outside, the sentry peering over the fence of the royal compound turns away to shake Mbopa's shoulder. The prime minister's been dozing, sitting upright against the fence. Drowsily, he listens as the sentry whispers that Pampata's at last managed to get Shaka back inside.

How much longer is this going to go on for? Mbopa runs a hand over his eyes. This isn't the first night his sleep's been disturbed by an anxious messenger come to tell him the King has left his hut – a euphemism, he's since discovered, that covers a wealth of strange behaviour. Sighing, the prime minister instructs the soldier to fetch his induna. The guards are to resume their posts.

Inside the royal hut, meanwhile, Pampata has filled a bowl with water and is gently wiping the dirt off Shaka's face.

2

The Milk And The Vessel

Pampata finds Mbopa watching the King's cows being milked in Bulawayo's large central enclosure.

He turns at her approach. Nods a greeting.

Soldiers stand motionless among the cattle; no one praises the King's beasts today.

"How is our Father?"

"He sleeps."

Mbopa shakes his head. Every day a large group of mourners gathers in the central enclosure before the cattle are brought in. They come from all over the kingdom, ordered here for this purpose – to beat their chests and ululate. This morning, however, Shaka seemed to have the energy only to stagger down to the ibandla tree and order the deaths of fifty, who he deemed weren't showing sufficient sadness, before returning to the royal hut.

Since Nandi's passing every dawn is an occasion of dread. A silence has settled over the capital; people move warily, quietly, for to catch the King's eye is to invite death.

Mbopa's tried his best to ensure that some form of governance is seen to be done. For a while, he and Shaka's councillors held court outside the capital, hearing the cases that were still foolishly brought to the King – although attendance eventually dwindled until the prime minister was able to order a temporary cessation. And not without a sense of relief: had Shaka heard about this callous disrespect, Mbopa and the councillors would've joined the bodies that litter the inner enclosure.

Oh yes – they're still there. Those whose execution Shaka ordered this morning and the others. The bodies lie where they fell and controlling the cattle is no easy task. Mbopa's taken to ordering the older bodies quietly removed every night. These are dumped over the cliff at the Place Of Execution. But it helps only a little. Bulawayo has been invaded by flies and the stench has spread everywhere – it can even be smelt from the huts built along the outer perimeter.

Shaka hasn't even ordered the bodies disembowelled, as is the Zulu custom. "Let the spirits stay trapped," he said.

And every morning Mbopa waits for the King to make his appearance, hoping today will be different, Shaka will have returned to usurp this evil impostor, this impundulu who walks in the King's stead.

And every morning, so far, the prime minister has been disappointed, has found the King in the same state.

Something has to be done.

Seeking a respite from the stench, Pampata's dipped her nose into the bunch of flowers she's carrying. Now she looks up, glances at Mbopa. "You spoke?"

Mbopa coughs. Spits. "I said: something has to be done."

Pampata watches a herdboy trying to milk an unsettled cow. Every time he squats with the pail between his knees, the cow shifts its flank away from him, so that the two are moving in a circle around the animal's front legs. Elsewhere, another herdboy struggles to control a cow that's wandered too close to a pile of bodies.

"I said –"

"I heard you," says Pampata, keeping her eyes on the cattle.

"Because," sighs Mbopa, "these brothers . . . I do not trust them."

Just as Nandi never trusted you, thinks Pampata.

"Especially the Needy One . . . And I ask myself how long? How long before Dingane makes his move?"

"The army . . ." begins Pampata.

The army has by and large escaped Shaka's enmity. But, notes Mbopa, they grow nervous, wondering when the King will turn on them as well . . .

"It is time," he adds.

"Time?" asks Pampata, looking at him.

"It is time," says Mbopa, "to seek out the King's Ubulawu."

He waits – but when no response is forthcoming from Pampata, and she raises the flowers to her nose and returns her attention to the milking, he continues.

"It is time to remind our Father of what the Truthsayer told him."

This turns Pampata's head. "Know you what the Truthsayer said?"

She's always thought she was the only one Shaka had confided in.

Mbopa grins. "No. But I am no fool. This was what he was going to ask the Truthsayer, was it not? Our Father told us this much. Perhaps he told you more . . ."

It's a reasonable assumption, but Pampata refuses to take the bait. "Perhaps you are right."

"Whether I'm right or wrong, we can't go on like this. You have the King's ear . . ."

Again Pampata contents herself with a nod. With the King gone mad everyone's status is in jeopardy, and she's loathe to admit that Shaka hasn't been as attentive to her as he usually is. Still, she *is* the only one he allows near him these days, so that's something.

"You have the King's ear," continues Mbopa, "you must remind him of the Ubulawu and what the Truthsayer said. He must have something to occupy his mind. Give him a campaign to plan and our Father will return to us!"

There's a sudden stiffening among the men in the enclosure. Then the soldiers are raising their shields and bellowing: "Bayede, Nkosi! Bayede!"

The King is coming.

*

In the days before Malandela, the father of Zulu, one of a king's most powerful weapons was a potion called Ubulawu – or the Froth. Using Ubulawu, the king could vanquish all enemies and even recover lost cattle. He'd mix the muthi in a sacred vessel at sundown, while praising the ancestors and speaking the name of the enemy he wanted to defeat. When lost cattle were being sought, dung and earth from the missing herd's kraal were added to the mix.

The king always used the same vessel. When he died it was destroyed and the heir had to "find" his own vessel; a process which could take years. It was said, though, that the king would know it as soon as he saw it. Emissaries from all over the kingdom would travel to the king's kraal with a selection of pots, hoping he'd "recognise" one of them, for it was a great honour for a clan to be the one who guided the king to his Vessel.

Over the decades, the vessel itself came to be called the Ubulawu. The Froth became almost of secondary importance. Eventually the Ubulawu stopped being a pot and became any artefact the king deemed a bringer of good luck – and so a potion became a talisman.

Senzangakhona's Ubulawu had been destroyed on his death and Sigujana hadn't had time to find his before Shaka had had him assassinated. For his part, Shaka professed disdain for the tradition. "Let my mighty army be my Ubulawu," he said.

Still, the more conservative of his councillors quietly hoped the day would come when Shaka found his Vessel.

Nandi also hoped her son would find his Ubulawu, which is why she urged him to seek out the Truthsayer. The fact that Shaka has never spoken about what the Truthsayer told him – except perhaps to Pampata – gives Mbopa some hope.

Like Shaka, he hadn't paid the tradition much attention. There was no reason to, the Zulu Kingdom was eating up everything – who needed a talisman? Now, though, in these dark days, the old ways have suddenly become more appealing. Maybe there's a point to them after all; the observances and rituals serving to hold the King in check as much as the people.

And there is this sliver of hope: Nandi had told Shaka to speak to the Truthsayer, reasons Mbopa, because she'd felt the Truthsayer could guide her son to his Vessel. Shaka spoke to the Truthsayer, but has said nothing of their conversation, made no attempt to seek out the Vessel.

Why?

He'd rejected the concept of the Ubulawu partly because he didn't believe in it. Like Mbopa, he refused to concede the King's power could rest on a mere thing. But he had Nandi pestering him, and agreeing to see the Truthsayer was his way of getting her off his back. Clearly, though, the Truthsayer's revelations had startled him – after all, he'd been in a foul temper for a long time after their encounter. And what could these revelations be? It had to have been something concrete to render Shaka silent on the matter. If the Truthsayer had merely told him yes, there was a Vessel out there for him, Shaka would have emerged from the hut mocking him. Instead, the Truthsayer must have told him what his Ubulawu was and where to find it. Why else would Shaka have killed the Truthsayer?

His natural stubbornness meant he would refuse to admit he'd been wrong to reject the tradition. He needed time to mull things over, to think and brood, before setting out to quietly retrieve the Ubulawu so it would seem as if he were acting of his own volition. And he had killed the Truthsayer to make sure no one else could discover the talisman's whereabouts, for in the hands of an adept sangoma it could be used as a powerful weapon *against* the King.

Other matters intervened, however, not least the landing of the White Men at Thekweni.

Now . . . well, now Mbopa feels it might be a good time to set about fetching the Ubulawu. It might just serve to remind Shaka of his responsibilities . . .

*

"Why do they not praise the cattle, Mbopa? The cattle low and praise the King. They must be praised in turn!"

Because, you insane baboon, if the men had praised the cattle you would've come here and demanded to know why they were making a noise – how dare they praise anything at this time!

It's Pampata who comes to Mbopa's aid. "But, Majesty," she says, "your soldiers are in mourning!"

"Mourning? Call you this mourning? And these herdboys – are they in mourning, too?"

Shaka points and bellows. "You! Boy! Yes, *you*! Come here!"

The herdboy had been trying to follow one of the anxious cows. Every time he crouched beside it, the beast moved away. In going after it, he almost tripped over a body, and leapt aside at the last moment, crashing against the cow with a shriek. Intent on the animal, his back to Pampata and Mbopa, he hadn't seen the soldiers raise their shields to salute Shaka . . .

Now he trembles before the King. Drops to his knees.

"Have you not – Look at me, Boy!" Tearful eyes meet Shaka's. "Have you not heard of my mother's passing?"

"Y-yes, Majesty."

"Yes? Do you say you have *not* heard?"

"No! No, Majesty!"

"Then do you think it is fitting you should mourn her passing by shrieking like a vulture? Hai! Then you may go join the other vultures . . ."

And before Pampata or Mbopa can move, Shaka's spear is embedded deep in the child's stomach. Raising his left foot, he pushes the boy backwards to free his blade.

"Mbopa!"

The prime minister hurries forward. He is to root out the herdboy's family. All are to be found and put to death – and not just the boy's parents and siblings, but the parents' parents and their families as well – uncles, aunts, cousins and grandfathers and grandmothers. "All of them!" growls Shaka. "I would see their bloodline obliterated, for who knows how deep this one's disrespect runs and when the boil will again fester. Let them all feed the vultures!"

The boy's body is glistening with blood, he has managed to fold his hands over the wound, and, in a series of ever-weakening movements, his heels skating over the dust, then digging in, he's managed to push himself further away from Shaka . . .

Aware of a shocked silence, Pampata tears her eyes away from the boy. Keeping her hand at her side, she surreptitiously signals that the other boys must resume their milking.

And not a moment too soon, for Shaka is striding forward. "What is this? Milk?" He kicks over a pail. "Hai, no milk! My Children do not deserve milk!"

Pushing aside cattle and boys, he moves among them, kicking over the pails, bellowing at his soldiers to do the same.

And Pampata's at the child's side. Crouching beside him, reaching for his hand. His eyes are wide, flickering in shock and fear. The wound in his stomach is a crevasse glistening in the sun; the blood seeping into the dirt forms a black crust, like wet ash. Pampata leans forward, whispering words of comfort into his ear. "Do not be afraid, Little One, the pain will soon pass and you'll be free –"

Yes, *free*, thinks Pampata, swallowing her tears, tears of rage and pain, free, while we are left here.

"Do not be afraid, Little One. The Great Journey and the ancestors await. You will never know pain again."

Mbopa stares at Shaka's back. The Bull Elephant has become an enraged rhino, stomping and kicking the pails. And the soldiers have joined him, mimicking his frenzy with sycophantic enthusiasm. And, truly, what choice do they have? These days no one wants to attract the King's attention.

Shudders pass through the boy's body; a sign that he's leaving. Pampata grips his hand tighter. Let the last eyes he sees be eyes of love. And let Shaka see her here. Let him berate and challenge her. Just let him!

But he strides past the two of them, his shins splattered with milk. Mbopa takes a deep breath and squares his shoulders.

"Milk!" says the King. "They would drink *milk*! I told you, did I not? I told you that now that we are rulers of all we see, my Children have grown effeminate. Weak! Let them taste hardship once again! My mother has gone and they would drink milk! I have given them a better life than my mother ever had – and they would drink milk! But they will suffer for their disrespect! Their laziness! Their spite!"

The cows have to be milked – obviously. But let the boys spill the milk on the ground. Let the ancestors have it – and may they praise Nandi for this sweetness proffered in her name! Mbopa is to get the word out to all the kraals: no Zulu is to drink milk until the King decides otherwise . . .

*

"And now," hisses Shaka, "do you comfort traitors?"

Pampata glares up at him. "He was no traitor. He was just a child!"

"An example must be made!"

Pampata grabs Shaka's elbow. "He was a child," she hisses.

"Unhand me, Sister!"

Her eyes ablaze, Pampata obeys.

Hunching his shoulders, Shaka brings his face close to hers . . .

. . . and there are those who say Shaka's looks belied his achievements. Although certainly strong, and able to lift a cow off the ground by its back legs, Shaka was not the noble warrior-king of legend, they say. Instead, he had a protruding forehead and buckteeth, and spoke with a lisp. Or was it a stutter? For while swimming with Magaye KaDiba-ndlela one day, did he not reassure his friend he could never kill him, because people would say Shaka was jealous of Magaye's good looks? Whatever the case may be, right now, glowering at Pampata, Shaka is ugliness personified . . .

"Know this, Sister," he says, spitting the words out, "there will come a time . . ."

Then he stops. And for an instant, Pampata sees the man she loves, but it's a passing vision, like a countenance glimpsed in flickering flames.

"You do not understand," he whispers. And turns away.

She moves off after him, keeping her distance. If she is to confront him once more, it is better to do so in the privacy of his hut.

*

Watching the two walk away, Mbopa finds himself thinking of the Needy One . . .

Leaving Shaka in Pampata's care, the prime minister had managed to sneak out of Bulawayo a few afternoons ago. Some hours of solitude sitting in the shade of a tree by a rushing stream was all he wanted. But he'd just settled down when he saw Dingane ambling along the path – and knew this was no accidental meeting.

The two men greeted each other: Mbopa's "Eshé!", weary; Dingane's response, "Eshé, ndoda!", nauseatingly bright.

Without waiting to be invited, Shaka's half-brother settled himself next to Mbopa. "Usaphila na?" *You are well?*

Mbopa shrugged. "Ngisaphila." *I am well.*

"And me," said Dingane, "I am well too. Given the circumstances."

Mbopa sniffed. Scratched his knee. "You have come to visit the King?" he asked.

A mild inquiry, but barbed for all that, since Dingane's presence at KwaBulawayo had not been announced. He was clearly there incognito, camped some distance away from the capital with his men.

"That was my intention," sighed Dingane. "To see whether he has recovered from his loss and whether I can be of assistance to him. But I fear I have wasted my time."

"Your spies keep you well informed."

"Not spies, Mbopa, just those who are concerned about the future."

"And you have allied yourself with these worried gentlemen?"

Another misleadingly mild inquiry. As a prince of the Bloodline, Dingane follows no one; let his pride force him to admit he's the leader of this group, guiding them in their "concern" as surely as any herdboy.

"Let us rather say that I listen to these loyal subjects."

Despite his annoyance at having his solitude disturbed, Mbopa had to stifle a grin. Loyal subjects? Whose? Does Dingane see himself as King already?

"And they *are* loyal, Mbopa," said the Needy One, showing that he'd read the other man's reaction accurately.

"If they are loyal why do they not take their concerns to the King?"

Dingane's laugh was the bark of a dog. "Now you mock me!"

"That is not my intention."

"You more than anyone else should know how things stand."

Mbopa contented himself with a shrug.

"These men," continued Dingane, "their loyalty lies with the tribe."

"Many have said that when they've sought to go against the King."

"But what if the King's actions endanger the tribe?"

"Should it ever dawn, that would be a day for hard decisions."

"Hai! That day is upon us. And it will be night before we even realise and where will we be, then?"

Now, watching Shaka stalk away, followed by Pampata, Mbopa hears Dingane's words once more.

"When the father goes mad he can no longer be head of the family," he had said, shifting position so he could face the prime minister. "Is it treachery when loyal men move to protect the tribe? What are they to do if the King's actions endanger the tribe?"

*

"What is it? What do you want?"

"Majesty . . ."

"You are like fleas, all of you! You are like fleas and I am the dog you torment! Am I never to be left alone?"

"Why must you fight us? We are your Children!"

"This I know, Sister! I also know that while I was winning a kingdom for you, you became lazy and ungrateful."

"This is not so!"

"Must you always contradict me?"

"Only when you are wrong!"

"I am the King! I am never wrong!"

"Then it is you who dishonour your mother's memory!"

"What?"

"Your hand is raised – slap me! It will not change the truth of my words. You destroyed those who mocked you and Nandi when you were a child and she was spurned by all – would you now turn on those who aided you, who were your friends? Has it come to this, Oh King Who Is Never Wrong?"

"Flea! Thorn!"

"For if you are never wrong what was the worth of Nandi's guidance?"

"Do not speak of her!"

"Why? Am I not worthy?"

"No one is worthy!"

"I loved her too! Did we not console each other when you were away at war? Yes, even when you were King! Better your fist, Father! Better that! Do not say I am not worthy!"

"Leave me alone!"

"I will, but we have important matters to discuss first."

"Do as you please! For that is your way, no matter what I say."

"Would you offer your enemies the same freedom?"

"Enemies? The People Of The Sky have no enemies. I have seen to that!"

"Not the people, Father. *You*! Have you forgotten the mambas within?"

"The Needy One? He doesn't scare me."

"But he scares me, Father!"

"Have you no faith in me?"

"The truth, Father?"

"Always!"

"Then no. For you are not yourself. You chastise your people for having grown lazy, but what example do they have to follow?"

"Are you calling me lazy, Sister?"

"Perhaps lazy is the wrong word."

"Ah! She backs down!"

"No, oh no, Father! I say that you have stopped caring – and that is why the people have stopped caring. They obey you out of fear, only fear, when they once respected you."

"The burden of respect!"

"Precisely! And respect is a burden only the man who is respected can cast aside through his own actions. And this is what you have done! But I warn you . . ."

"You? You dare to warn me!"

"Fear is a burden others can relieve. Let Dingane convince them he can allay their fears . . ."

"He is a coward."

"But a busy coward at the moment."

"Let him be so, it'll avail him nothing."

"And again you would ignore the mamba within."

"You say I have stopped caring and you are right. She has gone . . . Beloved, she has gone . . . And there is only emptiness. Let the Needy One and his creatures come, I do not care what happens to me. She is gone . . ."

"And she would want this?"

"What do you mean?"

"Would she want you to act in this way, Father, after all she endured?"

"You speak as if I have a choice in the matter!"

"Well . . . there is a way . . ."

"Are you about to pester me once more?"

"Yes, Father. He told you! He told you where the Vessel is. Now is the time to send your men to fetch it."

"You know this because I have spoken of it . . ."

"Yes, Father."

"But did I tell you where the Vessel is? Do you know where it is?"

"That you did not tell me."

"The Vessel is underground! The Vessel eats dirt while we speak. My mother! She was my Ubulawu!"

*

Pampata stares at Shaka. He sits on his sleeping mat with his head bowed. She stands. He lies back, rolls onto his side, facing the wall of the hut. She moves away, circling the fireplace.

"No," she whispers.

She raises her voice: "No, it cannot be."

"It can and it is," says Shaka, his voice muffled.

Then she's on her knees at his side, rolling him over and pummelling him with her fists. "No – no – no – no – no, it can't be! It can't be!"

He allows the blows to rain down upon him. Then, as she begins to tire, her anger and frustration turning to staccato sobs, he gently captures her hands.

"No," she weeps. "No, that can't be what he said to you!"

Shaka pulls her on top of him, holds her tight.

Later, just as she's about to drift into a tear-stained doze, he at last tells her what the Truthsayer had said, where he might find his Ubulawu, tells her about the Place Of Shame.

3
The Summons

It's early morning and the veils of Nomkhubulwana, the Princess Of The Sky, are draped at the Induna's feet. Yesterday afternoon a bird wandered into the doorway of his hut, pecking at some grain that had been spilt; now, seated on his favourite rock, the Induna awaits the visitor whose coming the bird presaged.

Below him lies a narrow ravine, with just enough space to allow huts to be built along the stream that follows its base; in fact, when they built the five new dwellings to accommodate Mgobozi's widows and children, they had to dig away a portion of the slope and reinforce the cutting with a woven latticework of reeds. The slope on the opposite side of the stream is almost concave, a shallow incline that suddenly curves up steeply to become a cliff face, and this is where they grow their crops and graze their cattle.

The Induna's rock is on the second ridge above the fields. From his vantage point, he can see over the ravine as it bends to follow the stream. The plain beyond is waving grassland with a few flat-topped trees dotted here and there, and he is easily able to spot anyone moving along the paths.

This seclusion means they've been able to disobey Shaka and continue to plant and harvest their crops. This was one of the King's first edicts following his mother's death. As a national sign of mourning, all crops were to be left unharvested and no new ones were to be planted. That the consequences haven't been as bad as they might have is down to Mbopa being able to persuade Shaka to make the war kraals exempt from this ruling. Now, quietly and whenever possible, these kraals dole out food to the surrounding villages. It's better than nothing, but since hunting has also been forbidden, the nation still exists in a state of virtual starvation – and Shaka's slayers roam the land checking that his new laws are being obeyed.

When it became apparent that Shaka's erratic behaviour was growing worse, Mbopa suggested the Induna heed the instructions he'd issued to the generals and their regiments. Except for those guarding the capital, all other amabutho were to remain at the war kraals – or return home for a rest period, if they were due one.

"Do likewise," the Induna was told.

While the storm of Shaka's sadness lasted, he'd batter everyone in sight, accusing those around him of being traitors, said Mbopa. "I can endure this without my bitterness making Shaka's words come true. You, too, will endure. This I know." But, shaking his head sadly, Mbopa had added that those who remained behind to serve the King would be forever tainted in Shaka's eyes.

"For this is the way of all rulers. What begins in jest often ends with the slayers sharpening their spikes."

The King spends so much time watching for plots, waiting for assassins to make their move, that once he's admitted the possibility of a trusted servant harbouring treacherous thoughts – and, truly, he doesn't even need the man's enemies to awake his suspicions with whispered lies – he'll always be wary, only too willing to read ulterior motives into the man's words and deeds . . .

"You who have served our Father so valiantly," said Mbopa, "I would not see you so tainted."

Besides, the time must come when Shaka decides he needs trustworthy men, men whose loyalty is beyond reproach.

"And I would rather you are the one he turns to," said Mbopa.

Initially, the Induna had wondered about Mbopa's motives. He was a cloudy man, who was sometimes harder to read than a sangoma's bones. Was he in fact trying to remove loyal men from the King's side in order to replace them with those who were wholly his own? These were perilous times – the river had become a rapid, the drizzle a thunderstorm – anything was possible. But then Shaka's own behaviour made it increasingly easier to take Mbopa's advice at face value. To retreat to one's own homestead at this juncture *was* a wise move.

Aiee, these are truly trying times.

The Induna rolls onto his back and gazes up at the sky. The sun has yet to crest the ridge and part of the rock is still in shadow. The air is cool, another one of Nomkhubulwana's gifts, to be savoured before the sun beats its drums and summons the great heat to stamp down on the land.

The fields on the slope below the Induna's rock are deserted. Kani, Mgobozi's wives and the other womenfolk are still busy with their household chores. They're singing. One will provide a verse, while the others share the chorus, then someone else will add the next verse. A song of love and death. "My love," runs the chorus, "he stayed in the west; my love, he slept in the west, slept softly; my darling, he walked to the west; so slowly he walked, thinking of me."

Voices joining in a soothing harmony.

When someone has died, it is said of him "Ushonile" – *He has set*, sinking in the west, like the sun.

The Induna sits up, the sky becoming green grass and brown stone. He swivels so he's facing the plain. The sun has climbed higher, the mist has disappeared, the visibility is better – and there, in the distance, moving along one of the paths, an iota that soon becomes a man-shape . . .

When it seems to the Induna that the man has two heads, he knows it's Njikiza, resting his club against his shoulder.

He stands, leaps off the rock. Kani will want to ensure they enjoy a hearty meal before they depart.

4
The Audience With The King

"So, Nduna, do you also say the King has gone mad and plot against me?"

"No, Majesty."

The Induna's sense of honour would have prompted him to give an answer devoid of bluster and denial no matter what the circumstances, but right now he's seething with rage, and it's a struggle to keep his voice level. He'd been hoping Njikiza was exaggerating – although that isn't the big man's way – but he's seen for himself the carnage that attends the mourning King. He's seen for himself the rotting bodies that litter Bulawayo's massive central enclosure. He's seen for himself the hunched shoulders and worried eyes of those still alive – faced with a dwindling food supply and a ruler suddenly grown capricious and vindictive. He's seen the holes ripped in the huts, the result of Shaka's latest ruling – no woman shall conceive during this time of mourning and the King's slayers roam the capital at night, peering through the holes to see if Shaka's edict is being obeyed.

"Aiee, there is a lack everywhere except in their ranks," said Njikiza, as they made their way to the capital. "Only their numbers grow, it seems. The crops wither and die, the people fade away, but every day there are more slayers to do the King's bidding."

"And Mbopa?" asked the Induna. "What does he say of this?"

Njikiza shrugged. "What can he say? Besides, they are the King's own men."

"I thought we, of the Fasimba, were the King's own men."

"We have been supplanted."

"For the moment."

"I hope you are right, Nduna."

Now the Induna stands with his shoulders squared in front of the King, hoping his anger doesn't show as Shaka regards him intently.

"It is so?" asks the King. "You are one I can still trust?"

"It is so, Majesty."

"A straight answer. So rare in these crooked times! But answer me this, Nduna: when all else is crooked, is not the straight answer the lie?"

"When all else is crooked, Majesty, the straight man carries the day."

Shaka grins mirthlessly and becomes a shadow as he settles himself on a pile of skins in the male side of the hut.

To reach the bowl at his feet, he has to lean into the firelight, tearing the shadow, leaving it to pool in his eye sockets.

"I have become a baobab," he sighs, the pot in his lap. "A baobab draped in vines and creepers who, in seeking to protect me, strangle me."

He raises the pot and tips the water over his head. The pot back in his lap, he runs a hand across his face. The dampness reflects the fire and it's as though he's wiping away the light.

The Induna waits, his back straight, his stance solid, his anger tempered by Shaka's pain. The King is truly not himself. He seems to have aged, speaks softly – almost mumbling – and his movements are slow, wavering.

"They do not know," whispers Shaka, staring at the coals in the fireplace. "They do not know, Nduna," he says glancing at the warrior. "They say it is time. It is time," his eyes return to the coals, "it is time you sent your finest men to fetch it. Your Vessel, they say, now is the time to seize it."

He shakes his head. Regards the Induna. "But they do not know, Nduna. They do not know that she was my Vessel, my Ubulawu."

Nandi, his blessed mother. All was done in her name; her praise was the only praise that mattered.

"There is an emptiness, Nduna. The skin has been torn, the drum is silent."

He runs his hand over his glistening face once more and this time the gesture heralds a change in mood, in tone.

"Do they think I need an Ubulawu?"

Anger.

"Do they think I am so weak I must put my faith in a *thing?* Is that it, Nduna? What say you?"

"Father, if your Children want symbols, let them have them."

"Do *you* think I require this thing?"

"No, Majesty. But your Children do. You know the truth, Father. That is enough."

"Their lack of faith angers me, Nduna."

"They are afraid, Father."

"Of me?"

"Of losing you, Father. For are you not the tribe? What will happen to the Sky when the Father Of The Sky is gone?"

"I am the Sky."

"Yes, Father."

*

The Induna finds it hard to follow the King's reasoning in this matter; the spoor runs across stony ground. Shaka is clearly at war with himself. Seeing Nandi as a crucial part of his success means his sense of loss is even greater. There are summer thunderstorms of rage and blazing hot days of stultifying apathy. Yet at the same time he's annoyed because his advisors suggest he find his Ubulawu, annoyed because they think he needs one. To the Induna it seems suspiciously like Shaka is using his veneration of Nandi as an excuse *not* to fetch the Vessel.

There's no doubt about it, the loss of Nandi has been a terrible blow to the King; the dead bodies and spiteful laws attest to that, are signs of a wounded elephant seeking succour in destruction, but never escaping the pain.

Mbopa and Pampata feel the Ubulawu will help the King to refocus his energies, regain his footing – and it might just work.

But is it only stubbornness that makes Shaka reluctant to accede to their wishes?

"Do they think I need an Ubulawu? Do they think I am so weak I must put my faith in a thing? Is that it, Nduna? What say you?"

But the Ubulawu is not a sign of weakness. Just the opposite: it is a talisman that strengthens the king. And the unspoken question that flits through the Induna's mind is: what is Shaka afraid of?

*

"You are one I can trust," says Shaka, on his feet, gripping the Induna's shoulders.

"There are others, Father."

"No. There were. But they are dead now. All gone. There is only you."

The King's eyes bore through the Induna. "Only you," he whispers.

"Speak and I will obey."

Shaka nods. He drops his hands. "They plot against me, you know that?"

"Yes, Father."

"Dingane and the others. Here, there, everywhere. They think I don't see," tapping the side of his head, "but I do."

"As do those whose loyalty lies with you, Father."

"For now."

Shaka smiles when the Induna makes no response. "See? You agree with me on this."

The Induna shrugs.

"But you, Nduna – you I can count on."

"As always, Majesty."

"Hmm . . ." Shaka turns away. Stands over the fire, his shoulders hunched; a man coming to a decision.

Outside night has fallen, a sweaty night, with sleep mere unconsciousness. People are eating their meagre meals and turning in, wondering what horrors the morrow will bring.

"You will choose as many men as you wish," says Shaka at last, keeping his back to the Induna, "but I'd suggest a group small enough to pass through the land more or less unnoticed."

He stands a moment, scratching his right elbow with his left hand, watching the coals change colour. Then he turns.

"You will go and fetch this Ubulawu. You and your men . . . you will go and fetch this Ubulawu at the Place Of Shame."

The Induna fights to retain his inscrutable expression.

The Ubulawu finds the king; he recognises it. The Ubulawu defines the king.

The Induna can suddenly see why the King was reticent in revealing what the Truthsayer told him, why he finds it easier to believe Nandi was his Ubulawu, why he hasn't sent his warriors to fetch the Vessel . . . That Shaka's Vessel is at the Place Of Shame is almost too shocking to contemplate . . .

*

In the event, the Induna decides to take Njikiza, Thando and Jabulani.

"These men?" inquires Njikiza.

The Induna nods. "Do you have anyone else in mind?"

"Perhaps."

"Is he at the capital?"

They must set off at first light tomorrow, they cannot delay their journey until a suitable candidate can get here from a distant kraal.

"No, no," says Njikiza, "he is here. He's just now arrived."

"And he is happy to leave again so soon?"

"Nothing could make him happier, Master."

"Where is he?" asks the Induna.

"He awaits your pleasure outside."

"Very well," says the Induna, indicating that Njikiza should go first, "show me."

But no introductions are needed. The Induna ducks out of the hut behind Njikiza – straightens – and stops.

A youth in his late teens strides forward. "Master, you cannot leave without your udibi!"

For the first time since his arrival, the Induna's grin is one of unalloyed delight.

"Boy," he says, his grin widening at the inappropriateness of the appellation, for his udibi is now almost as tall as he is, "should you not be with your regiment?"

"Njikiza said you might have need of my services and he spoke to Nqoboka on my behalf."

"But you are too old to be an udibi."

And the Induna has resolved to travel without udibis, for where they're headed . . . well, battles and skirmishes are one thing, this is quite another.

"Hai, Master! That just means I can carry more!"

"And may yet outpace us," says Njikiza.

"Yes, he has become a fine warrior."

"And he might yet be of some service, for he has learnt his craft from some of the nation's finest soldiers," adds the udibi.

The older men chuckle.

"Very well, then," says the Induna, extending his hand to the udibi, "you will join us – but as a valued warrior."

"I thank you, Master," says the teenager, as they shake hands in the Zulu fashion, by first clasping their right hands, palm to palm, then tilting their wrists up, so that their fingers fold around each other's thumb, before reverting to the initial clasp.

5
The Slayers

The five set off at daybreak. Only Mbopa and Pampata are there to wish them well, and the men collect their baggage and are gone before even the herdboys have stirred.

Each warrior wears the kilt comprised of the isinene with its weighted tassels and the calfskin ibheshu. A sleeping mat and a cowhide cloak are tied in a bedroll diagonally across his chest. Slung across his chest in the opposite direction are a food satchel and two waterskins. Each man also wears a calfskin pouch around the waist, containing flints, good luck charms and the like.

All except Njikiza carry an iklwa, with four more of the short stabbing spears and two or three longer hunting spears affixed to the inside of their shields. The Watcher has his trusty club and carries extra water-skins for the party.

Their first destination is the Kingdom's northernmost war kraal.

They leave KwaBulawayo brooding on the hillside, its many huts resembling half-buried skulls in the purple dawn. Once they are out of sight of the capital, the Induna sets a pace that's almost, but not quite, a flat-out run. The men respond eagerly – a sign they're pleased to be away from that grim place.

Rolling hills. Lovegrass – fragile brown stalks shooting out of a low tangle of green blades, the size of a man's fist – giving way to thicker thatchgrass, growing up to a metre high in some places. Acacias with their flat-topped crowns and light-yellow bark; buck browsing off the seed pods, darting away as they catch a scent of the men.

*

They are one river away from the war kraal when they encounter the slayers.

It's late afternoon. The river is a broad brown swathe. Shallow steps on either side show the height it reaches in times of flood. The muddy flanks between the banks and the water have been baked by the sun, but it's a thin crust, pitted and churned up where animals come to drink water.

The Induna and the udibi have moved forward to survey the crossing. They squat in the shadows of the bushes several metres from the bank. On the opposite side a herd of wildebeest has come to the water's edge. Out in the centre a hippo yawns, revealing its short, thick fangs. But there's no challenge; instead it settles back again, its eyes and snout drifting above the water, brown on brown and almost invisible. The udibi points. There and there: two more submerged hippos. Lurking, watchful eyes, flared snouts.

Orange smears cross the sky. The sun is lost behind a range of black mountains. They will not reach the war kraal before nightfall and the Induna's debating whether to risk a crossing at this hour, when the animals come to drink, or to make camp this side of the river. Then there's movement, the wildebeest saunter sideways, and two men come into view.

In addition to kilts, they wear monkey-skin headdresses that cover their ears and the backs of their necks. Each headdress is held in place with a leather thong; slipped into each thong is the long tail feather from an ibis. The men carry bedrolls and a spear each, but no shields. Without stopping, they plunge into the water some distance from the buffalo. The Induna signals to the udibi and they leave their hiding place to rejoin the others.

*

The two parties meet on the path beyond the bushes that shield the river from view.

There is no customary greeting. Instead one of the slayers, a short man with pockmarked cheeks, extends the tip of his spear. "What is that?" he hisses.

He's pointing at Jabulani, who's caught a small duiker for their evening meal and has the buck draped across his shoulders.

"What *is* that?"

The slayer turns to the Induna, who's stepped forward, thereby identifying himself as the leader of the party. Only the Induna's necklace signifies his rank, and if the slayer recognises him, he doesn't show it. If anything his hiss becomes more venomous, for an induna is a big catch.

"Do you not know Shaka's ruling? Hmm?" He comes in closer, crowding the Induna, or trying to, for he has to crane his neck to meet the warrior's eyes. "Do you not know he has forbidden all hunting?"

Hadeda heads with their long, sharp beaks still intact are tied to the slayer's ear flaps, and the Induna watches as they wobble in indignation.

It is Njikiza who speaks. "We are Fasimba," he says, "the ruling does not apply to us."

The slayer steps past the Induna.

"Ah, it is you, Dlani!" says Njikiza, casually resting his club against his left shoulder. "It is good to see you have at last sunk to your depth, for in truth you were a pitiful soldier. Better women and children to feed your assegai than men who'd fight back, eh?"

Dlani is too enamoured of his own self-importance to feel afraid, but the Induna notes signs of nervousness in his companion, who hangs back.

"He is our master, here," says Njikiza, indicating the Induna with his free hand. "He has only to give the command and we will fall upon you!"

"Treasonous lizards," splutters the slayer.

But the Induna ignores the angry face peering up at him. He is considering Njikiza's words, the course of action suggested.

"You will return with us to the capital," says Dlani. "We will see what Shaka has to say about such disobedience!"

Gazing at the slayer, the Induna nods. When he speaks, it's Njikiza he answers. "Yes," he says, "I think that will be a good idea."

He dodges sideways as Njikiza's club shatters Dlani's head – and charges the slayer's companion. But, on the opposite side of the path, Thando's arm is quicker. He accompanied Jabulani on the hunt and still carries his hunting spear. The incusa thumps into the other slayer's chest.

*

"Truly," says Njikiza, as they watch the other three drag the bodies deep into the long grass, "we have saved many lives today."

The Induna nods. And who knows how many deaths these two have already been responsible for?

They have removed the slayers' headdresses and buried them; hyenas will see to it that the bodies are never found.

6
The Barrier

Mdlaka, commander in chief of the Zulu army, is in residence at this, the northernmost war kraal in the Kingdom. Even he has felt it advisable to be away from KwaBulawayo at this time. But self-preservation isn't the only reason he's come here with two regiments to reinforce the garrison. It's to the north that the major threats to the Zulu Kingdom currently lie. To the northeast, there's Soshangane and his Shangane people, growing ever stronger; although, so far, he's directed his energies to harassing the Portuguese settlements along the coast. Directly above them, as it were, beyond the high country, there's the traitor Mzilikazi. Shaka was right to regard him so highly, for he's shown himself to be an apt pupil, swallowing up the tribes he comes across, obliterating those who will not join him, just as the Zulu King once did.

"They are no match for us," says Mdlaka, "yet! But who knows what will happen if the King continues to starve us."

The general lends the party a pair of guides, who'll lead them through the passes and up onto the plateau. Since the moon is full, they'll be able to travel at night. After resting for the remainder of the day the men set off that evening.

Higher and higher they climb, into Ukhahlamba, the Barrier Of Spears, the mountain range thrown up by volcanic fissures millions of years ago. Layers of basalt rest on sills of dolerite, shaped by rain from the east, run-off water scoring deep valleys, ravines and gorges. A 350-kilometre-long wall of peaks and pinnacles, hooking the clouds, causing them to bleed snow or to lash the rock with spears of rain and hailstones the size of eggs, leaving scars on the southern slopes, bare, crescent-shaped terraces. A place of mist and ghosts, filled with the wailing of those who've lost their way.

And then there are the Ancient Ones, who've sought refuge here, and who roam the slopes with the sure-footedness of baboons. Some say they steal the spirits of wayfarers, imprison them in the walls of their caves, where strange elongated markings can be seen; now, forever lost, those travellers have become mere husks, blown by the wind, bewailing their fate.

The Zulus travel through the night and into the next day, resting until sundown before resuming their journey. In the moon's silvery light, they traverse paths that are little more than narrow ledges on the basalt cliffs; their movement and the need to be ever watchful helping them overcome the cold.

It's tough going; a steep drop one misplaced step away, the air burning in your chest, your feet numb, the blood thumping in your ears like a drum.

And the cold wakes them first, followed by the Induna, chivvying the men along. Aching muscles have to be cajoled into movement. Although these are fit men, their thigh and calf muscles are unaccustomed to the gradient. But the cold is a whip, spurring them on. Linger and you, too, might become a shriek in the wind . . .

Another night and half a day, and they're atop the escarpment. The streams are frozen and frost lies in patches amid clumps of long-stemmed grass with curved flowers that resemble caterpillars. Lichens grow in yellow and orange patches on boulders. Everlastings add a touch of yellow. These plants have twig-like stalks and can be used as fuel, but at these high altitudes making a fire is an arduous process, soon abandoned. Their fingers rubbed raw from working their flints – amid much bickering and cursing – the men finally resort to bundling themselves up in their cloaks and huddling together for warmth.

Before he allows fatigue to claim him, the Induna watches a lammergeyer ride a thermal, the vulture's wings spread to their fullest extent. Something falls from its beak; a tiny dot the Induna surmises is a bone. He decides he doesn't want to speculate on whether it's human or animal. Best simply to take it as a reminder – and a few hours later, although barely able to bark his commands – he's so tired – the Induna has the men up again. They can't risk spending the night here.

Wearily, the Zulus force themselves onward, but soon the paths are leading downhill and the pace is quicker. By dawn the next day, they're over the mountains and the air's warmer.

7
The Ma-Iti

It was a boy called Mulumbi who saw them first (says the Induna). He was brave, as befits the son of a chief, but even he could scarce control his fear as he hid in the reeds. For what were these creatures? A glaring angry eye. A mouth curled in a snarl. A long beak sliding through the water. Had river monsters risen to the surface? Then he saw men were riding these creatures.

Later, he tried to draw their likenesses in the sand. Told the others of the figures he'd seen moving about on the giant canoes. Shaggy men in robes of blue and red.

*

Their guides have long since left them and, if the travellers are to make good time, they know they have to stick to the paths – even if the chance to slaughter a few Zulus who are far from home might be an irresistible temptation for young men whose tribes and clans have been harassed by raiding parties from the south.

They eat their first meal of the day at dawn, when the visibility is such that the slender streamer of a cooking fire will not be noticed in the haze. When they set off, they travel in the loping jog trot favoured by Zulu impis on the move, with two men scouting ahead. The pace is fast, unrelenting. When the sun is at its zenith they rest up in a hiding place far from the path. The heat is intense, but unlike the strength-sapping humidity of the coast, it's a dry heat, and a man can find relief in the shade after he's emptied his waterskin.

Two hours later, they resume their march, moving quickly again. As the sun begins to set, the Induna slows their pace. Jabulani and Thando start looking for game. The early evening is another good time to build a fire. After they've eaten, they travel for an hour before finding a place to bed down. It's a necessary precaution – eating in one place, sleeping in another – just in case the smoke from their fire's been spotted.

Their journey takes them through a ragged bushland of long grass and low stands of buffalo thorns, marula trees and tangled red bush-willows; they can't see far ahead, meaning that while they might be hidden, so might others. And all around, guarding, guiding their passage are the mountains, granite cliffs leaping out of crumpled, folded slopes, where the buffalo thorns and bushwillows are impenetrable.

*

Finally, realising his pride was at stake, the chief, Lumbedu, led a group of armed men to go and meet the strangers. The spears he and his men carried were flimsy sticks with points made of bone, and their circular shields were small and fragile. Yet they went forward to meet these strangers with the hairy faces and shining chests . . .

*

The Induna and the others clamber up the ridge to where Jabulani and Thando crouch behind a large boulder. Jabulani points with his spear. Below them a herd of zebra and impala are grazing. Or *were* grazing. For the Induna sees why the scouts have stopped. While some animals continue to pick at the grass, these are nervous nibblings, and the whole herd stands almost motionless staring in the same direction. The Induna's eyes sweep the grass, guided by the gaze of the animals – and soon he spots them. Two lionesses, crouched low in the long grass.

Panthera leo is colour-blind, and the black and white stripes of the zebras cause individual animals in a herd to blur into one, constantly shifting mass. If the lionesses charge first, they'll dictate the direction the herd flees, but the big cats are hesitant, loathe to lose their prey in the resultant movement when one animal becomes a haze of stripes.

Then, suddenly, it's as if a bowstring has been released. Perhaps the cats pick up the alien scent of the men, but suddenly they're bounding forward, huge paws closing the distance. The herd wheels, swings away, but the first lioness is onto an impala, pulling it down into the long grass, its massive jaws crushing the buck's windpipe. The second cat is after a zebra.

"That is a clever one," whispers Jabulani.

The Induna nods his agreement. Instead of going straight for the zebra, the lioness runs diagonally past it, putting itself between the animal and the herd. The zebra's front legs lock in a gasp of dust as it executes a tight turn. Now it's running away from the herd. The sharp turn involved it almost coming to a complete stop, and it's lost valuable metres. The other lioness simply ran in a wide arc, picking up speed, and it comes at the zebra from the side, leaping at its neck.

"Let's go," hisses the Induna. They will slip down the ridge and skirt the area where the lionesses are enjoying their victory.

Later, the Induna will curse himself for being so foolish. He should've known better and the need to keep moving is no excuse . . .

*

Although the old stories do not say as much, I believe those on the canoes wanted to be seen (says the Induna). This is why they lingered there. And Lumbedu and his warriors were surprised when the strangers revealed themselves to be friendly. Gifts were exchanged; Ma-Iti baubles for fresh meat and fruit.

After that the two groups met daily and, gradually, the strangers were able to explain what they were looking for. What they required. They built a kraal on the banks of the Zambezi and fired up their forges, and Lumbedu himself led some of the strangers to a stream in the mountains where the shiny stones the Ma-Iti sought could be found. In return, Lumbedu and his men were given weapons from the Ma-Iti forges. Swords for the chief and his eldest sons, spears with steel tips for the rest of the tribesmen . . .

*

Rustling movement.

Thando, bringing up the rear, turns.

They were so busy watching the lionesses, they must have passed within metres of the lion hiding in the long grass.

The men swing round to see the lion moving in for the kill. Shouting and banging their shields will do no good. The lion has eyes only for Thando. The Induna, the udibi and Jabulani instantly drop their iklwas and each unclips a long hunting spear from his shield.

Thando sinks into a crouch, throwing his assegai behind him as he does so, while Jabulani steps to the left of the path, the Induna and the udibi to the right. Njikiza strides along the track, moving closer to Thando . . .

Its mane pressed backwards, the lion's strides widen. Horror, come alive, given shape and form, it springs . . .

. . . and Thando kicks his shield at the animal, and rolls backwards. The isihlangu crashes into the lion's leap, knocking its paws askew, spoiling its trajectory, as three spears thud home, one in the cat's left flank, two in its right flank, pincers that seem to pinion it to the sky.

Amid the dust of its own leap, the lion tries to twist in midair, pain vying with the knowledge it can no longer be certain of its landing, and crashes into the ground a metre from Thando . . .

. . . who's rolled away, like a man on fire, and retrieved his iklwa. He rises into a crouch, even as the lion scrabbles to regain its footing, claws gouging the dirt.

Then man and beast throw themselves at each other.

As the lion's jaws swing open in a roar of pain and anger, Thando rams the iklwa into the animal's mouth and sails past the creature, hitting the ground in a roll that brings him back onto his feet.

By now the Induna and the udibi each have a second incusa ready. Jabulani crouches behind his shield, calling the lion toward him and away from Thando, who's unarmed, calling so the cat will turn and offer its spine to the assegais the Induna and the udibi have ready.

But Njikiza has something else in mind. He charges the dazed animal, swinging his club like a scythe, knocking the lion's head sideways.

"Brother!" calls the Induna as he tosses his spear to Thando . . .

. . . who catches the assegai by its haft and leaps at the stricken lion once more, sending the blade into the creature's neck.

A lone paw swats the sky and then it's over. The men are left panting, drenched in sweat. Thando drops to his knees, his eyes on the animal, as though expecting it to spring into life. Already crouching, Jabulani sags onto his backside, laying his shield down. The udibi moves to Thando, squats on his heels and hands the warrior a waterskin.

*

Later, when they stop for their evening meal, the udibi asks the Induna to tell them more about their destination. The Induna's been waiting for just such a question, and he suspects the encounter with the lion has forcibly woken them up to the fact that they are truly far, far away from home. If one of them is injured, he has only the others to rely on, for the chances of finding a trustworthy medicine man are slim indeed. The hardships they faced crossing the Barrier Of Spears were to be expected, and were anyway tempered by the fact that it's summer. All have made that journey before. But this is the furthest from home any have ventured. Although they will follow the Induna unquestioningly, they've realised it's time they start preparing themselves for what lies ahead.

"I will tell you," says the Induna, "but it's a long, tangled story, much like this land."

"Aiee, but we still have a way to go," says Jabulani.

"That is so," grins the Induna.

And he tells them of the coming of the Ma-Iti.

*

Others knew them as Sidonians and Canaanites. After Alexander The Great besieged Tyre, one of their great cities, they became Seleucids. During the Roman Empire, they lost all identity and came to be, to all intents and purposes, Syrians. When Homer spoke of them, he called them Phoenicians.

525

But Phoenicia, a narrow strip of territory on the eastern coast of the Mediterranean, was only their starting point. In becoming the greatest traders and seafarers the world had ever seen, their nation grew into a sprawling collection of city-kingdoms. From Sidon and Tyre, Simyra and Byblos, from Jubeil and Tripolis, Arwad and Berytus, their fleets sailed out, crisscrossing the Mediterranean and exploring the Atlantic Ocean. Trading colonies were established on the islands of Rhodes and Cyprus, at Tarshish in southern Spain, and at Utica and Carthage in North Africa.

They gave the world glass and the alphabet, and their industries, particularly the manufacture of textiles and dyes, metalworking, and, of course, glass-making, were renowned.

And sometime, five hundred years before the birth of Christ, some drifted down to southern Africa from the Red Sea. They were big men, big, hairy men, with strange eyes in shades of blue and green. Some wore armour – silver breastplates and helmets that glinted in the sun – and their weapons were impressive. Steel swords and sturdy spears . . .

*

The Induna tells of how a bargain was struck. If Lumbedu's people showed the strangers where to find the gold and diamonds they sought, and brought them ivory and skins, the Ma-Iti would give them weapons made in their forge.

And it wasn't long before Lumbedu and his sons got to thinking. These new weapons were fine for hunting, but they could be put to better use . . .

And, barely two moons after the Phoenicians' arrival, Lumbedu led his men against a neighbouring village.

"Was it a wealthy village?" asks the Induna. "No. Were its people belligerent? No."

Lumbedu and his men merely went to war because they knew they could win with their superior weapons.

And at the Phoenicians' urging, Lumbedu handed over those captives who would not swear allegiance to him.

And the Ma-Iti settlement grew, much of it taken up by pens housing the prisoners. Then galleys would arrive and the prisoners disappeared.

And there were more conquests as Lumbedu acquired an army equipped with the finest weapons the Ma-Iti could manufacture.

Soon he was the ruler of one of the largest empires the continent had ever seen. Ma-Iti galleys came and went; taking slaves, gold, diamonds and ivory and bringing more colonists. Long trains of heavily laden oxen, and even tamed zebra, wound their way eastwards toward the Ma-Iti citadel on the shores of Lake Makarikari, where they were loaded onto the galleys.

And all the while, Lumbedu's wild, undisciplined armies tore across the land.

And it was as the Ma-Iti had planned.

And the old stories claim that Lumbedu ruled for exactly a year and a day.

On that day, with the bulk of the emperor's army off on a campaign, the Phoenicians rode their zebras into the king's capital and chopped off Lumbedu's head, and killed all of his sons. When the army returned, it was ambushed by the Ma-Iti using to devastating effect the one weapon they had not given to the tribesmen: the bow and arrow.

The mighty empire, one of the largest the continent had ever seen, now belonged to the Ma-Iti.

And it was as they had planned: arm a tribe, set it to conquer the others and then all they had to do was subdue that one tribe . . .

8
The Thief

The land is deserted, forlorn. There are no plumes of smoke from distant cooking fires. No cattle are to be seen grazing in the distance. For a while now the Zulus haven't come across any other wayfarers. Yet, at some of the river crossings, the muddy banks have been churned up by the passing of hundreds of feet.

Around midday the travellers reach a fork in the path. One strand continues straight ahead, along the ridge they've been following; the second peels off, drops down into a ravine. There's the distant rustle of a stream, like rain heard from inside a cave. It's likely there's a village somewhere down there.

Normally, they'd continue on, straight ahead, but now the Induna tells Thando and Njikiza to settle themselves in the bushes higher up the ridge. He and the other two will go and find the village.

The younger men look confused – aren't they supposed to avoid umuzis? – but Njikiza nods like someone who's just had his own suspicions confirmed. Obviously he and the Induna have been building the same hut, weaving the signs – what they've seen and what they haven't seen – to come to the same conclusion.

*

It is the time of Mfecane. A time of upheaval and dispersal, with tribes trekking backwards and forwards across the hinterland of southern Africa, their numbers decimated by war and starvation. The land has become overcrowded; a tribe must fight and give no quarter if it's to survive.

Later, historians will try to lay the blame for the Mfecane at Shaka's feet. But, the truth is, it was Zwide's wars in the first part of the nineteenth century that sent refugees pouring over the Barrier Of Spears – where they carried on fighting to secure a foothold among the Sothos. Shaka's conquests merely swelled the numbers of those fleeing, set the likes of Soshangane retracing the footsteps of his ancestors and heading north again. At the same time, the interlopers upset the balance of power that existed among the Sotho tribes, and when they weren't fighting the newcomers, the Sothos turned on each other.

*

Initially, the three slip through the trees growing on the slope of the ravine; then, at the Induna's signal, they move back onto the trail and make their way toward the clearing.

Roundels in the grass where huts once stood. Weeds and bramble invading the space where the cattlefold used to be, battling through the decades-old accumulation of dung. Fragments of thatch. A broken spear. A discarded axe. Shards of pottery.

There's something gentle about how the land has set about reclaiming the settlement. It has waited, and when no one came to tend it, it began to move forward with diffidence in its slowness.

"Why would he do this?" whispers the udibi.

The Induna sighs. "Something tells me we'll have the answer to that question soon enough."

And indeed they do.

The following day.

*

He sits complacently on a huge flat boulder, watching them approach. A boy holds a shield to protect him from the glare of the sun. To the east, the ground rises up to a low bluff; in the west, the grassland gives way to bushwillows and other low trees. Without appearing to glance around, the Induna examines the terrain on either side, not liking the lay of the land – that bluff, like a huge python to his left; the bushes to his right, seeming to float in a lake of shadows.

No command is necessary. A few metres from the rock, the Zulus halt and spread out in a semicircle, with Njikiza and Jabulani on the left, the udibi and Thando to the right. The man says something to the boy as the Induna comes forward. The boy steps aside, lowering the shield, and Mzilikazi stands, leaps off the rock.

"Eshé, Nduna!"

"Eshé, ndoda."

"You are well, Brother?"

"I am well. And you?" The Induna grins. "You are well too, I think, for we have seen how *well* you live off this land."

"We did not choose to live like this. You know that. Besides, I am merely following the way I learnt at Shaka's side. The Zulu way."

"Then you are a poor pupil," says the Induna. "For Shaka's way is to unite the people like a clenched fist, so that all may live in peace. What I have seen in these hills and valleys is more akin to a famine, a plague that weakens and destroys – and nothing else."

"Yes," says Mzilikazi, grinning, "and how is the Father Of The Sky? I've heard strange rumours. The King has gone mad, they say, and uses his clenched fist to beat his own children. Indeed, some say this madness is very like a plague which, even as we speak, ravages the Sky People."

"The King is in mourning."

"And the people, united now, as you say, must share his pain with losses of their own. In which matter, the Bull Elephant would aid them. With enthusiasm."

"The King is in mourning."

"Hai! It is more the setting of the sun. For your sky is dark."

The Induna shakes his head. "And these are the words from one who was as a son to Shaka! Just think how great your herd would've been now, your wealth and status, had you paid your tribute! Is this not so, Brother? I think you know this now. I think the many days you've spent wandering back and forth across this land like outcasts has opened your eyes to your foolishness. You say the King, in his suffering, seeks to make his subjects suffer, but I see something similar, I hear the echo, here. Knowing you were foolhardy and wrong, you seek to take out your anger on all you come across! You, too, would shatter the bowl of self-restraint and see your suffering spill over the land to be tasted by all."

Mzilikazi grins. "Do you know what they call us out here? Abakwa-Zulu. The People Of Zulu. What does that tell you?" he asks.

"And until the very end Shaka stayed his hand. What does that tell *you*, Brother?"

"Stayed his hand, Nduna? I have many women and children who, if they were not back there eating dirt in your kingdom, might disagree with such a claim."

"You know well that you were betrayed by your own brother!"

*

Finally Shaka was forced to act; finally he gave in to the warnings of his councillors that such flagrant mocking of his authority could not, must not, be allowed to go unpunished. Finally, he sent his army against Mzilikazi and his followers, who'd left their home village to take refuge in a mountain stronghold.

And there are those who say Shaka stayed his hand yet again, allowing his favourite to make his escape even though Mzilikazi's half-brother had changed sides, come over to the Zulus and showed them the secret path that led to the top of the stronghold.

And it is true – Mzilikazi and his people, who would come to be called the Matabele, greatly contributed to the Mfecane, as they roamed the land, a tribe of nomadic bandits, practising the total warfare favoured by Shaka.

*

"Speaking of betrayal," murmurs Mzilikazi, "how is the Needy One?"

The Induna grins. "Plotting."

"Truly, these half-brothers have a way of getting underfoot."

"About all they are good for."

"And my cousin – she is well?"

"Kani is well," says the Induna.

"I wish it were otherwise."

"Meaning?"

"It makes killing you difficult . . ."

"You mean *trying* to kill me."

"Perhaps. But I love my cousin and I am loathe to see her bereaved."

"You speak as if the word is the deed," says the Induna. "Yet, here I stand." He turns his head to indicate the warriors behind him. "Here we stand."

"That can be remedied, Brother."

At a nod from Mzilikazi, the boy holds up the shield, holds it high above his head and faces east, then west. The Induna's eyes leave the servant to watch as a line of warriors move up onto the crest of the bluff.

Wheeling with the boy as he faces west, the Induna watches as another regiment detaches itself from the bushwillows. Spears and shields silhouetted against blue sky; spears and shields emerging from the shadows. Some three hundred men, the Induna reckons.

"Ho! Ho!" bellows Njikiza, striding away from the path and facing the warriors on the distant bluff. Raising his club, he spreads his arms wide. "Brothers," he says over his left shoulder, "these are mine! You will have to content yourself with what remains."

*

"I see he hasn't changed," says Mzilikazi.

Njikiza lowers his arms and faces Mzilikazi. "Neither have you, Brother – more's the pity."

"It is good to see you too, Watcher Of The Ford. And you, Thando, although from the look on your face I can see you'd gladly tear me limb from limb. You, too, Jabulani!"

"Looks can deceive," says the Induna. "I saved you once. To have to kill you now would be a pity."

"Indeed. Are you of a mind to attempt such a feat?"

"That is up to you."

"Well, this I know," says Mzilikazi. "You are no advance party. You have not come to seek me out, although I'm sure you knew our paths would cross."

"This is so," agrees the Induna.

"For Shaka has other things on his mind."

"Perhaps."

"Perhaps. Yes. Tell me this, Nduna: why do I think I know where you are headed?"

"You might be many things, Brother, but you are no fool."

"Which is why I will not set my men onto you. Or so you reckon."

"You are no fool, but then again the choices are limited."

"This is so. In which case, I have to ask you: are *you* a fool, Nduna?"

"I do not fear rocks and stones."

"Neither do I," says Mzilikazi. "But this place – it is more than that, is it not?"

"We shall see."

"I do not suppose you will tell me why you are going there."

"No," says the Induna. "But I will remind you of your own words: we are no advance party. You are dead to Shaka so long as you stay among the izilwane on this side of the Barrier."

*

"You are dead to Shaka . . ."

Had he seen a flicker of pain pass through Mzilikazi's eyes when he uttered those words?

Whatever the case may be, they talk a while longer, Mzilikazi describing to the Induna a route that will save them many days, then they take their leave.

"I may be dead to him, Nduna," says Mzilikazi, gripping the Zulu's hand, "but tell him he's never far from my thoughts. Every day of my own rule I realise how great his achievements are. Tell him that and tell him too . . . tell him I will do my best to stay out of his way."

9
The Shame

The Induna lays the bejewelled dagger near the fire. It's the weapon he got from Mabhubesi, the Lion, who sought to thwart Shaka's plans before Gqokli Hill by destroying the Inkatha.

"This is our shame," he says.

He regards each man in turn. Flickering faces; brows furrowed in concentration. His fingers touch the hilt of the dagger.

"This is our shame," he whispers. "That there were some of us who sided with the vultures from the north, who fed our people to the vultures."

The Induna shrugs.

"It could be they thought they were being wise. For did that clan threaten you? Well, then . . . feed them to the Feared Ones. They said they were using the Arabi as one might a weapon. And there – their own words betrayed them. For a weapon can only kill you, my Brothers. And when we have killed, we honour our enemy by setting his spirit free. Is that not our way?"

The others nod.

"A weapon can only kill you. What these Arabi did was far worse. And those who sided with them, those of our people who sheltered in their shadow, knew this. They could not even plead ignorance. They knew, my Brothers."

The Induna's hand closes around the hilt of the dagger, rubies and emeralds pressing into his palm. Raising the dagger he brings it down, impaling the dirt by the fire.

"They knew. They knew these Arabi would take their captives far, far away. Shackles were all they would know. And shackles were all their children would know, and their children's children."

The Induna sighs.

"This is our sin. Our shame. That too many sided with the Arabi, too many helped them, for in helping them, they enabled the Arabi's reign of terror to last even longer."

This Place Of Shame, he adds, is but one of many citadels the Arabi occupied. Yet, while the others have gradually been swallowed up by the land with the passing of the years, it has endured.

"Why is this?" whispers the udibi.

It's Njikiza who answers. "Because we built it!"

Surprised exclamations ripple around the fire.

"How can this be?" asks Jabulani. "Shaka, our Father, would not . . ."

"Fool!" hisses Njikiza. "We speak of a time long before Shaka. A time before Zulu, even."

"Our people," says the Induna, "our forebears built this monstrosity. The sweat and the foul intentions that went into piling the stones –

these combined to create a muthi that called forth the Arabi, brought them here, like wild dogs following the scent of a wounded impala. And no one moved to put an end to the madness before it was too late."

He throws some twigs onto the fire.

"Evil sired the Place Of Shame," he says, "therefore only evil could have come of it."

And they should've known better, he adds. For did they not have the old tales to guide them?

"This is why I have told you of the Ma-Iti, a story you already know," says the Induna. "The Ma-Iti were the seed of this shame."

*

Their empire, with its mighty capital on the shores of Lake Makarikari, flourished for many decades. Galleys came and went, laden with gold and diamonds and slaves. Then the Ma-Iti grew indolent. Soon the ships stopped arriving and the Ma-Iti cared only about making their own lives as luxurious as possible. They grew lazy and more spiteful. Slaves who annoyed their masters were put to death and replaced by others taken from the great pens in the city, where men lived off scraps and knew only the lash of the whip.

Finally, the remnants of the tribes Lumbedu once ruled – Lumbedu whose name was spoken only as a curse – could take no more. Led by Lumukanda they began to plot the foreigners' downfall. But how were they to breach the citadel's walls? Lumukanda laughed and said there was no need to. What was the one thing the Ma-Iti had taught them? What was the one craft they were still allowed to practise, virtual slaves that they were?

With their insatiable appetite for gold and diamonds, the Ma-Iti had taught the tribesmen how to burrow into the ground. Decades of forced labour had turned them into skilled miners.

And so it was, while the Phoenicians feasted and drank, Lumukanda and a handful of brave followers tunnelled under the mighty walls and freed the slaves. Within hours, the revolt was over and the tyrants were dead.

"Let this evil place vanish," said Lumukanda.

And the city on the shores of Lake Makarikari was razed. Almost all the Ma-Iti artefacts were destroyed, returned to the earth. The few that remained were zealously guarded by chiefs and sangomas lest they fall into the wrong hands. But the Ma-Iti city ceased to be.

*

The udibi jogs to catch up to the Induna.

"Master," he says.

"Yes?"

"We are following the path Mzilikazi told you about?"

The Induna nods.

"We can trust him?" asks the udibi.

"How would you answer that question?"

The udibi walks alongside the Induna in silence for several metres, stepping over clumps of grass, falling in behind him to dodge a thorn bush, jogging to catch up to him again.

"I think I would trust him in this matter, Master."

"Why?"

"He is in your debt, Master. You saved his life once."

"The same can be said of our Father. Did he not also save Mzilikazi's life when he sought sanctuary from Zwide?"

"This is so. But I also tell myself this: he has nothing to gain by leading us astray in this matter."

"And nothing to lose by sending us chasing our own tails."

"Yes, Master. But I also saw you reading the stars last night. You would not have taken Mzilikazi's advice without first checking to see if we were heading in the right way."

The Induna grins. "This is so."

"And it is worth the risk, Master, for . . ."

The Induna stops, turns to face the udibi: "For the men grow weary," he suggests.

"Yes, Master. It is not because we are weak, Master . . ."

No, says the Induna, it is to be expected. They have their rest days, but they've been on the move constantly for too many sunrises now, most of that through hostile territory – and the strain of being ever vigilant has also taken its toll. The short cut mentioned by Mzilikazi is indeed worth the risk.

10
The Stones

They should've known better . . .

But there was a bad man called Munumutaba who, as a child, had been shown some pebbles by a sangoma. These, the sangoma said, had come from the Ma-Iti citadel on the shores of Lake Makarikari. They were valuable and gave the owner great power, said the old sangoma. If he had meant to frighten the boy, who was an unruly child – a thief and a bully – he failed. For Munumutaba was already on the path of evil. That night he returned to the sangoma's dwelling, which was far from the village, killed the old man, stole his stones and whatever else caught his eye, and set fire to the hut.

Later, he'd boast he killed the sangoma because he felt like it, and the stones meant nothing to him. This was a lie. Soon, Munumutaba began to experience the power of the stones. Good fortune favoured him. He stole without being suspected, waylaid and murdered travellers without the finger of suspicion once pointing his way.

Was it the stones? Possibly. But it may also have had something to do with the fact that Munumutaba at this time was but thirteen seasons old. Who would expect such evil from one so young?

Yet it wasn't long before Munumutaba's name became known. Boys older than him were only too willing to serve him. Soon he had a formidable following, an army of bandits that terrorised the region, thwarting all attempts to capture them. Again, was this the work of the stones? Or was it because he had his hideaway where none would dare venture?

In his wanderings, Munumutaba had visited Lake Makarikari, which was now a treacherous saltpan. It was here he led his band when chiefs sent out warriors to track them down. And no one dared venture there, for all knew the stories about the city of evil that had once stood there. But for Munumutaba these stories were as beer to a thirsty man. They filled his mind with grandiose dreams.

He would establish and rule an empire to rival that of the Ma-Iti. These dead men, cruel slavers who stole our people, would be his ancestors, guiding his every action.

The stones did their work and Munumutaba's power grew. His gang became a legion, the legion became a tribe – and soon the bandit was a king. And in the fifth year of his reign of terror, when there was no one left to challenge his army, the captives of his last campaign were sent to Makarikari with oxen and large sleds. There, they loaded all the stones and boulders they could find. Hundreds of men died bringing the stones back, say the chronicles; hundreds of sweating, suffering men, and thousands of oxen. But Munumutaba was able to lay the foundations of the fortress that would become the Place Of Shame.

He had his slaves quarry additional rocks from the surrounding hills and the walls rose and the citadel was built.

Yet Munumutaba did not enjoy his triumph for long. It was almost as if the stones he still carried felt he had outlived his usefulness. He'd reawakened the evil of Makarikari, given it new life in the Place Of Shame, now the stones had no more use for him.

And so it was that, one day, while Munumutaba was standing atop the highest tower of the fortress, a rock slipped. Then another. And another. Until the tower collapsed, killing Munumutaba.

It is said that when he realised what was happening, he reached into the pouch around his waist, drew out his precious stones and clenched them in his fist, believing they'd protect him. And, as he fell, he dropped the stones. So that when the tower was rebuilt, rock piled upon rock, the stones became part of the tower, the fortress. In this way, the Place Of Shame acquired a life, a resilience, of its own.

They were the diseased soul, the rulers of the Place Of Shame were their bodies, their creatures. And it was rebuilt by the son of Munumutaba, who took his father's name and ruled as Munumutaba II, as sure a sign as any that his father's cruelty would live on, multiplied.

Then came the Feared Ones. The men from the north. The Arabi. They seemed puny under their flowing robes, but looks beguiled. They were strong men, whose strength was aided by guns and strange magic.

And Munumutaba II befriended these Arabi, with an ease known only to kindred spirits. They wanted gold and diamonds and human beings. Munumutaba II happily obliged. In return, his artisans were taught a little Arabi magic. And so history repeated itself.

11
The Ferryman

They have come far and their journey is almost over, for there below them is the mighty Limpopo. A green porridge of tangled trees and bushes fills the valley on either side of the languid brown waters; Mzilikazi, however, has assured the Induna the track will take them through this jungle with little difficulty. And beyond those hills to the north, lies their destination.

They rest a while to give the wayfarers ahead of them a chance to cross the waters. The Zulus have been tailing the two, forced to hold themselves back with an agonised restraint. There's nothing else for it, though. The travellers are both women and although they appear to be hurrying, their heads bowed, the young woman gripping the gogo's elbow, their slow pace traps the Zulus. It's too late to try and swing past them; attempting such a manoeuvre in the dense foliage with no other paths visible means they're likely to get lost and waste valuable time – and the Induna wants them to be across the river by nightfall.

It's mid-afternoon when they finally reach the banks and the ferryman's canoe is on the opposite side – as is to be expected. Over there, a wedge of grass pushes the trees apart and one can follow the path for a fair distance before it winds into the shadows of the undergrowth. Seating themselves on boulders in the shade of overhanging trees, they wait for the ferryman to make his reappearance. He takes his time and the Zulus grumble and slap at mosquitoes. The placid quality of the river turns out to have been an illusion created by distance. The Limpopo is in fact fast flowing, the waters keeping up a constant, pouring sound, like a thousand warriors all pissing at once.

"Master!"

The Induna rises. Moves to the water's edge. The ferryman is waving, showing he's spotted his new customers.

"Now what's he doing?" growls Njikiza.

The ferryman is paddling along the far bank, moving upstream, away from them.

"Watch," says the udibi, as the ferryman at last strikes out into the river. "See? Now he has no need to fight the current, it becomes his ally."

"Mark you his technique well."

"Master?"

"For you will be doing some paddling soon." Noting the puzzled expression on the warriors' faces, the Induna grins, and adds: "All in good time, Brothers. All in good time."

Practice has perfected the ferryman's aim, little exertion with the paddle is necessary, and the current guides the canoe diagonally towards where the Zulus are waiting.

At a signal from the Induna, Thando and Jabulani wade into the water, to catch the craft and hold it steady. Raising his oar, the ferryman seems somewhat unnerved by this politeness.

"Can you understand me?" the Induna asks, after the man's clambered ashore.

The ferryman nods.

"We will give you one good hunting spear if you take us across, yes? Good Zulu steel!"

The ferryman nods. A Zulu hunting spear is a desirable commodity.

"Then let us get started."

"Wait, Master," says the ferryman.

"You will get your spear, never fear!"

It's not that, says the ferryman. They are big men. He can only take one at a time.

"Hai, but we do not expect *you* to take us!"

"M-master?"

At a glance from the Induna, Njikiza's big hand closes on the man's shoulder.

"You will rest here, while we take ourselves across."

"But . . ."

The word becomes a howl of pain as Njikiza's grip tightens and the ferryman is pulled backwards. Losing his balance – and helped along by Njikiza – he drops onto his backside.

"Rest!" growls Njikiza, giving him a meaningful prod with his toes.

After examining the canoe – a dugout created from a single tree trunk – the Induna decides it should be stable enough to carry three men, despite the ferryman's protestations. Jabulani, Thando and the udibi will go first. They'll leave their shields here.

When the udibi returns, the Induna loads the shields and settles himself in the prow.

*

It doesn't take the men long to find what passes for the ferryman's dwelling. Branches tied together create a low tunnel that opens into a clearing amid a thicket of bushwillows. The leaves and branches shatter the sun into hundreds of fragments scattered about the bare earth. There's a fireplace in the centre of the clearing and two shelters on the fringes. The smaller one is a thatched lean-to and clearly where the ferryman sleeps. The second is a miniature hut, much like the ones the Zulus build to store grain.

Pointing to this structure, the Induna tells Jabulani and Thando to rip it open.

While the warriors hack at the thatch with their iklwas, the Induna examines the leather pouches; hanging all around the circumference of the clearing, at about the height of a man, they give off an acrid smell he can't identify.

Perhaps it's muthi to keep predators at bay.

Soon Jabulani and Thando have wrenched away enough of the covering to reveal the contents of the small hut.

Spears, axes, clubs, bundles, gourds, staffs, walking sticks, sacks.

With the tip of his spear, the Induna points to one of the bundles. Jabulani reaches in and picks it out. Carrying it to where the light is better, he drops to his knees and unwraps the skin.

Kilts, cowhide robes, the chest coverings married women wear, long skirts and a profusion of other garments.

At the Induna's signal Thando fetches another bundle and opens it. This one contains sandals.

A smaller bundle opened by Jabulani reveals a collection of bead necklaces and bracelets, bronze bangles and ivory pendants.

The Induna holds up his hand, silencing the puzzled exclamations of the other two. "Come," he says.

Out of the thicket, the noise the Induna heard is louder – a wailing. He looks around. Spots a pile of red sand some metres up the path.

Seconds later, the Zulus are gazing into a deep, rectangular pit, such as might be dug to trap an elephant. The two women are down there, the younger one cradling the grandmother's head in her lap.

Her eyes widen when she sees the Induna. He places a finger to his lips.

"Master!"

The Induna turns. It is Njikiza and the udibi. Big Njikiza is carrying the ferryman over one shoulder.

"I thought you had something in mind, Master," says Njikiza, dropping the man onto the grass, "so I made sure he would not be going anywhere while we rowed him across. Neither did I fancy him becoming anxious during our crossing, for truly, I felt like an ox on a leaf!"

He notices the pit. Its two occupants.

"Hai! He had something in mind too, I see!"

The Induna nods, tells Njikiza, Jabulani and Thando to help the women out of the pit.

Njikiza leaps in and gently disentangles the young woman from her grandmother. "We are friends," he says, relying on his tone to soothe her. "We mean you no harm. We will help you."

It seems to work. She lets him hoist her up to Thando and Jabulani.

Getting the older woman out is a little more difficult. Finally Njikiza lifts her above his head, his one hand between her shoulder blades, the other under her backside. Leaning forward, Jabulani slips his hands under the grandmother's shoulders, while Thando grabs her feet.

Carefully, they lay her down on the grass. Crouching next to her, the udibi examines her limbs for any broken bones.

Now Njikiza is stuck in the pit. Thando and Jabulani can't quite reach him. The Induna jumps in. Crouching by the wall, he tells Njikiza to climb onto his shoulders, then pushes himself up, thigh muscles bulging. The other two snatch at Njikiza's wrists and drag him out.

The Induna turns to examine the pit; runs his hands over the walls. A dull red, like the colour of a pot, the soil is dry. Baked dry. There are furrows and gouges all around. Some have hardened into the same colour and could be taken as natural imperfections in the walls; others are darker, the sand damp, a sign they've been made more recently.

And here – what's this?

Something is embedded near the top of a particularly deep set of parallel gouges. The Induna picks it out between thumb and forefinger. Examines it with a look of distaste, before tossing it aside.

The pile of sand he first spotted is almost consumed by weeds. There's also the state of the walls. They would only be exposed to the sun at certain periods of the day and then only for a short while; for them to be as dry as they are, therefore, means this pit has been here for a very long time.

And it was never intended to trap an animal.

No, it's for human prey.

The gouges carved by desperate, frantic fingers are testimony to that. As is the fingernail the Induna found.

Jabulani has returned to the ferryman's dwelling and fetched a rope. It's lowered to the Induna and the men pull him up.

"How is she?" he asks the udibi.

No broken bones, says the udibi. The gogo was only stunned by the fall into the pit.

"She didn't fall," says the Induna grimly. "She was thrown!"

The grandmother's companion has moved closer to watch the udibi's ministrations. She shrinks away when the Induna reaches out to touch her shoulder – but it seems as if she's decided they're there to help.

"Is that what happened?" the Induna asks. "Were you and her," pointing to the old woman, "thrown in?" He mimes the action, making as if he's tossing something into the hole; then he points to the ferryman: "Thrown in by him?"

The young woman nods vigorously.

Sitting up, rubbing his head, the ferryman catches the end of this exchange, but seeing the two women is enough to lift him to his feet. Turning, however, he crashes into Thando. Who pushes him back onto the ground.

Three paces and the Induna's standing over him. "How many? How many have you murdered and robbed?"

The ferryman glances frantically to the right and left. Njikiza, who's joined the Induna, kicks the man in the side. "Answer the question, crocodile!"

"Where are they?" asks the Induna. "Did you eat them?"

The ferryman shakes his head.

"What! How come? A man who would slaughter the weak and the helpless, those who put their trust in him, must get to thinking: why bother hunting? Eh? Why should I exert myself when I already have all this meat around? Is that not your way?"

"No, Master! No!"

"All this meat! And here I must tramp through the bush to feed myself!"

"No, Master! I robbed them, it is so – but not that. No!"

"On the other hand, we Zulus are honourable men. We do not lie and steal."

The Induna extends his hand. The udibi's anticipated him and hands over the hunting spear.

"We agreed that for taking us across this river you would receive Zulu steel. Here it is . . ."

The ferryman shrieks as the blade enters his guts. The Induna twists the shaft.

"Stand!"

He twists the shaft again.

"Stand!"

Gasping and panting, the ferryman pushes himself upright – and immediately grips the haft of the assegai.

"Back!"

The Induna lets go of the spear as the ferryman topples into the pit. It is, after all, his to keep.

12
The Evil That Endures

Later, the boy will ask him how he knew.

The Induna grins. "Something tells me you ask a question whose answer you already know."

"Perhaps, Master."

"Enlighten me, then."

It's early evening. The river is three hours behind them. They've just eaten and are looking for a place to bed down. The women are with them, the grandmother riding on Njikiza's back. She can speak their language and they've learnt they're going in the same direction.

Frowning in concentration, the udibi works through the reasons the Induna might have had to suspect all was not right with the ferryman. First of all, he was a shifty character with restless eyes. His obsequiousness on being confronted by armed Zulus seemed a little forced.

"For I do not believe he waylaid every traveller, just the weak ones," says the udibi.

The ferryman would take one person across, silence them, throw them in the pit and go back for the other.

"But with us there, he must have been very nervous," adds the udibi.

Although the pit was some distance off the path, he'd have been fearful of the strangers' curiosity, and the fact that the women might have regained consciousness and started calling for help.

Which is another thing. They could see the path from the opposite bank, and they weren't far behind the women – why did they not see them moving along the trail? After all, the ferryman must have just deposited them there when the Zulus arrived on the opposite bank; what's more, being women, the two would surely have dithered a while until they got their bearings.

"Yet we saw nothing," says the udibi, "and he was gone a long time."

"This is so," says the Induna. "But there is something else."

"Master?"

Laying a hand on the udibi's shoulder, the Induna explains how Mzilikazi had warned him about the ferryman. This is why the short cut was little used – because there were stories of travellers vanishing. Mzilikazi had surmised the ferryman might have been involved, assuming the stories were true, and the Induna agreed with him. Although in truth they had nothing to fear from one man.

The udibi chuckles and they walk on beneath an orange sky.

*

Their journey's almost over, and so is the Induna's story. This tale told around the fire while they wait for their meat to cook; after they've moved on and found a place to spread their sleeping mats; sometimes even late, late at night, when the men gradually realise everyone else is awake, and someone will say: "Tell us more, Master, about these strange days," and they'll move closer so he can keep his voice low . . .

*

Some say it was Malandela himself, the father of Zulu, who led the legions that overthrew the Arabi and the creatures who infested the Place Of Shame. But that's a tale for another time. What matters is that the evil endured and was allowed to flourish . . .

This is our shame. Our people built this place and no one moved to stop them. And when the invaders came, they were greeted with open arms. Yes, even after their intentions were obvious, they were welcomed! They were welcomed and we set upon each other, while they laughed and raped our land.

Where are those who were taken away? Where do their spirits roam, so far from home and the ancestors? I tell you this, my Brothers: our destiny is a river whose course has been forever altered by this great evil, this pile of stones. The echoes of their pain will reverberate down the ages. Your children's grandchildren and their children will hear those echoes. The way things are is not the way things could have been. And this evil and all it represents will continue to lead us astray.

13
The Doomed

The women run up the path, wailing. The Induna orders the warriors into a spearhead formation, with himself at the apex, Thando to his right, Jabulani to his left and Njikiza to the rear. The udibi will move ahead, keeping the women in sight, but never straying far from his comrades.

The village is nestled below a ridge, the twenty dwellings arranged in a semicircle on the gentle slope. To the left is a cattlefold, a rectangular corral surrounded by a fence made out of branches lashed together.

The path they're on comes up from the stream below the settlement, leaving the trees that follow the water's course to run through stands of maize. The incline is relatively steep so that the village takes one by surprise.

These huts are circular and comprise a framework of stout poles intertwined with thinner sticks laid horizontally and plastered over. The thatched roof is cone-shaped and rests on wooden supports planted outside the walls, leaving a space between the walls and roof for ventilation.

Njikiza and Thando are to search the dwellings; Jabulani will keep a lookout on the crest of the ridge behind the huts. The Induna moves to where the udibi and the women stand around an old man.

He has risen and is resting his weight on a staff. The younger woman is on her knees at his feet, bawling her eyes out. Ignoring her, the gogo is firing questions at the greybeard.

"What is it?" asks the Induna. "What is he saying, Ma?"

The old woman turns to him. "They have been taken."

"All of them?"

She nods.

"And this one?"

The greybeard wears a cowhide cape fastened across his chest with a leather thong. Age has bent his back and his knees are calloused. Sandals, and a headring woven from his own hair and similar to the Zulu isicoco, complete his attire.

"His name is Lakotse. He was in the mountains where there are hot springs. I know of these springs, Zulu. My mother would go there after the harvest to ease her aching bones. They are one sleep away."

"How long ago was this? When did he get back?"

The old woman switches to the local dialect. Lakotse addresses the Induna when he answers the gogo, making a curving motion with his left hand and pointing downward.

"He arrived back here yesterday afternoon," says the woman.

Still keeping his eyes on the Induna, for he is clearly the leader here, the greybeard rattles off some agitated sentences.

"Hai! No!" says the old woman.

"What did he say?"

The grandmother shakes her head. "No! It cannot be!"

Lakotse speaks again, emphasising his words by banging his stick against the ground.

"Ma," says the Induna, "do not try my patience!"

"That is not my intent, Zulu. But I . . ."

"What does he say?"

"He says . . . he says the Lords took them."

"Who are these Lords?"

"Evil men. Men who are not men."

The Induna grunts. Hardly a helpful answer.

"And they rule these parts," adds the gogo, noting the Induna's irritation. "All fear them!"

The woman's strength seems to desert her as the import of her own words strikes her. She'd left her granddaughter to dissolve into tears while she endeavoured to keep a clear head and ascertain what was going on; now she knows her granddaughter's premonition – so vivid and startling it had seen her determined to set out for the village, begging her grandmother to let her go – was a vision of things that have come to pass.

Responding to a question from Lakotse she switches back to the local dialect. The Nguni people passed through here on their trek southward, leaving relics of their language behind, and the Induna can make out certain words amid the exchange. The woman is telling the greybeard what she's just told the Zulus; the reason why they've come looking for her other granddaughter, who married into this clan. When she's finished, Lakotse nods vigorously.

He too had a premonition. That's why he returned early, coming via the ferry.

Just then Njikiza and Thando arrive. The place is deserted. The inhabitants were clearly taken by surprise and there's no sign of a struggle. A mass of overlapping footprints in the cattlefold show they were herded there with their livestock before being marched off.

Lakotse interjects with a flow of angry, impatient words. Something about a warning.

"What does he say, Ma?"

"He says he warned them . . ."

The village had had a good harvest and the young men had urged the chief not to pay the tribute owed to the Lords. The chief had bowed to their demands and allowed the young men to go and see the Lords. They were heavily armed and led by the chief's son and a younger sibling.

"He says he warned them, told them they were being fools."

Worse than that, they were endangering the whole village. But they wouldn't listen to Lakotse.

"He says he suspects it was the heir that was the current that guided these waters."

And they weren't seeking to free the village from the tyranny of the Lords. That was simply their excuse. They were out to steal some of the Lords' power for themselves.

The gogo shakes her head in disbelief.

"Go on," says the Induna.

"Aiee! How could they be so foolish!"

"Greed is a strong muthi. Think of what men do in times of famine. How much more will they do when they hunger for power?"

Led by the heir and his younger brother, the men went to pay a visit on the Lords. A few days later, the Lords returned the compliment.

"Where will we find these Lords?" asks the Induna.

"The place we do not speak of."

The Place Of Shame . . .

Lakotse speaks again.

"What does he say?"

"He knows a secret path to this place. A path from his boyhood when he was foolish enough to be curious about forbidden places. He says he will show you the way!"

The grandmother pauses while the greybeard tells her something else.

"He says that perhaps it is not too late, for the moon is still broken. The evil will occur only when the moon has vanished, for it cannot bear to look upon such things."

Lakotse speaks again.

"He says if you leave at first light you will be there by dusk."

"Very well, then," says the Induna.

*

A little later, after seeing to her granddaughter's needs, the old woman approaches the Induna.

"You will do this, Zulu? Go after our people and save them?"

The Induna nods.

"It is true then what they say about the bravery of Shaka's lions!"

"Yet I see by your eyes you are troubled, there is something else you would tell me."

The old woman nods. "It is so," she says.

He and his men would save the lives of these people who are strangers to them, and it is so, her other granddaughter is one of the doomed, and she praises the Induna's courage, but there is this she has to say . . .

"These Lords – they are many men and you are but a few."

The Induna grins.

"Yes," he says, "but we are Zulus and they are not."

14
The Venerated Houses

Behold – the Place Of Shame!

Overlooked by bare granite hills, walls curve and undulate sinuously, blending into the boulder-strewn savannah; a congress of stone drawn together as though by some mysterious force.

Zima-Mbje!

*

Lakotse wanted to stay, indicated he was willing to fight alongside the Zulus – but the Induna sent the greybeard away after he'd shown them the path to the top of the hill, pointed out the shadowed cutting they could pass through without being silhouetted on the crest of the summit. Then he and Njikiza crept forward to reconnoitre, found themselves an embrasure of rocks on a vantage spot that gives them a clear view of the plain below.

Spread over twenty-four hectares, the ruins are arranged on a north-south axis, but it's the large enclosure situated to the south that first catches the eye. It's as if the structure has gradually grown a part of, although apart from, the veld, and in growing has become stronger, sturdier . . . more adept. Starting at the northwest side, the stones are laid in irregular courses and the perimeter wall is only half as thick and high as its later sections. Along the eastern stretch, these finally reach ten metres in height and are five metres thick. Here the courses are smoother, more symmetrical, and where two walls meet, they abut each other with unbroken vertical joints.

From this enclosure, one's eyes are guided northward, where other walls curve and turn, ending abruptly, or describing fingerprint-like loops and whorls. Then the savannah rises to a koppie – and a hilltop citadel of sorts – where stone walls run from boulder to boulder so that the structures seem to become part of the rock.

*

Circular huts built from clay-like dagha stand among the low ruins between the giant enclosure and the koppie. Cooking fires throw up slivers of smoke; a work party is returning with firewood; the livestock pens are empty, with the cattle out grazing somewhere; men sit outside the huts working on their spears and shields . . .

Signs of normality, but a more lingering appraisal shows the Induna that the huts are shabbily built, the thatch unruly, and each dwelling is surrounded by a pile of bones and wood and broken pots, skins ineptly dried and now spoilt, weapons and shields dumped rather than neatly stacked.

There's something skeletal about the ruins and the huts, and the people are like flesh clinging to the bones. But it's as if the decay has been reversed and the flesh is growing, spreading to cover the bones. Because over there, and there, two new huts are being built.

A rebirth and a growth; the ruins in the process of becoming a city once more.

*

The Induna turns his attention back to the large semicircular stone fortress. The largest extant structure within the citadel is an enclosure close to the northern wall and it currently houses the villagers. The walls are too high for a man to climb without difficulty and where they have crumbled away to create an opening, thorn bushes have been placed to prevent escape.

A few metres away, in almost the centre of the main enclosure, the remains of what was once a tower form a circular platform. An expanse of hard-packed dirt aprons the raised area. Clearly, this is where the Lords gather to be addressed by their chief and where the ceremony Lakotse spoke of is likely to take place.

One of the enclosure's higher inner walls forms a backdrop of sorts to the platform. The chief's sons are here, or at least their bodies are, for it is obvious that their spirits have long departed. The Induna can't make out how they've been tied to the stones, but the two men sag between outstretched arms, their heads bowed, their legs bent, almost swallowed by the bushes growing along the wall. At least the Induna surmises they're the sons who led the raid because each is wearing a wildebeest cloak with the animal's skull as a headdress.

It makes sense. The warriors the Lords would have despatched without too much ceremony, but these, their leaders, they would have retained as an example to the captives in the smaller enclosure.

*

"This is not good," mutters Njikiza. "Not good."

Well, yes, there is this . . . A detail the Induna has pushed aside so he can concentrate on the layout of the enemy camp.

The Induna grins, nudges his big companion. He can understand Njikiza's misgivings. Seeing the Lords, seeing who – or what – they are came as something of a shock to him too, but in examining the movements down below he's also noticed something else.

"Look," he tells Njikiza. "Look there!" He points to where a man has come up to address a group of warriors. Can Njikiza spot the difference?

The big man nods after a few frowning seconds and the Induna can sense him relaxing.

*

Despite its proximity to the settlement no one ventures near the great citadel; even the paths the Induna can see loop around the perimeter walls in wide arcs. What's more, the men guarding the prisoners remain outside of the citadel, positioned at a wide opening in the perimeter wall through which they can watch the inner enclosure. Doubtless these Lords will move to defend it should it ever be threatened, but this is clearly a sacred place, a site of taboos, to be avoided.

And that gives the Induna an idea . . .

15
The Capture

Someone's shaking his right foot.

Sitting up, wiping his eyes, the udibi remembers – and remembers to stay calm and not lunge for his assegai.

Warriors wearing feathered skirts surround them.

The clearing the Zulus chose to bed down in is small, bordered by bushes, and from their smug expressions these ostriches are clearly pleased to have ensnared them without a rustling of leaves or a snapping of twigs giving away their intent.

"Perhaps we should have posted guards," chuckles Njikiza.

"Hai, but we were tired," says Jabulani.

"This is so."

Njikiza's eyes find the udibi's – a quizzical look that asks if he's now fully awake and possessed of his senses.

The udibi nods and Njikiza lets go of his ankle.

"Well?" The question's directed at a warrior trying very hard to loom over the big Zulu. "I hope you have a good reason for waking us."

No response, except for unwavering spears and eyes.

The Lords have painted their faces with wet dagha: one broad stripe down the centre, over the forehead and nose, and down the chin, and three horizontal lines, one across the forehead just above the eyebrows, one crossing the nose under the eyes and the third curving around the chin to join up with the second line on the cheekbones. But, truly, they have no need for such adornments.

Even though Njikiza and the Induna warned them what to expect it still required an act of will not to reach for his iklwa just now and, despite his current pose of nonchalance, distaste burns the udibi's throat like vomit.

Izishawa!

"Aiee! These are not pretty maidens!" Njikiza yawns, bending his arms in a muscle-flexing movement that causes the warriors to stiffen.

"Perhaps they have not been milked yet. That might explain why they are so restless." Addressing another of the warriors: "Is that it?" Njikiza's fists come up to pull on invisible teats. "Would you have us milk you?"

A crash of branches and the soldier standing at Jabulani's end of the clearing steps aside to allow a man to pass. And the udibi sees for himself what the Induna was talking about.

Obviously one of the Lords' generals, the newcomer wears a strange headdress made from a zebra hide. Held in place by a broad leather band, it covers his skull and drops down over his ears and shoulders, framing his face. A rough tunic of a material the udibi can't identify clothes the man's upper body and stretches to his knees. It's open at the sides, while the front and back are held in place by a cord tied around the man's waist.

Instead of the dagha marks, the newcomer has had mud of a lighter colour smeared over the portion of his face revealed by his headdress, as well as his arms and legs. The mud has cracked and peeled away where his sweat has run, so it's as if his limbs are covered by large, dark brown scabs.

He jabs his spear at Njikiza. "Your language I speak!"

He pauses, as though expecting the Zulus to be awed.

"And too well speak it you," says Njikiza.

"Still be!"

Njikiza shrugs. "Still be we."

Izishawa.

Albino babies are strangled at birth, for these are to be feared. Even their name, Izishawa, means Those Who Are Cursed.

And this is who they face – an army of albinos, which has arisen at the Place Of Shame.

Following the man who speaks their language, the three Zulus are led down a steep path to a shaded clearing on the edge of the plain. Here, encircled by spears, they find themselves facing two more of the strangely dressed men.

"Sho! But this is a snake whose face I think I recognise!" says Njikiza, as the Nightman steps forward.

"Where is your leader – and your other little playmate?" asks the Nightman.

"You get tree snakes, mambas, cobras, pythons," says Njikiza, "and while they might all appear different, they are really all the same when you get down to it – for aren't they all to be killed if encountered? Even if they're as entertaining as this one who now speaks our language."

The Nightman grins. Turns. Catches the spear thrown to him. And wheels around once more, ramming the sharpened point into Jabulani's stomach.

"No!" hisses the udibi, gripping Njikiza's forearm as tightly as the big man's muscles allow.

Jabulani takes a step back, folds – and drops onto his knees.

"No!" says the udibi again, conscious of the shifting behind them, as spears are readied to impale Njikiza. The Watcher must stay calm.

"Do you find *that* entertaining?" asks the Nightman. "Hai! Do not stand there grinding your teeth – tell me! I would know!"

As the Nightman makes to prod Njikiza with the tip of his spear Jabulani hoists himself upward and sideways. Realising the Nightman is out of his reach, he's settled for one of the warriors standing to his left.

Half-expecting a move like this from their mortally wounded comrade, the udibi throws himself onto Njikiza's back, his arm around the Watcher's neck – the only way he can restrain the big Zulu . . .

. . . who makes to lunge at the Nightman . . .

. . . who's almost as quick as the udibi in summing up the situation and darts backwards, putting himself behind the warriors who move forward to protect him . . .

. . . as the soldiers behind the two Zulus close in, their spears horizontal . . .

. . . and the man Jabulani's attacked goes down, blood spraying from a torn jugular, and the Zulu has his spear, and even as the soldiers impale him, he manages to stab another . . .

*

A silence of curled lips and narrowed eyes, eager spears and tensed muscles.

Then Njikiza taps the udibi's elbow, indicating he's calmed himself. Slowly, not making any sudden movements that might alarm their captors, the udibi slides off the Watcher's back.

"Now *that* was entertaining!" says Njikiza, straightening, his smile cold, mirthless.

557

16
The Setting Of The Sun

The Nightman turns away in annoyance. He's on the koppie and he looks out over the plain, where the great enclosure lies coiled like a giant snake. "So!" he says, his eyes on the stones. "You could not find them."

Standing behind him, Golden Mane and Red Spear both nod vigorously.

"We searched!" says Golden Mane.

"High and low," says Red Spear.

The Nightman swings round. "But clearly you did not search well enough, did you? For I do not believe those two would have gone far. They have to be somewhere nearby."

"Our sentries are vigilant," says Golden Mane.

"Don't you think this will have occurred to the Zulus? Don't you think they will have made allowances for the vigilance of our sentries?"

The Nightman dismisses them with a contemptuous wave of his hand. Let them go and oversee the preparations for the rebirth ritual. About all they're good for! Fools! Tomorrow morning he'll personally lead a group of hand-picked men to hunt down the remaining Zulus. It will be a pleasant diversion after tonight's labours.

And if the Zulus are foolish enough to try something tonight . . . well, they won't get far. He's had Njikiza placed with the other captives in the citadel; the younger Zulu he'll have with him while he performs the ceremony, and it's the younger Zulu who'll die first should the others try anything.

But if these particular interlopers pose no real threat, what they represent is more worrying. The Nightman and his generals have heard the stories flying through the bush, tales of tribes pushing north, seeking new homelands . . . and now the Zulus are here.

But is that not in itself a propitious portent?

"Let us think like the Ma-Iti, here," murmurs the Nightman to himself.

Perhaps the skirmishes with the incomers and the fear these have induced – for is it not said the migrating tribes are driven by Shaka's bloodlust, would now fight as viciously as his impis? – are signs that the time is at hand when they can at last emerge from the shadows to seize power while the other tribes kill each other?

Like the Ma-Iti we have stood back so that we might pounce when the time is right.

This place, this Zima-Mbje, is but the start. Soon its power, slumbering for so long, will grow and spread, seeding the land, so that, one day soon, other cities of stone will rise up over the veld . . .

17
The New Moon

Large fires burn in an arc around the platform. Beyond these have gathered the Izishawa. There's about two hundred in all – men, women and children, with males predominating – and all have dagha stripes painted across their faces and bare chests. Some of the women and older children hold blazing torches and the men are armed. Their weapons comprise an assortment of spears and axes. Some carry rectangular wooden shields reinforced with a leather covering.

The stones are the bones, they are the pale flesh, watchful, willing . . .

The Nightman emerges from a narrow passage between the smaller circular enclosure holding the captives and the high wall to the rear of the platform. Lord of the Lords, he wears a keffiyeh that's no mere zebra skin imitation – it's a zealously protected relic from a long-dead Arabi – and a skirt made from ostrich feathers. His face, body and limbs are covered with a light-coloured mud. Followed by Red Spear, he passes the bodies of the chief's sons where they sag, pinioned against the wall, and steps onto the platform.

The udibi is here and the Nightman pauses a moment, favouring him with a grin. The young Zulu's hands have been fastened behind his back and a collar woven from grass fitted around his neck. The leash tied to it is held by Golden Mane, who stands to his rear, clutching a spear in his other hand. Both he and Red Spear are wearing zebra skin headdresses and white tunics open at the sides. As with the Nightman, their limbs and faces have been covered with mud.

"So, Zulu," says the Nightman, "are you ready to see the future?"

"I have already seen the future that awaits you."

Chuckling, the Nightman approaches the broad, flat-topped boulder resting on the edge of the platform closest to the gathered albinos. When he reaches the waist-high rock, fires spring into life on either side . . .

The udibi, who has seen the Lord following the Nightman toss handfuls of something onto glowing coals hidden from the crowd to cause the sudden explosion, smiles to himself when he notes the response to this wizardry. Only the younger children hiss in appreciation. The adults remain motionless. Perhaps familiarity has dulled their sense of awe.

Yet, at the same time, the udibi can sense hunger in their gaze. An eagerness. Their eyes are fixed on the Nightman as he carefully removes the rhino skin from the object he's carrying and hands the covering to Red Spear.

Now there's movement among the watching Izishawa as heads rise to watch the passage of the Nightman's hands.

The iron ring glints in the firelight as the Nightman holds it aloft.

The udibi swallows. Could this be the Ubulawu? "You will know it when you see it," the Induna had told them.

Raising his voice, but not shouting, the Nightman speaks.

The udibi notes how the Nightman's arms tremble with the effort of holding the ring above his head . . . It's as if the ring is too heavy for him – another sign, surely, that this is Shaka's talisman. An Ubulawu only the Father Of The Sky will be able to lift; in his hands it will become as light as froth.

The Nightman raises his voice and his words are echoed by the warriors, who stab the night sky with their spears.

The udibi's own hands are numb from his bonds, but even he feels a vicarious relief when the Nightman lowers his arms.

*

He shuts his eyes, waiting for his muscles to stop burning. He presses the ring to his chest and the vision is there, as powerful as ever, lifting him above his fatigue. These faces floating beyond the flames, doubled and redoubled, and doubled again, a pale-skinned army marching forth, carrying the stones that will seed their new cities . . .

*

Placing the talisman on the altar, the Nightman turns to the udibi.

"Do you see this army who will one day rule this land?"

"I hear only your creaking muscles, your panting breath."

The Nightman chuckles. "It is true, Zulu, being a Lord can be arduous!"

Red Spear steps forward. "What is happening?" he asks, his voice low and urgent. "Would you talk this unbeliever to death?"

The Nightman grins. "At this point, if I were you, and given my success in tracking down the missing Zulus today, I'd seriously consider keeping quiet!" Turning to the udibi: "Do you see? There are numerous ways in which this business can wear one down!"

"It is tiresome being a god."

"Hai no! Do not think that! We are not gods! For where are the gods?" The Lord makes a sweeping gesture. "They are gone! We are something a lot more . . ." he grins, ". . . dangerous. We are men!"

"I agree with you there," says the udibi. "There *is* danger abroad to-night!"

"The more so since two of your number remain at large?"

The udibi shrugs, his attention focused past the Nightman's shoulder, where the Lord who interrupted them carefully places a large egg-shaped boulder atop the flattened stone.

"Hmm. But I do not think I need fear two Zulus tonight."

*

For a while after being forced to join the men, women and children in the smaller enclosure, Njikiza kept his distance while he did a circuit of the wall, examined the thorn-bush barricade. He soon realised, however, that none of the villagers would dare approach him.

Did they think that by avoiding him they'd regain the favour of the Lords?

With the passing of the hours and the fall of night, Njikiza's anger has been growing, fuelled by frustration and disgust.

Is this what it was like?

Is this what it was like in the days of the Arabi?

Those people stolen from the land of their birth and sent far away – is this how they sat?

See the hunched shoulders, the glum faces, the listlessness . . .

Why do they not fight back?

Truly, they're like those smelt out by sangomas, deemed abathakathi, believing themselves to be dead already.

There're a number of strong men here – why don't they do something?

And now that the ceremony has begun and their guards are distracted, trying to catch a glimpse of the proceedings, Njikiza moves among his fellow prisoners – interrogating and cajoling, cursing and mocking – what he has in mind, what he wants them to do is clear to them even though they don't speak his language, but they remain obdurate in their gloom.

*

And, able to see more than those gathered beyond the fires, the udibi sees how the Nightman raises the iron ring and brings it down against the egg-shaped stone. It's a controlled movement, the Lord simply touches iron against stone – but there's a loud clang. The sound reverberates across the plain, a blade slicing through the night's flesh.

Turning his head, the udibi can just make out the Lord standing in the shadows behind the platform, striking something against the long piece of metal dangling from his left hand.

This happens four times – the Nightman making as if he strikes the stone with the ring, while, out of sight of those gathered before them, the other Lord provides the sound.

Then, placing the ring aside, the Nightman folds his hands around the curved ends of the stone and, lifting it, holds it at chest height so that those watching can clearly see what happens next.

And their awe, their concentration is palpable, a wave of desire and expectancy that rolls up the hill. Then the Nightman twists his wrists, turning his left hand toward him, his right hand away . . .

. . . and the large egg-shaped stone breaks apart.

And able to see more, the udibi sees how the flames from the fires illuminate smears of brown on the fragments that drop onto the boulder. Clearly the stone was broken beforehand and put back together using mud.

As the Nightman holds each piece up, cheers erupt from the Izishawa.

And the cheers grow still louder when the Nightman holds the baby aloft, this squirming infant plucked from the stone . . .

18
The Rebirth

Izishawa.

Even the Zulus regard albino babies as a curse on the family, the clan, the tribe, to be despatched as soon as possible . . .

But some fathers are proud. Destroying the baby might remove the curse from the clan and the tribe, but the family who, even if only for a brief while, harboured such an abomination, would be forever tainted.

In which case, the Induna had suggested when he and Njikiza returned from their scouting mission and told the others what they had seen, it's possible that some fathers might seek to hide the fact that one of their wives has given birth to an albino.

"But what of the midwife who attends the birth?" asked the udibi.

The Induna nodded. "Yes, there you have it." The midwife's silence would be crucial. "It is the midwives who are feeding this army, filling its impis."

"I still don't understand," said Thando. "Why don't they just kill these creatures?"

The answer to that question was simple if one thought about it, said the Induna. In helping a father hide the birth of an albino child, the midwife placed her own life at risk. Should the birth be discovered, she'd face an even worse punishment than the family. That she helped hide the Cursed One is bad enough, but she'd have committed an even greater transgression in allowing the Isishawa to be despatched without the proper cleansing ceremonies being performed by the clan shaman and requiring the participation of the whole clan.

Instead, the albino baby is handed over to the Lords. There is then no grave to be accidentally uncovered and the curse is physically removed. And where the mother is party to such a subterfuge she would willingly acquiesce, for a mother's love is strong and any fate would be better for her child than death . . .

*

Izishawa.

Having been born once of parents who would shun him, this little one held aloft by the Nightman is now being reborn into the army of the Lords, another soldier who'll be raised to know only bitterness and hatred . . .

An army of albinos, suckled at the Place Of Shame.

But not all are Izishawa, are they?

*

And the udibi has seen how, as soon as the Nightman raised the stone, the Lord making the clanging sound laid aside his instrument and darted forward. Clutching a bundle now and crouching low, he scurried to the boulder, removing the gag that had kept the baby quiet.

And the udibi has seen how, when he'd finished breaking the egg-shaped stone and displaying the pieces, the Nightman was handed the infant by the other Lord hidden from sight behind the altar.

And now there's movement behind him. The leash goes limp as Golden Mane falls away and Thando is there, untying the udibi's hands, cutting the collar . . .

And before the watching warriors can recover from the shock of seeing the chief's sons come back to life, the Induna has his arm around the Nightman's neck, the Arabi dagger poised at his throat.

19

The Lords

"We meet again, Zulu."

"A not unexpected reckoning."

His chin pressed against the crook of the Induna's arm, the Nightman grins. "This is so."

As soon as the Induna grabbed him, he'd tried to twist out of the Zulu's grasp, but it was a brief struggle, the consequence of his being taken by surprise. Now he's relaxed. There's no need to risk his life – after all, the Zulus are outnumbered.

Thando and the udibi come forward, armed with the iklwas Thando and the Induna brought with them. Golden Mane, the Lord who was holding the leash to the udibi's collar, lies dead in the space between the platform and the rear wall; Thando has the other Lord covered.

"Where's Jabulani?" asks the Induna, shrugging off the wildebeest cloak.

"Dead, Master," says the udibi.

The Nightman gags as the Induna's arm tightens around his throat.

"Njikiza!"

"Here, Master!" comes the bellow from within the circular enclosure a few metres from the platform.

"You will know when!" calls the Induna.

"I hear you, Master!"

The Induna releases the Nightman and, his hand on the Lord's chest, gently pushes him away until he can feel the pressure of the udibi's iklwa against his spine.

They're standing sideways on to the gathering, so the men can see how close their leader is to death.

"Tell your slaves to remain calm," orders the Induna, indicating the bewildered faces of the gathering with the Arabi dagger.

His eyes on the Zulu, the Nightman makes a flattening gesture with his left hand. Raising his voice he speaks a command that seems to do little to calm the muttering Izishawa.

"Do not try to trick me," says the Induna. "It didn't work before and it won't work now."

"They will listen to me and curb their bloodlust a little longer. Never fear, Zulu."

"We have nothing to fear from one such as you. Hai! But do my ears deceive me – or have you decided you can speak our language?"

"Part of the subterfuge."

"If it can be called that."

"Yes. How did you know?"

"When you said you came back with the ferryman. We had met that creature and he would have found a greybeard like the one you pretended to be easy pickings!"

Lakotse bursts out laughing. "The man at the river, the one you call a creature, was one of my men, one of my creatures! Am I to assume he now eats dirt?"

"As you will, shortly."

"But you are outnumbered, Zulu – or are you blind as well as arrogant?"

"I see only you. What happens afterwards does not bother me. Although many of your men may yet learn to regret my lack of concern."

"Fierce words, Zulu."

"And fiercer the deed."

"And I say again: these are merely words! Tell me, Zulu: do you think you can stop the future? For this is what we deal in here! Do you not understand that these beautiful ones are the harbingers of our tomorrows? Or are you like the rest? Kill them! Kill these abominations! Is that what you say?"

"I say only that *your* future is here!"

"We shall see about that!"

"We shall," says the Induna, "but first let us see what these valiant soldiers you would throw at us will do when they discover what you are." Indicating the other Lord: "And him too."

Instinctively the Nightman makes to back away. Instead, feeling the tip of the udibi's spear press deeper into his spine, he's forced to arch his back.

"Yes," says the Induna, "you are right to be afraid. And you are right when you say there are those, and I number my own people among them, who see these Izishawa as abominations to be killed – but what will these Cursed Ones say when they see you are exactly the same as those who would hunt them down?"

Stepping forward, the Induna spits into his left hand and runs the palm across the Nightman's chest, wiping the whiteness off.

"Do you see?" he asks the gathered Lords, holding up his hand. "Do you *see*? He is not one of you!" He runs the hand across his own chest, leaving a smear of pale mud. "He is one of us! One of those you have been taught to hate!"

*

An army of albinos, suckled at the Place Of Shame. Raised to know only bitterness and hatred and keeping the surrounding villages in their thrall, the fear they engender only adding to their rage.

But not all are Izishawa.

The Nightman and his generals are not albinos. They merely attempt to mimic the skin colouring by smearing mud over their bodies. "And doubtless this is where their power comes from," the Induna had told the others. "They can change colour and move among us unnoticed! And this must seem a great feat to those they command. They are powerful wizards, able to control the curse, use it to their own ends."

"I have seen this for myself, for you have pointed it out to me, Master," said Njikiza, "but how can they not know their rulers are different to them, that their power comes from mud and nothing else?"

"They came here as infants, they do not know any other way." There is no reason for them to question why their rulers seem to be a little different from themselves.

"This is why I told you that they are as much captives as the villagers they terrorise," the Induna had said, before going on to outline his plan.

"We will let them find us." Grinning, he added: "Or some of us at least."

Allowing themselves to be taken prisoner would be the easiest way for Njikiza, Jabulani and the udibi to enter the enemy encampment – and the Induna was sure Lakotse would want to see all of the Zulus hunted down before making an example of them. At the very least he'd want to keep those he had captured alive until the ceremony he'd told them about.

And while the Lords were distracted, questioning the others, the Induna and Thando would enter the enclosure and take the place of the dead men against the wall . . .

*

"They are not the Lords," says the Induna, "you are, you and these two, and perhaps a few others. *You* are the true Lords, these others are just your slaves."

He runs his left hand across the Nightman's face, removing more of the mud. Again he raises the hand so the warriors beyond the flames can see.

"You!' he says, addressing the Lord guarded by Thando. "Would you live?"

568

Without daring to glance in the Nightman's direction, Red Spear nods. "Yes, Master!"

"Then tell them," says the Induna, indicating the anxious, confused faces before them. "Tell them of your trickery!"

Red Spear's voice is a quaver as he starts to address the Izishawa and the Induna tells him to speak up. Turning his attention to their audience he notes how heads are turning, as the men look to each other for confirmation that they're really hearing what they're hearing.

"Tell them they can see for themselves!" calls the Induna.

As Red Spear translates, the Induna signals the udibi.

"Wait!" says the Nightman, as the udibi prods him toward the Induna.

"What?" asks the Induna.

"Do you think they won't turn on you when they are finished with me?"

"We'll see," says the Induna. Snatching the Nightman's arm, he twists it and pushes the Lord off the platform. Men surge between the fires to pull him into their ranks; a maelstrom of clawing hands and stabbing spears.

*

Njikiza's been following the exchange on the other side of the wall of the smaller circular enclosure. As soon as he hears the shrieks, he tears the gate aside, ignoring the long thorns that pierce his hands and arms, and is onto the first guard before the man even has time to react . . .

*

On the platform, meanwhile, reckoning the Zulus to be distracted by the howling mass beyond the flames, Red Spear turns and grabs Thando's spear. But the latter is too quick for him. Even as Red Spear's fingers have closed around the haft just below the blade, the assegai is wrenched from his fingers.

"Finish with him," calls the Induna and Thando obeys, ramming the blade into Red Spear's chest and thrusting him off the platform toward the flames, where he too is drawn into the maelstrom.

"He was right," says the udibi, as they back away from the mob. "We'll be next."

The Induna nods. But they have some time, thanks to Njikiza. Taking the ring from the altar, he tells the others to follow him.

The darkness is a minor hindrance, more an ally than a foe. Because it is a sacred place guarded by taboos, he and Thando had time to explore the great enclosure once they had entered it and acquaint themselves with its passages and chambers. In one of these they found waterskins and sacks of the soil the Nightman and his generals used to make the pale mud with which they smeared themselves – another reason why they would want their followers to stay away from the citadel. In a second chamber they had hidden the bodies of the dead men when it had grown dark and the Lords were too busy calling the Izishawa to the ceremony to notice the swap.

When they reach the perimeter wall furthest away from the platform, the Induna stops. The udibi will take the talisman and make good his escape; they'll help him to scale the wall, then the Induna and Thando and Njikiza will face the Izishawa.

The young Zulu draws back.

"No, Master!"

*

Njikiza steps sideways. Grabbing the guard's spear, he wrenches it out of the man's hands and drives his own blade home. It's not as good as a Zulu iklwa, but it'll do. He throws the second spear behind him, onto the pile he's accumulated at the gate.

"Ngadla!" he roars.

He runs back, grabs the nearest prisoner: "Ngadla!"

Why won't these fools do something?

He wheels as another albino comes at him. Parrying the man's blade, he rams his right heel into the man's left foot, then brings his own spear into play . . .

"Ngadla!"

He managed to snatch the warrior's spear before he fell and now he forces the weapon into a prisoner's hands.

He grabs another's elbow, pulls him closer: "Ngadla!"

And again: "Ngadla!"

They must fight!

*

"No, Master," says the udibi again, as the Induna turns to him. "As your udibi I have never disobeyed you – but did you not say I was to join you on this expedition as a warrior? Well then – as a warrior I say no! And it is as a warrior I will disobey you."

Let Thando be the one who escapes. Let him be the one who delivers the Vessel to Shaka.

The udibi is fully prepared to face the Induna's anger, and is surprised when the older man says nothing.

Instead, it's Thando who speaks: "Would you deprive my iklwa?"

"No, Thando, it's just that you are the better man for this task! You will get the Ubulawu back to our Father. You will tell of what happened here better than I can."

Addressing the Induna, the udibi says: "They call me your shadow, well then – let me be your shadow in this matter. When first you chose me to be your udibi, there at the kraal of the Langeni, you said I would serve you well."

"That was not a command," murmurs the Induna. "I was merely describing what I saw foretold in your eyes. And you did not disappoint me."

"Then let me not disappoint you here. If we are to set today, let us end it as we began: side by side."

"You would disobey me?" asks the Induna, his voice low, his eyes fixed on the teenager.

"Yes, Master, and you will have all of forever to chastise me."

20
The Watcher's Last Stand

Stabbing left and right, Njikiza drops two men. But the one grips the haft of the Zulu's assegai as he topples backwards, leaving the Watcher momentarily unarmed. A third Isishawa seizes his chance. He's wielding an axe, comes at the Zulu with both arms raised – and runs into Njikiza's fist.

Now where did the axe fall? The Watcher twists as a blade scrapes his side, tearing flesh. He rams his elbow into his assailant's face, shattering the nose in a spray of blood, and grabs the spear. It's a better weapon than the axe, enabling him to keep his attackers at bay. Pain flaring up the right side of his body, he begins to back up to the gate of the enclosure. Where the weapons lie and the prisoners remain unmoving.

Hands grab at his ankles. It's the axe man.

Njikiza stamps down hard and again, even harder, when he feels his foot connect with the warrior's head.

Daren't look back or at the ground, got to keep his eyes to the front. Screams and shouts over by the bonfires, a confused milling.

He chances a glance over his shoulder. He's back at the gate. Biting down the pain the movement causes him he drops to his haunches, fingers fumbling until they close around the haft of a second spear. Straightening up, he's hit by a wave of dizziness. Blood is pouring from his wound. How long will he be able to last? He turns round, tosses the spear he picked up at the nearest man. "Fight!" he shouts. "Defend yourself!"

Movement behind him. He swings and ducks, the pain biting his side momentarily forgotten.

*

The Induna and the udibi help Thando clamber up onto the perimeter wall. Then the Induna hoists the udibi so that he can hand Thando the talisman. After he lowers the udibi, they both wish Thando well. The Vessel must be delivered to Shaka.

"I will do it," says Thando.

"Now go!" says the Induna. "Hamba kahle!" *Go well* . . .

The sky is purple, dawn is near.

"Salani kahle," says Thando. *Stay well* . . .

He slips off the wall and drops into the darkness beyond.

*

The assegai sails over Njikiza's head. He lunges forward, through the flames of his pain. A warrior's throat explodes in a spray of blood as the Zulu's spear strikes. But someone's managed to outflank him, and Njikiza has to bring his right shoulder forward to parry the man's blow as he disengages his own spear. The albino's assegai slices through the fleshy part of Njikiza's upper arm and carries on to gouge a furrow across the Zulu's ribcage. If he hadn't turned in time, he would have been impaled. He wrenches the assegai away from the warrior and sends his own spear into the man's face. But his left side is now exposed. If another assailant had been there to guide an assegai with sufficient force . . .

As it is, though, a spear thrown from a distance imbeds itself in the Zulu's shoulder. With a bellow of outrage, Njikiza rips the missile from the wound.

But something has changed . . .

There are others here.

With a frown of confusion shadowing his eyes, Njikiza drops to his knees and topples sideways.

21
The Gathering

Dingane scowls and pulls his cowhide cloak tighter. This is silly, he thinks, offering his shoulder to the wind. In fact, this is ridiculous.

He lets the wind turn him, so that he's glaring at Mpande, his younger brother, who acts as his udibi. And who can't seem to stop his teeth from chattering.

No, this is monstrous! Which is to be expected, he decides, allowing himself a self-congratulatory smile, since it's the consequence of a monster's twisted mind.

Realising his brother's eyes are on him – the soft eyes of a weakling, expectant now, wondering about his smile – Dingane tells Mpande to stop making a noise.

"But I'm *cold*," hisses the teenager.

"Be quiet!"

We are all cold, thinks Dingane, his features hardening once more into a sulky, sullen look. But don't give *him* the satisfaction. Oh no, don't let Shaka see how you suffer.

Offering his brother his back, he stares out over the inner enclosure. Gusting through the huts the wind stabs your ribs and shoulder blades, bites your neck and stings your eyes. One of *those* days; those dirty, muggy days, when the wind holds the rain at bay and a cold man will soon find himself sweating beneath his skins. Even now Dingane can feel prickles on his back, his chest, but knows that if he were to remove his cloak, he'd soon begin to feel chilly. One of those days, when the wind brings only headaches and bad moods. A nagging discomfort as irritating as a baby who won't stop crying, a companion with hiccoughs – or a brother whose teeth keep chattering.

A glare over his shoulder, met by Mpande raising his shoulders – a cheeky, provocative gesture that says: What? What? As if he's unaware of what he's doing to annoy his older brother. And Dingane returns his attention to the enclosure, where the inhabitants of KwaBulawayo stand in the wind. Wary and weary, thinks Dingane. Hai, but they would serve a monster.

A mad man.

*

Dingane and Mpande are at the end of the group that comprises Shaka's inner circle, advisors and family members, who stand facing the people, separated from them by the cattlefold. The Needy One takes a few unobtrusive steps forward, so he can glance down the line, gauge the mood of *these* sycophants. Bowed heads. No chatter, no catching the eye of one's neighbours. Each man stands alone, lost in his own thoughts . . . his own fear.

This lack of enthusiasm warms the heart.

It is good to see. Always good to see.

But he is as a greybeard taking stock of another family's children, a man admiring a neighbour's cattle. Fine cattle! Well-behaved children! But not his children, not his cattle.

Mbopa is the only one he has . . . what? "Approached" is too strong, too *dangerous* a word. And Mbopa was as cunning as ever; Dingane cannot say they have spoken – that would imply a degree of participation on the prime minister's part. Dingane would be in grave error were he to see their chat as a colloquy – and he knows that. He has spoken and Mbopa has listened. He has watered the seeds he knows have to be there, somewhere in the man's troubled mind. Mbopa is no fool, after all.

Yes, Mbopa is the only one of this herd he's spoken to. While their unease pleases him, he knows he cannot rely on their support.

Neither does he *want* their support. He has his own . . . allies. His own inner circle. It is sufficient to know that Shaka, through his own misdeeds, has begun to alienate his trusted advisors. For let us say something should happen to the King – perish the thought – these fools can beg and beat their breasts, but they will find themselves without an ear to whisper into, their day will have set along with the King's.

All of this being mere supposition, of course. Idle speculation. The kind of daydreaming any claimant to a throne might indulge in . . .

*

The Lion had listened when he spoke, and since Mabhubesi lived in Dingane's district they had had lots of time for idle speculation. And it was soon apparent the Lion and he were on the same path, and how much better, how much easier things would have been had the Lion's little fit of pique served to turn the army against Shaka.

My hands would have been clean . . .

Then again, perhaps it was for the best. There was the problem of Zwide and the Ndwandwes to contend with. Would he have been swayed if Shaka had been deposed? Probably not. Zwide was ravenous for conquest. And in his daydreams, a claimant does not see himself as a vassal. That would be even worse than waiting for the King to die!

*

What's taking the Beetle so long?

Zulus rule all they see, or so it is said; does Shaka really need such childish displays to remind himself of his power?

Yet here we wait . . .

The King has his Ubulawu! At last the King has found his Vessel!

And it's all so much froth!

*

Feeling the sweat between his shoulder blades and down his chest grow icy again, Dingane hopes he isn't coming down with a fever.

Or perhaps it's the niggling worry that this Ubulawu, this froth, might just be what Shaka needs to regain his status, his respect among the people.

A grim thought, almost as dour as this day.

22
The Dawn

"There are narrow passages here," says the Induna. "We could defend ourselves well."

"That is not the Zulu way," says the udibi, "let us go and join Njikiza and meet them out there."

The Induna nods. It is the answer he was expecting. He lays a hand on the udibi's shoulder. "I once told you that to die in battle while your iklwa feasted was but a paltry alternative."

"I remember. We were among the Fish Eaters. You said better a greybeard, cows to count and wives to tire out."

"I am sorry this future will not come to pass."

The udibi shrugs. "It is as the Great Spirit wills it."

"Yes. Let your arm be strong and your aim true."

"Never fear, Master, you have taught me well."

They make their way back to the platform.

And stop. The man standing there, his size seemingly doubled by the amashoba he wears, wheels round.

"Eshé, old friends!"

The udibi gapes, while the Induna merely smiles as Mzilikazi motions for them to join him.

The fires lining the platform have burnt down and mist lies across the plain in the grey dawn. It reaches up to the knees of Mzilikazi's men, who surround the surviving Izishawa.

"See?" he says. "I have left some of these lizards for you, although they are barely worth the effort. But this is the way of stories, is it not? The bulls are always bigger, the kings stronger, the soldiers braver with each retelling."

"Is that why you have come? To see for yourself?"

"Perhaps," grins Mzilikazi. He claps the Induna's shoulder. "Then again, I could not let you have all the fun!"

"I will not lie to you," says the Induna, "seeing you here, this morning, is one of the happier moments of my life."

Mzilikazi bows his head. "I thank you and, of course, I am glad that you are here to proffer such a generous compliment."

Turning to the udibi, he smiles. "And you, Little One, although, truly, you are not so little any more, let me answer the question I see in your eyes. The Watcher is still with us. Go with my udibi. He'll take you to where my inyangas tend to Njikiza's wounds."

"Master?"

"Go! Ask him why he loiters so."

"Hai!" adds Mzilikazi. "But do not piss on him again if he will not move, for he still has a lot of fight left in him."

*

After the udibi leaves, with permission to take some warriors to go and fetch Thando after he's seen Njikiza, Mzilikazi and the Induna stand a while gazing at the scene before them. The walls tear the mist, yet at the same time appear to be woven into the mist, so it's as if the mist is rising from the stones, like vapour from a sweaty body on a cold day. And these other bodies – the remaining Izishawa, sitting, squatting, sprawled splattered in blood before the platform and watched by Mzilikazi's warriors – they are like waterskins the stones have sucked dry and discarded. They are fading like the bonfires, collapsed into a handful of coals, encircled by grey ash.

For all this, Mzilikazi's men remain wary, for there is illness here, the disease of the Cursed Ones.

He will escort the Zulus back to the Barrier Of Spears, says Mzilikazi, breaking the punch-drunk silence. "But first let us finish with these abominations!"

"No."

About to give the order, Mzilikazi stops, his mouth agape. "Brother? What say you? They are cursed! We are at risk from their disease even as we stand here."

"Leave them to the Great Spirit, Mzilikazi. I do not think they will linger long here now. They will go and you will not see them again."

"But ..."

"How can these men, these women and these children harm you, Brother?"

"They are cursed!"

"If that is so, then it is we who have cursed them! It is we who have said you are born of Abantu, but you cannot be Human Beings! Let us lift the curse."

"Hai! They are abominations, less than human!"

"How can that be? They understood they had been tricked by Lakotse and his men – "

"And they were about to turn on you, Brother. Do not forget that!"

"That is so, but what else could they do? Hatred is all they know." The Induna moves closer to Mzilikazi. "Hatred, Brother! A very human trait. Does the lion or the elephant show hatred? And when the dog turns on his master it's because the master has taught the dog to hate!"

Mzilikazi stares at the wretched figures a moment. Grins.

"What is it?" asks the Induna.

Certainly, says Mzilikazi, in his experience, only humans can look quite so crestfallen, so pathetic.

"It is so," says the Induna. "There's been enough killing. Perhaps this is the way we will thwart, once and for all, the evil that's lingered here for so long – by showing mercy and letting them go."

Shaking his head, unable to believe what he's about to do, Mzilikazi agrees to indulge the Induna. He orders a regiment to watch over the Izishawa as they pack their belongings and then to see them on their way.

*

And so it was. And so it was not. For just as the stories about the power of the Lords were exaggerated with each retelling – faces quivering in the firelight with the glee of horrors recounted – so it was with the tales that told of their demise. And perhaps here was a sign that the evil of Zima-Mbje was not quite vanquished. For, in the retelling, it became the chief's sons who had miraculously come alive to defeat the Lords, leaping down from the wall after biding their time to wreak havoc on their oppressors. And the men of that village soon forgot their foolishness and cowardice, and grew proud and haughty and began to look upon their neighbours with covetous eyes. Dazzled by their own lies they might have set about emulating the rule of the Lords were it not for the fact that Mzilikazi and his people returned to forge their own empire in those parts. And so the Matabele became entangled in the legend, with some stories claiming it was Mzilikazi alone who defeated the Lords.

And it was as if the Zulus had never been there.

23
The Ubulawu

A bustle. A ripple, as heads lift. A stiffening. The King approaches.

Now we will see, thinks Dingane.

And to allow an outlet for his nervousness, he cuffs Mpande in the guise of getting him to straighten up.

Nervous? Of course the Needy One is nervous, for all his delirious scheming. The Bull Elephant remains a force to be reckoned with.

Walking to his right, several paces to the rear, are Mbopa and Mdlaka. To Shaka's left, moving parallel with the prime minister and commander in chief of the Zulu army, are the Induna, the udibi and Thando.

After seeing the surviving villagers safely to their umuzi, they were escorted to the Barrier Of Spears by Mzilikazi and his men. Njikiza, for all his assertions to the contrary, was barely able to make the journey. Consequently, once the men had crossed the Drakensberg, retracing their previous route, Thando was sent ahead to the war kraal, to fetch an inyanga to see to the Watcher's wounds.

With Njikiza remaining at the war kraal to recuperate, the other three set off for KwaBulawayo accompanied by Mdlaka and his ubutho, the commander in chief deciding this was an occasion that demanded he show his face. Shaka had his Ubulawu. Surely this heralded a new spring; a time of rebirth for the tribe, the homeland.

Despite the weather, Shaka wears only his isinene and amashoba today. His warriors – the Induna, Mdlaka and the other two – are likewise attired; only Mbopa wears a longer kilt and a springbok skin draped over his shoulders.

This homeland: rolling hills and tangled bush, hidden ravines and dense forests. This homeland: by turns fierce and gentle, brutal and hospitable, just like the people who inhabit it. And did not the Bull Elephant win this land for them? Did Shaka not succeed where others – noble men like Dingiswayo, greedy brutes like Zwide – failed? This will be his legacy . . .

Soldiers line the perimeter of Bulawayo's great central enclosure, members of other regiments mingle with the people. Now they raise their shields and spears. "Bayede, Nkosi! Bayede, Nkosi Yamakosi! King of Kings! Bayede, Sitting Thunder! Bayede, Bull Elephant! Bayede!"

A cynical observer – or should that be a perspicacious one? – would wonder about Mbopa. The others have chosen their attire according to Shaka's example. Not Mbopa. Dingane wonders if this is not a sign of rebelliousness. Having grown weary of Shaka's wilful ways, has Mbopa responded with a touch of his own wilfulness? Hai, but then again, he is not a soldier. In choosing to mimic the King and his men by dressing as a warrior he would have courted disdain . . .

"Shaka! Shaka! Shaka! Conqueror! Conqueror! Conqueror of Conquerors!"

There is another one who watches Mbopa, albeit fleetingly. It is Pampata. She stands with the others of Shaka's harem in a regiment of their own, formed up on the opposite side of the ibandla tree to Shaka's advisors and family members. For the occasion, the women carry small shields called amahawu and small, ceremonial spears.

Mbopa snags her attention as he strides by, clutching the talisman, but although Pampata hears Nandi's words once more – "He is not to be trusted, that one; I do not understand why my son has elevated him to such a position" – she soon shifts her attention back to Shaka, watching his broad shoulders with wet eyes.

The people have of course joined the soldiers in their salute. And perhaps they, too, have been struck by the thought that a renewal is at hand, for their shouts grow ever more enthusiastic.

Wet eyes . . .

The Induna couldn't believe what he saw as they drew nearer the capital. Having received reports, Mdlaka had warned him what to expect, but even the general grew silent at the sight that awaited them. For to know is not necessarily to see, and nothing could have prepared them for this.

Nothing.

Shaka passes under the ibandla tree.

"Bayede, the Liberator! Bayede, the Sitting Thunder! Bayede, the Bull Elephant! Bayede, the Cunning Leopard! Breaker Of Tyrants! Father Of The Sky! Bayede!"

He comes to a halt several metres ahead of the ranks comprising his inner circle. Facing the people over the fences of the cattlefold, he listens to their cheers while the men who have accompanied him form up in a line behind him.

Standing next to the Induna, the udibi wants to believe this is a return to old times. See their faces, glistening with joy! Hear their praises! But he can't stop remembering what lies beyond the walls of the capital . . .

"Bayede, Nkosi Yamakosi! Bayede! Bayede, Bull Elephant! Bayede!"

Shaka KaSenzangakhona raises his arms.

Silence, as shields and spears are lowered.

Silence.

With something of a start Shaka realises his mouth is dry.

He stands glaring at the crowd, his chin tilted toward his throat, his eyes lost in the shadows of his brow.

Another grey sky, a body in the rain . . . The Induna's thoughts slipping unbidden through the gates of his self-control, his loyalty.

Why does he waver? Pampata's thoughts as she silently urges – wills – Shaka on. Please, Beloved, please . . .

The Needy One, his eyes narrowed, is pondering the difference between wavering and hesitation, hesitation and the sudden, complete forgetfulness that will descend upon some old men. Aiee! The Bull Elephant has become a confused dog who's lost his way!

Watching his King, the udibi is thinking of a young boy, a child really, although he would have looked upon you with disdain had you called him that, in the middle of a battle – and the King who turned away from his brave soldiers and their feasting iklwas to take the boy's hand and direct his attention to a distant mountain where smoke was rising like the lourie feather from the King's headband: "Watch the smoke, Little One, watch the smoke . . ." But the old men . . . The old men and others, they intrude.

Why does he waver so? Do not waver, my Beloved, do not waver!

A confused dog, old before his time, but killing has this effect on one . . .

The body in the rain . . . What does it mean?

"Watch the smoke, Little One."

And now the smoke has shifted, Father, what am I to do?

Of their own accord, the udibi's eyes are drawn to the main gates.

A field of bones lies there, almost encircling KwaBulawayo. Skulls, ribs, femurs, sunbaked and brown, while others are still adorned with tatters of flesh. And, as the returning travellers drew closer to the entrance of the capital, they saw the fresher bodies. Bloated sacks of flesh and a stench as impenetrable as any jungle.

At last Shaka spreads his arms: "My People!"

Although he had heard of this hideous crop the King had sowed, ordering the death of all the old men in the Kingdom, because their doddering offended him, Mdlaka also had good news to impart. Mbopa had finally persuaded Shaka to lift his ruling about food and milk. The people are allowed to hunt once more and plant their crops and drink the milk from their cows. The ban on fornication still stands, but they can feed themselves. But, wonders the udibi, did not this – a field of bones – negate that, the lifting of laws that were anyway insane to begin with?

"My Children!"

"Father!"

"My Children, my People! Children Of The Sky! People of Shaka! You have pestered me! Your plaints have bitten at me, like ants! How you have battered your Father!"

Well, that's one way of looking at it, decides Mbopa. The Ubulawu rests on his palms. It's wrapped in a leopard skin . . .

*

"Is that what you have come for?" asked Mzilikazi.

As the Induna nodded, a sliver of unease suddenly trickled down his spine – what if Mzilikazi had saved them only to thwart Shaka? Their eyes met. Maybe Mzilikazi held the Induna's gaze as a mild rebuke, or perhaps the thought they shared had had a momentary appeal . . .

*

"But," says Shaka, "I have listened! I have listened even though your lack of faith has pained me – *pained* me, my Children! You would see a return to the old days when we lived in fear. So be it! You would see your King strengthened by a mere trinket. So be it! Seek the Vessel, you have said. And I have sought the Vessel. And I have found the Vessel. I despatched my finest warriors and they have brought it to me. All for you!" Shaka nods his head. "All for you, my Children!"

The response is a roar: "Bayede, Baba! Bayede, King of Kings! Sorcerer of Sorcerers!"

Pampata and the other women ululate and beat their spears against their shields.

Lightning to the south, slicing the sky. Crackling thunder, sounding like an avalanche. A sudden gust of wind, battering the expectant faces.

"Behold!" bellows Shaka. "Behold! Your destiny!"

He turns to Mbopa, who strides forward, pulling off the top layer of the covering.

Gripping the ring in both hands Shaka raises it above his head. "Behold!" he bellows. "The Ubulawu."

*

"Did you see it?" Dingane's voice is a near-hysterical hiss. "Did you see it?" he asks, gripping the Induna's elbow.

Singing Shaka's praises, the people have returned to their homes and the sentries have resumed their patrols. Dust devils spiral in the central enclosure; fence poles rattle.

"Did you see?"

After Shaka had raised the Ubulawu, he turned his back on the cheers. Passing by Mbopa, he'd rammed the object against the prime minister's chest, and stalked away to the royal hut.

"Did you see?"

"I have eyes," murmurs the Induna.

"Do you, friend of my youth? I am not so certain!"

The Induna pulls away from Dingane. "Leave me!"

He has his bedroll and his waterskin. He has said goodbye to his udibi, who will be returning to his own regiment, and was just about to depart when the Needy One accosted him.

"You would go – go, then!" sneers Dingane. "But do not tell me you have seen, for if you can turn your back on this, then you have seen *nothing*!"

The two men stand staring at each other. Dingane believes he can detect pain in the Induna's eyes; a flickering, wavering uncertainty. Shaka's half-brother takes a breath, makes an effort to calm himself.

"Have you not heard the old stories?" he asks softly. "Of course you have! How then can you . . . How can you tolerate this?"

"Not now, Dingane. No, not now! I would go home to count my cattle and lie between the thighs of my woman."

"Wouldn't we all, Brother? But that's a luxury we may not be able to enjoy for much longer."

"So be it."

Dingane feels the rage rising once more. "Did you not see it?"

The ring, this Ubulawu Shaka brandished, was a collar – the heavy steel collar the Arabi – and other Izilwane – would affix around the necks of their slaves.

"Is that how he sees us? As mere slaves?"

"Hai, perhaps the jealous heir sees only what he wants to see!"

"We all saw it, my friend, and there was no mistaking it."

"That is not what I was referring to."

"Well, it's the very thing I am referring to. And it cannot be ignored."

The Induna raises his hand. Turns.

Dingane lunges past the Induna, stops in front of him, his hands on the other man's chest.

"Nduna! Friend! This cannot go on. And I am not alone in knowing this."

The two men regard each other a moment, Dingane watching the warring emotions flit across the Induna's face, the Induna noting how what he has seen today has driven all guile and fear from the Needy One. His outrage is pure for once.

To Dingane it seems as if his friend is about to say something, then the moment is gone, like ash in the wind, and the Induna pushes past him.

*

He follows the road that leads away from KwaBulawayo, the hard-packed earth glistening blackly, like blood; and all around him, the field of bones. Walking with squared shoulders, his shield tipped sideways, his iklwa in his other hand, he doesn't look back. The wind has been tamed and the rain falls unfettered. It sweeps across the veld; stinging silver drops beneath a bruised sky.

Soon the warrior, this induna in the service of Shaka, has faded into the mist, in much the same way as history will sometimes blur into legend.

DURBAN

SOUTH AFRICA

2006

Acknowledgements

Although this is a work of fiction that ultimately exists for no other reason than to entertain, I have tried to ensure the reader will come away with a reasonably accurate picture of Zulu society. If a few misconceptions are challenged, so much the better.

Writing was unknown to the Zulus of Shaka's day, and although many books have been written about this phase of our history, all draw from the same primary core of texts. For historians this constitutes a major stumbling block. For writers, however, it's an invitation to play . . .

*

A key source for this novel, especially as regards Shaka's campaigns against the Ndwandwes and his run-in with the sangomas, is E. A. Ritter's much-maligned *Shaka Zulu*. Ritter's attempts to cast Shaka as a warrior-king in the Arthurian mould can be annoying, but the fact remains that writing in the 1950s, amid the birth pangs of apartheid, he was flying in the face of contemporary ideology. Making full use of the Zulu oral tradition (a fact his critics seem to forget), Ritter was trying to show Shaka as being more than a bloodthirsty savage ruling a primitive nation. In doing so, despite all his shortcomings, he succeeds in presenting us with a vivid portrait, an alternative history, if you like, of how things might have been. This work of fiction is unashamedly located in that world.

*

Ritter himself wasn't above taking a swipe at *his* contemporaries, constantly castigating them for exaggerating Shaka's cruelty – or distorting the "facts" in the name of "sensationalist fiction".

Could P. A. Stuart's *An African Attila* (Shuter & Shooter, 1927) be one of the books he's referring to? Whatever the case may be, I was gratified to stumble across a copy. After all, here was a writer who, more than seventy years ago, was attempting something similar to my own endeavours – and doing so in a first-person narrative. But the title says it all. Shaka is a villain and the narrator serves him despite the king's excesses.

*

That a boy growing up in Brooklyn in the 1930s should develop an abiding fascination with the Zulus is quite remarkable. Yet this was the case with Donald Morris. He served in the US Navy during World War II and went on to earn two combat stars in Korea. In 1956, he joined the CIA and would do tours of duty in West Germany (1958–1962), France (1965–1967), Zaïre (1969–1970) and Vietnam (1970–1972). He never lost his fascination with the Zulus – and the idea of writing a book about them came from a chance encounter with Ernest Hemingway in Cuba in 1955.

The result was *The Washing of the Spears*, which took Morris eight years to complete. Most of it was written during his time in Berlin, and the research was undertaken by correspondence with libraries and museums in Britain and South Africa. The book has since appeared in seventeen languages worldwide, and has never been out of print.

It was a seminal work that attempted to tell the story of the war from a balanced perspective and marked the beginning of modern Anglo-Zulu War studies.

These days, however, whenever Morris is mentioned he is almost always referred to as an "amateur historian" – a spiteful appellation that, while accurate, belies his contribution to the field, even if subsequent research has made parts of his book dated.

Although its focus is the war of 1879, the first section sifts through the myths and attempts to present a scholarly history of the Zulu nation. And it provided a good starting point for my own investigations.

*

Peter Becker, whose bestselling histories are now dismissed as "lurid", travelled far and wide, interviewing old-timers and praise singers in his desire to understand "black history". His key works attempt to tell the "other side of the story" and are a lot more balanced and insightful than many contemporary critics seem to realise.

Doubtless because of Ritter's *Shaka Zulu*, Becker never actually wrote about Shaka, but his biographies of Dingane (*Rule of Fear*), Mzilikazi (*Path of Blood*) and Moshesh (*Hill of Destiny*) all overlap with Shaka's life and times and proved valuable.

*

When it comes to Zulu culture, especially as it was in the nineteenth century, Eileen Jensen Krige's *The Social System of the Zulus* (first published in 1935) was simply priceless. As was J.D. Omer-Cooper's overview of the period, *The Zulu*

Aftermath, and John Laband's masterly account of the Zulu army, *Rope of Sand.*

For further information about the Ma-Iti, Arabi and Zima-Mbje, I point readers to Credo Mutwa's *Indaba My Children.*

*

Patient colleague Zanele Mbatha of *Bona* magazine helped me with various translations. Any errors are entirely my own.

The "Talking muthi" column in the magazine by Force Khashane, veteran journalist and practising sangoma, was a further source of valuable information.

Patricia McCracken gave me the names for the phases of the Zulu day, while Marie Gurr, Lorna King and Reg Vermeulen put up with my occasional "elusiveness".

Alan Cooper said this would make a good novel, while my "American friend", Norm Gillespie, kept me going with his insightful criticism.

Norma, meanwhile, provided a welcome distraction.

*

Finally, for the record, in addition to Shaka, his mother, Nandi, his half-brothers Dingane and Mpande and the Zulu King's revered mentor, Dingiswayo, Zwide (and the sons mentioned), Mduli (the uncle who sneered at reports of Nandi's pregnancy), Mdlaka, Mbopa, Mgobozi, Mzilikazi, Soshangane, Pampata, Ntombazi and Nobela were all real people.

As for the Induna, interested readers are directed to the second paragraph on page 42 of the 1984 Longman edition of Omer-Cooper's *The Zulu Aftermath . . .*

Select Bibliography

Becker, Peter: *Path of Blood*, Panther, 1966
  Hill of Destiny, Panther, 1972
  Rule of Fear, Panther, 1972
  Tribe to Township, Panther, 1974
Brownlee, W. T.: *Reminiscences of a Transkeian*, Shuter & Shooter, 1975
Bulpin, T. V.: *To the Shores of Natal*, Howard Timmins, 1954
  Shaka's Country: A Book of Zululand, Howard Timmins, 1975
  Southern Africa: Land of Beauty and Splendour, Reader's Digest, 1976
Kenney, R. U.: *Piet Retief: The Dubious Hero*, Human & Rousseau, 1976
Krige, Eileen Jensen: *The Social System of the Zulus*, Shuter & Shooter, 1965
Laband, John: *Rope of Sand*, Jonathan Ball, 1994
Lugg, H. C.: *A Natal Family Looks Back*, T. W. Griggs & Co, 1970
  Life Under a Zulu Shield, Shuter & Shooter, 1975
Michel, Aime: "Zimbabwe, Africa's Lost Civilisation", *The World's Last Mysteries*, Reader's Digest, 1977
Miller, Penny: *Myths and Legends of Southern Africa*, T. V. Bulpin Publications, 1979
Mitchison, Naomi: *The Africans*, Panther, 1970
Morris, Donald R.: *The Washing of the Spears*, Abacus, 1992
Mutwa, Credo: *My People*, Penguin, 1971
  Indaba My Children, Kahn & Averill, 1985
Omer-Cooper, J. D.: *The Zulu Aftermath: A Nineteenth-Century Revolution in Bantu Africa*, Longman, 1984
Pearse, R. O.: *Barrier of Spears: Drama of the Drakensberg*, Howard Timmins, 1980
Ritter, E. A.: *Shaka Zulu: The Rise of the Zulu Empire*, BCA, 1971
Rosenthal, Eric: *Encyclopaedia of Southern Africa* (first edition), Warne, 1961
  Schooners and Skyscrapers, Howard Timmins, 1963
Samuelson, L. H.: *Zululand: Its Traditions, Legends, Customs and Folklore*, T. W. Griggs & Co, 1974
Service, Alastair: *Lost Worlds*, Marshall Cavendish, 1981
Stuart, J. and D. Malcolm (eds.): *The Diary of Henry Francis Fynn*, Shuter & Shooter, 1950
Tait, Barbara Campbell: *The Durban Story*, The Knox Printing Co., 1965
Taylor, Stephen: *Shaka's Children*, Harper Collins, 1995
Woods, Gregor: "Flintlocks in our History", *Magnum*, 30, 1 (January 2005)

WALTON GOLIGHTLY lives and works in Durban, KwaZulu-Natal. This is his first novel.